WINDFALL

Cassia Fallon has been married for seven years when she inherits half a million pounds—a vast fortune in 1935. For the first time she is able to do exactly as she likes. She starts to re-examine her marriage, her past, her present, her future. The money gives her confidence, courage, insight. Within a short time she has resumed the medical career that was once of overpowering importance to her, shed some of her domestic burdens, re-formed old relationships. One of them of a most dangerous kind. Thus Cassia finds that her windfall is liberating—but also corrupting. Not least because the need to know where it really came from soon becomes overpowering . . .

WINDFALL

Penny Vincenzi

CHIVERS PRESS
BATH

First published 1997
by
Orion
This Large Print edition published by
Chivers Press
by arrangement with
Orion Books Ltd
2001

ISBN 0 7540 1624 2

British Library Cataloguing in Publication Data available

Printed and bound in Great Britain by
BOOKCRAFT, Midsomer Norton, Somerset

For Emily and Claudia with much love.

And gratitude for everything, especially for their inspiration over the coffee . . .

ACKNOWLEDGMENTS

Windfall has been a particular joy to write; but I am very aware that I do owe many thanks (as always) to a great many people for the help, guidance information and quite often inspirational advice that has been given (as always) so generously; and it is not an exaggeration to say that without the following, the book could quite literally not have been written.

Peter Townend; Felicity Green; Adrienne Spanier; Pierre Barillet; Ursula Lloyd; Noni and Roger Holland; Sir Peter Bristow; Dr Oliver Scott; Sue Stapely; John Lovatt; Peggy Doughty. Some particularly tumultuous applause for Gwendolyn Sparkes, Athena Crosse and Angela Fox for bringing the twenties and thirties, in all their gossipy glamour, most wonderfully alive; for Dr Joan Waters for a unique and extraordinary insight into the life of the medical student and young doctor at that time; and John Granger of the Brooklands Museum for his encyclopaedic knowledge and tireless enthusiasm. I have found several books quite invaluable: most notably *Edward VIII: The Road to Abdication* by Frances Donaldson, and *Elizabeth's Britain* by Philip Ziegler.

And at home, huge and heartfelt thanks to Carol Osborne for continuing to create calm and cheerful order out of frequently dreadful chaos.

I have also been—as always—wonderfully published by Orion; I'd like to thank particularly Rosie Cheetham, editor extraordinaire, for many inspiring things, but perhaps most importantly for that most crucial quality in an editor, appreciativeness, and of course a steely self-control in never, ever mentioning the l (for late)—word; Susan Lamb for unfailing emotional and practical support; Claire Hegarty for yet another glorious cover; Louise Page for yet more splendid publicity; Richard Hussey for supervising the production with tireless calm; Dallas Manderson, Jo Carpenter, and the rest of the sales team for getting the book Out There. And of course Desmond Elliott, so much more than agent, rather wise and witty companion and friend.

And finally, as always, my family, and in particular my husband Paul, so tirelessly and soothingly supportive through yet another long year.

CHAPTER ONE

JUNE 1935

Cassia Fallon was scrubbing the altar steps when she heard that she had inherited half a million pounds. She often thought afterwards, given the storybook nature of the whole thing, that it could not have been more auspicious; had she been doing one of the other things that typically filled her life—like bathing her children, or tending to her garden, or presiding over her dinner table, or seeing to the rota for the Women's Institute, or taking one of the hundreds of phone calls that came into her house every week, requesting her husband's presence at some sickbed or other—then it would not have made nearly so poignant a story. However, the juxtaposition of those two events, being down on her knees, scrubbing stone steps, for heaven's sake, and hearing that she had suddenly become extremely rich: that was worthy of the highest drama.

Of course it hadn't been quite as dramatic as she afterwards remembered it: Edward had simply arrived at the church with her godmother's solicitor, Mr Brewster, who had been very agitated to find her not at the house, given the importance of the news he had to impart. She had in fact arranged for him to come, only she had forgotten, and Edward, irritated by her inefficiency as usual, had brought Mr Brewster down to see her.

'Mr Brewster said it was vital he spoke to you himself, showed you the will. He's come all the way from London. I do think it's too bad of you to have forgotten,' Edward said.

Cassia apologised, and went to sit in the church porch with Edward and Mr Brewster. He was an extraordinarily dull-looking caricature of a solicitor, dressed in a dark grey suit, dark grey tie, black bowler, and carrying a rather battered black briefcase. His voice was equally dull, monotonous and slightly whining, but Cassia listened to it attentively while he read her the relevant section of the will, and explained it to her carefully. And when she had heard the extraordinary words, when she had told him that yes, she did understand, and asked him if there was anything she should do immediately, and he had said there was not, she asked if he would mind if she just finished washing the steps. Mr Brewster, who had clearly long ceased to be amazed by any behaviour, however eccentric, said that of course he would not, but Edward followed her down the aisle and stood over her as she started wringing out the cloth.

'You did realise what he said, didn't you?' Edward said. Cassia sat back on her heels. 'I mean the amount. You did hear him?'

'Yes. Yes, of course I did. Thank you.'

'Right. I just wondered. Your reaction does seem a little odd.'

'I'm sorry, Edward. What did you think I should do?' she said, smiling. 'Burst into song, or utter a fervent prayer of thanks?'

'No, of course not. You just seem so calm. I . . . well, I don't feel very calm.'

'Sorry,' Cassia said, not quite sure for what.

'And I do think you should come back to the house.'

'I ought to finish this. Really. If you take Mr Brewster back and ask Peggy to give him a cup of tea, I'll be back very soon.'

Edward stared at her, then pulled out his handkerchief and blew his nose. He always did that when he didn't know how to react. 'Cassia,' he said, 'I really do wonder if you've actually grasped—'

'Edward, I've grasped it perfectly. Thank you. I've been left half a million pounds. By my godmother. But it's not going to go away, and Mrs Venables will be furious if I leave this unfinished. There's a wedding tomorrow. And as Mr Brewster's come all this way anyway, I'm sure he won't mind waiting another ten minutes.'

'Yes,' Edward said, staring at her, as if he wasn't quite sure who she was any more—rather accurately as it happened. 'Yes, all right.' Then he turned his back on her and walked rather quickly back to the porch. She heard him talking to Mr Brewster, and then their footsteps slowly fading.

Cassia wiped the steps very carefully, making sure there were no streaks left on them, then she carried the dirty water out into the vestry and tipped it down the sink.

It was a lovely day; an appropriately lovely day, she thought, as she walked slowly back to the house, and then thought how silly that she should expect the weather to fit in with her extraordinary news. If it had been an unseasonably horrible day— or seasonably perhaps, given that this was June and England—wet and windy, that might have seemed quite appropriate too, for she could tell herself they could all go somewhere warm and sunny for a holiday, to the south of France for instance, and that might even be rather better.

Cassia wondered why she didn't feel more odd. Maybe she was in shock. When she had worked in Casualty, she had seen people quite literally with their fingers or toes cut off, sitting calmly waiting for the doctor, discussing the weather with whoever was sitting on the next chair. On the other hand, she didn't feel as if it had been a shock, and nor did she feel it couldn't be true, or that there had been a mistake.

The nearest she could get to defining how she felt, finding something to compare it with, was . . . what? When she heard she had passed her finals with exceptionally high marks? No, because that had been a result of her own work and cleverness. When Edward had asked her to marry him? Or rather told his father she was going to marry him? No, because that had been a rather more complex state of affairs. When Bertie was born? Or even William? No, that had been a pure wild happiness, nothing to do with this calm, warm acceptance.

Perhaps, though, when they had told her Delia was a girl. A nice quiet little girl, she had thought, smiling up at them through the clearing pain, a contrast to the awful, noisy, loveable little boys. That had been a sense of simple straightforward pleasure (not knowing, of course, that Delia was to be the nosiest of the lot). That was nearer, but it did seem rather awful to compare the arrival of a much longed for daughter with that of a large sum of money.

Cassia gave up. This wasn't like anything she had ever known. She didn't feel anything really, anything at all. Not yet.

*   *   *

4

It was a very nice walk from St Mary's to their house: Monks Ridge House it was called, being built high on the ridge above the village of Monks Heath, with its view right over the small valley, of the winding river, the tight complex of houses round the picture-book green, the church set at the back of it. Square, redbrick early Victorian, it was a classic West Sussex country house, with a very dark slate roof and an exceptionally pretty fanlight over the front door. However tired Cassia was, however discouraged by her failure to perform as the perfect doctor's wife, however cross or anxious over her unruly children, her heart lifted as she turned the last corner in the lane and looked at Monks Ridge. It was like seeing a friend waiting for her, uncritical, undemanding, pleased to see her. There was so much that was critical and demanding in her life, she found the house extraordinarily soothing.

Cassia had loved it from the first moment she had set eyes on it. You move in here, it seemed to say, and you won't get any trouble. And they hadn't. It was warm in winter, cool in summer; its pipes never froze, its fires burnt beautifully; its rooms were neither too large nor too small, its garden good tempered and undemanding.

There was a large extension at the side, not beautiful, added in the last year of the old queen's reign, which made a perfect surgery for Edward, and at the back, a small conservatory with arched windows where Cassia had managed to grow a vine, and where on summer nights when she couldn't sleep (usually because she was trying to soothe a crying baby) she would sit in her rocking chair,

5

watching the stars.

Cassia had always loved the stars: one of her very early memories was of standing in the garden at night, holding her father's hand and gazing up at the sky while he showed her the constellation after which she had been named. She could never actually work out the shape of a lady sitting in a chair, holding out her arms, but she pretended she could to please him. She liked too the story he often told her of how Cassiopeia had been sent to the heavens for boasting about the beauty of her daughter Andromeda.

Cassia loved the conservatory although Edward said it wasted heat and space. She could see his point about the heat, but the other objection was clearly nonsense: there was at least half an acre of garden beyond it, mostly grass, studded with shrubs and fruit trees.

Oddly (significantly even, she thought), she found Edward sitting in the conservatory now, with Mr Brewster.

'Hello. Sorry I was so long. Is Peggy making tea?'

'Yes, and I should be on my way. Lot of calls this afternoon. Can you manage now?' Edward said.

'Yes, of course. We can manage, can't we, Mr Brewster? I don't suppose there's a lot to manage. You can tell me a bit more, I expect, and I can listen.'

'Yes, indeed,' said Mr Brewster.

As Edward left them, Peggy came in with the tea tray, looking flustered. Strangers in the house made her nervous.

'Thank you, Peggy. Mr Brewster, would you like a piece of cake?'

'That would be delightful. Thank you.'

The cake wasn't delightful at all, of course, as Cassia had made it. It had sunk in the middle. But Mr Brewster ate it uncritically and accepted a second piece.

'Now, perhaps we should go over this again. So that you are quite clear about it all.'

'Yes, I'd like to look at it properly. Was anyone else left anything?'

'A few small bequests to servants and so on. Lady Beatty obviously felt you were the most worthy recipient. And having no children, and being estranged from Sir Richard . . .'

'Does he know about this?'

'Not yet. I will be informing him, as a courtesy, as they were married for many years.'

'Yes. I wrote to him when Leonora—Lady Beatty—died,' Cassia said.

'You were notified of her death by her brother, I imagine?'

'Well, actually by her brother's wife. Cecily Harrington. We have remained quite close. Nothing for any of them in the will?'

'Only a small bracelet for the eldest child.'

'Oh, yes, Fanny. Dear little thing, she is. Well, not so little now, she's nearly ten. I'm sorry, Mr Brewster, not very interesting for you.'

Mr Brewster smiled at her. 'I find other people's families of endless fascination.'

Cassia stared at the will, at the words: 'I exercise my power of appointment in relation to the Maple Trust, in favour of my goddaughter, Cassiopeia Blanche Fallon . . .'

'It doesn't say how much money it is, though,' Cassia said.

7

'That is because the money was invested by the trustees, and at the time the will was drawn up, it was not possible to say how much it would be worth. As it happens, it is worth a little more than five hundred thousand now, five hundred and eleven to be precise.'

'Goodness,' said Cassia. 'It grows, doesn't it, money?'

'Well invested, yes. Of course it can also shrink.'

'Why didn't she just leave it to me? I mean, why the trust and everything?'

Mr Brewster cleared his throat. 'I believe Lady Beatty was a little . . . extravagant. She explained to me that it was thought best to put the money in trust for you.'

'Yes, well, that's certainly true. I see. And the Harringtons, they don't know about this?'

'No indeed. I visited your godmother in Paris last March, at her request, to draw up the document. You are naturally the only person to have had sight of it. You and your husband, that is.'

'That was at the apartment in Passy, I suppose?'

'Indeed so. Very beautiful it was, I must say.'

'She must have been quite ill then?'

'She certainly did not appear to be in robust health, no,' said Mr Brewster, 'although she was clearly being very well taken care of.'

'Was she alone?'

'Yes. Apart from the staff in the apartment, of course, and I understood there was a resident nurse.'

'I see.' So at least Leonora had lived out her last days in comfort. Cassia had wondered—wondered and feared. 'Well, what happens now, Mr Brewster?'

8

'There are certain formalities. The money is not available for your use quite yet. As the executor, I have to obtain grant of probate, but you need have no concerns about it. Oh, and here is a letter, also lodged with me, from your godmother.'

Cassia took the envelope from him, opened it very carefully. It felt odd, almost as if Leonora had come suddenly into the room. Reading the extravagant writing, slanting loopily across the thick cream paper, was like hearing her husky, amused, voice.

'My darling Sweet Pea . . .' Oh, that ridiculous name, Cassia thought, and suddenly she was back there, on the terrace at the Ritz, twelve years old, led in by Benedict . . .

*   *   *

Cassia had come to London for the Peace March, invited to stay with her rich and glamorous godmother. She had only met Leonora a few times at that stage, and not at all for the last three years. Although she was very excited, she was also extremely nervous as she stood on the platform at Euston, trying to spot Leonora in the crowds of people, all arrived for this great national celebration.

After a very long hour it had been Benedict Harrington, Leonora's brother, who had appeared beside her, charmingly apologetic for his lateness. 'Leonora has been held up, God knows how. She phoned me out of the blue and asked me to come and fetch you. It must have seemed a very long wait, I'm so sorry.'

Benedict was tall and slim, golden haired and

rather unusually brown eyed, very handsome, Cassia thought, and most beautifully dressed in a dove-grey suit. She had smiled at him, and assured him she had been perfectly all right. He said she must, in that case, be extremely brave, that he would have been terrified at being all alone in London at her age. He had been instructed to take her to meet Leonora at the Ritz hotel, where she was having tea with some friends. 'She thought that would be more fun for you than just going back to the house.'

Cassia had said politely that it did sound great fun, although she would actually have preferred tea at home with Leonora.

As they travelled through the streets of a London turned red, white and blue, Benedict took out a gold cigarette case with a slightly shaking hand, and proceeded to smoke all the way to the Ritz, while pointing out to her the various London attractions they were passing. She wondered why he should be nervous, and decided it must be the thought of the march the next day, in which she knew he was to lead his regiment. Nervous or not, she liked him very much: he handed her out of the taxi as if she was an adult; picked up her shabby brown leather case and ushered her through the swing doors into the Ritz.

Inside, Cassia stopped and gasped aloud. Nothing she had ever seen could have prepared her for this place, with its tall, tall ceilings, its gilt chairs, its chandeliers, the unbelievably smart people everywhere.

'Come along, through here,' Benedict said. 'Oh, there she is, look,' and there Leonora was, coming towards them, smiling and holding out her arms.

'My darling!' she said, giving Cassia a kiss. 'How incredibly lovely to see you.' She led her up a couple of steps on to a wide terrace, set with tea tables and large palms, to a table where several other ladies were sitting. They were all dressed most wonderfully, Cassia thought, in pastel-coloured afternoon dresses with elaborate hats. Leonora's dress was apricot silk, and her hat a wonderful confection of roses and feathers. But it was the ladies' stockings that Cassia noticed first, for they were not black or even dark brown but very very light beige. She had never seen stockings like that, had not even known they existed.

Leonora put her arm round her and looked down at her. She was tall like her brother, with the same golden hair and brown eyes. 'How pretty you are!' she said. 'And very tall for your age. Now what am I to call you? Cassiopeia is a bit of a mouthful.'

'Most people call me Cassia,' said Cassia, smiling at her, 'but—'

'I don't like to do what most people do. Cassia sounds very dull to me. I shall call you—Sweet Pea. How will that do? A little bit of your name, and that is how you look: one of those flowers, very curly and colourful and delicate. Everyone! I want you to meet my goddaughter, Cassiopeia Berridge, but we shall call her Sweet Pea. Benedict, darling, have some tea with us, won't you?'

'No, Leonora, thank you. I have a great deal to do before tomorrow.'

'Oh, very well. Sweet Pea, darling, go and sit down next to the lady in yellow.'

Benedict smiled at Cassia, bowed briefly over her hand. 'Goodbye,' he said. 'I shall see you tomorrow after the march.'

11

'Thank you,' she said, 'and good luck tomorrow.'

'So divinely handsome, your brother,' said one of the ladies.

'Still not engaged, then?' said another.

'No, not yet,' said Leonora quickly. 'Now, Sweet Pea, would you like a cake or some sandwiches?' and she waved at a waiter.

And then, to Cassia's absolute horror, Leonora rummaged in her small bag and drew out a very pretty cigarette case and picked out a cigarette. The waiter was hurrying towards them, and Cassia felt sure he was going to ask her to leave the restaurant. Smoking in public was the most terrible thing a lady could do, she knew that. However, he did nothing of the sort, but produced a book of matches from his pocket and lit Leonora's cigarette for her.

In the corner of the terrace a pianist was playing 'If You Were the Only Girl in the World'. Cassia sat listening to it and gazing at these ladies in their light stockings smoking their cigarettes, and knew she had entered an utterly and most wonderfully different world.

* * *

Cassia wrenched her mind back from her memories, forced it on to her letter.

My darling Sweet Pea,

By the time you read this, I shall no longer be with you. Nasty thing that I've got, there is no hope at all, the doctors say. I just hope it carries me off quickly.

You are to have the money and to spend it not wisely—heaven forbid, darling—but well. Do anything at all you like with it—but have fun with it. Lots of fun. You were my dearest child, the one I never had. I've missed you horribly, more than any other person or thing since leaving England. Watching you grow up, having you to live with us, presenting you at Court, all those things made me terribly terribly happy. This is to say thank you.
Bless you, darling.
Best love, Leonora.

The letter blurred.

'Are you all right, Mrs Fallon?' Mr Brewster's voice was concerned.

'Oh, yes. Yes, thank you,' she said, fumbling for her handkerchief. 'It was reading the letter. It brought her alive again. I did love her very much.'

'Of course. She was a friend of your mother's, I believe?'

'Yes. She was much younger than my mother, but their mothers were great friends, and my mother used to treat Leonora like a doll—push her around in her dolls' pram, carry her about. Leonora adored her. Right to the end, they were friends—well, till my mother died—although their lives were so different. Leonora married twice, both times to terribly rich men in London; my mother to a very modestly paid librarian in Leeds.

'I lived with Leonora and Sir Richard all the time I was doing my medical training. She gave a dance for me, presented me at Court, oh, all sorts of wonderful things, but I first went to stay with Leonora in 1919, for the Peace March. I thought

13

I'd landed in Wonderland. I was a little girl from the provinces, very unsophisticated, only twelve years old, and there I was, in this great house, with servants, meeting all these wonderful exotic people . . . More tea, Mr Brewster?'

'Yes, please. Do go on. Tell me about the Peace March. My father was involved in that, but I didn't see it.'

'Oh, it was amazing. How sad you missed it. I shouted and shouted until I was hoarse. It went on for hours, all the noise and colour and pageantry. The King marched, of course, and the princes, and all the Heads of State, Haig, Admiral Beatty, Sir Roger Keyes, Field Marshal Smuts, the Old Contemptibles, all the bands, and horses, great groups of men, all marching down Whitehall, past the temporary Cenotaph, saluting it, saluting the glorious dead. And I thought, we all did that day, that to have died for your country was truly the next best thing to living. I'd lost three uncles in that war, and just for that day I felt it was somehow worth it. Only of course it wasn't . . .'

'My father lost both his legs,' said Mr Brewster quietly. 'Fortunately for him, for all of us, he had a small private income. But so many of those wretches have spent the next ten or fifteen years selling matches. It's a disgrace.'

After another silence he smiled at Cassia again, then said, 'Well, this won't do any good, will it? I mustn't take up too much of your time.'

'It's me taking up the time, Mr Brewster. I'm sorry. It just seemed . . . appropriate somehow. To talk about Leonora, and those days.'

'Of course.' He patted her hand. He really was a very nice man, Cassia thought, not dreary as she

14

had first thought. 'Now, if you have any more questions, do ask me. As soon as the money becomes properly available to you, then I will notify you. Otherwise, I should be getting back to London. I wonder if I could telephone for a taxi to the station?'

'Yes, please do. I'm sorry I can't take you, but Edward needs the car for his rounds.'

'Naturally. No, a taxi will do splendidly.' His face eased suddenly into a conspiratorial smile. 'You might consider buying a little car of your own now. Just a suggestion, of course.'

'Goodness,' Cassia said, 'yes, I suppose I might. We'll have to see. Anyway, I'll just go and phone.'

As she stood in the hall, waiting for the local taxi service to answer, she thought how very odd it would be to be able to consider buying anything at all for herself, of her own volition, without asking Edward, without having interminable discussions first.

It did seem a rather agreeable prospect.

*   *   *

After Mr Brewster had gone, Cassia went out to the kitchen and did a bit of clearing up. She never managed to get the kitchen properly clear, but she did like to keep trying. Actually, she didn't like it, she loathed it, but she knew it had to be done. Monks Ridge was much too big really for her to look after with only Peggy's rather incompetent help, especially with three small children. 'How you manage without a nanny, Cassia, I can't imagine,' Cecily had said once, and Cassia had replied quite briskly that she managed somehow, like everyone

15

else who couldn't afford one.

She looked at the clock: almost two. Delia had been asleep for much too long. She'd never sleep tonight. She'd have to wake her up and perhaps take her for a walk—that might be a good idea, because then she could think. Bertie wouldn't be back from his little school until four, and William had gone to play at the vicarage, so she and Delia could have the afternoon to themselves. Delia was always better when the boys weren't there.

She went to find Peggy, who was ironing Edward's shirts. Peggy liked doing that: she didn't do them nearly as well as Mrs Briggs, the daily, but it made her feel important.

'Peggy,' Cassia said tactfully, 'Peggy, do leave those, I'd much rather you got on with the supper. I thought we could have fish pie and I won't have the time to make it. I've got to collect William and—'

'It's all right, Mrs Fallon, I can do both,' said Peggy, smiling at her. 'I know the doctor's particular about his shirts.'

'Er . . . yes, he is, but—'

'Don't you worry, Mrs Fallon. Is everything all right? That wasn't bad news from that man, was it?'

'No, Peggy. Just a bit of . . . well, family administration.'

Cassia walked slowly up to the nursery. Delia was still very firmly asleep, her thumb stuck into her rosebud mouth, her fair curls coiled damply on to her head. She was so lovely when she was asleep, it seemed a terrible shame to wake her. But it had to be done. Cassia moved about the room, carefully noisy. Delia squirmed, opened her large dark blue eyes—her mother's eyes—and promptly started to grizzle.

'Darling!' said Cassia, deliberately cheerful. 'Hello. Time to get up. I thought we'd go for a walk.'

Delia shook her head.

'Well, I'm going,' Cassia said, feeling rising irritation, 'and you'll have to come with me. We can go to the woods, might see a bunny . . .'

Cassia carried Delia downstairs, gave her a drink, then strapped her in the battered old pram which stood in the porch. She told Peggy to take any calls very carefully, then called Buffy, a basset hound of quite extraordinarily sweet temper and set off down the lane. She sang 'One Man Went to Mow' loudly, trying to drown the sound of Delia's wails. She didn't feel very much like a half-millionairess . . .

*   *   *

Cassia was twenty-eight. She was arresting to look at, rather than conventionally pretty, with rich corn-coloured hair, very dark blue eyes, and a sensuously full mouth that curved upwards at the corners. She was slim and very tall—five foot ten—a factor which she claimed had had a great effect on her personality, leading people to assume from her earliest years that she was older than she really was.

She had been born in 1907, exactly nine months after her parents' marriage. Duncan Berridge and Blanche Hampton had fallen passionately in love over an overdue library book, and been married only eighteen months later, a hasty courtship by the standards of the time. It was a love affair that had never faltered in any way: each adored and

17

admired the other equally, and despite some rather dark prognostications by Blanche's father, who felt that the only daughter of a prosperous solicitor could have done rather better for herself than marrying someone he persisted in labelling a clerk. However, since Blanche was rather serious and didn't have a capacity for attracting large numbers of young men, and he had very little money to settle upon her, he agreed to Duncan's request for her hand.

Serious Blanche might have been, but she was beautiful, with heavy dark hair drawn back from a pale, oval face, and the startlingly dark blue eyes she had passed on to her daughter. Repressed by her four brothers and an oppressively dictatorial mother, she blossomed in her happy marriage and became, besides a supportive wife and talented housekeeper, a champion of women's rights. Some of Cassia's earliest memories were of her mother reading to her father reports from the paper of the Suffragettes and their battles, and expressing her admiration for them—an admiration which, most unusually for a man of his generation, he shared.

Cassia's birth, so soon after their marriage, had led Duncan and Blanche to expect a large family, but in fact for many years there were no more babies. This had a profound effect on Cassia: the absence of brothers led her to assume that there was nothing remotely superior about the male sex, and the absence of any rivals for her parents' affection gave her a serene self-confidence. She was also, as a result of spending a great deal of her time in their company, very mature for her age.

She was educated initially at boarding school. It was fairly unusual for a small girl in 1916 to be sent

18

away to school, and it was in some ways Cassia's misfortune that her parents, who loved her dearly, were so anxious to see her well educated. Her father had had to leave school at the age of fourteen and although he was well read and musically accomplished, he had no professional qualifications, and felt painfully disadvantaged in the company of those who did. Blanche, who had been the only member of her family deprived of a decent education, purely on account of her sex, felt her own daughter deserved better, so when Cassia was nine and there was no good prep school of any kind in their neighbourhood a solution was found in a small boarding school thirty miles away. A few decades later she would have been transported there and home again each day by a rota of parental chauffeurs, but in 1916 only the very rich had cars, and boarding school fees of twenty pounds a term seemed more affordable.

And so Cassia became a pupil of Hammond House, a large Victorian house on the outskirts of Leeds, filled with a lot of other generally friendly and jolly little girls. Miss Hammond, the headmistress, was an enlightened and warm-hearted woman, educated under the wonderful aegis of Miss Beale and Miss Buss at Cheltenham Ladies' College. She held a passionate belief that girls were not only as clever as boys, but could and should do as well in their chosen careers, and many of her students went on to the excellent Leeds Girls' High, Cassia among them. She also loved her girls and held tea parties every Sunday afternoon in her study, where the children sat in front of the fire toasting teacakes and drinking hot cocoa and were allowed to talk to her about anything at all. In

19

Cassia's case, this was very frequently of her absolute and unswerving determination to become a doctor.

*　　　*　　　*

When Cassia was ten, Blanche had enlisted as a VAD and worked as a nurse in a hospital just outside Finchfield. She had always wanted to nurse, and in some ways she had never been happier than she was then, setting off early in the morning on her bicycle for the three-and-a-half-mile ride, and returning late at night, her back aching, her legs throbbing, to tell Duncan of the events of her day. Blanche found herself totally unsqueamish, and with a genuine talent for her new task. She saw things which horrified her, heard things which broke her heart; but overall she felt properly fulfilled for the first time in her life.

*　　　*　　　*

The war had not entered Cassia's consciousness very strongly. Of course she knew it was going on: their prayers every day, and in church every Sunday, were for its satisfactory conduct and the welfare of the men at the Front. Every so often a girl would be called into Miss Hammond's office, and emerge weeping at the news that a brother or uncle or, most dreadfully, a father, had been killed or injured.

Cassia knew also that the fighting was very terrible, but that our men were very brave and were winning the war steadily and indisputably under the superb direction of their generals. Three of her mother's brothers were at the Front.

She was deeply grateful that her father was not fit enough to go to France, and glad too that he looked quite old, as it meant he wouldn't be handed a white feather in the street for being a coward.

*   *   *

One afternoon in the summer holidays in 1917, Blanche asked Cassia if she would like to come to one of the hospital concerts and sing for the men. 'Poor things, these concerts cheer them up so much. I've asked Matron and she is more than happy for you to do so. Your father will play for you.'

Cassia was more than happy too. She had a very pretty voice, and had performed in several concerts at Hammond House. She practised a few of the favourite war songs, like 'It's a Long Way to Tipperary' and 'Pack Up Your Troubles In Your Old Kit Bag', and a couple of more romantic favourites, like 'If You Were the Only Girl in the World' and 'Daisy, Daisy'.

Blanche told Cassia to wear her new white muslin dress with the frills and white stockings and shoes, and tied a white ribbon in her dark gold hair. The three of them set off together in the governess cart that one of Blanche's brothers had lent them, along with a rather lazy pony, for the duration of the war.

Cassia, who had never seen the hospital, felt suddenly nervous as they drew up outside its great, grim walls. The grounds were full of men, some of them in wheelchairs, others sitting with their eyes

21

bandaged, or walking slowly about on sticks or crutches, all dressed in the dark blue flannel suits of the wounded. Most of them looked at the cart and its occupants and smiled, and even waved at Blanche whom they recognised, but a few remained motionless, staring blankly in front of them with white, gaunt faces. Cassia knew they were suffering from shellshock. Blanche had explained it to her, and how its sufferers lived partly or totally withdrawn in a dreadful, haunted, half-real world, unable to communicate with anybody much of the time: 'In time, it is hoped, with good nursing and the love of their families, they will return to a proper life and rediscover themselves, but meanwhile, poor things, they are in a terrible way.'

Far worse, Cassia thought, were the men sitting in wheelchairs, with both legs amputated; and she was amazed to hear two of the blind men laughing raucously. It seemed almost impossible to her that anyone should ever smile, let alone laugh, with so much to endure. She would rather have died. But she smiled and waved back to them all, and followed her mother over to a few of them and said 'how do you do?' and shook their hands; 'bless her' she heard several times and 'pretty little angel', and she stopped being nervous and when it came to her turn in the concert, she greatly enjoyed standing on the stage and singing her songs, and when they were all cheering and shouting 'encore, encore' and Duncan beamed at her and nodded and started to play 'Are There Any More At Home Like You?' and they clapped even before she had sung the first note, she felt she had done something properly useful for the first time in her life.

Afterwards, Blanche left Cassia with Duncan while she had a discussion with Matron. They were standing in a corridor, waiting for Blanche to return, when they heard a dreadful groaning coming from a small side room. Cassia, drawn to it, she felt, quite against her will, ran over to the room and opened the door.

A man lay there in a high-sided bed, clearly in agony. He was writhing about, tossing his head like a terrified horse. His eyes were bandaged, his breath rasping, but as he heard the door open, he turned towards her. 'Please,' he said, 'please, I can't stand it. Please, for God's sake, help me.'

Cassia looked at him for a moment, then said, 'Wait, I'll come back, I promise,' and turned and collided with her mother.

'Mama, Mama,' Cassia said, clasping her mother's hands, pulling her into the room, 'this poor man is in the most dreadful pain. Give him something for it, please, please.'

'Cassia, I can't possibly give him anything,' said Blanche. 'That is not for me to do.'

'But you're a nurse! You must, you've got to, please, listen, he's crying—'

The man uttered a strange mixture of groan and sob, calling out again for help.

Cassia burst into tears. 'Why won't you help?'

'Cassia, he has gas poisoning. It's a dreadful thing. He's only just been brought here and—'

'But he is here, and you must be able to help him. That's what this place is for.'

Blanche looked at the man's notes, hanging at the foot of his bed, then drew Cassia outside the room, and closed the door on the man. His cries could still be heard as loudly.

'Mama, please. You're cruel, it's horrible. Why won't you—'

'Cassia, listen. It is not for me to decide what drugs he has. Only the doctors can do that. They know best, and they have decided he cannot have anything more until the morning.'

Cassia looked at her for a moment, trying to ignore the dreadful sound of the man's pain, and then turned and walked very determinedly towards her father who was standing talking to the matron: a tall, imposing woman, rather beautiful, with dark red hair and a very long, elegant neck. 'Ah, Cassia! What a pleasure your singing was. I was just telling your father how much you must have pleased the men—'

'Please,' said Cassia, 'please go and help that man in there.' She pointed towards the door. 'He's in such pain, and my mother says—' She stopped, tears spilling over her lashes, frightened, horrified tears.

'Yes? Your mother says what?'

'That only the doctors can do anything, decide what he can have.'

'That is quite right. A doctor saw him only an hour ago, and prescribed what he must have. He has had it, and is much better for it.'

Cassia stared at her. 'He's not better for it at all. He's suffering terribly, you know he is!'

'Cassia!' said Blanche, shocked.

'Cassia,' said Matron, kneeling down and taking her hand, 'I know how it must seem to you. And it's not that I won't help. I can't. We are doing all we can for that poor man. I'm sorry you should have

24

had to see him.'

'It doesn't matter that I've seen him,' said Cassia, pulling her hand free, 'just that he's in such a lot of pain. The doctor must have got it wrong, not realised how bad he was. I think you should tell him—' She brushed the tears from her eyes again.

'I'm afraid that's not how it works,' said Matron, looking less patient. 'It is not for us to question the doctors' decisions.'

'Well, I think you should,' said Cassia staunchly.

'Cassia, be quiet immediately!' said Blanche.

'Cassia,' said Matron, 'you are obviously a very kind, caring person, but you really do not understand this situation. Perhaps one day you can come back here and learn for yourself. And put your courage and your kindness to good use. As a nurse.'

Cassia looked at her. 'No,' she said, 'I really don't want to be a nurse. I want to be able to decide things for myself. I'm going to be a doctor.'

*   *   *

Only, in spite of that moment of vision, a passionate determination to succeed, and her graduation from one of the finest medical schools in the country with the highest possible marks, the nearest she had come to medical practice was acting as unpaid secretary to her husband, giving unofficial advice to pregnant and recently delivered young women, and making up cough mixture and bandaging the occasional knee as its owner sat wailing in the surgery. And that hurt, hurt very badly, every day of her life.

CHAPTER TWO

'This is very good fish pie, Peggy.' Edward smiled at Peggy over his empty plate. 'Is there any more?'

'A bit, Dr Fallon. I'm glad you like it.' Peggy blushed. She was devoted to Edward, and his praise was not easily won. 'Brain food, my mother always said it was, fish. I'll go and see if there's a bit more.'

She disappeared. She wasn't actually a very good housekeeper—which was what she liked to be called, but she was devoted to the Fallons. She didn't mind what she did, not even cleaning or washing nappies—although Mrs Briggs did most of the heavy work—and that, Cassia supposed, made up for a lot of her deficiencies. Peggy came back in with the dish and ladled more pie on to Edward's plate.

'Daddy doesn't need to feed his brains. They're absolutely huge already, aren't they, Daddy?'

'I hope so,' said Edward, smiling at Bertie, 'but I'm not over-confident about their size.'

'They must be, otherwise you couldn't be a doctor. Could he, Mummy?'

'No, of course not,' said Cassia. She smiled determinedly at her husband and her elder son, so staggeringly alike, with their straight brown hair, their brown eyes, their long faces, their thin bodies. Bertie was already the tallest boy in his class, already clumsy. William on the other hand was still slightly chubby, blond and blue eyed like his mother and baby sister.

'Oh God, there's the phone. Not another baby, please! Not tonight,' said Edward with a sigh.

'Are any due?'

'Maxine Foster is. Almost. Yes, Peggy?'

'It's Mr Harrington for Mrs Fallon.'

'Oh, tell him I'll call him back, could you? Explain we're having supper. And find out if he's in Devon or London.'

'Yes, Mrs Fallon.'

'What's he calling about?' said Edward.

'I've no idea,' said Cassia shortly. She wondered if Benedict had phoned about the will—he was Leonora's brother after all. They had been terribly close, he must have known about it.

She was beginning to feel extremely strange. Her prime emotion, she realised, was not excitement, but a great sadness. She had not known how ill Leonora had been, that she was dying, and so had not been to see her. She had missed the funeral in Paris, quiet, hastily arranged, and had consequently felt an appalling remorse as well as grief at the time. Somehow the day, the bequest, above all Leonora's letter, had made her freshly aware of it. She sat thinking of Leonora, of her courage, her silliness, her beauty, her capacity for fun—and realised afresh that she was gone, quite quite gone . . .

She lifted her head and saw Edward looking at her, sympathetic, concerned, and half smiled at him.

He smiled back, and said, 'Why don't you go and sit down? Have a rest.'

Sometimes, just sometimes, she remembered why she had married him.

*　　　*　　　*

27

As she sat by the fire, flicking through the *Telegraph*, Delia's wails trailed down the stairs. It was no use, no one else could calm her. She'd have to go to her.

She went and made Delia a bottle, gave it to her, settled her down again, then walked down the stairs. Edward was in the hall.

'I'm just going to phone Benedict back,' she said.

'Oh, all right. Don't talk too long, will you? I'm half expecting a call about that baby, and anyway, trunk calls are—'

'Expensive?' she said, amused, looking at him very levelly. 'Don't worry, Edward. Maybe I can help with the bill.' She always regarded that afterwards as an absolutely definitive moment.

Cecily answered the phone. 'Cassia. How nice. How are you?'

'I'm fine, Cecily, thank you. And you?'

'Oh, pretty well. Awfully busy, of course. It's Ascot next week and we're taking a house down there, and then soon after that we're off to the South of France, with the children and some chums. Actually, Cassia, why don't you all come and join us? It would be such fun.'

'Cecily, I really don't think we could. Much as I'd love to. Edward doesn't get what you might call holidays, and—'

'Well, come without him. Just for a few days. It would do you good. You looked so tired last time I saw you.'

Yes, I probably did, thought Cassia, I always do. I always feel tired, my life is totally, unrelentingly tiring. She had a sudden vision of lying by a pool in the South of France, somewhere near Nice probably. Benedict and Cecily took a villa there

28

every July, filled it with friends, with amusing, good-looking people. Cassia had gone once, the year of her finals. She had lain there in the sun, sipping cocktails, talking and listening to nonsense, playing bezique and backgammon, dancing at night by the pool to the gramophone, or going down to Nice to some night-club or other, and once to the casino. Leonora had arrived on Cassia's last day, full of gossip about Paris and Le Touquet, demanding gossip about London. It had been a magical, hedonistic, enchanted time and, like so much of her past life, seemed now an unbelievable, impossible dream.

'I don't think so,' she said. 'Edward does like to have me here, but thank you for asking me. Um, could I speak to Benedict? He phoned earlier.'

'Yes, of course. Just hold on a minute. And do think about coming to France. I'd love to have you there. It's going to be such fun.'

Dear Cecily: she was so genuinely affectionate, so irresistibly optimistic. She needed to be, of course: she might have a lot of life's goodies, but she certainly earned them.

'Cassia, hello. It's Benedict. I just wanted to let you know we're having a memorial service for Leonora. So many people missed the funeral, and it seems so shabby not to do what we can for her. We thought the end of this month. How would the twenty-eighth sound to you?'

'Fine. Where will it be?'

'St George's, Hanover Square. It's a lovely church and the vicar is a friend of mine. I don't suppose Richard will come, although naturally I shall ask him, and so many of Leonora's old friends have somehow disappeared—but a lot of the old

29

crowd will be there, and Harry of course. In fact I've asked him to speak. He said he would.'

'Oh good,' she said carefully, 'and what about Rollo Gresham?'

'I don't know,' said Benedict, almost too quickly. 'He's very elusive these days.'

'But he was her . . .' How did you describe exactly Rollo Gresham's role in Leonora's life? Her lover, yes, but more than that: she had lived with him for years, and although they had parted, it had been on amicable terms, Leonora always said. He had left her very well provided for . . . very well indeed, it seemed. 'I just thought he'd want to be there,' Cassia finished lamely.

'We shall see. Naturally I shall make every attempt to notify him.' Benedict sounded irritable. 'And I thought it would be nice if Rupert Cameron came. Leonora was awfully fond of him. Only I don't have an address or phone number for him, so if you could—'

'Yes, of course. It's a Brighton number, 427.'

'Marvellous. Do you think he'd speak? Or read something? That marvellous voice of his, it would be wonderful. What do you think?'

'It's a very good idea. And he'd like it, he was very fond of her too. He's resting at the moment, as they say in his profession, so I'm pretty sure he'd be able to be there.'

She smiled: Rupert would indeed like it. He had adored Leonora as she had him. And it would be lovely to have him there—she would feel very much alone otherwise, as Edward would inevitably make some excuse, as he always did on such occasions.

Benedict cut into her rambling thoughts. 'Good.

Well, I think that's all for now. I'll get on to Cameron. Oh, and I heard Cecily asking you down to France. It's a nice idea, we'd love to have you.'

'I'll think about it, but I really can't see how—'

How what, Cassia? she thought. How to get away, afford the fare, buy some clothes, leave Edward without his support system? But she could. At least consider it: it was all suddenly so much less impossible. Not for the first time since Mr Brewster's arrival she experienced the heady, almost shocking realisation that she could, actually now, do what she liked. She crushed it firmly: it wasn't fair; nothing had changed, not her relationship with, her loyalty to, Edward. Just because she had some money. That wasn't going to change anything important. She wouldn't allow it.

*   *   *

She went back into the drawing room where Edward was listening to a concert on the wireless. He turned the volume down. 'What did Benedict want?'

'They're going to have a memorial service for Leonora. He wanted to talk to me about it.'

'That's a nice idea.'

'Yes. You'll come, won't you?'

'Of course, if I can get cover that day. Not that it would matter much if I didn't.'

'It would matter to me.'

'Would it?' he said and smiled at her, the slow sweet smile that was there less and less frequently these days. 'Well, I'm pleased to hear it. But all those people—her friends, that lot. I won't be a very valuable addition, will I?'

31

'Oh, Edward, don't be silly. Please. Such a cracked record, that one.'

'I'll come if I can. All right?' There was a silence, then he said, 'Did Benedict know about you? And the money?'

'He didn't mention it, and I didn't feel it was appropriate to. Anyway, what was I going to say? Guess what, Leonora's left me half a million pounds?'

'Half a million pounds,' Edward said. 'It is an awful lot of money. I hope it'll be all right.'

'Edward, of course it'll be all right,' she said, half amused, half irritated. 'Why shouldn't it?'

She sat in an armchair; and thought about Leonora, wondering against the background of the music what happened to people that they could take a lovely, loved and joyful life, and fill it with fear and greed and distress? What had driven Leonora to do that? To throw everything away, in that dreadful madness? And it had been a madness. A sickness.

*   *   *

'It's an addiction,' Benedict had said to Cassia, on the dreadful day when Leonora had run away to France, away from Sir Richard, who had changed from loving husband to bitter jailer, away from safety and security, and into her new, empty, wretched life.

Cassia had been living with them, in the middle of her medical studies, and had come home to find the house silent, dead, Sir Richard locked in his study. She had gone round to Benedict and Cecily for comfort, had sat crying, staring at Benedict as

32

he struggled to explain. 'She's an addicted gambler. It's as much a sickness as cocaine or alcohol addiction; she can scarcely help it.' He had tried to help: first by trying to stop Leonora, to warn her against the associates who saw her and her wealth coming; then by bailing her out endlessly, paying off casinos, private gambling clubs, all her debtors; then when he could do no more, when Richard discovered what she was doing, standing by her as she faced her husband and struggled to redeem herself.

The final showdown had come when an antiquarian friend of Sir Richard's had come to dinner and asked if he might borrow a tiara that had belonged to Richard's grandmother. 'I've never forgotten it, it really is the most perfect example of worked gold, and the settings of those rubies, quite extraordinary.'

'Of course we'll lend it to you,' said Sir Richard. 'Leonora has it now, but it would be an honour, wouldn't it, my dear?'

'Yes, but . . . that is . . . when did you say . . .'

'Not until November, only I would like to have sight of it before then, so that it can be catalogued, and so on.'

'Well, no time like the present,' said Sir Richard. 'We'll get it and—'

With a loud crash, the chair Leonora was leaning on slipped from under her and she fell to the floor in a dead faint.

It had all come out: the tiara had been sold; all Leonora's jewellery had been sold, much of it heirlooms belonging to Sir Richard's mother. She had had very good copies made, and worn those, and paid her debts with the proceeds. It had been a dreadful, wretched time, and Cassia had never quite got over it.

Sir Richard had moved Miss Monkton into the house, to keep an eye on Leonora. Nominally a companion, actually a spy, Miss Monkton, with her thin wispy hair and her halitosis, was paid to watch her charge, to listen to her conversations, to go everywhere she went. Cassia had watched Leonora disintegrate under her misery, grow quiet, colourless, fat as she ate too much, her only remaining self-indulgence. Deserted by her friends—for who, after all, would wish to be associated with such very open disgrace? Cassia had had to endure living in a house that had become silent, miserable, full of hostility and harsh words. And to be denied an understanding of the reason, for Leonora would not speak of it, and Sir Richard could not. Almost two years later, she had come home to find Harris, Leonora's maid, weeping, Richard locked in his study, and Leonora gone.

Cassia had been to visit Leonora in Paris several times. She lived in a very grand penthouse apartment on the Avenue Foch—'We can almost reach out and touch the Arc de Triomphe, look,' she had said, leading Cassia out on to the balcony—with Rollo Gresham, a great slob of a man whom Cassia loathed. How could she? Cassia had wondered, before she came to recognise that Leonora needed money more than anything in the world, money from a source that understood her addiction—and Gresham had a very great deal. For five years they had lived together, while Sir Richard divorced her and married the blessed Margaret, as Rupert irreverently christened her.

Although finally Rollo Gresham left Leonora, she had been extraordinarily well provided for, and he had gone to enormous lengths, it seemed, to see that she had the best possible medical care. He had clearly been a much kinder, better man than she had given him credit for, Cassia thought now, thinking of poor Leonora, so brave, so lovely, so generous—so very, very generous . . .

*　　　*　　　*

Edward switched off the radio, and said, 'Let's go up, shall we? You look exhausted.'

'I'm not in the least exhausted,' she said, irritable.

'Well, it would be nice anyway.'

The smile again; the sweet smile. She knew what it meant, that smile, in conjunction with bed; that he wanted to make love to her. Well, that was all right. It happened less and less these days, and it was seldom more than just nice any more; but she still enjoyed it, still felt closer to him.

More loving, more forgiving. Forgiving: why, for heaven's sake, did she need to feel forgiving? It was nonsense. It wasn't Edward's fault that he was a doctor and she wasn't; not his fault that she was a lousy housekeeper and only a tolerable wife; not his fault that she was deeply, uncomfortably, discontented. If it was anyone's, it was hers.

'Yes,' she said, smiling back. 'Yes, it would be nice.'

*　　　*　　　*

She lay in bed watching him as he undressed,
35

folded his clothes neatly, brushed his hair and his teeth, got into bed naked, turned out the light. She was naked too; acknowledging, by the night-dress still in its case on the bed, that she was ready for him, wanted him. She was ready, very ready: she could feel herself reaching out to him, from hungry, unsatisfied depths, hoping, yearning that tonight, as there had not been for a while, there would be time, that he would wait for her, let her climb, soar, come. Often now, Edward's needs, suddenly, urgently felt, did not allow for patience, for her. She felt wrongly used in bed, as she was in the rest of their marriage: necessary, an important, a crucial requirement even, but not a recipient of proper consideration or care.

He began to kiss her, slowly, carefully, as he did everything. Her emotions intensified by the events of her day, she suddenly wanted him very much. She responded, with her mouth, her hands, her voice, telling him she loved him, wanted him. He didn't like that usually, was embarrassed, half afraid someone would hear, but tonight he seemed pleased, told her he loved her too.

He began to smooth her body with his hands, slowly, rhythmically, caressing her breasts, her stomach, her thighs. She rose within herself to meet him, feeling herself clenching, tautening, releasing in a smooth, mounting delight. It would be good this time, she told herself, it would be good, the long, sweet unfolding, her body would take its due from him. Even as she began to know within her the brilliance, the high peaks of pleasure, began to reach for them, to feel for them, to ride, she felt him change, tense, and knew he wouldn't wait, wouldn't take her with him, that yet again he would go on alone, leaving her behind, calling out to him, that it would be over for him, and she would be left there, disappointed, still hungry, and terribly, horribly alone.

*   *   *

Well, she said to herself later, sitting in the kitchen drinking a cup of tea (having left him snoring, smiling beatifically), perhaps that was what marriage was. That was what became of passion, became of the bright, brilliant thing that once was there; and then she thought (because such thoughts turned her to honesty) that there had never been any bright brilliance with Edward. It had always been sensible, warm, affectionate reason.

*   *   *

She had met Edward when she was at the university. He was two years ahead of her, doing his clinical studies, actually working in the hospital. It was such a huge step up from the three years of theory that preceded it. She could still remember seeing some of the students on ward rounds on her first day, distinguished from the real doctors by their short white coats, talking to patients, allowed to examine them even, under the watchful eye of their Honoraries. She remembered thinking how unimaginably far away such an achievement seemed. That first day had been the most terrifying, as well as the most wonderful of her life, she thought now with a smile. She remembered her seventeen-year-old self, standing in a vast room stretching into what seemed to be infinity, filled with large glass-topped tables, and on them, rows and rows of white-swathed objects.

The Dean had been standing in the doorway, directing Cassia and the other new medical students inside. 'Ah, Miss Berridge,' he had said, when she reached him, 'you go to table number twenty-four and take the left leg.'

The sense of nightmare had grown: these were the corpses, the cadavers, the Dean had just urged them to respect. Dead bodies, once people: and she had been given the left leg of one of them. She advanced to table twenty-four, looked at her body. The smell was awful, formaldehyde, she supposed. More awful still, the veins stood out, dark and red. For a ghastly moment, she thought she was going to be sick. She took a deep breath, then another.

Everyone around her had looked perfectly normal, cheerful even. A couple had already picked up their scalpels and were cutting into their corpses: Cassia had stood there, helpless, unable to move, wondering if it would be braver to leave then, to go home, or to stay and do what she was told.

'It's only dye,' an amused but kindly voice said. 'Don't worry. Come on, I'll show you what to do.'

Cassia looked up and saw another girl standing in front of her, smiling. She was short and slightly plump, with a riot of red curly hair. 'I'm Jenny Porter. You all right? You look terrible.'

'I feel terrible,' said Cassia.

'This is the worst bit, apparently. My father told me about it. He was—'

'Don't tell me, a student here. I must have the only father who wasn't. I'm Cassia Berridge. Okay, let's get it over with,' said Cassia, picking up her scalpel. She wondered if it was possible to cut into a vein successfully with your eyes shut.

*   *   *

Some weeks later, she was sitting in Casualty with a badly sprained ankle, sustained from slipping on a piece of liver, hurled by one of her fellow students across the lab at another.

Casualty wasn't too crowded. Jenny and Tom Cavanagh, who had brought her over, had left her to find themselves a cup of tea. The nurse in charge had a look at Cassia's ankle and pronounced it a sprain.

'It'll need strapping up. Here, you. Come and strap up this ankle.'

Cassia was bent over her foot, rubbing it to relieve the pain, and the first glimpse therefore that she got of Edward Fallon was of a pair of very nice hands, slender, with very long fingers. He had bony wrists, and wore a rather battered gold watch, and she noticed that his shirt cuffs were frayed. Not a rich student, then: maybe on a scholarship, like herself.

'Hello,' he said. His voice was very nice too, light, slightly diffident. 'I'm—'

'I can see,' she said, looking at his badge. 'Mr E. Fallon. How do you do? Cassia Berridge. First year.'

'Fourth. What have you done to your foot?'

'I slipped in the lab.'

'Oh dear. Liver or frog?' He grinned at her. He had nice teeth too, Cassia thought, a bit crooked, but very white. She took in the rest of him—slightly long face, wavy brown hair, hazel eyes, freckles,

39

nice, smiley expression—then pulled herself back to reality with an effort.

'Liver.'

'Dear, oh dear, these medical students,' he said. 'Right, then, let's get this on.' He started winding on the bandage, his head bent.

Cassia said, 'So is it fun, doing Clinical?'

'Wonderful. I'm really enjoying myself.'

'Was your father here?' she said.

'No, although my grandfather was. Was yours?'

'No. This must be a first, two students meeting, neither of them with fathers here.'

'Mine's a teacher,' said Edward Fallon, tucking in the end of the bandage. 'Prep school in Sussex. Yours?'

'Librarian. In Leeds.'

'Ah. So where do you live, in one of the hostels?'

'No, with my godmother and her husband.'

'Oh. Nice for you, that. Bit of homeliness. Digs are awful.'

'Yes,' said Cassia, thinking of the vast house in Grosvenor Gardens where she lived, the servants, the lavish meals; homely was hardly the right word for it.

'Well, that's done. How does it feel, if you put your weight on it?'

'Fine. Much better. Thank you. Now I have to wait for my friends.'

'Right-oh. Would you like me to get you a cup of tea? I can say you're suffering from shock, if you like.' He grinned at her.

'Oh, no. I'll just sit and watch. See what it's like to be a Casualty doctor.'

'It's okay,' he said. His voice was considered, careful. Cassia thought if you asked him if it was

40

going to rain, he would give the matter a great deal of attention before answering. 'As I said, I'm enjoying it all very much.'

'What branch do you intend going into?'

'Oh surgery, I think,' Edward said.

'Me too! I—'

'Mr Fallon! Over here, please. If you have a moment . . .' Sister's voice was sarcastic.

Edward Fallon gave Cassia a last, quick smile and hurried off. She sat looking after him thoughtfully. He seemed an awful lot nicer and an awful lot less arrogant than most of the male students.

*   *   *

She had almost forgotten about him when the sergeant on the reception desk at the university building called her over as she left one evening. 'Miss Berridge! I have a note for you. Left by a young gentleman.'

'Thank you.'

'Very nice young gentleman, he was. Student at the hospital. Aren't you going to open it?'

The message was written in a well-formed, neat hand: an invitation to the medical students' Christmas ball from Edward Fallon. Cassia wondered if her coming-out dress, almost two years old now; would appear seriously out of date. She decided Edward Fallon would be most unlikely to notice even if it did.

*   *   *

'You look absolutely beautiful,' said Edward Fallon

41

and blushed. He blushed a lot, and Cassia liked it. She liked everything about him: his rather untidy good looks (greatly enhanced by his dinner jacket), his slow, gentle voice, the slightly serious interest he showed in everything she had to say, his lack of arrogance, his passion for his medical career, his extremely old-fashioned good manners.

Edward had insisted on collecting her from the house on the evening of the ball, and had a taxi cab waiting outside; it was only later that she discovered he had walked all the way to Grosvenor Gardens from Camden Town, where his digs were, that being the only way he could afford a cab to take her home again.

He was very respectful, without being obsequious, to Sir Richard, who had insisted on meeting him, and charmingly courteous to Leonora. He was clearly taken aback by the house.

The dance was held at the Students' Union. The organisers, who included Edward, he told her proudly, had worked extremely hard, dressing it up with great branches of holly and yews and an extravagance of red ribbons. The tables were decorated with holly and Christmas roses, and at suppertime the central lights were turned down and candles lit on the tables.

Edward introduced Cassia rather formally to some of his friends, and then set her down at a table with them and asked her very seriously if she would like to dance.

'Of course I would!' said Cassia. 'Isn't that why we're here?'

He was not a good dancer, which she did mind a bit, because she was very good herself. However, he was extraordinarily generous about allowing her to

42

dance with his friends, although when she and one of them gave what amounted to an exhibition of the Black Bottom, and everyone stopped to watch, he stood on the edge of the floor looking rather lost, and she promptly felt rather mean.

He saw that her glass was carefully topped up, his own remaining at a steady level (again, because he could not afford more than one additional bottle of wine, the ball ticket covering the price of one half), and asked her several times if she was warm enough.

'I'm very very warm, Edward, thank you. Even in this rather revealing dress. It was my . . . well, I first wore it in the summer. Not this summer either,' she added hastily, for she had a terror of him thinking her rich, 'last.' Which was when he had told her she looked beautiful.

'Thank you,' said Cassia lightly, and smiled into his hazel eyes.

He looked at her intently for a moment and then said, 'I mean it, you are, I'm not just saying it. I don't just say things.'

'No,' she said, serious herself now, 'I can see you don't.' It was an oddly potent moment.

Now she took to the floor only with Edward and only for the safe dances—the waltz and the occasional quickstep.

'You've obviously done a lot of dancing,' he said, as they sat back at the table.

'Oh, I learnt at school, and I went to a few dances last year.'

'So where do your parents live?'

'My father lives in Leeds. My mother died a long time ago,' she added quickly.

'And is your father as rich as your godfather?'

43

Edward said, suddenly awkward.

'Goodness, no, he's very hard up. I'm on a scholarship. It was just that my mother and Leonora were friends as children. Father was happier about me being in London if I was safely under Richard and Leonora's roof.'

'My father isn't rich either,' Edward said, after a long, careful pause.

'No,' she said lightly, 'I can tell,' and could have bitten her tongue out, for he flushed and looked down.

'I'm sorry,' Cassia said, for it was too big a gaffe to ignore, and put her hand on his. He pulled it away and began fiddling with his cufflinks. 'Edward,' she said, 'please forgive me. You misunderstood what I meant.'

'I hardly think so,' he said. 'You meant it was extremely obvious that I was hard up. I'm sorry, I'm not what you're used to, I'm sure.'

'Of course it's what I'm used to,' said Cassia, in exasperation. 'Just because I stay in that . . . that silly house in term time doesn't mean our house is like that. Our house is a very ordinary one in Leeds and I went to the local girls' high school, where my very best friend lived over her father's greengrocer shop.'

He turned to her then, and smiled his slow, careful smile. 'I know it's silly of me to be so sensitive about it, but—'

'Very silly,' said Cassia, 'when it couldn't matter less and nothing bores me more than rich people and their silly nonsense and—'

And then it happened, absurdly, melodramatically on cue.

'Cassia! Darling! How lovely to see you. I

thought it was you, and in your coming-out dress too, how too sweet.'

She looked up, recognising the voice. It was Edwina Fox-Ashley, dazzling in a silver dress, a tall silver feather in her gleaming dark hair, hanging on to the arm of a red-faced boy who was clutching a bottle of champagne. 'Why are you here, darling, who brought you?'

'Edwina, can I introduce Edward Fallon, a fellow medical student. I'm doing my first year here.'

'Good Lord, are you really? I do remember you were rather serious, but I didn't think it was going to come to anything. Archie Symington, by the way, he's a student here too. Hates it, don't you, Archie? Only doing it to keen his pa happy. Listen, darling, we have to go now, but I'll catch up with you later. Kiss kiss; And you, Edward. Lovely to meet you.'

Cassia turned back to Edward Fallon and saw, as she had known she would, an expression very close to distaste in his eyes.

'Your coming-out dress?' he said. 'Did you do all that?'

'Well, yes, I did,' said Cassia reluctantly, 'but only to—'

'Keep your pa happy?' said Edward. His voice was very cold. There was nothing she could say or do to restore the evening to its earlier happiness: absolutely nothing at all.

*　　　*　　　*

Months had passed, and Cassia had put Edward out of her head, worked hard, had fun. And then her father had died—a dreadful, unexpected, unforeseen shock—of lung cancer. Only it wasn't

45

really lung cancer, or so Cassia had always felt. It was the result of the long, lonely years, struggling to bring her up and keep his job without the help and support of his beloved Blanche—to manage without the help Cassia could, and she felt should, have given him.

She had been at dinner with Cecily and Benedict when the news came, listening to a lot of silly gossip about the Prince of Wales.

The worst thing had been the shame and the guilt. Shame that she hadn't noticed how ill he was—or had she been careful not to notice?—guilt that she had left him when he was so patently frail.

'How could I have done that?' she said to Leonora, who had come up to Leeds with her. 'How could I have just gone off, back to my stupid, beastly, selfish life, not noticed how ill he was?'

'Because, my darling—come over here, sit down, come on, have a cuddle, that's right, that's better— because that was what he wanted.'

'But he didn't. He wanted me to stay at home and be a companion to him, and I just turned my back on him. I was impatient with him at Christmas—he was getting deaf, you know, and you had to say everything quite loudly, and in the end I didn't say anything much because it was so irritating. And on my last evening I promised to sit with him and listen to a concert on the wireless and he was so looking forward to it, and then some of the girls from school turned up and asked me to go out with them for a meal, and he said go on, off you go, I'll be fine. And I did. And when I left that last morning, he was coughing, and I should have stayed, I should, Leonora, and I—'

'Sweet Pea, stop it. Listen. He had cancer. Lung

46

cancer. He would have died whether you'd been here or not. And of course he didn't want you to stay at home with him, he would have hated it. And he was lucky: he died suddenly and quite painlessly. Very often it's months, months of terrible pain—'

'Leonora, don't try and make me feel better,' said Cassia, pulling away from her in a flash of anger. 'I don't deserve it and it's impossible. Oh God! I hate myself.'

*   *   *

She got through the funeral somehow. There was a small gathering at the house afterwards. Cassia looked round the drawing room and thought it would never again seem like home, and thought too that she had never felt so alone. Only Rupert, standing at her side throughout, holding her hand, seemed to be properly with her; the rest, even Leonora and Sir Richard, were distant, almost unfamiliar figures.

*   *   *

Her father's death did one thing for her: it reunited her with Edward. He had seen Cassia standing in the reception area of the hospital, waiting for Tom Cavanagh. Edward told her how sorry he had been to hear of her loss. 'It must be terrible.'

'Yes,' she said simply; 'it is. But one just has to come to terms with it.'

'Yes, of course. I thought of writing, but . . .'

'It was very nice of you to speak to me about it,' said Cassia. 'Most people are too embarrassed. They pretend nothing's happened, or that I've had a cold or something.'

'Really?' He looked genuinely surprised. There was a long, agonising pause, then, 'I was perhaps a bit foolish that night. At the ball. About your family.'

'Oh, I don't know,' said Cassia, carefully. 'I could quite see how it seemed.'

'Could you?' he said, blushing again. 'I do hope so. Anyway—' the words were rushing out now— 'anyway, maybe you'd like to go to the cinema one night. Or don't you like the cinema? If you don't, we—'

'I love the cinema,' said Cassia. 'Thank you.'

'That's all right. Saturday, then? I'll pick you up.'

*   *   *

Cassia had been in love before, with Rupert Cameron, so she knew what she felt for Edward Fallon was not that. It wasn't painful, it didn't leave her heart thudding and her stomach churning, and so far he had had no real effect on her senses. But then the nearest they had come to sexual contact had been a few rather hesitant, tentative kisses after visits to the cinema or Lyons Corner House when he had bought her supper, and, as summer wore on, after the picnics they had in Hyde Park by the Serpentine. What she did feel in his company, however, was a clear, easy happiness; for the first time in her life she was close to someone with the same concerns, interests, ambitions and hopes. They shared political views too, being gently socialist in their views, behind the miners, against the more rigorous manifestations of the English class system. They were both determined that when they were practising as doctors they would support any scheme for bringing medical help to those who at the present time feared to seek it because of its cost. Edward was even fiercely supportive of the infiltration of women into the medical profession.

'I think you'll make a marvellous doctor,' he said earnestly to Cassia one lovely summer's evening, 'really marvellous, and whether you're male or female is neither here nor there. Why should it be?'

'No reason at all,' said Cassia, 'but tell me, Edward, how would you feel if you actually had to work for a woman? I mean, have her telling you what to do?'

'That would be—different,' he said.

'Why?'

'Well, because I feel . . .'

'Men really are the more important sex?' she said, smiling up at him.

'Not more important, but perhaps more naturally in command. I mean, that is nature, isn't it? The male of every species is dominant.'

'That's mostly for physical reasons,' said Cassia. 'You don't think they're dominant because they're cleverer, I hope?'

'No, of course not, but more—well—authoritative.'

'I see. So in twenty years' time, when I'm an Honorary and I have medical students following me on my rounds, and I'm instructing them what to do, should I only take the female ones? Because I couldn't be authoritative enough for the males?'

'No, but—'

Cassia laughed suddenly. 'It's all right, Edward. I'm only trying to catch you out. I do happen to think there will be lots of women Honoraries, and

49

they will be very authoritative, but we can wait and see.'

'Tell me,' Edward said, slightly awkwardly, 'if you were married . . . Would you go on practising?'

'Yes, of course,' she said, astonished by the question.

'Even if you had children?'

'Yes. I hope you're not telling me, Edward, that if you were married to a doctor and she had children, you'd expect her to give it all up. Why should she? And what a waste.'

'Yes,' he said, slightly doubtfully, 'yes, I suppose so. It would be a bit hard on the children, though, wouldn't it?'

'Oh. I don't know. Obviously I'd have help. But a miserable, frustrated mother isn't going to be any good to anyone, is she?'

'Why should she be miserable and frustrated?'

'Because she's not doing what she wants to do,' said Cassia impatiently.

'Surely looking after children is more important, more fulfilling, than anything else?'

'I don't agree with you at all. No, I'd be a doctor first and a mother second. My husband would just have to recognise that.'

*   *   *

She and Edward were, by the end of June, accepted as a couple. Cassia herself was slightly surprised to find this, so informally and easily had it happened.

The occasional letter from Rupert, who had gone to Hollywood to seek his fortune and had found only a succession of starlets with whom he was having a succession of apparently disastrous

50

affairs, reminded her what passion actually felt like, but served to make her grateful that its discomfort was no longer a constant companion. She was very fond of Edward, and since she was hardly looking for a husband or even a lover, he suited her admirably; indeed, she sometimes wondered if he was capable of becoming a lover at all; so gentle and passionless did he seem. And then something happened which changed everything.

*   *   *

'I've failed. I've failed my finals.'

Cassia sat looking up at Edward; at his white face, at his hands, clasped together in some kind of supplication—and could think of nothing that she could say to comfort him.

'I told my father,' he said. 'I telephoned him straight away, and he was very nice about it. It's so hard on him, on both of my parents—they've made such sacrifices to keep me here. My mother was sweet, really sweet, as mothers are, just worried I'd be upset. She said I must go home and see them, and I will, straight away. I have to sort things out, decide what to do, and . . .'

'Edward,' she said, 'Edward, come here. Come and sit down here. Please.'

She was sitting on his bed, in the small room where he lived. She had spent a lot of time in that room over the past year. She was now a fully fledged medical student herself (having passed her Second MB top of her year), and it had become a kind of second home to her, with the encouragement of his rather liberal landlady who liked her and took a most motherly interest in

51

Edward. Cassia had studied there with him, read, chatted, listened to concerts on Edward's tinny radio there; eaten mountains of sandwiches, drunk gallons of tea; welcomed Edward back, grey with exhaustion, from forty-eight-, sixty-, seventy-two-hour stints in Casualty, Obstetrics, Surgical; helped him with his notes, his thesis, his revision.

Edward came over to her and she held out her arms. He sat down on the bed beside her and buried his head on her shoulder. He stayed there in total silence for quite a long time.

'I worked so hard,' he said suddenly, sitting up, 'so terribly, terribly hard. It's so unfair; lots of people who didn't work passed. I suppose I must just be very stupid. Is that the explanation, do you think? Just not clever enough, as simple as that.'

'Edward,' Cassia said, 'of course you're clever. You're just bad at exams. You get these dreadful awful nerves, it can't be helped—'

'No,' he said, 'it can't be helped, and look what's happened, as a result of that: I've failed, and I'll go on failing.' He was growing angry now, his voice rising, angry with her. 'It's all right for you,' he said. 'You're good at exams, you thrive on them. You don't know what it's like, sitting there with your brain like bloody scrambled egg, trying to make sense of the questions. You have no idea, and you ought to have. It's easy for you and—'

Cassia stood up. 'I'm sorry, Edward, but I don't think there's much future in this conversation. Not now. I'll come back later. When you're feeling calmer.'

'No,' he said, panic in his voice, 'don't go, Cassia, please. I'm sorry, don't go. I need you here, I really do. I love you so much and—'

52

There was an absolute silence. Cassia stood there, not moving, just staring at him.

Edward stared back at her. 'Did I say that? Did I really say that?'

'Yes, you did,' she said. 'You really did.'

'Good Lord,' he said, and his slow smile began to break. 'I can't believe it. I've been wanting to say it for so long, and I couldn't. Every time saw you I would screw myself up and tell myself that this time I would, and then I couldn't, and all the time in between I'd be cursing myself and promising I would next time.'

There was another silence, then he smiled, for the first time that day.

'I love you very much. Very, very much. Oh God. Now I've embarrassed you, haven't I?'

'No,' she said, 'not at all. It's lovely.'

'Cassia, you don't think, do you, that you might love me too?'

'Yes, Edward,' she said, realising with something of a shock that she might think that, think that she did love him. 'Yes, I really think I might.'

And then because she wanted to comfort him and make him feel better; she lay down on the bed and held out her arms to him. Everything became very confused after that: he was kissing her, kissing her and caressing her, and telling her how very much he loved her, and then he turned away from her with a great sigh and said, 'No, no this is wrong.'

'Oh Edward, but you know what I think about it,' she said, for they had had several fierce arguments, in which she had outlined her view that sex was about love and not marriage.

He said that whatever she thought, it didn't

53

change what he thought, which was precisely the opposite; and they lay there for a long time quietly, just holding hands.

*   *   *

The Dean said Edward could resit the exams in a year. 'I told you so,' Cassia said.

'Yes, but it's so hard on Father, another year of keeping me. I have to pass next time, and really well; I have to.'

His father was hoping Edward would take over the local practice. The GP, a great friend, was retiring shortly; it was a point of issue, Edward said.

'He just doesn't understand how much I want to do surgery. But after this perhaps I should give in, do what he wants.'

'On something as important as that,' said Cassia firmly, 'you must do what you want.'

Edward was going home for a couple of months: he couldn't start again until September.

'And I can spend some time with David Martin, that's the GP, accompany him on his rounds, help in the dispensary. It'll be good experience. I shall miss you terribly,' he said.

'I'll miss you too,' Cassia said and meant it.

*   *   *

Halfway through August, she got a letter from Edward: his parents had asked to meet her ('I've told them so much about you') and had invited her down for the coming weekend. 'It's lovely here, I so want to show it all to you. The weather is perfect, bring a tennis racket—we can use the school courts, as of course the school is empty at the moment—and a bathing suit, just in case we get to the seaside. I could meet you on Friday night at Haywards Heath. Do come. I love you. Edward.' Cassia wrote back that she would love to.

*   *   *

The Fallons lived in a rather forbidding small house, just on the edge of the school. Every wall was covered with photographs of small boys, in groups, with Desmond Fallon.

Desmond Fallon was a deeply serious man, pompous in the way of schoolteachers, openly proud of his son, although clearly embarrassed by his temporary failure. Mrs Fallon was quiet and shy, welcoming to Cassia, and seemed almost nervous of her.

'We had hoped so very much,' Desmond Fallon said, on the very first evening, at the very first meal, 'that Edward would have qualified by now, and that I could have retired at Christmas. But it was not to be, and I feel I must support him until he wins through, which I trust he will.'

'Of course he will,' said Cassia firmly, smiling at Edward, thinking that if this was the kind of thing he had to contend with, it was not surprising he found exams an almost unimaginable ordeal. 'He's going to pass next time. He does so well generally, he's extremely highly thought of—'

'Is that so, Miss Berridge?' Barbara Fallon leaned forward, her pale blue eyes anxious. 'So it really is only a temporary problem, you think?'

'Of course it is, Mrs Fallon, and please call me

55

Cassia. Everyone is convinced he's going to be a marvellous surgeon.'

'That's very nice to hear,' said Barbara, 'isn't it, Desmond?'

'Yes, although we are actually not quite so keen for Edward to be a surgeon, Cassia. We were very much hoping that he might go into general practice, here in the village. The present doctor is a close friend of ours and it would be very good to feel that Edward was the link between the past and the future.'

'General practice is excellent,' said Cassia carefully, 'but surgery is much more exciting.'

'I did not realise one went into medicine for excitement,' said Desmond Fallon dryly.

'Oh, Mr Fallon, it is the most exciting thing in the world. Getting a diagnosis right, solving a problem, saving a patient . . .'

'Indeed? I had not seen it quite like that. Edward is not quite as articulate as you are.'

Edward smiled slightly awkwardly at his father, then at her.

'Cassia is extremely articulate,' he said. 'I wish I shared that gift. But yes, that is why I want to go into surgery, for the drama, the—'

'Good gracious,' said Barbara Fallon, 'I had always thought the whole point about medicine, family medicine at any rate, is a lack of drama, simply a good, solid contribution to the community.' She looked at Cassia rather piercingly. 'And you, Cassia, surely you don't see yourself as a surgeon? Not the sort of field a woman would want to enter, I would have imagined.'

'I do, actually,' said Cassia, smiling at her. 'I would very much like to do surgery. Probably

56

obstetrics.'

'Indeed! It must be quite unusual, even these days, for a woman to be at medical school and with such ambitions.'

'Very. Only six in my year. Seven in the following one. Of course it's getting better all the time.'

'Whether better is the word is a matter open to discussion, I would have thought.' Desmond Fallon spoke mildly, but his eyes were probing. 'I happen to think this new desire among women to have careers, rather than regarding marriage as their vocation, could be destructive. Society is built on the family, and the woman, as wife and mother, is the lynch pin that holds it together. Too many women neglecting that role, and we shall be in very serious trouble.'

'I think we can do both,' said Cassia carefully. 'Work and support the family.'

'Oh, now there I would have to disagree with you,' he said. 'Marriage is a full-time job, and it cannot work any other way.'

'We mustn't get Cassia on to this subject,' said Edward, unexpectedly. 'She is inclined to become very excited.'

Cassia stared at Edward, faintly shocked, not wishing to be rude, but feeling an absolute compulsion to continue to state her case. 'The thing is,' she said, 'the world is changing. I think we have to be open minded about these things. Don't you?'

'Yes, of course,' said Barbara carefully, and then visibly seeking to change the subject, 'I believe your own background has been quite unusual, Cassia. That you lost your own mother when you were very young. So sad.'

'Yes, it was. She died in childbirth when I was thirteen. She was a wonderful woman,' she added. 'She managed to instil in me a belief that women should lead their own lives, follow their own hearts.'

Cassia felt disproportionately upset suddenly, the memory suddenly vivid, of being there in the tiny room at the hospital looking at her mother's body, trying to relate this still, silent being, so remote and so peaceful, to the vibrantly busy, indefatigable person who had loved, disciplined, inspired and supported her; who had been a companion and friend as well as a mother; who had above all made her feel there was nothing she could not do, nothing at all, if she wanted it enough . . .

'Much of what I've achieved, I've achieved for her,' Cassia explained rather lamely into the slightly awkward silence, and blew her nose hard.

'Indeed?' said Barbara Fallon. 'How very nice.'

Silly, buttoned-up woman, thought Cassia.

Then Desmond Fallon said, 'You live in London with your godmother and her husband. Quite well-off people, as I understand?' His eyes were suddenly sharper. Ah, thought Cassia, he likes the thought that his son has found someone with rich connections.

'Yes,' she said carefully, 'yes, my godfather has a large industrial company.'

'He was knighted, I believe?'

Now why on earth would Edward have told them that? 'Yes. For services during the war, manufacturing munitions and so on.'

*   *   *

58

Next day, Cassia and Edward went on a picnic. She listened as Edward talked for a long time about his parents, about their life at the school, their position in the local community, about how important it was to them that he should live up to what they saw as their own high standards.

Finally she said, 'Edward, this is very interesting, but let's stop talking for a bit, shall we?' and lay down on the bracken carpet of the woods while he kissed her for a long time, with his long, slow, careful kisses.

'I love you,' he said, 'very much. You do love me too, don't you?'

'Edward, you know I do,' said Cassia warily. She was beginning to understand how deep his insecurity must be, why he minded so much about such things as her background, her life with Leonora and Sir Richard.

*   *   *

The Fallons went out that evening—'to a party at the Manor House,' said Barbara Fallon, clearly anxious that Cassia should understand that they did indeed mix with the very best people in the neighbourhood. 'Doris has prepared a meal for you. Only cold, I'm afraid, but—'

'I'm sure it will be delicious,' said Cassia. 'Thank you.'

The cold meal was not at all delicious: slices of lamb, salad, and bread, followed by extremely small portions of trifle, and then biscuits and cheese. The memory came to her, unbidden, halfway through the trifle, of the wonderful meals at Grosvenor

Gardens, and she was horrified to hear herself sigh.

'Are you all right?' said Edward, and yes, she said, of course, just a bit tired. And then he said what was he thinking of, he hadn't even offered her a glass of wine. He would get a bottle from the cellar. 'Father won't mind, he's very generous like that.'

Cassia found it hard to imagine Desmond Fallon being generous about anything, but she smiled and said how very nice.

The wine was a nondescript red—but it had the desired effect, cheering her up and relaxing her, and after a while, when they had cleared away and washed up, she asked if they could go and play some gramophone records.

There were a few rather old-fashioned dance records amongst them and they danced. After another couple of glasses of wine, they started kissing rather enthusiastically on the sofa, but after a few minutes Edward sat back, clearly feeling awkward.

'I'm sorry. It's just that I think they might be back quite soon.'

'Well, let's go upstairs. To your room. Or mine.'

Edward flushed. 'Oh, well, I don't know. I mean—'

'Mummy wouldn't like it. Edward, for heaven's sake. You're a grown-up. Anyway, she won't know we're both in there. She'll just think we've gone to bed early—which we might . . .' She was rather drunk, she realised. She smiled at him, leaned forward, kissed him very hard on the mouth, her tongue searching for his.

He pulled back from her. 'Cassia, you know—'

She felt a stab of irritation. 'Oh, Edward. Yes, I

60

do know, and sometimes I wonder if you really want me at all.'

'You know I do,' he said.

'I don't know anything of the sort. Actually. Prove it to me.'

'Yes, all right,' he said, and his face changed suddenly. 'Yes, I will.'

And thus it was that somehow they were lying on Edward's bed, and he was kissing her, and she was returning the kisses, and great shards of desire were moving through her, and she was feeling for him, feeling into his trousers, feeling his erection, hard, trembling, and she wanted it, very badly, wanted it in her, and she told him so, and no he said, no it was wrong. 'It's not wrong, Edward,' she cried out in a passion of frustration, kissing him hard, frantically, and then he was kissing her back, one hand up her skirt, searching, feeling for her, the other on her breast, caressing it, working at it, and then just as he raised his head, looked into her eyes, said, 'Oh, God, I love you,' the door of the bedroom opened, and over Edward's shoulder she saw Desmond Fallon's face staring at her in a mixture of disbelief and distaste. And then heard, incredulous, Edward's voice as he rolled off her, struggled into a sitting position, Edward's voice saying, 'Father, I'm sorry, sorry if you're upset, but—well, we are going to be married.'

* * *

She would have thought, had she been asked, that she would have denied it herself, then and there, said no we're not, that has nothing to do with it, but she was so taken aback, so humiliated, so

61

absolutely diminished in herself by what had happened, that she went along with it.

Desmond said he was shocked that a son of his could behave in such a way, that he would like to see him downstairs, and left them.

Edward looked at Cassia sheepishly, and said nothing while she looked back at him, wanting to say that they were not going to be married, it was not true, but not liking to in the face of his embarrassment and distress.

Finally he said, 'Perhaps we should tidy up and go downstairs.'

'No, Edward,' she said, 'I am not going downstairs. I'm sorry to leave you to face them, but I feel upset. I am going to bed. Please explain.'

He said he would and left the room, looking utterly dejected. Cassia heard him in the bathroom and went along to her own room, where she crawled rather miserably under the covers. Greatly to her surprise, she slept.

*   *   *

In the morning she awoke to a strong sense of remorse, mingled with panic. Things had to be resolved.

She got up and had a bath, dressed and then packed her case. The best thing, she felt, would be to leave as soon as possible, first making clear that Edward's announcement of the night before had been in error. She went downstairs cautiously and into the dining room. Desmond and Barbara were not there but Edward was standing at the sideboard helping himself to bacon. He turned and smiled at her.

'Cassia. Good morning! Did you sleep well?'

'Yes. Thank you. Surprisingly so. Edward—'

He interrupted her. 'I had a very good conversation with my parents last night. They've been marvellous, quite marvellous. Very broadminded, even my mother. I think they think—well—' he smiled, slightly bashfully—'that I'm just a red-blooded young man. Doing what comes naturally.'

'But we weren't doing anything.'

'I know, but it was obvious what might have happened.'

'I see,' she said, her voice cool. 'And what am I if you're a red-blooded young man? A trollop?'

'No, of course not. They said, once they'd calmed down, they liked you very much. They are very impressed by you.'

'How nice,' she said.

'Yes,' he said, clearly missing the irony in her voice, 'and they said long engagements did put young people under a lot of strain. That they could remember what it was like to be young.'

'But there hasn't been a long engagement.'

'I know, but it helped to imply that there had. Unofficially, of course. And they seem quite happy about it.'

'Edward, there isn't anything to be happy about. We're not—'

The door opened, and Desmond Fallon came in. He nodded at her briefly, said good morning and that he and Barbara were going to church. 'It would be nice if you would join us.'

'I will, of course,' said Edward. 'Cassia? Will you?'

He looked so desperate that she said she would.

63

When they got back, she could sort things out.

The church was packed. After the service various friends came up to the Fallons. To her surprise they introduced her to all of them, very courteously, and in Barbara's case quite proudly; told them she was at the hospital studying with Edward.

'A couple of years behind him, of course,' Barbara added carefully each time, as if it was unthinkable that they should be at the same stage.

Desmond said each time, 'Very unusual for a woman to be studying medicine, of course.'

It began to occur to her that in the world in which the Fallons moved, a woman medical student was something rather impressive.

When they got back to the house, Desmond and Barbara disappeared.

'Edward,' Cassia said urgently, 'we must talk and then I want to go.'

'Go! Go where?'

'Back to London. I can't stay here. It's too difficult for me, besides—'

'Ah, there you are.' Desmond Fallon was almost smiling. 'Come into the drawing room, we'd like to say a few words.'

She looked desperately at Edward, but he was smiling encouragingly, had taken her arm, was ushering her into the room. Barbara stood by a side table; there was a bottle of champagne on it, and four glasses. Desmond went over and opened it with a flourish, poured it out, handed her one. It was warm, and very sweet; she tried to look enthusiastic.

'Well,' Desmond said, still looking at Edward, 'congratulations. To both of you. Of course you're very young, but you're obviously very serious about each other.'

'Mr Fallon—' Cassia began.

'No. Don't say another word,' Desmond said. 'Of course you have a long wait ahead of you. There can be no question of marriage until Edward is fully qualified. And—' he gave her a look that was almost conspiratorial—'I dare say your views on working women and marriage will change. So here's a toast. To the two of you. And the future.'

'The future,' said Barbara.

It seemed impossibly cruel to say there wasn't going to be a future. Or not of the kind they envisaged.

Edward took Cassia to the station later that day; Desmond lent him the car. They were early and sat waiting for the train.

Cassia took a deep breath. 'Edward, we're not engaged, and you know we're not. You should never have—'

'But we could be. We should be. All I've done is bring it forward a bit. I love you. Very much. And you love me.'

'Edward . . .'

'You do, don't you?' he said, and he looked so hurt, so anxious, that she was frightened. 'You said you loved me.'

'I do love you, but—'

'Well, then. What could be more wonderful and more natural than getting married? Cassia, if I have you, I can do anything, I know I can. I love you so much, and I'm so happy.' He smiled down at her. 'You know, it was just as well it happened like it did. I'd never have plucked up the courage to ask you in cold blood, so to speak. Oh, look, here's the train now. Let's find you a seat. Come on.'

There was a friend of his parents on the platform, a bluff, noisy man Cassia had met outside the church. He said he'd join her if she didn't mind. Cassia said of course she didn't, and gave up all hope of explaining to Edward until she saw him again in London.

And that had been the fatal, irrevocable mistake.

CHAPTER THREE

'My darling, you look simply wonderful.'

Cassia smiled up at Rupert, thought how untrue it was; thought he, on the other hand, did look rather wonderful, and how unfair that men, even when they were in their mid-fifties as Rupert most definitely was, could still be so extremely attractive while women at the same age were old.

And oh God, he was attractive. The silvery blond hair was as thick as ever, the blue eyes as brilliant, the wonderful, chiselled features as sharp, the tall body as slim. Somehow he always managed, even though he had never had very much money, to look as if he was in the hands of a good valet and a fine tailor. It was all part of his gift, part of his charm: the actor's charm. Just as he bestowed upon any gathering pleasure and humour, so he bestowed upon his surroundings an interest and a kind of grace. Today, he was wearing a dark grey pinstripe suit, which would have looked very ordinary without the striped black and pink silk tie—tied in the Prince of Wales knot, of course.

Cassia stood drinking him in, thinking how much

66

she still loved and missed him. 'Oh, Rupert,' she said simply, 'it's so lovely to see you.'

'And you, my darling. And you look quite marvellous. I love that hat.'

'Do you? I bought it early this morning. I thought I couldn't let Leonora down, so I went to Harvey Nichols as a sort of memorial gesture to her. Is it really all right?'

'It's perfect. It looks expensive.'

'It was. Very,' she said, and smiled at him. It was a reckless smile. She had felt reckless as she wrote the cheque, glancing constantly at the hat as it lay, still untissued, in its box: black straw, shallow crowned and huge brimmed, with a wide red ribbon, tied in a most outrageously theatrical bow.

'Where's Edward?'

'He couldn't come.'

'Well,' Rupert said, bending to kiss her, 'I shall play the role of husband-by-proxy. With the greatest of pleasure, I might add. How would that be?'

'It would be lovely, Rupert, thank you.'

'Right, then. Take my arm. Now shall we go inside, or are you waiting for Benedict and Cecily? I am very nervous about my reading, I can tell you.'

'Rupert, you don't know what nerves are,' said Cassia, laughing. 'What have you chosen?'

'The lovely thing from Revelations, you know?'

Cassia shook her head. 'No. I'm not very godly, I'm afraid.'

'Well, it will be a nice surprise for you. Ah, here is Benedict now. And Cecily. Will you excuse me a moment, darling, I just want to have a final look at my reading. I'll join you inside. Keep a place for me.'

'Cassia, my dear,' said Benedict Harrington, kissing her. 'How nice you look. Doesn't she, Cecily?'

'Marvellous,' said Cecily. 'Lovely hat, Cassia.'

'Do you like it? I thought it might be a bit frivolous.'

'Well, if it was, which it isn't, no matter. This is a memorial service, not a funeral,' said Cecily firmly, 'and Leonora's life was dedicated to frivolity.'

Cassia smiled at her, bent to kiss her. Cecily was at least six inches shorter than Cassia, deliciously, voluptuously pretty, her capacity for prattle a dazzling disguise for a sharp, clear intelligence.

Benedict was a most vivid evocation of Leonora: they were—well, had been—almost Shakespearean in their brother-and-sister alikeness. As she looked at him, Cassia drew back, shut out the associations, the memory of Harry Moreton at her coming-out dance, telling her the unspeakable, the shocking, spoiling what had until then been so perfect, so magical an occasion. She smiled at Benedict, determinedly blotting out the memory. 'This is a wonderful occasion, Benedict. I'm so glad you thought of it.'

'She deserved it,' he said simply.

'Yes, she did,' said Cassia, and surprised herself by kissing him again. She tended to forget, they all did, how much he had loved Leonora.

Benedict smiled down at her, then turned as he heard his name.

It was the Fox-Ashleys. Sir Marcus tall and elegant in his morning suit, his wife dangerously chic, her voice rising above the rest of the rather subdued chatter that was going on.

'Benedict, dear, what a turn-out. Of course

68

people never can resist this sort of thing, can they?'

'Can't they?' said Benedict, smiling at her with his unfailing courtesy. 'Well, I'm very pleased you couldn't, Sylvia. How lovely you look. Where is Edwina, by the way?'

'Oh, somewhere over there,' said Sylvia. 'She's in a frightful bait. Harry insisted on riding this morning. Edwina was simply furious with him, but don't worry, he'll be here. He's frightfully tickled about being asked to read, sweet of you.'

'He was Leonora's cousin, after all.'

'Yes, I suppose. So complex, your family. Oh, Cassia, I didn't see you. Lovely hat, dear.'

'Thank you,' said Cassia. 'Benedict, shall we go in?' She had only one wish in that moment: to be in her place, safely settled with the Harringtons, before Harry Moreton arrived.

*   *   *

The church was packed. She was surprised, as was Benedict; 'I didn't think so many would come. It's marvellous. Oh, Cassia, good heavens, it's Richard.'

Cassia felt tears sting behind her eyes. 'I'm so glad,' she said, staring at Sir Richard, with his new wife, Margaret, so unlike Leonora, so uncompromisingly sensible and clever.

Sir Richard came over to the pew, bent down and kissed her.

'Good morning, my dear. Lovely to see you.'

'Lovely to see you too, Godpa. I'm so pleased you're here.'

The organ began to play the wonderful lyrical ripples of 'Jesu, Joy of Man's Desiring'. He patted

69

her hand. 'See you afterwards.'

'Thank God,' said Benedict suddenly in her ear. 'Harry's arrived.'

With an extraordinary effort of will, she didn't look round.

There were prayers, hymns, the twenty-third psalm, then Rupert stood at the lectern and began, in his low, resonant actor's voice, the lovely lines from Revelations: 'And behold, I saw a new heaven and a new earth.'

As he finished, reading, 'There shall be no more death, neither sorrow nor crying,' Cassia felt her grief fill her, wound her. She bit her lip until it almost bled, to silence the rising sobs, grasped Cecily's hand, scarcely realising she did so, and she watched Harry Moreton walk to the nave, and turn to look at the congregation through a great veil of tears. His dark eyes fell on Cassia; recognised but did not acknowledge her, did not look away either. He stood there completely still, for a long time, and then finally opened the book he was holding, and began to read.

'Ecclesiastes,' he said, 'chapter three,' and paused for another long while. 'To every thing there is a season, and a time to every purpose under the heaven. A time to be born, and a time to die . . .'

His deep heavy voice was immensely moving. Cassia sat, her eyes closed now, remembering when their strange, dangerous, difficult relationship had begun; thinking of that tall, sulky boy brought to have tea and to play with her on her first visit to London.

*   *   *

70

'Harry is my second cousin,' Leonora had said. 'You'll get on with him awfully well.'

It didn't seem very likely, Cassia thought looking at Harry, dressed so oddly she had thought in a silk shirt and short trousers, his dark curls too long, his brown eyes heavy with distaste both for her and the occasion.

She had gone forward, smiling, and said, 'Hallo, I'm Cassia.'

Harry had shaken her hand but not returned the smile. He sat down in a chair and stared out into the garden.

'What would you like to do?' Cassia said.

'I really don't care,' he said.

'We could play Ludo. Or a card game. If you like.'

'I hate games' he said, picking up a copy of the *Illustrated London News* and flicking through it.

'We could go for a walk in the garden.'

'It's raining.'

She had given up at that, become cross. She sat down at the jigsaw-puzzle table and started to do one. After a while Jarvis, Leonora's maid, had come in and said would they like tea. Sitting at the table in silence, watching Harry eat his way silently through a pile of sandwiches, she tried again.

'This is very nice cake, isn't it?' she said through a mouthful.

'It's all right.'

'Are you on holiday from school, like me? Where do you go to school?'

'I don't go to school,' he said. 'I have a tutor. Until I go to Eton, of course.'

'Isn't that a bit dull? Lonely?'

71

'Not at all. I prefer adult company.'

Cassia had had enough. 'Aren't you a little old,' she said, 'to have a nurse?' He had arrived with a uniformed nanny.

'No,' he said. 'Someone has to take care of me.'

'What about your mother?'

'I don't have a mother. She died when I was born.'

Compassion filled Cassia. 'I'm so sorry, Harry,' she said, 'how dreadful for you.'

Harry Moreton looked at her, his expression more hostile still. 'Not at all,' he said. 'I never knew her, after all.'

'No, but what about your father? I suppose you spend a lot of time with him.'

'I don't have a father. He was killed at the Battle of the Marne. When I was eight.'

Cassia looked at him in silent horror for a moment, then stood up and walked out of the room.

'I just couldn't bear it,' she was to explain to him, years later, 'that you had to endure this awful thing, live in this awful way, and nobody had thought, bothered to tell me something so important.'

When Leonora came to find her on her return much later that night, she was extremely angry. 'Cassiopeia—' and that was a measure of her anger, using her full name—'how dare you treat Harry so rudely? I understand you left him at the tea table, never to return.'

'He was very rude to me. Very rude and unfriendly.'

'However he behaved, he was a guest in this house, and it was your duty to be courteous.'

'I did try. Honestly, Leonora. And why didn't

you tell me that he has no parents?'

'I didn't think it would matter to you,' said Leonora, 'one way or the other.'

'Of course it matters,' said Cassia, indignant herself now. 'It matters terribly. It explains such a lot. Who does look after him anyway?'

'Oh, servants,' said Leonora. 'There are plenty of people in the house.'

'No grandparents even?'

'Well, Harry's maternal grandfather does live there, but he has nothing to do with Harry. He has never forgiven Harry for killing his daughter, as he sees it. As soon as Harry goes to school, his grandfather will move back into his own house.'

'And he'll live alone? Just with servants?'

'He does more or less already.'

'Oh,' said Cassia. Her mind was whirling at the horror of Harry's wretched, lonely, unloved life. 'Leonora, I'm sorry if I was rude. I'll—I'll write to him, make my apologies.'

Cassia had written to Harry, a stumbling, awkward note. He had not replied, and she had not seen him again for two years.

*　　　*　　　*

'A time to be born, and a time to die.' Harry had read the words again at the end of his text, to make it the more poignant; he closed the Bible now, stood looking at them again, and then walked slowly back to his place by Edwina. As he passed Cassia, he looked at her thoughtfully, as if he did not know quite what to make of her. She met his eyes, those deep dark eyes, steadily, and did not look away.

73

A buffet luncheon was set out in the dining room at
Eaton Place, the French windows open to the warm
golden air. The garden was studded with small
tables, which were filling now with groups of
people, all chattering, laughing, kissing. Staff
moved through the crowd with trays of canapés,
filling and refilling glasses with champagne.
Vintage, thought Cassia, studying the labels with
open curiosity, marvelling at the sheer, absurd
generosity of it all.

'Godpa, hello,' she said, going up to Richard.

'My darling child, how lovely to see you. And
how well you look. Margaret has had to leave, one
of her charity committees, you know. I would have
preferred to go home, but I didn't want to appear
unfriendly. I was quite saddened, you know,' he
said, his fierce old face softened suddenly, 'by
Leonora's death. I had been so very fond of her,
and I felt perhaps I handled it all badly. I don't
know.'

'You did what you thought best,' said Cassia.

'Indeed, but what we think the best can be
actually the worst. I think I was the wrong husband
for her all along. Sadly.'

'Godpa, you weren't. She loved you very much. I
know she did.'

'Not as much as she loved you. You really were
the light of her life. The child she never had. Poor
Leonora . . . My dear, I must be going now. Come
and see me some time, won't you?'

'Yes . . . Um, Godpa?'

'Yes, my dear?'

'Leonora . . . I expect you know, she left me some money.' She felt she ought to tell him, that it would be somehow wrong not to; and then she looked at him, as she told him, and was disconcerted by what she saw: an expression of— what? Shock? No. Surprise? Yes. Disbelief? Almost. And then a careful ironing-out, a smooth, bland smile.

'How very nice. I'm delighted. I told you, you were the child she never had. Well, don't waste it, my dear. Put it towards a holiday, or some clothes, or a little car of your own perhaps. That's what she would have wanted.'

She felt awkward now, unable to say that he didn't understand, it had been a lot of money.

She stood watching Sir Richard's tall, beautifully dressed figure moving across the buzzing room, between all the other beautifully dressed figures, Thinking how very different this was from her life now; from what she had come to expect, to see as normal.

'Cassia?' It was Harry Moreton's voice behind her.

She turned round slowly, reluctantly.

'How are you?'

'I'm very well, thank you, Harry. I liked your reading very much.'

'Good,' he said carelessly. She felt, unwillingly, the tug, hard, harsh, deep within herself, towards him and his sexuality; tried and failed also to avoid his eyes. He smiled, recognising it, clearly savouring it.

'It's extremely good to see you,' he said after a charged silence. 'I was so pleased you could come.'

'Of course I came. And I thought the service was

75

wonderful. I thought perhaps that Rollo Gresham might have been here.'

'Well, you were wrong,' Harry said shortly. He was hostile to Gresham, and Cassia wondered why. 'Is the doctor not here?' he said suddenly.

'No, he had a baby to deliver,' she said shortly.

'How very exemplary. Well, now, tell me how it's all going: life in the country, the family, all of it.'

'It's all going very well,' she said, 'and the family's fine.'

'I'm delighted to hear it. And what are you doing with yourself? Any medicine?'

'Oh, there's no time for that,' she said, quickly. 'I have the house to run, and I'm very involved with village life, of course, the various committees and so on.'

'Oh, dear,' he said, 'that sounds a little worthy.'

'Harry,' she said, 'there is nothing wrong with worthiness.'

'I think I would disagree with you there,' he said, smiling, his eyes malicious. 'I think there is a great deal wrong with worthiness. Worthiness is tedious, dull, self-congratulatory. And unattractive.'

'And I suppose,' she said, 'that unworthiness has great virtues in your eyes, does it?'

'Oh, indeed it does. It's amusing for a start. Its practitioners have a certain charm. It could even be called challenging. And it certainly isn't self-congratulatory.'

'It isn't of much value either,' she said.

'I would disagree again. There is great value in amusement. And charm.'

'This is a ridiculous conversation,' she said; and then saw that he was grinning at her.

'Oh, I'd forgotten,' he said, reaching out his

76

hand, patting her arm, 'I'd forgotten how wonderful it was to tease you.'

'It's nice to see you,' she said suddenly, forgetting to be careful, surprised at herself.

'It's nice to see you too. Oh, Lord. Edwina's coming for me. We have to go. What a pity, when you've finally been allowed out for a day.'

'Of course I'm allowed out,' she said irritably. 'I just don't have that sort of time. Life in a country practice is very busy.'

'I see. Well, we had better part, I suppose.' He took her hand, and bent and kissed her cheek, then stood back studying her. 'That is a most wonderful hat, and it looks quite horribly expensive. I'm surprised a doctor's salary can run to such a thing.'

CHAPTER FOUR

'Cecily and Benedict have asked us to go and stay with them,' said Cassia. 'In the South of France.'

'France?' said Bertie. 'Can we go? We just started French at school and—'

'Bertie, of course we can't go. Any of us. Least of all you.'

'Yes, he could,' said Cassia quickly. 'He's invited. We all are.'

Edward flushed. 'Clearly it's out of the question.'

'Why is it out of the question?'

'Cassia, I can't possibly leave the practice. I can't afford a locum, and the fare to France for all of us would be very expensive. I—' And then he looked at her, and she knew what he was thinking: that she could pay for them, could pay for anything now . . .

'Yes,' she said quickly, 'you're right, I should have thought.'

* * *

Later that morning, surprising herself, she phoned Mr Brewster. 'I just wondered how long it might be before I could have access to the money. A bit of it, that is.'

'A couple of months, I should have thought. Why, did you have something particular in mind?'

'Oh no. I just wondered, that's all. I mean, we might be doing some work on the house and—'

'Mrs Fallon, any bank would make you a loan on the basis of the will. You have only to put them in touch with me, no need to wait. Really.'

* * *

Edward came in at lunchtime in a bad temper. 'Cassia, I would be grateful if you could be more available when I'm doing a big surgery like that. Twice I wanted something made up and you weren't around. It can't be so difficult to spend your mornings in the house, surely.'

'Edward, I had a lot to do this morning,' said Cassia.

'I can't see why any of that could not have waited,' said Edward. 'It's just a matter of organisation, surely. You used to be so good with your time.'

Cassia counted up to ten and then, feeling it was best got out of the way, added that she wouldn't be in the house the following morning either because of the dentist.

'For God's sake,' said Edward, 'is it really beyond the bounds of possibility for you to arrange such things in the afternoons? I cannot run this practice without your help and—Look, I have to go, I'll see you later.'

*   *   *

'Mrs Venables, I won't be able to do the flowers next week, I'm afraid. I'm going away.'

'Away, Mrs Fallon? Where to?'

'France.'

'Good gracious. The doctor didn't mention it when I saw him last night.'

'The doctor isn't coming.'

'Oh, I see,' said Mrs Venables.

You don't, you don't see at all, thought Cassia, putting down the phone and gazing at the threadbare carpet. She seemed to have spent a lot of time looking at that carpet over the past few days as she had made all her phone calls: to Cecily, to Mr Brewster, to the travel agent, to Harrods— Harrods for heaven's sake, ordering holiday clothes for the children. It was easier than taking them all shopping, dreadfully easy in fact. She had just opened an account, and given their sizes, and asked for a selection of shirts and shorts and swimsuits and sunhats, which had all arrived four days later. Then she had gone up to London for a dizzy day, feeling sick with guilt and excitement, to buy things for herself: a couple of linen dresses, some of the new wide slacks and loose knitted silk jersey tops, sandals, a new bathing suit, a huge-brimmed sunhat and a long pale pink crepe dress for the evening, just in case they went into Nice. It seemed an awful

79

lot of clothes for six days, more than she had bought in six years.

Mrs Venables couldn't possibly see what those six days represented, and indeed Cassia was trying very hard not to see it for herself: not just the taking of a well-earned rest, not even just a bid for independence, but a blow, a harsh, swift blow at the soft underbelly of her marriage, the first time in its six-year history that she had defied Edward, done what she wanted and what he did not want her to do. Edward would be fine: he would still have Peggy to look after him, and Mrs Briggs, and the whole village would rally round.

But of course it was to do with the money. That was what the row had been about: not that she was going, not that Edward would be left on his own, not that he had accused her of wanting to get away from him; not even, in his words, that he did not know why she should want to go without him. It was to do with the money. And Edward, sitting quietly, anxious to be conciliatory after his initial hostile outburst, at last said that he thought she did actually deserve a break, agreeing that yes, it was a good idea, had also known that it was to do with the money.

*   *   *

'Isn't it lovely?' said Cecily. She was standing by the pool with Cassia and Fanny.

'It's beautiful,' said Cassia, smiling, 'quite, quite perfect.'

The pool was built into a white-tiled terrace edged with olive trees and trailing bougainvillaea about a hundred yards below the house. The staff were preparing the area for the evening, lighting lanterns, setting small tables, carrying out glasses, cocktail shakers, a gramophone, records. Below the pool terrace a lawn reached out towards the sea, edged with tall pines and oleanders; the air was thick with the heavy scent of flowers, mingled with the lighter one of herbs.

'We usually have drinks here,' said Cecily. 'Our neighbours from the next villa are joining us this evening, terribly nice. Nothing formal. Then we have dinner up there.' Cassia looked up: more staff were setting a long table on a second wide terrace. The house was ravishing: palest pink, with curving balconies and an almost flat tiled roof.

Bertie appeared on one of the top balconies and waved. 'Mummy! Come up here, it's like a boat.'

'I'd better go back to them,' said Cassia. 'Delia's probably screaming her head off and—'

'Nanny will deal with Delia,' said Cecily. 'Fanny darling, you go and bring Bertie and William down here. They'd probably like a swim before they go to bed. Now, Cassia, sit down. Cocktail, champagne . . . you say.'

'Oh goodness. Champagne, please. If you'll join me.'

'Of course I will, although I mustn't drink too much. Doctor's orders.'

'Really? Why?'

'I'm in the club again.'

'Oh Cecily.' Cassia leaned forward and kissed her. 'How lovely. I'm so pleased. How do you feel?'

'Oh, not too bad. I just hope that this time it's a boy. Keep Benedict happy.' And there's a piece of irony, Cecily thought, reaching for her cigarette case and lighter. What a thing to say. How horribly, hideously appropriate.

She was lucky, Cecily knew, to have conceived again. The opportunities were few enough. Mostly she was very patient, but one night, a few months ago, she had become very upset. She hadn't said anything, of course, but she had heard him on the phone, having what seemed a rather odd conversation. As it turned out, it was perfectly innocent, but he had known why she was upset, had come to her room, had tried, silently, to comfort her, and she had suddenly wanted him very much and he had responded to her. He had lain beside her afterwards, holding her in his arms, telling her how much he loved her, how lucky he knew he was.

When she had told him a few weeks later she was pregnant, he had been, as always, wonderfully, overwhelmingly happy. Of course there was more than one reason for his happiness: it wasn't just because he loved his children, loved fatherhood—it was the fact that he could prove to the world yet again that here he was, a happily married, family man.

Oh God, thought Cecily, throwing back her head, smiling carefully at Cassia, a suddenly slightly blurred Cassia, how hard she earned all this: the beautiful houses, the servants, the luxurious background to her difficult, dangerous life.

'It's not easy, you know,' she said suddenly, 'what I have to live with. Always worried, always afraid. Thinking people know—I just hope that—' She visibly shook herself, smiled at Cassia. 'That it really is all over. That he's all right now.'

'You can't talk about it to him?'

'Oh, good heavens, no. It's always been my cardinal rule. Ignore it, pretend it was never there.

That's the only way he—we—can be safe. And I think it's all right. I think he's happy, don't you?'

'I think he's very happy,' said Cassia, 'thanks to you.'

'And you, Cassia, are you happy?'

Cassia was almost shocked by the question and its unexpectedness; called her face, her voice under careful, steely control. 'Of course I am. Terribly happy. How could I not be?'

'Oh, I just wondered. Not everyone is. And you do have quite a difficult life,' said Cecily quickly.

'Nonsense, it's not difficult at all. Oh, I know we don't have lots of money, and . . .' she paused, wondering if this was the moment to tell Cecily, or at least to find out if she knew, then changed her mind '. . . money and help and things, but that doesn't bother me. I'm very lucky and very happy,' she finished, hoping the speech didn't sound too carefully written.

'Good,' said Cecily lightly, 'that's what I hoped you'd say. It's lovely to have you here. Thank you for coming.'

'I'm loving it. Thank you for asking me.'

*   *   *

The days slid past: golden, idyllic, hedonistic. Three were gone before Cassia had begun to grow idle. However, she woke on the Sunday to find it already eleven, and the villa strangely quiet. She put on her bathing suit under her robe and went down to the first terrace.

Smith, one of the maids from the London house, smiled at her. 'Good morning, madam. Mrs Harrington asked me to tell you they have gone to

83

meet friends from the railway station. And Nanny has taken the children for a walk. Would you like some breakfast, madam?'

'Just some coffee.'

She sat sipping it, her face raised to the hot sun. God, how was she going to face real life after this? Even Delia had hardly grizzled once in the last forty-eight hours. In less than two days they had to leave, make their way home to England. Monks Heath. And Edward. Oh God. To Edward.

*   *   *

She had waited that autumn for Edward to come back to London, so that she could clear things up once and for all. Her life was clear, purposeful. This year she would do Casualty and Surgery or Obstetrics. She sat in her room at Grosvenor Gardens, ticking off the words, the magical words, over and over again.

The night Edward came back she went to see him. He was already tense, nervous: he had an interview with the Dean next day. 'A lot hangs on that. I have to impress him, make him believe I can do it.'

It didn't seem fair to have The Conversation, to worry him, make him more nervous.

The next day Edward was allotted a place in Casualty. He was on duty for seventy-two hours, without a break. When he came off he was grey with fatigue. She couldn't have The Conversation then either.

The pattern continued: always a reason not to speak, not to upset Edward. Constantly exhausted, with a clear need to study at the same time,

Edward was in no condition to discuss the future. When he was doing something slightly less stressful, then they could talk. There was no rush.

She got three days off at Christmas; Edward was on duty the entire time. They spent Christmas evening together, in his small room in Casualty, eating turkey sandwiches.

'I couldn't get through this without you,' he said, leaning forward, kissing her. 'I really couldn't. I love you so much.'

She couldn't spoil what pleasure there was for him in his Christmas.

*   *   *

Shortly after Christmas Cassia was moved on to a surgical ward. Her Honorary was Horace Amstruther, one of the most distinguished surgeons of his day, famously eccentric.

Cassia was extremely lucky, she knew, to have been allotted to him; nevertheless it was a terrifying ordeal, entailing long hours in the operating theatre, observing the great man at work, turning her observations into a written report, and frequently being subjected to a public humiliation across the table.

Nevertheless, Cassia loved the theatre: the intensity of the atmosphere, the fierce concentration, the ongoing danger, the terrifying discoveries. Her personal life seemed of very little importance.

In the spring, Edward was moved onto Obstetrics. His finals were looming, and he was in an appalling state, working ninety-six hours on occasion and trying to study as well.

Edward did pass his finals, but only just. Not well enough to win him a place as a houseman at St Christopher's, not well enough therefore for him to go on and do surgery. The best he could hope for was a post at a general hospital, and from there, general practice. He sat staring at Cassia, facing the dreadful disappointment of his future. That night, they made love for the first time; she felt it was the only thing she could do to comfort him. That too was a disappointment—to her. He lay in her arms, and alternately castigated himself and told her he loved her and that she was wonderful.

He got a job as houseman at a hospital in Harrow. He hated it. Cassia didn't see him very often, every third weekend at the most. It was a relief: because he was so unhappy; because she was so wonderfully, ecstatically absorbed, working in Obstetrics.

When they did meet, briefly, usually in his digs near the hospital, they talked little, and certainly not of the future, his being too uncertain, hers too threatening.

They made love whenever possible; that at least began to be good. Cassia, discovering her body, its hungers, its capacity for pleasure, could be uninhibited and demanding in bed at least. Edward was more tentative, still instinctively guilty, but became slowly skilful.

*　　　*　　　*

She discovered she was pregnant the week she began her finals. She was disbelieving, sure it was the stress keeping her period from coming, causing the nausea. She had always been so careful, had consulted a woman doctor who had fitted her with a cap and instructed her in the use of it.

*　　　*　　　*

'I'm pregnant,' she said, staring at him across his small room, wondering why he was smiling, looked so happy.

'I think I've got a practice,' he said, seeming not to have heard her. 'Not in our village, but near there. Father is lending me the money to buy it.'

'Good,' she said, 'I'm so glad,' and then, 'Edward, I'm pregnant.'

'That's all right,' he said, as if she had said she wanted a cup of tea. 'That's perfectly all right. We can get married now. It doesn't matter—in fact it's wonderful.'

And she had stood there, staring at him, wondering at his blindness, his stupidity, and much too unhappy for both of them to tell him she had passed her finals with outstandingly high marks and been offered a house job at St Christopher's.

*　　　*　　　*

And so the nightmare had really begun. She had thought, initially, she would have a termination— but the child was not just hers: it was Edward's, and she knew she must consult him. Edward was

87

deeply, horribly distressed.

'It's alive,' he kept saying, staring at her in disbelief, 'our child. You can't do that, Cassia, you can't just kill it. I cannot believe you could even think of such a thing.'

'But,' she cried out in agony, 'but there's my life, my career. I want to do surgery, and I can, I—'

'Yes, I know you can,' he said, looking at her, his eyes full of terrible pain. 'You can do what I can't. I know that.'

'Edward, it isn't like that.' God, how could she make him feel better, less diminished, less humiliated?

'Yes, it is,' he said, 'and you can't make it any different. You are cleverer than me, you can do better than me, you can do anything you want, and I can't. Well, how very nice for you, Cassia, how very, very nice.'

Edward's misery was shocking. 'You said you loved me,' he said, over and over again. 'What has happened? What did I do?'

'I do love you,' Cassia said, consumed by guilt, 'I do. I just don't know that I can marry you.'

'But why not? What's changed? You said you would.'

'No,' she said, 'I never did. Actually.'

'You never said you wouldn't. All I've done, all I've endured, this past three years has been for you. Loving you has kept me sane. You've no idea how often I nearly cracked, gave in. And then I just kept on thinking; no, one day it will be worth it.'

'Don't, Edward, please.'

'You can't shut me up,' he said, angry suddenly, 'just because it suits you. You have to know.'

88

*　　　*　　　*

She went to see Rupert, to discuss it with him, as she did everything in her life.

'You can't just do what you want,' he said simply. 'Life isn't like that. You have responsibilities—the child, Edward's happiness and ultimate success, your own. Go your own way now and you will wreck three lives.'

'It's all right for you,' she said. 'You're free, you can do what you want. You've never seen your career threatened.'

'Cassia, you're talking like a child,' he said, his face sterner than she could ever remember. 'You have to give in to life sometimes. Edward loves you, and you love him. That is what matters, that is what you must hang on to.'

*　　　*　　　*

In the end, worn out with guilt, self distaste, physical sickness and a longing to have it settled, she said she would marry Edward. She was mad not to, she told herself: Edward loved her, and of course she loved him. There was their child to consider. They were compatible in every single possible way; there was no reason not to marry him. And she was a qualified doctor, Edward told her, she told herself; in a few years, she could begin again, not as a surgeon, but in general practice, perhaps, specialising even in obstetrics. All was not lost; it was simply delayed.

*　　　*　　　*

She was married, perversely, from her grandmother's house in Halifax. It was the only way she could see to keeping it small, controlled. A handful of guests: none of the London people, just Rupert, a tiny group from the medical school, Benedict and Cecily. Leonora refused to come: she said she would be the spectre at the feast. Cassia pleaded to no avail.

Sir Richard gave her away and a month later they moved to Monks Heath, where she was known simply as the doctor's wife.

*   *   *

'Well, well, well, it's the doctor's wife.'

Cassia opened her eyes. The voice was instantly recognisable, the face, with the blazing sun behind it, a dark blur.

'You really shouldn't be lying there, in this sun, in that rather revealing bathing suit,' said Harry Moreton. 'Very pretty incidentally, but you're getting burnt.'

'I went to sleep,' she said, trying not to sound sulky, knowing he was right.

'Perhaps you should put a robe on. Here, is this yours?'

'Yes. Thank you. I didn't know you were coming today,' she said, pulling it on, wincing slightly, for her shoulders were indeed burnt. She was cross with Cecily for keeping his arrival from her.

'I didn't know either. We had planned to come next week. But then suddenly we thought we'd come today. London is deadly hot, nobody there. Got the Golden Arrow all the way. Marvellous trip.'

90

'Yes, I know. I came that way too,' said Cassia.

'Oh really?'

'Yes. Are you surprised?'

'No, of course not. Nothing you did would surprise me, Cassia.'

'I just might see that as a challenge,' she said lightly. 'Edwina, hello.'

Edwina Moreton was striding down the steps from the house. She looked tired and irritable. 'God, it's hot. Hallo, Cassia. You are terribly burnt.'

'Yes, I know,' said Cassia.

'I can't find anyone to unpack for us, and I want a drink, and—'

'Perhaps you could unpack for yourself. At least, as far into your luggage as your bathing things.' Harry's expression as he looked at Edwina was interesting, Cassia thought: absolute detachment.

'Harry, I haven't travelled for almost twenty-four hours to act as my own maid. I wish we'd brought Mildred now.'

'And I'm extremely glad we didn't. I'm perfectly happy to act as my own valet. I'll see you later.'

'Arrogant pig,' said Edwina. She sat down. 'Well, we're here, for better or worse. It seems pretty nice, I must say.'

'It's lovely,' said Cassia. 'I'm already dreading going home. I do love the sun, and as for having Nanny—'

'You mean you don't have one? How extraordinary. Some progressive new idea, or something?'

'No,' said Cassia, 'we can't afford it,' and then thought, as she seemed to keep thinking these days, that actually now she could—

'Cassia, do listen. I said, what time is lunch usually?'

'Oh, sorry. About one thirty. We have it down by the pool, very informal.'

'I think I might go and have a zizz. Oh Lord, here's Harry coming back. I'm going to nip up the other side before he gets down. See you later.'

Harry reappeared, dressed in a black towelling robe. 'I'm going to swim. Want to join me?'

Cassia shook her head, and put on her sunglasses. She lay back in her deckchair and tried not to watch him. She felt edgy, her easy pleasure quite gone. If she had known Harry was going to be here, she would not have come. Why on earth hadn't Cecily warned her?

He had taken off the robe, and was wearing a black bathing suit beneath it. His arms and legs were heavily muscled; he looked as always extremely fit, not an ounce of fat on his broad, powerful frame, and—Cassia averted her eyes from him and picked up her book. There was a loud splash as he dived in. She stared at the pages of her book, having no idea what she read.

*   *   *

That night, six more people joined them for dinner. 'I feel we have to amuse Edwina,' said Cecily, 'she's so very demanding. I'm sorry they're here at the same time as you, darling. I know how you feel about Harry, but I really couldn't stop them. They just phoned early this morning to say they were in Nice. Apparently Harry phoned Benedict earlier in the week to see if it would matter if they came early, and Benedict said no. Not a word to me, of course.'

'Cecily, if it's me you're worried about, it doesn't matter. I can cope with Harry quite well these days.'

'I know. Anyway, I must go and have a word with Cook. She says she doesn't like doing four courses on a Sunday. I mean why on earth not, how absurd . . .'

Cassia smiled at Cecily's bustling back.

*   *   *

The four courses were superb. And of course an endless progression of wines. Cassia, dressed in her pink crepe dress, sat between two extremely good-looking men—Cecily had carefully placed her as far from Harry as it was possible to be—her senses growing sweetly confused in the soft, scented darkness. The talk was amusing, self-indulgent gossip: about friends, parties, who was where.

'Marvellous spot, this, Benedict,' said one of the good-looking men, whose name was Max.

'Isn't that Gresham's place down there?' said Cassia's other neighbour, pointing out some lights shining far out on the promontory. 'We dined there a few years ago.'

'Was,' said Max. 'He's sold it now. Probably wanted to be nearer the casino.'

Everyone laughed. Except, Cassia noticed, Harry, whose expression was almost angry. She had never realised how antagonistic he was towards Gresham.

The conversation turned to the Prince of Wales and Mrs Simpson, currently holidaying together (although of course with a large party), about the progression of their affair, the old Queen's absolute hostility to her, about what Thelma Furness and Emerald Cunard and the Prince's old flame Mrs Dudley Ward had to say about it, about the chic of Wallis—'Too dazzling,' said one woman. 'She makes every other female in the room look dowdy.'

'But hard, don't you think?' said another. 'I always thought the prince liked pretty ladies.'

'Ah, but this one has very special skills, I'm told,' said Edwina.

'Oh, you don't believe all that nonsense, Edwina, surely?'

'Of course I do. Everyone knows he has a tiny problem and—'

'Tiny being the word,' said one of the men, laughing.

'Then how did he keep Freda with him all that time?'

'Oh, Mamie, who wouldn't stay with him, problem or not? Anyway, maybe *she* has the special skills too,' said Edwina, and then laughingly refused to disclose any more.

Harry was looking at Edwina, Cassia noticed, with the same expression of absolute detachment he had shown that morning. She was looking marvellous, in white silk wide-legged pyjamas, matching gold and emerald slave bangles on her thin arms, emerald clips in her dark hair. She was also extremely drunk.

'Well, I would like to see him become king soon,' said one of the handsome men. 'The country needs him; he will do a great deal for it.'

'I really don't see why,' said Benedict. 'He has shown no talent for anything at all except dancing

94

and playing golf.'

'Not true,' said Harry. 'He is marvellous with people.'

'Yes, and he seems genuinely concerned about the miners and the unemployed generally,' Cassia said. 'I think he feels very strongly for his people: all of them.'

'Do I detect the voice of socialism here?' said her neighbour.

She smiled her sweetest smile. 'Yes, I suppose you do, if socialism is caring about ordinary people with no wealth, no voice of their own to make heard.'

'They seemed to make their voices pretty clearly felt in the General Strike,' he said. 'And then all these absurd marches, virtually riots, in Sheffield.'

'Yes, but those people are desperate, hungry, and the government were threatening to cut what little help they were being given.'

'Yes, and they got their way, didn't they? The Minister of Labour, what's his name, Stanley, had to give in to them. The man on the Clapham Omnibus, or whatever you like to call him, seems to be doing pretty well to me.'

'Oh, Max, what a very simplistic view,' said Harry dryly, 'and how easy for you to voice it, sitting here, drinking Benedict's Premier Cru. And it's one of the reasons Baldwin doesn't like the Prince, the fact that he has so many of the people's hearts. He's jealous. I wouldn't be at all surprised if Baldwin blocked this relationship, if it came to any kind of a crunch, forced a constitutional crisis.'

'What nonsense, Harry, it won't come to that,' said Cecily. 'He's just enjoying himself, having fun while he can. Anyway, this is all getting terribly serious. Shall we dance?'

Cassia stood up; her head swam slightly. She went up to her room, brushed her hair, renewed her lipstick, sprayed on some perfume. She wanted to dance. Music was drifting up from the poolside, all her favourites: 'Just the Way You Look Tonight', 'Let's Face the Music and Dance', 'Let's do it' . . .

She found the table deserted, except for Harry; he was drinking a brandy, pulling on his cigar. He looked at her and smiled, indicated the chair next to him. She hesitated briefly, then sat down.

'Nice to find you on my side, for once,' he said.

'What? Oh, well, I did agree with you. I think he does have that gift.'

'But Wallis doesn't,' he said. 'Anyway, thank you for taking my side.'

'I wasn't exactly taking your side,' she said, laughing. 'I honestly think that, as you very well know.'

'Yes I do,' he said, suddenly serious. 'Tell me, Cassia, do you regret giving up your career, giving up helping those people?'

'Oh no,' she said quickly. 'Besides, I'm helping Edward to help them. It's one of the things we share.'

'I see,' he said. 'That's very commendable.' His eyes were amused. 'Tell me, have you enjoyed your evening? You certainly look very nice.'

'Thank you. Yes, I have.'

'And forgiven me for arriving?'

'Harry, don't be ridiculous.' And then because it suddenly, surprisingly, seemed important that he should know, she said, 'Leonora left me some money, Harry.'

'Oh, really?' He reached out, poured himself a

96

cup of coffee. 'Well, she was extremely fond of you.'

'Yes, and I was of her. I wish I'd seen more of her those last few months. I feel so guilty about it.'

'You didn't know,' he said, 'how ill she was. None of us did, really.'

'Not even you?'

'Not really,' he said, his voice, his eyes, absolutely devoid of emotion. 'Not until the very end.'

'But she was all right? I mean, she wasn't alone? I couldn't bear to think—'

'Cassia, she was very well cared for. I promise you that.'

'So you saw her?'

'Yes,' he said abruptly. He seemed upset: he and Leonora had been very fond of each other.

'You must miss her,' she said carefully.

'Yes, of course I do.' He said, his voice lighter, 'And what are you going to spend it on, this money? More hats?'

'Harry, it was quite a lot of money.'

'Well, I'm delighted for you. I hope you have fun with it.'

'That's exactly what Leonora said. In her letter to me about it.'

An almost imperceptible pause. 'Well, that's what money's for,' he said. Then he said, clearly wishing to change the subject, 'Well, no doubt you would like to go down and dance. You like dancing, don't you, Cassia? Rather good at it, as I recall.'

'Not any more, I'm afraid,' she said.

'Does the doctor not enjoy dancing?'

'Not much.'

'What does he enjoy, then? Food? Wine? His

97

work?'

'All those things,' she said briskly.

'And you, I hope. Does he appreciate you, Cassia, as he should?' The voice was light, carefully so.

'Of course he does.'

'Good. You are lucky, then. I don't think Edwina appreciates me.'

'I'm sure she does.'

'I'm afraid she doesn't,' he said, and his voice was harsh suddenly. 'Let us not have any foolish platitudes here. But then what could I expect, eh, Cassia?'

'I don't know,' she said. She was beginning to feel afraid of the direction the conversation was taking.

'Well, you should,' he said. 'Now, come along, let us go down to the pool.'

She would have danced with him; they might have talked more, grown closer in the next two golden, Mediterranean days. However, a message arrived from Edward, brought to her by the butler even as they walked down the steps. She was told, as she stood there, gazing out at the moon on the sea, the red oleander flowers disappeared now into the darkness, the white ones still shining, that his mother had died, and that Edward wanted her to come home immediately.

CHAPTER FIVE

Life was extremely difficult over the next few weeks. Edward was morose, and Desmond, having

98

initially refused an invitation to stay, proceeded to do so; for almost a month he was there, a depressive shadow hanging about the house. The children took advantage of everyone's distraction to be difficult, and it was impossible for her to do the right thing. Edward snapped at her, complaining about the children, the state of the house, his own crushing workload. When she pointed out, quite mildly she felt, that she could help a great deal with the workload at least if he would only allow her, he told her she had no idea what she was talking about and stormed out of the room, slamming the door.

And when Edward came back to say that he was getting very tired of her harping on about her own career instead of supporting him in his, she lost her temper and did what she always did when life got on top of her: went off to Brighton to see Rupert.

'And I've got something to tell you,' she said to Rupert, when she phoned to arrange it, 'as well as being in need of cheering up. Something important.'

'What a complex meeting we shall have. Darling, of course you must come over, and I'll take you out to lunch.'

'No, Rupert,' she said, 'I'll take you.'

How often had she dreamed of such a thing, she thought, as she sat on the train chugging along the Brighton line from Haywards Heath: dreamed of being grown up and glamorous and buying Rupert Cameron lunch. Or dinner. And then dreamed of what might happen next, of Rupert declaring passionate, desperate love for her and begging her to run away with him, and her saying, yes of course, and them finding themselves in some wonderful suite in some amazing hotel somewhere . . .

She told Rupert about it, laughing, as they sat eating enormous prawns and drinking some extremely good white Burgundy.

'I loved you so much,' she said, 'so terribly much.'

'Does that mean you don't love me any more?'

'No, of course not, but it's different. Obviously. I'm happily married.'

'I hope so,' he said, suddenly serious, stroking her cheek. 'I hope you are.'

'It's only these past few weeks that have got me down. You were right, telling me to marry Edward. I did what you said and—'

'Was that decision really based so much on my advice?'

'You did have a very big influence on it. On me. You always have. You know that. I suppose it— well, tipped the balance. I just needed you to point it all out. You know that we were so perfectly suited, that there was more to life than just doing what I wanted . . .'

'Oh God,' he said, 'You seem to remember every word of the bloody script.'

'I do. But only because it was such a good script.'

There was a long silence; then he said, 'Well, I hope he appreciates you.'

'Funny. That's what—' she stopped.

'Yes?'

'Oh—that's what Harry said. The other day.'

'You were talking amicably to Harry? Good heavens! And where did this polite conversation take place?'

'In France.'

'In France! Good heavens, whatever took you,

both to France?'

'Cecily. And Benedict. I went to stay with them.'

'How very decadent. I'm surprised at Edward.'

'Edward didn't come,' she said quickly.

'Oh, I see.'

'No, you don't see,' she said, 'and that's to do with my news.'

And then she told him. He was first surprised, amazed even, then delighted, then thoughtful for her, exactly as she had known he would be.

'How did Edward take it?'

'He was pleased,' she said quickly.

'Good.' He looked at her carefully. 'Good for Leonora, then. Knowing you were the person to need it most. And what are your plans for yourself, with this money? Long term, I mean? You could go back to your medicine, couldn't you?'

'Rupert, I couldn't,' she said, shocked by him saying the unsayable, the unthinkable even to herself. She had shunned that thought, refused to give it a moment's consideration.

'Darling, why on earth not? Surely that's exactly what Leonora would have wanted to have given you, the freedom to go back, to do what you always wanted.'

She stared at him. The argument sounded somehow prepared, well planned. 'She didn't talk to you about it, did she, Rupert?'

'No,' he said, 'I had no idea what she was going to do. It just seems so obvious somehow. There you are, with all that money, the wherewithal to have your dream, and you're turning your back on it. I mean, what are you going to do, for God's sake, spend it on frocks or something?'

'No. No, of course not.' She felt rather

101

emotional, suddenly threatened by his mood.

'I'm sorry, poppet. It's just that I care about you so much, and what happens to you. I always did.'

'Yes, I know you did,' she said, and she was back there again, back in that wonderful, magical, romantic time when he had first stayed with them, in the house in Leeds.

*   *   *

He insisted on taking them out to dinner, that first evening. He had come to the Leeds Playhouse with a repertory company and had looked her father up. Cassia had been just fifteen years old, and she had changed into one of the outfits Leonora had bought her on her most recent visit, a navy dress in fine wool, trimmed with cream ribbons. It was very flattering and quite grown-up looking.

Rupert had insisted on pouring her a glass of wine—'It will do you good'—and she learnt that he and Duncan had met at school; that he had been one of the ushers at Blanche's and Duncan's wedding, and then lost touch with them as he pursued what he swore was an unsuccessful career, but which sounded to Cassia wonderfully glamorous. He was to appear for three weeks at the Leeds Playhouse, opening with *Justice*, the 'social' drama by Galsworthy. He was to play the lead.

'Of course I'm a little old for it,' he said, smiling ruefully at Cassia, 'but for some reason I have got the part.'

'I don't think you look at all old,' she said, smiling back at him, 'I think you look very young. Actually.'

'What an extremely charming girl your daughter

102

is, Duncan,' he said. 'You must be very proud of her.'

'I am,' said Duncan, 'very proud.' She thought that for the rest of her life she would remember that moment, looking at them, enjoying their admiration, her father and this wonderful, handsome stranger, sitting there in the warm, golden candlelight of the restaurant, just slightly confused with the wine, but able for the very first time to recognise the flicker of sexual attraction within herself and to see it echoed in the eyes of a man.

'And where are you staying?' asked Duncan.

'Ah, now that is not quite such good news. The most terrible, terrible landlady is probably on the doorstep waiting for me with a rolling pin even now. The list of house rules in my room is so long it practically covers the entire wall. Breakfast is at seven thirty—can you imagine anything more dreadful? High tea is at six, but if we are even five minutes late we must go without. Baths can only be taken between the hours of eight and nine at night, and that by prior arrangement.'

Cassia was smiling at him and thinking he was charming and able somehow to make everything sound amusing and fun, when she heard her father speaking the wonderful words.

'Well, you must come and stay with us. We'd love to have you, wouldn't we, Cassia?'

'Yes,' she said, 'we'd simply love it.'

*   *   *

There followed three weeks of pure happiness. Rupert Cameron was, she swiftly discovered, not

103

merely charming, but possessed of a genuinely delightful nature, tirelessly good tempered, funny and fun and when she came home from school (earlier than she had done for months, hurrying up the street rather than dragging wearily along it) he was usually there and would make her a cup of tea, wanting to know about her day.

They had been to see him in *Justice*, and Cassia had thought him quite wonderfully good.

She never usually saw him when he came home at night, for it was late, and she was in bed, but one night when she couldn't sleep and went down to make herself a cup of cocoa he arrived home and came into the kitchen.

'Well met by moonlight, Proud Cassia,' he said. 'Make me one of those too, would you?'

Warm with pleasure, she made him a big mug and sat down with him while he drank it and chatted to her.

Finally he said sadly, 'I could sit here all night most happily talking to you, but I suppose your father would not like it.'

He got up and walked over to the kitchen door, then turned and studied her as she sat there, in her lumpy old dressing gown—if only she had known, she would have put on the beautiful silk one Leonora had given her. He blew her a kiss and then came towards her, bent over and kissed her again, very gently on the lips.

'How pretty you are. And what a lovely ending to my day,' he said.

Cassia sat there for over an hour, reliving every phrase, every word they had exchanged, remembering each smile, exploring the thud of pleasure that was half emotional, half physical, felt

104

deep within her body as he had kissed her. Then she crept upstairs, past his room and lay in her own, sleepless with pleasure for hours.

* * *

Rupert had left soon after that. He wrote occasionally, once with the news that he had gone to call on Leonora, as Cassia had suggested, and she had been wonderfully welcoming. He had met her brother, and liked him very much, and of course Sir Richard. Then many months later, he wrote again to say he was to appear in the *Merchant of Venice* at the Manchester Playhouse and he very much hoped that Duncan and Cassia would come to see him.

* * *

The tickets had been bought, an hotel room booked for the night for it was too far to travel back to Leeds late—and then on the morning of the performance Duncan had awaken with a severe migraine, unfit to do anything but stay in bed.

* * *

'So I just came on my own,' she said to Rupert calmly, over dinner in Manchester, after the play.

'But won't they be terribly worried?'

'No, not at all. Father has been given a sleeping draught and won't wake till morning, and Molly and Phyllis think I am staying with a friend.'

'I am deeply touched that you should have risked so much to see the play.'

'You,' she said firmly, 'not the play. And it was wonderful, you were wonderful, and it was absolutely worth it.'

'You're quite a determined person, aren't you?' he said. 'And how are the studies, and the plans for your future?'

'Not good,' said Cassia, and burst into tears. And tried to explain through them the appalling difficulties of being a very ambitious schoolgirl while being expected to look after a demanding father who could not see at all why she should not cook his supper each night and supervise the running of the household.

'Of course it is difficult,' Rupert said, tenderly, passing her a handkerchief, 'and I can see you need help. Perhaps I should try to explain to your father about your difficulties.'

'He wouldn't listen,' she said briefly, 'and he doesn't really want me to do medicine. He thinks I should leave school now and learn to be a secretary.'

'Well,' he said, laughing, 'if it came to a battle between your irresistible force against his immovable object, I know which side I'd stand on. In fifteen years' time, when I am really old and have all kinds of unpleasant diseases, I shall say, "Send for Dr Berridge, she will cure me," and I shall hope not to be disappointed.'

'Don't patronise me,' she said, angry suddenly. 'I'm an adult and I'm going to do what I want with my life, and nobody is going to stop me.'

'Tell me, Cassia,' he said suddenly, 'do you see me as very old?'

'No,' she said quickly, 'not at all. And what does age matter anyway when two people—'

'Yes,' he said, his voice very gentle, 'when two people what?'

She felt the wretched, uncontrollable blush of colour rise, and took a gulp of wine. 'Nothing. Nothing at all.'

There was a long silence, and then 'Look,' he said, 'it's very late. I have a duty to get you back to your hotel, and I am scared silly as to what your father is going to have to say to me about all this if he does find out—'

'What could he say?'

'Oh, my darling,' he said, half laughing, half deadly serious, 'if you don't know that, then you really are a child.'

'Oh,' she said, very quietly, and she knew then what he meant, and knowing was deeply and mysteriously exciting. She stared at him across the table, across the candlelit space between them, and could see her feelings for him, the warm, leaping, disturbing feelings, mirrored in his eyes. 'I do know,' she said quietly, 'and I don't care. I wouldn't care even if—even if what he might think were true.' For a moment she knew he was thinking, contemplating, that same thing, and she was ready for it, recklessly wonderfully ready. Then: 'Cassia, my darling,' he said very thinly, 'you do, you would care. Or you would tomorrow.'

'No,' she said, 'no, I don't. I wouldn't.'

'Well, I do,' he said firmly, trying to smile, 'and I am going to take you back now, and in the morning I think I should personally escort you to Leeds and brave the old lion in his den and assure him that nothing in the least unseemly took place.' He held out his hand. 'Come along; and we can discuss your future on the way.'

Humiliation filled Cassia. She felt hot, sick with shame. She had thrown herself at him, and he was embarrassed and miserable. She stood up, very quickly, and met his eyes quite steadily. 'Yes, all right. What a good idea.'

*　　　*　　　*

'Now then,' he said next morning, as they settled in an empty compartment, 'you are to listen to me very carefully. We don't have very long and it's important you should understand. I want to begin by saying how much I admire you,' he said. 'I think you're very mature, and very brave. And quite extraordinarily attractive. Which is why I am having to talk to you like this now. I have behaved appallingly. I have taken advantage of you horribly. I've flirted with you, and treated you as if you were a great deal older than you are, simply because I find you so attractive. I think you're absolutely glorious, Cassia. I could . . . well, never mind what I could do. I'm sure you can imagine. Perhaps you can't. I never know how much young girls know these days.'

Cassia dared a look at him. His eyes were fixed on her, and the expression on his face was so painstakingly honest, so helplessly remorseful that she almost laughed. 'Oh, quite a lot,' she said carefully, turning her attention back to her hands. 'We have studied a great deal of biology, I have no misapprehensions in my head about gooseberry bushes or storks.'

'Thank God for that at least,' said Rupert, with a heavy sigh. 'But my behaviour has been disgraceful. Having said all that, you see, I do want you to understand how much I was attracted to you. I don't want you feeling spurned and humiliated. It took every ounce of self-control I had last night to reject you. I have no doubt it was very good for me and went some way towards being a penance for my dreadful behaviour earlier. Kissing you, leading you on, when you are only fifteen years old, and a lonely, unhappy fifteen years old at that—I should be shot. I have the morals of an alley cat, and the only reason I got the better of them last night was because I like and respect you so much. You do understand, don't you?'

'I think so,' said Cassia.

'I just want you to know that, rotter or not, I can't help admiring you. Very much. Is that terrible, have I made things even worse?'

Cassia felt quite different suddenly, no longer a foolish, embarrassing virgin, but a desirable, self-confident woman. 'You've made them absolutely better,' she said, 'thank you. And I suppose I shall grow older, and then you will feel less guilty, and then who knows what may happen.'

He took her hand then and sat staring at it, his thumb massaging her palm, and then he raised it to his lips and kissed it, lingering on it with his mouth, turning it over then and kissing the palm for a long long moment, working on it. She looked at his bent head, concentrating on the moment, thinking that she must remember it, every tiny detail of it, for ever, and then he lifted his head and looked at her and his face was very solemn, very intense, and he said, 'Oh Cassia.'

Suddenly a leaping courage seemed to be taking her over, telling her what to do. She leant forward and took his head in her two hands, and pulled him

109

towards her very gently, kissing him on the mouth.

She felt his surprise, his shock, felt an initial gentle attempt to withdraw, but she resisted it, continued to hold him there, and then she felt a change in him, felt him pulling her towards him, very gently, felt his mouth on hers change, become harder than before, felt his lips move, his tongue beginning to explore hers, and it was wonderful, marvellous, and she felt a response to him, not just in her mouth, but a warm leaping, deep within herself, and as she pressed towards him, eager, longing for more, he set her back from him quickly, urgently almost, as if it must be done quickly, met her eyes with his own rueful, brilliant blue ones.

'I do deserve to be shot,' he said. 'Cassia, Cassia, you must forgive me, I—'

'Rupert,' said Cassia, half laughing now, 'stop being so very absurd. It was me, I made you do it and—oh God . . .'

The train had pulled into Leeds station, and standing in the corridor, staring into their compartment, clearly quite transfixed, and having seen every tiny detail of what had been going on, was Mr Devenish, her father's boss and manager of the Leeds Public Library.

*　　*　　*

There was the most appalling series of scenes.

Her father turned first white, then grey with horror at the story. Looking back, Cassia could see that the chief source of horror was that it had been Mr Devenish who had seen her (and who would without doubt spread his report all over Leeds before the end of the day). Second in this order

110

was what Leeds would have to say about it; third, that it was his own, oldest friend who had been involved in this dreadful thing; fourth, that Cassia could so thoroughly have deceived him; and very much last, what might or might not have happened to her during the night she had been away from him and in the company of the oldest friend.

Duncan was assured comparatively easily on this last point, Rupert having thrown himself into a display of dramatic remorse and painstaking detail as to what had actually taken place. More powerfully, Cassia told her father that if he did not believe them, he could take her down to the doctor's surgery and have her virginity confirmed there. He was clearly shocked at the frankness of this speech, but it served its purpose. However, the horror of having his daughter branded a trollop all over Leeds, the loss of the family's respectability, the dread that he himself might lose his job, was almost unbearable. Rupert was told to leave the house and the city at once and not to return.

Cassia's grandmother was sent for. She listened to the story, her lips folded tightly, and then said she should clearly move into the house permanently herself, to make sure that Cassia was properly supervised and chaperoned at all times in the future. She added that Cassia should leave school at once, be made to stay at home and do her duty as a daughter.

Cassia thought very fast and said that if her grandmother wished to come and live with them, that was entirely her affair. However, if they tried to force her to leave school, then she would see to it that the rumours about her behaviour and what had happened overnight in Manchester were greatly elaborated to extend to a full seduction and even a possible pregnancy—

Her father sent her to her room, but she knew she had won. He sent for her an hour later and said that he had decided she could stay at school, providing they would have her. 'It seems to me you may find yourself expelled if they come to hear of this, in any case.'

She was not of course expelled; indeed, news of her extremely modest misdemeanour never reached the headmistress. What did astonish and please her was how much the arrival of her grandmother in the household actually helped her. The old lady took over all her domestic duties, freeing her for her studies.

The night with Rupert had been a turning point in more ways than one.

*   *   *

And so he took his place in her life as chief advisor, mentor and lover-like friend. He argued, first quietly, then with increasing passion, with her father and her grandmother when they tried to block her application to medical school, and when Leonora had written to her father to propose that she should present Cassia at Court and pay for her to do a London Season—a prospect which pleased her father far more than the most brilliant medical career—Rupert talked her into that as well.

*   *   *

Looking back, she could see how skilfully he had guided her out of her early schoolgirl crush, into the loving, flirtatious friendship they had shared ever since. This had been finally accomplished by an experience so painful she was still unable to laugh about it.

When she was almost seventeen, still dazzled by him, he had invited her to come and see him in a musical in Manchester, and to have dinner with him afterwards. Excited, thinking that perhaps now, at last, he was actually going to declare his love for her, perhaps even consummate their relationship, she rushed round to his dressing room after the show.

'You were wonderful, wonderful,' she said.

'You *look* wonderful, wonderful,' he said, smiling down into her eyes, 'and so grown up, oh, dear Cassia, yet more temptation for me to resist.'

She had said, very serious suddenly, 'Stop resisting it, Rupert, please,' and pulled his face down to hers, as she had done on the train. She began kissing him rather intently on the mouth, so intently indeed that she did not hear the door open.

It was only a voice, sounding half amused, half irritable, saying 'Rupert, darling, I had no idea you were two-timing me,' that made her turn her head and see the leading lady, a glorious creature with dramatic dark eyes, and a pair of incredible breasts which were extremely visible since her silk robe was hanging open.

She had stared in horror for a long moment, absorbing the obvious intimacy between them, and that Rupert's face was a caricature of discomfort; and then she pulled herself away from him and ran as fast as she could down the corridor and to the safety of her hotel, where she lay sleepless almost all night, in a state of utter misery and humiliation.

He came to find her next morning, as he had the time before, and sat holding her hand as he tried to explain, so skilfully that at the end of the hour she was no longer angry, no longer embarrassed even, and had accepted the fact that however much he loved her, she must remain to him a very dear and precious friend.

'You are divinely attractive,' he said, 'but I am a dreadful old rake. I look to you for reform, not encouragement.'

Reluctantly, she had accepted it, and had come quite swiftly to enjoy what she could see was a unique place in his life, for he paid her the compliment of confiding in her as she did in him. She learnt swiftly too to regard the ceaseless procession of young women through his bedroom and his life with a lofty amusement, and to recognise that had she joined them, she would have lost him for ever.

He was still, to her, in many ways, the ideal man: she had always loved Rupert and always would because he was charming, easy and handsome, (albeit still capable of irresponsible, and even disgraceful, behaviour at times) that he made life colourful and amusing and fun and she owed him a great deal, since he had been the man who had first made her aware of her own sexuality and its considerable strength. Whoever she had loved and desired since, whoever she had married, to whomever she had borne children, Rupert still possessed the capacity to disturb, if not excite her, and he was arguably still the most important man in her life.

'Anyway,' she said now, leaning back, smiling at him, 'I feel I can thank you properly now at last, for all that you did for me all those years ago.'

'Darling . . .'

'Rupert, you once said you'd give anything to be able to put a play on yourself, that if only you could find someone to invest in it, it would make all the difference. Well, I could do that now. You saved my career, now perhaps I can save yours.'

'Oh, my darling,' he said, and his blue eyes were very brilliant suddenly, 'how sweet you are. How much I love you. I do appreciate it and the thought alone is quite enough—'

'No, Rupert,' she said firmly; 'the thought is not enough. I want to do it. Now promise me you'll think about it.'

He leant forward, took her hand, raised it to his lips. 'You're marvellous,' he said, 'and thank you. It could be wonderful. May I get back to you? And while we're talking careers, can I ask you to at least think about getting back to medicine?'

'I'll think about it,' she said, smiling, 'but I really can't see it's possible. For all sorts of reasons. Not least what my husband would have to say about it.'

'Oh, Cassia,' said Rupert. 'Whatever happened to the person who was going to do what she wanted with her life and nothing was going to stop her?'

'You know what happened to that person. And you of all people shouldn't reproach her for it.'

'No,' he said, very quietly, 'I know. I just wonder if I should reproach myself. That's all.'

The day after Desmond went home, Edward looked at Cassia across the breakfast table and smiled at her, rather shamefaced. 'Cassia, I'm sorry I've been difficult.'

'That's all right, Edward. I understand.'

'I hope so. Now look, I've been thinking. This house is in a bit of a mess, isn't it? It could do with some money spending on it. Painting it and so on. Maybe put in some central heating. It does need a new roof, and I'd really like to rebuild the surgery. Extend it. So I thought that's what we should do. As soon as possible, really.'

'Good idea. With my—that is, with Leonora's money,' she said, unable quite to analyse how she felt.

'I had thought of it,' Edward said, 'as our money.'

'Yes,' she said quickly, realising with horror that what she felt had been possessiveness over the money, her money, as she couldn't help thinking of it. How dreadful that she could be so mean, so ungenerous about it, to Edward of all people, who had always shared with her everything he had. To try to make amends, she said, 'Edward, you wouldn't like to buy a different practice, would you? A bigger one, perhaps?'

'Why on earth should I?' he said, astonished.

'I just thought perhaps a London practice, or—'

'Cassia, my medical career is my own. Something I've worked for, earned by my own efforts and merit. I don't want any fancy rooms in London.'

'I didn't mean fancy rooms. You know I didn't. But we always used to talk about the problems of people living in the cities, underprivileged people, wanting to help them.'

'No,' he said, his voice cold, 'I'm extremely happy here. It might seem a very modest practice to you, Cassia, but it affords me a great deal of satisfaction. And I think I give the same to my patients. Or perhaps you have reason to think otherwise.'

'Edward, you're choosing to completely misunderstand me. I never suggested the practice was in any way deficient. It's marvellous, and your patients all think you're wonderful. I only wondered—'

'If I might like something better.'

'No!'

'Well, I don't see how else your remark might have been interpreted. And I certainly don't want you offering to procure it for me. Now you must excuse me, I have work to do.'

She looked after him, feeling suddenly panicky, without being quite sure why.

*   *   *

'I've had a few estimates done,' he said a week later, a slightly uncomfortable, strained week, 'for the house.'

'Oh really?' She struggled to sound, to feel, calm, happy. 'I would have done that.'

'Well, you seemed a bit lukewarm, and what with getting the boys back to school and so on . . .'

He had never made those sorts of allowances for her before. She smiled at him uncertainly, knowing what it meant, that he was sorry for his outburst but didn't want to say so.

'So—' he reached for a file, pulled out some

pieces of paper—'for about two hundred, we can have a new roof. Then painting the whole house, inside and out, three hundred. And to rebuild and enlarge the surgery, five hundred. Very good, don't you think?'

'Yes. Very good.'

'Mr Cartwright's was the best estimate, and we know him, so I've told him to go ahead. He says the roof should be done very soon, before the winter sets in.'

'You've told him to go ahead?'

'Yes. And meanwhile, Mr Morris is going to get to work on the surgery. It means I'll have to move into the dining room, but it won't take long. By Christmas I'll have a spanking new place to work.'

Cassia sat and stared at him. 'What's the matter?'

'Nothing. It's just that . . . well, maybe we could have talked about it a bit more first.'

'But we have, frequently. Last week specifically. About the roof, about the terrible state of the surgery.'

'Yes, I know, but I mean about doing the work. I'd have liked to think about it a bit.'

'But why? What on earth is there to think about?'

'Oh, I don't know. You just seem to have gone ahead and taken decisions and—'

'Cassia,' he said, his voice infinitely patient, 'I just explained, you've been very busy and I really did want to progress it and—Dear God.' He stopped suddenly. 'This is about the money, isn't it? About it being your money.'

'Don't be absurd. It's just that we've always discussed everything very carefully before. Before

118

deciding on it.'

'You didn't discuss your going to France with me,' he said.

Careful, Cassia, be very careful; it's true, you didn't. 'That was different.'

'Why?'

'Well,' she said, smiling, trying to make it sound funny, light-hearted, 'we'd had a row, hadn't we? I said I was sorry. Said I was wrong.'

'Yes,' he said lightly, but his eyes were hard as he looked at her. 'It was quite wrong. So let's get it right with this work on the house. Our money, our house.'

She was sorry and she tried to make him make love to her that night, so that she could show him, but he wouldn't. He lay far from her, distantly thoughtful, even while he held her in his arms.

*   *   *

Three weeks later the house was in chaos: scaffolding all over it, full of dust, patients trooping through the hall into the dining room, which had become the surgery, using the cloakroom, those who knew her popping into the kitchen to say hello.

'It must be very exciting,' said Mrs Venables, pushing her aged mother down the passage in her wheelchair, 'getting all this work done. The house is going to look wonderful.'

'It is,' said Cassia, 'very exciting.'

'Such an expense, having work done these days, too.'

'Well, I was left some money by my godmother, you see, and that—'

119

'Really? Oh, I see.' Mrs Venables looked uneasy suddenly. 'I hadn't realised that.'

Now why did you have to tell her, Cassia? Why not let her think Edward was doing so well he could afford to pay for it? Why tell her it was your money, within your gift to do all these wonderful things to the house? It was mean, petty.

But she knew why. It had become very clear to her one night after he had been dismissive of something she had said about a breech birth, of the dangers, of the arguable need for Caesareans in all such cases. She had looked at her new freedom, her new power and felt better. It was her revenge for all the years of being the doctor's wife. Cleverer than the doctor, more highly qualified, but only his wife, with no acknowledgement from the doctor of that fact, ever. And now, richer than the doctor, able to pay for things herself, that the doctor couldn't actually afford. The revenge might be inappropriate, but it was something at least.

CHAPTER SIX

The money was there now, sitting in her bank account. Her own bank account. Her new bank account. It had been Mr Brewster's suggestion that she should have a special account for it: a high-interest bearing deposit account. She was going to see Benedict shortly, to discuss investment.

'And if I wanted to buy something, I can just make a transfer to my—our current account.'

'You mean something like a car?' he said, and his eyes twinkled at her. 'Yes of course. Not bought it yet, then?'

'I haven't bought anything very much yet. Only a new roof and a few clothes and things. And I might invest in a friend's play—only my husband doesn't know about that,' she had added hastily, 'just in case you see him.'

'Mrs Fallon, lawyers and doctors are, like priests, not given to divulging the details of their clients' lives. May I say how rare and refreshing it is to see such common sense, such a grasp on reality.'

'Thank you,' said Cassia, wondering if he realised how terrified she was of even starting to spend the money on anything, anything she really wanted, because of its implications on her life, on her marriage, on herself . . .

*   *   *

That evening, she did broach the subject of the car. She started by suggesting they bought a new family car: their own was three years old, and mostly used by Edward. What about a Daimler? she said. Nothing too expensive, that would take all the family easily, but would also be suitable for Edward and his house calls.

She was interested in cars, quite knowledgeable about them indeed. Sir Richard had been the first private car owner she had known, had taken her for a ride in it around London on her very first visit. A wonderful dashing thing it had been, an open cream-coloured Buick with wooden spoked wheels. Benedict had owned a Bentley, much more sedate, but very beautiful. Harry, of course, had had endless cars, wonderful things, their names forming a roll call of motoring glamour: a Delage, a Bugatti

121

and a Maserati—all of which he raced—a gorgeous Rolls, the Hispano Suiza which he had claimed did seventy miles an hour . . . Cassia wrenched her mind away from Harry's cars and waited while Edward pronounced on his own purchase.

It would be very nice, he said, to have a new one, and a Daimler was a good idea, but it was hardly necessary. She then said if he didn't want a new car, she did.

'Well, then,' he said, slightly impatiently, 'let's get one, then. I'll take a look at the market, see what's around.'

'What I also meant was I'd like to have one of my own,' she said, listening to her voice falling into the very still silence. Edward looked at her, his face blank, but his eyes sharp, and said finally that he really couldn't see that was at all necessary.

'Edward, it would make my life much easier, and I love cars, you know I do.'

'Well,' he said finally, 'if that's what you really want. But for heaven's sake, get something small and easy to handle. Get an Austin Seven, you can't come to much harm in that, and don't expect me to look after it for you when it breaks down.'

She had been so angry she went straight to London and bought a Jaguar SS 100. It was an enchantingly pretty sunshine-yellow convertible, with chrome wheels and trim, and a particularly pretty running board, curving up over the front wheels. 'It suits you, it's like a really nice hat,' Cecily exclaimed happily when she drove it round to the Boltons to show it off. It did at least sixty, the salesman told her, and it did indeed, she found, flying down the A24 towards Monks Heath that golden October day. When she arrived in the drive

122

at Monks Ridge it made such a noise that everyone in the house came rushing out to see it.

'Cripes!' Bertie had said, and 'Goodness gracious!' William had screamed.

'Oh, my Lord,' Peggy said, her hand on her plump bosom.

Edward was out, but Cassia was in the kitchen making some pastry when he got back, and his face thunderous with rage was enough, as Peggy had remarked to Mrs Briggs next day, to turn the milk sour.

'What in the name of heaven is that thing in the drive?'

'It's my car,' she said, smiling sweetly. 'I bought it today. Do you like it?'

'It's ridiculous,' he said. 'You can't possibly keep it. I told you to get an Austin Seven.'

'Perhaps,' she said carefully, conscious of Peggy's round eyes, 'we should go into your study. Talk about it there.'

He stalked out of the kitchen into his study, stood with his back to her, staring out of the window. 'What the hell are you playing at, Cassia?'

'Edward, I wanted a car, I've bought a car. It wasn't very expensive, a few hundred pounds—'

'A few hundred pounds!' he said. 'Not very expensive! And you dared to argue with me about the roof. God help me, what is happening to us?'

'I didn't argue about the roof.'

'Of course you did.' There was a long silence, then Edward said, 'I want you to take it back. Tomorrow.'

It was too peremptory, too arrogant. She met his eyes steadily. 'I'm not taking it back, Edward. Sorry. I know about cars, I like cars, I wanted this

123

one.'

'Yes,' he said, 'I know you know about cars,' and stalked out of the room.

*　　　*　　　*

Almost three years ago it had been, she thought, looking after him. Bertie had been three, William almost two.

Cecily had telephoned her a couple of days earlier, asked her to join them for a picnic. 'It'll be such fun, Cassia. We're going to Brooklands to watch the car racing. Of course Edward's invited as well. It's lovely there, and it's so exciting to watch. We have lunch in the club house, take a picnic tea . . .'

'Oh Cecily,' she said, 'I'd really love it, but what would I do with the children? They're too little to bring.'

'Ours will be coming down just for the picnic tea, Nanny will bring them. Why don't you bring yours here, and Nanny can look after them. If you come up on Friday, you can stay the night. Oh, go on, Cassia, neglect your duties just for once.'

'I'll ask Edward, and ring you back.'

*　　　*　　　*

Edward said he could think of nothing worse than sitting by a noisy racetrack for hours on end, and that anyway, he couldn't possibly get away. 'But if you really want to go, then of course you must.'

And so she had gone. What Cecily hadn't mentioned was that Harry Moreton was going to be there, racing his Bugatti.

＊　　＊　　＊

She had seen photographs of Brooklands, but nothing could have prepared her for the reality: the snaking track, the steep banked curve which the cars rode at terrifying speeds and angles, the relentless ebb and flow of noise, the smell of the exhausts, the sense of energy and excitement.

'It's wonderful,' she said, smiling from the top of the grassy bank near the entrance, already covered in picnickers. 'I'm so glad I came.'

'Thought you'd like it,' said Benedict. 'Now look, we can go down to the pits, see them getting the cars ready. Harry said he'd look out for us.'

'Harry?' she said, containing her voice with a great effort. 'I didn't know he was going to be here.'

'Oh, yes, it's a club day, and he's racing. Does it quite a lot.'

'Oh, I see,' she said, wishing suddenly, and hating herself for it, that she looked a bit smarter. Her cotton floral dress seemed very commonplace and dowdy, and she hadn't even thought to wear a hat. It hadn't really seemed to matter very much before but—

'Come on, Cassia, buck up,' said Cecily, pulling at her arm. 'It's great fun in the pits, honestly . . .'

It was; like something in a film, men in white overalls working furiously, often three to a car, people rushing about, shouting, engines revving, tyres being whipped off, replacements being wheeled across the area at a run like great children's hoops.

'Oh, there's Harry, look,' said Benedict, and

there he was, dressed in white overalls and a brown leather helmet, walking towards them, waving, smiling, a cigarette in his mouth, his goggles hanging from his hand, absolutely relaxed, as if he was going to do no more than stroll up to the club house with them, rather than take his car round the track at a hundred miles an hour.

'Good morning!' he said. 'And Cassia, what a lovely surprise. How pretty you look—blue always did suit you.'

'Thank you,' she said.

Why was it, how was it, that everything he ever said managed to imply a past, a shared past, tugging her back to it, disturbing her hard-won tranquillity.

'So when is your race, Harry?' said Cecily.

'Oh, not till three o'clock, so I'll be able to join you for lunch. Apparently Gresham's over from France, flying his plane into the Aero Village.'

'Where's that?' said Cassia.

'Over there, right on the other side of the track. He's got a Maserati here, and I've told him a dozen times the Bugatti's the better car, so we shall see this afternoon.'

'Leonora's not coming I suppose?' she said hopefully.

'No, sadly. Well, you must excuse me, I'll see you at lunchtime.'

'That should be interesting,' said Benedict as they walked away. 'There's a huge rivalry between those two where horsepower's concerned. I'd have thought the Maserati was the faster car myself, but we shall see.'

'Goodness,' said Cecily, 'a race within a race, how exciting. Shall we go and place our bets?'

The club house served a very good lunch, but Cassia was finding it hard to swallow. She was sitting next to Harry and the table wasn't really big enough for five—Edwina had arrived now—and Harry was pressed rather close up against her.

Edwina was looking dazzling in a white linen suit and a wide-brimmed black straw hat. She smiled graciously at Cassia and told her she looked tired. 'I'd have thought the country air would have been good for you,' she said. 'It's obviously very over-rated.'

'So where is the doctor?' said Harry, picking up his glass. 'This is very good claret, Benedict. Just what I need to steady my nerves.'

'You haven't got any nerves,' said Edwina, 'and I'm sure you shouldn't drink before a race, Harry.'

'Oh, nonsense. Helps on the bends. Yes, where is your husband, Cassia? Wouldn't he enjoy this sort of thing?'

'Yes, but he's working,' she said hastily.

'Really? Well, you know what they say, all work and no play . . . although I'm sure you don't find him dull.'

'Of course I don't,' said Cassia irritably. She moved her right leg, which was pressed very hard against his left one, away from him; he moved his slowly but very deliberately after it. She realised he was looking at her, his eyes very intent on hers.

'Are you all right?' he said suddenly. She felt his leg move again, felt the dreadful, treacherous stirrings deep within her, frowned at him.

'Don't you start telling me I look tired,' she said.

'I was only going to tell you that you look a little sad.'

'I'm not in the least sad,' she said, trying to smile as brilliantly as Edwina, and failing.

'I'd hate you to be sad. Even if—' He stopped suddenly, obviously reconsidering what he might have been going to say, then smiled, and said, 'Well, tell me what exciting things you've been getting up to. I want every tiny detail. Oh, Kay, hello! How are you? See you later.'

'Is that Kay Petre?' said Benedict.

'Yes. Pretty, isn't she? Doesn't look like a racing driver. Bloody good, she's beaten me twice. Oh look, there's Gresham's plane coming in now. Nice little thing, isn't it? Leopard Moth. I'm thinking of getting one myself.'

*   *   *

The cars lined up at the start at two forty-five, an extraordinary assortment of sizes and shapes. They were handicapped, the tiny Austins and Morrises moving off first, then the Rileys—one driven by Kay Petre in her trademark blue overalls—and the MGs. Finally the big boys, Harry's Bugatti, gleaming silver blue in the sunshine, and Rollo Gresham's black Maserati, somehow threatening, left almost together, Rollo a second ahead.

They were all standing watching on the girder bridge, over the great banked curve; Cassia felt very odd, the sexual disturbance of lunchtime somehow confused in her senses with the exhaust fumes and the vibration and the sense of vertigo that came from looking down on the cars.

'I don't think I can stand much of this,' said

128

Edwina. 'I think I might go and wait in the club house.'

'Don't do that!' said Benedict. 'You can't deprive Harry of your support at a moment like this.'

'He doesn't need it,' said Edwina. 'His ego is so huge it provides quite enough support for the whole—Oh my God.'

There was a sudden roar as the two cars swept under the bridge, the Bugatti fractionally ahead; it was at the very top of the bank, only just within the safety line, clinging to the track at its seemingly impossible angle. They swung round the curve, lower down.

'Why do they have that ghastly slope?' said Edwina irritably. 'What's the point? And why don't they fall off?'

'Braking device, in essence,' said Benedict, 'and centrifugal force. Anyway, two more laps, then it'll be over. Hold my hand, Edwina.'

'I don't need my hand held,' said Edwina. 'I'm cross, not frightened.'

Kay Petre's Riley and a couple of Rovers came under the bridge first on the second lap, and then hard behind her the Bugatti and the Maserati, lower down this time, Rollo ahead by feet.

'I hope to God Rollo doesn't win,' said Edwina. 'I shall have an appalling weekend if he does.'

The smaller cars were coming through now, people shouting, urging them on.

'Christ almighty, here they come again,' Benedict yelled.

The Maserati came through under the bridge, ahead by half a length; Harry's Bugatti, above it on the bank, suddenly moved higher still, right to the rim, and then like a horse that has been kept in

129

check, pushed apparently effortlessly forward, gravity helping him on the downhill stretch. Gresham shot very sharply into the bend, skidded slightly and for a moment looked as if he would crash hard into Harry. He righted his wheels and for several terrifying moments they were exactly parallel, not more than six inches apart. Their wheels apparently locked, sliding crazily together round the bend, then they were lost to view again in a scream of tyres.

'Jesus,' said Benedict, 'I think they've—'

'What?' said Edwina. 'They've what, Benedict? Not crashed? God, of all the stupid—'

'I'm not sure. Let me through, can I get through, please . . .'

*   *   *

Rollo Gresham won by a whisker. The two of them climbed out of their cars, grinning, stood posing for photographs for the cine-camera enthusiasts who lined the track.

Cassia and the others had run down from their vantage point to join them, Cassia on legs that were now suddenly weak, the panic that had risen slowly subsiding, Edwina and Cecily several yards behind.

'Jolly good race,' Gresham was saying, 'and you're buying me dinner, I think.'

'Dinner? What dinner?' said Edwina.

'We said the loser would buy the other one dinner,' said Gresham. 'Coming, Edwina?' He was grinning at her in his strangely insolent way. Cassia thought how much she disliked him and wondered how Leonora could possibly have chosen to live with him.

'Of course,' said Edwina, 'that's the least you can do for me, after practically killing my husband. Where shall we go?'

'Le Touquet. That was the idea.'

'Le Touquet! No fear! I hate those little planes. Why can't we have dinner in London?'

'Because I like Le Touquet,' said Gresham, 'and I won the race. Cassia, you're very pale. Are you all right?'

'Yes I'm fine, thank you,' she said slightly irritably, aware that everyone was looking at her, afraid they might know why. 'Is Leonora going to be in Le Touquet?'

'What? Oh, no. She's in Paris. She said to give you a kiss if I saw you, so may I?' He leant forward; he was very hot, and he smelt of sweat. He was a large man, good looking in a rather coarse way.

As she pulled back, she saw Harry's eyes on her, thoughtful, concerned.

She managed to smile at him. 'Is she well?' she said, turning back to Gresham. 'Leonora, I mean.'

'Very well. Looking marvellous. You must come and stay with us very soon. Edwina, are you sure you won't come? It'd be much more fun if you did. And Cassia, what about you? I've got room for four.'

'No thanks,' said Edwina.

Cassia shook her head. 'No, really, thank you, I have to get home. My children are arriving in a minute, and as soon as we've had tea, we'll have to be on our way.'

And there it might have ended, innocently, virtuously, only as the Harrington Daimler pulled into the car park, a cloud of steam shot out of the radiator and Preston got out, looking worried.

131

'She's been overheating all the way, Mr Harrington. Needs a bit of work done on her, I'm afraid.'

'Well, we're in the right place for that,' said Benedict. 'I'll go and borrow a mechanic.'

Nanny got out of the car, followed by the older children, and lifted William out. 'He's not very happy, Mrs Fallon, I'm afraid. He's got a tummy ache, and he's a bit hot.'

'Oh dear,' said Cassia. 'Come here, darling, let me—goodness, yes, he is. We'd better leave at once, I think, if Preston could—'

'What's the matter?' Harry had appeared with his mechanic.

'I need to get home rather quickly, William isn't very well. If the Daimler's out of action, maybe Benedict could take us, but—'

There was a pause so brief, so imperceptible no one else would have noticed it but she did.

'I'll take you,' said Harry, 'I'll take you now.'

'Oh, Harry, no, you've got your French dinner and I don't want to spoil your day.'

'It wouldn't spoil my day,' said Harry. 'And don't worry about the dinner, I can be back in plenty of time.'

Cassia looked at him. His face was grimy and streaked with sweat, his hair even wilder than usual, released from its helmet. She felt suddenly a surge of violent sexual excitement, careless, dangerous. She knew that she should refuse at once . . . 'That would be marvellous,' she said.

*   *   *

He had come in his Bentley, a huge cream thing,

132

with a brown soft top which Harry opened to the lovely afternoon air. She settled the goggle-eyed boys in the back, and said goodbye to the rest of the party.

After half an hour the boys both fell asleep. Cassia fixed her eyes carefully on the road, trying not to look at Harry, horribly aware of what she had done, aware that he knew too.

'How is that ridiculous marriage of yours?' he said suddenly.

'Harry, it's not ridiculous,' she said, laughing in spite of herself.

'Of course it is. Jesus, Cassia, I wish—'

'Harry, don't. Please don't.'

'Why not?' he said, and there was an underlying rage in his voice.

'Because there's no point. It's too—'

'Too what? Too late, you were going to say, weren't you?'

'Yes,' she said simply.

'Bloody criminal stupidity,' he said, glaring at the road. 'Marrying him like that, when we—' And then he stopped, turned his head and looked at her, very steadily. She met his eyes, just for a moment too long, felt the excitement again, smiled at him. She couldn't help it. 'Oh, Christ,' he said. 'Let's get off this bloody road.'

Half a mile further down the road, they passed a lane. He turned sharply into it, so sharply that the tyres screamed.

'You're not on the racetrack now,' she said.

'Sorry. Did you enjoy the racing?'

'I absolutely loved it. I thought it was terribly exciting.'

'I thought you did,' he said. 'It's exactly like sex,

133

the whole thing, I find,' and then turned the car again, down a track.

'Where are we going?' she said slightly weakly.

He looked at her and his face was absolutely intent on her, his expression almost hostile. 'Somewhere I can kiss you,' he said, 'somewhere I can get close to you for once.'

'What! Harry, the boys are—'

'Asleep. Shut up, or you'll wake them.' He slammed on the brakes, the car lurched violently, stopped.

'Harry, I can't.'

'Of course you can.'

And then she was in his arms, and his mouth, lazy, slow, confident, on hers, and she didn't resist, didn't protest, just kissed him back, on and on, in a sweet, urgent darkness. It was more than a kiss, more than an embrace: it was a long-kept promise, a long-planned rediscovery, timeless, endless. She felt his hands in her hair, on her neck, then moving to her breasts. Felt herself responding, swiftly, violently, knew what she wanted, knew she had to have it. It was as if the ferocity of the speed and the noise had somehow entered her, become part of her, and even as she recognised the danger, her fear, she would have ignored it, helpless in the face of such blinding, violent temptation.

She would have got out of the car and lain down on the ground, and taken him into her, there and then, but 'Mummy,' said Bertie, 'Mummy, where have we come to?'

*   *   *

He hadn't seen, she kept telling herself, as they

134

drove hard, silently on to Monks Heath, he hadn't seen anything, and if William had, he was too little to tell; but fear, blind, hot fear filled her. Harry, hostile at her anxiety, her insistence that they left at once, did not even look at her. It was very hot, and the lurching round bends made her feel sick. The boys loved it, squealing with delight, William seemingly quite recovered again. When they pulled into the drive at Monks Ridge, they leapt out, ran into the house calling for Edward. Harry sat, still staring straight ahead, and said, 'When will I see you again?'

'You won't,' Cassia said, restored to sanity. 'You mustn't,' and got out of the car herself 'Goodbye, Harry, thank you, I won't ask you in,' she said loudly, and looked at her house in all its dullness and its frustrations, and at Edward, walking out of the door now, his face set in disapproval. She walked up to him and kissed him briefly. She waved Harry off as he nodded at Edward in silence and then pulled, very hard, too hard, out of the drive again.

She was about to ask Edward how his day had been when Bertie's small voice said, 'He's nice. He kissed Mummy.'

'Edward, you are being ridiculous,' she said, as he faced her in the drive. 'Of course he kissed me: he kissed me goodbye, that's all.'

'I hope that's true,' he said. 'I hope that was all.'

The fact that she was lying, combined with her frustration and the turbulence of her day, made her more indignant, not less.

'How dare you!' she said. 'How dare you imply such a thing. I've spent a day with friends, a happy day which you were not prepared to join me in, however much I might have wished it.'

'I cannot stand those friends,' he said, 'any of them, you know I can't. How dare he drive away like that without even speaking to me, patronising me, in that ridiculous car.'

'He raced another car,' said Bertie, 'a big blue one.'

'Raced? He raced?'

'Yes,' she said. 'Harry was driving a Bugatti, and Rollo Gresham a Maserati. It was very exciting and—'

'And he had a plane,' said Bertie. 'The other man had a plane.'

'A plane. A Bugatti. A Maserati. And of course a Bentley. I see. How very fortunate for them all. Clearly, Cassia, you must find it very dull here.'

'Oh, shut up,' she cried. 'Your bloody jealousy spoils everything. What have I done, except enjoy myself for once—'

'For once. Well, I'm sorry your life here should be so unenjoyable, Cassia: It seems rather sad. I'm afraid I have to leave you now, I have work to do. Perhaps you should get the boys to bed, they look very tired.'

She followed him into the house, silent with rage, with misery, and did what he said, for the sake of peace, and because she had no option and was in any case to an extent remorseful. An uneasy truce was formed, but from that day on talk of cars was dangerous between them.

*   *   *

It caused a great stir in the village, her car. It changed the way people saw her. The women were

136

openly disapproving, the men patronisingly impressed, alternately offering condescending advice and flirtatious comment.

She loved her car: for it didn't only provide her with freedom, it symbolised it as well.

*   *   *

Benedict took her out to lunch to discuss investments. They went to the Savoy.

'I'd like to make a bequest,' she said, 'if that's the right word. I'd like to give a scholarship to be awarded annually at St Christopher's. Can I do that?'

'Of course you can, providing they're willing. Which I imagine they would be. Or a research chair, something like that. I would have thought the best person to talk to would be the Dean. I should go and call on him, he'd be pleased to see you.'

'Do you think? He was so angry when I told him what I was going to do, told me I was wasting myself and the hospital's money. I was very upset,' she said, remembering the awful scene.

'I expect he'll have forgiven you by now,' said Benedict cheerfully, 'especially if you're waving a cheque book at him. You write and tell him what you want to do, and he'll have the red carpet out for you, mark my words.' He hesitated for a moment, then said, 'You haven't thought of going back into medicine yourself? Now that you could.'

'Rupert said that as well. Are you sure you haven't been talking about this? No, it's all right, I'm only teasing you. I don't see *why* I could suddenly. What's changed? I'm still married to

Edward, still living in the country, still have three small children . . .'

'True, but you could pay for a good nanny. You qualified well enough, God knows.'

'Yes, but who would be interested in a woman who'd never done her house job? Wonderful as the thought is,' she added with a sigh.

'I think you should talk to the Dean about that as well,' said Benedict.

She was touched he should care so much. 'Benedict, I can't. Edward would find it— unbearable. Now look, can I order something off that wonderful trolley and then I must go. I have to catch the three thirty from Victoria, or I shall be in terrible trouble.'

*   *   *

'Any progress?' said Cecily when he got home.

'She wants to set up a scholarship at the hospital. But she seems very set against going back into medicine herself. Says it would be very hard on Edward. I don't see why.'

'Oh, Benedict, really! How would you feel if it was me? If I was a much better stockbroker than you were, and I was setting up in a rival firm.'

'Is she really a better doctor than he is?'

'Much better.'

'Poor Cassia. Very tough.' He looked at her. 'How do you feel, Cecily?'

'All right. A bit tired. Why?'

'I thought we might discuss Christmas. This party you've been talking about, the guest list and so on. I've drawn up mine. Here.'

She looked at it, and recognised most of the

138

names. 'Who's Dominic Foster?'

He was pouring himself a drink. There was a pause, just fractionally too long. 'Architect I met. Working on one of these garden city developments I've invested in. Nice chap. You'd like him. I was telling Cassia she ought to put some money into that field. Huge potential.'

'Oh,' she said. 'Yes, well, do let's invite him.'

He looked at her then and she could see that he had, as always, understood, that he knew what she was thinking. Whether she was right or wrong, she knew she was right to go on enquiring, being careful; making sure—and making sure he knew what she was doing. She had to: for both their sakes.

CHAPTER SEVEN

Cassia wrote to the Dean, and got a charming letter back. He would be delighted to see her. Would she not join him for coffee one morning to discuss her proposal?

Cassia walked slowly through the medical school, past the lecture theatre, past the labs; the smells, the noises, taking her back. She forced down the inevitable regrets, and knocked firmly on the Dean's door.

'You were very happy here, weren't you?' he said, his thick eyebrows meeting over his piercing dark eyes. 'Did well too. Damn shame. Oh, I know, you did what you felt you had to. More's the pity. Wanted to do obstetrics, didn't you? Instead of which, you had to have brats of your own. Dreadful waste. Dreadful. Well, there you are. Now then, what's all this about a scholarship or a fellowship or something?'

They decided a research chair in obstetrics should be set up, with an annual donation of ten thousand pounds.

'Jolly fine idea, this,' said the Dean, 'most generous. What shall we call it? The Fallon Chair?'

'No,' Cassia said quickly. 'I thought perhaps Beatty. That was my godmother's name, the one who left me the money.'

'Well, that's up to you. Husband know about this, does he?'

She met his eyes steadily. 'No. Actually, he doesn't. Of course I'm going to tell him.'

'Probably best. Not very bright, as I recall, your husband.' The eyes were more piercing still.

'He's very bright,' said Cassia, defensively. 'He just suffered horribly from exam nerves.'

'Funny how the really brilliant chaps always manage to overcome those. And I dare say he was touchy, you doing better than him. Probably just as well for him that you decided to get out, if you really had to marry him. Not for you though.'

'Yes,' she said, and then she took a deep breath and said what she had sworn she would never say, never ask, never think even: what chance would there be of her returning now?

'To come back here, absolutely none. You might persuade a general hospital to take you on, as a houseman. It'd be very tough, though. And you couldn't do that, could you? Move into a hospital, leave those children?'

'No, I couldn't possibly.'

'Well, tell you what you might do, if you're really

140

serious. These birth control clinics setting up all over the place now—more power to their elbows, I'm sure you'd agree. There might be a chance you could work at one of those. They want women doctors. It's pretty mundane work, but if you're serious, I know a few people in that field. I could arrange for you to see someone.'

'Thank you,' she said, and realised that the weight had lifted just a bit, that the coldness was easier. 'Thank you, yes. It's probably out of the question, and my husband would have to agree and—'

'For God's sake,' said the Dean. He slammed his fist down on the desk. 'What was I doing, giving a valuable place to you, just to hear that your husband will have to agree to your doing a bit of work? Well, I mustn't upset you, or you might change your mind about the Chair. And thank you for that. Thank you a hundred times. Give my regards to that husband of yours.'

'Yes, I will. Thank you.'

'Nice hat,' he said suddenly. 'I like to see a nice hat on a pretty woman.'

She was still smiling when she reached the street.

*   *   *

London was looking very Christmassy, lights everywhere, windows decorated lavishly. She wandered down Bond Street, enjoying it, and then started worrying about Christmas itself, about how she was going to get it right. She had thought she wouldn't spend a lot of money, that she would only buy everyone the sort of present she and Edward could afford together, nothing that he would find threatening. And then, as she had sat in her car, her ridiculous, lovely, rich-girl's car in the High Street in Haywards Heath and looked in the window of the bicycle shop and seen a gleaming red and chrome Raleigh bike with a three-speed and lamps, and thought of how much Bertie longed for such a thing, and thought also of the Meccano set (size 3) she had actually bought him, it all seemed extremely silly, if not downright mean. So she had bought the bike, a trike of comparable splendour for William and a wonderfully frilly dolls' crib for Delia.

She hid them all in the loft.

She had bought expensive presents for Peggy and Mrs Briggs too (knowing that they knew about the money, knowing they would find her mean if she did not): a soft lambswool shawl for Mrs Briggs and a pretty woollen blouse and skirt for Peggy, and hampers from Fortnum's for both their families. And then, while she was on the phone to Fortnum's, she had ordered one for themselves too. Edward could hardly expect them to sit down to a modest meal and a bottle of Burgundy while down the road his servants' families were downing the champagne and foie gras that his wife had provided.

Just the same, she realised, gazing into Asprey's vulgar windows, she was increasingly nervous. Perhaps she should leave all the expensive presents in the loft, and get out the Meccano sets and the rag doll she had bought in the first place. But that really did seem silly.

*　　　*　　　*

142

Cecily was enjoying her party; she always did. Apart from anything else, she liked just standing and observing it as it reached its peak, studying it, this creation of hers, this carefully choreographed company.

She was a natural hostess: generous, thoughtful, socially imaginative. Nobody at her parties ever had an empty glass, stood alone on the edge of a group, found him or herself rooted for more than a few minutes in uncongenial company. People always left happily, pleased with themselves as well as her.

The major part was inevitably made up of glossy London society, with even the occasional minor royal—she had twice entertained the Duke of Gloucester and his pretty duchess, and once the Princess Royal and Lord Lascelles—but she also liked to include members of the international set, women like Natalie Paley, daughter of the Grand Duke of Russia, Mme Martinez de Hoz, even once Diana Vreeland, her guest list a glittering roll call of the smart and interesting.

After the party, a couple of dozen—tactfully briefed—would stay for supper.

Tonight the family representation was small: Harry and Edwina Moreton, Cecily's parents, and Cassia Fallon. Edward had been unable to come, due to an influenza epidemic sweeping the Home Counties. The close friends included Rupert Cameron and the high-profile architect Dominic Foster and his wife Nicola, thin, dark haired, almost impossibly chic. Foster, tall, dark, languidly good-looking, was reputedly single-handedly responsible for converting a very large stretch of green countryside around the south-eastern edge

143

of London into suburban streets.

Nicola Foster had been talking for some time to Edwina Moreton: Cecily watched her, thinking how much she would like to look like that, with a boyish figure, a neatly cropped head.

Nicola was coming over to her now, smiling. 'Thank you so much, we've had a marvellous time, but we must go now. Where is Dominic? Ah, there you are. I must just go and powder my nose, and then we must move off.'

Dominic stood looking down at Cecily. He really was very good-looking, she thought, and his charm was undeniable.

'Cecily, goodnight. It's been the most wonderful evening. Thank you so much for inviting us.'

'Well,' she said, offering her face as he bent from his considerable height to kiss her, 'I'm so glad you were able to accept. You and your wife must come and dine with us one evening, after Christmas.'

'We should be delighted. Thank you. And a happy Christmas to you.' He half bowed, smiled at her, then turned away, went over to Benedict, who was sitting down, talking to her mother.

Cecily watched them closely: Benedict looked up at Dominic, smiled, stood up, shook his hand, and then, clapping the other arm on his shoulder, ushered him gently out of the room. It was nothing but the most urbane of gestures, and Benedict was back very soon. Within less than sixty seconds, he came over to her, sat down beside her, kissed her hand, told her how clever she was, what a wonderful evening it had been. Nevertheless, she knew. She always knew. And some dark, fearful instinct told her that this time she might very well not be able to do anything about it.

*   *   *

Cassia was sitting on the sofa with Rupert; thinking how much she loved him (while no longer being in love with him), watching the room, chatting idly about this person and that, envying and trying to analyse Edwina's chic.

'You look infinitely beautiful tonight, my darling,' said Rupert, smiling at her, and she smiled back, startled as always by his apparent ability to read her thoughts. 'Edward is very foolish to let you out on your own.'

'Rupert, I'm a hick matron of twenty-eight with three small children. Don't be so silly.'

'Twenty-eight I have to allow you, immense age that it is, but hick you are not. You look extremely stylish. That is a wonderful dress, black always did become you. God, I wish I was twenty-eight again.'

'What were you doing when you were twenty-eight?' she said curiously.

'Very much the same as I am doing now,' he said lightly, 'being an unsuccessful two-star actor, touring in various two-star companies, with a long string of disastrous love affairs already behind me. Only then I knew I was going to be successful one day—now I don't.'

She stared at him, shocked by the genuine sadness in his voice. 'Rupert, I've never heard you talk like this before.'

'I don't very often. Mostly I know I'm lucky to be working at all, to have survived the war, to be happy, to have friends like you, but turning fifty-five hurts a bit. Makes you think. But what I mind is never playing the West End. Not once. And never will now, I fear.'

'You might.'

'I don't think so. It would take a miracle to manage that. But enough of self-pity, my darling. Cecily looks wonderful, doesn't she? So serene. It suits her, pregnancy.'

'Yes, it does. Although . . .'

'I know. I saw it too. Nothing to worry about there. He's much too ambitious, that young man. Harmless in this context, I would say. I shall go and tell Cecily so right away.'

'Rupert, be careful. She doesn't like . . . well, you know, anyone knowing.'

'Of course she doesn't. When was I anything but the soul of tact?'

She watched him move over to the sofa, perch on its arm, start chatting to Cecily, obviously telling her some joke, then gossiping. And saw Cecily look up at him, startled, then smile, and visibly relax.

Much later, Cassia asked him what he had said.

'Oh, just that there was only one thing Dominic Foster really wanted and would stop at nothing to get, and that was a knighthood, and that his every action was directed at that.'

'Is that true?' she said.

Rupert hesitated. 'Not *quite*, but the end result will be exactly the same. He certainly won't do anything remotely risky. It was shorthand for that. And it made Cecily feel much better.'

'You're wonderful,' said Cassia, reaching up to kiss him, 'and I love you.'

*   *   *

Christmas passed with surprising ease. Cassia had,

with infinite care, put her case to Edward, had said how Scrooge-like it seemed not to buy everyone nice presents, had explained about the bicycles in the windows, and the dolls' cot and about Peggy and Mrs Briggs and the hampers and indeed their own, and he had accepted it all with a very good grace. On Christmas Eve she had given him his present—a very plain gold watch, which he was delighted with.

Afterwards she persuaded him to make love to her. It hadn't happened for a long time and lying with him now, afterwards, her body fallen sweetly into peace, she said, 'Edward, I do love you very much.'

'I know you do,' he said. It was an unexpected response; she was disconcerted by it.

'And I presume you still love me?' She was half nervous, smiling into the darkness, her hands still moving tenderly over him.

'Of course I do.' He leaned towards her and kissed her, then turned over into his sleeping position, his back towards her.

And she felt, in spite of the sudden closeness, his cautiousness was back, and knew she couldn't do anything about it, anything at all.

*   *   *

On 20 January, 1936 King George V died at Sandringham. The old king had scarcely drawn his last breath before Queen Mary kissed her eldest son's hand and said, 'The King is dead, long live the King.' The new reign had begun, and the new king was said to be possessed by a frantic grief. There was immediately across the country not only sadness, an echo indeed of that grief, but a sense of excitement at the accession of this new, young, charismatic king.

Next day Edward VIII travelled to London, to present himself before the Accession Privy Council and broadcast to his people, and the following day the Accession was proclaimed at four different points in London, the first being St James's Palace. A photographer caught sight of the king standing in the window just before he left the palace, talking to a slender, pale, dark-haired woman, still unknown to most of his subjects. Next day almost every newspaper carried that picture of the King and the unknown woman. She was not unknown for very long.

*   *   *

'I'm going to London on Thursday,' said Cassia at supper one night early in February.

'What for this time? More shopping?' Edward smiled at her, but his eyes were wary. 'I'm sure it will be very dreary up there, the capital must still be in mourning. Absurd, the whole thing.'

'What, that everyone should be sad the King has died? I don't agree with you.'

'Oh, I forgot you had met him,' said Edward, his voice heavy with irony.

'Mummy! You met the King!' said Bertie, his brown eyes wide with excitement. 'How, where?'

'At Buckingham Palace,' said Cassia quickly. 'It was just a big sort of party thing.' Edward was scowling at the newspaper.

'Golly! Mummy! What was it like?'

'Quite exciting,' she said, risking the scowl being

148

directed at her, resentful at it suddenly.

'Did they have their crowns on?'

There was a scrape as Edward pushed his chair back. 'I have to go,' he said. 'I have work to do. Why are you going to London, if it's not to join in the mood of national mourning?'

'I'm going to have lunch with Godpa and Margaret. They invited me ages ago, and I've put it off and off and now it seemed a nice idea. Is that all right?'

'Yes, if you can spare the time.'

'Of course I can spare it,' she said. 'I haven't exactly got a full-time job.'

'Well, things have changed rather,' he said.

'What do you mean?'

'I mean that you used to find it difficult to arrange to be here with me in the mornings even, because you were so busy with the church and the WI and so on, and now you seem to be able to dash off up to London at a moment's notice.'

'Boys, off you go,' she said, seeing Bertie's eyes watchful suddenly, less starry. 'Go and find Peggy, ask her to wash your faces.' And as they left the room she closed the door and said, 'Edward, that's not fair. I haven't been near London since before Christmas. I've chosen Thursday because you don't have a morning surgery, and Bertie's at school, and Peggy's happy to look after Delia and William.'

'I don't like her being in charge of them too much,' he said. 'She's very limited.'

'Edward, I don't call one day in a month too much.'

'I think it's rather more than that. Actually,' he said.

Cassia suddenly felt a spin of anger. 'It isn't.

Actually. I'll go through my diary if you like and prove it to you. Anyway, if you're so bothered, maybe we should think about getting someone less limited for them.'

'What on earth do you mean?'

'I mean a nanny.'

'A nanny! I don't want a nanny in this house, it would be ridiculous.'

'You might not, Edward. I might. And sometimes I think I want it very much. I have three children under six, one a very demanding baby. It's a lot of work. Most women in my situation have a lot more help than I do.'

'I don't seem to recall that many of my patients' doors are opened to me by a nanny, even if there are six children under six inside.'

'Oh, Edward, stop it. You know perfectly well what I mean.'

'Yes,' he said, 'I do know perfectly well what you mean. And I find it rather offensive. The implication is that I have never been able to afford to provide the sort of help you have a right to expect.'

'You are being childish,' she said, starting to unstrap Delia from the chair harness. 'Childish and—oh, never mind.'

'But I do mind,' he said, 'very much. Anyway, you go off and have your lunch with your rich relations. I'm sure it will be a lot more enjoyable than cold meat and salad here with me.'

'Oh, for God's sake,' she said, and left the room, slamming the door behind her.

He had still hardly spoken to her when she left for London on Thursday morning.

*　　　*　　　*

She actually caught a far earlier train than was strictly necessary: she just didn't want to be hanging around the house. Having consequently got to London far earlier than was necessary, she decided to go and do a little shopping.

London was very quiet. All the shop windows were draped with black, and many of the men wore black bands round their sleeves, but inside the stores it was more cheerful.

She went to Harrods and began to enjoy herself. Delia needed some new dresses and while she was in the children's department she bought a few things for the boys as well. She wandered down to the fashion floor and bought a couple of dresses for herself, one a day dress, in fine navy jersey which would be very useful, and the other a cocktail dress which certainly wouldn't, in black silk crepe, ankle length, with long narrow sleeves, scooped out at the back and with a long fall of the same fabric, reminiscent of a train, almost as long as the dress. Heaven knew when she'd be wearing it, probably not until Cecily's next Christmas party. And then because she had no shoes to go with it, she bought a pair of black suede shoes, elegantly narrow with slender heels, and a bag to match with a rhinestone clasp, and then found herself looking at hats, and trying on and finding it impossible not to buy a wonderful, ridiculous hat, broad brimmed and shallow-crowned, with a huge osprey feather set right across it.

She felt quite differently when she had finished her shopping. It was alarming how it could do that for her, shopping, she had discovered. She was able

151

to think about Edward more tolerantly: so tolerantly indeed that she bought him a new silk tie before visiting the flower shop and acquiring an armful of lilies for Margaret.

She went out of the back door of Harrods to hail a taxi and direct it to Grosvenor Gardens. There weren't a great many taxis about, and as she stood there waiting, she realised that she was standing opposite an estate agent, and for no reason at all, simply idle curiosity, she crossed the street, leaving her shopping in the charge of the Harrods doorman, and studied the houses on offer in the window. There was one that caught her eye, not for sale, but to rent, an enchanting little dolls' house of a thing, in Walton Street. 'Long summer let, drawing room, dining room, three bedrooms, staff quarters in basement, pretty garden. £250 per calendar month.' And because Walton Street was so near, and because she was still going to be a little early for her lunch, she walked the five minutes or so down the street and stood looking at it.

It was at the Harrods end of Walton Street, a tall, narrow little house, built in stucco and London stock brick, with steps with iron railings running up to the red front door. Cassia looked at it and smiled, for the house had charm and a certain aura of happiness about it.

She went back to Harrods, checked her parcels were still safe with the doorman and went into the estate agents, only really to confirm that the house was actually let.

No, indeed, it was not, said the rather middle-aged young man at the desk. It was a most delightful property, and ideal if madam was for instance thinking of taking a house for the London Season. If she was interested he could arrange a viewing.

Cassia had no thoughts of taking a London house for the Season, or indeed for anything else, and heard herself saying, to her own considerable surprise, that no, she needed a house for more than six months, unfortunately. Then, because the young man was so nice and so clearly disappointed, she allowed him to take her name and address so that he could inform her of any other properties which might suit her. She finally retrieved her parcels from the long-suffering doorman and allowed him to hail her a taxi.

And then, partly because sitting in a taxi on her way to Grosvenor Gardens, surrounded with bags and boxes of clothes, suddenly brought it rather forcefully back to her, and partly because of the conversation at breakfast, she found herself suddenly reliving that summer of 1924, when she had done the Season, been a debutante, presented at Court by Leonora, when, despite her reluctance, she had had such a wonderful time . . .

Cassia had been actually shocked to find how much she had enjoyed it, almost from the beginning.

Of course a lot of the girls had been silly, and a great many more of their mothers were terrible, but many of them were friendly. Leonora was immensely popular, which had helped to make Cassia more so, and insisting on giving her a cocktail party in April as well as her dance in June, had sent her status up, establishing her as one of the more important girls, one to be courted.

She would hardly have been human if she hadn't

liked, at the age of seventeen, the experience of being bought literally dozens of lovely dresses, of going to wonderful houses all over London, and in the country at weekends, and dancing night after night away, of finding herself clearly, and to her great surprise, attractive to young men—pretty silly some of them too, but some were quite good-looking and amusing—of finding her dance programme filled up quite early in each evening, of eating a lot of wonderful food and drinking a great deal of extremely nice champagne—too much, very often, but who cared how you felt in the morning, when you could lie in bed late, have breakfast there and wait to feel better.

The presentation at Court, which she had been particularly scornful of, had in fact been (she admitted to her diary) quite amazingly wonderful. From the moment she had stood in the drawing room in the house at Grosvenor Gardens beside Leonora, both of them in their white Court dresses with long trains, and the three white osprey feathers—the Prince of Wales feathers—in their hair, and seen Sir Richard's face tender with admiration as he raised yet another glass of champagne to them both, she had felt as if she were living some strange, enchanted dream.

There were over three hundred girls being presented that night, and there was a very long wait in the ante-room. She longed for the lavatory, but there wasn't one, merely a chamber pot in another small room, behind a screen, for those in the direst need. Cassia decided her need wasn't that dire, and distracted herself by reciting her Latin declensions. She felt quite sure none of the other girls would have even known what a declension was: for most

154

of them and their mothers, education was something almost entirely wasted on girls. Females were reared and prepared for a life of marriage, motherhood, and housekeeping at its loftiest level, and had no thoughts or ambitions beyond it.

She was just thinking that the most humble of her classmates at Leeds Girls' High, the ones on scholarships, were worth ten of each of these foolish, vapid, spoilt creatures, and wondering not for the first time in the past six weeks what on earth she was actually doing here, when she and Leonora were ushered into the throne room, and more appropriate thoughts immediately entered her head.

The throne room was vast and almost impossibly grand, all huge gilt mirrors and fine paintings and red velvet hangings and incredibly elaborate crystal chandeliers. There was a string orchestra playing in the gallery, and at the end of the room, under a gilt and velvet canopy, were set the two thrones. It was all more like a stage set than a stage set.

Their Majesties were both smaller than she had expected, but immensely, glitteringly imposing, Queen Mary's famously statuesque stance accentuated by her piled-up hair and impossibly deep pearl necklace. As Cassia made her deep, deep curtsy, her head bowed (terrified her feathers would somehow escape their moorings and fall off), she suddenly remembered Rupert studying a picture of her and saying he thought the Queen was probably not real at all, but stuffed, and felt a wild and inappropriate desire to giggle.

*   *   *

Cassia's own dance had been held in the second week of June. 'Before Ascot and Henley. People are beginning to get just a little jaded after that,' Leonora had said when the date was first discussed. There was to be a dinner party for twenty beforehand, in the dining room, and then the dance would begin at ten in the marquee. Four hundred people had been invited and every time she thought about it, Cassia felt a mixture of nerves and total disbelief. Her dress was gloriously simple, in palest blush-pink silk crepe—'It should be white, but let's cheat a little, and make you stand out,' Leonora had said blithely as they looked at endless toiles and fabrics. It was long-waisted, skimming over her slender body, hinting at, rather than outlining her small high breasts, with a softly tiered skirt falling almost to the floor and dipping into a slight train behind her. On her golden-blonde hair, carved now into a perfect, jawline bob, she wore a diamante bandeau, and her only other jewellery was her present from Leonora and Sir Richard for the occasion, a double string of pearls.

She had gone down the stairs and they had been waiting for her at the bottom, Leonora and Richard, and as she reached them, saw them looking at her in something more than admiration. She was no longer a pretty schoolgirl playing games at being a debutante, but a young woman, not only beautiful but sensuously aware of the fact.

And then Harry had arrived. She looked down at him, observing him in the simple act of handing his cloak to Jarvis, acutely and arrogantly aware of the sheer force of his own presence, and remembered afresh how much she disliked him.

He looked up and saw her, and bowed just

slightly, and as she reached the bottom of the stairs, he took her hand and kissed it. 'Well, well,' he said, 'how grown up you are. I would not have known you.'

'Nor I you,' she said coolly, and then she looked up at him and saw something at the back of his eyes, something reluctant, something she could see he found difficult.

He said, almost as if against his will, 'You look lovely, Cassia. Really very lovely indeed,' and she had remembered that moment for the rest of her life.

Harry had spent much of the evening on the sidelines watching, his expression brooding and slightly disdainful. He danced a few times with some of the more sophisticated girls, and once Leonora laughingly asked him to dance and impressed the two of them gave what amounted to an exhibition of the Charleston. The entire floor cleared and everybody watched. Harry danced extremely well, and she had been surprised: in her experience it was small slight men who danced well, not six-footers who looked like rugby fullbacks.

It was a perfect night: warm, brilliantly moonlit, the air thick with the scent of roses. She felt wonderfully, perfectly happy, as if some kind of seal had been set on her life: her charmed life.

And then Harry had come over to her, bowed briefly, said, 'May I have this dance?'

It was a waltz. She had moved, slightly awkward, into his arms. She had never been close to him before; he was very warm, and he held her very firmly. It was not an unpleasant sensation, and dancing with him was oddly sensual. For the first time in a year she felt the strange deep stirrings in her that Rupert had once inspired, and resented them. Those were for Rupert, the love of her life, she didn't want to feel anything for any other man, and certainly not for Harry Moreton, whom she disliked.

'Shall we slip away?' said Harry suddenly.

'I'm sorry?' She stopped dancing and stared at him.

'Go to a night-club. Maybe the KitKat. It's terrifically smart there.'

'Harry, you're suggesting I should leave my own dance and go to a night-club?'

'Just for an hour or so. No one'll know. Surely you've done that before? Edwina Fox-Ashley told me she hadn't spent more than an hour at any party this year.'

'Harry, I don't think I want to dance with you for a single moment more,' Cassia said. 'I'd like to go and sit down now. Perhaps you'd get me a drink. Before you leave.'

'Oh, for God's sake.' He looked irritated. 'It was only a suggestion. Yes, all right, I'll get you a drink. If that's what you want.'

She went outside the marquee and stood breathing in the cool, soothing air, reminding herself he was a stupid, spoilt, childish youth. When he found her he was carrying two glasses and a bottle of champagne, and was looking slightly uncomfortable.

'I'm sorry. If I upset you. Didn't mean to.'

'Well, you did. You'd better go if you want to, I should think. It's getting late. I'd hate to keep you.'

'Oh, no hurry,' he said. 'These places all stay open till dawn.'

He seemed genuinely unaware of how much he

had hurt her, and against her will she smiled at him.

She realised suddenly that he was very drunk. 'You do look very nice,' he said, and bent suddenly and tried to kiss her on the lips.

Cassia turned her head away, but he pulled it round sharply and kissed her again, holding her face still. His breath smelt of alcohol; she pulled away from him. 'Harry, don't. You're drunk.'

'Of course I'm not drunk. I haven't had enough to get drunk. Little Miss Goody Two Shoes,' he said. 'Just an innocent little girl from the backwoods, aren't you, Cassia? Dressed up as something quite different.'

'Don't talk to me like that,' said Cassia sharply.

'Why not? You really don't know how the world works at all. Or maybe you do.'

'Harry, would you please stop patronising me. I resent that, very much.'

'Well, let's see. Put you to the test.' He looked at her, an odd expression in his eyes, malicious, almost mean. 'Let's see how much you know about real life, shall we?'

That was when he told her about Benedict.

*   *   *

She had been horribly, hideously upset, had felt sick.

'Go away,' she said, half shouting. 'Get out of here, out of my dance. You've spoilt it, you spoil everything. You're foul and vile and I wish I'd never met you. Get out, get out of this garden, this house. Go, go go.'

Harry looked, for the first time since she had

159

known him, unsure of himself.

'I said go!' she shouted again.

She had no idea how long she stayed out there, trying to come to terms with what she had heard, trying to make sense of it.

For years she had been puzzled by it, by why he had done it; when finally she saw that he had found her rejection of him unbearable, had sought for revenge and found it in a piece of wanton cruelty, she saw also why he had felt her rejection so strongly. Only of course by the time she understood, it was too late. Much too late.

*   *   *

She had piled most of her parcels and boxes up on to the pavement, and was rummaging in her purse for money when she heard a voice, amused, that she knew very well indeed saying, 'An expensive morning, Mrs Fallon, I presume?'

She lifted her head, and because she had been thinking about him, or rather trying not to think about him, she found herself filled with all the old emotions, rather than the new, nudging towards friendship, and looked very coolly at Harry Moreton. 'No, not really, just a few things for the children.'

'Really?'

'Yes,' she said, bending to pick up the bags, and promptly dropping the hatbox, which he recovered for her—only not before the lid had slithered off and revealed the contents in all its absurd extravagance.

'An unusual hat for a child,' he said, 'but perhaps life in the country is more interesting than I had imagined.'

She looked at him, trying to summon up the carefully nurtured hostility, and then, because the situation was so extremely silly, smiled. 'I did think I deserved one thing for myself,' she said.

'I'm sure you do. And it is a very fine hat indeed,' he said, 'and I do hope you can find some suitable occasions for it. Not too many down in a Sussex village, I imagine.'

'I do occasionally leave the Sussex village,' said Cassia.

'As I see. With a slightly increased frequency, too, I fancy. Now let me help you in with those and—Do put the hat on, give Richard a treat. Margaret has many virtues, but she's not God's gift to the couturiers. I hear you are lunching with them. Sadly, I can't join you, I have a dreary assignation at the Reform Club. I've been discussing the new Waterloo Bridge project with Richard.'

'What are you doing to Waterloo Bridge?'

He stood staring at her, his face first surprised, then thoughtful. 'I'd forgotten what an unfeminine interest you take in such things,' he said slowly. 'It's rather nice.'

'Harry, really, that's a monstrously old-fashioned remark. Women do have much more in their heads these days than—well, than hats and the staff shortage.'

'Do they?' he said. 'I hadn't noticed. Anyway, Richard is involved in the construction of the bridge and I am investing in it. That is, my company is investing in it.'

'I didn't know you had a company.'

'There is a great deal you don't know about me,

161

Cassia,' he said lightly, 'to my regret. Anyway, let me help you carry all those clothes for your children.'

She was still laughing when Jarvis opened the door.

*   *   *

Harry was persuaded to join them for a drink before lunch, and then departed with huge expressions of regret.

Sir Richard was touchingly delighted to see her; Margaret in her undemonstrative way was also welcoming. She really could not have been a greater contrast to Leonora, Cassia thought, with her long, rather fierce face, her solid figure, her severely drawn-back grey hair.

'I'm afraid I have to leave you shortly after luncheon,' Sir Richard said. 'I've a crisis at the factory. Will you forgive me?'

'Of course.'

Lunch was delicious: clear soup, lamb cutlets, apple tart. It was, indeed, she thought with a suppressed sigh, much nicer than cold meat and salad. Afterwards they moved into the drawing room.

Over coffee, Sir Richard said, 'Well now, tell me more about this Chair you are planning to set up at that hospital of yours.'

She told him that it was to be a Chair of obstetric research, that she desperately wanted to do it, that it was the nearest she was going to get to doing obstetric research of her own now.

'Very sad, that,' Margaret interjected.

'Yes, well,' Cassia said, a little over-bright, 'I try

162

not to think about it too much. And I just might be able to do something else, it seems, something at least a bit medical. Anyway, back to the Chair. I want it to bear the Beatty name, in Leonora's memory, as I said on the phone.'

'Well, darling, it's very sweet of you, and exceedingly generous. I think you deserve to spend the money on yourself.'

'There's plenty left for me,' she said, laughing. 'It was half a million pounds, after all.'

There was a very long silence and then he stood up and came over to her, and bent and kissed her and said, 'My darling, how wonderful, I'm so very delighted for you,' but not before she had seen in his eyes an expression of such absolute and unmistakable shock that she was seriously shaken herself.

CHAPTER EIGHT

'Right, Mrs Moreton. Do get dressed and come back into the consulting room.' Then the nurse said very gently, as she did at this point to all Mr Fortescue's ladies, 'Can I offer you a cup of tea?'

'No,' said Edwina, 'no, thank you.' She managed a wry smile. 'A gin would be more like it.'

Mr Fortescue was sitting behind his large desk. His face was round above his multiple chins. He had assumed an expression of careful sympathy.

'Well now, Mrs Moreton,' he said, 'I'm afraid, as you suspected, that there is no sign of a pregnancy. Now, of course nothing is certain, and the human body and its reproductive capacity is not an exact

163

science. However—'

'I'm not ever going to be able to have children?' she said, forcing the words out.

'It seems unlikely. It would appear that you are simply not ovulating, and unfortunately the progesterone injections have not worked either. Which means—'

'I know what it means,' she said. 'No eggs. For the jolly little sperm to meet.' A brittle smile.

'Yes. Correct.'

'And there's no treatment for that?'

'I'm afraid not, no. We've been through this before, of course, but I would like to recap. You are quite sure you haven't had any infections, as far as you know? Of the uterus, or . . . well, of a gynaecological nature?'

'No,' said Edwina firmly. 'I haven't. So why do you think I've missed two periods when they're usually so painful and heavy?'

'I would say almost certainly for psychological reasons. You wanted to be pregnant so much you managed to persuade your body that you were.'

'Yes, I see.'

'It's a pity your husband couldn't come with you today,' said Mr Fortescue. 'I would have liked to talk to you both.'

'He's out of London this week,' said Edwina quickly.

'I see. How does he feel about your failure to conceive?'

'I don't think he minds. Very much.' That was a lie: Harry was beginning to mind very much indeed.

'Well, do tell him that if he has any questions, if I can give him any information, he is most welcome to come and see me.'

'Yes. Yes, I will.' As if Harry, who would not tolerate failure in any area, and in anyone, would agree to discuss his wife's infertility with a complete stranger. Even an expert on the subject.

*   *   *

It was growing dark when she emerged into Welbeck Street and there was a raw wind blowing up it; she felt tired and very depressed. If Harry knew about this, about her infertility, he would probably want to divorce her.

Perhaps it would be a good idea anyway; they had so little in common, were hardly happy. She should never have married him, really; she had known deep down it was a mistake, but he had been the most amazing catch—good-looking, sexy, charming, clever—and rich. So extremely rich . . .

So that when he had asked her, when he had said . . .

'Edwina, I'd like you to marry me.'

She had been sitting beside him at a table at a ball. She had thought at first he was joking, had laughed, (thinking at the same time she wouldn't have minded if he was not, he looked so absurdly handsome in his tails) and then seen that the expression in his eyes was very serious. Not exactly warm, not exactly lover-like; but serious. Almost desperate.

So she had sat back in her chair and looked at him, and said, 'I presume you don't actually mean that, Harry. Or do you?'

'Of course I bloody well mean it!' Then clearly realising that this was hardly lover-like behaviour, he pulled himself up almost visibly and said, 'I want

165

you to marry me very much. I think you're beautiful and extremely interesting and very very sexy and I'm sure we'd be happy.'

It was the word 'interesting' that did it: she had always tried to be interesting, and thought she had failed, that she was too empty headed, too concerned with trivia to qualify as such.

Beauty, she knew she possessed—her oval face, her creamy skin, her brown eyes and her gleaming dark hair—and she knew she was sexy too.

She loved sex, and indeed had discovered her body and the pleasure it could afford her when she was only fifteen and sharing a bed with a friend at an overcrowded country house party where her parents were guests. The girl, who had been making a great play of reading a story by Virginia Woolf in bed, had begun almost at once making advances towards Edwina, stroking her breasts and her thighs, and then when Edwina had to her own great surprise plainly liked it, had not withdrawn, but started kissing her.

Edwina had found the soft mouth on hers, its tongue seeking out her own, wildly exciting, and responded. Her delight when the girl began to feel between her legs, and thence further, seeking out an area of almost unimaginable sensation and pleasure, surprised but did not in any way repel her. She had grown up in the company of an outrageous mother: Sylvia Fox-Ashley had talked to her openly about sex, in all its manifestations and pleasures, from her earliest years. Lesbian and homosexual sex of all kinds had always interested rather than shocked Edwina.

An introduction to heterosexual sex a year later, with a sweaty Etonian after a New Year's Eve party

166

in Scotland, disappointed her, but she persevered, and several more experienced lovers later she was happy to accept that her true sexuality was of the more conventional kind; although she had continued over the years to enjoy the occasional lesbian encounter.

She had not slept with Harry Moreton until the night he had proposed to her so unexpectedly, and completely overwhelmed by him and the intoxicating prospect of marrying him, she had gone home with him to his great house in Lowndes Square and found herself experiencing such extraordinary and ferocious pleasure in his bed that for days afterwards her body continued to stir and throb at the memory.

She finally fell asleep to find him leaning over her, looking at her with a mixture of desire and a strange impatience; she smiled and he said, without smiling back, 'You haven't yet said if you'll marry me.'

She said of course she would; and then, greedy for more of him, pulled him down on to her and into her, and they did not talk any more.

*   *   *

It was days later, after a great many bottles of champagne had been drunk and congratulations received, that she realised that he had never said he loved her. Nor had he asked her if she loved him.

She buried the thought deep under a welter of plans and did not allow it to surface until long after the wedding.

When it had been hopelessly too late.

167

*   *   *

Edwina decided to go and see Cecily. It was, she knew, in some ways an unfortunate idea, as Cecily was now seven months pregnant, but Edwina was very fond of her. She was so kind and gentle and extremely easy to talk to, though she had had no intention of telling Cecily about her afternoon with Mr Fortescue, but sitting listening to Cecily talking happily about Fanny and Stephanie and how they felt about the new baby, she suddenly burst into tears and then found herself telling her all about it.

'Oh, darling,' Cecily said, putting her arms round her. 'I'm so, so sorry. I can't think of anything worse. Oh, dear, that's not very tactful, is it?'

'Don't be silly,' said Edwina impatiently. 'I can't imagine anything worse either.'

'What does Harry think about it all?' said Cecily.

'He doesn't know,' said Edwina sharply, 'and he's not to.'

'Edwina, you can't keep it from him. I mean, it's obvious, and—'

'Yes, yes, I know. But I don't want him to know there's no hope at all. He'd hate it. I know he would. Much better to let him go on thinking it might happen. And besides,' she said, distorting Mr Fortescue's actual words on the subject slightly, 'he did say there was some hope. Just that it was very unlikely.'

'Edwina, you could adopt.'

'Can you imagine Harry, with all that male arrogance of his, taking some other person's child into his life and thinking of it as his own? Look, don't start worrying about Harry,' said Edwina

168

fretfully, 'it's me who needs the sympathy. Harry has lots of other things in his life: his work, his paintings—God, the money he spends on those things, bought a Modigliani last week for thousands—his horses . . . at least he hasn't got a mistress. Yet. At least I don't think so.' She lit a cigarette.

'Oh, Edwina, of course he hasn't. Don't be absurd.'

'It's not absurd. Harry is rich, very attractive and getting bored with me. I know he is. So it would be extremely naive of me not to expect it.' She smiled, a quick, bright little smile. 'Anyway, when he does, of course, then I shall take a lover. Much better than making a fuss, don't you think? And much more fun as well.'

'Do you have anyone in mind?' said Cecily, laughing.

'There are lots of people I'd be happy to jump into bed with, if that's what you mean, but no one who's actually asked me. Seriously, that is.'

'Well, I hope they don't,' said Cecily, 'and I'm sure Harry isn't about to have an affair. I'm sure he loves you very much.'

'Cecily, he doesn't love me at all. Never has. Don't look like that. Oh God.' And the tears began again. 'What I need,' she said, blowing her nose, 'is something to do. I can't really devote the rest of my life to buying myself frocks and giving parties. God, I wish I'd been a bit better educated. Like Cassia.'

'A lot of good it's done Cassia,' said Cecily briskly. 'Completely wasted, thanks to that prig of a husband of hers.'

*   *   *

169

'Mummy! William's been sick. All in his bed and then on mine.'

'Oh God.' Cassia dragged herself out of sleep. 'I'm coming, Bertie, tell William to go to the lavatory.'

'He's in there already. He's crying.'

She went to find William, shutting the bedroom door carefully behind her. It was three o'clock. Poor Edward had only been in bed for an hour, after delivering a very reluctant baby.

An hour later she had changed William's bed twice more, and was sitting wearily beside him when there was a loud scream from Delia's room. She rushed in, to find Delia throwing up copiously all over her cot and the floor. By the time she had sorted her out, William had been sick again. And then Bertie started. It was a very long night . . .

*   *   *

By seven o'clock they were all three asleep, glassy pale, but the worst over. She crept in beside Edward. He groaned, looked at the clock, said he had to get up.

'They've all three got d and v,' she said. 'I've had a terrible night.'

'It was that mince they had for supper,' he said. 'I thought it smelt off.'

'Why on earth didn't you say something?'

'I thought you'd make your own judgement,' he said.

'Clearly I did. I thought it was off and I thought, oh, good, they'll all be sick. Thanks for your help, Edward.'

'You stay there for a bit. Get some rest. I'll see you later. Did you give them plenty to drink? It's very important to keep up their fluids.'

'Edward,' she said, trying not to shout, 'I do know about the treatment of d and v. Thank you; I just want you to know that everything, everything they had, including water, came right back up again. All right?'

'Yes, all right,' he said. 'I just thought I'd mention it.'

She hoped she could get some sleep; she felt slightly queasy herself. She heard the sounds of the household moving into action below her: Peggy clattering in the kitchen; Edward shouting at her from the dining room for his bacon—God, he was arrogant in his quiet way; Mrs Briggs arriving; Buffy barking at the milkman; Edward shouting at Buffy to be quiet. She tried to get comfortable.

Silence. Peace. Her mind began to spin woozily. Then, 'Mummy! I've been sick again.'

*   *   *

She was dragging the sheets off Bertie's bed when Edward came in holding some letters.

''Fraid Mrs Briggs isn't feeling too good, I've told her to go home. Maybe it wasn't the mince did for these three. So I'll have to haul you into the surgery later. Peggy said she had too much to do to help this morning. You all right?'

'Oh, everything's absolutely fine, Edward. I've still had no sleep, Bertie's just been sick again, and now you tell me Mrs Briggs is going home and you want me in the surgery. Why don't you tell Peggy to go to bed as well, just in case she feels ill later?'

171

'Don't be ridiculous. You all right, old chap? Try to drink some water. By the way, I brought you your post up.' He stopped, looking at her; there was a certain wariness in that look. 'There's something from St Christopher's for you,' he said. 'Any idea what it is?'

'Er, no. Reunion, I expect.' Damn, she should have told the Dean to write to her care of Cecily, but normally she managed to intercept letters.

'I haven't had anything from them.'

'Perhaps it's for both of us.'

'They wouldn't send it just to you, surely? Mind if I look?'

'Well, I—'

'Mummy! Sorry. Oh, sorry. All over your nightie.'

When she had had a bath and washed her hair, she walked wearily into their bedroom.

Edward was sitting on the bed; he looked very odd. 'What the devil is this about?' he said. 'This letter. From the Dean. About a research Chair.'

'Oh,' she said, 'that.'

'Yes. That. Cassia, what the bloody hell are you playing at?' He never swore: she knew it meant he was very upset. 'Does this mean that you've been to see the Dean behind my back, asked him to set up a research Chair at St Christopher's, at my hospital—'

'Mine too.'

'Don't play games, please. My hospital, without even discussing it with me. Have you any idea what sort of humiliation this represents to me, what the Dean must be thinking?'

'Edward, don't be ridiculous. Why should he be thinking anything? Except that he's grateful for the

172

money.'

'The money,' he said. 'Oh yes, that. The damn money.'

There was a ring at the bell. Peggy called up the stairs, 'Doctor! First patient's here.'

He stood up. His face was grey. He looked at her with absolute distaste. 'Please come down as soon as you can. I need your help. We'll talk about this over lunch. It has to be cleared up. And what's this nonsense about a family planning clinic?'

'I don't know. You haven't let me read the letter yet.'

She picked it up. The Dean had scrawled a postscript by hand: 'Spoken to my colleague about the family planning clinics. She'd be pleased to see you; discuss things. Her name is . . .'

She put the letter down. She felt very sick herself.

*   *   *

'I'm going to get a nanny,' said Cassia. 'I've decided.' She was sitting in her chair, on the opposite side of the fire from Edward, she doing some tapestry, he the crossword: a picture of domestic harmony, she thought. Who would think what a bitter battlefield their marriage had become in so short a space of time?

'And do I have any say in this? Since it is my children who are to be handed over?'

'Obviously I wouldn't hire anyone without your approving her. I'll do some interviewing, and when I've got a shortlist I'll ask you to see them.'

'I mean,' he said, 'do I have any say in the fact that you are intending to engage a nanny at all? I have to tell you I'm most unhappy about it. You are their mother. You should be looking after them.'

'You never minded Peggy looking after them. Peggy who is scarcely fit to look after herself.'

'You were never far away.'

'No, I wasn't, and as I intend to be at least a little away, some time in the future, I want someone more responsible to take care of them.'

'How extremely conscientious of you.'

'Oh, go to hell,' said Cassia.

He walked out of the room. She heard him going into his study and shutting the door, and tried to analyse what she felt. It seemed to be horribly little.

*   *   *

'That must have been very very hard,' said Dr Pamela Richards; her rather severe face was full of sympathy. 'To have come thus far, done so well— and then had to give it all up.'

'Well,' said Cassia carefully, 'I was pregnant. And my husband had bought the practice in Monks Heath. I felt I had to yield to those responsibilities.'

'I don't imagine the dean was very pleased. Or Mr Amstruther. I gather you were something of a pet of his.'

'He was furiously angry. Shouted at me for about half an hour.'

Pamela Richards smiled. 'As a wife and mother myself I can sympathise. Although it is a terrible pity you couldn't at least have done your House job. Then you'd have had a base to move forwards from. Anyway, you want to do something now, I understand.'

'Yes. So much . . .'

174

'Well, we do need women doctors. You'll have to do a course, naturally, but you won't find it very arduous. Can you manage that, get the children taken care of and so on?'

'Oh yes.'

'Good. Well, I'll put you down for the next course. It'll be in about a month, I think.'

'Wonderful.'

'I have to warn you,' said Dr Richards, 'this is not the most exciting work. Not for somebody with ambitions in obstetric surgery. But it would be immensely worth while.'

'I really don't mind. It will be a lot more exciting than manning the surgery and the pharmacy for my husband and doing the flowers in the church.'

Pamela Richards laughed. 'Yes, I daresay.' There was a pause. 'He's—happy about it, is he?'

'Oh yes. Of course. Absolutely.'

She almost believed it herself . . .

CHAPTER NINE

'Cecily's had a little boy,' said Cassia. She smiled at Edward, who managed a faint shadow of a smile back.

'How nice,' he said. 'If you'll excuse me, I must go now. I have a particularly large surgery this morning. You'll be able to help later, will you?'

'Yes, today, but you know I won't be here tomorrow? Or the rest of the week?'

'I was hardly likely to forget,' he said.

'But Janet can help you, can't you, Janet?'

'Of course. I'm looking forward to it.' Janet

Fraser beamed at her—she did a lot of beaming. She had been with the family for a month now and was generally a great success. She was twenty-nine, small and slim, with neat dark hair, large sparkling dark eyes and a wonderful wide beam of a smile. Nothing fazed her or seemed capable of even temporarily lowering her spirits, not Delia's tantrums or William's almost unbelievable messiness or the general chaos of the household. Her father had been a senior civil servant in the Foreign Office and Janet was both well travelled and highly educated.

'I especially don't want an old dragon,' Cassia had said to her confidingly when she was interviewing her. 'Just someone who can be part of the family.'

'That's what I want too,' said Janet Fraser. 'And yours is such a lovely family. So if you did feel I would suit you, it would be really very nice indeed.' That was the first time Cassia saw the beam.

Janet Fraser was Princess Christian trained, and although she wore the brown uniform and looked very efficient—as indeed she was—she had proved remarkably easy to live with.

Peggy had rather surprisingly taken to her and the children loved her.

Delia's behaviour had improved 'one hundred and fifty per cent', as Cassia told Cecily, half amused, half rueful, and the boys both said she was a jolly good sort. Although she was firm with them, she played all sorts of games with them, taught them card tricks, took them for long walks exploring the countryside and she didn't even mind Buffy's muddy feet.

Only Edward was resistant.

176

Cassia couldn't remember him smiling at Janet once in the month she had been there. 'I do wish,' she said at the end of the third week, 'you would be a little more polite to Janet.'

'Cassia,' he said, 'I didn't want her to come, I don't like her being here. I'm prepared to tolerate it, but don't ask me to make a bosom friend of her.'

'Don't be ridiculous, Edward, no one's asking you to be her bosom friend. Just a courteous employer.'

'Well, I'm not her employer, am I?' he said with the cold, hard look she had come to dread. 'And I don't want her driving my car. I don't actually like her driving yours.'

'She's not going to drive your car. And I can do what I like with mine.'

'As you do with everything else in your life.'

After a long silence Cassia said, 'Edward, this is so silly. Can't we be friends again? What's changed, what's different, except that life has become a bit easier for me?'

'You are changed, you are different,' he said, 'and life has become much more difficult for me. I can tolerate it. Just. But don't expect me to like it.'

She went out of the room and slammed the door. In the kitchen Peggy looked at Mrs Briggs and raised her eyebrows.

*   *   *

'Cecily is a very old friend,' Cassia explained now to Janet. 'Her husband is my godmother's brother.'

When Janet said, 'I expect you'd like to visit your friend and her new baby after you finish your course tomorrow, so if you're not back by seven I'll

177

make sure Mr Fallon's supper is served,' Cassia had great difficulty in not leaning forward to hug her.

*   *   *

'Mrs Moreton?'

'Yes, that's me.' Edwina pulled off one of her heavy Chanel pearl earrings as she answered the telephone, and sat down on the chair by her desk.

'You don't know me. Mary Whittaker's the name. I was given your number by Cecily Harrington. Such good news about her baby, isn't it?'

'Yes. Very good,' said Edwina politely.

'She said you were looking for something to do. Said you had some time and were prepared to do a bit of work. I'm on the management committee of St Christopher's Hospital. One of our other members has just left, and we need someone to help on the flag day sub-committee. How would that sound to you?'

'Well, I'm not sure,' said Edwina, to whom it sounded perfectly dreadful. 'I mean, I do have another—another thing in prospect, which I'm not sure about yet. Er, what exactly would be involved?'

'Well, organisation,' said Mary Whittaker, sounding mildly put out. 'I was told that was your forte. This is a countrywide event, in June, you know, and we need all our operators, collectors and so on, primed, briefed, deliveries of their flags monitored, that sort of thing. It really is most important work, and naturally we would give you some help. Lady Southgate is in overall charge, I expect you know her, everyone does, but, of course,

178

if you're not interested—'

'It's not that I'm not interested,' said Edwina, 'just that I might not have the time.'

'Oh, I see. Most unfortunate. How is your mother, by the way?'

'She's very well. Thank you.'

'I know her of course,' said Mary Whittaker, as if an acquaintance with Sylvia Fox-Ashley was an obligatory requirement. 'In fact, I shall be seeing her this evening. At a dinner party. Perhaps she will know someone with genuine time to spare.'

*   *   *

'Edwina?' Sylvia Fox-Ashley's voice was heavy. Edwina knew that tone, and sighed.

'Yes, Mummy.'

'Darling, black mark. You've offended Mary Whittaker, and therefore Sir Simeon, who's an important client of your father's.'

'Mummy, I didn't know. I—'

'Edwina, just for me, do it, will you? Anyway it's a very good cause. About time you did something with your life, if you're not going to start a family yet. No news on that front, I suppose?'

'No, Mummy. None at all.'

'Honestly, darling, much better have the children straight away, get it over with, and then get on with your lives. Take my advice, Edwina, and tell Harry you want a child as soon as possible. Or is he being difficult about it? Because if he is, then perhaps I should have a word—'

'No, Mummy, he's not and I forbid you to have any kind of a word about it. You're on very dangerous ground. I warn you.'

'All right, darling, keep your wig on. I wouldn't dream of interfering in anything so personal. Just the same, it would be very helpful if you could do this thing for me. Besides, those committees are a hoot, you know: lots of ladies playing God. It would amuse you.'

* * *

'I'm going to do some voluntary work,' said Edwina to Harry at the breakfast table.

'How exemplary. In what area?'

'Hospitals.'

'Very exemplary. Which one?'

'St Christopher's. That was Cassia's hospital, wasn't it? I've only just put two and two together.'

'Yes, it was.' His voice was courteously disinterested.

'Someone called Mary Whittaker's asked me to be on the management committee. To help run the flag day.'

'How very impressive.'

'Well, it's nice to know I have your support,' she said. His power to hurt her was always surprising.

'Sorry. Do tell me more. When does this begin?'

'Next week, I think.'

'You'll find it quite time-consuming,' he said, 'I warn you.'

'What on earth do you know about flag days, Harry?'

'One of my companies runs a contributory scheme for hospital care. Big business, the whole thing is, although St Christopher's has quite a struggle to make ends meet. It's not rich like Tommy's and Bart's and Guy's. Nothing like the

180

amount of property.'

She stared at him. 'What a lot of pies your fingers are in, to be sure.'

'Yes, well, if you took even the remotest interest in my business affairs, you might find it less surprising.' He stood up, looked down at her with the familiar mixture of affection and disapproval.

*   *   *

Cassia sat in a taxi on her way to Cecily's and Benedict's in an amalgam of excitement, exhaustion and severe self-doubt. Mostly self-doubt. She wondered how wise she had been to have embarked on this. On a return to the dangerous, potentially deadly world of medicine. She simply didn't feel equipped for it any more. Which was ridiculous, really; all that she would be required to do in the immediate future was to take a woman's gynaecological history, examine her, fit her with a contraceptive device and instruct her in its use: and she already found the prospect terrifying. Well, not terrifying, but certainly daunting. The contraceptives would fail, the women become immediately pregnant, some would seek abortions, unwanted babies would be born, marriages fail—and it would all be her fault.

Oh, for heaven's sake, Cassia, she thought, what has happened to the self-assured young woman, who had assisted in the operating theatre, delivered babies, sutured wounds, made diagnoses and never wondered for a moment if she might be in any way failing her patients? Or at least not doing the very best for them that she and modern medicine could? Gone for ever, she supposed, her identity blurred by years of marriage, of motherhood, of housewifery, of struggling endlessly to do something she was not very good at.

That was what had wrecked her confidence: failing, endlessly, depressingly, falling short of her own high standards, while knowing her real skills were being wasted, falling away—and minding so very much that they were.

Impossible to recapture those skills suddenly, that confidence; but she must just have faith in herself, somehow. The trouble was there was no one else who did . . .

*   *   *

'What a lovely baby,' she said, smiling into the blue-trimmed crib, at the squashed, ruddy, indignant features of Laurence Harrington, smiling across the room at Cecily, at Fanny and Stephanie lolling on their mother's bed, filled with quasi-maternal pride themselves.

'Isn't he? And so good.'

'And how do you feel?'

'I feel marvellous,' said Cecily, 'really quite well enough to get out of bed, but of course I can't. Ten days to go at least.'

'I did,' said Cassia.

'Really? How soon?'

'Oh, about three days after. Two, I think, with Delia.'

'What, actually out of bed?' Cecily looked shocked.

'Yes, of course. Well, there was so much to do. I didn't have much help, you know. And women in primitive communities don't lie about for a

182

fortnight after they've had their children, and nor do animals—they get up the minute they can.'

'But you don't know that that's good for them.'

'I can't see why it shouldn't be,' said Cassia, 'and nor does Edward, actually.'

'Does he advise it, though? To the women he delivers?'

'Well, so many of them are very poor, they don't have much option. But, yes, he does encourage it. After about a week, anyway.'

'Good gracious,' said Cecily, 'how very revolutionary. Girls, run along now and have your supper, it's well past the time.' The girls clambered obediently off the bed, kissed her, kissed Cassia and disappeared.

'I wish my children were that well behaved,' said Cassia.

'Well, mine have been raised by Nanny Hawkins,' said Cecily. 'How's your new nanny, by the way? Good decision?'

'Marvellous. She's absolutely wonderful. I adore her, the children adore her, even Peggy likes her.'

'Edward?'

'Oh, yes, he's getting to really like her too. And Benedict, is he pleased with his son?'

'Thrilled. But how is Edward, Cassia? Really, I mean. Does he mind what you're doing?'

'What, working? Yes, he's quite happy about it.'

'Really?' said Cecily. There was a silence.

Cassia said, 'No, not really. He's being ghastly. Hostile. Cold. I don't know what to do. Short of giving up before I begin.'

'Which you mustn't. You really mustn't. I think you've been self-sacrificing for quite long enough. I can't personally imagine why you want to do any sort of work, of course, when you can just stay at home with your lovely children and enjoy yourself, but I know how much you do want it, and how good at it you were going to be, and I think you deserve it.'

'Oh, I don't know,' said Cassia fretfully. 'All I'm doing is making Edward miserable, driving a great wedge between us. Maybe I should give up again.'

'No,' said Cecily, 'no, Cassia, don't.'

'But there's a horrible atmosphere in the house, he hardly speaks to me, won't touch me even. I suppose I have been rather tactless over it, over the money and everything, but I did want this so terribly much and I can't see why he couldn't be more generous . . .' She heard her voice shake, felt her eyes fill with tears, brushed them away impatiently. 'Sorry.'

'Darling Cassia, you cry if you want to. I feel terribly sad for you. It seems so unfair, after all you gave up for him. I think you deserve it, deserve a chance. Edward is very sweet, and I'm very fond of him, but he shouldn't sit on your ambitions as he has. You haven't seemed happy for quite a long time.'

'Haven't I?' Cassia said.

'No. You haven't. And it's sad. Very sad.'

'Well,' she said, with a sigh, 'I don't know that I'm making myself any happier now, but I'll go on a bit longer. See how things work out.'

'Good.' Cecily lay back on her pillows, smiled at her. 'I think that's the right decision.'

'You seem very concerned.'

'Well, I'm very fond of you. I mind that you're not happy. Cassia, do you still love Edward?'

A silence, then Cassia said, 'I think so. I hope

so.' And burst into tears, aching tears that hurt, were not a relief to shed.

Cecily held out her arms, as if she was little Fanny. Cassia went and lay on the pillows beside her. 'This is ridiculous,' she said.

'No, it isn't. Poor Cassia. I'm so sorry. I do so want things to be right for you. I owe you such a lot.'

'Oh, Cecily, don't be silly.'

'It was so wonderful,' Cecily went on, looking at her, her face very serious suddenly, 'what you did, all those years ago. I still owe you a huge debt.'

'Well, I certainly don't see it like that and I don't want you even to think of paying it,' said Cassia, blowing her nose. 'It was a pleasure. In a warped sort of way. Now look, I have to go, it's awfully late, and if I'm not home for supper Edward really will blow a gasket. I think your little Laurence is heaven. Absolute heaven.'

'Would you be his godmother?'

'Cecily,' said Cassia, the tears starting again, but easier, sweeter ones this time, 'I'd love it. What an honour. Thank you.'

CHAPTER TEN

Six months in Obstetrics and six months in Casualty had prepared Cassia for much of what she saw at the family planning clinic: women of thirty who looked fifty, pregnant with a tenth, or twelfth child, girls of eighteen pregnant with a third or fourth, girls of thirteen of fourteen just . . . pregnant. In Obstetrics they would be bearing the child, in

185

Casualty losing it, often bleeding to death as a result of a backstreet abortion. She was not even shocked by the signs of violence inflicted on these women, the bruising, the cuts, sometimes even broken bones. It was distressing, but she had grown used to that.

What she had not seen before was the crowds of small children, runny nosed, scrawny, with the greyish pallor of poverty that surrounded their mothers; and what she had not heard were the women's stories. Stories of hopelessness, until now, of grinding poverty, of crushing hard work, of perpetual poor health, all accentuated by the ongoing terror of yet another pregnancy.

She sat in her small room, and a seemingly endless procession of these women, women who might have lived in another age, another country from herself and her circle, trailed through it; her sessions began at two and were frequently still running at eight, for it was a point of pride with the Association that all who came were seen. They waited, patiently, the women, through the long afternoons, while their children whined and played and fought, and their babies were fed, sometimes twice or even three times, and while they waited they exchanged stories, sometimes sad, often bitterly humorous, of their husbands and the treatment they endured at their hands.

She imagined what it must be like to be one of those women, lying in bed, hearing heavy footsteps on the stairs, smelling drunken breath; waiting, dreading what was yet again going to happen—and its inevitable consequence. Time and time again she was told, often quite cheerfully, ' 'E's fine when 'e's not drunk, Doctor,' and, 'He won't take precautions, says it spoils things,' this followed by the equally cheerful, 'Then of course he gets mad when I tell 'im I've fallen again.'

She went home sobered by those experiences, ashamed of herself for complaining about her lot, for thinking Edward—always so kind, so considerate, so careful in bed at least—anything other than perfect.

She tried to tell him about it one evening, not just about the women but her gratitude, her remorse (thinking this at least might soften his hostility), but he listened politely for a while, then said, 'I saw plenty of that sort of thing in Harrow, of course. I'm sure I told you about it.'

'No, Edward you didn't,' she said (knowing all they talked about in the few hours they had was his work, his struggles, his exhaustion, and very occasionally her own), but he said perhaps, then, she had not been listening and would she excuse him now.

'Oh, for God's sake,' she said, 'no, I won't excuse you. I need to talk to you. I can't stand this, it's awful, we can't go on like this.'

'I'm surprised to hear you say that,' he said. 'The whole thing, all the changes in our lives, have been at your instigation, and if you don't like it—'

'What I don't like,' she cried in a passion, 'is your hostility, when all I am doing is just a little of what I have longed for ever since we got married. You should be glad for me, glad I am getting my chance—'

'I am very sorry,' he said, 'that you have been so unhappy in our marriage until now.'

'I didn't say I was unhappy. I said I was longing to work. As a doctor. As I have since I was a little

187

girl.'

'Ah,' he said, and his voice was icy, 'that old story.'

'What do you mean?'

'You're very fond of that bit of your history, aren't you, Cassia? The hard-working ambitious child, struggling against all those odds. We hear less about all the help you had, the input from your relations, your London Season, your rich friends. Just the sad little motherless soul up there in Leeds.'

'That is monstrous,' she said, standing up, physical violence rising in her, wondering if she should perhaps not resist it, hit him, whether that might bring home to him the strength of her feelings. 'Why are you doing this? Why are you so bitter, so angry?'

'I'm angry,' he said, 'because you continually imply that up to now you have had nothing, and I have had everything, when the reverse is a great deal nearer the truth. Now I do have work to do.'

He walked out of the room and into his study, and she heard the door slam. She sat staring into the fire, and wondered, not for the first time in those extraordinary months, that the money had not only empowered her finally to do what she wanted, but had also rendered her helpless to be the wife Edward wanted any more.

She didn't often think very much about the money at all; she did not allow herself to, knew if she did it would become an obsession. The small extravagances, self-indulgences, life changes that she had brought about for herself, were sufficient to satisfy her, to make her feel it was not being quite wasted. When she did contemplate it, as she was now, it was as something oddly abstract, a huge force, somehow threatening, irresistible if actually unleashed. Its power frightened her: she tried to keep it at bay, dammed up behind the wall of intense willpower and steely common sense that she had built up over the past few years, but she could feel it growing stronger now, forcing its way in small but inexorable forays into every corner of her life.

Contemplation about what she might do, could do, became increasingly irresistible; the knowledge that she could accomplish so much was frightening in itself. She moved from the professional, from wild thoughts of founding her own hospital, of setting up a medical foundation, to the personal, to taking her children and travelling the world, seeing its wonders, possibly for years.

And then there was what she had labelled the desire element, the least obviously hazardous, the easiest to fulfil: and thus the most dangerous. She thought of great houses, of fine furnishings, of beautiful pictures; she dreamed of exquisite clothes, of fine jewellery; she fantasised over yachts, racehorses, airplanes. All these things—or certainly many of them—she could have; but not within her marriage, not as Mrs Edward Fallon, not as the doctor's wife.

Were she to use the money, the great wealth that had become so absurdly hers, then she could see quite clearly her marriage must end, the marriage to the man she did not love, had never loved but who was the father of her children, central to all their lives and for whom and whose happiness she felt an almost unbearable responsibility. It would end not only in bitterness and hostility, but intense pain and humiliation on his behalf. It was impossible, given the condition of their relationship, that it could continue against the background of the money, her money. And so she waited, waited with her wealth walled up, to see what would happen, where it would end: and without quite even realising it, prayed that that end would come, somehow miraculously, through no fault or even action of her own.

*   *   *

Cassia looked at her watch. Almost five, but only three women left, Jane the secretary had said, so she should be away in about half an hour, and that would mean she could make the Savoy by six after all. She was doing an emergency cover at a clinic near the Elephant and Castle. She supposed she ought to go tonight. She had said that she'd be there unless Edwina heard otherwise. And it was to help St Christopher's, or so she had been told. But Edwina, of all people . . .

She forced her attention back on to the young woman sitting in front of her. 'Go on,' she said gently.

'You see, the thing is, Doctor, I really do need the help. I've had four babies now in five years. My husband doesn't like using things, you know, and the last little baby died.'

'Oh, I'm so sorry,' said Cassia. The girl didn't look more than twenty; she had said she was twenty-two. She somehow doubted that. 'What was it? Diphtheria, or—'

'No, she died at birth. They said it was partly due to her coming so soon after the other. Just ten

190

months, there was, between them.'

'Yes; that is very close,' said Cassia. It was actually an unlikely reason for the baby's death, but ten months! She thought of that baby's conception, the father who didn't like using condoms, and thought it was just as well for him that he wasn't there too.

'Of course you must have help. We can certainly prevent that happening again. Now I'm just going to examine you, and then I can fit you with a contraceptive, and explain how to use it. When was that baby . . . born?' It was so difficult sometimes, finding the right words to fit these sad, difficult lives. When was the baby born? When had it died?

'About six weeks ago.'

'That is a little soon. Your body will still be adjusting, returning to its normal shape. Internally as well. So we might have to do something temporary, ask you to come back.'

'Oh dear. But not—not the—'

'No, not the condoms.' She smiled at her. 'Possibly what we call a pessary. Then a cap later on. I'll explain. Now if you get undressed, and on to that couch over there . . .'

The girl, still tender from her baby's birth, shrank from the examination. Cassia's heart ached for her.

'Right,' she said, ten minutes later, handing the girl a neat packet and a leaflet, 'come back in three months. And good luck.'

'Yes, Doctor. Thank you so much.' Her eyes suddenly filled with tears, and she wiped them with the back of her hand. 'I'm sorry. I didn't mean to cry. It brought it back, you know, talking about it.'

'I know. You cry, I don't mind. Talk some more,

it might help.'

'Oh, no, it's all right. And I've got the others, I'm lucky. But it's a terrible thing, going through it, all the pain and that, and then seeing your baby, just . . . well, not alive.'

'I understand. Was your husband good about that? Sympathetic?'

'Oh yes, he's very good really. He just—well, you know what men are like.' She managed a watery smile.

Cassia caught the omnibus from the Elephant to the Strand; it jolted along quite fast, and she sat looking out of the window, hearing the girl's voice, remembering the baby that had died, remembering her distress, her guilt, remembering what had happened afterwards . . . Don't, Cassia, don't think about it now, not today, not this evening, for heaven's sake . . .

*   *   *

'Cassia, hallo. Sweet of you to come.' Edwina was looking dauntingly chic as always, in a black suit and a red hat, set dashingly over one eye. 'You must be exhausted after your work. I've ordered two martinis. I seem to remember you like them. Love the coat, darling, whose is it? Stiebel?'

'No, I got it in Selfridges,' said Cassia, 'and yes, a martini would be lovely.' She found it difficult to detach herself from the afternoon, acutely aware of the absurd contrast of poverty and martinis, stillbirths and couture.

'Good. Well, I just need a bit of help. I've been asked to do some charity work for St Christopher's, to help with their flag day in June, and I just

192

thought you could prime me a bit. I've got my first meeting tomorrow and I don't want to look a complete idiot. I was hoping for some background information. You know.'

'What, about the committee?'

'I think I know what they'll be like: perfectly ghastly. Mummy's warned me about them. No, I thought you'd be able to tell me about the hospital, you know. How long it's been going, how many wards, all that sort of stuff. And do you think I'll be expected to know anything about its medical work?'

'No, of course not,' said Cassia, laughing. 'I don't think you'd be expected to know how many wards there were either. But let me see, the hospital was founded in fourteen hundred and forty-two, it used to be near Smithfield, but got moved out towards Victoria in the early nineteenth century because there were Guy's and Bart's already in the City. They're not as rich as Thomas's, but—'

'No, that's what Harry said.'

'Harry? What on earth does he know about it?'

'Harry knows a lot about everything,' said Edwina vaguely. 'He runs some medical insurance scheme or something. I don't quite know.'

'Good Lord,' said Cassia. 'Anyway, although they do get quite a lot of legacies and so on, I do know it's an increasing struggle. So things like your flag days are vital. Oh; and they just might be impressed that you knew they were one of the very first hospitals to offer anaesthesia in childbirth. Let me see . . . oh, yes, the sisters are called after their wards, not their own names, and they're doing a lot of research into TB at the moment. How's that?'

'That's marvellous,' said Edwina. 'I knew you'd

be able to help. And how's the work? Are you enjoying it?'

'Yes, very much. Of course it's pretty mundane, but it's a start.'

'What is it, something to do with women?'

'Birth control clinics. It's a growing movement and—'

'It must be fascinating,' said Edwina, putting down her glass, examining her very long red fingernails. 'Do you want another drink?'

'No, really, I ought to get back.'

'Oh, come on. It'll cheer you on the long journey. Oh God, here's Harry. He threatened to come. I told him not to, but he obviously decided to ignore me. Hallo, darling.' She raised her face to be kissed. Harry bent over her, kissed her briefly, then looked at Cassia, and kissed her too. 'Hello, Cassia.'

'Hello, Harry. I'm just going, actually.'

'Charming as always,' he said lightly. 'Why not make a huge effort, stay for one drink?'

'Of course she will,' said Edwina. 'Harry, order them, will you? Martinis, we were drinking. I'm going to the cloakroom. Back in a tick.'

He sat down beside Cassia, studied her. 'How are you?'

'I'm very well, thank you, Harry,' she said, feeling the inevitable tug of sexual tension, situated so uncomfortably somewhere between her head and her heart.

'You look tired.'

'Well, thank you for that,' she said, hearing her voice sound defensive.

'Cassia, there's nothing wrong with being tired. Working too hard?'

'Not really.'

'But you are working? At your medicine?'

'Yes.'

'Good,' he said, sitting back into his chair, an expression of great satisfaction on his face. 'I heard you were. High time you went back to it.'

'Not you as well,' she said. 'Everybody says that, all the time, it's like some sort of conspiracy.' And then looked at him, and at the back of his dark eyes saw something she couldn't quite understand, a sort of wariness; then it was gone.

'And are you enjoying it?'

'Oh yes, very much.'

'Good. And can you help Edwina? With this new project of hers? I have to tell you I really don't see it lasting.'

'That seems a little unfair,' said Cassia. 'She's hardly begun and she's making a great effort.'

'Well, I have a great capacity for being unfair. As you know. Do you work every day?'

'No, only two afternoons. Quite long afternoons. Sometimes till about eight o'clock at night.'

'In London?'

'Not what you'd regard as London,' she said, 'but yes, on the outskirts of Brixton. Although today I was at the Elephant and Castle.'

'And then you have to do the long journey home. I'm surprised you don't get yourself a little house in town. Stay there on those late evenings and then travel down in the morning.'

'What a ridiculous idea,' she said, laughing. 'How could I possibly do that?'

'Quite easily, I would have thought. Now that you are a woman of independent means. Think of what it would save you: the clockwatching, the tension . . .'

'And what do you think Edward would have to say about that? Not to mention the children?'

'Edward could surely spare you a couple of nights a week. He's usually out delivering babies anyway, as far as I can make out. And I understand you have a nanny now, so the children would be perfectly all right.'

'Harry,' she said firmly, 'I'm afraid you don't understand me and my marriage at all.'

'No,' he said, looking at her very intently, his eyes thoughtful, 'I'm afraid I don't.'

*   *   *

She couldn't help it in the end. She sat on the train, staring out into the growing dusk, her head spinning slightly with the martinis, thinking, remembering, reliving it. That day. The girl at the clinic that afternoon and her baby. Her dead baby . . .

*   *   *

She had heard you never quite got over it, your first death, that it haunted you for the rest of your career. She could believe it: she would never forget, she knew, the sight of that little baby, dragged finally from its mother, poor, exhausted, terrified girl, only fifteen or so, and it was so clearly dead, an awful bluish-white colour.

Cassia had been on the obstetric ward for two months, had found it and all its attendant drama everything she could have hoped for. This was where she felt she belonged; where life began, was coaxed, eased, bullied out of struggling bodies, where every time, at every first cry, the joy was a tangible, vital force. Until then. Until that day. When that baby died. Cassia looked at it, its little face tranquil, almost smiling, its limbs limp and somehow heavy, and burst into tears.

'Now then, now then.' The midwife looked at her sternly. 'You're not going to get far as a doctor if you get emotional over everything. It's the poor young woman here who should be crying, not you. Miss Berridge, take this baby along to the sluice for now. I'll be with you shortly. Do stop screaming, dear,' she said to the mother, 'it's all over now.'

It was all over, thought Cassia, very much so; nothing to show for all these hours of pain but the tiny blue corpse. Suddenly she felt very sick. She laid the baby gently on a slab in the sluice, and although it was foolish, wrapped it in a towel and then threw up into the sink.

A student nurse looked at her sympathetically. 'It's awful, isn't it? Happened to me last week. Poor little chap.' She looked down at the baby. 'They're so bloody callous, these midwives, won't give the mothers anything to help the pain, seem to think they've a mission to make them suffer.'

'Last week,' said Cassia, smiling feebly, 'we delivered a baby to a midwife. I've never heard anyone scream like she did, and afterwards she said she'd never felt so ashamed in her life, remembering all the mothers she'd told to shut up. I've developed a great admiration for women since I've been here. Well, all women who've had children, anyway.'

*   *   *

197

She went home shortly after that. It was Friday night and she had been looking forward to the break. During the week now she lived in the hospital, in a tiny room next to the obstetric house surgeon's, but he had given her the weekend off.

Harris let her in. 'You look terrible, miss. Shall I run you a bath? Then I'm going out, it's my evening off. If that's all right. And Sir Richard's gone off to Norfolk. He told me to tell you.'

'Yes, Harris, of course it's all right. And I think I can manage to run myself a bath.'

'All right, miss. Well, I'll be off. Oh, and cook's gone to the pictures, as well, miss. Said to tell you she left your supper out.'

'Thank you.'

She ran a very deep bath, lay in it, soaking away her exhaustion, trying to forget the poor little blue corpse. She couldn't.

She climbed out of the bath, pulled on a light cotton frock and went downstairs to the dining room. She picked at the salad, then pushed it aside and walked through to the morning room. God, this was a huge depressing house without Leonora. She hadn't heard from her for ages; she hoped she was all right.

The bell rang sharply; Jarvis would get it. But he didn't. It rang again, and then again. Then she remembered: Jarvis was on holiday. One more peal and then hopefully whoever it was would go. One more peal came. And then another.

Cassia sighed, got up, went across the hall, opened the door. Harry Moreton stood there, wearing only a white shirt and cream linen trousers, with tall brown leather boots. His dark hair was more ruffled than she had ever seen it. He had a leather helmet under his arms, and some goggles swung from his wrist. He looked quite extraordinarily happy.

'Hallo, Cassia.'

'Oh, hello.'

'Can I come in?'

She made a huge effort. 'Yes. Please do. I'm afraid everyone's out.'

'How very compromising for you.' God, she hated his voice, that awful Etonian drawl. 'Well, anyway, I wanted to tell you something. Two things, actually. I have a present for you. From Leonora. I just went to see her in Paris.'

'Oh, Harry, how is she? Is she well? Oh, God, I'd love to see her, I miss her so much.'

'Yes, I expect you do,' he said, just slightly impatient. 'She's fine. She said to tell you to go and visit her. And then I have some news.'

'Yes?'

'I got a First,' he said. 'I just heard.'

She was thinking how typical, how arrogant of him to come and tell her *that*, of all things, when she looked at him, at his eyes, searching hers, at his face, oddly uncertain. She realised that he had no one else to tell, no parents, no brothers or sisters, Benedict and Cecily were away in France, she really was the only person he could tell, who was in any way connected to him. She said, with genuine warmth, 'Harry, that's marvellous. Really marvellous. Well done. You must be very pleased.'

'Well, you know. Pretty pleased, yes. I hate to admit it, but I did work quite hard in the end. Even my tutor seemed a bit surprised,' he said, and grinned again.

'I expect he did,' she said, and grinned back. 'Look, this is worth a drink. Jarvis is away, but I'll go and fetch some champagne from the cellar.'

'No, I'll go,' he said. 'I know where it is.'

He returned with a bottle of Krug and two champagne glasses; opened it with a great flourish, poured her a glass.

'Here's to you,' she said.

'And to you. To success.'

'Success.'

That reminded her rather sharply of Edward, who was not a success, who had passed his exams so conspicuously badly (having needed to pass them so well and so much more than Harry did). She sighed.

Harry looked at her. 'You look all in,' he said, 'really rotten, in fact.'

'Thank you,' she said, the old tartness in her voice, suddenly aware that she had no make-up on, that her hair needed cutting.

'Now don't get defensive,' he said. 'I suppose you've been overdoing it, working too hard?'

'Yes, I suppose I have. Well, not too hard, but very hard.'

'And what thrilling things have you been doing today? Who have you been snatching from the jaws of death?'

'No one,' she said, 'no one at all,' and thought of the little baby, lying very much in the jaws of death and her eyes filled with sudden, hot tears.

'Cassia,' he said, and his voice was very gentle, 'Cassia, what is it? What's wrong, what happened?'

'Oh,' she said, 'a baby died today. It was born dead, you know, and the midwife gave it to me and told me to take it to the sluice, the sluice of all places, as if it was a—well, as if it was waste. And I—'

'Cassia,' he said, and she looked up and he was looking at her with the most extraordinary expression on his face: concern, and horror and a sort of wonder. 'Cassia, do you mean to tell me you have to do such things? That you're actually there, with women giving birth, that you have to handle a dead child?'

'Yes, of course I do,' she said, half amused. 'How else would we learn, what else would we do?'

'I don't know,' he said, still looking very shocked. 'I suppose I thought you'd just learn about it. Not have to do it, be confronted by it. It can't be right, someone like you. How old are you? Just twenty-one. It's appalling.'

'Harry, the mother of this baby was fifteen. Now that really is appalling. We do all that: deliver babies, observe operations, dress hideous wounds . . .'

'How brave you are,' he said, still in the same gentle voice, 'how very brave.'

'But I'm not,' she said. 'I wasn't very brave today, but it was my first, you see, my first death, and—oh, dear. I'm sorry, Harry.'

She sat down on the sofa, sobbing helplessly; he'd probably leave in a minute, he'd be horribly embarrassed, and she was being such a total idiot, but: 'Come here,' he said, and sat down beside her and opened his arms. Too distressed even to think about it, she did what she most wanted at that moment and moved into them.

His white shirt was very crisp cotton and she could feel her tears soaking it, turning it limp; he smelt slightly of sweat, but it was fresh sweat, and

201

of the Turkish cigarettes he smoked. It was a surprisingly agreeable mixture; it was a surprisingly agreeable place to be. Slowly the tears ceased.

'Here.' He fumbled in his pocket for his handkerchief, dried her eyes, smiled down at her. 'That's better.'

'I must look awful,' she said, sitting back from him, sniffing.

'Cassia, you look perfectly all right. But I do draw the line at sniffing. It's disgusting.'

'Oh, sorry.' She blew her nose on his handkerchief, managed to smile at him. 'That was a bit more like you.'

'What do you mean? Like me?'

'Well, critical.'

'Oh. What else is like me?' He was smiling at her.

'I don't want to say now. Not when you're being so nice.'

'Aren't I always nice?' he said, handing her her glass of champagne. 'There, finish this, it'll do you good.'

'Thank you. And no,' she said, smiling again, 'you're not always nice.'

'Since this conversation seems to be cheering you up, shall I tell you what you're like?'

'Yes,' she said, quite distracted by this thought, 'I'd like very much to know what I'm like. How I seem to you.'

'Fierce,' he said. 'Very fierce. And cross, quite a lot of the time.'

'Cross! That's not fair. Most people say I'm very good tempered.'

'Well, most people must be luckier than me. That's what I see. Self-opinionated. Tough.

202

Awkward. Defensive. And incredibly sexy.'

'Thanks a—' she started, and then thought she must have misheard the last. 'What did you say?'

'I said you were self-opinionated and tough and awkward and defensive and incredibly sexy.'

'Oh,' she said. 'Oh, yes, I see.' She sat back and looked at him. She felt very odd: confused, shocked, absolutely vulnerable, and—

'You're blushing,' he said gently, and reached out and wiped a last tear away with his finger; then put the finger in his mouth and licked it.

She went on staring at him, and although he was not even touching her, she felt a stabbing deep within her, a harsh, strong movement that she knew was desire. A desire stronger, more powerful, more invading than anything she had ever felt before. He didn't move; just studied her, his eyes moving over her, very slowly, her hair, her eyes, her mouth, then down, down to her breasts.

And then he moved near her; and without touching her began to kiss her, very tenderly at first, his mouth, his tongue, exploring her upper lip, then within her mouth, very slow, very careful, and as it moved, the desire moved too, travelled deep within her, great sprawling tendrils of it, reaching, probing at her, and she moved with it, shifted, became closer to him. He pulled back then and smiled, just briefly, and then put his hands on her shoulders and began to smooth, to stroke them, and then, gradually, moved to her breasts, and all the time working at her mouth with his, and as his hands began to fold round her breasts, to hold them, his thumbs outlining her nipples through her thin dress, she couldn't help it, she moaned, aloud; pushed her own tongue under his and she could

203

feel his response to that moan. He smiled; she could feel the smile, and she smiled herself in return, and he unbuttoned her dress then, and bent to kiss her breasts, licking the nipples, his tongue slow, terribly slow and lingering.

She looked down at his head and tried to think that this was Harry, her enemy, Harry whom she had hated since she had been a child, and tried to think of Edward, Edward whom she was supposed to love, and more than anything in the world she wanted to be in bed with Harry, with him naked beside her and around her and inside her, and then she thought, with one last despairing and detached look at him and at herself, that she could not, must not do this thing and then somehow, just in time, she sat back and held Harry's face in her hands and told him he must go away.

It took a long time to persuade him. He said, first amused and indignant, then disbelieving, then hurt, then finally angry, that he could not, would not go, that there was no reason for it, then again, finally, that she was a foolish, prudish virgin. She clung with something approaching terror to her decision, came close to giving in to him, to her own desire for him, several times, felt literally sick with distress, with misery; only that last, furious insult saved her, made her angry, convinced her she was doing the right thing.

'How dare you,' she said, dashing away the tears that had begun again in this extraordinary, complex amalgam of passions, 'how dare you say that to me, when—'

'Well, is it not true?'

'No,' she cried, and that was her great, her terrible mistake, 'no, it is not true.'

There was a very long, still silence.

'Ah,' he said, 'so there we have it. The doctor, I presume. The wheyfaced medic. Well, I doubt he is very skilful. Whether you have experienced much pleasure at his hands. No wonder you don't wish to—'

Rage swept over her then: rage and outrage. 'You are disgusting,' she said, 'to talk like that, of such things.'

'Such things!' he said. 'What an expression. How ladylike, how unlusty. Fucking, that's what I'm talking about, Cassia, fucking. You do know that word, do you? Fucking, fucking, fucking. You fucking the doctor. How very uncarnal that must be. Do you lie there, under him, as he plunges up and down, do you lie there, waiting for it to end, thinking of England? I would have given you other things to think of, Cassia, I do assure you. But I dare say—'

'Harry!' she shouted, and it was almost a scream now, the tears pouring down her face, sweat breaking out not just on her forehead but in her armpits, her back. 'You are disgusting. Totally disgusting. Get out. Get out of this house. And never, ever come near me again.'

'I won't,' he said, fuming to the door. 'You can be sure of that.'

*   *   *

But he did: the night before she left for Leeds, for her wedding. He appeared, pale, grim, at the door, asked if he might see her just for five minutes. She said he might, and led him into the drawing room. He had lost weight, seemed somehow hollow, slightly less substantial. He looked at her and said, 'I told myself I wouldn't, couldn't come, but I had to. I can't believe you're doing this, Cassia. It's not too late, don't, please don't. I—'

She knew she must stop him saying whatever it was, fearing, knowing, she would hear the one thing she could not bear. 'Harry,' she said, 'I have to. I have to do it. I am—'

'Yes?' he said 'You are what?'

'I am pregnant.'

There was a silence. He stood there, studying her, his eyes moving over her, lingering first on her breasts, then her stomach, staying there for a long time, then moving up again to her face, to her eyes.

'Is that all?' he said. 'Is that the only reason?'

'No,' she said, quickly, too quickly, 'not the only reason, but—'

'Do you love him?' he said. 'Because that's the only reason. The only real reason. If you tell me you love him, I shall leave you alone, now and for ever.'

'I . . .' There was an endless pause while he stood there, his eyes probing hers, seeming to break into her, and somehow she said, and it was as if she was saying the words against a great physical force, 'I do . . . love . . . him.'

'Good,' he said matter-of-factly, and turned on his heel and walked out of the door and her life. For several years.

CHAPTER ELEVEN

The eyes boring into Edwina's were cold, disapproving, filled with something close to dislike. She looked down nervously at her hands and said, 'I'm sorry. Really. I've just been rather busy lately.'

'Mrs Moreton, we're all busy. But here we are, almost into April, and you tell me you haven't sent the letters out yet to the regional organisers. It's very disappointing.'

'I can see that. But I can get them out in a couple of days. Is that soon enough?'

'It will have to be. I think perhaps you need someone to help you. I'll ring Jennifer Barling, see if there's something she can do. This is very serious.' Her voice was genuinely angry.

Edwina felt a stab of panic. This was worse than if she'd never started. But it really was so tedious, and writing a hundred letters did take an awfully long time, and—

Mary Whittaker was talking again. 'In fact,' she said, 'I think perhaps I should ask Jennifer to take over from you altogether. We simply cannot afford to have people not pulling their weight.'

The panic grew; if news of this got back to her mother, she really would fly off the handle. 'Oh, no,' she said, quickly, 'I want to do it. It's just that this isn't quite my thing. Not really.'

'I can see that, Mrs Moreton.'

And then out of the ether, inspiration came: blinding, brilliant. 'Lady Whittaker, there was something else I did want to talk to you about. You see, I was thinking there was something I could do, something much more . . . me, if you like. I thought I could put on a fashion show for the hospital. A charity one, you know? I have a lot of contacts in the fashion business, a great chum works on *Vogue*, and masses of my friends would model. We could put it on in one of the big hotels, the Dorchester would be terrific, that new ballroom where the ice-rink used to be, and it would raise a lot of money. Another friend, Venetia Hardwicke, I expect you know her—' Mary Whittaker shook her head coldly. 'Well, she did one for St Thomas's, and it was a huge success.'

Mary Whittaker said, with extreme reluctance, 'I did hear that the fashion show for St Thomas's raised a lot of money. We did discuss the possibility of having one for St Christopher's, but we have no one on the committee with the necessary knowledge.'

That was painfully obvious, Edwina thought. She smiled encouragingly at Mary Whittaker. 'Well, now you do. And I really would throw my heart into this one, Lady Whittaker. Give it my all. I swear.'

'Well, I shall speak to the committee and come back to you. Meanwhile, will you *please* get on with those letters.'

*   *   *

Cassia had woken up that same morning feeling rather cheerful. Things seemed to be settling down. Her clinics were going well; the children were happy; Janet continued to be a joy, and even Edward had admitted, grudgingly, that she was very good with the children. Best of all, his attitude towards Cassia had suddenly eased. He had been more friendly, and last night, for the first time since Christmas, he had made love to her and her body had gratefully, joyfully, gone to meet him.

It hadn't been a total success; she hadn't quite managed to come, and afterwards she lay in his arms quietly as he drifted rather noisily off to sleep, thinking about herself and their marriage, wondering why she was so pathetically grateful for his changed attitude towards her, for his seeming to want her again.

Guilt, she supposed; she started to drift off to sleep, thinking that perhaps, after all, their marriage might be restored, in time, to its former self.

*   *   *

It was early when she woke. She heard the children getting up, heard Janet talking to them. God, it was wonderful to have her. She got dressed, ran downstairs smiling.

The postman had just arrived. There were several letters for Edward and two for her: one typed with an SW3 postmark, one in Rupert's florid hand. She started to open Rupert's then found her knees being tackled in a bear hug.

'Mummy, guess who?'

'I can't. Delia.'

'No.'

'Bertie?'

'No.'

'Um . . . not William!'

'Yes.' He laughed and as she looked down at him, she thought how much she loved him. Janet

209

came down the stairs smiling, with an also smiling Delia, and Bertie slid down the banisters.

Edward appeared, looking flustered. 'It's late. Any post? Ah, yes. Thank you. Good morning, children.' He didn't look at the letters, she noticed, just stuffed them into his jacket pocket; that was odd.

They went in to breakfast.

*   *   *

The letter from SW3 was from the estate agents near Harrods. Several particulars of houses fell out, including those of her house, as she thought of it, in Walton Street, and a note from the earnest young man.

'Dear Mrs Fallon,' it said, 'With reference to your enquiry about the house in Walton Street, this is still available and we are now able to offer it for a longer let than six months; I wonder if this might be of interest. I also enclose details of several other properties. I remain at your service, for D. S. Pritchard, E. Throgmore.'

Nice Mr Throgmore, she thought, he deserved to do well. She didn't think, however, that Edward would appreciate Mr Throgmore or her enquiries, and placed the letter in her bag, which was hanging on the back of her chair.

The second letter, from Rupert, was more interesting. 'Darling,' it said, 'if you still fancy joining the angels, I have a tiny project. Give me a ring if you want to talk. Best love, Rupert.'

She looked across at Edward. He was reading his letters now, frowning.

'Goodness,' she said, looking at her watch.

'Nearly half past eight. Janet, I'll take the boys.'

When she finally got home it was after ten: Edward's car was gone.

'Peggy, where's Mr Fallon?'

'Mrs Clark's gone into labour early. Doesn't look too good. Sent the patients home, the doctor has.'

'Oh dear, poor Mrs Clark. Well, I'll be in the dining room. I've got lots of letters to write.'

She went into the dining room, sat down at the table, and then caught sight of Edward's letters on the sideboard. There had been something about his face, the intensity with which he had been reading them, which had bothered her. She went over and picked one up.

It was in a neat hand, the postmark Brixton. Brixton! Maybe it had been for her, this one, from one of her patients or something; making that her rationale, she picked it up, turned it over and with slightly shaking fingers, pulled it out . . .

'Dear Dr Fallon,' it said, 'With reference to your advertisement for an assistant . . .'

*   *   *

It was a long hour and a half before Edward came back. He looked rather pleased with himself.

'Hallo, Edward. How was Mrs Clark?'

'Oh, fine. Baby's fine too. A month early, but perfectly all right. Now, I wonder what to do about surgery. I had to cancel it, you know . . . Silly situation, isn't it? Not having any kind of back-up.'

'Is that why you're advertising for an assistant?'

He flushed: a deep, dark red. 'Have you been—'

'Reading your letters? Yes, I have. A bit underhand, I know, but they were lying there on

211

the sideboard. Not as underhand, though, I'd say, as your doing this behind my back.'

'Don't be so ridiculous.' His voice was louder than usual. 'It was not behind your back. It has nothing to do with you.'

'Nothing to do with me! Edward, how can you say such a thing? Your practice, in this house . . .'

'Well, of course I was going to talk to you about it. Lots of times. But you're always so busy.'

'Busy! For God's sake. When I sit in that damn room every night, after supper, trying to resist the temptation to do my own work, so that I'm available for you—'

He did look shamefaced briefly, then said, 'Very good of you.'

'Edward, how do you think it makes me feel, knowing you were planning this, had already gone to these lengths to get an assistant when—'

'I'm sorry,' he said. 'I can see I should have talked to you, but what difference is it going to make to you?'

'What difference!' Her voice rose now. 'What difference, when you know I'd give my soul to do that job myself? You know that, Edward, we used to talk about it. One day, you said, one day . . .'

He looked at her awkwardly. 'I really don't remember. And it hardly seems practical, Cassia, does it? Besides, I thought general practice was something you regarded as very second rate. I thought you would only settle for surgery—'

'Ah, yes, but I seem to remember giving that up, for some reason—what was it now? Oh, yes, to get married.'

He brushed that aside. 'And you have the children, your own work—'

212

'As if I wouldn't give up my two pathetic birth control clinics to work here with you! Edward, why didn't you talk to me about it?'

'I was going to,' he said, looking more awkward still, 'I really did intend to tell you what I had decided.'

'Oh, I see. Not even a discussion. Just a decision.'

'You've done a few things without discussion,' he said, 'over the past six months. The nanny, your car—'

'Those are hardly comparable.'

'The Chair . . .'

'Oh,' she said, 'the Chair. That really hurt, didn't it, Edward? Really, really hurt.'

'It made me angry,' he said. 'I wouldn't say it hurt. Exactly.'

'Well, this has made me very, very angry. Are they any good?'

'What?'

'The applicants. Are they any good?'

'I haven't had time to study them yet. You can help me make that judgement if you like. Having read the letters.'

She ignored that. 'Well, I'm very glad the practice can support an assistant. What will you have to pay him, five hundred a year?'

'About that. But—well, with your money, certain worries have . . . eased, haven't they?'

'So I am to subsidise this appointment.'

His face turned very white. 'That was a foul thing to say,' he said.

She flushed, horrified that she could have said such a thing. 'I'm sorry. It's none the less true. It would have made it all the more reasonable for you

213

to have discussed it with me, don't you think?'

'Not really. No.'

She felt sharply, horribly guilty; tried to lighten the mood, be more conciliatory. 'Let me ask you something, Edward. Now that you know how I feel, would you not consider taking me on as your assistant? Or at least—' she managed a smile now—'at least giving me an interview? I could take on the women, maybe, and the children's clinic—'

'Oh no,' he said sharply, 'that would never do, not taking things on, taking them over—' and stopped, realising he had made another mistake.

'God, you're pathetic,' she said. 'You can't bear to lose the tiniest little bit of your position here, can you? The doctor, the wonderful, all-powerful doctor, whom the whole village doffs its cap to, that's what it's really about, isn't it? You want a new, lowly assistant, who can be seen as such, stamped as such, not any kind of an equal.'

She stopped again, remembering the previous night, the sudden desire to make love to her after so long a time.

'Dear God,' she said. 'You've even dragged our sex life into this, haven't you?'

'Be quiet,' he said. 'Peggy might hear—'

'I don't care who hears. Is that why you fucked me last night, Edward? To make me happy, feel better towards you, so that you could broach the subject of this—this . . . Oh, you're disgusting!'

She walked out of the door and slammed it, went out into the drive, and got into her car. As she drove viciously out of the gate, she looked back and saw him, still standing there in the dining-room window, staring blankly in front of him.

'Cassia's taking a house in London,' said Edwina. 'What do you think about that?'

'Is she?' said Harry. His voice was light, but there was an underlying note of self-satisfaction in it. 'Well, I suggested that to her. The other night.'

'Really? It seems rather odd to me. I can't think what she's going to do with it.'

'Live in it perhaps? That's what people usually do with houses.'

'Oh Harry, you know perfectly well what I mean. What do you think Edward will have to say about it?'

'Whatever it is, I am sure it will scarcely bear listening to. He is the epitome of dullness.'

'Yes, he is. Harry, could you do this up for me? The clasp is so stiff.' She held out a marcasite bracelet to Harry. He fixed it on to her wrist and then kissed her hand casually, his eyes moving over her. 'You look very nice,' he said.

He didn't often compliment her; his praise was hard earned, and when it did come, it was always minimal.

'Now I want you to pay particular attention to Binkie Norton tonight and his tedious wife. I'm trying to persuade him to join one of my boards. Bloody clever, and very good connections.'

'Yes, all right,' said Edwina. She would have preferred to go on talking about Cassia and her new house for a little longer—it really did intrigue her—but Harry always avoided the subject of Cassia; the old animosity between them had continued down the years. She had never properly understood it: chemistry, she supposed.

*   *   *

'I'm dining with Dominic Foster tonight,' said Benedict, walking towards the door. His tone was light, casual—too casual. Cecily looked at him sharply. She was feeding Laurence in bed; Benedict had come up to say goodbye.

'Benedict . . .'

'Yes?' he said, and then turning, saw her face and flushed deeply. 'Cecily,' he said, 'for God's sake. Dominic Foster is married.'

'So are you,' she said briefly. He went out and slammed the door.

Cecily sat there, thinking about Benedict, Benedict and the long, worrying, difficult years.

*   *   *

She had been very young when they had been married, not quite twenty. He had been thirty-five, and considered a great catch: immensely rich, charming, amusing, sophisticated. Cicely had fallen in love with him the very first time they had met, at a party given by one of her friends' mothers.

She was amazed when Benedict asked her to marry him. She had thought, hoped indeed, that he more than liked her, but she had had no idea that his feelings were sufficiently strong to inspire thoughts of marriage. Nevertheless, when he had turned up at her parents' house late one afternoon, bearing a box with an exquisite ring in it which had belonged to his grandmother, and told her he loved her and would be most honoured if she would consider marrying him, she did not pause for a

216

moment, merely flung her arms round his neck and said that she didn't need to consider it, she would love to.

The wedding was a huge success, proclaimed one of the finest of 1923. For their honeymoon they went to Egypt, took a cruise up the Nile. It was extremely romantic, and the thing that had been worrying her considerably, sex, largely due to her mother's rather doomy prognostications, proved to be at least not as bad as she had feared. On the other hand, it wasn't very good either. She assumed this must be her own fault: Benedict was terribly sweet and kind, comforting her when she apologised in the early days for not being more responsive, remaining tactfully silent later when she turned from him in tears after some increasingly unrewarding episode, even when it should have surely been getting better. It was just that it was always over so quickly: she had imagined wonderfully long-drawn-out closeness, holding and kissing and caressing, before anything actually happened.

On the nights when Benedict seemed to want her, he would turn to her, almost impatient, with his thing—she hated the technical term—already hard, and it was as if he had to get it into her really quickly. And she wasn't ever ready; not really, and he would plunge away for a bit, up and down into her, and she would try, so hard, to feel something, and there was nothing, nothing at all, certainly not the rhythms, the ebb and flow spoken of so lyrically by Marie Stopes in her book, *Married Love*, and then she would feel his thing shuddering into her, and he would kiss her and tell her he loved her and quite often just fall asleep and snore. She would lie

217

there, feeling sore and miserable, and wonder what she ought to be doing to make it better—for both of them.

And then she had become pregnant, and everything had changed. Benedict was pleased, unbelievably pleased. And he had cancelled so many social engagements without a word of reproach because she simply didn't feel up to going anywhere, and kept telling her he was only concerned that she should rest and take care of herself and their baby.

He had taken a job now, at a large firm of stockbrokers and she had seen this as a sign of his increasing sense of responsibility and was delighted.

Fanny was born in September, after a long tough labour which Cecily had endured with great courage. Benedict told her had never loved her more or been so proud of her. She said nervously she hoped he didn't mind the baby being a girl, and he had kissed her again and said he had always thought girls were much much nicer than boys.

She adored motherhood. Her relationship with Benedict had shifted from its slightly uneven nature: she no longer felt a foolish child living with a sophisticated man, but a woman, a grown-up, competent woman. She was very happy.

Shortly after that, Norman Duvant had entered her life.

He had written to her first, such a nice charming letter; she had been touched by it, had shown it to Benedict.

'Benedict, this is so sad. It's a begging letter, I suppose. From a Mr Duvant.'

'Let me see it, please. Please.' His voice had a

tremor in it. She handed it to him, watching him as he read the letter. 'Have you had any others? From this man?'

'No.'

'Are you sure?'

'Benedict, I would have remembered if I had. It's such a sad story, his mother dying and him losing his job. How do you think he got my name?'

'Oh, out of the society pages, I expect. These people feed off those. I will deal with it Cecily, and any others like it. You must inform me immediately if there are any more, do you understand?'

'Yes, Benedict, of course.'

'Or if this person tries to contact you in any way.'

'Yes, Benedict. I'm sure he won't.'

'I hope not,' he said, and stuffed the letter into his pocket and walked out of the room.

She had felt bad about poor Mr Duvant for a few days, and then forgotten about him. Then one late autumn day, soon after Fanny's first birthday, when she was having tea in the drawing room, Susan came in. 'It's a gentleman, madam, says you'll know his name, wants to see you.'

'Well, what is his name, Susan?'

'Duvant, madam, Norman Duvant.'

'No, I don't think—Oh, yes, of course.'

'He said he had something he'd like to talk to you about, madam. What shall I do?'

Benedict had been so clear that she was never to see or communicate with Norman Duvant, but she had liked his letter very much and here they all were, so happy and so fortunate, and what harm could it do just to see him and perhaps offer some advice?

'Show him in, Susan. Tell him I have fifteen

minutes or so. Bring another cup and a plate. And be sure to come immediately if I ring.'

*   *   *

She liked Mr Duvant immediately: he was polite and well spoken, surprisingly well dressed and very deferential. He was in his early thirties, rather good-looking, with light brown hair and grey eyes.

'What a lovely room,' he said, looking round. 'I am most grateful to you, Mrs Harrington. You'd be surprised how few people welcome us.'

Cecily looked doubtful.

'Oh, I'm sorry, I should have explained. I am forming an association of unemployed ex-soldiers from my own regiment which was your husband's own, of course. I don't know if he ever mentioned me . . .'

'No,' she said, feeling upset that Benedict had not, when Norman Duvant's letter had come. 'I'm sorry.'

'Well, why should he? Anyway, this association is more of a social thing than anything else. Time hangs heavy on our hands, you know, especially those of us who are young and active, and that is a bad thing. I have found a hall, in Paddington, where we can meet every day, where anyone can come. Just for a cup of tea and a chat. You'd be surprised how it keeps people's spirits up.'

'What a wonderful idea!' said Cecily.

'Indeed. But that costs money. The rent, heat, lighting, and then, although someone supplied us with tables, I have had to buy a few second-hand chairs and rugs. And of course cups and saucers and so on. I'm not asking for a gift, but some of the men have carved some small wooden toys—look, I have some samples here—and I thought you might be interested in buying a couple. I know you have a child and—'

'How do you know that?' said Cecily, slightly sharply.

'I saw the announcement in the regimental newsletter,' said Duvant.

'Oh, yes, of course.' She felt ashamed of her suspicions. 'Yes, naturally I'll buy some toys, they're charming. Why not let me give you a subscription as well? To put towards your expenses.' Benedict surely couldn't disapprove of this: it wasn't as if the man was begging. In any case, there might be no need to tell him. She could take the money out of her own bank account.

'That is extremely kind of you, Mrs Harrington. I am most grateful. I wonder if I might leave this letter for your husband? It's simply a copy of our own newsletter. I thought he might be interested in what an ex-comrade-at-arms might be doing with his life.'

'I'm sure he will be,' said Cecily.

He left quite shortly after that, and then Nanny arrived with Fanny, and she went up to watch her have her bath. She took her downstairs to her sitting room to give her some milk and a cuddle.

The letter from Norman Duvant lay on her small table still. Clearly Benedict had to see it: he would be very cross if he knew she'd kept it from him. On the other hand, he'd be furious if he knew she'd entertained Norman Duvant in his house.

Well, she thought, she would put it away safely somewhere for a day or so; it could keep.

'Rock-a-bye baby,' she sang very quietly, rocking

221

Fanny in her arms. Fanny reached up a small hand and touched her face. Cecily felt a sudden and very intense happiness. She was so very lucky, really.

The phone rang suddenly. She reached out to answer it, knocked the letter without realising it on to the floor.

It was Benedict. 'I wondered if you'd mind organising a dinner party tomorrow or the next night for a couple of Americans. I realise it's short notice, but I'd like to offer them some hospitality.'

Fanny wriggled off her mother's lap and started crawling round the room. She saw the letter under the table and smiled; she liked trying to get things out of envelopes. A tug from her sharp little teeth ripped off a corner of the envelope, and then it was easy to get a finger inside and pull the contents out. By the time Cecily had finished talking to Benedict, the letter was in three large pieces on the floor.

*　　　*　　　*

'But Benedict, this is blackmail! Can't you get that into your head.'

'Of course I can get it into my head. Don't speak to me as if I was a child.'

'You're behaving as if you were a child. And a very stupid one.'

'Oh for God's sake!' said Benedict wearily. 'Just stop it.'

'I stop it! I make this—this horrifying discovery about my own husband—'

'I told you,' he said heavily, 'never to have anything to do with that man.'

'Yes, well if you'd explained why—' She stopped, realising how impossible such an explanation would

222

have appeared.

'You should take notice of me anyway,' he said.

'Why? Because I'm in some way subservient to you? I'm sorry, Benedict, but that just doesn't seem quite right. Under the circumstances.'

'I—don't know what you mean,' he said.

'Well, let me explain. I discover that you have been having some kind of a relationship with a man. Which, whatever form it took, clearly has served to convince him he had some hold over you. A man, moreover, you have known for years. Whose presence in your life has given you cause for great anxiety—and which you have handled extremely ineptly, if I may say so.'

'Cecily, please be careful what you say to me.'

'I will say what I like to you,' said Cecily, 'and if you don't like it you are at liberty to leave. Although if you do I shall go straight to the police.'

'The police!'

'Yes, of course. That's what you do with blackmailers. You tell the police. It's a crime—and it's what you must do.'

'So is what Norman Duvant is accusing me of,' said Benedict quietly.

'I realise that.'

'Should we perhaps—talk about that?' he said.

Cecily looked at him, at the husband she had loved and thought she knew, whose child she had borne, whom she had promised to love and cherish and obey, and knew that they had to, to talk about it.

'Yes, perhaps we should,' she said after a long silence. 'Yes, of course . . .'

He spared himself—and her—nothing; Norman Duvant had been not merely in his regiment, but

223

his batman. Their affair had not begun until after the war, when Benedict had helped him to get a job in a bank, taken an interest in him, helped him along.

'Because you . . . were attracted to him.'

'Yes,' he said, very quietly.

She tried to understand. Her knowledge of homosexuality was extremely hazy, but of course she understood it: it was a condition, an illness, that afflicted some men, usually rather weak ones—she had heard it could be cured—and it was absolutely illegal. She listened in horror to stories of letters, dinners, then weekends in the Devon house, expensive gifts. He had even bought Duvant a house.

'Benedict, how could you?' she said, looking at him in horror. 'I know, I know,' he said, burying his head in his hands, 'but it was when he had begun to blackmail me. I thought it would finally shut him up.'

Only of course it hadn't.

'So that was why you married me? To shake this spectre off?' She hadn't thought anything could ever hurt so much.

'It was one of the reasons,' he said, harrowingly honest.

'Oh! So there were others. I suppose you thought I was naive enough, stupid enough, for you to get away with it. For me not to guess, not to work it out.' He didn't look at her. So something *could* hurt as much, hurt more even. Cecily closed her eyes, wondering how she could bear it.

'Didn't you love me at all?'

'Yes, of course I did. I do!' said Benedict. 'You have to believe that. I love you very dearly. I think

224

you are beautiful and sweet and a wonderful mother to our daughter and—'

'Well,' she said, 'that all sounds very satisfactory, I must say. What a fool everyone must think me.'

'Cecily, of course everyone doesn't think you a fool. Everyone doesn't know.'

'But some people do?'

'There was gossip, at one time, but since our marriage it has entirely ceased. You have to believe that.'

The pain deepened, ground into her. 'Does Leonora know?'

'Yes, she does,' he said, very quietly. 'She has tried to help. In various ways.'

'And Richard?'

'I think not.'

'And have there been others?'

'Occasionally. Not for a very long time. I have struggled, Cecily, tried so hard ...'

'Look at me, Benedict!' The words roared across the room, startled, almost frightened her. 'Have you ever, ever desired me?'

A long silence, then, 'I have loved you,' he said.

She stood up, unable to bear any of it any longer. 'I'm going to bed,' she said. 'I have to think. About all of it. But there is one thing you have to do, Benedict, and that is go to the police. That creature will just go on getting more and more horrible, more and more dangerous. And if you don't go, I will. I have this letter, and it is evidence enough. Goodnight.'

She looked back as she left the room. He was staring at her, his face filled with a terrible remorse, and something else: an appalling, naked fear.

'I mean it,' she said. 'It has to be done. For all our sakes, not just yours. Mine and Fanny's too. You have to be brave. For us.'

He did not go to the police, but he did go to Maurice Castle, a lawyer whom Leonora had put him in touch with, an interview with whom he reported back very fully to Cecily. A certain calm had filled her, and she found herself able to listen to the most unsavoury details with surprising detachment.

Castle had been soothing, competent, thorough: how much evidence could Duvant actually produce? Were there letters, copies of cheques, anything like that? Benedict had said yes, there were letters—although nothing really explicit. Castle was concerned that Duvant had been taken to the country house, asked if the servants had seen anything, witnessed a sharing of a bed. Benedict had said he thought almost certainly not.

'Castle said he thought it was most unlikely that Duvant would go to my business associates, which was his main threat. Or to anyone, really. He said that these fellows never seem to grasp that they are guilty of the crime as well. Or rather more to the point, perhaps, they bank on their victims not grasping it. He too would be tried and, if found guilty, imprisoned. It is all a bluff, and he said I should call it. And if he did talk, then I should deny it. It would be my word against his. He also said that if there was no real evidence then Duvant would really have lost in every way. The source of money would have dried up and he himself would be under investigation.'

'Indeed.'

'And then he said—' He looked at Cecily rather

226

warily, then for the first time there was a flash of humour in his voice. 'He said that if he were Lord Chancellor, he'd make the whole thing legal.'

'Legal!' said Cecily. 'What, homosexuality?'

'Yes. I don't expect you to agree, but he says the current situation simply leads to further crime. If it was legal, that would stop.'

Cecily said, 'That would never happen. The British public would never accept it. Not in a thousand years. Nor should they.'

Benedict said nothing, just looked at her, helpless.

'And what,' she said, a tremor in her voice, 'and what sentence might there be? If you were tried and found guilty?'

'Life imprisonment. No doubt about that.' He looked at her again, the shadow of amusement back in his eyes. 'It was a hanging offence, you know, until the middle of the last century. At least I won't be—'

'Benedict, please. It isn't amusing.'

'I know. I'm sorry.'

She had fretted, sleepless, for what seemed like weeks, then one day in late November, she had been sitting, trying to read, when Cassia had arrived unexpectedly. She was in her second year at medical school and was radiantly happy, Cecily had always been fond, but slightly in awe of Cassia, of her fierce ambition, her clearly brilliant mind. She wasn't sure if she could cope with her at this particular point in her life. She smiled at her rather weakly.

'Sorry not to warn you,' Cassia said, kissing Cecily, 'but I was passing on my bike, and I realised I didn't have a lecture till eleven, and I thought I might just see Fanny for a minute. Do you mind?' She adored Fanny, loved to come and play with her.

'I'm sorry,' said Cecily, 'Fanny's fast asleep. She's got a bit of a cold.'

'Oh, I'm sorry. Well, I'll just go away again.'

'No, don't,' said Cecily with a great effort. 'Stay and have a cup of tea or something. What would you like?'

'Hot chocolate, please. It's awfully cold out there.' She looked at Cecily sharply. 'Cecily, are you all right? You look awfully pale. Not having another one, are you? Oh, sorry, how awful of me, I shouldn't have said that, how rude. Cecily, don't cry. What is it? What's the matter?'

And astonished that she was able to do such a thing, Cecily managed, somehow, to get the dreadful words out, to tell Cassia what Benedict was.

Cassia was not in the least shocked; she came over to Cecily and put her arms round her and gave her a hug. 'How sad. How very sad for both of you. I'm so sorry.'

'Is that how you see it?' said Cecily. 'Just sad?'

'Yes, of course,' said Cassia, 'and only sad because of the attitudes of everybody. Making it a crime and all that nonsense.'

'You don't see it as one?' said Cecily.

'No. How could it be? Do you?'

'I don't know. I don't know about anything at all any more.'

'Why don't you just talk about it?' said Cassia. 'All of it. And remember I'm a scientist and thus completely unshockable.'

And suddenly she had been able to talk about it,

228

not her own sadness so much, her own humiliation, but the nightmare situation—the blackmailing, Benedict's refusal to go to the police, Maurice Castle's advice, her own instinct in the matter. 'What can I do, Cassia?' she had said, grasping Cassia's hands in her own. 'What on earth can I do?'

And that was when Cassia had made her offer.

*   *   *

Norman Duvant's house was halfway down a small, neat street in Ruislip; they found it quite easily. Cecily parked her Morris, and they sat looking at it: at its pretty, flower-filled front garden, its bright red front door, its muslin curtains blowing in the breeze.

'I know what you're thinking,' said Cassia finally.

'What?'

'That it doesn't look like a blackmailer's house.'

'No, it doesn't, does it? If it was horrible and dingy, I might feel a bit braver.'

'I'm feeling very brave,' said Cassia, getting out and slamming the door. 'Come on.'

'Oh dear,' said Cecily, 'I'm beginning to—'

'Well, I'm not. Look, you start the conversation and I'll just back you up. And if you feel your courage waning, just think of Fanny. None of it's her fault.'

'No. No, all right. Do I look frightened?'

'You look magnificent,' said Cassia firmly.

It was actually quite easy. Cecily was surprised to find a very strong, firm little speech had formed itself in her mind, which, confronted by Norman Duvant's complacently patronising face, made itself

229

very clearly felt.

The front room was pin-neat, oddly impersonal. There were several vases of flowers, some rather bad water-colours, and a few photographs, all of Norman Duvant as a small child with his parents.

'Well now,' Norman Duvant said, sitting down, 'to what do I owe the honour of this visit?'

The speech came out almost without pause. Cicely told Norman Duvant exactly what she thought of him, and of what he was doing; that she knew all about his relationship with her husband; that she also knew that he had been blackmailing him.

'Which puzzles me,' she said, 'since you must realise that if he were arrested, so would you be. I can't believe you are quite that stupid, Mr Duvant. I have taken legal advice and I am assured that there is no way you would avoid criminal charges, should any be brought against my husband. If, in the extremely unlikely event of my husband being sent to prison, and your remaining outside, any money you might have been extracting from him would stop immediately. Which really wouldn't do you any good at all, either. So I think the best thing you can do is leave him alone, forthwith. Neither of us has any intention of ever seeing or speaking to you again. If you value your own security you will remove yourself from our lives. If you continue to pester us, we shall take legal measures against you.'

Norman Duvant was silent for a while, then he said, 'I wonder how your husband's employers at the Stock Exchange would view any of the information I might give them.'

'Mr Duvant,' Cassia said, very cool, crossing one long leg over the other, 'I really very much doubt if they would give you the time of day. Mr Harrington is an extremely valuable partner in his firm, with a fine record. I do assure you that is of more importance to them than anything you might try to tell them.'

'Well, I shall write to them with a very full report this evening.'

'Of course you are at liberty to do so, but I would remind you again of the blackmail laws in this country. Now you must excuse us. Come along, Cecily, we have other, more important claims on our time.'

Cecily stood up, smiled radiantly at Cassia. 'Indeed yes,' she said, pulling on her gloves. 'I have shopping to do for a start. Good morning, Mr Duvant. I hope we shall not meet again.'

Cecily was astonished at herself; in that moment the entire thing seemed worthwhile. Enjoyment was slightly too strong a word, but she felt at the same time that she could, had the requirement been expressed, have flown through the air, walked on water, or done any other number of hitherto unimaginable things.

They left him then, walked out of the front door, down the front path, out into the car; Cecily started the car, put it into gear, drove it very fast and competently to the end of the street. There she stopped suddenly, leant out of the door and was violently sick.

'Sorry,' she said, 'sorry, Cassia.'

'That's all right. Here, take my hanky. You were magnificent. I was so impressed.'

'You were wonderful too. I hope it works, that's all. I can't believe it'll be that simple.'

'I think it will be,' said Cassia. 'It was the point

231

about blackmail that really got through to him. Didn't you see his face? So, as long as Benedict doesn't give in to him, I don't think we'll hear any more from him. You must tell Benedict what you've done. Otherwise he may do something off his own bat.'

'Well, if you think so. Thank you, Cassia. For everything. I'll never forget it. Ever. Most of all not minding about it, you know?'

'Yes. Yes, I think I know.' Then she said, very casually, 'What do you think you might do next?'

Cecily knew what she meant. 'I shall just go home and continue. Unless something very dreadful happens.'

'With everything just the same?'

'Why ever not?'

'Well, I don't know. I just thought perhaps—'

'Cassia,' said Cecily firmly, 'if you were thinking I might divorce Benedict or leave him or something, you couldn't be more wrong. He needs me. He needs me more than ever. I'm going to make our marriage work. I know I have to and I know I can.'

'So you still do love Benedict?'

'I love him more than ever. And he needs help to overcome this . . . this problem, and I'm going to give it to him. I'm not going to fail him now.'

'That's . . . wonderful,' said Cassia. She smiled at Cecily: a quick, slightly awkward smile.

Cecily could tell she wasn't entirely convinced, but she knew she could do it. What Benedict needed was a great deal of help and sympathy and understanding, and she could, in time, see him through this whole awful thing. It was, after all, only an illness of a sort—a psychological illness—

232

and people did get over illnesses.

She would learn to be more what he wanted in bed, less inhibited; that must have made things more difficult for him. They could rebuild their marriage and have more children, and in a few years the whole thing would seem like a terrible nightmare . . . Together they could face all the problems. That was what marriage was all about. For better and worse. The worse was over now, hopefully, and they could put it behind them.

However, in a way it had not been over, and for the rest of her life she knew she must live in fear of it starting all over again.

CHAPTER TWELVE

'The man's gone mad,' said Harry.

Edwina looked at him. 'Who's gone mad?'

'The King. He gave an official dinner party last night at St James's Palace, it's reported here; entertained the Mountbattens, the Baldwins, Diana and Duff Cooper, and the Simpsons, for God's sake.'

'What's wrong with that?'

'Oh, Edwina, really! Can't you see what he's doing? Trying to inveigle that woman into his official life by the back door. Hoping we'll all just come to accept the whole thing, just because she's got her elegant feet under the same table as the Prime Minister.'

'But she's married to Ernest.'

'I'd put a lot of money on that changing soon.'

'Oh, I think he'll get tired of her like he does of

everyone else, in time. And even if he doesn't, he can't marry a divorced woman. He's the King of England, Defender of the Faith and all that.'

'And terribly in love. Diana Cooper told me last week he really seems to feel he can't face life without her. Edwina, this is horrible coffee. I can't believe this is freshly ground. I don't ask much from you, but—'

'You ask a great deal, and I'm sure it is fresh. I'll check with Cook, don't go on about it. Anyway, the King doesn't have to face life without Wallis. She can stay there in the background, playing hostess at Fort Belvedere, waiting for him to get back from the royal duties.'

'He's going to want more than that. And this dinner party proves it.'

'Well we shall see,' said Edwina. 'I must go, I'm terribly busy today.'

'With which branch of your life? The medical? The pseudo theatrical? I'm getting quite dizzy with it all, Edwina.'

'Oh, go to hell,' said Edwina good-naturedly. 'The fashion show, actually, if that's what you mean by theatrical. I have a meeting with Leon de Rosay this morning, and then after lunch I'm seeing Venetia and Rose at Victor Stiebel's to discuss the possibility of him supplying some evening gowns for the show. And then—'

'You must forgive me, I'm finding this all a little too complex, fascinating as it is. I'll be late tonight myself, dinner at the Sporting Club. So I'll see you this time tomorrow, probably. Goodbye. Don't work too hard.' He got up, bent briefly to kiss her.

*   *   *

234

'Leon, that is the most marvellous coat. Could I order one for me while we're about it? And that suit, please, in wine. I just adore the padded shoulders. Only maybe just a little longer. And—'

'Mrs Moreton, I thought this was your business meeting. If you want me to summon a vendeuse, of course I will, but I cannot concentrate on two things at once.'

'Leon, don't be tedious. You're going to sell hundreds of extra things through this show of mine. De Rosay is going to be as big a name as Stiebel in six months' time. But I do want the suit. Please. Don't forget. There's no need to get some stuffy vendeuse in.'

'But—'

'Leon, concentrate. Now, let me see. You'll do six suits, four cocktail dresses and a few evening gowns. Which is all wonderful. And you need to have the girls in as soon as possible for fittings. That's no problem. And you can get Maria Guy to do some hats?'

'I think so.'

'You're an angel. Goodness, this is exciting. I'm loving it. Are you hungry? Because I could eat a horse.'

'Perhaps a tiny foal,' said Leon de Rosay, smiling at her. 'Shall we go and find one?'

She stood up, thinking how much she enjoyed the company of homosexuals: so amusing, so interested in one, so undemanding. And Leon was so good-looking too, with his chestnut hair and his wonderful aquiline nose. He had come a long way from Leonard Rosewall, born and bred in Clapham. She had been introduced to him by her

235

friend Venetia Hardwicke, who worked on *Vogue*: 'You'll adore him, Edwina, and his clothes are exactly you. I want to help him along a bit, we're featuring one of his suits in the August issue. Buy something of his and wear it around a bit, darling, just for me. Get people noticing.'

She had bought one of Leon's dresses. He was a brilliant tailor besides having a penchant for showy evening gowns. Harry had liked it; she had bought more, taken her friends to the next collection. He was being generous with her fashion show: it was a lot of work for him, and would cost him money, but it was no more than her due.

He took her to a small French restaurant, round the corner from his salon in Sloane Street; it was small, dark, intimate, every table a tiny, dimly lit island.

'Leon, this is so romantic. What a pity we're not having an affair.'

'Mrs Moreton, if that is what you want—'

'You tart!' said Edwina affectionately. 'You'd even do that, wouldn't you, if you thought it would make your name even bigger?'

'I would try,' he said, and kissed her hand.

'Well, you don't have to. I adore you as you are. Now look, let's order and then Leon, what's through there?'

'Another, smaller dining room. For even more private affairs than our own. Why?'

'Oh, nothing.'

But it wasn't nothing. A man had just walked quickly through the main restaurant into the small, inner room, and had been greeted with a warm handshake by another man, rising half from the table. She recognised very well the man sitting

236

down. It was Benedict Harrington.

*   *   *

She would have left, quickly, before he had seen her, but Leon was in the middle of a long funny story at two-thirty, when the first man left, alone. She recognised him at once: Dominic Foster, the architect. He didn't see her.

Leon recognised him too. 'Now there's a man of the moment,' he said. 'He even got a write-up in *Vogue* last month.'

'Well!' said Edwina briskly. 'What an accolade for an architect.'

This was wasted on Leon; he smiled at her. 'Yes. He designed an amazing set of studios in Pimlico. A friend of mine is taking one. Quite gorgeous they are, almost entirely glass—walls, roofs. Only problem, which no one thought of, is the pigeons . . .'

'Oh, yes?' said Edwina abstractedly.

Benedict had just emerged from the inner room. He saw her, was clearly shocked, then recovered, came over and kissed her. She could feel the tension in his body. 'Edwina! How nice!'

'Hello, Benedict. Have you met Leon de Rosay? The most brilliant couturier in London at the moment. Leon, Benedict Harrington. My husband's cousin.'

'How do you do, Mr Harrington.' Leon stood up, held out his hand.

She could see him taking Benedict in, reacting: not sexually, of course, but emotionally. They always knew one another straight away. Or rather about one another. The famous coded question

237

they were supposed to ask 'Are you a friend of Dorothy's?'—was so terribly unnecessary. Only for someone like Benedict, maybe it wasn't. Poor Benedict.

She smiled at him, her heart aching at his patent misery. 'Leon is helping me with a fashion show I'm organising, in aid of St Christopher's, aren't you, Leon?'

'Mrs Moreton,' said Leon, with a sigh, 'if you will excuse me, I simply must go. I have a client arriving in three minutes, a difficult client, not in the least like you.'

'Of course you must go. Thank you for a wonderful lunch and all your help.'

He half bowed to them both, walked out, signing the bill at the desk on the way.

Benedict looked at Edwina, clearly miserably anxious.

'Benedict,' she said firmly, 'sit down a minute. Let's have a glass of wine.' He sat down, and she signalled for the waiter. 'Two glasses of champagne,' she said briskly, and then, 'I always think champagne is the best thing after lunch. After anything really, of course. Or before it. Don't you?'

'Oh, yes. Thank you.' The champagne had arrived. 'To you, Edwina,' he said, and raised his glass, then virtually drained it.

'Edwina—'

'Benedict,' she said, 'Benedict, I promise I won't say a word to Cecily. Or anyone. About you being here. Don't worry.'

'Oh, it's perfectly all right,' he said. 'I wasn't going to—' and then met her eyes with his own and looked first resigned, then amused. 'Yes, I was. Well, I was going to try. To ask you that. So thank

238

you. It's just that—well, Cecily doesn't like Dominic Foster very much. I can't think why.'

'Benedict, please!' she said, the exasperation so clear in her voice that he looked startled. 'I might find myself having to tell Cecily after all if you're going to treat me like some sort of constipated idiot. I'll never, ever, say a word to anyone, you know I won't, but of course I know why Cecily doesn't like Dominic. And why you're here with him. Let's at least be honest with each other.'

He looked at her, then he said, 'Thank you. I didn't mean to offend you.'

'Well you did. Benedict, you know I don't care. Have you really forgotten that evening?'

'No,' he said, 'no, of course not. And you were wonderful then. But—'

'Well then. Just relax.'

'Thank you,' he said again, and smiled at her.

She was silent a moment, remembering the evening: she had left a night-club in a rage, stalked off into the night, having had a row with Harry, who was still inside, drunk and belligerent. She had found herself in a tiny street in the maze behind Park Lane, and as she walked down it looking for a taxi, she had seen Benedict suddenly leaving a house a few doors in front of her, taking his leave of a man.

They were not in any kind of physical contact, but it was so clear, simply from the expression on Benedict's face, and the way he was looking up and down the street, checking it for witnesses, what he had been doing there.

He saw her, of course, and it was almost funny, so appalled, so absolutely defeated did he look. Then he managed to smile, came over to her, and

239

said, 'Hello, Edwina.'

She said, 'Hello, Benedict. I'm trying to find a taxi. Would you like to help?'—more to give him something to do, to ease his wretchedness, than anything else.

'Yes, of course, I'll go and get one. You wait here.'

She had slipped her arm through his and said, 'No, don't be silly, we'll walk together.' They had walked along, and into the agonising silence she had said, 'Benedict, it's all right. Please, please don't worry about it.'

After a very long silence, finally he had said, 'Did you know . . . before?' and she had said, yes, she had, and it was fine by her and she could be as silent as the grave when required, only nobody would ever believe it. 'Where's Harry?' he said, and she had explained that Harry was probably even now under a table in the night-club and needn't ever know they had met at all.

'Of course he knows,' Benedict had said abruptly. 'He's always been marvellous about it.'

Edwina had said there was nothing to be marvellous about, in her opinion. 'And now look, there's a cab, I'm going to jump into it. Goodnight, Benedict, thank you for your help.'

And they had never mentioned it again, until now.

'I'm sorry,' he said again, 'I always forget how different you are.'

'Well, that's one way of looking at it,' she said, draining her glass.

She talked to him about her fashion show, saw him slowly relax. At half past four they were still there, and he was doing a wonderful imitation of his secretary looking first at the office clock, then

240

her watch as he came in late from lunch.

'I'm sure she's the only person who cares,' said Edwina.

'Yes, but Cecily might phone.'

'Are you so frightened of Cecily?'

'Not frightened of her, but I am afraid of troubling her.'

'It's such a shame,' she said suddenly, 'that she can't accept it. Just a little.'

'Edwina! How could she?'

'Oh, I don't know. But a little less . . . rigidness would make you both happier. You've loved her and stayed with her for a very long time, after all.'

'Yes, but she worries about me being caught. The disgrace. It's still a crime, Edwina, you really mustn't forget that.'

'It's so ridiculous, it makes me livid,' said Edwina. 'My own first sexual experience was a lesbian one. It was wonderful. I shall never forget it, ever.'

'Is that really true?' he said. His expression was odd, not shocked, not surprised even, but intently, almost fervently relieved.

'Of course it's true. And it wasn't just once either. Took me a while to adjust to the other way, I can tell you. I still sometimes see a woman and think ooh, yes, she'd be interesting. Chemistry, you know. But of course you do know,' she added, laughing. 'Anyway, I haven't for years. Now then, this is all getting a bit disgraceful. Another glass and I'll be jumping on you. That'd be interesting. Don't look so frightened, Benedict, I'm only joking. Oh, God, look at the time, I should have been at Stiebel's half an hour ago. I must dash. Bye, Benedict, darling, and please don't worry, I swear I

241

won't say a word. To anyone.'

*   *   *

Cassia kept telling herself that it didn't mean a thing, any of it, not really; she might have taken a house—a very small house—in London for a year, but it wasn't in any way significant. It might have been a little bit extravagant, just to sleep in for two nights a week, but she didn't have to worry about extravagance, thanks to Leonora, and Leonora would certainly have approved of this manifestation of it. It was just so much more sensible, every Tuesday and Thursday, simply to get into her car and be in her—the—house in less than half an hour. And every Wednesday and Friday morning, she would leave Walton Street at six and be home by half past eight and be able to take the boys to school. It wasn't going to make the slightest difference to them: all three children were fast asleep when she got home after the clinic, and she never saw them until the morning, anyway.

They were all rather excited about her taking the house, quite unmoved by the news that she would be away for two nights a week.

'We're in bed, anyway,' said William.

'London! Can we all go and stay,' said Bertie. 'Go to the zoo?'

'Yes, of course.'

'And Big Ben?'

'Yes, and Big Ben.'

They were all going to come up for Saturday, this very week, to see the house and stay the night. There was room, which had been another reason for getting the house, rather than staying in a hotel.

She didn't want the children to feel her life in London was somehow removed from theirs. It was part of her life as a doctor, the house, she explained to Bertie, who was the only one old enough to understand.

Janet had said she thought it was a splendid idea, getting the house. She worried about Cassia doing that drive late, she said, and so did the doctor, although he had never actually said so, but she could tell, he was always edgy until he heard the car in the drive. Now they would all be able to relax those evenings.

And Edward had seemed to understand about the house: what it represented. Which had been very important too. He certainly didn't see it as a threat. He'd just nodded when she'd told him, said, 'good idea,' and hardly listened as she explained about getting back before breakfast and taking the boys to school. He hadn't expressed any interest in coming to see it, he was terribly busy, but there was plenty of time for that. 'You do whatever you think best,' he'd said. Very rational. The whole thing was very rational.

Only of course that wasn't why she'd taken the house at all.

Maureen Johnson had come for her interview two days after her letter of application had arrived. Edward asked Cassia to meet her from the station; incredulous at his insensitivity, she sent Janet instead and greeted Maureen with her on the doorstep, dressed in a new and very expensive dress from Harvey Nichols. She had no idea why, it just made her feel better.

Maureen was pleasant looking with neat brown hair, scrubbed skin and rather small blue eyes; she also, Cassia noticed with some satisfaction, had very thick ankles. Maureen treated Cassia with a mixture of the deference due to a prospective employer's wife and the superiority of the professional woman over the housewife. She was, she explained to Cassia, fresh from a two-year house job at Kingston hospital in Surrey; she had actually trained at University College Hospital. Cassia smiled as sweetly as she could and asked Maureen why she was going into general practice rather than taking up a hospital position. Maureen told her she thought there was more scope in general practice for a woman. 'But were you not invited to stay at UCH?' said Cassia, and knew from Maureen's flush that she had not qualified for that particular honour and, moreover, that Maureen knew she knew.

Edward had interviewed her for over an hour and then taken her out with him on a call to a child with suspected diphtheria. They came back engrossed in a discussion about inoculation which continued through lunch. Cassia sat and first tried to smile, then flicked through the latest copy of *Vogue*, and finally asked them to excuse her as she had to collect William from school.

When she got back, Edward was in the surgery with Maureen. The door opened abruptly and he said, 'Could you possibly see your way to taking Maureen back to Haywards Heath?'

The sun had come out and Cassia wound down the hood of the Jaguar. It was, despite the brilliance of the day, very cold and windy, and she watched Maureen Johnson's neat hair grow tangled with some satisfaction.

'Goodbye,' she said graciously, as they reached

the station, 'it's been lovely to meet you. I still think you should have stayed on at UCH, done paediatrics there. I was asked to stay on to do obstetrics at St Christopher's after my finals, and I found it absolutely irresistible. Only, of course, Bertie came along and I had to say no in the end.'

The expression of confusion and dislike on Maureen's face stayed in her memory and helped her through Edward's fulsome praise of Maureen, his decision to take her on, his request that Cassia should look for rooms for her in the village, and his enthusiasm at Maureen's suggestion for a regular children's clinic every Wednesday afternoon in the surgery. Cassia tried to remind him pleasantly that she had mooted it several times herself, heard the venom in her own voice and gave up. 'And I do hope,' Edward said, 'you'll be able to help Dr Johnson to settle down, introduce her to everybody in the village, perhaps even be available in the background for a few of her early surgeries, so you can tell her who people are, give her a bit of background. Only don't get involved in anything medical, obviously.'

'Obviously,' said Cassia.

That was the day she phoned the estate agents and asked to see round the house in Walton Street. And had stood there, in the pretty first-floor drawing room, feeling dangerously, powerfully independent, and said that she would take it.

*   *   *

The clinic finished particularly late her first evening there, and it was almost nine thirty when she left Brixton; it helped with the justification of taking the house at all. She pulled up outside and sat looking up at the windows; she had hired a woman to clean it and keep an eye on it, and come in at tea time on her working days, light the fire and switch the lights on. The house looked warm, welcoming, pretty; she smiled up at it, pleased, as if it were a new and very charming friend.

She felt rather odder when she got inside, as if she was acting a part, not living real life at all; she seemed to be watching herself as she took off her coat and hat, and laid them down on the hall chair, and walked upstairs to the drawing room. It was a very pretty drawing room: she supposed if it was really her own, she might have done it differently, but given that it was a stage set, it was a very nice one, all shades of cream and blue. The fireplace was carved wood, with a pretty cast-iron grate and some hand-painted tiles, and on either side of it, floor-to-ceiling bookshelves set in alcoves. The shelves were bare, and so were the walls; she would have to fill both, but that would be fun. She would bring some photographs of the children up—that would help make it more hers.

She got up and went down to another part of her stage set, the little kitchen, and made herself a cup of coffee. Mrs Horrocks, the daily woman, had left her a fruit cake and a tin of biscuits. She was hungry, she realised, and sat at the small kitchen table, eating biscuit after biscuit. She was just going upstairs again to see if Mrs Horrocks had turned down her bed as instructed, when the phone rang. It was Edwina.

'Darling, how thrilling to have you in London. I'd simply adore to have a little house all to myself, get a bit of peace and quiet.'

246

As Edwina had her own very large house to herself a great deal of the time, this seemed to Cassia a rather extraordinary comment, but she didn't say so. 'That's not the idea at all, Edwina,' she said. 'It's just that my clinics finish so late and then it's such a long drive home. This seemed more sensible.'

'Well, if that's your story, Cassia, I certainly won't tell anyone any different. But presumably you'll use it other times as well. Look, I'm giving a dinner party a week next Wednesday, and I want you to come to that.'

'Edwina, I can't, you don't understand, I've no intention of—'

'Of course you can. There'll be lots of interesting people for you, including Leon de Rosay, he's a couturier, up and coming—oh, you know, do you? Sorry, I always forget you're not quite the bumpkin you were. Anyway, I'm putting on a fashion show in aid of your hospital—did I mention that?'

'No,' said Cassia, genuinely interested.

'Well, I am. So you ought to come. Mummy and Daddy will be there because she's helping with tickets, and you know how Daddy adores you, and then I wondered if we could ask Rupert. He could help with the actual staging, I thought. Could you ask him, darling, please?'

'Well—'

'Good. That's settled, then. Now I must go, and congratulations again about the house. I think it's marvellous.'

Cassia went back upstairs to the drawing room again, switched on the wireless. There was a concert on: a Bach organ recital. Edward didn't like Bach, always asked her if she would turn it down. Not off, of course, down. She loved Bach; she turned it up. God, this was wonderful.

She sat down on the sofa and put her feet up, and looked about her, savouring the peace, the Bach, the guilty happiness. Of course she'd much rather be at home, only even now, she thought, looking at her watch, she wouldn't be home, she'd still be driving anxiously fast, through the winding lanes. So it was all right; and she shouldn't feel guilty. The Bach and the peace were a bonus.

The walls were very bare; she would have to fill them quickly. Only you couldn't buy pictures quickly—it took time, and care. Suddenly she remembered her room at Grosvenor Gardens; she had several pictures there that Leonora had given her. She wondered if Sir Richard would mind her taking them. She went over to the telephone and dialled his number.

'Godpa! It's me.'

'Darling girl, how nice. How are you, where are you?'

God, more explanations. She made them quickly, smoothly, not giving him time to interrupt. 'You must come and see it very soon. Maybe on Saturday, I'm bringing the boys up. Come to tea, bring Margaret.' (This was fun too.) 'The thing is, I have some very bare walls. And I wondered—well, would you mind terribly if I at least borrowed a few of the ones from my room there? They were mine, I think.'

'Darling, of course you can. Any time. Saturday would be fun, yes. Thank you.' There was a pause. Then, 'It sounds a splendid idea, your little house. Very sensible.' She could tell he didn't think anything of the sort.

248

It was going to be quite difficult, making people understand. They would all think the money was finally going to her head, that she was going off the rails, setting up a new, shinily independent life, where she could do what she wanted, what indeed she had always wanted. As Leonora had, perhaps intended . . .

Well, they might think that, but it was quite quite wrong.

CHAPTER THIRTEEN

Edwina had planned with enormous care the dinner party which would launch her fashion show. She loved drawing up a guest list, pulling together disparate yet somehow compatible people, doing the *placement*, working out menus, ordering the flowers, planning what she should wear. And this one was particularly important, even the guest list had proved challenging, adjusting the balance of the fashion, business and social element. She looked at Harry at breakfast on the day slightly nervously.

'Harry, you won't be late tonight, will you?'

'I'm afraid I can't guarantee being back before nine,' he said, 'if then.'

'But Harry, it's such an important evening for me, please.'

'Edwina, I do have slightly more important things to do than fill my allotted position in your table plans.'

'Harry, you are the absolute limit. I really—'

He was smiling at her. 'Edwina, of course I'll be

here. I'm impressed by this new entrepreneurial spirit of yours. What time is curtain-up?'

'Well, they're asked for seven thirty,' she said, not sure if relief or irritation was stronger, 'but if you could be ready by seven I'd be grateful. Yes, Bishop?'

'Telephone, madam. Lady Bushnell.'

'Oh God,' said Edwina, hurrying out of the room. She came back looking cross. 'Bloody woman can't come. My perfect seating plan, all to pot. Harry, it's not funny. Why can't you, just for once, do something to help me with my life?'

*   *   *

He phoned her an hour later. 'I've replaced the Bushnells. Benedict just rang me about something, he and Cecily are free, and prepared to fill a chair. Or rather two. I hope you're pleased.'

'Oh, Harry, no! Not them, not tonight.'

'Why on earth not?'

'Harry, you don't understand. Oh God, why couldn't you have asked me? Now get off the line. I have to ring Leon de Rosay.'

But Leon de Rosay was not in his salon; he was out of town, the directrice told her, and not expected back until after four.

'Then get him to ring me, will you, please?' said Edwina. 'It's really very, very urgent indeed. Don't forget.'

*   *   *

Cassia decided to spend the morning at Grosvenor Gardens, sorting out her pictures. Sir Richard and

Margaret were both going out, Margaret had told her, but Jarvis was expecting her and she was to make herself at home.

'Richard said to tell you there were a couple of pictures of Leonora's own that you might like. I'll put them in your room as well. Just leave them if you don't want them.'

It was still referred to as her room: Cassia found it very touching.

It was very strange to be there, alone in the house, in the great hall. Leonora haunted it, an oddly vivid ghost.

'Oh, Leonora,' she said aloud, hearing the catch in her own voice, 'I do miss you.'

'Would you like some tea, miss? Or some coffee?'

It was Harris. Cassia was always 'miss' to Harris. She smiled at her and said tea would be lovely, and could she have it in her room.

'Of course, miss. I'll bring it up. You must miss Lady Beatty,' she added, looking at Cassia's face. (Damn, now she was crying.)

'I do, Harris, yes.' She rummaged in her bag for a handkerchief, half amused by Harris's clear view that it was Leonora who was Lady Beatty still, wondering how she saw Margaret. 'Anyway, it's nice to be here.'

'How are the children, miss?'

'All very well. Thank you.'

'I do miss having young people in the house. It's not the same at all. They were happy days, when you and Mr Moreton were children—what a funny child he was, so serious, like a little old man.'

'Yes, he was rather. Well, he seems younger now.'

251

'Oh, he's a lovely gentleman. Always sends me and Jarvis a Christmas present.'

'Does he?' She was amazed that Harry should show such consideration.

'Oh yes, miss, always. And when I was ill in hospital, he sent me some lovely flowers.'

'Good heavens. That is very nice.'

She walked upstairs, wondering at a Harry Moreton who could be so rude, so difficult, so absolutely ruthless, and yet who sent presents and flowers to elderly servants; a Harry Moreton who still, clearly, she hardly knew.

*   *   *

It was exactly the same, her room: even her night-dress case on the bed, some of her books on the bedside table.

The pictures were still hanging on the wall, and the two which Sir Richard had thought she'd like propped against the bed. They were very pretty early Victorian portraits, perfect for her new drawing room. One was of a small boy and a very large dog, the other a little girl sitting in a dog cart: they would sit very happily on either side of the window. They were in very nice maple frames, although one of those would need fixing. She turned it over; the backing was completely unfixed on one side and bulging a bit. There seemed to be something inside. Cassia pushed her fingers in carefully, and a sheaf of papers fell out.

They were pawnbrokers' tickets: dozens of them. Mostly for jewellery, but there was also one for a 'mother-of-pearl picture frame', another for some hat-pins—God, Leonora must have been desperate.

They were all dated from very long ago, some as early as 1920. Never redeemed, of course: and everything long sold, no doubt. She looked at the addresses: all over London, places like Paddington, Croydon, Golders Green. And one in Leather Lane, 'just off [it said] Hatton Garden'; that was the photograph frame.

The frame sounded very pretty. She wasn't far from Hatton Garden and the date on the ticket was only 1928. Well, it was ridiculous. That was eight years ago. Of course it wouldn't be there. But something tugged at her. She would just check . . .

*   *   *

There was a young man at the pawnbrokers' counter, impatiently half polite. When he saw the dates on the ticket he smiled, a rather condescending smile.

'We wouldn't keep anything that long,' he said, 'especially not something like that, valueless, you know.'

'Yes. Well, I just wondered—'

'Got a problem, Mr Taylor?' A much older man had appeared from the back of the shop.

'No, no problem,' said the young man. 'This lady seemed to think we might keep things for nine years or more.'

'Well,' said the old man, smiling at her, 'it's been known. What is it you've got?'

'Just this ticket. Practically an antique in itself, actually.' She smiled at him; she liked him. 'It was my godmother's.'

'Let me see.' He took it. 'Oh, yes, I see. Mother-

253

of-pearl frame, eh? Unusual. Hard to sell, I'm surprised I bought it. She must have been a very regular customer. What did she look like?'

'Very pretty. Fair, blue eyes. Very well dressed. Loved hats. And big fur collars with the foxes' heads. About forty. She probably brought you lots of things.'

'Oh! Mrs Jarvis.' So she had used the butler's name, Cassia thought, touched yet further by this illustration of Leonora's dangerously secret life. 'Yes, she was a very regular customer. How is she? Haven't seen her for a little while.'

'Sadly, she died last year.'

'I am very sorry to hear that. She was a great lady. Always gave me a little gift for Christmas. I wondered why not last year—'

'Last year? But . . .' Leonora had been in Paris for years; how extraordinary to remember her pawnbroker.

'Yes, that was the first time she forgot. Well, of course she didn't forget, poor lady. Now you wait there, and I'll just go and see if I can find that frame.' He disappeared upstairs. Cassia sat on a hard chair and waited.

After ten minutes he came down, shaking his head.

'No frame, sadly. But there is this.' He held out a gold filigree bracelet. 'This was hers, she was very upset at parting with it. Her mother's, she said. Well, I could afford to keep it, I thought she might just be able to redeem it one day.' He shook his head. 'Lovely, isn't it? Beautiful piece of work, done in India, she said.'

'Yes, it is lovely. Could I buy it now? Redeem it, I mean. I'd like to.'

254

'Of course. Let's see . . . a hundred pounds. That's less than I gave her, but I was sorry for her. Sorry to see her come back.'

'Back? What do you mean?'

'Well, it was after she'd gone abroad. I thought with the new life she'd be all right.'

'Oh, but she was.' It seemed important that he should understand. 'She was living in some style, in Paris. Honestly.'

'Really?' He looked at her doubtfully. 'Well, she was desperate for the money for this, I can tell you that. Desperate. That's why I gave her so much.'

'And when was this?' said Cassia. She felt rather odd suddenly, slightly scared, she had no idea of what.

'November 'thirty-four. That's when she gave me my Christmas present. "I'm sorry it's so late, Mr Fisher," she said, "but better late than never," and gave me a little box of truffles. I felt bad, because she clearly couldn't afford it, if she was selling her mother's bracelet, but she insisted . . .'

*   *   *

Outside, she hailed a cab, sat in it, looking at the bracelet. Trying to work out some kind of explanation. Because if Leonora was still desperately pawning things six months before her death, how in heaven's name could she have had half a million pounds to leave to Cassia? However carefully it had been put in trust? And surely the interest earned on that sort of money would be very considerable indeed?

It simply didn't make any sort of sense at all.

By four o'clock, Leon de Rosay still hadn't phoned Edwina.

She decided to ring Benedict to warn him that Leon was coming, but he wasn't in his office. 'He's gone home early, Mrs Moreton,' said Mildred Waters. 'Stephanie is singing in a school concert, and he has gone to hear her.'

She tried the house; neither Benedict nor Cecily was there. She left a message asking for Benedict to phone her.

*   *   *

Cassia phoned Mr Brewster when she got back to Walton Street. He wasn't there, but his secretary said he would be back at five and she would ask him to ring her then. 'Is it urgent, Mrs Fallon?'

'No,' said Cassia, 'not exactly. But I would like to talk to him very much indeed.'

*   *   *

The phone rang. It was Cecily. 'Edwina, did you want me?'

'Well, no, it was Benedict, about some . . . stock I'm interested in.'

'He's playing with Laurence at the moment. Shall I get him to ring you?'

'Yes please. If he's got time.'

*   *   *

'Edwina wants you to ring her,' Cecily said. 'It's

256

about some stock she's thinking of buying.'

'Oh Lord,' said Benedict, 'surely it can wait. I've promised Fan I'll play the piano with her. I'll see Edwina tonight. Did you think it seemed urgent?'

'No. Not urgent at all.'

*   *   *

Mr Brewster phoned Cassia at a quarter past five; he had been in court all day. 'Is there a problem, Mrs Fallon?'

'No,' she said, looking at Leonora's bracelet, sitting now on her own wrist: she liked it being there, something so personal; it brought Leonora back to her just a little. 'Well, not really. I just wanted to discuss something with you. That's all.'

'Do you want to come into the office?'

'Yes, please. If that would be all right.'

'Of course. Tomorrow morning? Half past ten?'

'Fine. I shall be in London. You have got a copy of the will there, haven't you?'

'I have, indeed. Well, until tomorrow, then. Good evening, Mrs Fallon.'

Cassia put the phone down and sat staring at it. There must be some kind of an explanation for it all; and if he didn't have it, maybe he would know where to find it.

*   *   *

'Edwina, that dress looks quite ghastly on you, absolutely the wrong colour. Why don't you go and change it quickly before anyone else arrives?'

'I don't want to change it, Mummy,' said Edwina firmly, 'and I think it's absolutely the right colour.

257

It's called shocking pink—Schiaparelli invented it.'

'You can't invent a colour, Edwina.'

'Well, Schiaparelli did. Anyway, it's Leon's version of it.'

'Marcus, do go and find me a drink, and where's Harry, Edwina?'

'Late,' said Edwina briefly.

She had hardly been able to speak to Harry when he phoned to say that he would be late. 'I'm sorry, Edwina, I really cannot help it,' he had said. 'I have a huge deal going through, and the chap who is organising the finance has been held up at the Bank of England.'

'He really is the limit. Do you think he's got a mistress?'

'I don't know, Mummy, it's really not the sort of thing I'd want to discuss with him, is it? Daddy, can I have a drink too? I'll have champagne. What about you, Mummy?'

'No, dry martini for me. Vodka, Marcus, don't forget, not gin. Who else is coming to this dinner, Edwina?'

'Mummy, I told you. The Whittakers, obviously, which is why I've asked you and Daddy, and Venetia and Paul Hardwicke, and Cassia, and—'

'Oh God, not that terrible husband of hers. Tedious little man.'

'No. But Rupert Cameron.'

'I like Rupert. He's so charming, always so interested in one.'

'Yes. And Benedict and Cecily, and Leon de Rosay, as I said. But the main thing is to keep Mary Whittaker happy, and impress on her how hard I'm working on the fashion show, so she won't be too terribly cross about my flag day.'

'How is your flag day, darling?'

'Flying at half mast. Someone else has taken over.'

'Edwina, that is very naughty,' said Sylvia Fox-Ashley severely. 'Oh, now here is Rupert, and Cassia too. How lovely to see you, Rupert. Come and tell me all about your madly glamorous life . . .'

*   *   *

Edwina was getting rather drunk. She had invited everyone for seven thirty, with a view to serving dinner at eight; at eight fifteen Harry had still not arrived. God, she could kill him.

He walked in, outrageously cool, at eight twenty, kissed her, kissed her mother, bowed to everyone else and asked them to excuse him while he changed into his dinner jacket. 'Five minutes, I swear. Why don't you all go and sit down? Really, I won't mind a bit.'

'Do let's, Edwina,' said Sylvia. 'I'm simply starving and your father will fall over in a minute, he's so tight.'

'All right,' said Edwina, 'let's go in.' Leon de Rosay had not arrived either. Her evening seemed doomed.

She had placed herself on the opposite side of the table from the door, next to Sir John Whittaker; it would be doubly difficult to jump up and intercept Leon when he came in. She'd put him as far as possible from Cecily, in between Cassia and Venetia; he would enjoy them both, and hopefully become so engrossed in conversation about the fashion show that he wouldn't say anything to Benedict. There was nothing more now

259

that she could do except pray.

Harry came in, looking sleek and slightly complacent in his dinner jacket; he smiled at everyone. 'Sorry again. Edwina will have me flogged later.'

'Sounds fun,' murmured Venetia. 'Harry, have you heard the latest on the little man and Wallis?'

'Depends which latest.'

'He's taken legal advice from Walter Monckton. About Wallis's divorce.'

'Yes, I had heard that,' said Harry. 'Beaverbrook told me.'

'Extraordinary, isn't it?' said Sylvia Fox-Ashley. 'I simply do not understand it. Why can't he just live with the woman quietly, instead of going in for all this nonsense?'

'He's supposedly in love with her,' said Venetia.

'And what does that have to do with it? He can still be with her, whenever he's out of the public eye. I've no patience with him.'

'How very unusual,' muttered Edwina.

Harry turned to Cassia, who was sitting next to him. 'And what do you think about our beloved King and his behaviour?' he said quietly, his eyes dangerously brilliant.

'I don't have many views on the matter,' she said.

'Really? I'm surprised. The conflict between love and duty: I would have thought that would have been right up your street.'

'Harry, please—'

'You look so very charming when you blush. Anyway, this is a nice surprise. I didn't think we'd get you swept up into our modest little parties quite so quickly after your return to London. I was extremely flattered, by the way, that you took up

260

my suggestion.'

'Harry, I haven't returned to London. I'm simply spending two nights a week here after my clinics. And what suggestion, anyway?'

'That you should get a little house up here. Surely you remember, we were in the Savoy, and—'

'Harry, it was my idea to get the house. So I don't have the long drive home after my clinics.'

'Did you have one today? A clinic?'

'Well no, but—'

'There you are, then,' he said, sitting back, an expression of great satisfaction on his face, 'not just for the clinics. For you as well. And why not? You look very nice, by the way. Lovely dress. Vionnet?'

'Yes, actually,' said Cassia, slightly unwillingly.

'New? I imagine you can't wear anything quite that stylish in the country.'

'Not very,' said Cassia, who had bought the dress the day before with the dinner party absolutely in mind, 'and of course I could wear it in the country. We don't actually walk round with straw in our hair, you know.'

'You surprise me. Incidentally, you realise what a huge responsibility you have, sitting there, don't you? Next to our guest of honour. Who doesn't seem to have had the courtesy to turn up.'

'He's been held up, apparently, buying silk or something. And I do realise the responsibility. I'm sure I shall enjoy it.'

'Well, you look a lot nicer than Edwina does, I must say. She's wearing something of his.'

'You're very interested in clothes, aren't you?' said Cassia curiously, confident that this was a safe topic. 'What is it you like about them?'

'I'm very interested in women,' said Harry,

261

leaning back, his eyes moving over her face. 'That's what I like about clothes. What they do for women. How they work. How women choose them and for what reasons. To make themselves look sexy, or chic, or whatever, to show themselves off or to hide behind—it's a very fascinating psychological game. Take you, for instance. What you use your clothes for.'

'Harry, I don't use them, I wear them,' said Cassia irritably.

'Ah, but you're wrong there. I know exactly what you use them for.'

'Oh, you do?'

'I do. To disguise yourself.'

'Disguise myself! That is really ridiculous.'

'The woman we see, these days anyway, is chic, stylish, very cool, very in control. Which, of course, is nonsense.' He grinned at her, picked up his glass. 'You're not drinking; this is excellent wine.'

'Why is it nonsense?'

'Because chic and stylish though you may be, you aren't in control at all.'

'Is that really so?' she said, praying her voice would stay steady.

'Absolutely so. You're positively careering along, driven by the most fearsome passions. Much more interesting.' He smiled back at her.

'How nice it must be for you to be able to read everyone so expertly, Harry,' she said. 'Do you never make mistakes?'

'Very, very seldom. And certainly not about you, I know you much too well.'

Sensing the danger, she decided to change the subject. 'Harry, I want to ask you something. It's about—' She had been going to say Leonora, but at

262

that moment the door opened.

'Leon!' Edwina got up, walked round the table, kissed Leon de Rosay where he stood in the doorway, ushered in by Bishop. 'How wonderful of you to come after your dreadful day. Do come in and meet everyone.' The introductions went round the table, Leon smiling, bowing, shaking hands, kissing cheeks.

Cassia watched him, thinking how handsome he was, that he was almost certainly a homosexual (although most soberly and carefully dressed and most modestly behaved), observing people reacting to him, admiring Edwina's élan as a hostess that she should invite him to her dinner table with people like the Whittakers. But of course, in his role as couturier, that was all right: he was simply a turn, the star of the evening, served up for everyone's amusement.

She watched Rupert greeting him, so easily charming, Cecily smiling, but oddly watchful, and then, oh God, then heard him say, into what seemed a very big silence, as he was introduced to Benedict, 'Yes, of course, we met the other day, did we not, at lunch?'

'Really?' said Cecily, smiling more sweetly than ever. 'Benedict, you didn't tell me.'

'Yes,' said Benedict, and he was just very slightly flushed, Cassia noticed, but immensely, intensely casual. 'That's right, so we did, at—oh, now where was it?' He paused, waiting, probably praying, she thought, but his prayers were not answered.

'Chez Victoire,' said Leon de Rosay. 'So amusing there, isn't it? And such wonderful food. You were with Dominic Foster. Such a very clever man, isn't he? An artist friend of mine has bought one of those wonderful studios in Pimlico, really quite extraordinary they are. Such great style he has. Not quite le Corbusier, perhaps, but still . . . Now, please, do all sit down and continue with your meal.'

*   *   *

'What a nightmare,' said Edwina. She was sitting at her dressing table, brushing her hair viciously.

'Oh, I don't know,' said Harry. He was lounging in a chair, smoking, watching her closely. 'I thought it was rather fun.'

'Yes, well, it might have seemed fun to you. And your being late didn't exactly help. The partridge were hopelessly overdone. And then Cecily sitting there, hardly talking, looking as if she had a golf ball up her backside, after Leon's little announcement.'

'You could have warned your friend Leon, for God's sake. Told him not to say anything. I really didn't like him, by the way. I'd rather you didn't ask him again.'

'Harry, I was trying to get hold of him all day to warn him. I couldn't. And whether you like him or not is immaterial.'

'It's not immaterial when he's sitting at my dining table,' said Harry. His voice was hard.

Edwina changed the subject. 'And then Benedict getting so drunk and practically climbing inside Venetia's dress, I suppose to show us all how normal he is, and Mary Whittaker giving us all a moment by moment account of last year's flag day. It's the last time I try and help anyone, that's all I can say.'

'Let's go to bed,' said Harry. 'It wasn't really that bad, and you carried it off extremely well. As usual. You really are extraordinarily competent, Edwina. So very good at taking control. Of everything.' He stood up suddenly, came over to her, put his hands on her shoulders, moved them down towards her breasts, kissed her hair.

Edwina looked at him warily in the mirror. 'Harry, please don't. I've got the curse and—'

'Again?' said Harry lightly. He moved away from her. 'It seems to happen with great frequency these days.'

'Yes, well, it is a regular occurrence, Harry, in case you didn't realise.' There was a silence. Then: 'Edwina, I've been thinking. It's about time that we had a child. What would you say?'

'I don't know. I haven't really thought about it very much at all.'

'No? Well, perhaps you could begin. Thinking about it. I find I rather like the idea of a son and heir. Suddenly.'

'And what if I don't?'

'I'd see that as rather unfair. Actually. We've been married quite a long time. Five years. I've been very patient. Now I find I'm getting rather impatient. All right?'

Edwina was silent.

'So perhaps you'd stop using whatever it is you do use, and start keeping at least one of your marriage vows. Goodnight, Edwina. I'll see you in the morning.' He picked up his brandy glass and walked out of the room, closing the door rather firmly behind him.

Edwina looked after him and sighed: a heavy, almost tearful sigh. She felt a bit sick. It really hadn't been a good evening—in any way at all.

CHAPTER FOURTEEN

Cassia had just turned her light out when the phone rang. She picked it up, her heart beating very fast, terrified it was Janet, or even Edward, to say that one of the children was ill, missing, the house was on fire, Edward himself had had a car crash . . .

'Cassia? It's Rupert. Darling, I've missed my last train. Could you give a poor vagrant a bed for the night?'

*   *   *

'This is lovely,' he said, looking round the drawing room. 'What fun, Cassia, I do envy you.'

'I feel awfully guilty about it, but . . .'

'Why on earth should you feel guilty? Silly girl. You've got all that lovely money, and Leonora wanted you to enjoy it. You must do that, for her.'

'You're right, I am being silly. Anyway, it's only to help me do my work.'

'What does Edward think about it?' said Rupert casually. 'Was he very cross?'

'Not really. He's treading a bit warily at the moment, what with Maureen Johnson and everything. Incidentally, Rupert, what do you think about this? It's really worrying me.'

She told him about the pawn tickets, about Leonora, about her own bafflement. 'She'd pawned this bracelet. Look, I bought it back today. From this place in Hatton Garden. It was her mother's, apparently. Her mother's! Who would pawn something of their mother's unless they were desperate?'

'I shouldn't worry, darling. You have to remember it was a sickness she had. It's not like you or me pawning something of our mother's. She'd obviously got herself into a mess, didn't want to tell Rollo.'

'Yes, but how could you be in a mess if you had the sort of money she was leaving me?'

'It was in trust, wasn't it? That was the whole point, I thought. She couldn't get at it.'

She was too tired to begin to make sense of it. 'It just worries me, that's all. It doesn't feel right. Did you see Leonora at all, during the last year or so?'

'Once,' he said.

'Where did you see her, though? In London?'

'Yes. She came over to see a doctor here. Thought he might be able give her better, different news.'

'Oh God, I wish I'd known. Why didn't anyone tell me?'

'She made us all promise not to—'

'All? Who's all?'

'Oh,' he said easily, 'me, Harry, Benedict. She thought you had enough to cope with. If the news had been good, then she'd have rung you up, asked you to lunch, taken you shopping, I expect. As it wasn't . . .'

'You all still seem to think I'm a child,' she said sulkily. 'It's so unfair.'

'Cassia, we don't. But you were—well, your life wasn't easy.'

'Don't make it sound as if I was living in some

kind of a workhouse,' she said, angrily, 'I was—' she corrected herself—'I *am* perfectly all right. I'm very happy. I have a good marriage, I have three lovely children, we have a nice house—of course I could cope with Leonora being ill. It's ridiculous. I could have comforted her, been with her, helped her. There are all sorts of new ideas about cancer treatment. I might even have been able to help.'

'She had the very best treatment,' he said firmly, 'that money could buy. The best doctors, the latest drugs.'

'Organised by Rollo?'

'I suppose.'

'Even though he'd left her?'

'He was most concerned that she should be properly cared for. He visited her, right up to the end.'

'How do you know that?' she said curiously.

'Harry told me. And I believe Harry saw him too. He did a lot for Leonora, you know, Harry. He was . . .' He hesitated. 'He was with her when she died.'

'I didn't know.' She was almost shocked. It took a particular kind of courage, that, a willingness to confront pain; and he had never told her, never sought to impress her with it. Yet again her view of him shifted; yet again that was uncomfortable.

'So you see, she was as well looked after as she could possibly be,' said Rupert.

'Yes. Yes, I do see,' she said. It all seemed to make sense: perfect sense. She just didn't feel quite easy about it, that was all.

'Talk to your solicitor chappie again about it.'

'Yes, I'm going to. Thank you for listening. As always.'

268

'My pleasure, darling. Funny evening, wasn't it? A bit tense.'

'Just a bit. Clearly Cecily was very unhappy about the lunch.'

'Well, we saw it coming, didn't we? At Christmas. And she can't fight it. Neither of them can. Oh, dear. What a mess. Poor Benedict.'

'Poor Cecily too. The thing is, Rupert, she just doesn't understand it at all. She sees his homosexuality as a mixture of a crime and an illness. She's forced him to have some awful treatment. They show these poor chaps pictures of pretty boys and then give them an electric shock. Or sometimes an emetic. It's supposed to cure them.'

'Jesus,' said Rupert.

'I know. Hideous. But I suppose it is so hard for her. Poor Cecily.'

'Yes.' There was a silence; then he said, 'Harry was very good, I thought. Smoothing things over quite brilliantly, changing subjects like mad. I was very impressed, I'd never seen him as a social lubricant before.'

'No. Nor had I.' She could hear her own voice, cool, half hostile.

Rupert looked at her, half amused. 'You still feel very ambivalent about him, don't you?'

'Who, Harry? No, Rupert, I don't feel in the least ambivalent. I still find him rude and difficult. In fact, I quite dislike him, most of the time.'

'All right, darling. Have it your own way. I must say I'll never forget your performance at the Embassy. It was very dramatic.'

'Oh, don't,' said Cassia. 'I've worked very hard on forgetting that.'

'You shouldn't forget about it, you were magnificent. If a little terrifying. Oh, now talking of dramatic and, indeed, magnificent, I think we might have a leading lady. For *Letters.*' Rupert had found what he thought was the perfect vehicle for Cassia to back.

'It was that miracle I was talking to you about.' he'd told her. 'A producer actually wants to put on a show that would suit me. Very low-key, not Shakespeare or Gershwin. Or one of these ghastly comedies I seem to be saddled with. Just a very simple thing, a play by some young chap consisting entirely of letters between two old friends—well, old by the end of the play. They are found when one of them dies, by a granddaughter. Tracing a love story, over fifty years, of meetings and partings, the war comes into it of course, and the depression, all the things that will touch people's hearts.

'It's a lovely story! They both marry other people, the wrong people; she thinks he's been killed in the war; he makes a lot of money and loses it again in the depression; her husband dies, his wife leaves him—and they arrange to met. But at the last moment the wife comes back and he feels he must give her another chance.

'Real tear-jerking stuff. Although sometimes it gets very funny. And they sit either side of the stage, reading the letters to one another; very simple, very cheap to produce.'

The leading lady was called Eleanor Studely. 'She's beautiful, intelligent, a very fine actress and we can afford her. She's never quite made it in the top league. Best of all, she'd love to do it. So the whole project gets a bit nearer.'

'Rupert, I'm so pleased. Just let me know when you need something from me, won't you? Now look, I really must go to bed, I'm all in. Your room is all ready for you. It's up there on the top floor just opposite mine.'

'Darling, how exciting. To be sleeping so near you. I think perhaps we should keep quiet about this little assignation, don't you?'

'What assignation?' said Cassia, laughing. 'Rupert, you are ridiculous.'

'No, I'm not,' he said, and she could see that he was quite serious. 'I really don't think it would be a good idea if your husband—or, indeed, Edwina Moreton and her set—knew we had spent the night together under the same roof. You know how gossip flies about.'

'Yes, but—' She stopped, suddenly seeing it from other people's perspective: a young wife, a rich young wife, taking a house alone in London, away from her family responsibilities, and an old flame, one she had been famously devoted to for years, suddenly staying at her house. It was a strange and oddly disturbing thought; not just in its implications but in its possibilities.

'Maybe you're right,' she said, standing up quickly, 'however absurd the idea. Yes, all right, it shall be our secret. Goodnight, Rupert.'

'Goodnight, Cassia. Sleep well.'

*   *   *

But she couldn't sleep. The discovery of the pawn tickets, the oddly moving revelation that Harry had been with Leonora when she had actually died, Rupert's reference to what he called her performance at the Embassy, had all disturbed her. She opened her curtains and sat up in bed, staring out at the London skyline, thinking about all of it, remembering that night, remembering her performance, half ashamed even now at how she had behaved.

*   *   *

It had been Cecily's birthday, the year before Delia had been born. Benedict had telephoned and said he was going to take a party of friends to the Embassy to celebrate, and that Cecily had particularly requested that Cassia and Edward were there.

'We're going there because it happens to be a Thursday.'

'Oh I see,' said Cassia, laughing. After four years of country-based domesticity she still remembered Thursdays at the Embassy, the night when everyone—'but everyone', as Edwina would have said—was there. 'It sounds a lovely idea, Benedict, and thank you for asking us, but we can't possibly come.'

'Why not?'

Why not? So many reasons. She had nothing to wear. Edward's dinner jacket, the one he had had as a medical student, was so shiny now with wear it attracted jokes even amongst their friends in the village, and, besides, the Embassy was white tie. Edward would, in any case, refuse to go; or if he did, under enormous pressure, would spend the evening sulking silently until she wanted to hit him. They couldn't afford it, the inevitable expenditure, however much it was presented as a party and they

272

as guests: taxis, at least one lot of drinks for everyone, baby-sitting, a present for Cecily, her hair would need cutting . . . and Harry would be there.

'No, I'm sorry, Benedict, we really can't. Don't ask me why, we can't. I'm sorry,' and she put the phone down and burst into tears.

Five minutes later Cecily phoned. 'Cassia, please come. Don't say a word, just listen. Bring the children with you, of course. My hairdresser is coming here, he'll do your hair. Wear that black dress you wore last Christmas, it was divine. I'd give anything to be able to wear clothes like you do. If you want to bring me a present, nothing could make me happier than some cuttings of that perfect white rose for my terrace. Come without Edward, if he doesn't want to come. I want you here, it's my birthday, and you'll spoil it if you don't.'

Faced with such graceful, tactful, loving hospitality, how could she give the one remaining, overpoweringly important reason for her not going?

*　　　*　　　*

It had been fine at first, absolutely wonderful. There had been twelve of them. Rupert had come with his latest love, a very pretty girl called Yolande, who would have made Cassia jealous, and spoilt her evening, had she not told Cassia she was about to go to Hollywood with a three-year contract with Selznick.

They had found a partner for Cassia, a rather nice and funny man called Patrick Compton whom

273

she had met before at the Christmas parties. He had sat next to her at dinner at the house and made her laugh so much she had twice choked and had to have her back banged rather over-heartily by an already drunk Benedict. Harry had been sitting at the other end of the table and had hardly spoken to her; he and Edwina had clearly had a row and he was not speaking to her either.

They had piled into cars at half past eleven and driven to Bond Street. The entrance to the Embassy at the Piccadilly end was down a long passage where a man stood all night selling gardenias to the guests. Patrick Compton bought Cassia one.

Luigi, the *maitre d'*, greeted Cassia by name, which gave her a disproportionate amount of pleasure, and showed them to a pair of sofas, with ice buckets set beside them; she found herself settled between Patrick and Benedict, a glass of champagne in her hand topped up so regularly that she became swiftly confused and thought she couldn't be drinking any at all.

Patrick Compton was not a good dancer, but he continued to be funny, even on the dance floor; she danced with Benedict, who was superb, and then Rupert who was, of course, even better.

'You look marvellous,' Rupert said, kissing her hand tenderly as he led her back from the floor. 'Really very, very lovely. You light this dreary old place up, you know.'

'Oh, Rupert, honestly,' she said, looking around, laughing, 'dreary old place, indeed. It seems like heaven to me, absolutely packed with good-looking people, look at them all. You don't know what dreary is, Rupert. You should come to a social evening at the village hall, then you would.'

'If you were there it would be wonderful,' he said. 'Now let me give you some more champagne, and then I think the dashing Lord Wynford is waiting to claim you.'

Lord Wynford did indeed, and then another man and yet another. She felt dizzy, drunk with pleasure and the champagne and the freedom from her workaday life. And then finally, just as her pleasure peaked, she looked up and saw Harry Moreton standing in front of her. He half bowed.

'May I have this dance?'

'Yes, of course,' she said, taking the hand he held out, carefully not meeting his eyes.

He led her on to the floor; the band was playing 'Nice Work If You Can Get It'. That was good, that was safe. Nothing slow, nothing dangerous. She always forgot how well Harry danced, his heavy frame becoming somehow lighter, swifter, his sense of rhythm faultless. She told him so.

'I never forget how well you dance,' he said, and smiled at her. 'Or anything else about you, for that matter.'

The number ended. She pulled away from him, said thank you, made as if to leave the dance floor. The music began again, slower, more dangerous: not good, not safe. Harry pulled her back towards him, took her in his arms. She moved carefully, cautiously, holding herself just away from him.

'You can't do it, Cassia,' he said.

'Can't do what?'

'Avoid me. It doesn't work. Come on, why don't you just enjoy yourself? And me. Just for once.'

'Harry, I'm not avoiding you.'

'Of course you are.' He drew her closer, his arms

very strong, their pressure impossible to resist. She gave in. He was very warm, as he always was; she felt alarmingly safe and happy suddenly. She smiled at him.

'That's better. Do you realise I haven't seen you since that rather exciting day at Brooklands?'

'Yes, Harry, I do.'

'I'm sorry about that.'

'There's nothing to forgive.'

'I mean I'm sorry we had to go home.'

'Harry, of course we had to go home.'

'We didn't have to. We didn't have to at all. But what I meant was, I'm sorry we had to go home too soon.'

'It wasn't too soon,' she said primly. 'It was hardly soon enough.'

'Don't be ridiculous, Cassia. You know what I mean.' He pulled her closer still, his mouth now in her hair. She began to give in to him, to the music, the sentiment, the nonsense—and the emotion, the longing, her own greed for him. She did know what he meant; and he realised it.

'We have to do something, you know,' he said suddenly, as the music changed again. 'Just the Way You Look Tonight': more dangerous still.

'What about?'

'About us.'

'Harry, I really don't know what you mean.'

'Of course you do. I really cannot contemplate spending the rest of my life entirely without you. It's a monstrous prospect.'

'Don't be absurd,' she said, half amused, half irritated. 'How can it be monstrous? We're both married now.'

'Well, that's your fault,' he said.

276

'Oh, Harry. You are ridiculous.'

'It's you who is ridiculous. Cassia, look at me.'

He had almost stopped dancing; his face as she looked up at it was as still as his body. Still, expressionless, except for his eyes searching hers. She felt them, those eyes, felt them as a physical force, deep within her, a powerful, probing energy. She was silent.

'Cassia, please! Stop running away from me. I can't stand it.'

Anger flooded her suddenly, anger mixed with frustration and a dreadful regret. 'Why do you do this to me?' she said, her voice very low. 'Why can't you accept it? Why won't you leave me alone?'

'You know why,' he said, 'and I can't and I won't.'

She wrenched herself free from him then, stood back from him filled with a blind rage that shut out everything but him; shut out the other dancers, the people watching from the small tables at the edge of the floor, the band . . . 'You have to,' she said, 'you absolutely have to. It's awful what you're doing to me, Harry, horrible . . .'

'It's your own fault,' he said then. 'You should have had more sense, more courage.'

And then she did lose her temper entirely, raised her hand and struck him very, very hard across the face. The sound was drowned by the music, but it could be seen, that blow, seen in the oasis of stillness, of violent emotion they had created on the crowded floor; everyone saw it, the whole place saw it. And mercifully misread it.

She had left him there, gone swiftly over to their party, holding the tears back somehow. 'Sorry,' she said briefly, smiling rather fiercely. 'Lost my

277

temper. Sorry, Edwina, your husband said something that offended me. Very much. So silly of me. Sorry, Cecily, Benedict. Rupert, shall we dance?'

And Rupert, dear Rupert, already half standing up to greet her, his eyes anxious, careful, took her hand, led her back to the floor, where they danced for a long time, where slowly she calmed down, where carefully, tactfully, he asked her no questions of any kind. Harry Moreton had disappeared.

*   *   *

'Yes, all right, Cecily. I did it. I committed this terrible crime. I had lunch with Dominic.'

'Don't try and make it sound innocent, Benedict. I know it isn't.'

'For Christ's sake,' said Benedict. 'Foster is working on a housing development in which my firm, and indeed Harry's, has an interest. It was just a business lunch.'

'Really? In a small intimate restaurant in Chelsea? Why not Rules, the Savoy, somewhere nearer your office, or your club?'

'Because . . . Jesus, Cecily, what is this, an inquisition?'

'Yes, it is,' she said, her voice rising. 'I want to know.'

'You don't want to know at all. You want the usual soothing platitudes. You've no interest in what I'm really doing, really feeling.'

'And what are you really feeling?'

He hesitated, almost caught in his own trap, then he said, 'I just told you, you don't actually want to know. What I feel is of no interest to you, providing I behave exactly as you want me to behave, toe whatever line your crazed imagination might have drawn. But I will tell you. I feel desperate, Cecily, stifled, hardly able to breathe. I can't react naturally to anyone, for fear of what you might think. I can't have the most light-hearted conversation with a man, make the most informal of arrangements, enjoy the most pleasant exchange. I do warn you, if you were seeking to drive me out of the house, you could not be going a more cast-iron way about it.'

'Oh, for God's sake,' she said. 'If you're going to—'

'No, Cecily, let me finish. I do everything you ask of me: I'm a devoted father, a loving, loyal husband. I submitted to that appalling treatment for you, I have never asked you for a moment's sympathy or consideration for my own feelings—'

'Sympathy!'

'Yes, sympathy. Do you really think it has all been easy for me, that I have never felt any distress, any confusion?'

'Of course I don't. That's unfair. I forgave you, totally—'

'It's not forgiveness I want, Cecily. I want understanding. And I have never ever had that from you.'

He left the house after that; she heard the front door slam, his car drive away. She tried to turn her mind away from where he might have gone, and lay for the rest of the night, staring into the darkness, wondering where it would all, finally, end.

*　　*　　*

279

'As I told you,' said Mr Brewster, 'I visited your godmother twice in Paris: once to receive her instructions, that I might draw up the will with the power of appointment; once to obtain her signature and that of the witnesses, of course. Who, as you will recall, were her doctor and the priest from the neighbourhood church which she had been attending.'

'Yes, of course. I remember being a bit surprised by that. Leonora was never a churchgoer.'

'The most ardent atheists can become believers, confronted by their own mortality, Mrs Fallon.'

'Yes, I suppose so. And this was in . . . ?'

'Late March. I could check.'

'No, it doesn't matter. And how did she seem?'

'Well, clearly she was a very sick woman, but her spirits seemed good. As good as they could be under the circumstances, that is.'

'And she was being well looked after? There was no suggestion that she might have financial problems?'

He smiled at her almost reprovingly. 'She could hardly have bequeathed to you what she did, had she been hard up, could she, Mrs Fallon?'

'No, of course not. And this was in Passy?'

'Yes. As I told you, the most beautiful apartment, on the top floor of a building in a very pretty small square. I can give you the address, should you want it. And yes, there was a nurse in attendance day and night, as well as a personal maid. I really don't think she could have been better cared for.'

'And she had been there for some time?'

'As far as I know. And she died there, of course.

Mr Gresham, who set up the Maple Trust, wrote to inform me of the fact. He had spent quite a lot of time with her in those last few weeks, or so it seems. As had her cousin, Mr Moreton.'

'Yes, I had heard that. Poor Leonora.'

'Indeed. But may I say she was in many ways fortunate. So often these days the old are neglected by the young.'

'I would not have neglected her either,' said Cassia, a sudden lump in her throat, 'had I known how ill she was. But for some reason, it was kept from me.'

'Your godmother's own wishes, I believe.'

'So I'm told. Absurd. Anyone would think I was a child.'

Mr Brewster smiled at her. 'To our parents, and their generation, Mrs Fallon, we are always children.'

'And the trust, which actually held the money, what about that? Do you know who set up this Maple Trust?'

'You mean the trustees? I don't have their names immediately to mind, although I could check. But they were appointed by Mr Gresham.'

'You know that for a fact, do you?'

'Yes, of course. I had to have sight of the terms of the trust and the document granting your godmother the power of appointment before I could draw up the document by which she could exercise it.' He smiled almost apologetically. 'I'm afraid it is very complicated.'

'So who did you deal with?'

'Mr Gresham's solicitors, who appointed the trustees.'

'So he had set up this trust, giving Leonora the

power of appointment to leave me the money.'

'Yes,' said Mr Brewster carefully. 'I thought I had explained this before, Mrs Fallon.'

'You had. I'm just trying to get it straight in my mind. Then presumably there would have been interest from the trust fund?'

'Yes, indeed.'

'Which was payable to my godmother?'

'Yes. That was within the terms of the trust.'

She sighed. 'Well, it all seems perfectly straightforward.'

'It is, Mrs Fallon, within the parameters of a certain complexity. Is something troubling you?'

'No,' she said quickly, 'not really.'

Only it was, she thought, as she drove back to Walton Street; she didn't know what, but something was. She was aware of a tiny, but persistent fear that wouldn't go away. Something was not quite right, didn't exactly fit.

*   *   *

The clinic was particularly busy that night: after three hours Mrs Barker, the receptionist, came in to report a waiting room 'still half full'.

Rupert had asked her if he could stay another night; he was seeing Eleanor Studely and Jasper Hamlyn for a drink that evening, to discuss the possibility of her doing *Letters*, and in the morning the three of them were seeing the management of the Second House theatre where they were hoping to put it on. 'I'm sorry to ask, darling, but it would be so much easier than going up and down to Brighton two more times. And I'll have a lovely supper waiting for you, like a good wife.'

282

'Don't talk about good wives,' Cassia had said with a shudder.

Now, the thought of him being there and the supper he would prepare—Rupert was an excellent cook—were the only things getting her through the endless evening.

On these occasions, particularly when she was tired—and she was very tired—Cassia began to feel she was hallucinating as the endless stream of women—mostly young, a few older, all with problems—came into her room. She only saw the more difficult cases: Nurse Hampton dealt with the straightforward ones. At about eight, there was a knock at her door.

'Dr Fallon?' said Joan Hampton.

However tired she was, being called Dr Fallon never failed to revive her. She smiled. 'Yes?'

'Bit of a difficult case here. Young woman in tears. She's got an infection, I think.'

'Send her in.'

The girl who came in must have been about nineteen at the most.

Cassia smiled at her. 'Sit down. What's your name?'

'Jane Ford, Doctor.'

'And what's the problem, Jane?'

'Well, it all hurts, Doctor. Really badly.'

She knew what 'all' meant. She smiled at Jane Ford encouragingly. 'How long has it hurt for?'

'Well, since I—I lost the baby, Doctor.'

'And when was that? And how far gone were you?'

'It was six weeks ago, Doctor. And I was almost three months.' She looked down, fiddled with her hands.

'Tell me about it. Did you just start to bleed? Did you have a fall?'

'I just started bleeding. Really badly.'

'Did you call a doctor?'

'No. My mum was with me, she said there was no need.'

'I see. And were you in a lot of pain?'

'Yes. Quite a lot.' She still didn't meet Cassia's eyes.

'And then what happened?'

'Well, after a while the baby just . . . just came.'

'Poor you. And did you go on bleeding a lot?'

'Yes, Doctor, quite a lot. It eased after a few days, but it's never really . . .' Her voice tailed away, she didn't look at Cassia.

'But you still didn't go to a doctor?'

'No.'

'And now you're in pain. Have you resumed intercourse with your husband?' She knew the answer to that one.

'Yes.'

'And it's very painful?'

'Yes.'

'Well, let's have a look at you. On to the couch here. I'll be as gentle as I can.'

The girl gripped the sides of the couch; Cassia began by palpating her abdomen, to relax her. She was hot; Cassia took her temperature. 'Jane, you've got a fever. A hundred and one. How do you feel generally?'

'Rotten, Doctor.'

She hardly needed to examine her any further; it was horribly clear. The cervix was inflamed and damaged; she was still bleeding slightly. She had obviously had an abortion.

'Jane, I'm sorry, but I really think you need to go to hospital. Don't look so frightened.' (As if she didn't know the reason for the fear.) 'Nobody will hurt you. I think you need some quite urgent medical treatment, possibly minor surgery—under anaesthetic naturally.'

'Oh I can't do that,' said Jane Ford. 'Can't you just give me something for the pain and the bleeding? That's all I want. My husband's getting very—well, upset.' (Yes, he would be, thought Cassia.) 'He's been away a lot, you see, he's a commercial traveller and—'

'Jane, if you want to talk about this, you know it's all absolutely confidential. I mean, if there's something more I should know. It won't go any further and nor would it if you were to go to hospital.' Jane looked at her, and her lips folded very resolutely. 'No. There isn't any more, Doctor.'

Cassia gave up. 'Well, all right, but it's vital you don't even try to have any intercourse for at least two months. And you must rest, and pay very strict attention to your personal hygiene. Take these iron pills, and I'm going to give you what we call a douche, to use at least twice daily. I want you to come back in two weeks . . .'

'That one'll never come back,' she said to Nurse Hampton, who had come in with the news there were still three more cases she'd like her to see. 'I'd bet everything I've got on her having had a little fling with someone else while her husband was away, got pregnant, went to a backstreet abortionist. Now she's in ribbons, she's got a bad infection, and she'll probably end up sterile if she's lucky. If she's not, she might even die. If only there was something we could do for these infections as

285

well; they're so terribly hard to treat. Oh, Nurse Hampton, sometimes I think we aren't making any progress at all.'

'Of course we are,' said Joan Hampton stoutly. 'At least we're here. And she might come back. Now, can you really cope with these last three? It's after nine . . .'

'Yes, of course I can.'

*   *   *

She got home at a quarter past ten. Rupert was in the drawing room reading. He came down to greet her, settled her at the table and dished up a delicious fish pie.

'You look all in. Here, drink this. It's a very nice wine, I bought it this afternoon from Berry Brothers.'

'Oh, Rupert, this is absolutely wonderful. Thank you.'

'Edward phoned,' he said.

'Edward!'

'Yes. Is that unusual?'

'Quite. Is there something wrong?'

'I don't think so. He sounded quite calm. Something about tomorrow?'

'I'd better ring him. Oh dear.'

*   *   *

Edward sounded coldly, horribly furious. 'Why is Rupert Cameron there?'

How could she begin to explain? 'Because he needed a bed for the night. And I offered him one.'

'How good of you. How convenient for him.'

286

'Oh, Edward, please! I'm exhausted. I've just done a six-hour clinic. Look, is there something wrong, otherwise—'

'Nothing really, no,' he said, clearly controlling his voice with a great effort. 'Maureen's father has been taken ill, she can't do her mother and baby clinic in the morning. I wondered if you could help, just with—'

Rage ripped through Cassia: fierce, dangerous. 'Just with what, Edward? Checking them in? Weighing the babies? Or something more difficult, like prescribing gripe water for them?'

'Cassia, please! God, I wish I'd never rung you.'

'So do I, Edward. But yes, I'll be there. Goodnight.'

'Bastard,' she said to Rupert.

He looked at her in silence, then said, 'Cassia, it's nothing to do with me, but—'

'No,' she said, 'it *is* nothing to do with you. Let's talk about something else, something more pleasant. How was Miss Studely?'

But it was hard to concentrate and she went to bed as soon as she had finished her supper: only to wake at two with indigestion and a terrible sense of unease.

*　　　*　　　*

'I'm going down to Devon for a few days,' said Benedict.

Cecily looked at him. 'Alone?' she said coldly.

'For heaven's sake, Cecily! Of course I'm going alone. I want to have some time to think.'

'About what?'

'About my life. Is that permitted?'

287

'Yes, of course.' She suddenly felt ashamed of herself; maybe he was right, maybe she was driving him away, putting him more at risk. 'I'm very sorry,' she said gently. 'I know I overreacted. It's just that—'

'I know what it is, Cecily, and I understand. But it's very hard to cope with. Very hard indeed. I wish you could trust me a bit more. That's all I ask.' Benedict looked at her. 'I think it's all been said. Over and over again. Anyway, I'm leaving tonight. I'll go straight from the office.'

'You haven't forgotten your son's christening, I hope? On Sunday week.'

'Of course I haven't bloody forgotten it,' he said. 'What do you take me for?'

'I wish I knew,' she said, and then would have given anything to be able to take the words back. Benedict looked at her in silence for a long moment, then walked out of the room, his face set, slamming the door behind him.

Fanny, who was running along the corridor to say goodbye to her mother before she went to school, bumped into him and was very surprised when he told her sharply to look where she was going.

She went into Cecily's room. 'What's the matter with Daddy? He looks very cross.'

'Oh, he's just worried about his work. Nothing serious. Come to give me a kiss goodbye?'

'Yes. Are you all right, Mama?'

'Absolutely all right, darling. See you later. Mind you don't forget your gloves.'

'I won't.' She gave her mother a hug, then picked her hand up and kissed it.

'I love you very much,' she said gravely.

'I love you too,' said Cecily.

If anything happened to Fanny, she thought, looking after her as she went, she would simply want to die. She loved all her children very, very dearly, but Stephanie was very often extremely silly, and Laurence too tiny to be—well, to be anything very much. Fanny, with her sweet seriousness, her gentle ways, her generosity of spirit, was, she knew (and admitted to herself, very occasionally), her favourite, a reflection of all that was best, and none that was worst, in herself. Just contemplating the intensity of her love for Fanny brought tears to Cecily's eyes.

She pulled herself together. She was overwrought because of Benedict and everything; it was just like the over-intense woman she had become, to start weeping over a happy, healthy little girl whose only problem in life was a very slight tendency towards plumpness. As had been her mother's: and still was, Cecily thought, slipping out of her night-dress, getting into the bath that was waiting for her. She must take herself in hand now that Laurence was being bottle-fed and there was no excuse for her to have second helpings of everything. She would begin eating less and doing some exercises that very day. No wonder Benedict hadn't been near her bedroom at night since Laurence had been born.

*   *   *

Perversely, Cassia was rather enjoying helping with the mother and baby clinic. It was all so cheerful: gurgling babies, happy mothers (even if they were tired), rosy toddlers. It seemed a very sharp contrast to the night before, and the pallid, hopeless women, all with seemingly insoluble problems. And the women seemed so pleased to see her, although a few, worryingly, seemed surprised.

'I haven't been away,' she said to one girl who actually told her it was nice to have her back.

'Haven't you? Everyone said you were living in London, gone to work there.'

'I'm only in London two nights a week. Who told you that, anyway?'

The girl looked awkward. 'Nobody actually told me, Mrs Fallon, everyone just seems to know.'

She knew she couldn't blame Edward, or even Maureen, for that; it was simply the rolling avalanche of village gossip.

'All right?' Edward came in, looked at her slightly warily at the end of the morning.

'Yes, fine. All gone now. No serious problems, except the couple I sent in to you.'

'Oh, yes. Davey Mortimer. He does seem to be quite seriously deaf. I can't think why his mother hadn't noticed.'

'Self-deception,' said Cassia briskly. 'No mother can bear the thought that her child is anything but perfect. And he was very good at lip-reading, didn't you notice?'

'No, I didn't.'

'Dear, oh dear.' She shook her head at him, pretending disapproval. 'Fine doctor you are. Just a joke,' she added hastily.

He even managed a smile. 'Thank you so much for doing that for me,' he said.

Cassia smiled back. 'It was a pleasure. Honestly.' It was nice to say that and mean it. It had been a long time, she feared, since she had given him anything but pain.

CHAPTER FIFTEEN

The main topic of conversation at Laurence Harrington's christening (to his mother's considerable irritation) was not how beautiful he had looked in the frilly christening robe that had been worn by Harringtons for five generations, nor how perfectly he had behaved, even at the moment the vicar tipped the water over his small head and intoned his four names—Laurence Henry St John Benedict. Nor was it of how exquisite the flowers had been in the church, how interesting a line-up the godparents were—an American merchant banker, a barrister, a countess, and a lady doctor—nor even how devastatingly pretty the baby's two sisters looked, dressed identically in lemon-coloured silk dresses. It was of what many had perceived as an assassination attempt on the King's life at the Trooping of the Colour the day before, and his great courage in carrying on with the ceremony after it, as if nothing had happened.

'We saw it,' said Bertie, jumping up and down with excitement, recounting the great adventure to Fanny. 'We were standing quite near the King as he rode past on his huge big horse, and we saw the man pointing his gun at the King and the police knocking it out of his hands.'

'And then what happened?'

'Well, then he just rode on,' said Bertie, clearly aware that the ending of the story was inevitably

291

something of an anticlimax, 'but Daddy said it was really brave of him. Of course, if he had been shot,' he added, seeing a chance to create a finale, 'Daddy could have got the bullet out and saved his life. Couldn't you, Daddy?'

'Bertie, don't be silly,' said Edward shortly. Cassia was in another room with the parents and other godparents while the official photographs were being taken; Edward was standing with the boys, trying to restrain them, without a great deal of success, from eating too many of the sandwiches, sausages and other savouries that were being brought round by the staff. It was very plain that he was not enjoying himself.

On the other side of the room, standing near the christening cake, Sylvia Fox-Ashley looked at him and sighed. 'Such a dreary little man, Cassia's husband. Marcus, why don't you go and talk to him?'

'Why me?' said Sir Marcus, mildly indignant.

'Well, somebody has to. It might as well be you. Do go on, Marcus, it's so ill mannered leaving him there like that.'

'I will in a minute,' said Sir Marcus with a sigh. 'Just let me get my glass refilled. Edwina darling, how are all your projects going?'

'What? Oh, you mean my fashion show. Quite well. We've got the venue and most of the mannequins now. We need some music, I think.'

'Maybe I can help you there. I met an awfully nice chap the other night who plays the trumpet—'

'Marcus,' said Sylvia Fox-Ashley, having organised the refilling of his glass, 'will you please go and talk to Edward Fallon. Where's Cassia? She ought to be looking after him.'

'Being photographed,' said Edwina, 'with all the other godmums and dads. She's certainly looking very good these days. The money suits her.'

*　　*　　*

The speech by the major godfather, the American banker, was long and tedious. Cassia glanced worriedly over at Edward. He was looking what she could only describe as difficult, standing next to Sir Marcus Fox-Ashley. She'd have to go and rescue him; maybe once the cake had been passed round they should go.

It had been a difficult weekend: he had made a great performance about getting Maureen Johnson to cover for him over the whole weekend, although that was exactly what assistants were for; had patently found her Walton Street house very hard to admire; had turned down her suggestion that they should all go and have lunch at Lyons Corner House at Piccadilly Circus, after the Trooping of the Colour, had refused to go with the boys to the zoo, and had sat all evening reading up in the drawing room while she and the boys played Snap and Beat your Neighbour and Ludo on the kitchen table.

'The doctor doesn't seem to be enjoying himself over much.' It was Harry, smiling down at her.

She smiled back at him rather uncertainly. 'No, I'm afraid not.'

'Shall I send my wife over to talk to him?'

'Oh no, I really don't think that would be a good idea,' said Cassia hurriedly.

'Oh really? Why not?'

'Harry, you know why not.'

'No, I don't,' he said, although of course he did. He knew that of all the people in the room, Edwina was the least likely to make Edward feel better, with the possible exception of her mother. 'She can be very charming when she wants to. And she flirts rather well, when she can be bothered. It's one of her few accomplishments. A great art, flirting, wouldn't you say, Cassia?'

'I really don't know, Harry, I'm afraid.'

'No, I wouldn't say it was quite your thing.'

'Thank you,' she said, slightly coldly.

'No need to get miffed. Women like you don't need to flirt. Another lovely hat. Really, Cassia, there'll be none of that money left soon.'

'Which would probably be no bad thing,' she said, and sighed suddenly, sharply, looking at Edward.

'Now why do you say that? It's not causing trouble between you and the doctor, I hope?'

'No, of course not. I—' She stopped, remembering suddenly her interrupted conversation with him at the dinner party, about Leonora. 'Harry, can I ask you something?'

'You can ask. I may not answer.'

'It's just that—well, Rupert said you were with Leonora when she died. That must have been terribly comforting for her.'

He looked down into his glass, clearly embarrassed at being caught out in a good deed. 'That's not a question,' he said finally.

'I know, but I hadn't realised. I just wanted to say thank you, I suppose. I wish I had been there too.'

'I felt I owed it to her.' There was a long silence, then he said, 'So what's the question?'

294

'All that time, when she was ill, before she died—was she being well looked after?'

'Yes,' he said, slightly impatiently. 'I've told you all this before. She had devoted staff, excellent medical care, and was as comfortable as could be expected.'

'So . . . not in financial trouble?'

'Of course not. Why?'

'Well . . . oh, it doesn't really matter.'

'Yes, it does. Tell me.' He sounded genuinely concerned.

She told him about the pawn tickets. 'It just doesn't add up with her leaving me all that money.'

'Which was how much exactly? Or should I not ask?'

'It was half a million pounds. Well, a bit more, if you're asking exactly.'

'A tidy little sum. Well, Rollo was—is—frightfully rich.'

'I know, but he'd left her.'

'He was very fond of her, wanted to see her well cared for. And he did see her well cared for. She had round-the-clock nursing, everything.'

She tried to feel comforted, to tell herself that she was worrying about nothing. 'Do you know where Rollo lives now?' she said.

'Haven't the foggiest. He keeps moving around. I think there was some rumour he'd gone to Venice.'

'But he went to Leonora's funeral?'

'In Paris? Oh, yes.'

'I see. Oh God, Edward is looking thunderous. We'll have to go.'

'What a shame. Well, goodbye, Cassia. I should stop worrying about Leonora and all of that, if I were you.' He bent suddenly, kissed her on the cheek. 'You look better every time I see you. It suits you, that money. We must go too—I'm flying to Le Touquet in the morning.'

'What for?'

'I'm building a hotel there. It's a lovely place. You'd like it. Want to come?'

'Harry, of course I can't come.'

'Why not? It's not a clinic day, is it?'

'No, but I have things to do.'

'For the doctor, no doubt. Very worthy. Well, I'll have to take you another time. I've just bought a very nice little plane. Ah, Edward. I was just telling your wife how very lovely she was looking these days. What a fortunate man you are. You must excuse me, I have some champagne to drink.'

Edward looked after him, his face distasteful. 'Can we please go?' he said. 'I've got a terrible headache.'

'So have I,' said Bertie, 'and I feel sick. I've been drinking that fizzy stuff. It's very nice, though.'

'Oh, Bertie,' said Cassia, 'you are dreadful.'

*   *   *

They drove home in silence in Edward's car. His black mood was infectious: not even William could surmount it. When they got home, the boys went to find Janet to tell her about their weekend; Edward went into his study.

Cassia looked after him, anger rising suddenly in her. She followed him, knowing it was a mistake, knowing it would lead to trouble, feeling unable to help herself. 'Edward, do you think you could possibly tell me what the matter is?'

'The matter is, as you very well know, I had to go to that absurd affair today. I loathe all those people.'

'Well, if I didn't know it before, I certainly do now. I should think they do too.'

'Don't be ridiculous! As if they'd notice anything I said or did.'

'They wouldn't notice anything you said because you didn't say anything. I was embarrassed. It was just rude.'

'Rude! I think your friend Mr Moreton was pretty rude, walking away as soon as we had arrived, saying he had to go and find some champagne.'

'Yes, well, Harry was born rude,' said Cassia, 'but everyone else was making a huge effort—dear old Sir Marcus, and . . .' Her voice trailed away.

'Yes. And who else? Next time, Cassia, please don't even try to make me come.'

'Next time I won't want you to come.' She walked out of the room and slammed the door.

*   *   *

'That went off awfully well, I thought,' said Cecily. She and Benedict were in the drawing room after dinner; she doing her tapestry, he working his way through a file of papers.

'Yes, I thought so too.'

'Laurence was as good as gold, and the girls looked so sweet.'

'They did.'

'I thought John Fisher's speech was a little dull.'

'A little.'

There was a silence. Cecily said, 'Benedict?'

297

'Yes?'

'Benedict, I am very sorry.'

'About what?'

'Well, that I was so angry about your lunch. With Dominic Foster. It was wrong of me. To make so much of it.'

'That's quite all right, Cecily.' He still sounded very distant; hardly smiled at her.

'Please forgive me.'

'There is nothing to forgive.' There was a smile then: a brief, courteous one. Cecily tried to see it as something more than courtesy and failed.

'Benedict—'

'Cecily, forgive me, but I have to get through these papers this evening. Perhaps I should go to my study.'

'No, please don't. It's nice to have you back. I've missed you.'

'I'm sorry, my dear, but I have to go away again. To Paris. Only for a week or ten days. One of the other partners in my firm, the stockbroking firm, that is,' he added carefully (he's making sure I don't think it's anything to do with property, anything to do with Dominic Foster, Cecily thought), 'is interested in forming a relationship with a French company. We're going to have a look at a few, talk to some of the people over there. He particularly wants me to go as I speak French.'

'Yes, I can see that would be an advantage,' she said lightly, smiling. 'What fun, of course you must go. I wish I could come with you.' She waited for him to say (as he would have done once) that perhaps she should—could do some shopping, some sightseeing—but he was silent and then said, 'I wish you could too,' making it clear that closed

298

the matter. 'Well, I will go to my study, I think, if you don't mind,' he said after a pause. 'See if I can make some headway with this.'

'When are you going?'

'On Tuesday. We'll take the night train.'

'Yes, I see. Well, I'll see you later.'

'Oh, I'll be working quite late. I'll sleep in my dressing room. I won't disturb you.'

'I don't mind you disturbing me, Benedict,' she said, but he was already piling up the papers into a file, reaching for his cigarette case; either he had not heard her or he had chosen to pretend he had not. Cecily went back to her tapestry, but it was rather difficult: the small flowers she was working on had become very blurred.

*　　*　　*

Edward had left the dining room before Cassia and the children started their breakfast in the morning.

'The doctor said he had to get on, and to excuse him,' said Peggy, coming in with a dish of bacon and eggs. 'Now, do you boys want porridge? Because there's some in the kitchen if you're really hungry.'

'I'd love some porridge, Peggy, if it's not too much trouble,' said Janet Fraser. She was sitting with Delia, spooning Farex into her. 'It reminds me of being at home, and yours is so delicious, the best I've tasted outside Scotland.'

Peggy flushed with pleasure and went off to fetch the porridge.

Bertie picked up the paper Edward had flung down. 'Oh, look, Mummy, here's a picture of Uncle Benedict and that nice man with the cars and

299

someone else. Look, here . . .'

'Where? Oh, yes. Goodness, they look awful. Like a police line-up. What does it say?'

The article accompanying the picture informed her that the Moreton Construction Company, the chief officers of which were Mr Harry Moreton and Mr Benedict Harrington, both major investors in the Waterloo Bridge project, had just signed a very large contract to build a new 'Garden City' in the borough of Guildford. The architect for the project was Mr Dominic Foster, also pictured.

She remembered Dominic Foster now from Cecily's and Benedict's Christmas party, his dark good looks, his tall graceful body; remembered afresh Cecily's face as she had watched him then, her patent discomfort at Edwina's dinner party, when she had heard of the luncheon between him and Benedict. He was certainly alarmingly handsome: but homosexual? Who could possibly tell? Poor Cecily; her ongoing, near neurotic anxiety—totally understandable under the circumstances, but unfortunate none the less— must make life at best endlessly uncomfortable, at worst terrifying.

There was a scrunch on the gravel; Cassia looked out of the window. 'Bertie, there's the post, can you go and get it?'

There was the usual large pile: mostly circulars for Edward, a few now addressed to Dr M. Johnson, which afforded Cassia some pain, a couple of ordinary letters for Edward, and one for her, typewritten, postmarked London. She tore it open; the name and address of St Christopher's jumped at her from the top of the paper. It was from the Dean.

300

Dear Mrs Fallon,

I trust you are well. We are planning to make an announcement shortly about the inauguration of the Beatty Research Chair and there may even be a small ceremony; naturally, if that were so we would like you and your husband to be present.

I hear from Dr Richards that you are doing some very good work at the Brixton clinic. I wonder if you would like to come and see me? We have been discussing the possibility of expanding our postnatal surgeries, which we now hold weekly, to include some kind of contraceptive advice where it is felt medically necessary. It is only very tentative at the moment, but I felt you would be uniquely placed to be involved, given your experience with the Brixton clinic and your working knowledge of this hospital and the obstetric unit, and indeed some of the staff here. Naturally, I would stress, your role would inevitably be of a rather junior nature, but on the other hand, it would bring you back into contact with the hospital.

If you would care to write or telephone my secretary, an appointment could be arranged.

'Mummy, are you all right?' said Bertie. 'You've gone ever such a funny colour.'

CHAPTER SIXTEEN

It must be a mistake, Edwina thought: or a practical joke. 'Perhaps you could repeat that. About when you'd like to see me.'

'Miss Le Page is free on Thursday morning, or Friday. But would that give you time to do your critique?'

'Oh, yes,' said Edwina airily. She had no idea what a critique was, but she could do most things quickly. 'Thursday would be fine.'

'Splendid. Eleven, then. With the critique, of course.'

'Yes, of course. Goodbye.'

She put the phone down, phoned Venetia Hardwicke at her office at *Vogue* immediately. 'Venetia? It's Edwina. Look, Did you really tell those people to phone me? From *Style*?'

'I did, actually. One of their editors said they were looking for someone well connected to do the shopping page. I told her about you and she sounded rather impressed. I didn't tell you before because I thought you'd be disappointed if it didn't work out. It's a piece of cake, Edwina, honestly. You just pick out a shop, or rather they'll pick it out for you, it'll be one of their advertisers, and you go and choose some things to write about and get them photographed. They need editors who can get into people's houses and wardrobes and so on. I thought you'd be right up their street. And I've been awfully impressed by what you've done with the fashion show so far.'

'Oh,' said Edwina, 'Well, I'd love to do it, but I

don't know whether I could. And what's a critique? And could I do it by Thursday? I said I could.'

'Edwina, you are priceless,' said Venetia. 'It's a criticism. I expect they told you to do one on the current issue? Yes, well, you go through it, bit by bit, saying which things you like and which you don't, and why, of course, and making suggestions for a couple of features.'

'What's a feature?'

'An article. Would you like me to come and help you?'

'Absolutely not,' said Edwina. 'I can perfectly well manage now I know what it is. What's she like, Miss Le Page?'

'Oh, terrifying. Works at being it, of course, as they all do. Absolute stickler for form, been known to sack a girl for not wearing a hat out to luncheon. But that's why she'll approve of you.'

Edwina went out and bought a copy of *Style*: it was like a cross between *Vogue* and *Tatler*, a fashion paper with lots of pictures of people at parties. She rather liked it, although the party section looked very stilted, no one looked as if they were having a good time. She picked up her pen and the large pad of paper she had bought, and settled happily at her desk. This was going to be fun.

*   *   *

'What on earth are you doing?' said Harry. He had arrived home to find Edwina scribbling furiously at her desk, great piles of paper all over it, the wastepaper basket spilling on to the floor.

'Writing a critique,' she said loftily. 'Of *Style* magazine. They want to see me about a job.'

303

'A job? What sort of job?'

'Shopping editor.'

'Shopping editor! You! How absurd.'

'Harry, you're such a beast. Why is it absurd?'

'One, you've never done a day's work in your life, you completely lack the discipline. Two, you have no idea how a magazine works. Three, and much more importantly, I don't like the idea. You're my wife. I don't want you doing some damnfool job.'

'Well, that's very unfortunate,' said Edwina coolly, 'because if I'm offered it, I shall certainly take it.'

Harry walked out and slammed the door. She looked after him and made a face.

*   *   *

Cassia sat in the dentist's waiting room and tried to distract Bertie from the ordeal which undoubtedly lay ahead of him. He was only six and his teeth were terrible; he already had three fillings.

Mr Rankin's door opened; the patient, a rather pale-looking woman, was ushered out. Bertie looked at her, envy burning in his eyes. Cassia sighed.

Mr Rankin beamed at them both. 'Ah, Bertie. Come for a ride in my chair?'

'Come on, Bertie,' said Cassia brightly, 'in we go.'

'Mrs Fallon, I think perhaps it would be better if you wait outside. Children are often better on their own, I find.'

Bertie allowed himself to be led in, with a last desperate look at her.

Cassia sat down with a pile of tattered magazines and tried not to listen to the sounds coming from behind the door.

There were the usual hotch-potch of publications from the usual hotch-potch of dates: *Good Housekeeping*, *Home Chat* and *Country Life*. Cassia started leafing through *Country Life*, and became engrossed in the advertisements for houses.

There was a rather ugly castle for sale in Scotland and a sprawling bungalow in the Scilly Isles and then a house which seemed somehow rather familiar. It was very large and grand and extremely beautiful, a Queen Anne mansion in Wiltshire, set in what the writer of the advertisement described as several hundred acres of rolling parkland, with outbuildings, fine stable block and several staff cottages. It was advertised for sale by auction.

She sat staring at it, trying to work out why it was familiar, and then, as she heard Mr Rankin saying, 'Well, that wasn't so bad, was it?' and the door handle turned, she realised. It was Rollo Gresham's house.

Rollo Gresham selling his lovely house! Why? He had been so proud of it, Leonora had said. He had held the most lavish parties there, even while he and Leonora had been living in Paris—food and wine brought down from London, guests flying in from all over Europe in private planes, on to the airstrip he had had made for his own plane, car races on the track he had also had built there, a string quartet playing at meals.

His paintings alone had been worth a fortune. Surely, even if he did spend most of his time

305

abroad now, he would want to keep so lovely a base in England? But maybe it cost a lot to keep going for the occasional visit, even for someone as rich as Rollo.

Guiltily, quickly, and without really knowing why, she folded the magazine over and pushed it into her basket, and stood up smiling at Bertie as he came through the door. He was white and drawn-looking.

'Three fillings, I'm afraid,' Mr Rankin said. 'Never mind, very brave.'

Bertie was resentful and tearful; she took him home and made him a hot drink and then sat reading to him and cuddling him, and forgot all about the copy of *Country Life* until the next day, when she found it in her shopping basket, couldn't quite think why she'd wanted to keep it in the first place, and tucked it into a drawer of her dressing table in case she remembered.

*   *   *

'This is very interesting, Mrs Moreton.'

'I'm so pleased you think so.' Edwina relaxed a little, allowed herself a sip of the lemon tea Miss Le Page had had brought to her. Miss Le Page herself was drinking only hot water, making Edwina feel that the infusion—even of a little Lapsang Souchong into it was an act of the grossest self-indulgence.

She studied Miss Le Page as she flicked over the pages of her critique; she was tiny, birdlike in every way, with little fluttering movements of her hands punctuating her speech. She had very dark hair, framing a face of porcelain whiteness; her eyes were huge and dark, her mouth a scarlet gash. She was dressed entirely in black, apart from a red hat which exactly matched her lips.

Edwina wondered if either the hatter or the cosmetic chemist had been briefed on that match. It seemed quite likely, given Miss Le Page's power. Only *Vogue* and *Harper's Bazaar* could challenge *Style*'s authority. The battle waged between the three of them for advertising revenue and readers was savage; the three editors never spoke, never communicated apart from the briefest of nods as they took up their places at the couture shows. They each had their strengths; *Vogue* being the fashion bible, *Harper's* a slightly greater breadth of vision, *Style* the additional input of the social pages. This had been the inspired notion of Aurora Le Page herself; the mixture it offered of gossip and fashion was irresistible; the editor of *Vogue* might pronounce it as common, the editor of *Harper's* denounce it as mindless, but its readers loved it.

There were rumours that Drusilla Wyndham, the gorgon-like social editor, not only received invitations to parties and weddings with ten pound notes fastened to them, she was frequently approached in restaurants, shops and even, famously, on her way back from the altar after taking communion at Chelsea Old Church, by mothers desperate to have their daughters' coming-out dances recorded in her column. Edwina had met Mrs Wyndham several times at functions, and rather liked her.

She looked up now as Aurora Le Page put her critique down.

'Quite interesting,' she said, 'considering you have no real idea what you're talking about.'

'No,' said Edwina cheerfully, 'how could I?'

'Absolutely. But I like some of these ideas. I believe you know Mrs Wyndham?'

'Yes,' said Edwina, 'we've met several times. At parties. She came to my dance, actually.'

'Yes, so she said. She said what a charming woman your mother was.' Which said a great deal about both of them, Edwina thought. 'Well, I certainly haven't seen anyone else who had any ideas at all. And you're clearly not unintelligent. How soon could you start?'

'Tomorrow?' Edwina said.

*　　　*　　　*

'Edwina, I forbid it,' said Harry, 'absolutely.'

'Well, that's fine by me,' said Edwina. 'I'm going to do it. If you don't like it, Harry, you can—well, what can you do? Divorce me? Hardly grounds, I'd have thought. Leave me? Perfectly fine. I mean, where are you living, in the Dark Ages? I'm not your chattel, I don't belong to you.'

'You know perfectly well why I don't like the idea.'

'Yes, I certainly do. You don't like the thought of me being just a tiny bit important. Having a life of my own, something to do other than run your household and trail around in your wake.'

'Edwina, that's not true. I have no quarrel with women working. But I don't want you to work at the present time because I want a family. Soon. As you very well know.'

'I didn't know that working prevented conception,' said Edwina coolly. She hoped he couldn't hear her heart pounding, prayed her colour wasn't mounting.

Harry had been standing by the door. He came over to her then, took hold of her wrist. His face was taut with rage. 'Edwina, if I find out that you are in any way avoiding pregnancy, I do assure you I will divorce you.'

'On what grounds?'

'Oh, never fear,' he said, 'I will find them. And they may not be very pleasant for you.'

When he had gone, Edwina reached for her cigarette case; her hands were shaking so much it was difficult to work the lighter. 'Oh God,' she said, leaning back in her chair, looking out at the golden summer evening that seemed to have grown suddenly darker. 'What am I going to do?'

*　　　*　　　*

'So sorry to have kept you,' said the Dean. 'Do sit down. Now then. An involvement with the postnatal clinic. How did that sound to you?'

'It sounded wonderful,' said Cassia simply.

'I thought it was a good notion. Mr Scarsdale and Sister Rigour tell me these clinics are proving extremely beneficial, and that there is scope, indeed need, for this area of yours. Of course it would have to be on a trial basis. It might not work.'

She was almost afraid to ask, but clearly had to. 'And where did you see me fitting into this scheme?'

'Well,' he said, 'you're a doctor, aren't you? You passed your obstetrics rather well. You've had some experience now in the field. I thought it perfectly feasible you should be the doctor in charge. Of that side of things, that is. Naturally I'd have to clear it with the Board and Sister Rigour, it is a rather— what shall we say—revolutionary notion. Most of my colleagues at other hospitals are very sceptical, but I think that's largely due to the rather eccentric views and behaviour of Dr Stopes. No doubt you are familiar with all of that.'

'Yes,' said Cassia. 'We're actually much more influenced by Dr Helena Wright and her work in the Birth Control Association.'

'Ah, yes. She's a splendid woman. Although there again, you know, medical people are very sceptical. But we are lucky to have a pioneering spirit on the board in the form of Lord Crowthorne, whose wife was a midwife for several years. It's given him a rather enlightened view of such things. Also, Mr Amstruther was interested in both the idea and your involvement when I mentioned it to him. In time, who knows, it might be possible for you to do some of the postnatal work yourself. But that would be up to Mr Scarsdale, obviously.'

'Yes, of course,' said Cassia, trying to sound and appear calm. She felt literally physically dizzy. Mr Scarsdale had been the obstetric surgical registrar when she had been a student; famous for his sarcasm even then. 'Were you thinking of getting that baby out today, Miss Berridge?' he had said to her once, as she had hesitated to turn a small pair of shoulders which had refused to follow the baby's head. 'Or shall we all go home and have a good night's rest and come back in the morning?' Now he was an Honorary and she could not imagine what he would have to say to the notion of her performing the most humble of tasks.

310

'Scarsdale was talking about you only the other day,' said the Dean suddenly, 'saying what a shame it was we'd lost you. He's pretty receptive to all this as well. Well now, I suggest you make your way up to Rigour, see if you can find Sister, have a word with her about it: I have mentioned it to her.'

Cassia couldn't think of anything worse than being confronted by Sister Rigour. She, of all the sisters, had been particularly hostile to the infiltration of women into the hospital. Cassia had actually been on duty one day, and had overheard Sister Rigour on the internal telephone, an acute emergency on her hands, saying, 'I need a doctor, but don't send Berridge.'

* * *

Rigour ward was quiet, three women lying in the peculiar rapture of the newly delivered, the remaining twenty-one reading, knitting or chatting cheerfully, and Sister had personally that afternoon managed the manipulation of a breech without recourse to any doctor. She was consequently in a mood of glowing self-satisfaction.

'Miss Berridge!' she said. 'How nice to see you.'

'I'm Mrs Fallon now,' said Cassia. 'I expect you remember my husband, he trained here as well.'

'I don't think so, no,' said Sister. 'Of course I only remember the outstanding ones. And the women, naturally.'

'Yes, naturally,' said Cassia, swallowing this double insult with good grace.

'I hear there's some question of a birth-control clinic here. I'm not very sure about the logistics. How it would work. But I certainly don't think it would do any harm, to put it mildly. I delivered a woman last week, sixth baby in five years. Her uterus is exhausted. And it's not as if she's a lone case. Anything that can improve that situation would be welcomed by me. I'm just not sure it has a place in the hospital. It would take up a lot of administrative time.'

'As I understand it, it would only be on a trial basis,' said Cassia, 'and it would contain its own administrative work, to a large extent.'

'That could be dangerous too,' said Sister Rigour. 'Autonomy has no place in a hospital. Still, we shall see. Now you must excuse me, I have a woman three weeks overdue to see to. No problems, apart from her blood pressure. OBE, I think, don't you?'

'Without seeing her, I wouldn't like to make a judgement,' said Cassia carefully, 'but, yes, it sounds like a good idea. If you think so, of course. And the baby's in a good position? Otherwise, if the induction makes labour faster, couldn't it be more difficult? Well, that's what we were always told,' she added hastily.

OBE stood for Oil (Caster), Bath and Enema. She had had one with Bertie and could still remember the misery. But she knew she would never hear the expression again now without a thud of sheer pleasure—at being caught up, for the first time for seven years, in hospital matters and at being asked, however cursorily, for her opinion.

* * *

'Edward, I have to talk to you,' she said, when she got home.

312

'Yes?' He looked at his watch. 'I may be called out. Old Tom Rickards is dying. I promised to go if he needed any morphine.'

'Oh, poor old Tom. I'm very sorry.' She was very fond of Tom: he had done some work in their garden; had played patiently with the boys; showed them how to whittle a piece of wood nail-sharp; how to blow birds' eggs.

'Yes. Very sad. Anyway, what was it you wanted to talk about?'

He was extremely annoyed, annoyed and hurt. She had expected the annoyance: the hurt took her by surprise.

'It's this Chair nonsense,' he said. 'You've bought yourself back in.' He was very white. 'I've got to go. I don't think there's much more to say, do you? Another day's absence from here each week won't make much difference, and no doubt you'll do what you want anyway. I'll see you in the morning. Goodnight.'

*   *   *

'I think you should tell him,' said Sylvia Fox-Ashley.

'Mummy, I can't. He'll kill me.'

'Why should he kill you? It's not your fault.'

'It's not my fault I'm sterile. Obviously. But I've known for quite a long time now. I should have told him. I've deceived him. Nothing makes Harry more angry than lies.'

'Can't you just tell him you're worried, you think you ought to see someone?'

'I could for a bit. But then he'll want to know what investigations are being done, and he's quite capable of coming with me, asking questions. And

313

our own doctor knows I saw Mr Fortescue.'

'You're making a terrific meal of all this, Edwina. Look, I'm sorry, darling, but I do have to change. We're dining at the Forty Three, have to leave in half an hour.'

Edwina was half relieved the conversation had been finished, even though she had intended to take it further: it was quite a difficult thing to tell your mother you'd had a pregnancy terminated three weeks before your wedding. Even a mother like Sylvia.

CHAPTER SEVENTEEN

'Odious woman,' said Mrs Wyndham. 'So vulgar.'

'But immensely chic,' said Aurora Le Page. 'Last time we ran a double page spread on her, we were spoilt for choice.'

'She's frightfully good at Canasta,' said Edwina. She had been discussing some ideas for her first shopping page with Miss Le Page when Drusilla Wyndham had stalked in with her social page photographs; talk had inevitably turned to Mrs Simpson and the King. They both stared at Edwina.

'How do you know that?' said Aurora.

'My mother played with her. Last summer. In Biarritz. She was there in a party. The men were off all day playing golf and she was left with Mrs Simpson, so that's what they did.'

'How fascinating,' said Mrs Wyndham, 'but I'm not really surprised. It's a rather vulgar game.'

'You don't happen to know what Mrs Simpson

314

might be doing this summer, do you, Mrs Moreton?' asked Aurora Le Page.

'My mother might. I'll ask her.'

'Please do.'

*   *   *

Edwina went back to the desk in the main fashion office which she shared with six other women. A gentler spirit than hers might have wilted in such an environment: Edwina's was thriving. The obsession with style, with originality, with the vital importance of the tiniest detail in a dress, a hat, a pair of shoes, a feather even, a deep conviction that not the deepest political crisis, the most momentous international event, could compare in significance with the latest collection from Monsieur Dior, the most recent pronouncement from Mr Hartnell: all these things seemed to her entirely reasonable and indeed sensible.

She felt herself, for the first time in her life, properly at home, careless of the often spiteful atmosphere. Acutely self-confident in any case, she accepted all criticism as constructive, saw most hostility as temporary.

She loved the job, which was not nearly as difficult as she had feared. By the end of her first month she felt herself quite on top of the whole thing. And happier than she could remember for a very long time: apart from the ongoing anxiety over Harry, her absolute inability to give him what he wanted, and what he might do when he found out.

*   *   *

'Cassia, I want to talk to you.'

'Don't you have to go into morning surgery?'

'Maureen's taking it today. What I have to say to you is too important to be rushed.'

'Oh.' She felt nervous suddenly. Her mind ranged over the events of the past three weeks: she hadn't been away more than usual; the children had been apparently quite happy; she hadn't gone to any parties or christenings in London or, more importantly, asked him to attend any.

She had most carefully not mentioned her work—not even the day when Dr Rivers, the obstetric registrar, had succumbed to influenza, Dr Simmonds, the junior houseman, was assisting Sister Rigour with the delivery of premature twins, and the staff nurse in charge of the postnatal clinic had been called over to assist in the labour ward, where no less than three other mothers were delivering. Cassia had therefore single-handedly taken the clinic, with the assistance only of a student nurse. It had been the hardest thing she had ever done, not talking about that; the day she knew she would look back on for the rest of her life as the one when she had actually returned to medicine. It had all been very mundane, of course: conducting pelvic and vaginal examinations, palpating breasts, checking general health. But she had spotted one breast abscess, one inflamed pelvis and diagnosed what she was convinced was appendicitis, not what the patient told her were her monthlies returning. She had put in a call to one of the doctors on the medical ward and he eventually came over and confirmed it. Arriving back in Walton Street at seven o'clock, exhausted, she had thought she could not remember feeling so happy for a very long time.

'I've been doing some thinking,' Edward said abruptly now, 'and I feel that neither of us is very happy with things. I realise that I haven't always behaved very well. Recently.'

'Well,' she said, anxious to be generous, 'neither have I. Not always.'

'It's been very difficult for me.' He smiled at her suddenly, a rueful, almost embarrassed smile. 'The thing is, I want to do something. Something very important to me.'

'Well then,' she said, carefully light hearted, 'you must do it.'

'Yes, but I would need your co-operation. Your support. You see . . .' He looked at her awkwardly. 'You're not the only one with thwarted ambitions, Cassia. Mine have been too. I always wanted to be a surgeon. I buried that, under this practice. I told myself this was what I wanted.'

'But you did want it. This practice, I mean.'

'I know, I know. And it's been very good. I've enjoyed it. But now I want to do something more. I want to go back to medical school.'

'Medical school! But—'

'Yes, I want to study surgery again, get my MRCS. I had never dreamed such a thing might be possible, but because of your legacy, things are different now.'

She was too astonished, too confused even to think. She had always assumed that Edward was perfectly content with his life, his medicine, with the position he held in the village, the respect and esteem it afforded him in the community.

It seemed barely credible that he was prepared to sacrifice all these things for the harshly

317

demanding life of a medical student, where he would have no authority, no respect, where his every utterance and, indeed, judgement would be challenged, questioned, often ridiculed. She had no doubt that given his extra maturity, and self-confidence, he would manage the work, would pass his exams well, would become a perfectly respectable surgeon. But the cost to himself, it seemed to her, would be inordinately high.

He was looking at her, an expression of impatience in his eyes. 'You look doubtful.'

'Oh, no. Well, not exactly. Go on.'

'In principle, though, do I have your support?'

'Yes,' she said, managing to sound positive. 'Yes, of course. You know your career was one of the things I first thought of, when I—we—got Leonora's money, that you could do something like that with it. Of course you have my support.'

'Good. Because, you see, I've already applied for and got a place.'

'You've got a place? Where, how, why didn't you tell me before . . .?' Her voice tailed away; she knew the inevitable answer to that one, didn't want to hear it.

'I've got a place,' he said, and the expression in his eyes was very strange now—wary, almost hostile, 'at University College Hospital, Glasgow. You may remember I went up there for a conference a few months ago. I got on very well with the Dean, it all went on from there. I did apply to a couple of London hospitals, but didn't get a place, and in any case, I liked Glasgow, the hospital, so very much. I start—well, I hope to start—this autumn. For two years. And obviously I'd want you and the children to move up there with me.'

The words didn't mean anything, not at first. They were just words, sentences, put together: strange, odd. He couldn't really want her to go up there: there was the practice, Maureen, the new surgery. She said so.

'I've thought about that. Originally I did think I'd sell it, but I don't think that's wise. I'll get a locum in to run it. Make Maureen a junior partner—she's exceptionally competent. And I thought she could live in the house. It would be better than it being left empty. Of course she may want to leave.'

'Have you discussed it with her?' she said.

'No, of course not. I wanted to tell you first.'

'Yes, I see.' She tried to smile, to appear at least mildly enthusiastic, while thinking wildly, wretchedly, what it would mean to her: giving up her clinics—well, no doubt there would be one in Glasgow, that might not be too bad—but her postnatal work, her path back into St Christopher's, over almost before it had begun. And the house—no, the houses, she would have to leave Walton Street as well—and Rupert and . . .

'How long have you been thinking about this?' she said, playing for time.

'Oh, several months. I've actually been making applications to various places.'

'And there wasn't anywhere in London, or down here?'

'Nowhere in London, no. And naturally I want to be somewhere with a reputation. If I'm going to do this, it's got to be properly, I don't want it going off at half cock. I mean, there's no point my going to Haywards Heath Hospital for instance.'

319

'No, of course not.' It was important she appeared positive, only put up reasonable objections. 'But what about the boys? Their school?'

'Well, Bertie will be off in a year to prep school. William can go to school up there. It's not a primitive community, you know.' He sounded bitter suddenly, bitter and cold.

She looked at him and saw that he knew she didn't want to go, would find every excuse she could not to. And wondered suddenly why Glasgow, why now.

There was a long long silence. Then he said, forcing his voice to sound cheerful, almost jovial, 'Well? What do you say?'

She said, quietly, carefully, 'It's a big decision, Edward. Very big. For me and the family.'

'I don't see why,' he said, dangerously quiet now.

'Oh, don't be absurd,' she said. 'Everything would change, everyone's lives—'

'Not drastically. The children would go to new schools. We would have a new house, make new friends. These are not unprecedented changes, Cassia. Many families make them, every year.'

'But the practice, suppose it didn't work out, suppose your locum didn't run it properly, then what would you do? You've put your life into that practice, Edward, you can't just throw it away.'

'Cassia, what are you trying to do, throw me on the scrap heap before I've even begun? If I do well, I won't come back to the practice: Perhaps you think that's unlikely.'

'Edward, of course I don't.'

'Just because I didn't do particularly well in my finals doesn't mean I'm incompetent.'

320

'I don't think you're incompetent. I'm just trying to think of everything. And all your patients in the village, they love you, and trust you, you're letting them down if you leave them.'

'Cassia, my patients will be fine. They're not going to be abandoned in some way, left without medical aid. Any other objections?' he said, after a pause.

She hesitated. 'Well, it's a risk. A big risk, for you.'

'For me!'

'Yes. Suppose you don't like it, suppose you find returning to student status more difficult than you think?'

'Cassia, I think I'm mature enough to cope with it. Given the importance of the end. And in any case, that's precisely why I'm holding on to the practice. It seems to me,' he said, 'you're not prepared to support me.'

'Edward, of course I am. That's not fair.'

'It doesn't sound like support. I'm disappointed in you, Cassia.'

She looked at him sharply, expecting pomposity, but he looked genuinely upset, hurt. Remorse hit her. 'Edward, please! Give me time. To adjust to the idea.'

'I didn't expect this,' he said, 'or perhaps I did. Let us say I hoped you'd be behind me, one hundred per cent. As I would be for you.'

'That's not true,' she said. 'Were you behind me when you took on Maureen as your assistant? When I told you about the clinic at the hospital?'

'That's quite different.'

'Why?'

'Surely you can see why. This is my entire career

321

we're talking about, not a few trifling clinics.'

'They are not trifling to me,' she said, and was shocked at the passion in her own voice, 'they are everything to me. My way back, my—'

'Ah,' he said, 'yes, I see. There we have it. This would interfere with your very important work, wouldn't it? Quite badly. All this touching concern for the practice and the village and the children. That's not what you're worried about at all. It's yourself and your own work and your bloody research Chair and your smart London friends—'

Suddenly she looked at him. There was grief on his face, grief and uncertainty. It was a long time since she had seen that; she felt, very surprisingly, tears behind her eyes. She got up, went over to him, tried to put her arms round him, but he pushed her away.

'Don't,' he said, 'please don't.'

'Edward, I didn't mean to upset you. Really. And I do admire what you want to do, and I admire you. Enormously.'

'Oh, for God's sake,' he said. 'How can you? I'm not successful, that's why this is so important to me, doing this. I'm not even particularly clever, I'm not certainly not witty and charming like—'

'Oh, stop it. Please. Stop being so sorry for yourself.'

'I feel sorry for myself,' he said quietly, 'desperately sorry.' And he walked out of the room and closed the door.

She heard the front door slam and watched him walk up the drive and out of the gate. He looked utterly dejected, his thin shoulders stooped, his head somehow sunk between them, his step slow and lifeless. She felt terribly ashamed of herself—

and very, very unhappy.

* * *

Benedict turned away from Cecily. 'I'm sorry,' he said.

'It's all right. I understand.'

'Oh God,' he said, 'I wish you did.'

'Benedict, I do. Look, in future, perhaps it would be better if you always slept in your own room. This is wretched for us both.'

'Very well. If that's what you want.'

'It's not what I want. It's what seems best. To me.'

'Fine. Shall I go now?'

'No. I love you being here. Here, put your arms round me.'

'It's very hot,' he said. 'Let's just stay like this.'

Tears stung Cecily's eyes; she blinked them away. She couldn't ever remember feeling so humiliated, so wretched. And he must feel the same.

What a wreck it was, this marriage of theirs, a hopeless, battered wreck There seemed absolutely no hope for it, for them, no prospect of them saving it. And Benedict probably didn't want to. She wasn't even sure, these days, if *she* did.

'What are you thinking about?' he said.

She searched frantically in her mind for something positive to say, found it, said in a desperate attempt to sound friendly, light hearted, 'I was wondering about the holidays. It's getting rather late to take the villa.'

'Much too late. Yes.'

'I wondered if we could go to Devon.' She wasn't

usually very keen to go to Devon; that grieved him, she knew, he loved the place so much.

'Oh, I don't think so,' he said. 'The place is in a bit of a state. We must get it redecorated. And the gardens are running to rack and ruin, they look dreadful.'

'All the more reason to go there. I can set some work in motion.'

'Look,' he said, 'can we not discuss this now? I'm pretty tired. I think I will go to my own room. If you don't mind.'

'Of course not,' she said, and cried herself to sleep.

*   *   *

In the morning he was contrite, anxious to be placatory. 'I thought Scotland would be nice for a few weeks,' he said. 'We could go and stay with Jock Danvers at Ord. The children would love it, and so would I. I could do a bit of fishing . . .'

'I'm sorry Benedict,' she said. 'I hate Scotland and even more I hate listening to Letty Danvers talking all day while you and Jack go off killing things. I'd rather stay in London. You go if you want to.'

'No, no,' he said, 'I'll stay here too.'

But that night he said he had decided after all to 'go up for the Twelfth. It's so truly glorious up there, those first few days. If you don't mind'.

'I don't mind,' she said. 'We might go to my parents' house in Hampshire. Fanny loves it there, and she and Stephanie can have some riding lessons in the Forest.'

'Good idea.'

'Edward,' said Cassia. She had been screwing up her courage for days to have this conversation.

'Yes?' He didn't even look at her.

'Edward, I've been thinking. About Glasgow.'

'You have?' His voice was lighter, hopeful even.

'Edward, if I decided I couldn't come . . .'

'Yes?'

'You could still go, couldn't you? You could take a house there, come home when you could. It might even be better, you could concentrate more on your work. Not many medical students have wives and families, after all.' She smiled, a bit too brightly.

'Oh, no,' he said, 'no. I wouldn't even think of that. I've told you, Cassia, I need your support. Your full support. Either you come with me, or I don't go.'

'But—'

'I can't do it without you,' he said. 'I need you with me, I really do. That's all there is to it. I hope very much you'll feel you can.'

It was almost dark in the room now; she couldn't see his face any more, but she could hear the genuine pain in his voice. 'Yes, I see. Well, I shall have to make a decision very soon, then.'

'Yes, you will,' he said.

That had been her last hope: and it had been very fully and dreadfully dashed.

CHAPTER EIGHTEEN

'It's blackmail,' said Harry briskly. 'He could perfectly well find a hospital much nearer London. Or he could perfectly well go without you.'

'I don't think he could. He lacks self-confidence, he's not a bit like—well, like you.'

'I devoutly hope he's not. Come on, let's go and dance.'

She hesitated.

'Come along. We can talk about it more later. I'm getting bored.'

What was she doing here, she thought wildly, following him on to the floor, here at the Four Hundred Club, alone with Harry Moreton? Had she gone absolutely mad?

He had phoned her at six thirty; she had just got in. 'Cassia? It's Harry. Look, how would you like to come to the theatre with me? I've got two tickets for *The Barretts of Wimpole Street*. It's supposed to be rather good.'

'But can't Edwina—'

'Edwina can't, no. She's got some damn fool photo session this evening.'

'I see. Goodness, she's taking this very seriously, isn't she?'

'Yes,' he said shortly, 'very. Anyway, I didn't want to waste the ticket, so I thought of you, thought you probably wouldn't be doing anything.'

'I'm sorry you should view me as a social disaster. I'm sorry, Harry, but I'm really very tired.'

'Oh, nonsense. It'll do you good. Get yourself ready, I'll be round at seven.'

She put down the phone and looked at it thoughtfully. She wasn't sure if the ease that was growing between her and Harry Moreton was safer or more dangerous than the highly charged antagonism that had been there before.

* * *

She thought the play was rather good, although Harry hated it and in the highly romantic third act, she suddenly felt something heavy fall on her shoulder: it was his head. She heaved it up.

'Do wake up,' she whispered fiercely, 'otherwise I'm going.'

'Let's both go. Come on, I've booked a table at the Ivy. We'll get there before the rush.'

* * *

And after the Ivy he insisted on taking her to the Four Hundred. They arrived just before midnight; it was only beginning to fill. The *maitre d'* bustled over to them. 'Mr Moreton, good evening. And madame.'

'Evening, Rossi. I trust you've got my table, we're in very good time.'

'Of course, Mr Moreton. Some champagne?'

'Please.'

The table was to the right of the door: Harry settled her at it, then sat down himself and smiled at her slightly complacently. 'People kill for this table,' he said, and just for a moment he was the pompous spoilt small boy again, demanding and acquiring everything he wanted. She told him so.

'Oh God. I was truly obnoxious, wasn't I?'

'Truly. I often wondered,' she said, sipping at her champagne, 'what it was that changed you, made you human. I mean, you went up to Oxford fairly awful still.'

'Thank you.'

'And then you changed, completely. Well, a lot, anyway.'

'Sex,' he said, leaning back in his chair, looking into his glass. 'I had the most amazing love affair with a woman quite a lot older than me in Paris; she showed me what a frightful little prick I was, taught me to laugh at myself.'

'Oh, I see,' she said, slightly uncertain of how to react to this.

'And she taught me a lot of other useful things as well,' he said, 'things best left to the imagination. For now, anyway.'

She was silent.

'Anyway, I'm glad you think I've changed, although I'm still extremely spoilt, of course. Good at getting what I want. And this is the best table in the room, famously so. Good for seeing from. And being seen at.'

'Oh, Harry. What on earth will Edwina say?'

'Not a lot. She knows how cross with her I was.'

'Not as cross as Edward is with me,' she said, rendered indiscreet by the second—or was it the third?—bottle of champagne. Harry had drunk most of it, but still . . .

That was when she told him about Edward and her dilemma. And he made his pronouncement.

'I hadn't thought of it like that,' she said later, as they sat down again.

'Thought of what like that?'

'Edward's behaviour. As blackmail.'

'Well, it seems perfectly obvious to me. Rather clever, in fact. Machiavellian. I wouldn't have thought he had it in him.'

'Maybe there is an element of that, but he does genuinely want to go. He's always wanted it.'

'Why didn't he do it before, then? When he was a medical student?'

'He didn't do quite well enough in his finals.'

'Ah. So there we have it. And you did? Extremely well, I seem to recall.'

'That hasn't got anything to do with it.'

'No?'

'Harry, that's very unjust. Very unjust indeed.'

'Well, you know him better than I do. I'm happy to say. Anyway, I do hope you're not going to agree to go with him.'

'I don't know what I'm going to do.'

'If you do go,' he said, and his voice was very serious now, his eyes on hers heavy, thoughtful, 'it will be the end of you. You know that, don't you?'

'That sounds very melodramatic. Not like you at all.'

'It's not melodrama,' he said, 'it's the truth. After all this time, you're beginning to get back, back to your career and your real self.'

'I'm also a wife,' she said, 'and a mother.'

'Yes, well, that can't be helped. But don't do it, Cassia. Don't give in to him. It's very wrong, what he's doing. Very.'

*   *   *

They arrived back at Walton Street at four, in Harry's latest motor car, an extremely large black Buick.

329

Cassia laughed as they pulled up outside the house. 'This car practically fills the street. It looks like a hearse.'

'Thank you for that notion. I suppose if I lost all my money, I could hire it out for funerals. Now I must go. I have to be at the Bank of England in just over three hours' time. Please excuse me. And thank you for a very nice evening.' He leant forward suddenly, kissed her very gently on the lips. 'Don't do it, Cassia. Don't give in to him.'

She sat staring at him, confused by the sudden change of mood, by his words, most of all by the kiss. Then he smiled, was himself again.

'I shall be away for three weeks,' he said. 'When I get back, I shall expect to hear that all is well with you. And if not, I may even go and see the good doctor myself.'

He got out, opened the door for her, kissed her again, this time on the cheek, and then he was gone: leaving her more confused, more afraid than ever.

*　　　*　　　*

Cecily sat in the great family Daimler on its way to Devon, hoping that Stephanie, who was always prone to car sickness, was not actually going to throw up, and trying to hear the more scurrilous details of Edwina's conversation with the photographer, which seemed to centre largely around whether Aurora Le Page actually kept cocaine in the cigarette box on her desk or not.

The photographer, whose name was Justin Everard, was a rather pale young man, dressed in black linen trousers and a cream linen shirt, with

330

over-long pale brown hair that fell on to his open collar. Cecily decided she disliked him intensely.

'I tell you,' said Edwina, 'I looked in that box the other day and it was full of cigarettes. Turkish ones,' she added, as if that was relevant.

'Oh, darling, you're so naive,' said Justin Everard. 'Of course there are ciggies on the top of the box. There's a false bottom to it, everyone knows that.'

'Oh,' said Edwina uncertainly. 'Cecily, look out, I think Stephanie's going to be sick. Oh God, how disgusting, darling, not into my Hermes bag, there's a lamb . . .'

Why on earth had she agreed to it? Cecily wondered, frantically mopping Stephanie and the mess up as best she could, calling to Preston to pull over; if she'd only said no, she'd be safely in Lymington by now, at her parents' country house; but somehow, the thought of having the house in Devon featured in *Style*, as the background to some wedding dress photographs, with her two little girls as bridesmaids, had been irresistible.

'They want somewhere with the sea as background,' Edwina had said. 'We were hoping to go to France, but Miss Le Page suddenly said there wasn't time—I think actually she didn't want to spend the money—and I thought of your house straight away. I mean, too perfect.' And anxious to have a diversion from her unhappiness, her loneliness, and with the added bait of Edwina's suggestion that the girls should be in the pictures too, Cecily had agreed.

Edwina had then proceeded to volunteer Benedict's Daimler in which to transport herself, the photographer and the clothes—'Well, it is so

331

wonderfully big, and much more comfortable for us all.'

Cecily had been surprised to find Edwina doing something so important as organising the photographs for what seemed to be a major article, but it turned out that the editor responsible for wedding dresses had been ill and Edwina had been co-opted on to the job largely because of her ability to produce a large and beautiful house by the sea. 'But the Fashion editor herself will arrive tomorrow and then we must all kiss the ground she walks on.'

'I hope not,' Cecily had said briskly, 'not when it's my own ground.'

There hadn't been time to contact Benedict, who was at a high-level conference in Munich, so she had just crossed her fingers and told herself that in any case he would be very proud to see his house all over the pages of *Style* magazine. She had telephoned the staff and they were preparing the house; and the girls were hugely excited at the prospect of being there, and bathing in the sea, never mind that of being photographed as bridesmaids.

*   *   *

They didn't arrive at the house until after six. Mrs Goss, the housekeeper, greeted them at the front door. She was round and rosy, with an accent like golden butter; Cecily was very fond of her.

'Hocking's just finishing in the dining room now,' she said. 'He'll take your luggage, meanwhile I'll show you to your rooms. Hallo, my lambs,' she added, taking Fanny and Stephanie to her cushion-like bosom, 'lovely to see you.'

332

They both kissed her. 'I was sick,' said Stephanie, 'all over the car.'

'It smells disgusting,' said Fanny.

'Poor little blossom! No appley dumplings for your supper, then . . .'

'Oh, yes, yes, I'm perfectly all right now. Come on, Fanny, let's go and see the cows.' They disappeared.

Cecily smiled at Mrs Goss. 'It's lovely to be here,' she said, 'and I'm sorry it was such short notice. You've met Mrs Moreton before, I believe.'

'Yes, I certainly have,' said Mrs Goss, bobbing briefly to Edwina, who managed the faintest of smiles before moving off round the house, peering up at it as if she were a highly critical prospective buyer. 'And this is Mr Everard,' said Cecily, glaring after her. 'He is taking the photographs tomorrow.'

Mrs Goss looked at Justin Everard slightly doubtfully, bobbed again. 'If you all follow me, I'll show you to your rooms. I'll feed the blessed lambs in the kitchen, if you don't mind, Mrs Harrington, and Hocking said to say dinner could be any time after seven thirty. Oh, and drinks are set out in the conservatory.'

Cecily led her guests into the hall and then let Mrs Goss take them upstairs. She went through into the drawing room and stood at the window looking out at the sea.

Merlins had been built two hundred years earlier, by the younger son of a Lord Jefferies, who had employed a highly imaginative draughtsman, and told him he wanted the dramatic coastline, with its constantly changing mood, echoed in the house. The result had been a very fine but rather eccentric Georgian house, its interior fairly

333

conventional apart from a panelled circular dining room, but with great windows almost the full height of the rear rooms, a vast conservatory forming what amounted to a semi-circular wing running cliffwards on the west side of the house, and a look-out tower on the east side, with a rotunda-style roof. Not only could the southern coast of Wales be seen from the tower on a clear day, but there was a breathtaking view at night of the heavens. Beyond the house, the lawns ran down directly into the heavily wooded cliffs; at the foot of the cliffs was a sweetly curving bay, from which the family bathed and sailed.

It was a beautiful evening, windy but brilliant; the girls were running down towards the woods, shouting loudly, excited by the sudden freedom. She smiled at their pleasure.

'This is a beautiful house, Mrs Harrington.' It was Justin Everard, down from his room, carrying a small camera in his hand. 'So unusual, such a very special atmosphere. May I take just a few snaps, get the feel of it all before dinner? And should we dress for dinner? I wasn't sure.'

'No, we don't very often dress down here,' said Cecily, smiling at him, at his appreciation of the house, 'only when we have very grand parties, which is about once every ten years. Please do, go ahead: or will you have a drink first? We always have drinks in the conservatory before dinner.'

'So enchanting!' said Justin. 'And look at those marvellous Lloyd Loom chairs. All of it, a fairytale palace. No, I'll wait for the drink, if I may. Those little girls are enchanting too, just look at them, lucky, lucky us.'

Any moment, thought Cecily, he's going to clap

his hands. She supposed he must be queer, and wondered why the usual combination of distaste and panic didn't fill her. Probably because he was a photographer, which, being artistic, somehow made it seem all right.

* * *

Dinner was rather fun; Edwina complained briefly and tactlessly that the house looked rather shabby, and she didn't know what Camilla Marsden-Rose would say, but Justin assured her (equally tactlessly) that the shabbiness wouldn't show in the photographs, and then turned his attention to Cecily, demanding to know as much of the history of the house as possible. She said she knew very little, whereupon he said, 'Well, let's make some up, then,' and they took it in turns to add ever-increasingly extravagant and unlikely stories. Justin's were much the best: he added an errant princess, a ghostly mermaid and a shooting star to establish the exact site of the foundation stone of the house. Edwina's were quite good too, and Cecily managed a bolt of lightning, thereby necessitating the rebuilding of the stables (a genuine puzzle, since they were very much Victorian in design).

Before they went to bed, Cecily led them up to the rotunda and studied the stars. 'Cassia should be here,' said Cecily, 'to show us her constellation.'

'Who is Cassia?' said Justin.

'Oh, a relative. Well, almost a relative—a friend.'

'How very confusing. And why should she be here?'

'Her name is Cassiopeia, and there is a group of

stars called after her.'

'I should like to meet her,' said Justin. 'I've never known anyone with a constellation named in her honour.'

'Well, of course it's the other way round, really,' said Cecily, blushing, feeling suddenly silly.

'I prefer it your way. A better story, since this is the occasion for good stories. Well, I must go to bed. We have a long day tomorrow. Camilla threatened to be here at nine, which probably means eight. She's coming down in her own plane, so terrifically smart, don't you think? Goodnight, ladies, I'm off to the Land of Nod. Thank you again for your hospitality, Mrs Harrington.'

'Please call me Cecily. It makes me feel old, being Mrs Harrington.'

'You couldn't possibly ever be old, you look eternally young,' he said, and kissed her hand.

'Goodness,' murmured Edwina, as he disappeared, 'you have made a hit. He's frightfully hard to please usually.'

'I expect I remind him of his mother,' said Cecily tartly.

'Don't be so touchy,' said Edwina.

* * *

Camilla Marsden-Rose arrived at seven thirty, landing her plane in a nearby field and striding across the lawns of Merlins in jodhpurs and a leather helmet, followed by Angela, the model, who looked green and very shaky.

'Too Amy Johnson,' said Justin, cramming the remainder of his toast in his mouth and rushing out to greet her. 'Camilla, darling, how wonderful you

336

look!'

'Don't start that, Justin,' said Camilla Marsden-Rose. 'This house is an absolute gem, too marvellous of Mrs Moreton to have found it. Pity it's so shabby, but maybe it won't show in the pictures. Can you get this wretched girl a drink of water, she's been frightfully sick, and is there someone here who could clean out the plane?'

Cecily, who had followed Justin out to greet her new guest, thought that working on *Style* was hardly going to improve Edwina's manners.

It was a very long day; they had to photograph four different wedding dresses and sets of bridesmaids' dresses in four different locations. After the first one, Cecily retired to her sitting room to read and write letters; everything she suggested in the way of locations, and even the way the little girls had their hair done, was crushed most witheringly by Mrs Marsden-Rose. By lunchtime (delayed until three) Justin was flagging visibly, Edwina looked almost chastened and the children were bored and fractious.

'Fashion is a tough job,' said Camilla, bolting down an extraordinarily strong gin and tonic, and holding out her glass for a refill, 'not for the faint hearted. Is it, Angela?'

'No, Mrs Marsden-Rose,' said Angela, managing a smile, 'nor the faint stomached.'

'Oh God, don't remind me.' She started eating from the buffet Mrs Goss had set out in the conservatory, adding that Angela was not to eat anything at all until the day's work was done. 'Your stomach is quite prominent already. Any more and you'll look as if you had to get married. And besides, I don't want you vomiting on the way back.'

*   *   *

Mercifully, Camilla left at six, bearing the unfortunate Angela with her. The rest of them collapsed in the conservatory and Cecily told Hocking to bring up some champagne from the cellar. 'I think we've earned it.'

The two little girls were highly relieved their day was over: 'She was so rude, that lady,' said Fanny. 'She said my face was too round, and she told Mrs Goss to get out of her way without even saying please.'

'Oh, she makes an art form of rudeness,' said Justin. 'I always expect to hear she's going to be exhibited at the Tate. The funny thing is to see her with Drusilla, though, isn't it, Edwina? She's such a monstrous snob, so keen to get in Drusilla's pages, she becomes frightfully deferential, seventeen thank yous a minute.'

'What does deferential mean?' said Stephanie.

'Extremely silly,' said Edwina briskly.

Cecily sat back in her chair laughing; she couldn't remember feeling so happy for months. 'I'm so glad you all came,' she said. 'You really have brightened my life considerably.'

'How sad it should need brightening,' said Justin. 'Now are you sure you want us to stay another night?'

'Oh, yes please.'

'Then consider your life further brightened. If you'll excuse me, I'm going to go up and have a deliciously long bath before dinner.'

'Of course. If you use the nursery bathroom, for

some reason the water is hotter. It's up on the top floor, next to the playroom, where you were this afternoon.'

'The nursery bathroom it is,' he said, and stood up. 'I'll see you again down here at seven thirty.'

She was to remember that moment for the rest of her life.

*   *   *

Cecily was the first down in the conservatory. She had found a dress in very dark aquamarine silk that she particularly liked, and had forgotten about, very flattering, it made her look quite slim—she really wasn't doing terribly well with her figure, she must try a bit harder—and had pulled her hair back off her face with the aquamarine clips Benedict had given her the night they had become engaged, and which for some reason she kept in Devon. She smiled at her reflection in the mirror, sprayed herself lavishly with the Arpege that she loved, and wondered why she was going to so much trouble for Edwina and a homosexual photographer. Well, if the evening was half as much fun as last night, it would be worth dressing up for.

She was sipping her martini, mixed with surprising skill by Hocking, when Justin arrived, carrying his small camera. He smiled at her, kissed her hand.

'You look wonderful!' he said. 'I love that colour on you. May I take a picture of you, sitting there?'

'If you really want to,' she said, laughing. 'I don't think I can quite compare with Angela.'

'Of course you do. She's a model, and a rather stupid one, you're a real woman, a mother, a

339

homemaker. And much more attractive, if I might say so. Now, just relax, that's right, and look at me . . .'

He took several pictures. Fanny appeared behind him and stood watching. 'Will you take one of me and Mummy?'

'Yes, of course. Go and stand behind her chair, put your arm round her, that's right. Now turn and rest your head on hers. Beautiful, enchanting . . .'

He took several more, then put the camera down on the low table. 'Right, I've earned my drink, I think. What a day. Oh, by the way, I found this up in the bathroom. It had rolled under the bath, came out when I tugged at the bath mat. I expect it's your husband's. So annoying to lose just one.'

Cecily held out her hand, and he dropped a cufflink into it. It was very heavy gold, rather large, flamboyant even. It wasn't the sort of thing Benedict would wear.

It wasn't Benedict's. And the initials embossed onto it were certainly not Benedict's either: not BH, however much she stared at them, and tried to make them so. They were something quite different, horribly, brutally different.

They were DF.

* * *

A dreadful sound came through the study door; muffled, but still audible. It was Edward, weeping. Cassia stood outside for a while, praying it would stop, knowing it wouldn't, dredging up the courage from somewhere to go in, to comfort him, afraid to do so lest, confronted by his pain, she gave in, told him what he wanted to hear. Finally, gently, she

340

tried to open the door; it was locked.

'Edward!' she said. 'Edward, please let me in.' There was no answer; the sound stopped briefly, then started again. 'Edward! Please.'

Abruptly then it did open; he stood there, in the doorway, his face ashen, tear streaked, filled at the same time with both grief and rage. 'Just fuck off,' he said, in a low voice. 'Leave me alone, go to your own bloody bed.'

She knew then, from the language, how unbearably she had hurt him.

*　　　*　　　*

She had not actually known she was going to refuse to go until she was sitting down with him, across the table, trying to force food down a throat that seemed dry and swollen, trying to postpone the moment, asking him about his patients, the progress (as if she could not see it) of the beech hedge he had planted.

Finally he set down his knife and fork and said, 'Cassia, let us stop this absurd conversation. What have you decided? I really need to know.'

She had sat there for a long time, in absolute silence, and as if she were watching a film, every detail of it clear, saw her life, the life she would have to lead if she went with him. She saw the house—very nice probably, she would be able to see to that at least, and with as much domestic help as she had now, only without a nanny, for why should she need such a person?—in a strange new city, where she had no friends, no contacts, no life of her own whatsoever, merely a pleasant, bland day-to-day emptiness. Where any friendships and

341

contacts would be forged entirely through Edward and his life at the hospital, and where her role would be once again entirely supportive, entirely subordinate.

And then she looked at her own life now, as it had become over the past year, in all its exhausting, challenging richness, and the scales tipped so devastatingly and with such speed that she closed her eyes, shocked at herself. For it was not just her work which mattered so much to her, and the subsequent soaring of her self-esteem, the fading of her misery and resentment—that was perfectly right and proper, that was by any standards absolutely acceptable—it was all the other things, bought at such cost, such emotional cost, her freedom, her house, the time on her own to be herself, the return of fun to her life, with Rupert and his probably vapid play, Edwina and her certainly foolish fashion show, things which she knew she should not value in the least and which she could see she was enjoying very much and valued very highly.

She had become herself again in the past year, with all that had been good and bad about her: strong, independent, clever—well, that was fine, that was good—but also opinionated, wilful, self-indulgent: and that was bad, it was appalling. And what she actually realised in those long moments was something infinitely frightening and fundamental: not so much that she had a great deal to give up, and it meant a great deal to her, but that she could not possibly love Edward, for if she did, then none of it would have meant so very much to her at all. She would have been deeply sad, horribly regretful: but she would, should, still have set it all

342

aside.

And still she did not really know, was fighting the new Cassia—or was it the old?—trying to be noble, trying to be good, when Edward said, 'Look at me, Cassia,' and she had looked at him and he had said, 'You won't do it for me, will you, you won't come?' and that had shown her, given her the courage to say no, no she couldn't, she was sorry, she would do everything in her power to support him from here, but she could not relinquish her own life to him when—and at this point she heard Harry's voice in her head, telling her she was being blackmailed over it, lending her courage—she knew it wasn't actually necessary.

'I simply do not believe,' she said, 'that you need me, all of us, to be there, living with you. I cannot see that, Edward, I really cannot.'

'Well,' he said, very calmly, pushing his chair back, standing up, 'at least I know where I am with you now. I think this time last year, Cassia, the answer would have been very different. You are not the same person, not the same person at all.'

'No,' she said, 'that is true, but I am the person you first knew, Edward, and that is greatly to the point, it seems to me. I have to be true to that person, not the one I had become. I'm sorry, but there is nothing more to be said. Except that I hope and pray you will still take this place at Glasgow.'

'How can I?' he said. 'How in God's name can I?'

'Very easily. We would all of us, the children and I, be behind you, all proud of you—'

'Don't start preaching family values to me,' he said, his voice quietly violent, 'you with your nanny, your job in London, spending half the week away from us all, going about with your wretched friends up there, involved with people like Cameron, the Moretons—'

'Edward,' she said, 'that has nothing to do with it.'

'Don't lie to me, Cassia,' he said, and his voice was so full of genuine pain that she felt sick. 'I am not quite as stupid as you so clearly think. Goodnight.'

CHAPTER NINETEEN

Cecily fought to keep her voice calm, level. 'Mrs Goss,' she said, 'last time Mr Harrington was down here . . .'

'When would that have been, Mrs Harrington?'

'A few weeks ago.'

'Oh, well, now I wasn't here, Mrs Harrington, I was on my annual leave, went to stay over with my sister in Tiverton. But I do feel quite sure he was well looked after. May was here, of course, and Hocking, and—'

'Mrs Goss, I'm quite sure of that, of course. It was just that a friend of his came too. Or so I understand. And lost a cufflink. He asked me to have a look for it. I just wondered if . . .'

'Now where would that have been?' said Mrs Goss, her rosy face anxious. 'In the guest room, where he slept, I suppose. What would have been the name of this friend, Mrs Harrington? I could ask Hocking.'

'No, no, don't worry, I'll ask him. When my guests have finally gone. They're just packing now and I'm taking them to the station. Well, Preston is, and I'm going too.' God, she was rambling. Hardly surprising: she felt as if she was delirious, after a nightmare evening, pretending at first that nothing was wrong, then saying that she had a migraine and had to go to bed, a totally sleepless night, a growing sense of nightmare.

Mrs Goss smiled, picked up what was left of the breakfast things.

'I'll ask Mr Hocking,' she said, 'and then when you get back maybe the mystery will have been solved.'

'Yes,' said Cecily, 'maybe it will.'

*   *   *

She waved Justin and Edwina off at Exeter; Justin bowed and kissed her hand elaborately on the platform. 'It's been too wonderful,' he said, 'and thank you so much for your hospitality. Your house and your children are divine. I absolutely insist we meet in London.'

'That would be very nice,' said Cecily, looking nervously up and down the platform lest she saw anyone she knew, 'and thank you for being so appreciative. I'm sorry about last night.'

'Don't even mention it,' said Justin. 'Edwina and I were exhausted and quite pleased to have an early night. Weren't we, Edwina?'

'What?' said Edwina. 'Oh, yes. Cecily, I'll see you when we get back to London. Harry and I are off to Cannes in a couple of days. Thanks so much for everything.' She was looking strained, and pale; she had the curse, she had told Cecily, appearing after breakfast, terrible cramps, refusing everything

345

but coffee, and swallowing what appeared to be a handful of aspirin; but she also seemed very distracted, Cecily thought, not herself at all. She wondered if she had told Harry yet about her inability to have children; she rather suspected not.

It was after eleven when they got back to Merlins; she went into the morning room and rang for Mrs Goss.

'Some coffee please, Mrs Goss, and could you ask Hocking to come in.' Better to get it over, she couldn't stand the suspense any longer.

Hocking came in looking anxious; he said he hadn't been able to find any cufflink.

'Look, you mustn't worry about it, Hocking, it's not particularly valuable, it's just that I told him I'd have a look while we were down here. It's probably in the room where he . . .' She hesitated. 'That is, where Mr Foster slept.'

'Mr Foster, madam? There was no one here by that name.'

'Really? Are you sure?'

'Perfectly, madam, yes. Mr Harrington's guest was a Mr Fraser. An old school friend, Mr Harrington said. A very nice gentleman.'

Cecily sat staring at him, momentarily taken aback, hopeful even; then, hating herself, she said, 'Oh, how silly of me, yes of course, why on earth did I say Foster? Mr Fraser, yes. Tall and dark . . . ?'

'Yes, madam.'

If she had needed any proof, any proof at all that Benedict had been feeling guilty about Foster's visit, anxious even, it was that he had sought to disguise it, given him a false name. And then discouraged her from coming down here, possibly for a year while work on the house was carried out.

346

It was so clever, so devious, so horrible . . .

*   *   *

'I'm sorry, Harry. I just don't think I can go tonight.' Edwina looked in her dressing-table mirror, saw her own face, glassy pale, saw Harry's beyond it, impatient, distasteful.

'What's the matter, why not?'

'I've got the curse and—'

'Oh God. Not again.'

'Harry, I can't help it.'

'I hope not.'

'What do you mean, you hope not?'

'Oh, nothing.' He looked at her, clearly trying to compose himself, to be more sympathetic. 'I'm sorry, you'd better go to bed. Shall I get Mildred to call the doctor?'

'I don't need a doctor. There's nothing seriously wrong with me. I just suffer from very bad menstrual cramps. I always have.'

'Yes but—'

'But what?'

'Oh, nothing. Forget it. But I think you'd better see a doctor anyway. It does seem to be rather bad. Most women don't have to take to their beds every month, like some sickly Victorian heroine.'

'Yes, well, other women are luckier. God, you're a bastard,' said Edwina. The pain was very severe; it was making her feel sick. And she knew what he was driving at: her failure, yet again, to conceive. That made her feel sick as well.

'I'm sorry,' he said again, 'sorry you feel so rotten. But I'd like you to try and sort it out. The whole thing. Now I'd better go, it's already after seven. I'll probably be late back. I'll see you in the morning.'

'So sweet of you to sympathise,' said Edwina under her breath as the door closed behind him. She climbed into bed and rang for Mildred; she felt too bad even to get undressed. 'Bring me a hot-water bottle, will you?' she said. 'And a hot drink, and some brandy, and some more aspirin.'

She lay down, turned on her side, pulled up her legs so that she was in the foetal position. The foetal position: that was an irony. God, it hurt. Harry was right about one thing: it was getting worse. Well, she knew what it was, Fortescue had told her, and there was nothing to be done about it, short of having a hysterectomy, and Harry certainly wouldn't agree to that. And it was all her own stupid, bloody fault. The pain suddenly worsened, shot through her, raw, piercing; she groaned aloud. And there would be hours of this before she felt better, most of the night, in fact. It wasn't fair: it just wasn't fair. Whatever she'd done. Other people got away with it, Scot free: why not her?

*   *   *

For the first time, Cecily was thinking quite seriously about a divorce. She had always resisted it before, not least because in spite of everything, she genuinely loved Benedict.

She and Benedict got on very well, although they had little actually in common: he was so very clever, and she knew she was not; his idea of an enjoyable evening was the opera or a chamber concert, hers the cinema, or a musical comedy; he read Proust and Dickens and such modern writers as Spender and Cecil Day Lewis, she devoured Galsworthy, Daphne du Maurier and her new favourite, Angela Thirkell. But they both loved their children, enjoyed family life, were interested in their houses and in decor, looked forward to their holidays; in fact, she had often thought in the past, as she contemplated her marriage, it was no less, and possibly in many ways more, satisfactory than those of many of her friends.

And divorce was still considered fairly scandalous, it would be appallingly bad for the children, and her own life, as a woman on her own, would be difficult and lonely.

But, she thought, tossing endlessly, night after night, in the four-poster bed in their room in Devon, the marriage was a failure. Benedict preferred men to women, and at any one time, no doubt, one specific man to her: the treatment had been a failure, her own efforts to cure him with love and patience had been a failure, she was a failure. That last was the worst: the humiliation was intense, far more so, she was sure, than if she had discovered he was in love with another woman. It was a total rejection: he didn't prefer someone else to her, he found her very essence, her womanhood, distasteful, unattractive, undesirable.

Given that fact, it was very hard to hang on to any sense of self-esteem, self-respect even. Maybe she was only attractive to homosexuals, she thought, remembering Justin Everard and his very insistent, albeit charming attentions. That was a frightening thought in itself. But then what man would find her attractive? she wondered, studying her reflection in the mirror one morning after her bath, hating the plumpness, turning herself away

349

from her own body, the full, heavy breasts, the rounded, loose stomach, the dimpled thighs. And no wonder Benedict of all people found her revolting. A man whose preference was for men, lean, taut men was hardly going to find any pleasure in her. Perhaps if she was more boyish, more like Edwina, Cassia even, it would be better. She kept meaning to eat less, to try really hard, but when you were unhappy, hunger was a most dreadful companion.

It was three days since Edwina and Justin had left; Benedict was due back from Munich in another two. He had no idea she was in Devon; she had decided to let him find out for himself. She almost enjoyed the thought of how terrified he would be to learn she was here. She would sit it out, his terror, wait and see what he did. She wasn't going to make it easy for him; she would force him to come to her. Only she had no idea what she would do after that: no idea at all.

*   *   *

For the first time in as long as he could remember, Rupert Cameron was feeling that most agreeable of emotions, self-respect. For much of his life he had done nothing he could be proud of: leads in light comedies in repertory in his youth, second leads as he had grown older, the occasional West End understudy, middleweight billing in provincial musicals, cabarets on ocean liners, so many Dandinis and Buttons in pantomimes, he had literally lost count. None of it added up to anything he could be pleased about, lived up to the early promise of the golden boy who had won the

Shakespeare trophy at drama school.

Now, suddenly, there was *Letters*—a fine piece of writing, an original concept, a demanding part, and a production of very real quality—and it was making him very happy. He found it oddly moving that he had Cassia to thank for much of it, Cassia, who was the person he loved best in the world.

He phoned her one morning in late summer, choosing the time when he knew Edward would be entirely occupied with his surgery, to ask if he could, once more, stay at the house in London for a few days.

'I'm sorry to keep asking, but I'm a bit short of the tuppenny at the moment and—'

'Rupert, of course you can,' said Cassia. 'If I'm not there, Mrs Horrocks will let you in, she's there every morning from ten to twelve.'

'Bless you, darling. We're going to do the first full read-through of *Letters* on Wednesday, if you want to come along.'

'I'd love to, Rupert, but I don't think I can. I've got to go and see the Dean about the announcement of the research Chair, and then I'll just stay on and do my clinic in the afternoon.'

'All right. Probably better not, anyway, until we know a bit more what we're doing. Are you all right, sweetheart? You sound a bit subdued.'

'Oh, yes,' she said quickly, 'I'm fine. Just a bit tired.'

'I think you're overdoing it. I shall take you out to dinner on Wednesday evening—or perhaps cook you dinner—and talk to you like a Dutch uncle about it.'

'I'd like that,' she said, 'thank you. But it isn't work that's making me tired.'

Rupert had known that, of course: he knew exactly what was making her tired, wearing her down, hurting her; he had watched it, helplessly, for years. And the worst thing was that he felt, to some extent at least, to blame.

* * *

Cassia had hardly put the phone down that same Wednesday morning when it rang again; it was Edwina.

'Hello,' she said. 'I hope this isn't too early for you.'

It was so unlike Edwina to say anything remotely considerate that Cassia was quite startled. 'No, it's fine. Honestly.'

'Good. I need a bit of advice.'

'Advice!'

'Yes. Gynae advice. I thought that was your sort of thing.'

'I'm not actually a gynaecologist,' said Cassia.

'No, but I thought you might be able to tell me who I could talk to. I mean, you all know each other, you medical people, don't you?'

'Edwina, I'm not even on nodding terms with any of the sort of doctors you would want to see.'

'Oh, how boring,' said Edwina. She was clearly very put out: and she sounded something else, Cassia thought, slightly distraught.

'Edwina, is there anything wrong? What's the matter? Why do you want to see a gynaecologist?'

'Oh, just some rather bad curse pains recently. Harry's getting awfully fed up with it.'

'Harry's fed up with it! That is the limit,' said Cassia. 'Edwina, I don't wish to speak ill of that

352

husband of yours, but I don't really think he deserves any sympathy over your pain.'

'No, but I keep having to not go out and—'

'So it's really that bad, is it? Doesn't sound quite right to me.'

'Well, obviously it's that bad or I wouldn't be ringing you,' said Edwina irritably. 'Anyway, you obviously can't help, so—'

'I'll do some research. I'm working at the hospital this afternoon. I'll see what I can come up with, and ring you this evening, maybe?'

'Oh, that'll be much too late, we're going away tonight. I was hoping to get it organised before then. Look, you're obviously no use to me, I'll have to ask someone else.'

'If you're going away, you can't see anyone anyway,' said Cassia. 'I'll get a couple of names for you before you come back from holiday. Have a good time.'

'Yes, all right,' said Edwina, and put the phone down.

'Such pretty manners,' said Cassia lightly into the now dead receiver, and turned her attention to the day ahead.

*   *   *

The Dean was in rather high spirits; he said he had had dinner the night before with Sir William Beveridge and that they had had what he called a fine old fight. 'He's got all these ideas about what he called a National Health Service, whereby free medicine, or rather medicine paid for by the state, would be available to everyone. Well, he's a politician, so what would you expect?'

353

'I can't see what's wrong with that,' said Cassia. 'It sounds splendid to me.'

'The principle's all right, but how is it going to be administered, eh? We'd all have to be employed by the government or the civil service or whatever, and what understanding would they have of medicine? No, it couldn't work. We'd all be tied up in red tape before you could say consultant. Oh, now that reminds me. Mr Amstruther was asking me about you, saying if you ever wanted to go with him when he takes his students to one of the municipal hospitals he's consultant to, you're to ask him about it. It would be interesting for you, wouldn't it? Get another perspective on the field.'

'That would be wonderful,' Cassia said. 'How very kind, thank you.'

'Not kind,' said the Dean. 'Nothing to do with me.' But she knew it was.

*   *   *

She went to seek out Mr Amstruther when she left the Dean's office. He was operating that morning, she was told, but was due to finish at lunchtime; she should be able to catch him before he left for his consulting rooms. She waited patiently outside his room off the long corridor leading to theatre. Amstruther didn't emerge until almost two. He came striding towards her, scowled as he realised she wanted to speak to him.

'Can't stop now,' he said, 'I'm very late.'

'I'm sorry, Mr Amstruther, but the Dean said I could ask you to take me some time with your students to one of the municipal hospitals.'

'Good Lord, did he? Yes, well, I can't see any

354

problem with that. We're going over to Balford on Friday morning. Big obstetric ward there. That suit you?'

Cassia thought swiftly. Friday morning! When she went home. It was sacred, the children looked forward to it, she looked forward to it; lately in the school holidays they had developed a tradition whereby she took them all out to lunch, Janet as well. She really shouldn't. On the other hand, it was an incredible opportunity. If she said no, he probably wouldn't offer again. She'd have to make it up to them some other time. She took a deep breath.

'Yes,' she said, 'yes, that would be wonderful. Thank you.'

*   *   *

Her afternoon clinic was long; she arrived back at Walton Street after seven to find Rupert waiting for her in the kitchen.

'Hello, darling. You look tired. I've cooked us a little chicken casserole.'

'Goodness, what a treasure you are,' said Cassia. 'How was the read-through?'

'Promising. Eleanor is quite brilliant and Jasper Hamlyn has so many wonderful ideas. I really have very high hopes for this. Thanks to you.'

'Not just me, Rupert, I hope,' she said, laughing.

'No, of course not, but—well, I hope you know how grateful I am.'

'Of course I do. And anyway, I am looking for a return on my angelic money.'

The casserole was delicious; and after that he produced a large bowl of raspberries and a jug of cream.

She sat back, smiling at him across the table. 'I feel much better. Thank you, Rupert.'

He looked at her. 'Want to talk about it?'

'What?'

'Whatever it is. That's making you sad.'

'No. Yes. Oh, I don't know. I'd better ring Janet first anyway. I have some slightly awkward news for her.'

Janet, being Janet, took the awkward news extremely cheerfully. 'Friday will be fine, Mrs Fallon. Of course you must go, it sounds like a wonderful opportunity. We'll all go off on our bikes. I've had a little seat for Delia fitted on the back of mine. She loves it.'

'Janet, you are wonderful. Is everything all right down there?'

'Oh, perfectly all right, Mrs Fallon, yes. Dr Fallon is very busy, of course. He went straight from the surgery into his study, told Peggy to bring him his lunch in there, but he does that sometimes when you are away.'

'Does he? Oh, Janet, I am sorry.'

'Whatever for? It's very understandable he doesn't want to eat with me and the children, it's a bit of a strain, not to mention a bear-garden. But apparently he's going to be out all day tomorrow. Leaving Dr Johnson in charge.'

'Poor Maureen,' said Cassia absently. 'How odd. I wonder where he's going. And what about the children?'

'Absolutely splendid. Bertie spent the afternoon with a little friend, riding. Says he wants to be a jockey. I said he'd have to ask you,' she added, laughing.

356

'Tell him he can't,' said Cassia, 'but he does love riding. I think he might like to have a pony. What do you think, Janet?'

'I think it would be a wonderful idea, Mrs Fallon. He has a natural seat.'

'Oh really? Well, I'll think about that one. Please give them all my love.'

'Do you want to speak to Dr Fallon?'

'No, I don't think so. He's obviously busy. Goodnight, Janet. And thank you.'

'She's wonderful,' she said to Rupert, putting down the phone, 'just one of the nicest people I've ever met. And Edward is so foul to her. It's embarrassing. He resents her being there, you see. Well, I can understand that, but it's not her fault and she never takes offence, just goes on and on being nice back. Anyway, I'm thinking of buying the boys ponies. Bertie would love it so much and, by some strange coincidence, the paddock next door to our garden is for sale. Good idea?'

'Yes, I'm sure. What does Edward say about it?'

'Edward doesn't say anything about anything to me, Rupert,' she said, and then burst into tears.

*　　　*　　　*

It was almost teatime when Cassia pulled into the lane leading to Monks Heath the next afternoon.

It had been a very long week, and she was tired. The morning at Balford General Hospital had been fascinating but gruelling; she had tacked quietly on to the back of the crowd of students and followed Mr Amstruther's stalking figure into the vast, gloomy obstetric ward, and stood silent while he alternately bullied and coaxed them into their diagnoses of the conditions of silent, frightened women, who had already been through the trauma of describing the most intimate details about themselves to at least four different doctors.

The nursing staff were of an interestingly lower calibre than those at St Christopher's; harsher in their approach to the patients, less competent with their procedures. She watched one clumsily attempting to withdraw a catheter from a tearful young woman who had had a hysterectomy two days before, and had found it extremely difficult not to go up and show her how to do it properly, and listened in horror as Sister told a deeply wretched old lady she was going to give her an enema in front of all the students if she didn't stop complaining about her pain. Only the knowledge that it was strictly against medical practice and that Mr Amstruther would never ask her to join his round again kept her silent.

Mr Amstruther was, as always, rude to the nurses, and humiliated his students—'Mr Ford, if you are of the opinion this lady has an ovarian cyst, why are you examining her in the area of her bladder?'—but surprisingly gentle and tactful with the patients, apologising if he hurt them and asking them if they minded the students examining them.

None of the patients objected, of course: apart from one feisty old lady who said she'd never had a man inside her yet who didn't know what he was doing and she wasn't going to start now, and cackled at him through her almost toothless gums. Cassia smiled at the memory, while thinking sadly at the same time that even that spirit was not going to withstand the onslaught of learning that she had a malignant tumour in her uterus, with secondaries in her spine; the most radical surgery could not help her, and the best that could be done was radiotherapy, to alleviate—in some small way—the pain.

She pulled into the drive at Monks Ridge, and Bertie came running towards her, shouting so excitedly that she could not distinguish one word of it. She got out, holding out her arms, picked him up, held him to her, burying her face in his soft hair, drinking in his warmth, and the sweet, fresh-air smell of childhood.

'Slow down, darling, start again, I couldn't hear you at all.'

'I'm going to school in September!' he said.

'Well, Bertie; of course you are, it's a new term. What's so exciting about that?'

'No, no, you don't understand. To my new school, to boarding school, next term. Isn't it exciting?'

'What? Bertie, don't be silly, of course you're not, not for another year, you're not nearly old enough.'

'But I am, you see, I really am. I can go, straight away. Daddy's arranged it.'

She set him down then, icy cold in spite of the hot sun, and looked towards the house where Edward was standing in the doorway, an expression of chilling satisfaction in his eyes.

CHAPTER TWENTY

Benedict had gone again, after a dreadful, hideous agony of a row that had raged for hours.

Once, little Fanny had appeared at the door of their room, her face frightened; Cecily had hugged her, told her to go and find Mrs Goss, that she and Daddy were talking.

'That's not talking,' Fanny had said, 'that's fighting,' and had pulled herself away, estranged from them for the first time in her short life. They looked after her, united, just for a moment, by remorse, sadness for their child, but the violence of the battle was too great to be contained. It gathered again, rose, engulfed them.

'I'm going,' he said, finally. 'I cannot and will not endure this any longer. I will be at the house if you want me.'

'Want you!' she had said. 'You can be sure of one thing, Benedict, and that is that I shall never want anything to do with you ever again.'

The expression in his eyes was so terrible, so filled with desolation and despair that even then she would have forgiven him had he not said, 'Well, in that case we are in accord at last. Goodbye, Cecily.'

After a long time Cecily pulled the heavy curtains across the windows, crawled into her bed, pulled up the covers and prayed for sleep. It did not come until the dawn had broken, filled with birdsong, and dancing sunlight, when she dozed briefly, fitfully.

*　　　*　　　*

Laurence Harrington, who had been left in London in the care of his nanny, wasn't very well. Nanny called the doctor . . .

360

*   *   *

Dominic Foster was having a problem with the design of the new development. He needed to discuss it urgently; Harry was away, and that meant Benedict. He'd try the office; if he wasn't there it would have to be the house. Besides, he had another, more pressing reason to speak to Benedict. He would really like to see him, talk to him . . .

*   *   *

Nanny saw the doctor out and then went to the telephone. Mrs Harrington sounded very strained, she thought, not at all how she should be after a week by the sea; and she was clearly upset by the news about Laurence's measles.

'I'll come up at once, Nanny. I think the other children should remain here, don't you? To avoid any risk of infection. Now if there's anything you need for him, do get it, and naturally you must inform my husband. Or has he gone to the office?'

'Your husband isn't here, Mrs Harrington. I didn't realise he had returned to the house.'

'Well, maybe he hasn't got back yet. Stayed at a hotel, possibly, on the way. Perhaps you'd let me know when he does get back, Nanny.'

'Certainly, madam.'

Cecily put the phone down, and went to find Mrs Goss. She was very sorry Laurence was ill, of course, but it was a relief to have an excuse to leave Devon and the children. The scene with Benedict had changed her perception of the house quite horribly, made it seem hostile and alien to her, and

361

the children, even Fanny, were grating on her raw nerves.

'Laurence is ill, developing measles, and naturally I must go back to London. I would greatly prefer it if the girls could stay here. I don't want them catching it, if I can help it. Now, is it too much to ask you to look after them, just for a few days?'

Mrs Goss said it would be a pleasure.

The girls were in the stables; Stephanie was being a pony and Fanny a rather bad-tempered groom. 'Keep still,' she shouted. 'Keep bloody well still.'

'Fanny, darling,' said Cecily gently, 'that's not a very nice word.'

'You used it,' said Fanny, her small face hostile. 'And Papa did. I'll say it if I like.'

'Fanny, I'm sorry about last night. If you were upset . . .'

She tried to put her arms round Fanny, but she pushed her off. 'It's all right. Leave me alone.'

Cecily sighed and told them she had to go to London, that Laurence had the measles. 'I don't want you getting it, so you're to stay here with Mrs Goss. That'll be fun, won't it?'

Stephanie beamed at her and said, 'Goody, goody.' Fanny stared at her, morose, silently.

*   *   *

Cassia sat in the study, staring at Edward. He was ignoring her, coldly and thoroughly, leafing through *The Times*; every so often he would look up and give her a look of such intense hostility she felt it as a physical blow.

362

They had scarcely spoken for days; she had gone into the house with Bertie, that Friday afternoon, holding his hand, listening to his excited chatter, had smiled, said how exciting, had not hinted for one moment that she did not think it was exciting too, had sat right through supper doing the same thing, and it was only when they had gone to bed that she had said to Edward, fighting to keep her voice non-combative, 'Edward, why have you decided on this?'

He had said, not looking at her, 'I think it's time he went away, he's getting very mollycoddled here.'

'Edward, how absurd! He's only tiny and—'

'He is not tiny. He's almost seven and he's treated like a baby.'

'Bertie is not treated like a baby. St Joe's is splendid, he's playing games—'

'I don't like him being looked after by that nanny of yours,' he said. 'I think she babies him. With you away so much, I think he needs school.'

'Ah,' she said, 'so that's it. The nanny. And me being away.'

'Partly. But in any case, I have made the decision. And I would advise you very strongly against undermining my authority in the matter in any way.'

'Of course I won't undermine it.'

'Really? I wonder why I find that just a little hard to believe. When you undermine most of my authority these days.'

'That's a lie.'

'Indeed? I rather think not. Well, please don't do it in this case. It would be very bad for Bertie, confusing for him. He's excited, he's looking forward to it, I don't want him upset.'

'You don't want him upset? Then don't send him away. Do you realise how lonely, how homesick, how frightened he's going to be? Cut off from us, from everything he knows and cares about, subjected to all kinds of things he's not ready for—'

'Don't be absurd. I was only just seven myself, when I went.'

'Yes, and you've told me about the crying under the blankets, the homesickness so bad you couldn't eat, the bullying by the bigger boys—'

'It didn't do me any harm,' said Edward shortly.

'I think it did you a great deal. Actually.'

He shrugged.

'You are monstrous,' she said suddenly. 'Don't think I don't know precisely what you are doing, Edward, and why. I'm going to sleep in the spare room.'

Now it was Tuesday afternoon and she was frantic, with suppressed rage, frustration and a determination to have the matter at least discussed.

Suddenly she lost her temper, walked over to him and snatched the paper from his hands. He looked up at her, his face thoughtful, and then he began, very slowly, to smile, and just for a moment he was the Edward she had once known and persuaded herself she loved: and she was stopped in mid-emotion, shocked at the vividness of the memory and the sadness at how far they had both travelled from it. Then she looked again at him, and saw the smile was quite, quite different: not loving, not tender at all, but complacent, strangely triumphant. At that moment, and in this matter, he had won.

'It's no good, Cassia,' he said. 'I want him to go and he's going. The school will take no notice if you try to change anything. I am his father, you see. In their eyes at least, the head of the family. I make the decisions.'

'It's so cruel,' she said, 'such an awful thing to do, just to hurt me.'

'Well,' he said, 'perhaps it's my turn,' and then just for an instant, remorse hit her, remorse and again sadness.

'Edward,' she said, 'what about Glasgow, what are you going to do?'

'I have turned it down. The place. I have no intention of going on my own. Now if you will excuse me, I would like to finish reading that article. It's most interesting.'

'I won't excuse you,' she said. 'I want to discuss Bertie. I want you to change your mind, I want him at home for at least another year, I don't see why you won't at least discuss it.'

'Really? Then you really have become very blind.'

'You don't think it will be good for him at all, really, do you? You don't care about him in the least. You haven't even considered him. If I thought you had, I wouldn't mind so much but—'

'Cassia,' he said, 'just stop it, will you? You are not achieving anything.'

And then Cecily rang.

*   *   *

'Cassia? Look, I'm sure this must sound stupid to you, but you haven't heard from Benedict, have you?'

'No,' she said. 'Why should I have?'

'Oh, nothing. I mean—well, Laurence has

365

measles, and I'm still not home, just travelling up from Devon now, we went down for a few days, I've stopped for tea. I thought he might have rung you, if he was worried, as you're a doctor and everything . . .'

Her voice tailed away; Cassia heard the fear underneath it, misunderstood it. 'Cecily, you mustn't worry about Laurence. Measles is nasty, of course, but he's a tough little chap, he'll be fine. Just make sure he's kept in a dim room because of the danger to his eyes, you know, and Nanny's so good . . . Cecily, are you there?'

'Yes,' said Cecily. Her voice was very quiet.

'Look, I'll come and see him tomorrow. Just to put your mind at rest. Would you like me to?'

'Oh, yes please. I'd be so grateful.' She hesitated. 'If you do hear from Benedict, you will let me know?'

'Yes, of course. Why? Has he—'

But Cecily had put the phone down.

*   *   *

Dominic Foster phoned the house at about the same time. Benedict had told him not to ring the house, but since the wife was in Devon, there seemed little problem.

*   *   *

Cecily arrived home at eight, exhausted and anxious. Adams let her in, told her that supper was waiting if she wanted it.

'No, not now, thank you, Adams, I'll go straight up to the nursery. Has my husband returned?'

366

'No, Mrs Harrington. Not yet.'

'Thank you, Adams. I'll be upstairs if he does.' She crushed the anxiety, and went up to the nursery.

*   *   *

In the morning, Laurence was worse: his little face scarlet with the high temperature he was running, his eyes hard and bright. He was covered now with the rash, and he cried endlessly, a croaking wretched cry. Nanny had been bathing him hourly with bicarbonate of soda; she looked exhausted.

'Nanny, go to bed for a while, have a proper sleep,' said Cecily, who had hardly slept either. 'I will see to him, and the doctor will be here soon after nine. Go on, off you go.'

There was still no word from Benedict. Carefully careless, she had phoned the house in Devon. The girls were being as good as gold, Mrs Goss said, and had been with her to visit her daughter and her year-old twins. 'I hope that's all right, Mrs Harrington. Oh, now there was a phone call, from a Mr Foster. Looking for Mr Harrington.'

'Oh, was there?' said Cecily. A hot tide of rage and disgust rose in her throat. 'What did you tell him, Mrs Goss?'

'Well, that Mr Harrington wasn't here,' said Mrs Goss. 'He seemed a bit put out. Very worried, I'd say. He said it was about business and if Mr Harrington did appear, could I tell him. I said I would. That wasn't wrong, was it, Mrs Harrington?'

'No, but if he rings again, perhaps you could tell him to ring my husband's secretary, not the house.'

Phoning the house! How dared he! How dared Benedict even allow him to think that he could? Tears of rage, of exhaustion, came into her eyes; she dashed them away.

'Anything wrong, madam? Master Laurence isn't worse, I trust?'

'No, Adams, thank you. He'll be fine. Adams, did a Mr Foster phone yesterday at all? For my husband?'

'He did, madam, yes. He left a number, would you like it?'

'No, it's perfectly all right.'

She stood there, trying to cope with this new assault upon herself and her dignity, when the phone rang sharply.

Adams answered it. 'Oh, Mr Harrington. How nice to hear from you, sir. Yes, she's here.' He held the phone out to her. 'He says it's very urgent, madam.'

Cecily took the phone. 'Thank you, Adams. That will be all for now.' He went out, closing the door behind him. 'Yes?' she said, hearing her own voice very cold.

'Cecily?' His voice was raw, exhausted. It seemed to echo her own feelings. 'Cecily, I must talk to you. I must.'

'I don't want to talk to you at the moment, Benedict. I really don't have the strength. I'm sorry.'

'Would you consider coming to see me, meeting me?' She hesitated.

'Please,' he said, 'please, Cecily.'

He sounded dreadful. Then she thought of

Dominic Foster, given their telephone numbers, given leave, still, to phone the house, and the fury rose in her again.

'I'm sorry, Benedict. I really find it impossible to contemplate. Besides—'

She had been going to tell him about Laurence, but he interrupted her. 'Very well, then. Goodbye, Cecily.'

She couldn't even bring herself to say goodbye; after a moment he put the phone down.

*   *   *

Cassia was with her when the police came, in the late afternoon, to say that Benedict's car had been found, parked in some woods near Camberley. He had been sitting in the driving seat, shot through the head; the pistol was still in his hand.

CHAPTER TWENTY-ONE

There was an inquest of course; a verdict of suicide was brought in—'while the balance of the mind was disturbed'.

Cecily gave evidence very calmly; she said that her husband had had a lot of worries of a business nature, but that she would not have described him as depressed. The coroner asked her if their marriage had been happy; she said it had been very happy.

Harry Moreton, as Benedict's major business partner, broke his holiday to attend the inquest. He stood, looking pale and rather angry, and said that to the best of his knowledge, there had been no reason for Benedict to take his own life, but that he was quite a volatile character.

'What precisely do you mean by volatile, Mr Moreton?'

'He was very sensitive. He took things hard.'

'But he had no business worries? As far as you know?'

'Not so far as our own business affairs were concerned. Of course nothing involving venture capital is free from anxiety; some of us weather that sort of thing better than others.'

The coroner said that was indeed the case, and after a very short period of deliberation, brought in his verdict.

*   *   *

Cassia had sat in the courtroom, holding Cecily's hand. Afterwards, they all went back to the house, and Cecily went upstairs to lie down.

'That was mercifully brief,' Cassia said to Harry.

'Yes, I put a word in a few ears.'

Cassia stared at him. 'Is there anyone you can't manipulate, Harry?'

He half smiled for the first time that day.

'You,' he said.

*   *   *

There was a very small funeral at St Luke's in Chelsea. Just Cecily, the two girls, Cecily's parents the Forbeses, the Moretons, Rupert Cameron, and Cassia and Edward. Cassia had been surprised when Edward agreed to her request to come, but

370

he had appeared badly shaken by Benedict's death, said he would like to come and pay his respects. Sir Richard and Margaret also came; this too was a surprise to Cassia, who had always observed Sir Richard's distaste for Benedict. But he said to her, as if sensing her question, 'He was a good man at heart, I think. And very good indeed to Leonora.'

She reached up to kiss him. 'I'm glad you're here. It helps. Both of them gone. It seems unbelievable.'

'Those poor little girls,' said Margaret, looking over at them, their small faces white under their black hats, their eyes huge and tear stained. Stephanie was clinging to her mother's hand, but Fanny stood slightly apart, her expression somehow defiant.

'Yes,' said Cassia. 'He was a wonderful father. Very sad. Oh dear, I'm afraid Mrs Forbes isn't helping Cecily much. I do think it might be better if she stopped crying.'

'Dreadful woman,' said Sir Richard. 'If Cecily can control herself, then surely *she* should.'

'She likes drama,' said Cassia, smiling at him. 'But I believe Stephanie is very fond of her, she might help her at least.'

'And how are those offspring of yours?' said Sir Richard. 'Doing well? The eldest must be . . . what now?'

'Bertie is nearly seven,' said Edward, suddenly taking part in the conversation.

'Good Lord, going off to school soon, then?'

'Yes. This September actually. We thought it was about time, didn't we, Cassia?'

'Yes,' she said and turned away from them all, unable to continue with the conversation, unable to

371

pretend she was part of this decision. She saw Harry standing on his own, his face dark and heavy. She went over to him. 'Are you all right?'

'Yes. I just can't believe they've both gone, though.'

'No,' she said, 'neither can I. I remember the day I first saw them together at the Ritz. I thought they were the two most beautiful people I'd ever seen.'

'And the most doomed,' he said, and sighed.

Cassia looked across at Cecily; she was talking to Edwina now, who was very pale and drawn, clearly shaken.

'Is Edwina all right?' she said. 'She looks dreadful.'

'Oh, yes, I think so. She was awfully fond of Benedict.'

'Yes,' said Cassia. 'She seemed to . . . well, understand. About him.'

There was a silence: small, heavy.

'I was a little afraid,' Cassia said then, 'that . . . well, someone unsuitable might have turned up.'

'I told him not to, if you mean Foster.'

'Is he very upset?'

'Yes, of course he is,' he said shortly, 'and can't show it, poor devil.'

Cecily came over to them. 'I wonder if you'd like to come back for a drink and something to eat?' She seemed perfectly composed, almost cheerful, not the grief-stricken wraith Cassia would have expected. 'My parents are coming back and—'

'Perhaps very briefly,' said Harry.

Cassia turned to Edward. 'Would you like go back to Cecily's for a short while?'

'No, I don't think so,' he said. 'I have to get back. Are you coming?'

'Yes, of course. What else would I do?'

'God knows,' he said and then bent and most surprisingly kissed Cecily on the cheek. 'Goodbye,' he said. 'Let us know if there is anything we can do.'

Cassia was astonished; she had expected the most token politeness from him. He seemed genuinely upset. She said as much on the train, but he looked at her blankly.

'I like Cecily,' he said. 'I feel very sorry for her.'

'Did you . . . realise, then?' she said, very quietly. 'About Benedict?'

They had never discussed it: Edward was fiercely judgmental in such matters; and she had always been careful to keep any suggestion of it from him, fearing it would add to his distaste for Benedict in particular, and her friends in general.

He stared at her for a moment, as if he found it hard to believe she had asked the question. 'Yes, of course I did,' he said finally. 'Did you really think I wouldn't?'

'And was that why you disliked him so much?'

'It was one of the reasons,' he said, and then got out his paper and read it for the rest of the journey.

*   *   *

'You look upset,' said Eleanor Studely to Rupert after rehearsal that day.

'Yes. I went to a funeral this morning. Old family friend.'

'And was he? Old?'

'No, he was quite young, younger than I am anyway, three small children. It's very sad.'

'I'm sorry. What did he die of?'

373

'He killed himself, I'm afraid. A direct result of some of the barbaric laws in this country.'

'Oh, Rupert, I'm so sorry. How dreadful.'

'Yes. He was . . . do you mind hearing all this?'

'Of course not.' She smiled at him. She was by any standards a pretty woman, with dark hair and creamy skin, and very large hazel eyes, but two things turned that prettiness to beauty: one was her smile, which was very wide and sudden, transforming her rather serious face, and the other was her voice, which was low, husky, intensely musical. She could work magic with that voice, make her audience cry, laugh, think, reflect, empathise with her; at this very moment it was soothing Rupert, easing his pain.

'Oh, darling, you're sweet. Well, you see, he was a homosexual, covered it up successfully for years, at Christ knows what cost to himself, and his wife for that matter.'

'Did she know?'

'Oh, yes. What did for him, I truly believe, was the strain, the long years of pretending, and of fear.'

'It's appalling,' she said, after a silence, 'all those lives wrecked, so needlessly. Why should he have had to marry, make her unhappy too? They have to change those laws, something has to be done.'

'Yes, but you see it's different for us. I mean, there are so many in our business, we understand it, see it for what it is. To his mother-in-law, for instance, his brother-in-law indeed, it would be something disgraceful, shameful, something he should be cured of, punished for.'

'And the wife? How did she see it?'

'I think she . . . well, let's say she tried. Very

374

hard. To understand.'

'Poor woman,' said Eleanor Studely, her lovely voice vibrant with sympathy. 'And was he related to your Cassia?'

'Only by God. He was her godmother's brother. And she's not my Cassia, as you put it.' For some reason the description irritated him: or did it make him anxious?

'Darling Rupert, I was only teasing. But you do seem terribly fond of one another. Jasper hinted that there was something going on between you.'

'Well, Jasper can mind his own bloody business,' said Rupert crossly.

*   *   *

Nicola Foster stood outside her husband's door. She knew what grief, what agony lay behind it; knew also how helpless she was to comfort him. Just the same, she could not leave him there, the grief unacknowledged; she cared for him too much.

'Dominic,' she said, knocking gently, 'Dominic, please let me come in.'

There was a long pause; then she heard his footsteps, and the key turning in the lock. He stood there before her, ashen, his eyes red and swollen. Nicola put her arms round him; silently, he responded to her.

'I've brought you some coffee. Here, come and sit down.'

'If only they'd let me go,' he said, 'to the funeral, if only I could have said goodbye.'

'Dominic, think of the wife. How impossible it would have been for her. I'm sure Harry was right. Here, drink your coffee.'

She poured it out and watched him: thinking how much she loved him, her husband, her best friend; thinking how well they suited one another; how lucky she was.

And how unlucky Cecily Harrington.

* * *

'Letter for you, Mummy.'

'Thank you, Bertie darling. Oh, it's from Sir Richard. You remember him, he lives in London in that great big house. My godfather. Sort of, anyway. He wants to come and see us, isn't that nice?'

'I thought you were looking a bit peaky at the funeral,' said Sir Richard, when she phoned him to say of course he must come to lunch. 'I hope you're not working too hard.'

'No, of course not. Anyway, I'm on holiday at the moment. We'd love to see you.'

'Good. I shall look forward to seeing the nippers. All right, my dear, we'll see you on Thursday.'

* * *

Just occasionally, Cassia let herself think about life before The Money. It was dangerous, because she had made so many decisions, taken so many irrevocable steps; there was no way now that she could step backward, become once again the woman who had had what seemed to be a good marriage, who had lived perfectly happily with her husband and her children, who had run the house adequately at least, who had been part of village

376

life, who had turned her back on her own ambitions and desires and directed herself and her formidable energies towards the making of a happy family.

She had been perfectly all right, that woman; she had had her frustrations, her problems, her regrets, but in no way had she considered herself unhappy. And certainly none of her family had been unhappy. She had not been estranged from her husband, nor parted from her children almost half of every week, and nor was she about to be wrenched from her small son against her will. She had known more freedom, fewer responsibilities, less anxiety. And a great deal less guilt. That woman slept soundly, if exhaustedly, and woke every morning with only the day's duties and concerns in her head, not a mounting crescendo of conflict and self-reproach.

Today, because Sir Richard and Margaret were with them, because she was concerned only with domestic matters, and now, lunch over, was simply sitting in the garden in a deckchair, watching the children play, because everyone seemed happy, at ease, she did allow herself; and the view back across the dangerous divide looked golden, untroubled, sweet. She sighed suddenly.

Sir Richard put his hand on her knee. 'You happy these days?'

'Terribly happy,' she said, and of course that was true too: returned to her medicine, to old friends, granted freedom, power to do what she wished, and lovely, expensive toys, clothes, houses and cars to play with. 'Leonora would be very pleased with what she had done for me, I think.'

She smiled at him, meaning it, then remembered

Benedict. 'But oh, Godpa, how terribly terribly unhappy she would be. About Benedict.'

'Yes,' he said and then, echoing Harry's words, 'doomed, they seemed, the pair of them, God knows why.' He sighed, looked across at Margaret, who was rather surprisingly taking part in a game of cricket with Bertie and William. 'I don't suppose you can understand it, but I do still miss her. In spite of everything. And I feel very remorseful about how I managed the whole thing. But what else could I have done?'

'Nothing,' said Cassia, and in that moment at least meant it. 'It was an impossible situation. Except you might have spared her the awful Monk,' she added, laughing. 'That was mean.'

'I know. Terrible woman, in her way. But you know, she kept in touch with Leonora, went to see her in Paris even. Felt it was her duty. Who would have thought it?'

'Who indeed?' said Cassia, and felt her heart quicken suddenly. 'How very sweet of her. Do you know, I think I might write to her, or at least send her a Christmas card. Could you give me her address?'

'Yes of course. Before we go. Oh, well held, young fellow. I think I might join in this game myself, get into the slips. Will you excuse me, my dear?'

Well, thought Cassia, lying back, closing her eyes, maybe Miss Monkton was finally going to be of some use after all . . .

*   *   *

Cecily took a deep breath and knocked, very

378

gently, on the door. There was no answer. She turned the handle very gently, pushed at the door, but it was locked.

'Go away, *please!*' Fanny's pretty voice was harsh with grief and hostility, 'I don't want to talk to you.'

'But darling, why not? I want to talk to you, especially as you're so unhappy.'

'Well, you can't help with that, can you? Not at all. Now go away and leave me alone. I'm not coming out, not opening the door.'

Cecily turned away, walked back along the nursery corridor. On the way she saw Nanny, carrying a pile of nappies into Laurence's nursery.

'I just came up to see Fanny,' she said, 'but she—well, she won't let me in.'

'She's very, very upset,' said Nanny. 'I've never seen a child in that sort of condition.'

'What sort of condition, Nanny?'

'I'd say she was shocked, madam, more than anything. And very angry. I heard Stephanie saying her prayers the other night and then Fanny said, "I'm not praying to God any more. I don't believe in him."'

'Oh, Nanny. It's terrible. I want to comfort her so much and . . .' She felt her own tears rising suddenly and bit them back: the tears she couldn't, wouldn't allow, for grief she had no business with.

*　　　*　　　*

Dominic Foster sat in his office, smoking endless Turkish cigarettes and drinking very strong coffee; he also would not allow himself to cry. Once he began, he would not, he knew, be able to stop. The guilt was the most terrible thing: knowing it was his

379

fault . . .

*   *   *

August was nearly over: Cassia watched the golden days, days where she could keep Bertie safe, unhurt, happy, slipping past, each one shorter than the last.

She hardly spoke to Edward, such was the frighteningly cold distaste she felt for him; he did not seem troubled by it, hardly seemed to notice.

Cassia had taken an extra week off, jealous of the time she had left with Bertie. She surrendered herself to amusing him, determined his last few days should be filled with pleasure. They went to the seaside, picnicking on the beach, savouring the delights of Brighton Pier, drove to London and stayed at the house, saw the Changing of the Guard, Madame Tussaud's, the Tower of London.

They actually saw the little princesses one day, scrambling out of their car followed by their nanny, and running into the house, 145 Piccadilly, where they lived. They were dressed alike in pale blue coats, white socks and button-up shoes, with straw flower-trimmed bonnets on their fair curls.

'They look very ordinary,' said William, 'not like princesses at all,' but Bertie said he thought they were pretty, especially Margaret.

The princesses' uncle David was due to go up to Balmoral for the annual family holiday. Private gossip at the inclusion of Mrs Simpson and several of her friends on the guest list was intense, but the English papers were still held silent on the subject.

*   *   *

Harry Moreton was reading *The Times* in the sunken garden of his country house one particularly beautiful morning when Edwina came flying out waving a magazine at him. He had been concerned about Edwina recently: she did not look well, pale and even thinner than usual, her lovely face drawn, almost angular. And she had been listless, sleeping badly. Harry did not love Edwina, but he was very fond of her. She was sexy and amusing and a clever hostess, and he certainly wished her no ill. He set down his paper and said, as indulgently as he could, 'Whatever have you got there, Edwina?'

'It's the latest issue of *Style*. It's got my first article in, look.'

Harry looked. It was only three quarters of a page, a survey of the accessory shops in Knightsbridge and Bond Street, but it had her name at the top of it. He studied it for a few moments before smiling at her and handing it back. 'Well done,' he said. 'I had no idea how clever you were.'

'There's no need to be so unpleasant.'

'Edwina, I'm not being unpleasant. I am genuinely impressed by this. It's just that I don't want to read it in detail. Not quite my subject. But I can see how satisfying it must be to you: especially to have your name at the top of the page.'

'So you've changed your mind about me working, then? You said you were very opposed to me doing a job. When I first got it.'

'The reason for my opposition was not to your working *per se*. I told you, I think it is excellent for women to work. I like intelligent women and I am a great supporter of women's rights. As long, of course—' he paused and grinned at her—'as long as it doesn't distract them from their duties to their husbands, in any way. Which was precisely my objection to this job of yours. It was because I felt your energies should be channelled into having a family. Have you seen anyone about that yet?'

'No. But I will. The minute we get back to London. I promise,' she said quickly: too quickly, he thought.

He frowned. 'Please do.' He went back to his paper.

*   *   *

'Cecily dear, are you listening to me?' said Ada Forbes.

'Oh, yes. Sorry, Mother.'

Cecily turned a cheerful face to her mother; they were sitting in the morning room, and Cecily was leafing through a magazine. Mrs Forbes had been up to stay for a few days: 'To try and take your mind off your grief,' she had said to Cecily when she had arrived, but so far she had observed little sign of grief in her daughter. Really, Mrs Forbes thought, it was as if she hardly cared that her husband had died.

'No, Mother; I quite agree. I really am perfectly all right,' said Cecily.

'I can see that,' said Ada Forbes. 'Your father and I have a cabin booked on the *Queen Mary*, sailing to New York in a couple of weeks. Naturally I had told him I would not be going with him, that I felt my place was with you, but I really feel—'

'Mother, of course you must go,' said Cecily.

382

'Such a shame to miss the trip, you'd enjoy it so much. Just bring me a nice new hat from Bonwit Tellers, I'm told they are the prettiest in the world, and I shall be perfectly happy.'

It seemed a very odd thing to say, as Mrs Forbes remarked to Mr Forbes when she telephoned him later that day while Cecily was out, seeing the lawyers about Benedict's will, but she had to agree that Cecily certainly seemed well able to manage without her.

*   *   *

After Harry had gone to meet his business contact, Edwina telephoned Cassia; Peggy told her she wasn't there that day. Assuming she must be in London, she rang the Walton Street number.

Rupert Cameron answered the phone. 'No, Edwina, she's not here. Can I help?'

'Rupert, whatever is going on between you and Cassia? You seem to practically live with her these days. No, you can't help, I'm afraid. I need some advice from her. In her medical capacity. Nothing serious. Bye, Rupert. Don't get too carried away, will you?'

*   *   *

Later at dinner she said to Harry, 'Rupert seems to have taken up permanent residence at Cassia's new house. I'm beginning to think that's why she got it in the first place. They've always had a thing about each other, haven't they?'

'I really couldn't say, I'm afraid,' said Harry. He had been drinking from his claret glass; he set it

383

down rather hard and the slender stem snapped. The glass fell over, spilling its contents all over the tablecloth.

He was in a very bad temper for the rest of the evening; Edwina presumed his business meeting must have gone badly. She knew better than to question him about it.

*   *   *

Bertie looked up at his mother, his small face fighting tears. 'Goodbye, Mummy,' he said politely.

Cassia bent down and took Bertie in her arms, felt his small, skinny body shaking with terror now at the ordeal that confronted him, kissed him tenderly on the cheek. She felt him clinging to her briefly, in panic, and pulled him closer, fighting back the tears. One fell suddenly, treacherously on his face, and she felt him recognise it, look up at her startled, saw him blink fiercely, and then they both smiled brightly, bravely, at one another, while she still held him, still wondered why she was doing this, why allowing it, why she had not fought it harder, and knew it was partly at least a result of her own guilt, her own sense that in this one way at least, Edward should be allowed some authority, some dignity.

'Come along now. Time to go and meet the other boys. Shake hands with your father,' said Mr Donaldson, in the voice of one who had absolute control—and of course he had now, over Bertie, over his life and everything to do with him, for most of the time and for many years.

Bertie pulled away from her and held out his hand to his father. 'Goodbye, Daddy.'

'Goodbye, old chap. Have a good term. You'll have the time of your life here, I certainly did.'

And Cassia smiled down at Bertie again, hearing Edward's voice telling her of all that he had endured at St John's, and how it had hurt him, damaged him, and wondered which of them was actually going mad.

'Right, well, shall we see your parents off?' said Mr Donaldson, and put his hand on Bertie's shoulder, as if to assert his ownership of him.

Cassia got in to the car, put on her sunglasses so that no one could see the tears which were now streaming down her face.

'Bye, Mummy,' came the small, slightly shaky voice; he was smiling again now, very bravely, and waving. She managed to call, 'Bye, darling,' and smile, and to wave too, and then another car pulled in front of them, removing him from her vision for a moment, and when it had gone and she looked again he was being walked towards the school by Mr Donaldson, his head held staunchly high beneath the grey cap, his shoulders, in their stiff new grey jacket, bravely square, in the face of his misery and fear.

'Oh for God's sake,' said Edward, as she removed the glasses, wiped her streaming eyes, blew her nose. 'He'll be fine, he'll have a wonderful time.'

'I hope to God you're right,' she said, her voice raw with hostility, and then, turning round to put her jacket on the back seat, saw Bertie's teddy, much loved, hugged half bald, lying there, and picked it up. The boys were allowed, officially, to bring their teddies; but Edward had said, very firmly, that he thought it was not a good idea.

The pain in her grew harder, coming in waves now, and she swallowed, hugged the teddy closer.

* * *

The boys of St John's sat at supper and it was discovered that one of the new boys, the very thin one, was having some difficulty eating his food; and when told firmly by the master on duty, the dreaded Mr Bosworth, that it all had to go, the boy gave him a desperate look and said something in a low voice.

'I'm afraid we don't allow that sort of fussiness here, Fallon,' he said. 'You're not a baby any more, you're at school, and at school we eat everything. It's good discipline. You are not excused anything that is served.'

The new boy managed to eat a little of the particularly disgusting gristly mince, but then suddenly rushed outside retching.

Later, as the bigger boys passed the lavatories, they heard vomiting sounds and Fallon came out, green faced, his lashes wet with tears. He smiled uncertainly at the boys, and said simply, 'I hate gristle, it always makes me sick.'

'Ah, diddums. Is Baby missing Mummy, then? Did she let him leave his nasty food? Poor diddums. Next time we'll get some extra for you, Fallon, get it put on your plate. Now get out, the bogs are ours until bedtime. Unless we call for you, and then you come jolly fast.'

Bertie's boarding-school career had begun.

CHAPTER TWENTY-TWO

Somewhere someone was screaming. Loudly and persistently, a dreadful wailing scream. Everyone in the house heard it.

The screaming came from the main bedroom. Nanny got there first, found her mistress lying on the bed, purple faced, punching the air, the bedclothes, anything within reach, which fortunately did not include Fanny, who cowered, terrified, against the window.

'She just . . . started,' she said, hiccuping breathlessly, 'I don't know why.'

Nanny pulled Cecily up to a sitting position and hit her hard, across the face.

The screaming stopped abruptly and there was absolute silence; then Cecily gasped, and burying her head in her hands, began to sob less hysterically, but just as persistently.

'Fanny, run downstairs at once, tell Adams to call Dr Rushton. And then go up to the nursery, I've left Laurence with Stephanie. I'll be up in a minute.' She looked down at Cecily's dark head, drew it to her large bosom, as if she were a child, rocking her, saying soothingly, 'Now, Mrs Harrington, hush, hush, you've been so brave, so very brave, you mustn't let yourself go now.'

However, Cecily continued to sob, loudly, frantically; it was only when Dr Rushton arrived and gave her a sedative injection, and Susan and Nanny tucked her tenderly up in her bed, and drew the curtains, that quiet fell on the house again.

'I fear she may be on the verge of a nervous

breakdown,' said Dr Rushton quietly to Adams (he being the person of highest authority in the household), 'and if that is so, she will need very careful nursing. It may even be necessary for her to go to a nursing home for a while. Clearly I should discuss that with someone, as she is quite unable to take any such decision for herself. I wonder who you would suggest?'

'I would imagine, Dr Rushton, that her parents would be the best people to talk to. I can give you their address and telephone number.'

*　　　*　　　*

Ada Forbes arrived next morning, bearing a rather formidable bunch of flowers and a large basket of fruit. She brushed past Adams and went straight up the stairs to her daughter's bedroom, dismissed Susan, who was sitting by the bed, and settled her own stout body there instead, holding Cecily's hand and weeping. After an hour of this, during which time Cecily neither moved nor spoke, she came downstairs and telephoned her husband to say that she was extremely sorry but she was clearly not going to be able to accompany him to New York after all. 'My duty is here, with Cecily. I'm very sorry, Gerald.'

Gerald Forbes said that of course Cecily was far more important than he was; and after waiting for what he felt was a decent interval, he sat down and wrote a letter to a certain Mrs Hardacre, a wealthy New York widow, to the effect that he would be alone in the city for a few weeks during November and would hope to be permitted to call on her.

Later that morning, after a rather longer session at Cecily's bedside, Ada Forbes came out of the room, dabbing at her eyes, to find Nanny waiting in the corridor.

'I wonder if I might have a word with you, madam. It's about Fanny.'

'Yes, Nanny. Is there a problem?'

'There is, madam. She is very withdrawn, hardly speaks, and is refusing to eat. She was there, you see, when Mrs Harrington first—well, when she became so very upset, and she was already quite disturbed by her father's death.'

'Surely it's natural she should be upset?' said Mrs Forbes. 'I'm sure she will get over it soon, Nanny, and of course she must be made to eat. I will personally sit by her and feed her myself if necessary.'

'The doctor says we should not do that, madam, that we should leave her for a few days, see how she gets on.'

'Well, I suppose he knows what he's talking about, but I would tend to disagree. I will talk to her, we have always got on extremely well, I have a rapport with all children, and see if I can find out what is troubling her particularly.'

Nanny went on down to the kitchen, feeling more anxious than ever. Her observations of Fanny's behaviour did not encourage her to think that the kind of coaxing Mrs Forbes clearly had in mind was going to help. It was five days now since Cecily had collapsed, and all that had gone into Fanny's little body since then had been water.

Upstairs, Fanny lay in her small bed, wondering

how long it would take before she could actually start to die, and also when the hunger pangs which assaulted her night and day would begin to ease. She hadn't thought fasting would be quite this painful; but at least the terrible discomfort in her stomach was a distraction from the much worse one in her heart.

*   *   *

Being regarded, however inaccurately, as Cassia's possible lover, was worrying Rupert. Light-hearted gossip had a way of becoming serious slander and, given the unhappy state of her marriage, he felt it was dangerous. It had also had another, absolutely unexpected effect; there was, he discovered, an erotic element in the rumour. It had aroused certain feelings and curiosities about her that he had thought long dead.

He thought of her a great deal, more intently indeed than he had for years—her slender body, her deep blue gaze, her shining corn-coloured hair, and her rather fierce seriousness, her absolute integrity, her courage.

She was, he thought, throwing stones into the sea one golden evening, a dangerous woman these days, and she did not quite yet know it: lovely, fashionable, sensuous and—the greatest change of all—absolutely independent. She could do whatever she chose, go wherever she wanted, have whoever she desired.

She had not yet taken any real advantage of that independence, but she was undoubtedly aware of it. And in the light of that freedom, and people's knowledge and perceptions of it, the fact that she could now find herself cast as his lover was truly dangerous.

*   *   *

'Mrs Moreton, Miss Le Page would like to see you in her office. Immediately, please.'

God, what had she done? It occurred to Edwina, as she walked just a little too quickly along the corridor towards Aurora Le Page's office, that it was faintly ridiculous that here she was, the wife of one of the richest men in England, suddenly returned to schoolgirl status.

She decided she must restore some balance to her relationship with Miss Le Page; indeed, it seemed absolutely reasonable that she should do so. She walked straight in, smiling blithely at the secretary, a creature almost as awe-inspiring as Miss Le Page herself.

'Good afternoon, Miss Singleton. Here I am. Miss Le Page sent for me.'

'It was I who sent for you, Mrs Moreton,' said Joanne Singleton, sternly, 'if we are to be precise.'

Her sternness immediately crushed Edwina's resolution, turned the cheerful smile to a nervous smirk.

'Please wait. Miss Le Page is on the telephone to New York.'

Edwina sat down and waited.

*   *   *

Cassia had wanted to go straight to London after taking Bertie to school that Friday, so angry did she feel with Edward, but she knew that would be hard on William, who was missing his big brother. Just the same, when Tuesday came, she left with relief.

The clinic was a long one, which pleased her, for she needed to be exhausted—sleep had eluded her since Bertie had left—and she wasn't back at her house until almost eight. She had forgotten all about Rupert's visit until she was driving down Knightsbridge; damn. He'd probably have left again in a huff. But as she pulled up in front of the house, she saw that the light over the door was on; and before she could even pull her key out of her bag, Rupert had opened it, was ushering her in, was kissing her on the cheek.

'You look tired.'

'I am tired. Rupert, can I smell supper? You are an angel, really, the people in this street must think we're married. Or that you're my lover at least. Oh, sorry, not funny.' She laughed, put down her bag, went into the kitchen. The smell of something wonderful reached her from the oven. 'Duchesse potatoes, my favourite,' she said, and turned to kiss him; he was looking at her slightly oddly. 'What's the matter, don't you love me any more?'

'Yes, of course I do,' he said, and smiled quickly. 'Come on, sit down, have a drink. Gin and tonic, martini, what?'

'Not gin. It makes me so melancholy, and I feel bad enough already. Let's have a glass of wine, and I'll sit and watch you make the omelette.'

'Why are you melancholy?' he said, taking a bottle of wine out of the fridge. 'Is it Bertie?'

'Yes, I miss him so much and I feel so angry with Edward, I can hardly bear to look at him, it was such an awful, horrible thing to do.'

'Revenge,' said Rupert. 'Not pretty.'

'I suppose. Oh God, what a mess. Unhappiness everywhere—think of those poor little things of Cecily's, of Cecily herself.'

'Yes, it seems she is very unwell,' said Rupert. 'Edwina was here earlier—'

'Edwina. How extraordinary, why?'

'She said she wanted to ask you something. She said you'd know what it was about.'

'Oh God, yes, I do, and I keep forgetting. Oh dear. What was it about Cecily, then?'

'She's had some sort of nervous collapse, apparently. And Fanny is very upset still, scarcely eating, apparently.'

'I'll go and see them in the morning. Poor little Fanny, she loved her father so. Oh Rupert, what a mess.'

'I'm afraid so,' he said and sighed.

Cassia looked at him.

'What is it?'

'I'll explain later. But it's complicated. Now hold out your plate. Shall we eat in here?'

*   *   *

'Are you all right?' said Harry. His expression as he looked at Edwina was impatiently concerned.

'Yes. No. Well, you know. It's the usual. Christ, it hurts!'

'Oh God,' he said, and then, clearly sensing his reaction was harsh, 'Here, let me get you up to bed.

'I thought you were going to see someone about this,' he said, trying not to sound irritable, as she lay back on her pillows, holding a hot-water bottle to her stomach.

'I am. I've asked Cassia to suggest someone. She

393

said she'd find out. I called at her house tonight on my way home, to remind her, but she wasn't there. Rupert was,' she added, swallowing a handful of the pills he handed her.

'Rupert? At Cassia's house?'

'Yes, he's always there these days. Anyway, he said he'd get her to ring me. Harry, do stop glaring at me, I've done my best. Oh, God, this is awful.'

'I'm not glaring at you,' he said, and turned and stalked out of the room.

Edwina clenched her fists, wondered how much more of this she could stand. They said childbirth was like period pains, only ten times as bad. If that was so, then perhaps it was just as well she wasn't ever going to have to go through it.

*   *   *

'Oh, Cassia, what have we done?' said Rupert.

She smiled at him across the pillow, her face peaceful, her eyes very large, very dark blue. 'What I've thought about for most of my life,' she said.

'Yes, but . . .'

'But what? Rupert, don't look like that, it's not so very dreadful. Or was it?'

'No, of course it wasn't. It was lovely . . .'

*   *   *

It had all been so totally unexpected. They had had supper and finished one bottle of wine and she had felt suddenly better, braver about Bertie, more hopeful about Edward. 'I think,' she had said, 'perhaps we should have another of those. In fact, why not some champagne? So we can toast the

394

future. Whatever that might hold.'

'All right,' he had said, 'and then I must go.'

'I wish you wouldn't. You're making me feel so much better. And it's getting awfully late.'

'Well, we'll see,' he had said.

There was a bottle of champagne, but not in the fridge. It wasn't cold enough and it was too sweet, not sufficiently sparkly. Cassia drank a glassful, failed to enjoy it, drank another and felt her own temporarily high spirits go as flat. She sighed. 'Oh, Rupert. I feel so . . . so sad.'

'Poor darling.'

'No, I don't deserve any sympathy. It's all my own fault. I pushed Edward out, don't you see, I got that money, that wretched money. I must talk to you about that, Rupert, as well, there's something . . . Well, anyway, I got it and I started spending it in my own way, doing what I wanted. I didn't share it with him, not as I should have done. I took this house, that was a terrible thing to do. I didn't need it at all. But I'd found out he'd taken on that awful Maureen, when he knew I wanted to work with him one day, and I did it as revenge, to get back at him.'

'Well, he should have considered you more.'

'Rupert, don't make excuses for me. And the car, I bought exactly the sort of car I knew would make him angry—flashy, obvious—and I started seeing all of you again, in London.'

'Cassia, we're your friends, of course you should see us, he had no right to stop you.'

'He didn't stop me, he just wasn't comfortable with you, don't you see? He's shy, awkward with people, especially . . . well, especially rich people, he can't help it. I've estranged him absolutely, refused to go to Glasgow with him—'

'He should never have asked you to do that.'

'Why not? Don't answer, I know what you're going to say, and it's not true. I should have gone. And now this minute Bertie, poor little fragile Bertie, is lying in some cold, horrible bed, far away from me, and it's only happened because I've been so selfish, so thoughtless.' She was crying now, tears streaming down her face.

'Cassia, you're talking nonsense. Come over here, and have a cuddle.'

A cuddle: that was a safe word, a nice safe thought, cosy, unsexy. She joined him on the sofa, crawled into his arms, lay with her head on his chest, hiccuping gently. 'I'm sorry, Rupert.'

'Don't be sorry. It's sweet you're so remorseful. But quite unnecessary. For seven years, you had none of your own way. You lived with Edward, doing your wifely duty, gave up all your hopes for yourself, all your ambitions—'

'I had to marry him! You know I did. I was pregnant. And you said at the time, when I asked you—'

'Yes,' he said, very quietly, 'I know what I said. And I feel a heavy burden of guilt about everything that's happened to you since.'

'Good heavens! Have you really?' She sat back staring at him; her face was tear stained, her hair ruffled.

'You look about fifteen years old,' he said simply.

'I was fifteen when I first met you.'

'And I was an old man of forty something,' he said with a sigh.

'I thought you were the most handsome, the

396

most dashing thing I had ever seen.'

'Yes, I know you did. And I took the most appalling advantage of it.'

'Rupert, you didn't. I wanted you to, my God, I did, but would you? I remember kissing you on the train—it set the standard for all the kissing I did for years. And no one ever came up to it.'

'No one?'

'No.' She flushed. 'And now I've just wrecked everything. Everyone's lives that I care about.' She had started crying again. 'Oh, Rupert. Do you think I'm very wicked?'

'No,' he said, and meant it, 'I think you're rather good.'

'Good! That sounds so boring.' She took another swig of the flat champagne. 'I do feel rather drunk suddenly, though. It's all the emotion, I suppose. So, darling Rupert, my lovely dashing love from the past, do you think I'm boring?'

'No,' he said, and suddenly common sense was gone, caution was gone and all he knew was that he wanted her, fiercely and ferociously, as he had once, many times, had denied as many times. He looked at her, at those large, dark blue eyes, wet with tears, at her mouth, that full, sensuous mouth that he had once so long ago kissed and he needed, more than he had ever needed anything, to make himself her love now, to feel young again, wanted again . . .

He had intended just to kiss her, quite briefly, but her response was so lovely, startled for a moment, then so warm, so tender, so deeply sensuous, that he could not stop.

He went on, and the warmth became heat, their mouths harder, their tenderness sharply and

397

dangerously desire. He moved one hand, felt for her breast; beneath her silk blouse, her thin chemise, the nipple was outlined, firm, erect; he felt her moving against him, closer now, determined almost, felt his own response, knew he must stop, must not, could not go on—and went on.

It was very lovely: she was at first tender, sweetly welcoming; became greedier, more passionate. He entered her quickly, the danger driving him; she began to move beneath, against him, he followed her, sensing a nervousness, an anxiousness almost. He felt her begin to rise, to climb to her climax quite swiftly; she was still suddenly then; he waited, and quite soon after that she did come, her body arched, he felt her spasms, heard her gasps, then her groans, and then as she eased, stilled, and his own climax began, her sigh. And then it was over: their sweetly gentle, deadly dangerous act, and he thought as he lay there, holding her, feeling her, smelling her, that they had truly found themselves in a new country, new territory, and could not decide whether they had left or entered Eden.

*   *   *

Mrs Forbes went up the stairs to Cecily's room. She was beginning to dread these encounters. Cecily would turn her head and look at her, then return to her habitual pose, staring out of the window, with dull, glazed eyes. She had not eaten or left her bed, except to have it changed and to allow Susan to help her wash, for over a week. Even when she did that, she clung to one of her pillows as if it were a child, refusing to surrender it; it was becoming grubby, but she would not have the slip changed. She no longer wailed, or even cried; she just lay there.

'Good morning, dear!' Ada Forbes still managed, with a great effort, to sound cheerful and positive; nobody seemed to understand what a great effort she was making both with Cecily and Fanny. It really was a little unfair. Still, she had to struggle on for both their sakes. 'Such a lovely one, here, let's open the curtains a bit wider, maybe even the window. How are you today? Have you got a smile for Mother? Come along, dear, just a little one. No? All right, then.' She sat down in her chair by the bed, and smiled even more brightly. 'Now Dr Rushton is coming this morning, and I do want you to make an effort for him. Otherwise, I'm afraid, dear, you may have to go to a nursing home. That won't be nice, will it?'

Cecily stared at her briefly, then turned her attention back to the bed-hangings over her head. Ada felt a stab of violent irritation.

'Cecily, dear, I do think you might make a little effort. We all have to endure things, you know, I certainly have in my time, and it's no use just giving in. It's selfish and very immature. Now come along, dear, do try to be a little bit more positive. Here, let me sit you up higher, and maybe I could brush your hair, it really does need washing, Cecily, I've always told you not to let your personal standards drop, it's the beginning of the end, standards, keeping up appearances is everything, in my personal opinion, it really is, and . . .'

At this point, as she explained to Dr Rushton, Cecily suddenly opened her mouth and started screaming again, 'and hitting me, with her fists, it

399

was actually quite painful. I really can't be expected to put up with this sort of thing, none of us can.'

Dr Rushton agreed, sedated Cecily and telephoned the nursing home in Richmond, saying that she would be arriving by lunchtime and that he was arranging for a private ambulance to bring her.

*　　*　　*

When Cecily had gone, Ada stood in Cecily's room, weeping quietly.

She rang for Susan. 'This bed should be changed again, Susan, and particularly this pillow. Take it.'

'Yes, madam. Oh, there's a letter here, tucked inside it, look, addressed to Mrs Harrington. I wonder if—'

'I will take that, Susan, thank you. And deal with it appropriately. Thank you, you may finish now.'

*　　*　　*

Later that afternoon, Dominic Foster received a phone call from a Mrs Ada Forbes, who told him she would like to come and see him. She added that she was Mrs Benedict Harrington's mother, and that her daughter had been removed by ambulance only that morning to a nursing home.

'As you were such a close friend of my son-in-law's, or so I gathered from your letter, I expect you might like to send her some flowers, so I will give you the address.' Dominic took it down meekly and arranged to see Mrs Forbes the following day.

*　　*　　*

Florence knocked at her mistress's door. 'Excuse me, madam, Mrs Fallon is downstairs. She'd like to see you. I explained you weren't well, madam; but—'

'Oh, I really can't—Well, maybe. All right, Florence, ask her to come up. Bring a tray of tea, would you, for two.'

'Hello,' she said listlessly to Cassia, as she entered the room. 'I'm not very good company, I'm afraid.'

'Edwina, I don't care. I'm not here for company.' She was looking very pretty, Edwina thought detachedly, it really had done a lot for her, getting that money. 'What's the matter, same old thing?'

Edwina nodded. 'It really is pretty bad.' She turned in the bed, winced. Cassia looked at her sharply. 'Edwina, have you told your own doctor about this?'

'Well, yes, of course I have.'

'And what does he say?'

'That it'll improve when I have a baby.' She laughed shortly. 'That's a joke.'

'Why is it a joke?'

'Oh, doesn't matter. Christ, I feel awful. Sit down, Cassia. I only came to see you because I thought you might have the name of someone I might see.'

'Yes, I have now. I'm sorry I've been so long about it. A wonderful woman called—'

'Oh, I can't go to a woman doctor,' said Edwina.

'Why on earth not?'

'Because Harry doesn't believe in women doctors.'

'Well, that's very enlightened of him,' said Cassia coolly. 'I can't wait to ask him why not.'

401

'Yes, well, I can't help what he thinks. The point is, I've got to see someone to shut him up. Otherwise Oh God . . .' A knife-edge of pain shot through her. The combination of the pain and her misery at what she had to keep from Harry, what he was going to say when he finally found out, brought her very uncharacteristically to the edge of tears; she reached for a hanky, wiped her eyes. 'Sorry.'

'Edwina, this is not right. Honestly. Would you mind if I had a look?'

Edwina submitted herself to Cassia's attentions resignedly.

'That hurt there?' Cassia pressed gently. It did: horribly. 'Edwina, I think you've got an ovarian cyst. I can't imagine how your doctor could have missed it. Did you describe all these symptoms?'

'No,' said Edwina. 'It didn't seem very important.'

'Well, it was very silly of you,' said Cassia briskly. 'But he should have examined you. It's quite obvious to me, the pain, the swelling—'

'Oh, don't start a medical lecture, for God's sake. I don't need it. Anyway, what is an ovarian cyst?'

'It's a growth on the ovary. Usually harmless, but horribly painful, and can cause all these problems you've been having. Anyway, it ought to be removed, and all these awful symptoms will stop. I really can't believe no one's spotted it. Have you ever seen a gynaecologist about—well, about anything? In the past year, I mean.'

'No,' said Edwina firmly.

'Well, you must. Go and see this woman, please, she's awfully good. Or if it must be a man, there's

402

Mr Amstruther at St Christopher's. He has rooms in Harley Street. But he's a bit of a bully.'

Edwina hesitated, then she said, 'Oh, to hell with Harry. Yes, all right, arrange it will you? Er, Cassia . . .'

'Yes?'

'Could one of these cysts stop you getting pregnant?'

'It could certainly lessen the probability. Why?'

'It's the last thing I actually want, it's just that I suppose I've got to think about it one day, that's all.'

'Well, you can talk to Miss Gerard about it. Now look, put that hot-water bottle back on your tummy and have some nice hot tea. I'll ring Miss Gerard straight away, shall I? When could you go, next week some time?'

Cassia stood at the telephone by Edwina's bed, waiting to be put through to Miss Gerard's secretary, and smiled down at Edwina. She really did look very good, Edwina thought, glancing at her own haggard reflection in her mirror; better than she'd looked for years, and it wasn't just the clothes. She looked really young and sort of lit up. A bit as if she was in love, or at least having a really good affair: now there was a thought. She certainly deserved it, after all those years with that dreary husband of hers. Well, perhaps her half-joking remarks about Rupert were accurate . . .

*　　　*　　　*

Fanny lay on her bed motionless, face down, willing some kind of unconsciousness to come over her. It did not. All she felt was a terrible gnawing remorse, even worse than the gnawing hunger pangs. The door opened and Nanny came in. 'Just go away.'

'Fanny, listen to me. Please. You really must try and eat something. You're making yourself ill, and Dr Rushton says—'

'I don't care what Dr Rushton says. I don't care what anyone says. Go away, Nanny, please.'

She heard Nanny sigh as she closed the door; she didn't want to be unkind to her, but really nobody could help. Her mother had killed her father—or certainly caused his death—and now she had killed her mother. She had to die herself, that was only fair.

*   *   *

'Right, Fallon. In you come.'

Bertie stood in the doorway of the lavatory. He was shaking with terror.

'Ah, look, Mummy's poor little baby boy is frightened. Is he missing Mummy, then? We did hear he was crying in bed last night.'

'I wasn't,' said Bertie, staunchly.

'Course you were. Pathetic little squirt. Anyway, we've got a cure for crying, haven't we? Every time you cry we're going to do this to you.'

'What?'

'This,' said Collins, the biggest boy. 'Come here, squirt, bend over. Right, now put your head into the bog.'

'No,' said Bertie, 'I won't. It's disgusting.'

'Go on!' Collins pushed his head in, until his forehead and his nose were submerged in the water; he struggled, but it was no use, they simply pushed harder. 'Right,' said Collins, 'pull, Parkins.'

There was a rushing sound, a terrifying pressure up Bertie's nose, as Parkins pulled the chain and the water flooded into the lavatory pan. For what seemed an eternity they held him there, then as the water slowly ebbed away, they released him. He came up gasping and fighting for breath, shrank against the wall of the lavatory.

'He's going to cry, I think,' said Collins, 'poor diddums. I hope he won't cry tonight, don't you, Parks?'

'Oh, I certainly do,' said Parkins.

'Otherwise we'll have to do it again. Only next time, Mummy's boy, we won't clean the bog first. We'll find one with some shit in it. Or maybe we'll make you shit first. Wouldn't be difficult, pathetic little squirt like you.'

'Collins! Parkins! Matron's coming.'

'Quick,' said Collins, disappearing into the lavatory, 'And you, Parks. And don't you say a word,' he said to Bertie, 'or you'll be really sorry. Not just a bit sorry, like you are now.'

*   *   *

That Friday, Cassia went to have tea with Miss Monkton.

The village in which Miss Monkton lived was near Petworth, less than forty minutes away, but it was an Indian summer's day and the roads were hot and dusty. Cassia nearly hit a cyclist coming in the other direction: she would have to be more careful, concentrate a bit harder. She was finding it hard to concentrate on anything at the moment, ever since Tuesday night; the memories and implications of it, both good and bad, obsessed her.

For about twenty-four hours she had felt wonderful: sweetly happy, for the first time for years. And then reality had hit her, and with reality guilt and fear.

The only thing she was sure about was that she and Rupert had done something extremely dangerous and that life could never be the same again. The fact that it had been, at the time, very pleasurable, had seemed, had been indeed, absolutely irresistible, had nothing to do with the implications, which were terrifying.

In the first place, she was not in love with Rupert now, and she knew she was not. Oh God, she thought closing her eyes briefly in anguish, she loved being with him, still found him attractive, still adored him even; but she was not in love with him.

He was her confidant, her best friend, the person with whom she felt, probably, happiest in the world: but his place in her life was not as her lover. And she simply did not know what to do about it: neither of them did. The worst thing of all about it, she thought fretfully, was that because of what had happened, she had lost her best friend.

And if Edward even suspected what had happened, he was quite likely to insist on a divorce, on taking the children away.

No, thought Cassia, trying and failing to crush the panic, her whole life was threatened by this awful, reckless, stupid thing; she still found it hard to believe she had done it. Or that Rupert had done it, given what he had told her about all the snippets of gossip he was hearing about the two of them.

For the first time she felt she could agree with Rupert, when he had embarked on his routine of self-flagellation, started saying how he should have been shot, strung up, whipped. He should. But Rupert was helplessly, hopelessly fragile where sexual temptation was concerned; she knew that as well as anyone. It was actually part of his charm, his rueful, irresponsible, little-boy charm.

That apart, she should have known better, she was the sensible one; but she had been so low, so miserable about Bertie, so in despair about her marriage—and yes, all right, so sexually hungry. Being suddenly confronted with the temptation of Rupert was like being offered some succulent meal after a long period on bread and water.

'So what happened to self-control, Cassia?' she said aloud, drumming her hands on the steering wheel; and then realised she had arrived at Miss Monkton's cottage and that for a while at least she would have to stop thinking about the hideous tangled mess she had got herself into.

The cottage, as she would have expected, was not pretty and the path from the gate to the door was ramrod straight. Miss Monkton appeared at the slate-grey door.

'How nice to see you, Mrs Fallon.' She seemed much the same, the hair perhaps a little thinner, the hands just slightly more clawlike, and she was even wearing a dress that Cassia remembered, droopier and shabbier than ever, in black wool, with a lace collar and cuffs.

They went into the front room; it smelt appallingly stuffy, and was rather sparsely furnished. There were at least three fly papers, all covered with very dead flies, and several rather dismal pictures showing wildlife in various stages of death and decay.

'Now do sit down, Mrs Fallon. Perhaps you'd like a barley sugar sweet, so refreshing, I always think.'

'Oh, thank you,' said Cassia, who was longing for a cup of tea, 'that would be very nice. Er, I expect you saw in the paper that Mr Harrington had died.'

'I did, poor soul. I could only think how thankful I was that Lady Beatty had not been alive to see that. It would have broken her heart. So sad, the pair of them gone. Mrs Harrington must be very upset.'

'Yes, indeed, and the children, of course.'

'I was so sorry not to have come to Lady Beatty's memorial service,' Miss Monkton said. 'Mr Harrington did invite me, but I have very bad arthritis these days and there is no train station for many miles.'

There was a long silence, then Cassia said, 'We live not far from here, you know. Near Haywards Heath. My husband is a doctor.'

'Yes; I had heard that. It must be wonderful, I think, to be a doctor, to be able to heal the sick. You never completed your own studies, I presume?'

'Oh, yes,' said Cassia, 'but I didn't practise. I married Edward and the children came along.'

'A pity that,' said Miss Monkton, surprising her. 'I would like to see more women in the professions myself. I wanted to be a nurse, you know, but my poor father could not afford the training. I had to go straight into my work as a governess, after I had left school.'

'What a shame,' said Cassia, 'which reminds me, Miss Monkton; one of the reasons I wanted to come and see you was so that I could thank you personally for going to visit Leonora in Paris.

When she was ill. I know she was well looked after, of course, but it must have been wonderful for her to see someone from home. Something of a daunting journey for you, I would imagine.'

'Not really,' said Miss Monkton, surprising her again. 'I had been several times before. You shouldn't assume that just because I am an impoverished and unmarried Englishwoman, I have never set foot outside these shores.'

'Miss Monkton, of course I didn't think that,' said Cassia, flushing, feeling foolish.

'I worked for a diplomatic family, when I was much younger, and we spent some time in Paris. And I had a cousin who lived there permanently. She is now deceased, very sadly. I used to visit her every two years or so. I know the place quite well.'

'Yes, I see,' said Cassia. It was hard to imagine anyone less like a practised visitor to Paris than Miss Monkton.

'So when I knew that Lady Beatty was there, I naturally went to visit her. I was fond of her. And very relieved, of course, that I did go. Considering the circumstances in which she was living.'

'What circumstances?'

'Well, Mrs Fallon—oh dear, she would have hated you to know, but I suppose now that she has passed away, it doesn't matter. It was after Mr Gresham had left. She was in serious difficulties. And not well. Anyone could see she was not well, although she sought to hide it from me at first.'

'You mean she was hard up?'

'Extremely hard up, Mrs Fallon. Living quite alone, in a very modest place. I only discovered this from visiting her at the old address, near the Arc de Triomphe, when I was redirected.'

'And when was this?'

'It was January 1935. It was bitterly cold and wet, which made Lady Beatty's situation worse. The apartment was cold and—'

'Miss Monkton, how long had she been there?' The panic over Rupert was nothing compared to this.

'Oh, only a few weeks, she told me. "Purely temporary, this is, Miss Monkton," was what she said. "Just till I get back on my feet."'

'But didn't Mr Gresham—I mean . . .'

'Mr Gresham was living abroad by then, I believe, possibly in Cairo.'

'Yes, actually, I have a poste restante address for him in Cairo, but I don't know if he's still there. I knew he'd gone, but I thought he left her well provided for.'

'I'm very much afraid he lacked the wherewithal to do that. Mr Gresham had also become rather hard up.'

'But how could he have been? He was so extremely rich.'

'As I understand it, he had the same . . . what shall we say . . . affliction as Lady Beatty. He gambled, relentlessly. He had lost almost everything, I believe. They had been reduced to considerably straitened circumstances; Mrs Fallon, considerably.'

'Oh God!' It was the heat in the room, of course, the stuffiness, the hideous fly papers that had made her feel so light headed, was making the floor heave slightly under her feet, not what Miss Monkton was saying, not what it meant.

'Mrs Fallon, are you all right, do you feel faint? Here, put your head between your knees.'

Cassia felt her cold, clawlike hands on her neck, forcing it downwards; it added to her sense of nightmare. She struggled against it, against the hand, the nightmare, then said, 'I'm sorry, Miss Monkton, I must have some fresh air.'

Cassia stood up, went out of the cottage door, sank down on the dried-up lawn. It was warm out there, she could feel the sun on her face again, hear the reassuring sounds of a car driving down the lane, cows mooing, birds in the hedge, a lawnmower in the next-door garden. Gradually the nausea, the faintness, eased. She sat back, took a deep breath and managed to smile at Miss Monkton, who had followed her.

'So sorry, Miss Monkton, to have worried you.'

Later, she learned a little more: that Miss Monkton, distressed at what she had found, seeing Leonora clearly ill, had urged her to seek help.

'What sort of ill, Miss Monkton?'

Miss Monkton flushed. 'Her illness was of a . . . a female nature, Mrs Fallon.'

'Yes, I see. Did she tell you that?'

'Er, yes. And there was some evidence of it, in the bathroom, a pile of laundry . . . oh dear.'

'You mean she was bleeding a lot?'

'Yes,' whispered Miss Monkton. 'She said it was—well, her age, you know, nothing to worry about. I begged her to see a doctor and she said she couldn't afford it, that it wasn't necessary.'

'Did you tell anyone?'

'She made me promise not to tell any of you about any of it. "Death rather than dishonour, Miss Monkton," she said, quite gaily. She was very brave. I said I wouldn't and I kept my word. I bought her a few things I thought might help her,

411

some patent medicines, and so on, but I did tell my cousin in Paris, said it was quite desperate. She contacted her own doctor and he apparently went to see her. And quite shortly after that, I got a letter from Lady Beatty, from quite a different address, really a very nice district, the sixteenth arrondissement, near Passy, saying that she was fine, feeling much better, that an old friend had turned up and lent her some money and thanking me for my help . . .'

Cassia drove home, feeling a weight occupying the area somewhere between her head and her heart, that had nothing to do with Bertie, with Edward, not even with Rupert; she could not analyse precisely what it was, but she did know that it contained a very large element of fear.

CHAPTER TWENTY-THREE

'So how well exactly did you know my son-in-law, Mr Foster?' Ada Forbes's expression was rather stern.

'Oh,' said Dominic Foster, tempted wildly, just for a moment, to tell her exactly, 'pretty well. We worked together, but we were friends as well.'

'Quite. Well, it was tragic. Tragic. And my daughter is absolutely devastated. She's had a complete nervous collapse, you know, is under permanent sedation for the time being, in a nursing home. And the children . . . well—one of them in particular—quite distraught. Poor little thing, refusing to eat, there is quite a lot of concern about her.'

'Oh, God.' He felt a stab of pure, stark remorse. 'Fanny?'

'Yes. She was his favourite.'

'Yes, I know. He told me.'

'How extraordinary. You really must have been very good friends.'

'Yes, we were. Which is why—why I wanted so very much to see your daughter. As I said in my letter. You see, we had talked a great deal, Benedict and I, the last few days before he died. I wanted to tell her about it. I thought it might help. That's all.'

'That is quite out of the question as she is so very ill. Are you—' she leant forward—'are you saying you think you might know why he did it?'

Dominic said simply, 'Yes.'

'I see.' She was clearly desperate to ask him more; he sat, firmly silent. 'Well, all I can do is to tell my daughter, when she is better, what you have told me, ask her if you may go and see her.'

'Yes of course, what I have to tell her may help her a little. Even now.'

'Well, I think we are going to have to live with that, don't you? She is certainly far from reach to both of us at the moment. Poor soul.' She dabbed her eyes, then smiled rather weakly at him. 'Well, I must be going now, Mr Foster. I will certainly pass your message on to my daughter. Good afternoon.'

He saw her out of the office and then went back and sat for a long time, staring into the space which she had occupied, thinking of Benedict, seeing him again, his tall, languid grace, his sudden brilliant smile, hearing his voice, easy, amused, amusing— and hearing his own, heavy, wretched, that dreadful night, telling him what he had decided, telling him

413

the one thing that, clearly, Benedict had not been able to bear.

*   *   *

Cassia sat with her arms round Fanny, holding the pathetically thin little body, feeling the great sobs wrack through it. She was actually on her way to see Harry Moreton in his office, but having heard Cecily had been admitted to a nursing home, had decided to visit the house and see how the children were.

Adams had welcomed her in, almost effusively, Susan practically fell into her arms, saying, 'Oh, madam, I'm so pleased to see you,' and Nanny came running down the stairs and ushered her into the morning room, telling her she had never been more relieved to see anyone in her life.

'I did think of telephoning you, madam, but Mrs Forbes was against it. She feels she is the best person to cope, and of course she must be, but—'

'Cope with what, Nanny? The children, I suppose?'

'It's Fanny, she is totally withdrawn, won't speak to any of us, and is refusing to eat.'

'Refusing to eat! How long for?'

'Well, she's had precious little since Mr Harrington died, but since her mother had her breakdown, nothing. Dr Rushton is in despair, says we shall have to force-feed her soon—'

'Surely not. Where is she? Do you think she'd see me?'

'I really don't know, madam. She won't see her grandmother, that's for sure.'

'Go and tell her I'm here and I'd really like to

414

see her. Tell her Bertie's gone away to school and I'm really missing him and seeing her would cheer me up.'

Five minutes later, there was a gentle knock at the door and Fanny stood there. Cassia was shocked. She wasn't just thin, she was emaciated. Her little face was waxy pale, her brown eyes huge and dark shadowed; her dress hung loosely about her, her legs, in their black stockings, stick thin.

'Hello, Fanny,' she said, hoping her shock didn't show on her face, 'how are you?'

'All right,' said Fanny, and then half ran across the room, and fell into Cassia's arms, crying.

'Promise,' she said through chattering teeth— she was very cold, Cassia noticed—'promise you won't mention food.'

'I promise. Why should I anyway?'

Fanny looked at her, and her eyes were very sharp. 'Don't be silly, Cassia. You know why.'

'Sorry. Yes, I do. But I promise I won't. What's the matter?'

'I—I made Mama ill. That day. It was my fault. And now she's going to die, and—'

'Fanny, who told you she was going to die?'

'She did.'

'Fanny, are you sure?'

'Yes. Quite sure. I heard her, I was there. And it was my fault. You see, I gave her a letter. I saw it lying on the table and Stephanie said should she take it up to her, and Nanny said no, Mama was still asleep, she was very tired, and she needed lots of rest, because she was so upset. And I thought that was silly. Because she wasn't upset. She was perfectly all right, she didn't care about Papa dying at all, she hadn't even cried.' She stopped.

415

Cassia took a deep breath. 'Fanny, sometimes people are too unhappy to cry. I felt like that when my mother died. Did you know my mother died when I was only a little bit older than you?'

'No,' said Fanny, 'I didn't.' She nestled closer to Cassia, sensing sympathy, understanding.

'She died, having a baby. The baby died too. And I couldn't cry, just couldn't. I stood there looking at her, and I couldn't cry, it was too awful, too sad. And I know your mama was terribly unhappy about your father dying.'

'No she wasn't. It wasn't like you—I can imagine that, I felt like that about Papa for a while—but Mama was happy about it, always on the phone, laughing with her friends. Don't tell me she was unhappy, she wasn't.'

'All right.'

'So I took the letter up, and she was sitting in her bed, reading a magazine. And she smiled and held out her hand and I knew she wanted to kiss me, and I—I threw the letter at her and said, "This came for you," and stood watching her. And she looked at it for a long time, and then she said, "I don't think I want to read this now," and I said, "Well, I'm going to read it to you, then". I picked it up and she snatched it from me and I tried to get it back and then I said go on, open it, and she did, very slowly, and read it a bit: and then she suddenly started screaming and screaming, it was so horrible, she went all stiff, and I went over to her bed and said, "What's the matter, what does it say?" and tried to get it again, and she said, "You can't have it, you can't, you should never have brought it," and then she said, "This is going to kill me," and she started screaming again. Then they all came

416

and—and then . . .' The sobs were racking her again, the skinny little body convulsed.

'Shush, Fanny, it's all right.'

'It's not all right. If I hadn't brought the letter, and made her read it, she wouldn't have done that, she'd have gone on being happy. And now she's going to die.'

'Fanny, your mother is not going to die. You've got to believe that.'

'Well, what did she mean?'

'Darling, I don't know, but it wasn't what you thought, I promise you. People say all sorts of dreadful things when they're upset. I spoke to Dr Rushton this morning and he said she's had something called a nervous breakdown. Nobody ever died of that. She will be in the nursing home for a long time, but she is very slowly getting better.'

Fanny looked up at her. 'Is that really true?'

'It's really true.'

Fanny got off her knee, went over to the bookshelf. 'What are you doing, Fanny?'

'I'm getting the Bible. I want you to swear on it.'

Cassia sat there, her hand on the Bible, and swore that what she had told Fanny was true.

'Thank you,' said Fanny. She took a deep breath. 'Don't take your hand off yet. Did you really want to see me because you were missing Bertie? Not because they told you about me not . . . not eating?'

'No,' said Cassia, smiling at her, her heart lifting at the sight of a small upturn at the corners of Fanny's pretty little mouth, 'no, I'm afraid that wasn't quite true. I was worried about you, but I am missing Bertie terribly and so is William. I tell you what, if your grandmama agrees, how would you

417

like to come and stay with us for a few days?'

'Oh,' said Fanny, her voice resonant with longing, 'oh, Cassia, I'd *love* it.'

*   *   *

Ada Forbes was initially resistant to the idea. She owed it to her daughter, she explained to Cassia, to run the household and care for the children, indeed she had promised her that, even as Cecily was being lifted into the ambulance. Handing over Fanny, hugely agreeable as the prospect seemed, was not quite part of that agreement. 'I'm not at all sure that would be best,' she said. 'This absurd refusal to eat, we have to overcome that. I certainly don't like the idea of her being away from Dr Rushton, and—'

'My husband is a doctor,' said Cassia carefully, 'so she could still receive medical attention if necessary, and—' inspiration came to her: inspiration and the memory of Mrs Forbes's frequently expressed view that London was no place for children to grow up—'the country air would surely do Fanny good. London is not healthy, and at the moment it can't be helping.'

She watched Mrs Forbes accepting this with patent relief. 'Well, that is certainly true,' she said. 'Well, perhaps it would be a good idea. I really do feel I need the break. I have slaved for this family over the past few weeks, literally slaved, and had no thanks for it. Yes, I think I might accept your offer. Providing Dr Rushton agrees, of course. Thank you, Mrs Fallon, it's very good of you.'

'Not at all. I'm terribly fond of Fanny. Er, Mrs Forbes, Fanny mentioned some letter that had

418

upset her mother. Do you know of any such thing?'

'No,' said Ada firmly, 'I don't. I have checked through all my daughter's correspondence, each day, and I have seen nothing that could remotely be described as distressing, I assure you.' It was one thing having Mrs Fallon become involved in Fanny's care; quite another in her daughter's affairs.

*   *   *

Cassia was late for her appointment with Harry. He was clearly in a very bad temper when his secretary showed her into his office.

'You're very late,' he said.

'And I'm sorry. I went to visit Cecily's children—Fanny isn't at all well.'

'Poor little thing,' he said, surprising her. 'What's wrong? Apart from what amounts to losing both her parents.'

'She isn't eating,' said Cassia, 'or sleeping properly. Anyway, she's coming to stay with us for a few days.'

'How nice for her. How very good of you.' He looked at her again with something close to distaste.

His secretary, Miss Murray, came in with a tray of coffee and biscuits. Cassia accepted the coffee, waved away the biscuits, took a sip, and then said, 'Harry, is something the matter?'

'No, not really.' He made an obvious effort to be more friendly. 'I hear you've kindly arranged for Edwina to see some woman doctor.'

'Yes, Monica Gerard, she's a very fine surgeon and gynaecologist.'

'Well, as long as she can sort Edwina out. I obviously wouldn't have chosen a woman myself, but—'

'Yes, Edwina said you had some strange prejudice against women doctors.'

'No, no, of course not,' he said. 'It's just that—'

'You think men are likely to be better. Really, Harry, I'm surprised you don't employ a male secretary.'

'Oh, that's quite different,' he said, grinning. 'Secretaries play a supportive role. One women are better suited to. No, Cassia, I do assure you I have no quarrel with women having careers. I think it's splendid. In theory.'

She sighed. 'Well, anyway, I think Edwina does have a problem, but it's hopefully not very serious. I only wish she'd seen a gynaecologist before.'

'Yes, well, she didn't. Now what can I do for you? I really haven't got very long.'

'Yes. Yes, of course.' She took another sip of the coffee; it was very strong, but delicious. It would be: Harry was notoriously fussy about coffee, it had to be freshly ground, very strong, very hot. He was fussy about most things; Edwina's life couldn't be easy.

'Harry,' she said, fixing her eyes on his face, 'I'm sure you told me Rollo left Leonora well provided for.'

His dark eyes did not even flicker. 'I did indeed tell you that, because it was patently true. When Leonora died, she was living in a luxurious apartment in Paris, cared for by highly qualified staff, and with an extremely expensive specialist overseeing her case.'

'I went to see Miss Monkton the other day,' she

420

said.

'Oh, the Monk. Yes. Why on earth did you go and see her?'

'Because Richard told me that she'd been to see Leonora in Paris. I was very surprised, because I thought she disapproved of Leonora so much, but he said she had been very kind to her. So I wanted to thank her. Anyway, she said that . . . she said that Rollo was very hard up. That they had lost almost everything. He had left Leonora and she was living in very modest circumstances indeed.'

'Oh no,' he said lightly. 'Modest perhaps, compared to Miss Monkton's view of her London home, but—'

'Harry, she was living in poverty. That was Miss Monkton's word. All alone. And ill. Unable to pay for treatment.'

He did not move, did not seem in any way discomfited; he seemed completely relaxed, even mildly amused. 'Well,' he said finally, 'and then what happened? How was it, do you think, that by the next time I saw her, Leonora had come to be living in such pleasant and agreeable circumstances?'

'I don't know, Harry. Leonora told Miss Monkton that an old friend had turned up and lent her some money.'

'Well, there you are, then.'

'No, if the money was only lent, that wouldn't explain the luxury, as you put it. She wouldn't have spent a great deal of it, would she?'

'No. Possibly not. But then Gresham came back to her. Even he had some conscience. And I really cannot accept that he was penniless; it's absolutely inconceivable he had lost the lot. Look,' he said

421

suddenly, 'why don't you come out with it, ask me what you really want to know. I loathe prevarication. Otherwise, I really don't have time for all this.'

Aware that she was still avoiding the real issue, her real fear, she said, 'It's just that I thought she would have told you everything that had happened.'

'Cassia, you must know that people are not entirely lucid when they are dying. Especially when they are heavily drugged with morphine, surrounded by large numbers of medical staff.'

'No, I realise that. But—' She stopped again.

'But what, Cassia?'

'Well, what about the money she left me? It was an awful lot, Harry. Surely if she'd been desperate she'd have spent some of it on herself.'

'Oh, Cassia, for heaven's sake. The money she left you was in trust. Have you no idea how hard it is to break a trust? That's the whole point of the things.'

'What about the interest? Mr Brewster said she was getting that—'

'And no doubt seeing it off at high speed.'

She sat staring at him, cursing his ability to unsettle her, make her angry, lead her into a tortuous maze of inconsequential argument.

'Look, Cassia,' he said, 'I don't quite know what you're trying to prove, but whatever it is, I don't think I can be of any use to you. I'm sorry.'

'You could be of use to me,' she said, taking a deep breath, 'if you told me the truth.'

'And which particular bit of that rather dubious commodity would you like? Perhaps you'd tell me.'

'All right. Did you know Leonora was living

422

there, did you rescue her from that place, that apartment? The one Miss Monkton found her in? And take her to the other one?' It was the most she dared to ask him, the rest was too dark, too dangerous even to reflect upon in that moment.

He looked at her, and his dark eyes were thoughtful. It was very quiet in the room, and utterly still; she could hear the clock ticking, even the creak of the radiators. Then he pushed back his chair and said, 'No, Cassia, I did not. Will that do for you? Now then, perhaps you'll be kind enough to leave this whole matter alone, and let me get on with some work.'

She stood up, afraid of asking more, afraid of not asking more. Finally she said, 'Thank you very much for seeing me, Harry. For your time.'

'That's all right,' he said, 'but I do wish you'd stop all this nonsense, just let things rest.'

*   *   *

Walking down the street away from him, in the confused state of sexual tension and emotional outrage he always seemed able to arouse in her, she knew she had learnt absolutely nothing, gained precisely no ground, indeed had quite possibly lost some, for now he was on his guard against her, would be anticipating any future moves. 'Damn,' she said aloud, 'damn damn damn.'

On the other hand, he had never actually lied to her, it was not in the nature of their relationship. Perhaps it was all true, perhaps Miss Monkton had exaggerated, perhaps it had been a temporary problem.

After all, if Rollo Gresham had abandoned her,

423

left her unprovided for, he would hardly have come back. And Harry would hardly have lied about that.

* * *

'Have you seen anyone else about this?' said Miss Gerard.

'No,' said Edwina. 'Well, not recently.' She wasn't sure how much she should confess to this strange, brisk, rather likeable woman.

'Not about the dysmenorrhoea?'

'I'm sorry?'

'The painful periods.'

'No. Well, my GP said that would clear up when I had a baby.'

'A very unrealistic attitude, in my view,' said Miss Gerard coolly. 'Besides, with a cyst such as this, your chances of conceiving would be considerably reduced.'

'Really?' A flood of relief overwhelmed Edwina: here was the explanation that she could offer Harry; not her fault, surely, this time, it couldn't be traced back to her . . . 'And what causes the cysts?'

'We don't quite know. They just happen, some women are more prone to them than others. They are most commonly the result of the egg-producing follicle enlarging and filling with fluid.'

'But not—not an operation of some kind?'

'An operation? Good heavens, no. What sort of operation?' Miss Gerard looked at her, and Edwina could see that she had quite suddenly realised what she was actually talking about.

'Mrs Moreton, if there's anything you want to tell me, you can. It would go no further, ever. A doctor's consulting room is like the confessional.

424

We are bound never to divulge anything that we hear.'

'Oh, no. No, there's nothing.'

'Good. Of course you can always talk to me again, if you have any anxieties. Now then! that cyst must be removed, and the sooner the better. I could fit you in next Friday, or the following Wednesday. Which would suit you better?'

'Oh, Friday, I think. Yes. How long would I be in for?'

'Three or four days. Incidentally, this friend of yours, who spotted the cyst, is she a doctor? Or a nurse?'

'She's a doctor. Well, she trained as a doctor,' said Edwina, 'at St Christopher's.'

'Oh really. What's her name?'

'Cassia Fallon.'

'Well, she obviously knows her stuff. It really isn't that easy to spot, not when comparatively small, as this one is. Tell her from me she's a clever woman. Well, good afternoon, Mrs Moreton. I'll see you next week.'

*　　　*　　　*

Bertie lay weeping in his bed, a sock stuffed in his mouth to muffle the sound, lest anyone should realise and exact retribution for it, and wondering how he was going to endure the five and a half weeks, or forty days, or 960 hours, until he went home for half term, and how even then he was going to manage not to tell his parents and his brother and sister that life at St John's was a painful, wretched, day-by-day torture and that death seemed preferable to spending the next

425

seven years there.

CHAPTER TWENTY-FOUR

'He sounds quite happy,' said Cassia, passing Bertie's letter to Edward over the breakfast table.

'Of course he's happy. Plenty of other boys to play with; all the games he wants, how could he be unhappy?'

'Can I see Bertie's letter?' said Fanny, as Edward left the room.

'Yes, of course, darling.' Cassia smiled at Fanny. After only five days she looked a different child, still very thin, but with some colour in her face and more importantly some life in her eyes.

'Telephone for you Mrs Fallon,' said Peggy, coming in with her tray. 'It's Mr Cameron. Can I clear, please?'

'Yes of course.' She could feel her face burning, absurdly, her heart thudding; any mention of Rupert now filled her with a panic-stricken guilt. 'You children help Peggy, and then, William, we must go to school.'

Rupert wanted her to attend a rehearsal of *Letters*. 'I just haven't quite got it,' he said. 'Please come and watch a rehearsal, let me know honestly what you think. You're a fresh eye. And Jasper would love it, he wants to involve his major backer. Please, darling, do come.'

She hesitated. She had told him several times she thought they should see nothing of one another for the time being, but he had been hurt, upset: 'I will, of course, get some digs for myself, but I can

426

surely go on seeing you. I don't think one indiscretion should wipe out a lifetime's friendship. That would make me very unhappy. Don't you feel my friend any more?'

'Yes, of course I do,' she had said quickly, but it wasn't quite true. The old ease was gone, the happy flirtatious companionship, and with it trust.

Maybe, she thought now, standing there in the hall, maybe through the play they could draw together again, and so she agreed to come.

Besides, she thought as she put the phone down, she wanted to tell him about Miss Monkton, her revelations about Leonora and her situation, Cassia's growing conviction that the money had come from another source—a dreadful, dangerous source . . .

*   *   *

Ever since she had first seen Miss Gerard, Edwina had felt she knew what the word light-headed meant. The thought of being able to tell Harry that she was never going to be able to have children through absolutely no fault of her own was intoxicating; of course he would be disappointed, but he'd get over it and there was absolutely nothing she could do about any of it. She could get on with her life, untroubled by guilt; she had not realised how bad that guilt was, how deep her fear of discovery, until it confronted her.

There was an editorial conference that morning, in Miss Le Page's office. The biannual circulation figures had come in the day before, and *Style*'s had gone down.

'Which means,' Francis Stevenson-Cook, the

publishing director, had told her in his own deceptively languid tones, 'as of course you know, Miss Le Page, that advertising revenue will drop. And after that who knows what will follow it: editors perhaps? Mmm?'

Francis Stevenson-Cook (born Frank Stephens) had risen from the ranks of office boy at *Style* to governing the empire which owned it and its sister magazines *Home Style*, *Wedding Style* and *Country Style*.

He was a bisexual, extremely handsome, and very stylish; it was said that the Prince of Wales himself had on occasions followed his lead. All his suits, superbly tailored, were in shades of grey in varying patterns and tones, all his shirts cream, in finest lawn, or silk; he wore his wavy brown hair a little long, flopping over his brilliant blue eyes, bow ties whenever he felt the occasion would permit it, and carried a silver-topped cane wherever he went.

He admired and appreciated women as much as he did men and had an extraordinarily finely honed instinct as to their taste; no one could spot a trend in a fashion collection, a colour in home furnishings, a concept in a garden, more swiftly and reliably than Francis Stevenson-Cook. He was brilliant, amusing, charming—and absolutely ruthless.

He lived in a flat in Mount Street, refurbished and, to an extent, refurnished in a most lavish style every two years for nothing, by whichever interior designer was most eager to curry his favour. He owned an equally lavish apartment in Paris, threw the most outrageously extravagant parties, and was to be seen around London's smartest restaurants and night-clubs with a procession of beautiful young women.

His sexual proclivities were a most bountiful source of gossip; his butler-cum-secretary, who lived with him and ran his life with steely efficiency, was widely rumoured to be also his boyfriend (a rumour which Stevenson-Cook encouraged in a mixture of mischievousness and pragmatism), but the fact was that that relationship was entirely platonic and he actually had lovers of both sexes. He was not, however, promiscuous (although he encouraged a rumour to that effect also); sex was actually a rather low priority in his life, and he preferred to conserve his considerable energies for his work.

All his editors were terrified of him with the exception of Drusilla, who pronounced him common (a fact which he had once told her he accepted wholeheartedly) and who he in turn recognised as the only member of his staff who was genuinely irreplaceable. Fashion editors came two, or at least one, a penny, as he was fond of saying; a woman who was on first-name terms with almost every titled personage in the land did not.

He was sitting in on the conference that morning, his brilliant eyes moving from face to face as its owner spoke, speaking only occasionally himself, and then to request that he might hear the utterance, whatever it was, again. The explanation given for this was so that he might consider it very carefully; in reality it was to impress upon the speaker that what he had heard was scarcely credible in its crassness.

Camilla Marsden-Rose had just finished describing her main fashion features for February for the second time that morning, in tones rather less firm than usual, when Edwina realised that Francis Stevenson-Cook's eyes were on her; she met them coolly.

'I think we have not been introduced,' said Stevenson-Cook, smiling just very slightly. 'Miss Le Page, could you . . .'

'Yes, of course,' said Miss Le Page, interestingly flustered, Edwina thought. 'This is Edwina Moreton, a recent addition to our staff. Mrs Moreton is in charge of the shopping pages.'

He bowed over his cane to Edwina; she smiled slightly, and inclined her head at him. 'Mrs Moreton,' he said, his eyes on her face rather intently, 'tell me, what in your view is the most important facet of the spring look?'

Edwina hesitated; she knew if she merely echoed Camilla Marsden-Rose she would sound foolish, especially as she did not quite agree with her; but if she did not, then retribution would be exacted for the rest of her stay at *Style*.

Then inspiration came to her. 'Charm,' she said firmly.

'Indeed? And how would you see this quality embodied in the clothes? As described by Mrs Marsden-Rose?'

'Well . . . their essence. Of course in all the fabrics Mrs Marsden-Rose mentioned, the gauzes and organzas and so on, and the more feminine designs, but I think it's also a feeling in the air.'

'Do go on.'

God, what had she let herself in for? She smiled at him very slightly.

'I think women are ready to appear more feminine again, Mr Stevenson-Cook. More what men might like. That's what the new clothes are

430

really all about. It isn't change for change's sake. As Mrs Marsden-Rose said,' she added hastily.

'Well, she didn't quite, but let it pass. Very interesting, don't you think, Miss Le Page?'

'Oh, yes,' said Aurora Le Page. Her voice was very cold.

There was a long silence, then he said, 'I agree with you, Mrs Moreton. I would suggest your pictures get that feeling across, Mrs Marsden-Rose.'

'Well, naturally they will,' snapped Camilla. 'I had every intention of that.'

'Yes, no doubt, but I would have men in at least some of the pictures as well. Being . . . what was the word, Mrs Moreton? Oh, yes, being charmed.'

'But surely, Mr Stevenson-Cook, that could look rather cheap?'

He looked at her distantly, then smiled. 'That must surely depend on how you handle the photographic session. Which is in turn surely your job. Anyway, naturally, this is only a suggestion. The final decision is yours. I would not dream of dictating to you. As you know. Now can we turn our attention to the advertisers? They are going to need considerable pampering in the next six months . . .'

Edwina looked round the room filled with women, absurdly overdressed, or so most people would consider, for an office meeting, several of them in hats, all exquisitely made up, their hair beautifully done, looked again at Stevenson-Cook himself, with his silver-topped cane, his just slightly foppish bow tie, his elegantly autocratic bullying, and thought that for all its absurdity, it made for her a sort of sense. You could not dictate on style if you did not possess it. Francis Stevenson-Cook did not only run a magazine empire, she realised that morning, he was the head of what amounted to a school of style. And she liked that. She liked it very much indeed.

*   *   *

Cecily lay and looked out of the window of her room overlooking Richmond Park.

She wasn't desperate any more, not violently wretched; she was in a condition of heavy, black lethargy, which held her in thrall and from which she could never imagine any kind of release.

She knew that for as long as she lived, she would remember Fanny's little face, angrily hostile as she tried to hold her, comfort her after the funeral, telling her to leave her alone, and knowing why she had said it, knowing she blamed her for Benedict's death—and of course she deserved that blame, she had earned it very well—or Fanny's voice, harsh with rage as she thrust the letter at her, the awful letter, saying, 'Go on, read it, read it.' Fanny would not forgive her; Fanny should not forgive her, and in time Stephanie and even little Laurence would learn what she had done and would not forgive her either.

Her mother's visits were interminable torments, sitting there for as long as she was allowed—mercifully only thirty minutes, during which time Cecily's eyes never left the clock.

The children were not allowed to come, but the little notes and drawings sent by Stephanie were a torture, accentuating as they did the absence of anything similar from Fanny.

Edwina had written, asked if she might come, and Cassia; so, rather to her surprise, had Harry. The nurses read her their letters, in bright, encouraging voices, saying wouldn't it be nice to see them, and she always said no, she didn't think so. And she was tired: she could not sleep without pills, and even then the few hours granted to her were filled with demons, some foul and faceless, some recognisable. Those were the worst: hideous nightmares from which she awoke screaming, to find herself in the soothing, useless arms of the nurses.

She was having various treatments: pointless, exhausting treatments with drugs, with analysis, with sleep therapy. It all seemed absurd, the doctors persisting in their view that there was something wrong with her, while she knew there was nothing, nothing wrong with her at all. It was merely that she had done something utterly terrible, and for the rest of her life she was going to have to live with the fact, and she didn't see how that would be possible.

There was a new treatment being mooted, which frightened her: electric shock treatment. She was not supposed to know about it, but the doctors had discussed it with her mother, who had told Cecily, using the threat as a tool in her own amateur therapy, 'Very effective, but really rather unpleasant, dear, I believe. Now if you could only pull yourself together, get home, take up your responsibilities to your family, who do need you, then it would be far, far better for all of us, especially me. It's very hard for me to see you like this, you know.'

Her doctor had clearly been angry when he had

discovered Cecily knew, when he had found her crying quietly and shaking with fear, and had promised he wouldn't use it without her consent, but she didn't quite trust him.

Every day now she felt less in control, less connected with the person who lay in the bed, with her face and her name, and wearing her clothes. She hated her so much, that person, that person who had killed her husband, sent him to his death, hated her and was afraid of her, but she couldn't get away from her; she was chained to her for the rest of her life.

She ought to die, it would be much for the best; she deserved to die. Only actually she didn't even deserve that: dying was too good for her.

*   *   *

After a working lunch in Harry Moreton's office that day, Dominic Foster finally asked how Mrs Harrington was progressing.

'Oh, pretty well, I think,' said Harry, who actually had no idea, beyond the bland assurances passed to Edwina by Ada Forbes. 'The treatment they're giving her seems to be successful.'

'Good,' said Dominic, 'that's splendid.' At least if Mrs Harrington was recovering, he had a little less to reproach himself for, a less urgent need for him to talk to her, explain to her what had happened.

*   *   *

'My darling.' Rupert's voice filled the darkness. Cassia stiffened, tried to relax, wondered what she was doing here, why she had been persuaded to come. 'How wonderful it was to get your last letter. Life is so absolutely appalling here, so near to hell, we stand in mud all day, those of us who are still alive, and lie in it all night. The rats are our constant companions—'

'Rupert, you're overplaying it a bit.' The director's voice cut through the darkness. 'You're writing this letter in a state of exhaustion and terror; remember that. Very low key, a bit flatter, all right?'

Rupert began again.

It was actually very intriguing seeing the play in the raw, watching it carved into shape. Not that there was a great deal of shape, with just two actors and almost no scenery. She hoped it was going to work; not for her own sake—she had no interest in seeing her investment pay off—but for Rupert. This was his big chance, and he needed it very badly. More now than ever, she thought, and sighed aloud.

'Mrs Fallon?' A voice came from the seat behind her.

'Yes?'

'I'm from the *Daily Sketch*. Could we have a quick word?'

'A word? What about?'

'Your involvement with this play. I understand you've invested some money in it. Mr Cameron said I could speak to you about it.'

She remembered now: Rupert had asked her, several weeks ago, had said the man was going to write an article about the play, that the publicity would be invaluable. 'I'd love it if you could say a few words, darling, just about how long we've known each other, why you decided to put the money into *Letters* . . .' She had said that of course she would.

'All right, go on, ask me whatever you like. Only could I read it first, before it's published?'

'Yes of course,' he said, getting out his notebook. 'Now then, what appealed to you about this play . . .'

She was clearly not going to get a chance to talk to Rupert today about her anxieties about the money—and Harry . . .

*   *   *

That night, Cecily carefully swallowed two of her pills, and then tucked the third into one of the lace hankies she kept in a small pile by her bed, and later transferred it to her washbag. The idea had come to her while she had heard two of the younger nurses discussing an overdose patient who had been brought in. 'She only took ten hypnotics,' said one, 'and that nearly killed her. Another two or three and she would have died.'

Hypnotics were what she was given every night with her warm milk. It really wouldn't be so difficult to save a dozen or so up, and then swallow them all at once. And then it would be over: no more guilt, no more hatred, and she would be able to get away from the horrible, hideous person who inhabited her now scrawny body. She couldn't imagine how she could have failed to think of it before.

*   *   *

436

'Well now, Mrs Moreton.' Miss Gerard's face as she looked down at Edwina was expressionless. Edwina, still feeling sick from the anaesthetic, tried to smile at her and failed. 'The cyst has been removed and sent for a biopsy, but I really don't think there is anything to worry about there.'

It was the 'there' that worried Edwina.

'However,' said Miss Gerard, 'if you have had trouble conceiving, it is very plain why.'

'The cyst, I suppose?' said Edwina hopefully.

'No, not the cyst. I'm afraid the surgery has revealed a far more serious problem.'

'What?' said Edwina. A cold tentacle of fear was creeping into her head.

'Mrs Moreton, I'm afraid your Fallopian tubes show extensive damage. Quite clearly blocked. And there is considerable adhesion between the adjacent tissues.'

'Which would mean . . . ?' said Edwina.

'Which would mean conception will be virtually impossible for you, I'm afraid. Yes?' She turned, frowning; the door had opened.

Harry stood in the doorway, holding a very large bunch of roses. He scowled. 'I'm Harry Moreton. This is my wife.' He went over to the bed, bent and kissed Edwina. 'How are you, Edwina?'

'I'm fine, Harry. Thank you.' She managed to smile at him. He turned back to Miss Gerard. 'And you are . . .'

'I am Monica Gerard, your wife's surgeon, Mr Moreton. Sister really should have asked you not to come in just yet.'

'She did,' said Harry, and smiled at her. Edwina knew that smile; his most dangerous, his most challenging. Miss Gerard did not return it.

437

'I see. Well, perhaps you could be kind enough to step outside, just for a moment. I am in the process of a post-operative examination, and I would rather—'

'You appeared to be merely talking to my wife, Miss Gerard. I cannot imagine that you could be telling my wife anything that I am not intended to hear. Now then, did you discover anything disagreeable, Miss Gerard? Any complications? Or can I assume my wife will make a full recovery?'

'A perfectly full recovery, Mr Moreton, yes. The cyst was, as far as I am able to tell, benign, and although it has caused your wife problems, they should now be a thing of the past.'

'Good. I'm delighted to hear it.' He gave her one of his piercing stares. 'I heard you mention conception, did I not?'

Miss Gerard stared back at him. 'Yes, Mr Moreton, you did, but I really think this is not the best time to pursue this particular matter. I really would rather finish this consultation with your wife before any further discussion can take place as to her condition.'

'And I would rather you didn't,' said Harry.

Edwina struggled through the fog of her panic. There would be a hideous scene if she did not take charge.

'Miss Gerard,' she said, summoning all her considerable courage. 'Of course I would like my husband to hear whatever it is you have to tell me. Please do go on.'

Miss Gerard looked at her; her eyebrows raised just very slightly. It was more a warning than a question. 'Very well. I was just telling your wife, Mr Moreton, that her Fallopian tubes are clearly dysfunctional. That means there can be virtually no chance of her conceiving a child. I'm sorry.'

'I see.'

There was a long, intense silence. Edwina was aware of her own breathing, of the clock on the wall ticking, of a trolley moving down the corridor outside the room, of a car hooting in the street below. Then Harry spoke again.

'And is there no treatment?'

'I'm afraid not, Mr Moreton. The damage is too extensive.'

'Damage? This is not an inherent . . . defect?' The word was harsh, ugly; the look he gave Edwina the same.

'I would not quite describe Mrs Moreton's condition as a defect, Mr Moreton.'

'Indeed? What other label would you pin on to sterility?'

'Infertility—as I prefer to call it—is a most unfortunate thing, Mr Moreton. I would not call it a defect.'

'Well, I would. Anyway, what has created these dysfunctional tubes?'

Now, thought Edwina, closing her eyes, waiting for the blow to fall on her, now what will she say? And heard, to her quite extraordinary, exquisite surprise, 'Mr Moreton, medicine is not an exact science, although we would all like it to be. There are any number of factors which could have caused this condition in your wife. I could not possibly be expected to answer that question without extremely extensive investigations into her history, general health . . .'

'I would have thought you would have done that already, Miss Gerard.'

'Well, Mr Moreton, you would have thought wrong. Removal of an ovarian cyst is a straightforward procedure. Investigation of infertility is not. Now, if you would be kind enough to step outside the room for a few minutes, I would like to examine your wife.'

'Thank you,' said Edwina feebly as the door closed behind Harry, 'thank you very much.'

'As I said to you before, Mrs Moreton, the doctor's consultation room can be compared to the confessional. And I do not take very kindly to being pressured. But your husband is not a stupid man.'

'I'm afraid not.'

'Oh, come now. Very boring, stupid men.' She pulled the bedcovers back up, and smiled at Edwina. 'I would advise you to tell him the truth. In as palatable a form as you can find. That the damage could only have been caused by a pelvic infection, probably resulting from . . . a surgical procedure. Of course you need not tell me anything at all, but if it would help, then I am happy to listen.'

'I would like to, actually,' said Edwina, 'but perhaps not just now. I'm frightfully sorry, Miss Gerard, but I think I'm going to be sick.'

*　　　*　　　*

Cassia was about to telephone the Harley Street clinic to see if she might visit Edwina when there was a thunderous knocking at the door. She opened it, half alarmed, half irritated.

Harry was standing there. He looked appalling, white-faced, dishevelled, and clearly extremely angry.

440

'Harry! What on earth is the matter? It's not Edwina, is it? She isn't—hasn't...'

'She's fine,' he said, walking past her into the kitchen, sitting down at the table, his head in his hands.

'Well, what?'

'She's had this bloody operation. As you know. I saw the bloody stupid woman who performed it. The one you recommended.' He glared at her.

'Whatever else she may be, Monica Gerard is not stupid.'

'No, I know. I'm sorry.'

Cassia tried and failed to remember Harry having used the word 'sorry' during the past ten years.

'Anyway, she's removed the cyst. That was all absolutely fine. But as I arrived, she was talking to Edwina.' He said nothing for a moment, looking defeated, utterly low. Then he took a deep breath. 'Cassia, Edwina can never have children.'

'Oh,' said Cassia. 'I see.'

'Is that all you have to say?' he said, scowling at her again.

'No, of course not, I'm sorry. And I am so very sorry to hear that. It's terrible. For her, for you.'

She looked at him, sitting there, somehow too big for her small kitchen, his head bent, his distress a tangible thing, and felt an almost overwhelming urge to go and put her arms round him. To counteract it, she sat on her hands.

'Did... did Miss Gerard give a reason?'

'She said Edwina's Fallopian tubes were blocked. Very seriously dysfunctional, I think were her exact words. That there was nothing that could be done.' He looked at her. 'You know about these things,

441

Cassia. Is there really nothing that can be done?'

'Harry, without seeing the damage for myself, knowing more about it, I really can't answer you. But—' She stopped.

'But it's unlikely?'

'Well, yes. I would think it probably is. I'm so sorry.'

'So what would cause that?' he said abruptly.

'Harry, I honestly don't know.' She sensed danger, swerved to avoid it. 'I keep telling you, without knowing more about it—'

'You're all the fucking same,' he said suddenly, knocking a glass off the table with a violent fist. It fell, shattered on the floor; she stared at it, shocked.

'I'm sorry,' he said, pushing his wild hair back. 'Here, let me clear it up.'

'No, it's all right. I'll do it.'

'Oh Christ.' He put his head in his hands. 'Could it have been an abortion?'

'What?'

'You heard me. I think she's had an abortion. I think she's probably had more than one.'

'Harry, that's absurd, why should she?'

'She doesn't want children, she's never been keen on the idea, she probably thought it would wreck her figure, more recently interfere with that damn job of hers.'

'Oh, don't be absurd. She would never have . . . You're over-reacting.'

'I don't think so,' he said. 'I told her a long time ago to stop taking precautions. Nothing's happened, and it seems to me more than possible that she's taken some active steps herself.'

'That's an outrageous thing to say. If her tubes

are blocked, she can't conceive. It's as simple as that.'

'Yes, but why are they blocked? Answer me that.'

'Harry, I don't know. I have no idea. What I do know is you're talking absolute nonsense. Unfair, dangerous nonsense. I know you're upset, but . . .'

He sat there, glaring at her. 'Well,' he said, finally, 'we shall see. I intend to find out. Anyway, whatever the reason, it seems we are destined to be childless. And I—oh God, help me.'

She couldn't help it then: she put out her hands, took one of his. She was surprised at his intense distress, and said so.

'You don't understand me at all, you see,' he said, staring down at her hands wrapped round his. 'I wanted children very much indeed. I see them as the only reason for getting married. I wanted to see my line continue. I like children, although I can see that's a bit hard to believe. And I had that ghastly, filthy childhood, I wanted to have some children and give them a good one.' He looked up at her, and his dark eyes were so full of pain, she winced.

'Oh, Harry,' she said, helpless in the face of the pain, 'what can I say to you? That there are other things, that often childless marriages are very happy—'

'Jesus Christ Almighty,' he said, staring at her. 'Happy! Me and Edwina! Dear God in Heaven. How could you possibly think such a thing? How could you even suggest we were happy?'

She stared at him, genuinely shaken by the violence in his voice. 'I—well, I hoped you were.'

'You hoped!' he said, his voice ugly with rage. 'You hoped that we were happy! That I could be

443

happy with Edwina! Dear sweet Jesus, Cassia, you know why I married her, for God's sake. Don't you?'

She realised suddenly, with a sense of slight shock, that she was still holding his hand. The physical contact, so gentle, so tender, was oddly at variance with the violence of his mood. She looked down at them, at their hands; felt afraid, tried to move one of hers away.

'Don't,' he said sharply. She put it back and was still. 'I married her,' he said, very slowly and distinctly, 'simply because I could not marry you. No other reason whatsoever. As you very well know.'

This was danger: terrible danger. She was afraid to speak, afraid to move, feeling in some strange confused way that if nothing was disturbed, if the silence could continue, they might move away into safety.

After a long silence, he said, his voice steadier, 'You did know that, didn't you, Cassia? Yes, of course you did. You knew it then, and you know it now. So please don't start mouthing obscene platitudes about us being happy, because I don't think I can bear it. Not today, today of all days.' Still she was silent.

Suddenly he stood up, wrenched his hand away from hers, brought it down violently on the table. 'Damn you,' he said loudly, 'damn you, Cassia.'

'Don't,' she said.

'Why not? Can't you see that I have an absolute right to be angry with you?'

'No,' she said, 'I don't think I do. And I think perhaps you'd better go.'

'Oh no,' he said, 'I'm not going. You're always

444

telling me to go, Cassia: you told me to go that night when I came to Leonora's house and first kissed you; you told me to go the night when I came to tell you not to marry Edward. And I did what you said, I went, and both times you were wrong and I should have stayed. You're very fond of saying I'm arrogant, but in fact you are immensely arrogant yourself, probably far more so than I.'

'I'm not arrogant.'

'Oh, but you are. You know so well what's best for you, best for me, best for everyone. You're arrogant, and you're stubborn, and you're ruthless and—'

'Stop it,' she said, standing up, 'stop this. I will not listen to it, and if you won't leave, then I will.'

'Don't be absurd,' he said, pushing her back into her chair. 'And that's something else: you only hear the things you want to. I would like you to hear this, Cassia, and I would like you to reflect upon it. Here we are, the two of us, locked into miserable marriages—'

'Mine is not—' she started, and then stopped.

'Of course it is,' he said. 'Don't lie about that, of all things. It's miserable, desperately so. You should never have married him, it was an appalling mistake, and you should at least have the grace to admit it to me.'

'I won't admit it.'

'Very well. As I said, you are appallingly, dangerously stubborn. And had it not been for that stubbornness, we could have been perfectly happy. One happy marriage instead of two wretched ones.'

'Oh, now, Harry, that is really absurd.'

'Is it? Why?'

'Well,' she said, aware that as always he was getting the better of her, 'you can't blame me for you marrying Edwina. You didn't have to marry anyone.'

'Oh, but I did,' he said. 'Because I wanted to hurt you. I wanted to hurt you more than anything in the world; indeed, it was the only thing I wanted.'

'That is an appalling thing to say. To have done,' she said, genuinely shocked.

'Really? Why? When you were wilfully hurting me.'

'This is ridiculous. I wasn't marrying Edward to hurt you, I was marrying him because I was pregnant with his child. I told you that. How could I do anything else?'

'Easily,' he said, 'very easily. That was no reason to marry him, when you loved me. We could have solved that problem, very minor in comparison with—'

'Minor! A child!'

'Cassia,' he said, and his voice was very low, but still violent, 'Cassia, I would have taken Edward's child. Not easily perhaps, but I would have done it. I would have seen it as a small price to pay for you.'

'Oh,' she said, 'oh, I see.' She felt devoid of emotion; an empty, shocked shell.

'I hope you do,' he said. 'I hope you believe me.'

'But if—'

'Yes? If what, Cassia?'

'It doesn't matter. It really doesn't.'

If you knew I loved you, she had been going to say, why did you let me do it, let me go? But she knew the answer, and she did not want to hear it again: it was her own arrogance, her own

446

stubbornness, her certainty that she knew best, knew what had to be done; she would not have listened to him. How many women, pregnant with one man's child, would have listened to another when he said he loved her, that he would take her, even with that child, would have admitted that she loved him?

She felt grief fill the empty shell of her, a dreadful, hungry grief; felt tears rush to the back of her eyes. She dashed them impatiently away, looked away, at the blank wall, fighting down the sobs.

'Now, you must not cry,' he said, his voice gentle suddenly, reaching out as he had done once before, so long ago, arresting a tear in its journey down her face, looking at it on his finger, 'not unless you want me to stay with you. You know what happens when you cry, don't you?' And again, remembering, showing her that he remembered, he raised the finger to his lips and licked it, very tenderly, his eyes fixed on hers. 'I find your tears absolutely overwhelming, Cassia. And I wouldn't leave you this time, you know. I wouldn't and I couldn't.'

And she sat there, staring at him through her tears, and felt the emptiness filling swiftly, with something quite different, something very strong, very dangerous, a desire so violent, so intense it was pain, so urgent that she moved, curved her body towards him, and then she reached out both her hands, across the table and took his face between them and leant forward and kissed him, on the mouth, very hard, very deliberately, her tongue seeking his; and then pulled away as swiftly and said, 'No, Harry, don't go, please don't, please

447

stay.'

He stood up then and held out his hand, his face strangely expressionless, his eyes fixed on hers, and led her out of the room.

*　　　*　　　*

What happened between them then, passed everything she had ever known, every expectation she had ever had. She had no idea how long they were there, in her bed, for darkness fell and the street lamps came on. She heard once through the tumult the phone ringing, and once a knock at the door, and it meant nothing to her, nothing at all: her entire being, not just her body, but her mind and her heart and what she supposed she would call her soul, was focused on Harry, on how much she loved him, on what was happening between them at last.

So frantic was she, so desperate for him, that at first she could not, would not wait, lay there like a whore, arms held open for him, legs splayed, ordering him into her. She could not have begun to imagine that moment; as he entered her, she felt not only herself, but her life, all the years behind her, filled. Her climax began almost at once, rising, clenching, pulling at her and 'Wait,' he said, easing himself up from her, 'wait a little.'

'I can't wait,' she said, 'I can't,' and felt it immediately break, shatter deep, deep within her, heard herself cry out, in a long harsh cry, fell half sobbing; half laughing back on to the bed.

'Oh God,' she said, 'Harry, I'm sorry, so sorry.'

'That's what the man is supposed to say,' he said, smiling down at her. 'I told you you were arrogant.

448

Are you always like that?'

'No,' she said, smiling back, 'no, I am not always like that, I am never like that.'

'Well now,' he said thoughtfully, looking at her, tracing the shape of her breasts, of her pubic hair, with his finger, 'well now, let us see.'

He began again, then; lay away from her, kissing her, kissing her mouth, her ears, her throat, her hair, moving down to her breasts, her stomach, her thighs, settled into her with his tongue; she held his head, pushing it into her, feeling the bright, brilliant darts of pleasure, moaning at times, crying out at others, climaxed slightly, sweetly again.

'You are having this all your way,' he said then, and moved into her, heavily, slowly, and with infinite care; she lay there, feeling him, deep, so deeply into her that his body became a part of hers, every movement, every tremor; she felt herself lost then, in a strange, wild new country, her progress measured only in the great swooping arcs of pleasure that she rode, now moving forward, now circuiting back on herself, and her body did not only feel, it could see and hear, it knew darkness and brilliance, noise and silence. She came not once, but several times, always higher, deeper, fiercer, the echoes each time fading only as the next began; she felt him come, heard him call out, cry her name, a great primeval cry, and when at the end she finally lay still, exhausted, and at peace, new knowledge, new instincts within her body, her prime emotion was awe at the pleasure they had known, and their power to unleash it.

She fell asleep then, briefly; and awoke to find him watching her, his eyes thoughtful.

'Now what are we to do?' he said.

449

CHAPTER TWENTY-FIVE

Cassia thought at first she must be mishearing; Janet was telling Edward something about William wanting to play cricket on the football pitch, and Edward was laughing. She wasn't sure which was the more welcome fact; that Edward should listen sufficiently courteously to Janet, or that he was capable of laughing these days.

She took a deep breath and pushed open the door, smiling determinedly herself. Edward's expression froze and he promptly disappeared behind the *Telegraph*. Janet smiled back at her.

'Mrs Fallon, good morning. I was just suggesting to Fanny here that we should maybe read some poetry together this morning. It's dull for her when William is at school. She was telling me how much she enjoyed the Edward Lear verses. I love them too. So later on, when Delia is asleep, and if it's all right with you, Mrs Fallon . . .'

'Janet, of course it is. It's sweet of you.'

'I'm not too keen on Lear myself,' said Edward suddenly from behind the paper. 'Lot of bloody nonsense.'

'But, Dr Fallon, that's the whole idea,' said Janet, her pretty mouth twitching.

He looked at her and smiled his slow reluctant smile—God, thought Cassia, what that used to do to me, that smile—and said, 'Yes, I suppose so. Touché. Well, I must get into the surgery, I can't sit here talking all day.' The implication that they all could was very strong.

'Now,' said Janet, advancing upon Delia and the

450

hideous mess she had made on the tray of her highchair—'let's get this mess cleared up and then I think I might take you out for a bit. Do you want to come, Fanny?'

'Oh, yes please. That'd be lovely. I do like the country.'

Cassia looked at her fondly; she was almost herself again now, although still quieter than she had been. 'You don't feel . . . ready to go home yet, darling?'

Fanny shook her head violently, and her large dark eyes took on their haunted look. 'No, I don't. I love it here so much, Cassia, please let me stay.'

'All right, Fanny. You can stay.' But not indefinitely, she thought, walking out into the hall to greet the postman. She would have to go back to London one day, when her mother came home perhaps. Poor Cecily; really, she ought to go and see her—she *would* go and see her. But not just yet. She couldn't think about it yet.

She couldn't think about anything at the moment: except Harry. He occupied all her senses, every waking moment of the day and most of her dreams as well. Even her work seemed unimportant, not quite real. She had stopped fretting over Bertie, her marriage, Rupert: none of it mattered. Only Harry. Harry and being with him.

*   *   *

'Mrs Moreton, good afternoon. I trust you are quite well again.'

Edwina looked up startled from her desk: Francis Stevenson-Cook stood in front of her. He was looking particularly resplendent, in a suit in very dark grey wool under an even darker grey overcoat, with a velvet collar.

'Good afternoon,' she said, 'and yes, thank you, I am quite well now.'

'Excellent. I came to ask you to have luncheon with me tomorrow. Are you free?'

Edwina knew that if Stevenson-Cook asked you if you were free, you were free. 'That would be delightful,' she said. 'Thank you.'

'Good. If you come downstairs at twelve forty-five, my driver will take us to the restaurant. Good afternoon to you.' He turned and left the office with a wave of his hat.

Edwina sat staring after him.

'Don't get excited,' said Betty Farquarson, the accessories editor, coolly, 'he takes everyone to lunch at least once.'

Edwina knew this was not true, but she smiled sweetly at Betty and said, 'I do realise that,' and picked up the phone to cancel her lunch with Justin.

'And how is your delightful friend?' he said after agreeing to come to the office for the meeting instead.

'My friend? Oh, you mean Cecily. She's not at all well, I'm afraid. She's had a nervous breakdown.'

'Oh, how frightful. Poor her. I shall send her some flowers.'

'Justin, how terribly sweet of you.'

'Well, I liked her very much. And I thought she was very attractive. Beautiful, and really rather . . . sexy.'

'Justin! Surely not.'

'Surely, indeed. Well, perhaps sexy isn't quite the word. Sensual. Yes, that's better. You stick-insects

452

of ladies shouldn't dismiss her type. We poor men rather like it.'

*   *   *

She left for home a little early; she was tired. It was a fortnight since her operation and although she felt quite recovered, she did seem to need rather more rest than usual.

She had had a long conversation with Monica Gerard the next day, and told her everything. Miss Gerard had been totally pleasant and non-judgmental, but said that she was afraid Edwina's history did confirm her original opinion. 'Your tubes really are damaged beyond repair, and the infection you describe, following the termination of pregnancy, would have accounted for it.'

'Yes, I see,' Edwina had said with a sigh. 'I suppose I'd have quite liked a sprog or two, but I've got loads of other things to fill my life with. My husband's rather more keen, I'm afraid.'

'Well, I would advise a frank conversation. He is obviously an intelligent man. Presumably this operation took place before your marriage.'

'Oh, yes. Yes, of course,' said Edwina hastily.

Miss Gerard had looked at her sharply. 'I feel sure that it did. Quite a few years before. That will naturally make it rather more acceptable to him. Now then, if I could just examine those stitches . . .'

And so she had returned home, braced for an inquisition, and found none. He greeted her kindly, but abstractedly, told her she must be sure to take things easily, and after seeing her into her bed, disappeared to his club.

Since then she had hardly seen him. It was a

453

huge relief; but it was none the less still rather odd.

*   *   *

Francis Stevenson-Cook took her to lunch at the Caprice; he had inevitably his own table, tucked into a corner. There was a bottle of Veuve Cliquot in an ice bucket beside it.

Edwina, who had a strong head, drank three glasses before the first course arrived, a fact which appeared to give Stevenson-Cook great pleasure.

'I admire women who can drink,' he said, 'but now that the food has arrived, we will leave the rest. Nothing worse than ruining champagne by disturbing its taste. They do a very fine white burgundy here, I think we will have that. So vulgar, this restaurant, isn't it? All the pink? But I do rather like it.'

'I quite enjoy vulgarity,' said Edwina, 'providing it's terribly, terribly expensive.'

'What a very interesting view. I think I agree with you. Well, it is certainly terribly terribly expensive here. And certainly the food is not vulgar in the least.'

He was a charming and attentive host; regaled her with gossip—including the news that Mrs Simpson had introduced the three-decker toasted sandwich to the King's guests at Balmoral and that Prince Aly Khan now kept three mistresses at the Ritz on three separate floors, laughed at her jokes, and admired her dress and particularly her hat.

'Do you like it? One of Miss Swirling's creations,' said Edwina.

'I thought it might be. Such fun, isn't she? The last time I walked down Bond Street—a very rare occurrence—I did think of going to see her, but I feared I might be interrupting a session with a client.'

'I'm sure she wouldn't have minded,' said Edwina. 'Hard to imagine an interruption she'd like more, in fact.'

'Maybe, but I do have a great respect for people in their working environment, Mrs Moreton. I feel it's rather vulgar to intrude, to trade on one's position. Don't you agree?'

'Oh, absolutely,' said Edwina. It seemed to her that of all the people she had ever met, Francis Stevenson-Cook traded on his position most thoroughly and ruthlessly.

On the way back to the magazine offices, he said, 'I understand you are mounting a charity fashion show.'

'Yes. In just over a month's time. Of course it won't interfere with my work at *Style* in any way.'

'Are your plans for it complete? Is it all under control?'

'Well, more or less,' said Edwina carefully; in fact, she was horribly behind with the arrangements, and had even wondered, since her surgery and consequent tiredness, if she should cancel, or at least postpone it.

'And which charity is it in aid of?'

'St Christopher's Hospital. A very close friend of mine works there, and she—'

'She? Is she a nurse?'

'No, she's a doctor,' said Edwina, who had always been a trifle hazy about Cassia's role at St Christopher's.

'A woman doctor! How very unusual. She must be extremely clever.'

'Yes, she is. Anyway, it's being held at Grosvenor House. In the Great Room. The one that was the ice-rink, you know.'

'I do know. I went to the Halloween fancy-dress party there in 1930. I went as a mermaid. Of course that made skating impossible, but I was on a sleigh.'

'How glorious,' said Edwina, genuinely entranced by this picture. 'I do wish I'd seen you.'

'I have some photographs. I'll show you some time. Now, back to your fashion show.'

'Well, we have the clothes all organised, and the mannequins—a few professional, and some friends—'

'Oh dear,' said Stevenson-Cook with a very slight sigh. 'Amateur mannequins are always a disaster in my view.'

'Oh, no, they're all quite good. I have a lot of very stylish friends,' she added with a touch of complacency.

'I don't doubt it. And is your friend the doctor taking part?'

'Yes, she's modelling.'

'Modelling! So she is elegant as well as clever. What a paragon. I should like to meet her. I shall meet her. Now I should like to propose that *Style* becomes involved in this show of yours.'

'Oh!' said Edwina. She was astonished: astonished and wary. 'Well, that would be very nice, but Miss Le Page feels—'

'I know what Miss Le Page feels,' said Stevenson-Cook, 'and I happen to feel differently. This will clearly be a very superior affair. Association with it can do us nothing but good. I would propose that the magazine takes a table at

456

the event, and advertising space in the programme. We could give copies of the magazine to each lady present. And I imagine there will be a tombola of some kind?'

'Yes. Very important, always raises lots of money.'

'Then a year's subscription to each of the magazines as prizes. How would that be?'

'That would be splendid,' said Edwina. 'Thank you, Mr Stevenson-Cook. Thank you so much.'

'Don't thank me, Mrs Moreton. I see this as something of mutual benefit. In more ways than one.'

* * *

'You must leave him,' said Harry.

'I will leave him. But not yet.'

'Why not yet? You've wasted quite enough of our lives, Cassia, I can't allow it to go on.'

'Harry, I haven't wasted our lives!'

'Of course you've wasted our lives. Entirely your fault.' He grinned at her. 'I seem to be able to forgive you, God knows how. Tell me why not yet.'

They were lying in bed together in the house in Walton Street; they had an arrangement to meet there for lunch each of the days she was in London.

'Lunch?' Cassia had said when he first proposed it, smiling at him. 'That seems rather a waste of time. Especially as I seem unable to eat at all at the moment.'

'Lunchtime, then. We shall take a little nourishment to replenish our energies. I shall see to that. You are to be ready for me when I arrive.'

And she was, each time: lying naked in bed,

457

feverishly impatient. He would appear in the doorway, his arms full of flowers, presents, champagne, would hurl them down, tear off his clothes, and join her there. Join his mouth to hers, her body to his; join thoughts, hopes, fears, laughter; join their lives.

They would stay there for an hour, two if they each had time; they would eat a sliver of cheese, strawberries, some ice-cream; she stocked her kitchen with fresh coffee beans, the variety that Harry preferred, and bought a grinder. Harry would drink champagne, and she would drink the coffee while she opened her gifts.

He bought her wonderful things, some rare and thoughtfully chosen books: an antique history of medicine; a first edition of *Gray's Anatomy*; some modern, lavishly illustrated books about India, Egypt, China, all the places he said he would take her; poetry books from which he made her read to him; the complete works of Pliny, Socrates, Virgil, from which he read her fragments.

And he bought her jewellery, a triple length of pearls—'which you are to wear always, you were wearing pearls when I first realised you were so beautiful, at your dance, remember? When I behaved so appallingly? Yes, of course you do'—a diamond watch and clips, an emerald necklace, a set of three gold bangles.

He bought her other things—silk negligee, scarves, robes. 'These are mistress's things, Harry,' she said, laughing.

'Quite right,' he said, 'for that is what you are, just for the moment. You know what the proper definition of mistress is? I looked it up today.'

'No,' she said, 'what?'

'A woman with power to control. That is what you have, Cassia, the power to control. To control me. It's a rare talent, don't waste it.'

'Of course I can't control you,' she said, half irritable, 'nobody can.'

'Oh but you are wrong,' he said, pushing her gently down on to the pillows, kissing her breasts, 'you do control me, you always have. There have been times when I have tried to take control of you, but failed. From the first moment I saw you, standing there considering me, in that tartan dress and black stockings, your hair hanging down your back, you have controlled me. I have not done a single thing, since that day, without considering you and how it might or might not please you. If that is not control, tell me what is.'

She didn't argue—she could not, he was too clever for her; merely pulled him down on to her and kissed him. But his words—the brilliant, beautiful words with which he courted her, made love to her—moved her, moved her physically as much as his body, his mouth and his hands.

'Why can you not leave the doctor yet?' he said again, picking up a strawberry and examining it.

She hesitated. 'It's all so . . . difficult now. We have to think of how best to manage it all. Edward is so hurt, so unhappy already—I've done him so much wrong.'

'Indeed? How? He's had seven years of you, more in fact, you've given him three children—'

'Which I plan to take away from him.'

'He can marry again, have more. He can marry that other appalling-sounding doctor person.'

'If we are not very careful, I will lose the children. He's already sent Bertie away from me.'

'Cassia, I will hire the best divorce lawyers in the land. You will not lose your children. I promise you that. Next? You haven't convinced me yet. I may have to pick up the phone and instruct my lawyers now, before I leave.'

'Oh, Harry, really!' She smiled at him. 'Please, please be sensible. We must take our time. And besides, there's Edwina.'

'Oh, she won't mind,' he said easily, 'as long as she gets enough money.'

'Of course she'll mind. She's very fond of you.'

'Only quite, I would say.'

'Why did she marry you then?'

'She was dying to marry me,' he said. 'She knew I didn't love her and she didn't hesitate. She was getting my money, my houses, my position, my cock—'

'Don't!' she said. That had hurt her.

'Oh, don't come over all virginal; Cassia. The good doctor got you in all your loveliness—' he stroked her thighs tenderly, bent and kissed them—'and Edwina got me. There is no sense in pretending none of it happened, that we remained in some strange way chaste for one another. Is there now?'

'No,' she said quietly. 'No, of course not. Anyway, we have to be careful, cautious. Please, Harry, be patient. There are so many dangers.'

'Very well. Just for a little while. But not for long. There you go, you see, controlling me, as always. I told you you did that.'

She looked at him sharply, the fear surfacing suddenly, the half formed fear she kept so well buried, that she had thought was buried. 'And have you never tried to control me? In any way?'

460

'Good Lord no,' he said. 'I know my limitations.'

*　　*　　*

Nanny was finding life extremely difficult: difficult and worrying. Mrs Forbes was a nightmare, never stopped criticising her, her and all the staff. And Stephanie was missing her sister and her mother and was behaving extremely badly. Only the baby was cheerful.

She also found herself in a position of strange authority; not only Susan, but the rest of the housemaids looked to her for direction. They were miserable at what had happened to the household; it was difficult to keep their morale high.

Even Adams was low; he confided to Nanny occasionally over their late-night tipple of whisky in hot milk that he was not sure how much longer he could consider remaining in the house.

And then things began to get worse.

'My daughter is not to know this, naturally,' Mrs Forbes said to her, one evening, 'but they were talking about electro-convulsive therapy for her again at the nursing home today. Most extreme, and very unpleasant, of course. It is a measure of how seriously they are taking her illness.'

She then went on to describe electro-convulsive therapy to Nanny in some detail; she listened in horror.

'If only there was some key. That is what the doctors are looking for,' Ada said with a sigh, 'some slight thing, that might lift this terrible depression. Guilt, you see, over poor Mr Harrington's death. She blames herself, which is absurd, but natural, all widows feel it apparently, the doctor was telling me about it. Of course my daughter is very sensitive, she gets it from me . . .'

*　　*　　*

'Cassia?'

She had been sitting in the dining room, writing to Bertie—only a week now till half term—safely, virtuously contained in her other life. Her real life. His voice was a physical shock.

'Harry!' She crushed the instinct—the incriminating instinct should she be overheard—to tell him he must not do this, must not phone her at home, and said, her voice pleasantly level, 'How nice. How are you?'

'Lonely. Miserable. Concupiscent.'

'And how is Edwina?'

'Do you know what concupiscent means?'

'No.'

'So ignorant, you are. It means lustful, filled with desire. What are you doing?'

'I'm writing to Bertie.'

'How very virtuous. I'm flying to Le Touquet tomorrow. I want you to come.'

'That would be very nice, and please thank Edwina for inviting us,' she said, acutely aware of the many people who might be listening to this conversation, 'but I'm afraid we can't—'

'Of course you can. If you don't I shall come down and tell the doctor some of the appalling things you've been doing over the past few weeks. A beautiful Indian summer's day is forecast and you are to come. I want to fuck you on French soil. Find some excuse. I'll collect you from your house in London at six.'

462

'I'm afraid it will be quite imposs—'
The line had gone dead.

* * *

'Edward, I'm so sorry, I have an urgent extra session tomorrow. In the morning. One of the other doctors is ill. It means my going up to London tonight, I'm afraid.'

'Fine. Don't worry about us.'

She wondered why she had even bothered to tell him, and went to warn Janet.

She went down to the post office to make the next call: to tell Mrs Jennings, the secretary at the clinic, that she had a domestic crisis and simply couldn't make the next day's session.

'That's all right, Dr Fallon. It looks like a quiet day, anyway. I hope things get sorted out for you soon.'

'Thank you. I'll see you on Thursday, then.'

* * *

She could hardly believe her own irresponsibility and wickedness. She told Janet she would collect William from school and spent the entire evening doing all the things she most hated, as a sop to her conscience.

* * *

Ada had gone out, to meet Stephanie from school and take her to a party.

Nanny was enjoying the peace and quiet when the phone rang in the hall. It was Edwina Moreton.

463

'Oh, Nanny. I need your help. Look, before Mrs Harrington was—well, ill, she was selling some tickets for me. For my fashion show. Anyway, I need to know how many tickets she's sold. She'll have a record of it somewhere, in her desk, I expect. Could you go and have a jolly good look for me, please, and then ring me back? I'm at *Style* magazine, Regent 444. Got that? And then ask for me. Thank you, Nanny.'

Nanny went into the morning room, and started rummaging through Mrs Harrington's desk, but there was nothing at all connected with a fashion show.

She went up to Mrs Harrington's room. There was a small escritoire in the corner; that might produce something. But it had been used for sewing; not a scrap of paper in it.

She left the room, and wandered out on to the landing, where she found Susan with some flowers.

'Oh, hello, Nanny. Everything all right?'

'Yes. Well, Mrs Moreton just telephoned me, about some fashion show she's running. Apparently a list has been mislaid, of the number of tickets Mrs Harrington has sold. I have searched her desk, and it's not there: is there anywhere else she might have kept papers?'

'She sometimes used the little rolltop in the guest room,' said Susan, 'the one where Mrs Forbes is sleeping. You could try there. And Mrs Forbes is out at the moment.'

'Good idea,' said Nanny. 'Thank you, Susan.'

She knocked at Ada's door, just to make sure she wasn't in the room, and went in. The little rolltop desk was open.

This was better: lots of correspondence in Mrs

Harrington's writing, with correspondence from friends, all neatly slotted in, in alphabetical order. Nothing that looked as if it was connected with the fashion show, but she could try the drawers: the top one yielded a small accounts book, some bank statement and—yes! A file labelled 'Fashion Show'. She pulled out the contents: it was all there. A list of people approached, neat ticks by the ones who had bought tickets, a second list headed 'Table guests?', again with ticks. Mrs Moreton would be very pleased. She slid the drawer shut again carefully, and in the process dislodged one of Ada's piles of papers. They fell on the floor in a flurry.

'Damn,' said Nanny, and bent down to retrieve them. She tried not to look at them, of course, but she couldn't help it. There were a couple of letters from Mr Forbes which began 'My dearest Ada', and which contained details of his trip to New York. More letters, mostly from Mrs Forbes's friends, telling her how wonderful she was. That was about all. Oh no, there was another. Nanny pulled it out from where it lay under the foot of the desk.

She recognised the name on the top of the letter heading: it was the architect Mr Harrington had been working with, he'd telephoned the house a couple of times, Dominic Foster. What on earth was he doing, writing to Mrs Forbes? Then she saw the letter was to Cecily.

Dear Mrs Harrington,
I was so desperately sorry to hear of Benedict's death. It goes without saying that my thoughts are with you at this sad time.
I would very much like to come and see you.

465

I realise you might not find this a welcome prospect, but there is something I would like to talk to you about, in connection with Benedict, and the time leading up to his death. I do realise this might be painful, but I think—in the long run—you might find it helpful. If you can find it in your heart to allow me to visit you, I would be so very grateful.—Yours sincerely,
      Dominic Foster.

'Poor man,' said Nanny aloud, 'what a sweet letter.' She put it back carefully, wondering if Mrs Harrington had indeed seen him.

*   *   *

She almost had enough tablets now, Cecily thought: ten. To be on the safe side, she would get twelve, then there would be no chance of her being brought round. If she took the twelve pills plus her own three, at bedtime, and no one checked her until morning, there would be no point pumping her stomach, because she would be quite, quite dead. Dead and safe.

*   *   *

Cassia ate supper with the family, pressing a monosyllabic Edward for details of his day, listening to Fanny as she recited the Edward Lear poem she and Janet had read together that day, and finally, after tucking William up in bed and taking Edward his coffee, kissed everyone goodbye and said she was so sorry to have to go tonight, but she had a very early start and it would be impossible to get there in time through the ever heavier rush hour traffic. That at least, she thought, was true.

*   *   *

Only four more days, Bertie thought, burying his head underneath his pillow (not that it was necessary any more, he was past crying, past anything except an exhausted, resigned misery), and then he would be home for half term. Home to his mother, to William, to love; home to his father; to safety, to warmth; home to food he did not have to finish, to a bed where he could sleep in peace; home to Buffy, to Peggy, to freedom. Home. He fell asleep smiling.

He awoke as the bell went, hot, itching all over, everywhere, stumbled into the bathroom scratching, feeling dizzy, looked in the mirror.

'Chicken pox, you've got chicken pox; Fallon, I'm afraid,' said Matron firmly. 'Come along with you; up to the san. Bad luck, you won't be able to go home for half term with that. Still, never mind, there's a few others up there, you won't be on your own. Now come along, don't cry, great boy like you.'

*   *   *

Cassia was waiting for Harry on the doorstep when he arrived, wearing a beige gabardine jacket and jodhpurs with high brown boots, a cream silk shirt and his pearls around her neck.

'You look beautiful,' said Harry.

He kept his plane at a small airfield in Heston,

just off the Bath Road in West London; walking towards it, observing how small it was, feeling his arm heavy, on her shoulders, she felt, irresistibly, like someone in a film.

'It's very . . . nice,' she said doubtfully, as Harry demanded her admiration for the plane, studying its worryingly lightweight-looking wings, the curved hood over the cabin. 'What make is it? And what are those things fixed on the wheels?'

'It's a Vega Gull Gypsy Six. And those things are called spats. The longer ones, like those over there, are called trousers. They're for streamlining.'

She climbed into the cabin, settled herself into the passenger seat, buckled herself in. Harry got in beside her, started fiddling with the instruments, checking them, shouting at the mechanic down on the ground. He switched on the engine; the plane filled with noise, and then moved slowly forward across the grass. She felt briefly scared, thinking how irresponsible she was being, thinking of the considerable risk she was running, the risk not only to herself, but her family; and then that lifted with the plane, became excitement, freedom, a sense of heady, wonderful adventure . . .

*　　　*　　　*

It was extraordinary going up, just rising through the air so easily, so smoothly, moving towards the blue sky, watching the ground shrinking beneath her, watching trees, houses, roads, become tiny toy things. She gazed down at them enraptured, feeling dizzily safe.

'It's wonderful,' she said, smiling at Harry. 'I can't believe it.'

'Glorious, isn't it? You feel so free up here.'

They reached the coast, and she looked down at model cliffs, tiny ships, a sea even bluer than the sky. 'I love it,' she said.

Harry reached across, took her hand and kissed it. 'I'm glad you do. I might have gone off you if you hadn't.'

The French coast appeared with astonishing speed. They flew into the shining day, following the line of the sea, and then Harry suddenly said, 'There's Le Touquet now. Pretty, isn't it?'

It was very pretty: a vast and beautiful beach, the great stretches of impossibly perfect green golf courses, glorious maritime pines.

'It's known as Le Touquet Paris Plage,' said Harry, 'because it's so chic that half Paris is here on the beach. And half London as well.'

They turned into a wide estuary; the plane banked, then settled again. The grass of the airfield seemed to reach up to them suddenly, and then they were down.

'Welcome to France,' he said. 'I hope you enjoy your stay.'

'I'm sure I shall,' she said, smiling.

There was a car waiting for them, with an English driver. 'Morning, Mr Moreton. Good flight?'

'Excellent,' said Harry.

'Where to, sir?'

'The Links Hotel.'

*   *   *

In the suite at the Links reserved for his exclusive use, he ordered coffee, orange juice, champagne,

469

ran a bath. 'Take that lovely suit off and come and join me.'

She sat in the bath with her back to him, his arms round her, holding her breasts. He began to kiss her shoulders, her neck; she dipped her head, kissed his arms, his hands.

'I love you,' she said.

'I love you too.'

He lifted her very slightly, in the water, settled her on to him; she felt him sinking in her, felt strangely taut around him in the hot water.

'You're beautiful,' he said, 'so beautiful,' and began to move, lazily, easily. She felt her own rhythms begin, gently, almost reluctantly at first, then growing in strength, in violence. She leant back against him, her arms flung wide, her head turned to the ceiling, and felt him pushing into her, harder now, urgently. Rippling circles of her own, deep within her, echoing the ones in the water, began to spread, reaching through her, outwards, upwards: she tensed, was still, and then quite suddenly came, in huge, hot breaking waves of pleasure, and cried out again and again as she did, as he came too, that she loved him.

*   *   *

'Well,' he said, passing her a glass of champagne, 'that is the first objective of the day accomplished.'

'Having a bath?' she said, smiling.

'No,' he said. 'I told you I wanted to fuck you on French soil.'

'But it wasn't soil,' she said, 'it was water.'

'You are appalling,' he said. 'A literal-minded pedant. I don't know that I can spend the rest of

470

my life with such a person.'

She shrugged. 'You must please yourself, of course.'

'That is exactly what I am doing,' he said, coming over to kiss her. 'Pleasing myself. Pleasuring myself.'

'And pleasuring me.'

'Naturally. That is part of the pleasure. You have not had enough of it, of pleasure. I intend to see you get a great deal more.'

'Well, that will be very nice,' she said.

'I trust it will be more than nice. You really must try to extend your vocabulary, Cassia,' he added, laughing at her. 'I am going to buy you a *Roget's Thesaurus* as soon as we get back to London, and make you learn ten new words a day. Don't look so cross, you know I don't mean it. You are quite, quite perfect. Well, almost, anyway . . .'

* * *

Nanny was haunted by the letter from Dominic Foster. If Mrs Harrington was really as bad as Mrs Forbes said, then it would be wrong not to make sure at least that Foster had been allowed to speak to her. Bravely, she broached the subject early next day.

'Mrs Forbes, I wonder if I might have a word.'

'Yes, Nanny?'

'I do hope you won't think this . . . interfering, and I do apologise for what might seem a breach of etiquette, but I was looking for something of Mrs Harrington's yesterday, something to do with Mrs Moreton's fashion show . . .'

'Oh, yes?' said Mrs Forbes. She didn't like

Edwina Moreton, Nanny knew. 'And did you find it?'

'Yes, I did. I had to look through the desk in the spare room, though. I do hope you don't mind—'

'Well, that was very wrong of you. Many of the letters in there are private. I am surprised at you, Nanny.'

'I'm sorry, Mrs Forbes, but Mrs Moreton was in a considerable hurry and—'

'Mrs Moreton is always in a hurry. It's a very unattractive quality. Anyway, do go on.'

'Well, I did find the file. About the fashion show. But I couldn't help seeing a letter to Mrs Harrington from—from Mr Foster.' Oh dear, this was beginning to go really badly: Mrs Forbes had an ugly flush on her face, and her eyes were very hard and glittering. 'It sounded as if—well, as if he might be able to help Mrs Harrington. Make her feel better. And I thought—as she was so very ill— that anything . . .' Her voice faltered.

'Nanny, I am very shocked by your behaviour. It was very wrong of you to go through my desk, and even more wrong to read my personal correspondence.'

'I'm sorry, Mrs Forbes. Very sorry. But . . . .' Indignation gave her courage: it wasn't Mrs Forbes's desk; it hadn't been her personal correspondence, far from it. 'But it just seemed too important to ignore. I mean, did Mr Foster go and see Mrs Harrington? Because I really think—'

'Nanny, I am not in the least interested in what you think. I am very disappointed in you. When my daughter is better, I shall certainly see it as my duty to inform her of it. But since you ask, I told Mr Foster there was no question of him seeing my daughter at the moment, she is far too ill. And he was quite happy to accept my decision. Now perhaps you should go to the nurseries and confine your energies to your duties. On all future occasions.'

'Yes. Mrs Forbes. I'm sorry.'

Nanny left the room near to tears; in the ten years she had worked for the Harringtons, in the twenty years she had worked for the family before that, she had never been spoken to so harshly. Of course she had overstepped the boundaries of her position—she was aware of that, had apologised profusely for it—but the situation was serious enough and her affection for Mrs Harrington deep enough to warrant it; moreover, she had no intention of stopping now.

But who could she go to? She could ring up Dominic Foster herself, of course, but he was hardly going to override any decision of Ada Forbes. Then she thought of Edwina Moreton. She was very sensible really, related to Mrs Moreton by marriage after all, she would care, she would be able to help. Yes, that was a good idea. She'd telephone Mrs Moreton once Mrs Forbes had finished her breakfast, and retired to the lavatory for her daily session there.

But Mrs Moreton was neither at home, nor her office. She was out for the day, the secretary in the fashion department said, on a photographic session.

Nanny sighed; it would just have to wait. At least until the evening. She wondered wildly if she should ring Mr Moreton, but she was much too frightened of him to contemplate it seriously. One more day wouldn't matter, surely.

Harry and Cassia walked along the wide promenade of Le Touquet, holding hands. It was a glorious day, white and blue and becoming windy; the air was headily clear.

'This is lovely, so lovely,' she said. 'I feel . . .'

'What do you feel?'

'Perfectly, absolutely perfectly happy.'

'Good,' he said briskly. 'That's exactly what I want you to feel.'

Later they had lunch in one of the small streets of the town and the restaurant, small, dim, seductively rich smelling, was wonderfully welcoming.

'I've turned into such a wicked person,' she said suddenly with a sigh, reaching for his hand, stroking it across the table.

'Really? In what way?'

'Oh, selfish, deceitful, irresponsible, all the things I most disapprove of.'

'And what has brought about this change in you? I hope you are not laying the blame at my door.'

'No, of course not,' she said. 'This—us—is merely the manifestation of it. Of the wickedness. No, it was the money, I'm afraid. It has done terrible things to me.'

'Nonsense,' he said briskly, 'that money has only done one thing to you: given you courage to be yourself. I'm delighted with it, your money.'

'I dare say you are,' she said, looking at him thoughtfully, grateful for the slightly confusing effects of all the wine she had drunk, that she could allow her brain to pursue this. 'So are you implying

474

I was always wicked, always deceitful and selfish?'

'I think,' he said, raising her hand to his mouth and kissing it, 'I think you are neither entirely wicked nor entirely good, merely interesting. Extremely interesting. And the interesting person was being stifled, crushed. Now she is emerging, in a most satisfactory way. How does that sound?'

'Totally unreassuring,' she said, laughing, 'but I'm too drunk to argue with you.'

'It's never a good idea to argue with me, drunk or sober. I always win,' he said, waving at the waiter, asking for the bill. 'And now you must excuse me, I have my business meeting. Will you be all right? Go and look at the shops, they're quite wonderful. I'll meet you back in the hotel at four. Then we can have tea, before going back.'

'I don't want to go back,' she said. 'I really don't want to.'

'That's because you are not being sensible, and coming to live with me. I have no sympathy.' He reached to kiss her across the table. 'Goodbye. I'll see you later.'

Cassia wandered out of the restaurant, bought herself a silk sweater and a white silk scarf for Harry, then walked back in the direction of the promenade.

She stopped at a café for a hot chocolate, then reached for a guide book she had picked up in the hotel. And read of the casino, a very fine casino (it said), and found the thought absolutely irresistible. The Casino du Palais, one of Leonora's old haunts.

She went out of the café, found a taxi.

*   *   *

She hadn't meant to go in, merely to look at it, but admiring its splendour, trying to imagine Leonora, her friends, Rollo Gresham, in there, she did walk in through the door, stood slightly uncertainly in the foyer, looking round her.

A man came over to her, clearly some kind of hall porter.

'*Madame, je regrette, c'est fermé.*'

'Oh, no matter. Do you speak English?'

'A little.'

'I thought you might remember my godmother, Leonora Beatty. She came here quite often, I believe.'

'Ah, Lady Beatty. A most beautiful and very lovely lady. I was so sorry to hear that she had died. Yes, she would come here, in a big party in the old days, with Monsieur Gresham and their friends. She was always very kind to me.'

'She was always very kind to everyone,' said Cassia. She was surprised to find tears at the back of her eyes. She smiled at the man. 'And do any of them come here now, her friends, Mr Gresham perhaps?'

'Not Mr Gresham. We have not seen him for some time now.'

'Oh really? I wonder why not.'

'I really could not say, madame.' He seemed embarrassed, suddenly. She was intrigued.

'Is he in trouble?'

Another man, in morning dress, clearly more important, appeared through a door in the foyer. '*Est-ce qu'il y a un problème, Henri?*'

The doorman spoke rapidly to him in French, looking sideways at Cassia from time to time. She heard the names Beatty and Gresham, and suddenly felt rather sick.

The second man looked at her slightly coldly. 'Madame, good afternoon. I understand you were enquiring about Monsieur Gresham?'

'Yes. He was a great friend of my godmother, Lady Beatty. She has died, as I believe you know, and I have heard nothing from Mr Gresham for quite a while. I just wondered if he might still come here.'

'No, madame. We also have not seen Monsieur Gresham for some time.' There was a note in his voice, heavy, almost hostile.

'Oh. Oh, I see.' She waited. There seemed to be no more to come.

'Is there anything else I can do for you; madame?'

'I was hoping to make contact with Mr Gresham. I have written to him, at the only address I have, but received no reply. I thought perhaps you might—'

'I know nothing of Monsieur Gresham's whereabouts, madame. Unfortunately. I would suggest you ask his friends, perhaps.'

'I can't really do that,' she said, aware that she sounded foolish. 'I don't know any of his friends.'

'Well, then I'm afraid I really cannot help you. And now if you will excuse me . . .'

'Yes, of course. I wonder if I could leave my card here. You could give it to one of these . . . friends. Ask them to contact me.'

He took it, turning it over in his hand.

'Of course, madame. If I do see any of them.'

'Thank you.' He bowed to her. 'Good afternoon, madame,' he said, and disappeared back into his office.

Cassia thanked the man on the door and turned away. She felt odd: physically and mentally. A second wave of nausea hit her; she looked round for a chair, saw one by the door and sank down, and put her head between her knees.

The porter hurried over to her, looking concerned. 'Madame, can I get you anything? A glass of water, perhaps? Call a taxi?'

'No, no, it's quite all right.' She'd probably caused the poor man enough trouble. 'Just a dizzy spell. I'm fine now.'

'May I suggest, madame, the café, just down the street. You could get a coffee there perhaps, a brandy.'

'Yes. Yes, I'll go there, thank you.'

'And madame—' he hesitated—'the patron there, he knew Monsieur Gresham well . . .'

*   *   *

Sitting in the café, sipping iced water and strong coffee alternately, she felt better. When the waiter came for the money, she said, 'Is the owner of the restaurant here? I would like to speak to him, if he has time.'

'One moment, madame. I will ask.'

They all spoke English so well, she thought irrelevantly.

'Madame? You wished to see me. No problem, I hope?' A short, stout man, the patron had dark hair and black eyes, and had clearly been rather good-looking in his youth. He smiled at her.

She returned the smile, said 'No, no problem at all. But the man at the casino, he said you might have some news of a friend of mine. Well, not

478

exactly a friend. A lost acquaintance . . .'

'Indeed, madame? And what is the name of this acquaintance?'

'Gresham. Mr Rollo Gresham.'

'Ah, Monsieur Gresham. We miss him, he was a very . . . cheerful gentleman.'

'He was indeed,' said Cassia politely, trying to equate the loud vulgarity of Rollo Gresham with cheerfulness. 'So he never comes here now?'

'No, madame. He never does.'

'You don't know why that is?'

The same awkwardness again, then he said, 'Well, madame, he—well, he had some problems. But you will know of them, I expect.'

'No,' said Cassia, her heart beginning to race uncomfortably. 'What sort of troubles? Were they—were they financial?'

He hesitated. 'It is really not for me to say, madame. I'm sorry.'

'Please!' she said. 'It's important to me. My godmother, Lady Beatty, you know, she was . . . with him, for the last few years of her life.'

'Ah, Lady Beatty. So beautiful a lady, so kind. I was so sorry to hear she had died.'

'Yes,' she said, 'yes, thank you. But you see, she died in Paris, and I didn't know until it was too late, and I am trying to find out what happened to Mr Gresham since then. If he's really in trouble I need to know.'

'He was in some financial trouble, madame, yes. He had—what is the word, *il manque de l'argent*— ah yes, debts. Everywhere here. Many people knew that, there is no harm my telling you. I do not know the size. I can only tell you there was a problem, that we do not see him any more.'

479

'Yes, I see,' said Cassia again. She was finding it hard to say anything remotely coherent. 'And how long has it been since you have seen him? Can you remember?'

'Oh, a year . . .' He paused. A year would be all right, she thought, a year would be perfectly all right. 'No, it must be two years. It was the summer the Prince, your King now, of course, was in Biarritz. Monsieur Gresham and Lady Beatty had met him there, I remember Monsieur Gresham telling us.'

Two years . . . the time ground into her brain. 'And you haven't seen him since?'

'Oh, perhaps a little, madame. But not . . . not as we did.'

There could still be explanations, Cassia, of course there could; temporary difficulties, they did happen, and then people recovered again. She heard a voice from the past year, at Benedict's and Cecily's villa in France, a man's voice saying, 'Isn't that Gresham's house down there?' and another answering, 'He's sold it now.' And the house in England, the one in *Country Life*, that too on the market . . .

'And you don't know where he is now?' she said, her voice sounding loud with fright.

'I believe he is living in North Africa, madame. That was the last story I had heard.'

'North Africa! Goodness, why?'

'It is not such a strange idea for a man who loves France,' he said quickly, smiling at her. 'The food is French, or some of it, French is spoken in all the cities, many many French people go there. And it is very beautiful . . .' He smiled.

'Yes, I can see that. But you don't have an

480

address for him there?'

'No, madame. I do not. I'm so sorry.'

'Well, if you see any of his old friends, perhaps you could ask them to be in touch with me? Here's my card, look, there are two addresses.'

He bowed. 'Thank you, madame. I will do my best. And now, madame, another coffee, a brandy perhaps? You look a little pale.'

'A coffee perhaps, thank you. And thank you for your help. I'm so grateful.'

She sat there for a long time, trying to make a little sense of it at least, to persuade herself that sense could be made of it: trying and failing.

*　　*　　*

'You're very quiet,' said Harry. 'What's the matter?'

'Oh, nothing. Honestly.' She smiled at him. They were in the car, driving back to the airfield, through wide streets set with huge villas. It was cloudy now, stormy-looking, and her mood had changed with the day, with what she had learnt.

'Cassia, if there's one thing I cannot stand, it's being told there's nothing the matter when there clearly is. Especially by a woman. Now what is it?'

'I just don't want to go back,' she said.

'Oh Christ.' He had been sitting with his arm round her; he withdrew it, pulled away from her.

'What? What have I done?'

'Told me a lie.'

'I haven't told you a lie,' she said. 'I don't want to go back.'

'You have told me a lie. That's not the problem. Not this one, anyway. Now please can we get it out

481

of the way, or shall I just get on with some work? I have no intention of sitting here trying to coax something out of you.'

'I'm sure you don't,' she said shortly, 'and there's no need. Could we perhaps discuss the weather or something straightforward like that?'

'It's not straightforward, as a matter of fact,' he said, looking out of the window, up at the sky. 'It looks quite stormy. It might be a difficult ride back.'

'I don't care,' she said, and meant it. A difficult ride would suit her mood.

It was almost five o'clock. The sky was extraordinary, rolling black clouds, drenched with great shafts of light here, poured over with red and orange there, and occasionally stretches still of pure aquamarine blue.

They skimmed across the airfield, took off in an easy, smooth lift from the ground, seemed to slide through the lower clouds into the drama beyond. It was like another country up there, another landscape, such as Cassia had never seen. She clapped her hands with pleasure at the sight of it: great cliffs and seas of clouds, grey and orange waterfalls tumbling into black, sudden sheets of white, an apparent infinity. It was as if they were on a great highway, the great banks and cliffs of cloud landmarks; Harry sat at the controls, absolutely absorbed and intent, and she thought that she had only seen that look before when they were in bed.

There was a huge engulfing flash of light and a monumental sound that seemed to enfold them, swallow them up in itself, and they dropped suddenly, in a perpendicular descent that left her shocked, physically and mentally. He put out his hand, briefly, clasped hers. 'It's OK,' he said, 'only a storm, don't be frightened.'

'I'm not,' she said, and she wasn't, she was excited, exhilarated, intensely alive.

On they rode, through the churning clouds, the noise, the dazzling light, and it was like sex, she thought, exactly like sex: an endless series of peaks and swoops, brilliant light, then shadow, then greater brilliance still, and more than once she heard herself, as she did in bed, cry out with the strange, fierce pleasure of it.

It was over in the end, and, also as with sex, they moved into quietness, a clearer, simpler sky. She could see now the field below them, the colour somehow strange and unfamiliar after the country they had left behind, and the plane landed lightly and with extraordinary ease. And as it came to rest, she looked at Harry, and he at her, slightly shaken, both of them, at what they had shared. They smiled at one another and Harry reached out again and took her hand as he had earlier and lifted it to his lips and kissed it.

'Dear God, I love you,' he said.

CHAPTER TWENTY-SIX

'Where the hell have you been?'

'You know perfectly well where I've been. I told you. I've been to Le Touquet.'

'I mean this evening. You said you'd be back for dinner. I waited over an hour and a half, I wanted to talk to you about something.'

'I've been in the office. Anyway, what did you

want to talk about? Your fashion show? Your job? Your next dinner party?'

'No,' said Edwina, 'Cecily. Her nanny telephoned this evening. She'd been trying to get hold of Cassia, but apparently she wasn't either at her house or the clinic. The point is, Nanny was worried. Apparently, she found some letter that Dominic Foster had written to Cecily, asking her if he could come and see her, to talk about Benedict's death. He seemed to think it was important, that it would help. Anyway, Nanny asked the dreadful Ada if he had been to see Cecily and she said no.'

'This is all extremely interesting, Edwina, but I do have other things to attend to.'

'Harry, don't be so bloody callous.'

Just for a moment he looked contrite, then he said, 'Well, what would you like me to do?'

'I do think, given that Cecily is so very ill, about to have this horrible treatment, we should at least find out what it is that Dominic has to tell her, don't you? I mean, it might help. Nanny thinks it's important. She's got into frightful trouble with Ada, doing all this. It's a measure of her devotion to Cecily she's carried on with it. And I can see why.'

He looked at her sharply. 'You really are worried, aren't you?'

'Yes, I am, and if you don't talk to Dominic, I will.'

'All right. I have to phone him anyway, about a new project of mine in Le Touquet. Can you ask Bishop to bring me a brandy? I'll be in my study.'

*   *   *

484

Edward's voice on the telephone was coldly polite. 'I tried to get you at the clinic, but I was told you weren't there this afternoon.'

'No,' she said quickly, 'I was at another one. I told you, it was an emergency.'

'Ah, yes. So complex, all your arrangements. Now, I'm afraid I have some slightly unfortunate news. Bertie has chicken pox. He won't be able to come home for half term.'

'Not come home? But Edward, why not? It's not a dangerous illness. I can collect him in the car and—'

'Cassia, the school rule is that anybody with an infectious illness must remain in the sanatorium until quarantine is over. However, they have said that we may visit him.'

'Well, that's extremely kind of them.'

'So I told Matron that you would phone and make the necessary arrangements.'

'Don't you want to be involved?'

'I will join you if I can.'

'Yes, all right, Edward. I expect I'll go tomorrow.'

'Surely you have a clinic tomorrow?'

'I can cancel it. Easily. Bertie is much more important.'

'How very curious your work seems to be, Cassia. One clinic is so pressing you have to leave the house the night before to be there on time, another of so little importance you can simply cancel it at a moment's notice.'

She was silent; she dared not start an argument over this of all things. 'I'll phone you, then.'

'Very well.'

*   *   *

She phoned the school. Matron said Bertie was very uncomfortable and miserable, but, as of course Mrs Fallon would know, her husband being a doctor, chicken pox was the least serious of all the childhood illnesses.

'I am also a doctor, as a matter of fact, Matron,' she said, unable to help herself.

'Indeed? I had not realised that.' She sounded disapproving. 'Well, be that as it may, I do know your son would like to see you. He's very upset about not coming home for half term.'

'Yes, well, I'd like to talk to you about that. Could I come tomorrow?'

'That would be perfectly all right, Mrs Fallon. In the afternoon perhaps?'

'Yes, fine. Goodnight, Matron. Please give him my love. Tell him I'll see him tomorrow.'

*   *   *

Rupert read the article first. He had woken early and gone for a walk, down towards the Embankment. He stood there on Albert Bridge, oddly calmed by the loveliness of early morning on the Thames, the mist rising off it, the eerily beautiful light, the heavy industrial craft working their way slowly through the water, the great stretch of buildings on the banks, the Houses of Parliament gleaming in the sun.

It was a cold morning, as well as a beautiful one, and after a while he bought himself a cup of tea from a stall, and then saw a newspaper stand just beyond it and saw on the front page of the *Sketch* a strapline advising him that they had done a round-up of all the West End shows, both new and long-standing, in an easy-to-view guide.

Maybe, maybe they would have mentioned *Letters*. His friend had promised he would get the piece in if he could. He had.

CHILDHOOD SWEETHEARTS UNITED IN WEST END VENTURE, Rupert read (the headline set above smudgy photographs of the childhood sweethearts in question), and then in growing, crawling horror, an account of Cassia's involvement with *Letters* that implied a relationship between them at least as passionate and illicit as that between Laurence Olivier and Vivien Leigh:

Rupert Cameron, star of the highly original new production *Letters*, has been the most important figure in Cassia Fallon's life since she was an impressionable young girl of fifteen. He was her father's best friend, and she used to long for his visits on tour to Leeds, the city where she grew up, so that she could see him on the stage, and even more excitingly, in his dressing room afterwards. He stayed in the family home when he was playing in Leeds, rather than in theatrical digs, and was a thrilling addition to family life for the young girl, who would wait up for him to come home, while the rest of the household was asleep, to ply him with hot chocolate and to hear his stories of the night's performance. He was her confidant and mentor, encouraging her to train as a doctor, and although she is now married and has a young family, it is Mr Cameron she regards as her 'very best and dearest friend'.

Recently, Mrs Fallon came into a large sum of money which enabled her to invest in *Letters*, the play in which he is finally launching his West End career. As the major backer, she is an important part of the production, which is an unusual show, tracing the close relationship between two people who have loved and remained faithful to one another over a span of many years, despite marriages to other people. There could be echoes here of real life for Mrs Fallon and Mr Cameron!

When I arrived at the theatre, I found Mrs Fallon sitting in the empty stalls transfixed by her 'dearest friend's' performance. She told me it was her greatest ambition that the play might be successful and Mr Cameron become a star. 'It is so very exciting to think that I have been able to help make this possible.'

Mrs Fallon, who is a very attractive young woman, and was a leading debutante in her day, now lives in the country with her family, and also has a house in London where she spends much of the week: 'This makes it possible for me to see more of Rupert—and the rehearsals, of course,' she added with a gay laugh. 'But of course we are only good friends, nothing more than that.'

Letters opens in a week's time at the Second House theatre on the Embankment. Mrs Fallon will, of course, be at the first night, although her husband, who works hard in his country practice, is not expected to be there.

'Oh my God,' Cassia half whispered, looking at Rupert across the kitchen table. 'This is appalling. How on earth did it happen? I said so little.'

'Did you?' he said. He was white, shaking, smoking cigarette after cigarette. 'Did you really? So how did he know all this rubbish, about you and me being alone in the house, when everyone else was asleep, and you living in London, away from your husband? And where on earth did they find that photograph?'

'I don't know: some old copy of the *Tatler*, I suppose, I was only about eighteen. And I suppose I told him those things. But they were so unimportant, meant to be funny, some of them. He's twisted them, made them into something quite different. We can sue them, can't we? I'll ring a solicitor, there's surely something we can do.'

'There's nothing we can do, Cassia. There's nothing here that's not true, and nothing you didn't tell him.'

'It's so unfair,' said Cassia, 'so terribly unfair. I was only trying to be helpful, and he promised to let me read whatever he'd written. I'm going to complain to his editor.'

'Cassia, they always promise to let you read it. Oh God, I should never have let you talk to him—'

'Let me! Rupert, you made me talk to him, you asked me to because you said it would help.'

'I know, I know. I'm sorry.' He pushed his hands through his hair. 'Whatever will Edward think?'

'God knows. Or what he'll do, and as for—'

'As for who?'

'Harry,' she had been going to say, bit the name back. 'Oh, you know, Janet, the village, the children, all our friends. Maybe they won't see it,

Rupert, maybe—'

'They'll see it,' he said. 'They'll see it all right.'

* * *

'Cassia?' It was Harry. 'What is this wonderful story in the *Sketch*? I love the vision of you as a theatrical angel, buying some illicit passion.' He was laughing; she supposed that at least was something to be thankful for.

'Harry, it isn't funny.'

'Isn't it? I find it extremely funny. Can I have lunch with you somewhere very public, gain notoriety from my association with you?'

'No, you can't,' she said irritably. 'I'm keeping very well out of sight, and besides, I'm goings down to see Bertie at school this afternoon, he's got chicken pox.'

'Poor little brute. Can I come too?'

'No, Harry. Don't be ridiculous. I've got enough problems . . .' She heard her voice shake; heard his own change to one of concern.

'You're really upset, aren't you? It isn't so very important. Particularly under the circumstances.'

'What circumstances?'

'Well, you hardly want to preserve your marriage, do you? This could be quite helpful if it was read out in your divorce suit, I'd have thought.' He was laughing again.

'Oh, Harry, don't! Please don't.'

'All right, I'm sorry. Incidentally, talking of divorce, did you see another item in the newspaper? Mrs Simpson was granted her decree nisi yesterday. At Ipswich Crown Court. Now we shall see feathers fly. Look, meet me at the

490

Dorchester for a quick drink before you go—give you Dutch courage to face the doctor.'

*   *   *

One of the younger nurses at the nursing home saw the article, recognised Cassia Fallon's name as that of the lady who had brought over several things for Mrs Harrington when she had first been brought in and had telephoned several times since, and read it excitedly to her colleague over breakfast.

'She seemed such a nice lady. Who would have thought it? She didn't seem that sort of person at all. And her husband a doctor. Poor man.'

'What difference does that make?'

'Well, I don't know, it just seems more . . . wrong somehow. A leading debutante, she was, you know what that means, very spoilt—'

They were interrupted by Sister, who had come in in a very bad temper, having received a dressing-down from Matron in her turn, to complain about the state of the linen room. 'You can put that newspaper away, Nurse, and go up and see to Mrs Harrington. I want her bed changed. She's got two visitors coming this afternoon, two gentlemen Mr Moreton and Mr Foster—but you're not to mention that to her, Mr Moreton said when he telephoned.'

'Yes, Sister. No, Sister. Certainly, Sister.'

As if it did any good saying anything to poor Mrs Harrington: she never took anything in.

*   *   *

Cecily had not, of course, seen the article; but she

491

was taking little in that day. She felt strangely elated, almost happy. She had saved enough pills now, and tonight she would take them. This was her last day; it was almost over.

* * *

Nanny saw the paper lying in the kitchen when she went down to fetch Mrs Forbes a cup of herb tea after breakfast. Poor Mrs Forbes was not feeling at all well, said she could feel one of her bilious attacks coming on; so great was her misery that she had clearly decided to let bygones be bygones with Nanny. Or rather, Nanny thought grimly, so that she could use Nanny to run around after her, nursing her.

Cook had been reading the article about Cassia and Rupert aloud to a goggle-eyed Susan when they heard Nanny's footsteps on the stairs. Cook threw it hastily down on the table and attacked a ball of pastry with her rolling pin. Nanny, waiting for the kettle to boil, managed to read the entire article upside down. She was very shocked.

* * *

In the village of Monks Heath, there was talk of little else, every inhabitant, from Milly Hascombe, who took in washing, to Mrs Venables, reading her cook-general's copy while pretending not to, much as Nanny was doing in London, was consumed with excitement by it. 'Poor doctor,' was the phrase on everyone's lips, followed by some variation on the observation that everything had been perfectly all right until Mrs Fallon had come into that money.

492

*　　　*　　　*

Dr Fallon conducted himself with great dignity; only Maureen had witnessed him cracking a cup as he set it down with quite extraordinary violence on his desk in the study, and hurling a copy of the *Sketch* into the waste paper basket—and more poignantly, dashing a brusque hand across his eyes as she asked him if he would prefer to take surgery, or go down to Mr Harrison in the Drift Cottages, who was complaining of violent chest pains and difficulty breathing. Wisely, she thought, he opted for Mr Harrison. There were at least five copies of the *Sketch* being read in the waiting room.

*　　　*　　　*

Francis Stevenson-Cook also saw the article. He made it his business to skim through all the papers before leaving for the office. It was Rupert Cameron's name that actually attracted his attention, for he remembered Edwina telling him that Rupert had choreographed some of the fashion show. He read the piece with interest and growing amusement. She sounded a rather interesting person, if a naive one; he looked forward to meeting her, and picked up the telephone that stood by his bed.

His unfortunate secretary, whose working day began at any time from seven onwards, said that yes, she would certainly arrange for Mrs Moreton to be available for lunch that day.

*　　　*　　　*

'The only thing I mind,' said Harry, raising his glass to Cassia, 'is having Rupert established as your childhood sweetheart. When really of course it was me. Perhaps you could ask the *Sketch* to publish a correction to that effect tomorrow.'

'Oh, Harry, please! It isn't funny.'

'I think it's extremely funny. So does Edwina. She phoned me from the offices of *Style* to make sure I'd seen it.'

'Oh God!'

'What do you think the doctor will have to say?'

'I don't know. He doesn't say anything much to me at all these days.'

'Well, I think he might break his rule about this. Pretty distressing stuff, I'd say, for a husband to read over his breakfast egg.'

'Do you really think so?'

'Well, of course I do. It does more or less describe an adulterous passion. The irony being, of course, that your adulterous passion is for someone quite different.'

'Yes,' she said listlessly, 'I suppose so.'

'The other irony is,' he said, leaning back in his chair, his eyes amused, 'that a few weeks ago I was extremely irritated by a suggestion of Edwina's that you and Rupert were having an affair.'

'Oh, really?' said Cassia. The dizziness and nausea of yesterday seemed to have returned. She finished what was left of her martini rather too quickly and tried to smile at Harry.

'Yes. I tried to be grown up about it, of course. To tell myself you were after all childhood sweethearts, as the *Sketch* expresses it so elegantly. And then a couple of days after that she mentioned she'd called at your house one evening and that Rupert had been there. She saw that as proof positive; and I must admit even I found it a little unsettling. Then things took a rather different turn, as you know, and I forgot all about him. Until today. Poor old Cameron. One of life's losers, I'm afraid. Is this play any good, incidentally? We ought to attend the opening night, I think. Show some solidarity. I'll tell Edwina to get some tickets.'

'Yes, it seems very good. What I saw of it.'

'Ah yes, at the rehearsal. Where you were . . . what was the word? Transfixed. You see how I have committed the article to memory. Well, it must be good to transfix you.'

'It is,' said Cassia again, 'very good.'

'You really are worried about it, aren't you?' he said suddenly. 'You shouldn't, you know, nobody really takes any notice of the tabloid press.'

'It seems to me, Harry, that everyone takes a great deal of notice of it,' she said.

'Oh, not really. A little cheap amusement, and then tomorrow, someone else.' He leant forward, took both her hands in his. 'It's nonsense, that's all, a bit of fun. Try and see it like that. Amusement for the masses. And as there's absolutely nothing in it, what can—' He stopped quite suddenly, just sat there, absolutely still, his eyes fixed on hers.

She looked at him, and she could see his expression change. And in spite of the warmth of the Dorchester Hotel bar, of her new sable coat, bought in a fit of sexually induced extravagance the day after she and Harry had first made love, she shivered.

'There isn't anything in it, is there?' he said after a long silence. 'You're not in love with him?'

'No, of course I'm not.' She smiled, hoping, praying he would leave it, leave the subject. He did not.

'And you haven't . . . had an affair with him?'

She was silent.

'Recently?'

She sat there, her eyes meeting his steadily, not moving, not speaking.

'Dear sweet Jesus,' he said, 'you have, haven't you? You've been to bed with him. Edwina was right. Well, haven't you? Answer me, Cassia, please.'

'Yes,' she said, her voice very low, 'yes, I have. But it wasn't like you think.'

'Oh, really? Is that really so?' His expression, his voice, were calm; just for a moment she was hopeful, hopeful that he would believe her, would listen to her. Then he leant forward, grabbed her wrist, twisted it upwards, and sat there holding her by it.

'Do tell me how it was not how I think. I would very much like to know. Does his cock grow backwards? Does he make love standing on his head? Or is—'

'Harry, please! Please!'

'You are disgraceful,' he said, standing up, releasing her wrist with a violent gesture. 'Disgraceful. I would not have believed it of you. Can this be the woman who expressed great distress the other day at the notion of me sleeping with my own wife?'

His face was white; his eyes, brilliantly dark in that whiteness, were full of a dislike and distaste so strong she could feel it like a physical force.

'Well', he said, 'I have clearly been deluding

496

myself. Aided and abetted by you. It seems that even my wife's morals are of a higher calibre than your own. Goodbye, Cassia. I do hope very much we never meet again. In fact, I feel a very strong compunction to be out of this building immediately, if you are going to remain in it. Perhaps you would be kind enough to settle the account. Whores are very highly paid these days, I do believe. But, of course, you would know that . . .'

CHAPTER TWENTY-SEVEN

Dominic Foster was trying to concentrate on a drawing, to distract himself from his natural nervousness at the prospect of visiting Cecily in the nursing home that afternoon, when Harry Moreton phoned him. He sounded extremely strained.

'Dominic? Look? I'm sorry, I can't make this afternoon after all. I've asked Edwina if she'll go with you, but she's got a luncheon or some bloody nonsense. Can we postpone it?'

'I'd rather not. Actually. I think it's very important. Could we go later?'

'No, I really can't, not today. You could go on your own, of course.'

'I can't do that, Harry.'

'Well, it'll have to wait, then. Sorry.' And he put the phone down.

Dominic was torn between relief and a sense of anti-climax . . .

*   *   *

Cassia drove much too fast towards St John's school and Bertie. She felt in some strange way she was putting a distance between herself and her unhappiness, and going there, visiting him, was the one thing she could do that was useful, helpful, that would not hurt anyone.

She was, of course, going alone. An icily courteous Edward had said he was far too busy to come.

'Yes, I see. But Edward, we do need to talk, when I get home.'

'Oh, you're coming home, are you? How very good of you. Do I take that to mean that you have no rehearsals to attend?'

'Edward, that is just so much nonsense, that article, so ridiculous.'

'Indeed? I had thought it was I who was ridiculous. Or rather had been made to look so. Yes, I agree, we do have something to talk about. Several things.'

*   *   *

'Company for you, Fallon,' said Matron, smiling. 'One of the big boys has got chicken pox now. Come along, Collins, into bed here, beside Fallon. You can cheer each other up.'

Bertie looked through crusty eyes at Collins, who was smiling bravely up at Matron. 'Thanks, Matron. I feel a bit sick, could I have a bowl, please?'

She bustled off, and Collins looked at Bertie.

'You little turd,' he said, 'this is your fault I'm here, it's your filthy germs I've got. You see that pot over there? I'm going to fill it up with pee and

498

make you drink it, you little piece of shit. Oh, thank you, Matron, thank you very much. Don't worry about me, I'll be fine now, I feel a bit better now I'm lying down. Me and Fallon'll be fine, won't we, Fallon?'

Bertie didn't speak; he just lay looking at Collins, in a state of terror so abject he actually felt as if he was going to mess the bed.

Matron hesitated. Then she said, 'No, I think I'd better stay for a bit. In case you are sick.'

*   *   *

'Hello, Bertie.'

She looked so lovely, so much more beautiful even than he remembered. Her lips as she bent to kiss his hot, itching face were so cool, her hair as it fell on to his forehead so soft, she smelt so lovely. It was more than Bertie could bear. He burst into tears, careless of Collins's eyes on him, and sat up, winding his arms round her neck.

'Mummy,' was all he said, over and over again, repeating it like a mantra. He felt not happiness, but as if his heart was going to break.

Cassia sat holding him, her face buried in his soft brown hair, noticing his extreme thinness, his burning temperature, the frantic clasp of his arms. Something wasn't right; she knew it.

'I'll get you a cup of tea, Mrs Fallon,' said Matron, who had been watching this scene with a touch of disapproval. 'Come along now, Fallon, be a big boy, let your poor mother sit down.'

As Cassia sat down, a very good-looking boy in the next bed, much older than Bertie, smiled at her.

She smiled back. 'Hello.'

499

'How do you do, Mrs Fallon. Aren't you going to introduce me to your mother, Fallon?'

'Oh, yes,' said Bertie, brushing away his tears. 'Mummy, this is Collins. He's probably going to be head boy next year.'

'How very important,' said Cassia.

'I've been keeping an eye on Fallon,' said Collins, 'as he's so new. Tried to help him a bit. Haven't I, Fallon?'

'Yes,' said Bertie.

'How very kind of you.'

'Oh, not really. The least I could do. And it's really lucky there's two of us in here, to keep each other company. Isn't it, Fallon?'

'Yes, it is.' His voice was low, slightly shaky.

Cassia looked at him thoughtfully. He didn't seem himself. Well, he wouldn't be, he clearly wasn't at all well. A couple of the spots on his face were slightly infected; she remarked on this to Matron.

Matron clearly saw this as a reflection on her professional skills. 'Naturally I am aware of that, Mrs Fallon. I have been attending to them.'

'I'm sure you have, Matron. It's just that there's a danger of scarring with chicken pox. That would be a shame.' She smiled encouragingly at Bertie; he stared back at her, trying to smile and failing. She put out her hand, took his, pushed back his hair. Even his scalp was covered in spots.

'Poor old chap. Look, I've brought you some fruit and a few books. Would you like some grapes now? Collins, what about you?'

'Oh, that would be awfully kind of you, Mrs Fallon.'

She sat there for an hour or more, chatting to

Bertie, reading him a story. He remained tense, watchful, his eyes huge in his blemished face. She felt increasingly uneasy.

'Darling, I'll be back in a minute. I'm just going to have a word with Matron.'

She found Matron sorting what looked like an impossibly complex pile of socks. 'What a job!'

'Indeed,' said Matron. She was clearly still feeling stung by Cassia's criticism.

'Matron, I really would like to take Bertie home. He does seem absolutely wretched. I know it's against the rules, but I can't quite see why, to be honest. It is half term, and extra work for you. I just wonder what the point is of him staying here. I'd love to have him home with us, and I'm sure it would do him good. Of course you're looking after him beautifully, but there's nothing like your own family when you're ill. And he does seem very . . . tense.'

'Well, he is a very highly strung child, Mrs Fallon.'

'I know that. All the more reason to have him home, nurse him back to health there. Look, could I have a word with the headmaster? I can see it's not your decision.'

'If you wish, of course. But I'm quite sure he will agree with me.'

*   *   *

The headmaster did. Politely, firmly, very slightly patronisingly, he told her it was out of the question, that other boys' parents were less willing, less capable to care for sick children, that it was far better to have one rule for all, that justice might be

501

seen to be done. 'I'm sorry, Mrs Fallon, but in the long run, it could make life more difficult for your son if he is allowed to break the rules.'

Cassia sighed. She could see the logic of that if nothing else.

She went very slowly back to the sanatorium. Bertie was alone; Collins had disappeared.

'Hello, darling. I'm back.'

'Mummy?' He put out a hot little hand, held hers. 'Couldn't I possibly come home?'

'Darling—'

'Please! Please!'

'Fallon,' said Matron, coming in again. 'Don't upset your mother. You know the rules.'

'Look,' said Cassia, hating herself, 'look, darling, school rules have to be kept. They really do. They can't make exceptions for one small boy. However miserable. Can they, Collins?' she said to Collins who had come back into the room.

'No, of course not,' said Collins.

'I've got to go now, darling, but I will come back in a day or two. Maybe even tomorrow.'

'Mummy, please!' There was a desperation in his voice, in his eyes.

She struggled, managed to hold firm. 'No, darling. Now I must go. I've got to go home and see the others and Daddy, of course. I'm sorry.'

She bent to kiss him again, felt him turn from her, heard him stifle a sighing sob. It hurt; it hurt horribly. She stood up, quickly, before she weakened, said goodbye again, waved quite gaily to Collins and half ran from the room.

*   *   *

Bertie looked helplessly at Collins. He could feel the hot tears running down his face; he couldn't help it, he didn't care. He didn't care about anything any more.

'Diddums,' said Collins very quietly, 'poor baby diddums. Come on, over here, have a nice drink, that'll make you feel better. I've been piddling all afternoon, just for you. Matron's gone to take supper. Come on, in with your head . . .'

*　　　*　　　*

Cassia was halfway down the stairs, when she realised she had forgotten her gloves. She thought at first she would leave them, didn't want to upset Bertie by returning. But it was a frosty evening, and her car was very cold. Reluctantly, she turned and went back upstairs . . .

*　　　*　　　*

'What on earth is he doing here?' said Edward, as she carried Bertie into the house, wrapped in blankets. 'I thought the rules at his school were—'

'No longer his school, Edward,' she said. 'He's left it. As of this afternoon. And don't even try to argue with me, please. I've told the headmaster that he and the matron and Bertie's housemaster, and quite possibly a few of the parents, will be extremely fortunate not to find themselves the subject of a further interview with me in the *Sketch* newspaper. A copy of which I found, somewhat to my distress, on his desk. That is, if we don't receive a very full written apology, a confirmation that a boy called Collins and his cohorts have been

503

expelled, and a full refund of the term's fees. Janet, would you help me get Bertie up to bed, please?'

*   *   *

'I'm very tired,' Cecily said to the nurse who came to ask her what she would like for supper. 'I really don't want any supper. Could I just have my hot drink and settle for the night early?'

The nurse went to ask Sister, who said that it was just as well Mrs Harrington's visitors hadn't come, she really wouldn't have been up to seeing them.

'Take her her hot drink at eight 'o clock, Nurse, please, and her pills. But try and persuade her to have a little supper in the meantime. It will do her good and it helps the pills to work.'

*   *   *

Dominic stayed in his office, working, and then at six o'clock went over to the cupboard where he kept a bottle of whisky and poured himself a large one. He and Benedict had often sat at the end of the day, at this window, overlooking the Thames, drinking whisky; Irish whiskey it was that they both liked, whiskey spelt with an e, Benedict called it. They both took it the same way: with just a little very slightly warm water, and they drank it slowly, savouring it, and nibbling at salted almonds. The other drink they both liked was white port: Benedict had some friends in Oporto, and they had introduced him to it.

God, he missed Benedict . . .

He thought about Cecily lying in her nursing

504

home, sick and alone, and felt very remorseful suddenly. He should have gone today; he really should.

It had been cowardly of him not to. The worst that could have happened would have been that Cecily would have abused him, ordered him out. He could have survived that. He really could. And he might have been able to help her.

He looked at his watch. It was still only half past six . . .

*   *   *

Edward was waiting when Cassia came down from settling Bertie.

'Please come in here,' he said, leading the way into the sitting room. She followed him in and shut the door.

'Have you gone quite mad?' he said quite quietly.

'No, Edward. I have come to my senses.'

'You kidnap a child from his school—You listen to some no doubt exaggerated story about his bad experiences there, make a complete fool of yourself in front of the headmaster—'

'Edward—'

'Now what do you think is to become of him? Where is he to go now? Who will take a child who has been taken out of a perfectly good prep school halfway through the term just because he's homesick and can't cope? Perhaps you'd like to answer me that.'

'Edward, that is not a perfectly good prep school. It's an appalling place. Shall I tell you what they were doing to him? Holding his head down in

505

the lavatory and pulling the chain. Every night. Threatening him with worse if he told. Told anyone. Today, one of them was forcing him to drink urine, out of a chamber pot. Actually in the sanatorium. And no one keeping an eye on a small boy, a new, very small boy, the youngest in the school, to make sure he was all right. Now don't tell me nothing like that had ever happened before, Edward, that they should not have been alert to it, and don't tell me that is a good school.'

He was silent for a long time. Then he got up, went over to the fireplace and stood there, staring in at the blazing spitting logs. 'Oh, God.' He looked across at her, his face drawn. 'What have we done to him?'

'Well,' she said, choosing to ignore, with agonising generosity, the 'we', 'of course you thought it was for the best, but he can't go back, Edward, he really can't.'

He looked utterly exhausted; his thin shoulders drooped as he stood there, his face etched with new, deep lines, his eyes sunk beneath his bony forehead. She felt stricken suddenly: she had done that, or much of it, and he had not deserved it.

'If we were divorced,' he said suddenly, 'I could probably get custody of the children. Have you thought about that?'

Cassia's guts literally lurched. 'Edward, why are you talking about divorce, for heaven's sake?'

'Because I've been thinking about it.'

'Because of this nonsense in the paper?'

'Is it nonsense?' he said, his voice heavy. 'Is it really nonsense?'

Another deep breath. 'You know it's nonsense. The only real truth in that report was that I've

506

known Rupert all my life. Everything else was innuendo, they distorted what I said. You must see that.'

'Oh, I suppose I do, yes,' he said, surprising her. 'But I have been thinking about at least separation for some time. It has nothing to do with Rupert Cameron, or indeed anybody else. It's that I don't really see any future in our marriage. You have no time for me, no interest in me—you're so wrapped up in your own life you won't even consider making a temporary move in order that I can get a qualification that would transform my career. Is that really so very much to ask?'

'No,' she said quietly, 'not if you put it like that. And I would love you still to do that, you know I would. But you could have got that qualification anywhere, Edward. In London, quite possibly. It really wasn't necessary to uproot us all, was it? Edward, I know I've not always behaved very well. Since—well, since I got the money.'

'I think that's an understatement,' he said. Thank God, she thought; he didn't know how much.

'Yes, I suppose it is, and I'm very, very sorry. But I just want you to try and see it from my point of view. It may be that our marriage is over, but if it is, then we should approach that constructively. It won't do us or the children any good not to.'

'Perhaps you should tell me,' he said, his voice heavy, dark, 'about your point of view.'

'I'd like to. It might help. Might make you feel less hostile to me. I wasn't really properly happy. Before. Oh, Edward, I wanted to work so much. So so much. I could have been such a good doctor. I know I could. But I gave up any chance I had, came

507

here with you, lived with you, as your wife—'

'Very good of you,' he said.

'Please listen. I gave up my dreams of surgery, of obstetrics, for you and our future. Not easily, of course, but I was very happy to do it. And anyway, there was Bertie. But I could have worked locally, on a part-time basis, I could have helped you, here, in this practice, only you wouldn't let me. That hurt me so much. There I was, running, or trying to run the house, doing something I hated badly, when I could have been doing something I loved well. Only you wouldn't let me. Why, Edward, why?'

He was silent.

'And I did miss my friends, they were so important to me, Leonora, and Cecily and Benedict and—'

'Harry Moreton?'

She felt herself flush. 'Yes Harry, of course, and Edwina. They were my family, really, as Rupert was. And you kept me from them, too. You always refused to come and see them with me, made it awkward for me to see them, were hostile if they came here. I was lonely and frustrated and bored, Edward, even if I did have the children and you. And so when I could take things for myself, I'm afraid I was tactless and impatient and greedy. And when you took Maureen on, I could hardly bear it. It was so unjust, so cruel. Or it seemed so. I'm sure it seemed different to you.'

Still he was silent.

'That was why I took the house, you know, to hurt you back. And so it went on from there, Edward, didn't it? I hurt you and then you hurt me. That was why you sent Bertie away, really, wasn't it? To hurt me . . . But I still want you to get that

508

qualification, Edward, I really do. I'd love you to do it in London, or at least somewhere nearer, so you could come home often. I'd support you in every way I could, but don't ask me to give up what shreds of my own career are left. Please.'

He stood up. 'I'm going for a walk now,' he said. 'I need to be on my own. I'm very sorry to have been such an unsatisfactory husband. Sorry you've been so unhappy.'

'Edward, that's not what I said. You're distorting it. Please, please, try to understand it.'

'Oh, I do,' he said, 'I do. It reinforces my own view of myself, which is not a pretty one. God in heaven, Cassia, do you think I'm so stupid that I couldn't see all those things for myself? Do you think I'm proud of myself for sending Bertie away, for my jealousy of you? My inability to relate to your friends? Of course I'm not, but—' He stopped; she realised there were tears in his eyes.

Remorse moved in her, a great raw wound. 'Oh, Edward,' she said, moving towards him, wanting to hold him, to comfort him, as if he were one of the children.

'No,' he said, moving away from her, 'no, don't. It's too late, Cassia. Too late for both of us. We can't negate everything that's happened. There's no future for us together any more.'

She stood there, staring at him, feeling guilt and misery settling into her, heavy, inescapable, staring at the ending of her marriage, listening to its death knell.

CHAPTER TWENTY-EIGHT

Sister stood in the hall, looking at Dominic rather severely. 'It's rather late,' she said, 'for visiting.'

'Yes, I'm extremely sorry. Mr Moreton, Mrs Harrington's cousin, you know, was called away suddenly, and I was held up in the office, but I would still like to see Mrs Harrington. If at all possible. I think,' he said, 'I really think I can help her. I knew her husband very well, I have some knowledge of what was in his mind when he, well, when he died. Please let me see her.'

Sister hesitated. She looked at her watch. It was after seven thirty; Mrs Harrington had been bathed, her bed changed, she was virtually ready for sleep. A visitor now might upset her; and in spite of what he might think, whatever it was he had to say could upset Mrs Harrington rather than cheer her up. It seemed very unwise.

'I'm sorry,' she said, 'I really don't think it's a very good idea. Another day, perhaps, and if you could try to come earlier . . .'

'Yes,' said Dominic humbly. 'Yes, of course. Well, perhaps you could give her these.' He handed Sister the bunch of white roses he had brought and he went out of the front door.

The nursing home was on Richmond Hill, near the gates of the park.

It was quite dark now, and a full moon was rising; against its brilliance in the frosty sky was etched the shape of the great Cedar of Lebanon that stood just inside the gates. It was hauntingly beautiful. Benedict would have loved that tree,

510

Dominic thought; he adored trees, had spent a lot of money planting them down in Devon. 'These are my immortality,' he had said to Dominic, once, 'here to look at for centuries ahead.'

Dominic had parked his car under the tree; he walked over to it, wondering if he would ever be able to forget what he had done, forgive himself; if Benedict, wherever he was, would forgive him.

He looked up at the nursing home, wondering which room was Cecily's; and saw the curtains being slowly pulled half aside at one of the first-floor windows, and then Cecily's face at the window, looking out. He could see her quite clearly. She was wearing a white night-dress; and her dark hair was loose, hanging over her shoulders. He could not see the expression on her face, of course, but her stance, the despairing droop of her shoulders, the way she leant her head on the windowpane, spoke of an intense and dreadful misery. Then he saw a figure come up behind her, a nurse, saw her put an arm round Cecily, draw her away from the window, close the curtains.

Afterwards, things seemed rather hazy to Dominic; he remembered running back to the house, ringing urgently at the bell, remembered a nurse telling him that visiting time was over, remembered even moving her gently but firmly aside. He could just remember racing up the stairs, hesitating on the landing, working out which was Cecily's room; could just remember her face, white, horrified, frightened, remember her shrinking back on to her pillows. After that, no details, no details at all.

*   *   *

'It was really awful,' Nurse Jenkins related to a breathless common room. 'I was in the corridor, and I followed him in, of course, and he went over to the bed, poor Mrs Harrington was so frightened, and then she did start to scream, and he put his hand over her mouth, and I almost screamed myself then, I thought he was going to rape her, but I didn't, I stayed calm somehow. I just pressed her bell, you know, and then went over and tried to pull him off her, and then I heard him shouting something at her, saying it had been all his fault that her husband had died, and she just went all quiet, and lay there staring at him, and then she started to cry, but not that awful screaming she does sometimes, just ordinary crying, and he sat down on her bed, holding her hand, and saying, "There, there." Then Sister and Matron arrived, and the porter, and told him the police were on their way, and she said in a really strange voice, "There's no need for that, no need at all," and then he got off the bed and knocked over her tray and I went for a towel from her bedside cupboard and, of course, that was when I found all the pills . . .'

*   *   *

'I thought we might go to the Forty Three later,' said Francis Stevenson-Cook. He and Edwina were dining at the Savoy; had been dancing in between courses.

'I'd adore to go to the Forty Three,' she said.

'It really is the best music in London, don't you think? And the best cocaine as well, of course, if you want it.'

'I don't,' she said firmly. She had tried cocaine a few times and had enjoyed it, but it was not something she was going to reveal to a virtual stranger, and particularly one who was her boss.

'Nor me,' he said lightly, 'I don't enjoy anything of that sort. I like to stay in control. At all times.'

'I had noticed,' she said, 'that you don't drink very much. Is that for the same reason?'

'It is. How about you?'

'Well,' she said laughing, 'as you know, I drink rather a lot. I adore it.'

'Of course. But I meant, do you prefer to control or to be controlled?'

'I'm not sure. Actually. I have a very controlling husband.'

'Indeed?'

'Yes. I suppose being controlled absolves one of responsibility.'

'It does indeed, but that also implies a certain— what shall we say—frailty of will. I would not imagine your will to be frail, Edwina.'

'No,' she said, 'no, I don't think that it is.'

'That is a wonderful dress,' he said suddenly.

'Thank you. Hardy Amies.'

'Do you not patronise the Parisian couturiers?'

'Not really,' she said. 'To be honest, I don't know any of the houses there.'

'I think you should buy in Paris,' he said suddenly, 'it would suit your style. Are you going to the collections in January?'

'What, for the magazine? Goodness, no, I'm not nearly important enough, you should know that.'

'You are quite important enough,' he said, 'in my opinion.' He picked up her hand suddenly and kissed it, his brilliant blue eyes fixed on hers. 'I should like you to go. I would like to go with you, I think it would be fun. We shall see. Now, shall we have coffee, or go on to the Forty Three? That won't cause problems with your husband, will it?'

'Oh, no,' said Edwina vaguely. 'Anyway, he's abroad.'

'Good. I don't like upsetting husbands. I do pride myself on my sixth sense on a marriage, though. I have rarely found myself entertaining a truly happily married lady.'

'Oh, really? So I'm not truly happy? Is that what you are saying?' She laughed, took out her cigarette case, offered him one.

'No, thank you. I smoke only in bed. And yes, I would say you are not truly happy. In your marriage, that is.'

'Ah,' said Edwina.

*   *   *

The Forty Three was packed. Everyone was there: the Mountbattens with Charles Chaplin, Max Aitken, Penelope Dudley-Ward, the Sweenys . . . 'Did you know,' Francis hissed in her ear, as he smiled and bowed across at the ravishing Margaret Sweeny, 'that she'd had twenty-one affairs by the time she was twenty-one?'

'Is that all?' said Edwina.

There was a sudden stir through the place; not a sound, not even a movement, just an almost imperceptible concentration on the entrance.

'It's the King,' said Francis. 'Look, he's just joined the Mountbattens.'

'Good heavens. But not her.'

514

'No, apparently he's been told not to be seen in public with her. Not in the week of her divorce, at any rate. I'm told, though, that things are reaching something of a climax. Scenes with the Queen, talks with Baldwin, with the Archbishop . . .'

'He can't actually think he can marry her, surely?'

'I imagine,' said Francis soberly, watching the King move on to the dance floor with Mrs Dudley-Ward, 'he thinks he can't do anything else.'

*   *   *

Cecily woke up feeling deeply, terribly sad. It was so different, that sadness, from the other wretched emotions that she had lived through during the past weeks: the rage, the horror, the remorse, and the dreadful, horrible guilt, that it seemed almost sweet. She lay there, on her pillows, thinking about Benedict, remembering him, the way he had been, so kind and gentle always, so good a father, so loyal a friend—and so good in so many ways a husband, and it was the purest pleasure to be able to do that.

She was forbidden visitors that day, for which she was grateful; it was explained to her that she had had a shock from which she needed to recover and she said that she understood, that she did not, in fact, feel quite up to seeing anyone, even (least of all, but she did not say so) her mother; but she also said that she might like to start seeing people quite soon now, as soon as they felt it might be possible, she would like to see her children very much, all of them, and Mrs Fallon, and she would like to see Harry Moreton.

She didn't think she would like to see Dominic

515

Foster again, or not for some time; his courage in coming to see her, in confessing, with all its attendant risks, had impressed and moved her greatly, but her prime emotion towards him was still hostility, jealousy that it had been Dominic's faithlessness that in the end Benedict had been unable to live with, rather than any failing of her own.

She had still been, she knew, intolerant, uncompassionate even, and at the last, unforgiving. She would carry that and her memory of it with her for ever, she knew. But as she had sat there, hearing Dominic telling her, in a quick, urgent voice, that Benedict had always, in his way, loved her, loved her very much, had wanted to continue with their marriage with all its failings, had even at their last meeting talked lovingly and gratefully of her, the worst of her remorse, her self-hatred, had fallen away.

Something else came into her consciousness too, for the first time, something healthy and strong: anger at Benedict that in taking his own life he could have subjected her and their children to such horror and such pain.

*   *   *

She also realised, as the medical staff told her she should see no one that day, that they had a problem themselves: in enabling her to hoard and, hide her pills, they had been guilty of a lack of proper supervision, a kind of neglect. If that were revealed, there could be serious trouble, and she did not wish that for them.

After lunch that day (having eaten almost half a

516

plateful) she asked to see Matron, and the doctor if possible. Matron came in, looking sternly uneasy; Cecily smiled at her and told her how much better she felt, and that there was no need for the story of the pills that she had forgotten about to go any further, as far as she was concerned, she didn't want people to know she was so stupid, and she would be grateful if Matron would convey that to the doctor and also to any of the other staff who had come to know of it.

'It was certainly through no fault of anyone here that I became so absent-minded; and since I never wish to see another sleeping pill as long as I live, I see no risk of it ever happening again.'

Matron said she was extremely glad she was feeling so much better, and that she was grateful for the kind words expressed by Mrs Harrington, which she would pass on to the doctor.

Later the doctor himself came to see her and said that although medical etiquette required him to say in his report on her that she had not always taken her pills and that they had been found in her room, he was satisfied himself that no more than absent-mindedness was to blame, and that she herself, he presumed, would not wish her family to suffer any more than they already had from a mistaken idea that she might have planned on taking an overdose.

'And I will explain this to the rest of the staff, particularly to Nurse Jenkins, who found the pills.'

'Thank you. Now I am very tired and . . .' She felt her eyes fill suddenly, with exhaustion and the strain of the two interviews, as well as sadness. She swallowed hard, reached for a handkerchief. 'I would like to sleep: for a while. But there is no

517

need for Nurse Jenkins to continue to sit with me, Dr Meredith; I really can be quite safely left, and I do value my privacy at the moment.'

Dr Meredith patted her hand and said that as from that moment, she should have it, 'on condition that you notify me immediately if you feel any return of the old symptoms. The mind does not recover quite as steadily as the body, and you may have setbacks.'

'I don't think I will,' said Cecily politely, wiping her eyes, 'because a major reason for my symptoms has gone. Of course I am still very unhappy, but I can see now that I shall in time recover.' She closed her eyes. 'How I could ever have needed to have pills to send me off to sleep I find it hard to imagine.'

She woke up three hours later, in the early evening dusk, to find a very large bouquet of roses in a vase by her bed; the card read simply, 'Thank you for listening to me. Dominic.'

In a few days, when she really felt stronger, she would write to thank him.

*　　　*　　　*

Cassia had not gone to work that day, had phoned the clinic, citing the same domestic crisis that she had on Monday, able to elaborate on it quite truthfully that day, saying she would come in on Friday instead; and serve me right for lying about such a thing, she thought gloomily, putting down the phone, they'd sack me if there was any justice.

She could hear nice Nurse Hampton frowning sympathetically down the phone, shocked to hear of Bertie's misfortunes, reassuring her that she must only come back when he was quite well enough to be left. Which was probably in about ten minutes, Cassia thought, listening to the shrieks of laughter that were coming from Bertie's bedroom—such normal, happy sounds.

The clear sense of happiness reached out to her, clearing just for a while, at the sense of panic that had taken over her life. It was stronger than anything else, that panic: stronger than sadness, remorse, stronger even than the raw, wracking misery that had filled her ever since she had watched Harry walking away from her in the Dorchester, heard his voice over and over again, calling her a whore.

As long as she lived she would never forget that moment, never even begin to forget it. It had provided a scourge with which she chastised herself, night and day, over all her behaviour: not merely the foolish fatal incident with Rupert, the all-consuming selfishness of her adultery with Harry, but—perhaps most—the savage wilfulness with which she could see, and with horrible clarity, she had destroyed her marriage. She loathed herself for her cruelty, her selfishness, her rejection of the kind, gentle, loving man she had married, married so wrongly, and the brutality of her behaviour to him. That was what created the panic: not that her marriage was ruined, Edward damaged beyond repair, Harry and her chance of happiness lost to her for ever, but that she could actually be the creature who had wilfully, knowingly, brought about all those things. A creature she had to live with for the rest of her life.

*　　*　　*

519

She went upstairs and into Bertie's room. Fanny was sitting at the end of his bed, and Bertie was lying back on the pillows. Tears streamed down both their faces, not of misery, but laughter, and William had collapsed upside down on to the floor, his legs and arms helplessly entangled with Delia's and those of Buffy, who had followed Bertie up to his room when Cassia had carried him there last night, and had been there, with occasional forced absences while William marched him round the garden, ever since.

'Hello, Mummy.' Bertie managed to stop laughing for a moment. 'Can I have some more toast?'

'Of course you can. You're obviously feeling better.'

'I'm feeling much better. Hardly any itching and not hot at all. Just starving, starving.'

'Starving,' said William, beating a rhythm on the floor with his feet. 'Toast for me too, please.'

'Starvy,' said Delia, 'toasty, toasty.'

'All right. I'll be back in two ticks.'

'Two tickles, you mean,' said William, giggling at his own wit. 'Two chicken poxy tickles.'

'Chicken tickle,' said Delia, 'chicken tickles, chicken tickles.'

Cassia went downstairs smiling.

She took the toast back upstairs; Bertie was quieter now, told her to sit on the bed. She did and he took her hand. 'Don't I really have to go back to that school? Never?'

'Never,' said Cassia, 'never, never.' She held out her arms.

He cuddled up against her. 'It was horrible,' he

520

said simply.

'I know. I'm so sorry.'

'Wasn't your fault. Or Daddy's,' he added firmly. 'He thought I'd like it. I thought so too.'

How generous children were, she thought, turning her head, resting it on his, how quick to forgive. 'I know, darling. We made a mistake.'

'Yes, well, it doesn't matter. It's worth it to be home again.' There was a silence, while they watched Delia feeding Buffy her toast.

'Mummy?'

'Yes, Bertie?'

'What does shagging mean?'

'What?' She was half shocked, half amused.

'Shagging. What does it mean? Because Collins said there was an article in the paper, that said you were shagging some bloke who wasn't Daddy.'

Cassia looked at him, at William who was looking at her enquiringly, and prayed for inspiration. It did not come. 'Well,' she said finally, 'if it was the article I'm thinking about, it was a very silly one. It was about how I've lent some money for Rupert's new play. And then it was about what good friends we are, which is true, of course, but the reporter got a bit carried away and seemed to think I was his girlfriend.'

'What, you and Rupert?'

'Yes.'

'So is shagging being someone's girlfriend?'

'Sort of, yes.'

'Well, that's really silly,' said William. 'I mean you can't be anyone's girlfriend, because you're married to Daddy.'

'Yes, of course. I told you it was silly.'

There was a silence, then Bertie said, 'Two of

521

the boys at school, their parents were divorced. I suppose then you could shag someone else, if you were divorced?'

'Well, yes, I suppose you could. Incidentally, Bertie, shagging isn't a very nice word. Not one I'd use.'

'OK,' he said cheerfully. 'Anyway, you're not divorced, are you?'

'No, of course not.'

'I'd hate that so much,' he said, burying his head against her again. 'I'd rather go back to that school than you get divorced, you and Daddy, I really would.'

CHAPTER TWENTY-NINE

Harry glared at Edwina across the dining table. 'I am not going to the bloody thing, and that's the end of it. Please don't mention it again. Take your new boyfriend. He'll probably enjoy it. Now I'm going to the office. I don't know when I'll be back.'

Edwina looked after him thoughtfully. He had been in a filthy temper for days. Not that that was anything unusual; but she did wonder if his remark about Francis was a clue. She'd told him about dinner and going to the Forty Three when he'd got back from Munich, simply because he always got so angry if he discovered such things for himself. He hadn't seemed remotely interested; hadn't seemed remotely interested in anything she'd said or done for weeks. In a way the bad temper was a return to normality.

Well, if he wasn't going to come to Rupert's first

night, she certainly was. She'd promised Rupert and, apart from anything else, she needed to keep him on her side because of the fashion show. But it certainly didn't look as if it was going to be the theatrical event of the Season; the bookings were very modest, even for the first week.

She wondered if she might actually take Francis, or at least ask him if he wanted to go. It was quite a good idea of Harry's.

She'd spoken to Rupert at the weekend and he'd sounded utterly distraught, said the whole thing was going to be a disaster; but then that was probably the artistic temperament. She'd seen a great deal of the artistic temperament since she'd been working at *Style*, and felt she absolutely understood and sympathised with it. If you were struggling to do something superbly well, it created huge tension and strain, which inevitably surfaced. Just the same, the play could be dreadful: maybe it wasn't such a good idea to ask Francis.

In the event Francis raised the subject himself. He'd phoned her about the fashion show and then asked when Rupert's first night was. 'Tomorrow,' she said. 'He's frightfully nervous.'

'Well, he's chosen an auspicious day. London will be packed. The Jarrow marchers are arriving, poor desperate things, there's a Communist rally, and it's the Opening of Parliament. The new King's first performance. Oh, and the forecast is heavy rain. Is Rupert getting a full house?'

'Very poor bookings, apparently. I honestly don't know that it's going to be very good.'

'Poor fellow. We ought to support him, don't you think? Specially as he's doing such sterling work for us. Look, can you get me a ticket or two? I could bring some chums along.'

*   *   *

Cassia was taking Fanny and Stephanie to *Letters*; Edward had, of course, refused to come. Afterwards, Rupert had suggested they all went out to supper together, 'And I can either drink champagne or a phial of poison.'

'I might join you in the latter,' said Cassia.

*   *   *

A letter came for her that Monday morning, from M. Jean Berrez, the patron of the café in Le Touquet. He had seen one of Rollo Gresham's old friends, and had managed to get an address for her: he was living in Marrakesh. 'It seems M. Gresham has not been well, so he would, I am sure, like to hear from you.'

Cassia sat down and wrote to Rollo Gresham immediately . . .

*   *   *

The November morning dawned, as Francis had said it would, to torrential rain. It did a great deal to depress everyone's spirits, that rain: Rupert's as he lay, awake from dawn in an agony of terror, listening to it lashing against his windowpane; Cassia's as she drove up to London with Fanny, forced to take a circuitous route to her house, on account of large areas of London being cordoned off for the state procession to Parliament; Harry Moreton's as he stood scowling at his office window, staring out at it whilst shouting instructions at the unfortunate Margot Murray; those of the loyal subjects of His Majesty who had been waiting patiently for several hours to see the state procession and to wish him well on his way to his first parliament; and of all the weary men who had been marching for over a month now from Jarrow and had chosen that day to present their petition to Parliament, that it should 'recognise the urgent need that works should be provided for the town'.

It did not help anybody either that the King cancelled the state procession and travelled to the Houses of Parliament by car (thereby making the detours virtually unnecessary, and the loyal waiting totally pointless), although the men of Jarrow were able to watch the arrival of the King at Westminster from a good vantage point (where, with the good nature that had characterised the entire march, they cheered him most enthusiastically).

Cassia, who had stopped off at Eaton Place to leave Fanny with Nanny, arrived rather late at her clinic, to find Nurse Hampton's patience with her and her unreliability finally bending, if not actually snapping.

'I'm so sorry,' she said humbly, 'so very sorry. It's just that—'

'Never mind what it is, Dr Fallon. It's a relief that you're here. Now, shall we get started? We've a lass in there with five children under six, all with her, all creating, so the sooner she's seen the better.'

Sometimes, Cassia thought, putting her head round the waiting-room door and asking the mother of five—who was clearly a great deal younger than she—to come into her consulting room, just sometimes, she wondered if her job was worth it. Then she looked at the girl's greyish-white face, at her thin hands, clasping her youngest child in his distinctly threadbare shawl, listened to her voice, tired, anxious, explaining how one more and she thought she'd go mad, and knew it was.

* * *

The Second House theatre was not exactly packed. Cassia and Rupert's mother, a most daunting old lady who had defied her doctor and her Brighton nursing home to attend, together with Stephanie and Fanny and Eleanor Studely's daughter, a rather serious little girl with her mother's dark beauty called Portia, sat alone in the front row. Mrs Cameron kept looking behind her with an expression closer to anger than anxiety and said to Portia, who was doing much the same thing, 'Don't worry, people always come late to first nights.'

'It's such a pity Uncle Edward couldn't have come,' whispered Fanny to Cassia. 'It would have helped. And Janet would have liked it.'

'Yes,' said Cassia, who wished she'd thought of inviting Janet herself, 'yes, it's a terrible shame.'

The Horrockses, to whom Rupert had given complimentary tickets, sat in the row behind them, with six people who seemed to be friends of Eleanor's, and there was a group of Rupert's theatrical chums up in the front row of the circle. Two couples, one of whom Cassia recognised as the other backer, joined them in the front row; a few more distinctly damp, and what Mrs Cameron described in a loud whisper to Cassia as arty-

526

looking people took their places halfway down the stalls.

Jasper Hamlyn, a greenish-pale James Piggott, and a group of friends came down the side aisle, talking and laughing loudly and bravely. Jasper came over to Cassia, kissed her hand and told her theatrical history was about to be made, before leading his friends to their seats. Two men, who were obviously journalists, arrived and complained about the seats they had been given. Jasper Hamlyn moved them into the second row, next to the Horrockses.

And that was all.

Cassia looked at her watch; it was already seven forty. Curtain up couldn't wait much longer. She felt sick; a small trembling hand slid into hers. It was Portia's; her own, responding to it, squeezing it comfortingly, was clammy with sweat. It just wasn't fair. Poor Rupert, he'd be going through the tortures of the damned backstage. And where on earth was Edwina?

And then, just as the lights were going down, there was a great noise outside, the doors opened and at least two dozen people came in, headed by Edwina and an exotic-looking man wearing a scarlet-lined cape, and carrying a silver-topped cane. They all looked as if they were going to a party, the men in dinner jackets, the women in long dresses; they seemed to illuminate the drab little theatre, fill it with excitement and pleasure.

'Can't possibly find our seats in the dark,' the exotic man said in a whisper that could be heard throughout the theatre. 'Let's just sit where we can.'

They seemed to fill the stalls, those few people,

separating into small groups; Cassia saw Mrs Cameron's stern face relax, felt a lump in her own throat, then turned her attention and determined to concentrate very hard on the play. In the event it was not in the least difficult.

*   *   *

From the moment the curtain rose on the two of them, Rupert and Eleanor, sitting on chairs on either side of the stage, the set a simple Victorian-style drawing room, cleverly designed with a few items of furniture—a jardinière, a chair, a low table, to make a division of sorts in it—to the moment when it fell an hour and a half later (there was no interval), the entire theatre was utterly silent. Nobody shuffled their feet, nobody coughed, nobody rustled sweet papers; the story, so simply, so movingly, at times so wittily told, took hold of the fifty or so imaginations laid before it and did not release them. It smiled, that audience, it sighed, it wept, it held its breath; and when the last letter was signed off in Rupert's beautiful voice— 'All my love, for what I truly believe to be eternity'—and the curtain came down, there was an absolute silence for what seemed a long time, before applause rose, its noise out of all proportion to the size of the audience.

In the balcony Rupert's friends stamped their feet: Portia looked back up at them, her small face flushed with joy, and then joined in, the other children following her lead. One of the journalists shouted 'bravo', and clearly wishing to set his own mark on the occasion, Francis Stevenson-Cook rose to his feet and clapped more loudly still. Other people followed him, until the entire audience was standing; Cassia watched Rupert holding Eleanor's hand and taking bow after bow, his face raised into the spotlight, his eyes brilliant with tears. There were cries for the author, the producer; in all they took nine curtain calls. And at the last Rupert looked out into the front row, where they sat, and blew Cassia and his mother and the children a kiss.

*   *   *

'Marvellous, wasn't it?' said Edwina, linking her arm through Cassia's as they walked round to the stage door. 'What a triumph. Cassia, this is Francis Stevenson-Cook. Francis, my frightfully clever friend, Cassia Fallon. You could say she made this evening possible,' she added carelessly, and then disappeared into the mêlée of people kissing Rupert.

'Ah, the famous doctor!' said Stevenson-Cook. 'I am delighted to meet you at last. I've studied your picture in the paper, heard of your huge success in your career—'

'Oh heavens,' said Cassia, half irritated, half amused, 'no success at all, and it was a very old picture.'

'Well, you look every bit as beautiful now. If I might be allowed to say so.'

He was very good-looking, this friend of Edwina's, although possibly, she thought, a homosexual; it had been he, she realised, who had led the crowd of people in late, the crowd who were now fluttering and swooping about the corridor kissing everyone within reach, the immensely stylish crowd, overdressed for the

529

occasion, but bestowing upon it a chic, a sense of social importance, that had undoubtedly contributed to its success.

'It was very nice that you all came,' she said suddenly. 'Thank you so much. Rupert will be terribly grateful.'

'Our pleasure entirely. It was marvellous. And one must look after one's own, after all. Now tell me, how was it exactly that you made this evening possible?'

'I just put a bit of money into it.'

'Oh, yes, of course. I remember the article. And is your husband here?' he said carelessly after a moment.

'Oh, no. No, he's working. As usual.'

'I see. How sad he should miss such a success.'

'Terribly,' said Cassia, and then in an effort to escape what was clearly to develop into an inquisition, 'You must excuse me, I have three little girls here, all in need of supervision.'

'I adore children. I'd love to meet them,' he said, surprising her.

'Of course, I'll round them up and bring them over.'

*   *   *

They never reached a restaurant. After a while, the Stevenson-Cook crowd departed 'for another party, too boring', although he and Edwina, of course, remained. They all moved to the stage; more champagne was brought in, and a hamper of food materialised apparently from nowhere: canapés, tiny sausages, smoked salmon sandwiches—
'Francis's idea,' said Edwina to Cassia. 'He had it in

the car, said we might need it.'

'He's very nice,' said Cassia, 'and this is all terribly generous.'

'Don't you adore him? He's such fun, and really been so kind to me.'

Cassia hesitated. 'No Harry, then?'

'No, he's been in the most frightful bait for days. Refused flatly to come, even though he had told me to get tickets. I'd have been quite sunk without Francis this evening, been here on my own unescorted like you,' she added, 'but, of course, it doesn't matter for you.'

'No, I suppose not,' said Cassia (wondering why not: too dull? too unattractive?).

'Who are those extraordinary people standing over there, next to old Mrs Cameron? Isn't she marvellous?'

'Oh, they're the Horrockses,' said Cassia, laughing. 'She does for me, in London. I suppose Rupert invited them.'

'Too heavenly of him, but they do look a bit out of it. I'll go and talk to them for a bit, put them at their ease. I'm marvellous with working-class people, it's a knack I've picked up from Mummy.'

Mr Horrocks, who had had several glasses of stout before he had even left the house, and several of champagne since, found himself having a rather bewildering conversation with Edwina.

'I thought you looked a bit out of your depth,' she said, smiling at him sweetly, 'but really no need. It's too thrilling you're here, and it's marvellous to think people like you can enjoy the theatre. Do you get up this way often?'

'Not very often, no, but Mrs Horrocks does, of course, looks after Mrs Fallon's house for her.'

531

'Yes, so I understand. She must enjoy that. And Mrs Fallon is a charming person. I've known her since we were debutantes, you know.'

'Is that so? Well, she seems very nice. And Mr Cameron, he's a charming gentleman.'

'Oh, you've met him, have you?' said Edwina. 'Here, have some more champagne. It's a tiny bit warm, but I don't suppose you'll mind too terribly much.'

'Not too much, no,' said Mr Horrocks. He drained the champagne glass, held it out slightly uncertainly to Edwina for refilling. He gave her a wink, drained the glass again. 'Mrs Horrocks has met Mr Cameron a lot more often. He's at her house all the time. Stays the night quite often.'

'Really?' said Edwina. 'Are you sure about that?'

'Course I'm sure,' said Mr Horrocks. He grinned at her. 'Well, they're all the same these theatricals, aren't they? No better than they should be. It's the artistic licence, Mrs Horrocks says, don't you, Bets?'

At this point Mrs Horrocks dug him hard in the ribs. 'Time we went home; Alan,' she said, 'you've had far too much of that stuff. Come on, let's go and find Mr Cameron, say thank you.'

Edwina watched the Horrockses weave their way across the room, and then stood looking at Cassia thoughtfully. How very interesting. Goody goody Cassia. So the article hadn't been so far wrong. You never could tell with people. She couldn't wait to tell Francis.

*   *   *

The party finally ended after one.

'Come on!' said Cassia, clapping her hands, beckoning to the children. 'It's terribly late.'

There were violent protests; Edwina told her not to be such a prude, and said why didn't she and Rupert come to the Embassy, with her and Francis.

'No, I don't think so,' said Cassia. 'I am responsible for these two, and what are we going to do with your mother, Rupert? I thought she was supposed to go to a friend in Victoria at the end of the play?'

'Oh, she can come back to my digs,' said Rupert. 'I can settle her there, and then I'd love to come to the Embassy. Eleanor, why don't you come with us?'

Eleanor, who was clearly longing to go, said what about Portia, and Cassia said that was fine, she could stay with them. 'One more little girl won't make any difference.'

'Yes, but then where can I stay? I can't go all the way home to Croydon tonight.'

'You can stay at our house,' said Edwina. 'We'd love to have you with us. All right? Come on, everyone. Francis, you ready?'

Cassia took the children back to Walton Street alone; in spite of her pleasure at the night, at Rupert's success, she felt suddenly rather depressed.

*　　　*　　　*

She was woken by a small hand tugging at her sleeve. It was Fanny. 'Cassia, wake up. Portia's terribly worried, she says she has to go to school, she's got to play in a lacrosse match, she's lacrosse captain in her year. Her mother's at Aunt

533

Edwina's, isn't she? Could you ring her, Cassia, please, or do you know where Portia's school is?'

Cassia didn't; through a considerable haze of pain from a throbbing head, she dialled Edwina's number. The butler answered the phone.

'Oh Bishop. Sorry to bother you, but could you possibly ask Mrs Studely, who is staying there, to come to the phone? It's rather important. Only tell her,' she added hastily, 'tell her Portia's perfectly all right.'

'One moment, madam, please.'

A long pause, then a sleepy voice came on to the phone. She felt briefly guilty, then thought that Eleanor really should have remembered her daughter's lacrosse match.

'Oh, God,' she said, 'oh dear, how awful of me. I did forget; I can only plead temporary insanity. Brought about by my considerable anxiety. Oh dear, Cassia, is she terribly upset?'

'Well, a bit,' said Cassia, looking at Portia's anxious little face. 'Where does she go? Shall I take her?'

'Oh, no. She's at St Margaret's, in Clapham. I'll get dressed quickly, come and fetch her, in a taxi. Oh, dear, how dreadful of me.'

'Look,' said Cassia, her heart going out to Eleanor in her guilt-ridden anguish, 'if she has to get to Clapham, I'll drop her over to you, that'll save you at least quarter of an hour. And then you can have the taxi waiting. And don't start putting on your sackcloth and ashes yet,' she added, 'I've done much worse than this to my children.'

'Have you really?' said Eleanor. 'Thank you so much for saying that.'

534

It wasn't until she and Portia were in the car that Cassia realised where she was going: to the Moreton house. The thought of seeing Harry was literally terrifying. Well, maybe Eleanor would be waiting outside. Or Harry would still be asleep—it was very early.

The Moreton house looked blessedly dark and slumbering; Eleanor was not, however, outside. Cassia waited a few minutes, then knocked gently on the door and ran down the steps again, like a naughty child. Eleanor was probably in the hall. At worst, Bishop would open the door.

Harry Moreton opened it. He was fully dressed, his overcoat slung round his shoulders, carrying his briefcase. He looked down at her, his face initially startled, shocked even, then coldly, horribly distasteful. 'Why are you here? he said.

Cassia felt horribly sick. Then she swallowed hard, and said, 'I've come to collect Eleanor Studely.'

'Who the hell is Eleanor Studely?'

'She's a friend of Rupert's. An actress.'

'And what is she doing in my house?' It was an expression of such hostility, such disgust that anyone connected with Rupert, or indeed her, should be within any property of his, that she winced.

'She stayed here. She was out with Edwina and her friends last night. It was after the play. You know.'

'Oh, that. Yes.' Again the absolute distaste. 'Well, you'd better go in and find her. I'm leaving.'

He stood aside so that she could walk into the

house; as she passed him, the sense of him, this man whom she had known so intimately, whose body had become so utterly familiar to her, pulled at her, and she felt it, that remembered intimacy, that pleasure, felt it as a violent physical force.

She looked up at him then, she couldn't help it, looked at his face, at his eyes; they met hers, and she could see, just for a moment, that he felt it too, the pull; and then it was gone and the dark eyes lost everything, even hostility, became utterly, deadly blank.

Eleanor suddenly appeared. 'Sorry, Cassia, I'm so sorry. Oh, good morning, you must be Mr Moreton, do forgive me . . .'

Harry said nothing more to either of them, ran down the steps, and got into his car, drove away, the tyres screaming through the morning silence.

'Oh dear, he seems very upset,' said Eleanor.

Cassia didn't even try to answer.

*   *   *

Later that morning she went to see Cecily. The news that Cecily was better, wanted to see her, had touched her deeply. She decided not to take Fanny and Stephanie, and drove them over to Eaton Place to Nanny. They were still high with pleasure at having been at such a dazzling affair as the party on stage the night before. Rupert had telephoned to say that Saturday night was already a sell-out. 'So you'll get your investment back at least, my darling, and probably ten times over.'

Cassia told him rather wearily that that was the last thing on her mind, but she was very, very happy for him. The thought of having any more money, she realised, made her feel sick.

Cecily was sitting up in a chair at the window when Cassia arrived. She turned and smiled at Cassia, held out her hand. 'It's so lovely to see you,' she said simply.

'It's lovely to see you too,' said Cassia, shocked at her appearance: she must have lost two stones at least, the creamy skin was parchment dry and pale and the dark eyes sunk deep into her face. But they were serene eyes, they had lost the frenetic brightness that had been there at the funeral, and the dreadful staring vacancy of the morning of her breakdown.

Cecily smiled, clearly reading her thoughts. 'I look awful, don't I? But you should have seen me a week ago. This is fat by comparison. Fat and rosy.' She laughed. 'I never ever thought I'd be trying to put on weight.'

'Cecily, I'm so pleased you're better.'

'I do feel better,' said Cecily, her voice slightly surprised. 'It's lovely. I—well, I really did want to die, you know. Until the other day. Now I'm just sad, sad and lonely and full of regrets; but not frantic any more, not in despair.'

'What happened? To make you feel differently?' said Cassia.

'Dominic Foster came to see me.'

'Dominic Foster!' said Cassia, trying not to sound too astonished. 'But, Cecily, I thought—that is, you—'

Cecily smiled. 'I know what you thought. But he—well, he told me something that made all the difference. He was very brave, actually. He came here, and insisted I saw him. He told me lots of things, actually, but one in particular and I—well, I

537

realised it wasn't all my fault. It wasn't all his either, of course, which is what he thought—we both contributed—but most of all I realised it was the awful conflict Benedict just couldn't cope with. The conflict with himself, with me, with all of us, with his—his instincts, but most of all, what society does to him, him and people like him. I never thought I'd come to think this, Cassia, but you know I do now agree with you about the laws about—' She hesitated, obviously finding it hard to say the word; Cassia waited. 'About homosexuality,' Cecily said finally. 'I have come to see it's dreadful that they drive people underground, make them subject to blackmail, all that sort of thing. Think of that awful Norman Duvant, what he was able to do to Benedict.'

'Yes,' said Cassia quietly. 'Just think.'

'I mean I still feel odd about it all. I still see it as an illness, a sickness, which I know you don't. But maybe you're right, and maybe I'm getting there. I'm trying to, anyway.'

Cassia leant forward and kissed her. 'You don't have to feel anything, get anywhere,' she said.

'No, but can't you see? That's part of feeling better. It's hard to explain. Anyway,' she smiled again, 'thank you so much, so very, very much for everything, but most of all for looking after Fanny all this time. I know it must have been difficult.'

'It wasn't,' said Cassia truthfully, 'not in the least. She's a darling child. I do think, though—' she hesitated—'she's ready to come and see you now, to talk. I think it's a bit like you and Dominic and everything: she can see she might have got it wrong, but she needs to be helped to work out how and why. And she does miss you. Terribly.'

'Yes, well, I want to see her too. I've already seen Stephanie and darling Laurence, that was easy. Fanny did seem more of a problem. She wouldn't even speak to me, you know.'

'I do know, but I think that's over now. She'll just be pleased to see you, be with you,' said Cassia, 'and she's got such a lot to tell you, which will help—she's very full of Edwina's fashion show. They're going to be in it, you see, her and Stephanie and little Portia—she's Eleanor Studely's daughter—'

'Cassia, you're going too fast. Who's Eleanor Studely?'

'Oh, Rupert's leading lady. So nice, and so beautiful. She's a widow.'

'Do you think he might fall in love with her?' said Cecily hopefully.

'No, no chance at all. You know he likes little starlets.'

'He likes you, darling.'

'No, he doesn't,' said Cassia firmly—too firmly. Cecily looked at her thoughtfully. 'Not like that. Of course he doesn't. But anyway, back to Fanny. I do think she could go back to school as well now. She's much much better.'

'When is it? The fashion show.'

'Pretty soon. Three weeks, Saturday the twenty-eighth. Edwina's got the most extraordinary man helping her with it, well he's her boss, actually. I can't make out if he's—' She stopped suddenly, aware that Cecily was far from ready for a discussion about whether Edwina's new escort was a homosexual. 'If he's in love with her or not.'

'In love with her? Cassia, what are you talking about? What about Harry? She hasn't left him, has

539

she?'

Cassia looked out of the window, felt herself flush, aware that she had been foolish, and more than foolish, expressing a dangerously strong bit of wish-fulfilment. 'Of course not,' she said hastily. 'You know Edwina, the way she exaggerates, rambles on about things.'

'Yes, I suppose so. Goodness, I can see I have a great deal of gossip to catch up on. Incidentally, it was so sweet of Edward to send me those flowers. Please tell him I'll write to him when I feel better.'

'Edward! Sent you flowers!'

'Yes, didn't you know? He sent me two lots, actually, one just after the funeral, and one while I was ill. And a sweet note, too.'

'Oh, yes, of course, he did mention it,' said Cassia hastily. She could hardly have been more surprised if Cecily had told her Edward had come in to see her wearing an evening dress and high heels. And then thought that would really have been very inappropriate indeed and giggled.

*   *   *

Edwina looked at Harry slightly nervously across the dining table. He was eating silently, rather fast, studying some papers as he did so. She cleared her throat and said, trying to keep her voice light, 'Harry, I'm so sorry to interrupt your reading, but I would like to speak to you just for a moment. If you can spare the time?'

'Yes?' he said.

'We want to do some photographs next week, of some thick stockings, country shoes, that sort of thing.'

540

'We?'

'The magazine. And the idea I had was that we should use cars. As background.'

He frowned. 'You're planning to hang stockings over cars? It sounds a little bizarre.'

'No, of course not. No, models will be wearing them. But standing on running boards, getting into the cars, that sort of thing.'

'Oh, I see. Yes. Well, it could look quite interesting, I suppose. Is that all?'

'Not quite, no. The point is, I wondered if we could use a couple of your cars? The prettier ones. The Hispano, for instance, it's so lovely. And the Delage. Possibly the Bugatti . . .'

'Oh no,' he said, 'not the Bugatti. But yes, the others, if you like. On condition Manning is there. And I don't want anyone else driving any of them. Certainly not you.'

'Yes, of course,' she said. She was amazed at the ease with which he had agreed. 'That's very good of you.'

He shrugged. 'It's no great hardship.'

'Well, thank you,' she said again, and then, feeling she should show a little interest in him, out of gratitude said, 'What are those papers you're reading?'

'Oh, company reports. Very dull. Coffee?'

'Please. The play went off very well last night.'

'Oh, really? And then where did you go? You weren't at the theatre, I imagine, until after three. Unless it was an extremely long play.'

'Oh, at the Embassy. With some friends. Rupert Cameron and his leading lady—'

'Yes, I saw her, unfortunately. This morning.'

'Oh, did you? She's rather beautiful, didn't you

541

think?'

'I really hadn't noticed, I'm afraid. More cream?'

'No, thank you. Incidentally, I heard the most delicious bit of gossip last night. About Cassia.'

He said nothing, merely sipped at his coffee.

'You know what that article in the paper was saying? About her and Rupert?'

'I seem to remember something, yes.'

'Well; it does seem as if it's true. Her char was there last night, don't ask me why, but her husband said—'

'Cassia's husband?' His eyes were watchful suddenly.

'No, the char's. He said that Rupert stays at Cassia's house all the time. Isn't that extraordinary? Well, you know what they say, no smoke without fire.'

'Indeed not,' said Harry.

*   *   *

Cassia was trying to concentrate on some reports she had to write for the Birth Control Association next morning when Edwina arrived at the door. She felt a wave of terror at the sight of her, as she had ever since the first night with Harry, terror and guilt, but Edwina looked perfectly cheerful and friendly.

'Can I come in? I want to ask you something.'

'Yes, of course. Why aren't you at work?'

'I am, sort of. I wondered if I could borrow your car next week?'

'My car! Why?'

'For a photograph. It's so pretty, that wonderful yellow, and we're already using two of Harry's,

542

both blue. I thought it would complete the set. Would that be all right? I'll take great care of it, of course. In fact, I'll get Manning to pick it up, and drive it and so on, he's seeing to Harry's, naturally.'

'Well, yes, of course you can. If you want.'

'Thanks. Wednesday, it'll be, you're in town, aren't you? I can lend you my car for the day in its place if you like.'

'Oh, I don't think that'll be necessary. There's a rehearsal for the fashion show that evening, isn't there?'

'Yes. At Style House, in the studio. Such a godsend, that. Francis is being such an angel about it all.'

'He's very nice,' said Cassia carefully.

'Isn't he? I just adore him, such fun, always in a good mood—or nearly always. Unlike my own dear husband. Who is being—well, vile is the only word for it, at the moment. I don't know, Cassia, I sometimes can't see the point of our marriage at all. Specially now he knows about the children.'

'What children?'

'That I can't have any.'

'Oh, I see,' said Cassia. She struggled to sound merely polite, lightly interested. 'When did you find that out?'

'Ages ago, actually. But I hadn't told Harry until I had that op. you know? Your Miss Gerard pinpointed the reason, actually. She's awfully nice, Cassia, I must say. Blocked tubes, apparently.'

'Blocked tubes. Oh, Edwina, that's very unlucky . . . Why on earth should you have blocked tubes?'

'Oh, I suppose I might as well tell you. We're such old friends, after all. And you're not going to tell anyone, are you? Medical etiquette and all

543

that.'

'No, of course not,' said Cassia. She didn't think it necessary to explain to Edwina all the ramifications of medical etiquette.

'I had an abortion,' said Edwina casually. 'Well, I had two actually, but the first was when I was only sixteen. Anyway, that was all right, but the second was just before I got married.'

'Just before?' said Cassia. 'You mean it was Harry's baby?' She knew pressing Edwina like this was dangerous, but she simply couldn't help it.

'No, that would have been all right. Obviously. No, Harry had been away, in New York. I had dinner one night with Roddy Buchanan, you remember him, such fun, I always had such a thing about him, cried buckets when he married Yolande. Well anyway, he was terribly miserable, said he'd made an appalling mistake, that he should never have married her, and we both got fearfully drunk and—well, one thing led to another, and a couple of weeks later I realised I was in the club. There was nothing else for it, I had to get rid of it. Harry would have known, and anyway I couldn't possibly have—well, anyway. So I had an abortion. And I got an infection of some sort. I felt lousy for weeks. It was hell on the honeymoon, I can tell you: I had to pretend to Harry I'd got flu and a really bad curse. Anyway, that was what did it, apparently. Simple as that.'

'Terribly simple,' said Cassia. She felt rather dazed, as if everything in the world had shifted.

'Anyway, it does seem to have taken a lot of point out of the marriage, really. Specially for Harry, it seems. We never were madly in love, just rather fond of each other, I suppose. And we suited each other. And got on pretty well. Now we don't seem even to do that. On the other hand . . . oh, I don't know. I don't really fancy divorce, do you?'

'I haven't really thought about it,' said Cassia faintly.

'Oh, you must have done surely. Specially now, with all this about Rupert and so on.'

'Edwina, that has been hugely exaggerated. Honestly.'

'Oh, really? Not entirely, though, as far as I can make out. Come on now, has it?'

'Well,' said Cassia helplessly, 'not entirely, no, but—'

'Oh, darling.' Edwina looked at her and smiled. 'No need to cover up to me. Specially not after what I've just told you. Anyway, I won't say a word, obviously. It's entirely your affair. Literally.' She leant forward, patted Cassia on the arm. 'Look, I must go. Thanks so much about the car. Terribly sweet of you. See you soon.'

Cassia stood staring out of the window for quite a long time after the sound of Edwina's high heels clacking down the street had faded. She felt absolutely shattered, rather, she imagined, as one might after struggling to stay on a very wild horse for a long time, before falling off on to very hard ground. Her life generally seemed to resemble a very wild horse at the moment. She really wasn't sure how much longer she could continue to ride it.

But one thing at least had changed, importantly: any guilt she had felt about Edwina in connection with her affair with Harry had completely disappeared.

CHAPTER THIRTY

Such tiny threads, our lives hang on, Cassia reflected, as she edged her way across London towards Balham in the grey November mist: a mist that was already thickening into a dark, woolly fog. Sixty years ago, her grandmother had met Leonora's mother at a tea party; without that tea party, Leonora would not have become her godmother, she would not have met Harry, would certainly not have inherited the money.

A tiny thread was at that moment linking another life to hers, starting on another complex weave of events: Barbara Perkins, a twenty-two-year-old mother of three who had been putting off her visit to the birth control clinic for some time, largely on account of it being against her husband's wishes, decided, when her mother arrived unexpectedly allowing her to leave the children with her, that a visit to the clinic was more important than her own nervousness or her husband's objections.

She'd been feeling rotten all day; the pain which had accompanied her period had been quite bad and was still with her, and she felt oddly shaky and weak.

She got to the clinic feeling so nervous she forgot about the pain; a young, rather smartly dressed woman followed her in, rummaging frantically through her bag as she did so. Barbara was very surprised to hear the large, cosy-looking nurse who sat in the waiting room saying that no, Dr Fallon, she hadn't seen the keys to the store cupboard anywhere. Well, she couldn't be much of a doctor, Barbara thought, hardly older than she was, and might have made that the excuse to leave again, had not a fresh wave of intense pain suddenly struck her and left her leaning on the cosy nurse's desk, trying to breathe deeply as they had told her she should when she was in labour.

'Are you all right?' It was the doctor, her face concerned.

'Yes,' Barbara said, 'I'm fine, just a bit of indigestion.'

'Here,' said the doctor, producing a tablet from her bag, 'chew this, they're really good. I'll try not to keep you waiting long, shouldn't be too busy this afternoon, with the fog and everything.'

Her indigestion tablet didn't do much good— about as much good as the deep breathing had in labour; by the time she was finally called in to the doctor's office, she was feeling so bad she thought she might actually faint or be sick.

*   *   *

'Right,' said Cassia, 'do sit down, Mrs Perkins. Now just let me get a few details—address, age, and I presume you're married.'

'Too bloody right,' said Barbara.

Cassia looked up at her in amusement and saw that the face in front of her was very white, and that she was biting her lip. 'Are you all right?'

'Think so,' said Barbara Perkins, 'just got this pain still.'

'Where is it? show me.' Barbara indicated her lower abdomen. 'Is it very bad?'

'Quite bad, yes. It'll go, it was bad this morning

547

as well.'

'Come and lie down on the bed. That's right. Now can you just pull your panties down a bit, so I can feel your tummy . . .' She palpated Barbara's tummy gently; it was clearly very tender. There was a slight swelling on the right-hand side, almost imperceptible, in the area of the ovary; as she pressed that, Barbara winced. 'Sorry. Does that hurt a lot?'

'Yeah. A lot. And I feel a bit sick.'

She had an appendix scar: it wasn't that, then. 'When did the pain start?'

'Oh, about a fortnight ago. On and off, not like this.'

'Have you had a period recently?'

'Yes, doctor. About two weeks ago.' Not a miscarriage threatening, then.

'Was it heavy?'

'No, not very bad at all. It was a relief, though. I did think—' She hesitated.

'Yes?'

'I did think I might have fallen again. We'd— well, you know, we'd . . .'

'Had intercourse?' said Cassia helpfully.

'Yes. At the wrong time. And he doesn't like— you know, the . . . things.'

'No, they don't,' said Cassia. 'Well, you're in the right place to get everything sorted. I think you could have something called an ovarian cyst. It isn't serious, but it can cause bad pain. I'd like to refer you to the hospital, you might have to have a very minor operation. Don't look so worried, a great friend of mine had it done recently, and she was back at work in a week or so. Anyway, let's get the other business sorted out and I'll give you a letter for the hospital.'

She measured the girl for a diaphragm, trying not to hurt her, worrying about the intense pain she seemed to be in. 'Right, then, get dressed and then come and sit at the desk again. I really think—'

There was a loud crash: Barbara Perkins had fainted. Cassia yelled for Nurse Hampton, lifted Barbara on to a chair, bent her forward, put her head between her knees.

Barbara Perkins yelled out.

'I'm sorry,' she said through chattering teeth, sitting up slowly, throwing her head back, 'it's bloody agony. It really is.'

Cassia looked at her; she was sweating, and a ghastly colour. 'Barbara, when did you have this unprotected intercourse?'

'Seven, eight weeks ago. God almighty, this is horrible.'

Cassia thought fast. 'Excuse me a moment. Nurse will look after you.'

She went to the outer office, dialled St Christopher's, asked to be put through to Mr Scarsdale. He was taking a clinic, a fact of which he informed her in an extremely impatient voice.

'Mr Scarsdale, I'm terribly sorry to bother you, but I need your help. I'm in my clinic in Brixton. I've a young woman here, and I'm pretty sure she's got an ectopic pregnancy . . . What? Severe abdominal pain, tenderness, she's sweating badly, her pulse is a bit fast. Temperature slightly up, just under a hundred. BP's OK at the moment. Oh God, hold on a minute . . . Yes, Nurse Hampton? Sorry, Mr Scarsdale, apparently she's just started bleeding. No, not a lot. No, it's not an appendix, she's had that out. Of course. Would you? I'd be so

549

grateful. Thank you. Yes, I'll call for an ambulance from here. Thank you so much. About twenty minutes, I suppose. Although with this fog . . .'

She rang for an ambulance, then went back into her room. Nurse Hampton had laid Barbara Perkins on the bed, was holding her hand, wiping her sweating face.

'I think you just might have something called an ectopic pregnancy, Barbara,' said Cassia. 'That means the baby is growing not in your womb, but in one of your Fallopian tubes. Unfortunately, it can't possibly survive there.'

'Thank Christ for that,' said Barbara, her eyes meeting Cassia's with a flash of humour.

'Well, yes,' said Cassia, smiling back at her, 'maybe. But it could be dangerous unless we get you to hospital very soon. I've called an ambulance, and I'm going to come with you to St Christopher's Hospital. It's not the nearest, but it's very, very good and I trained there. Just hang on, and in an hour or so the worst will be over.'

The phone rang; Nurse Hampton went to answer it. 'I'm afraid we have a problem,' she said. 'That was St Christopher's. Because of the fog, ambulances are having a lot of trouble getting anywhere at all. It doesn't seem like a very good idea, taking Mrs Perkins over there.'

'Where's the nearest, then? Thomas's is not a lot nearer. Oh wait, there's Queen Alexandra's, we can take her there ourselves, probably quicker than waiting for an ambulance. Barbara, if you lean on us, do you think you can walk out to my car?'

'I think so. Just.'

Cassia looked at her again; her colour had worsened. 'I'm just going to have another look at your tummy, if you don't mind. And take your blood pressure.'

The blood pressure was lower; she felt Barbara's abdomen carefully. It had changed; become hard, rigid even. Which pointed to a haemorrhage into the abdominal cavity. It must be an ectopic, couldn't be anything else. And if it had ruptured it was life threatening. She smiled at Barbara, patted her hand.

'You'll be fine. Come on, let's get you into my car. The hospital's very near.'

*   *   *

The fog had slowed the traffic to a crawl. They settled Barbara on the back seat, and Nurse Hampton crouched on the floor beside her. She was still only bleeding a little, but her teeth were chattering.

'Pulse?' said Cassia briefly.

'Quite steady,' said Nurse Hampton in a bright tone.

It wasn't actually a very long journey from the clinic to the Queen Alexandra Hospital. In normal circumstances it would have taken ten minutes, fifteen at the most. But these were not normal circumstances. It was extraordinary how swiftly you became disorientated in the fog: Cassia could have sworn she should have passed that school, King George's Infants, about quarter of a mile before, and there it was now, looming up. And surely there was another left turn she could take almost immediately: it seemed to have totally disappeared. No, there it was. Thank God. At least the streets were virtually clear, and strangely silent,

551

movements slowed, sounds muffled by the fog.

'Shan't be long now,' she said cheerfully, into the driving mirror. 'Two or three minutes at the most. How's the patient?'

'Pulse just a tiny bit unsteady,' said Nurse Hampton, her voice quiet with suppressed panic.

Cassia glanced over her shoulder. 'Blood pressure?'

'Ninety over sixty.'

'Bleeding?'

'About the same.'

Someone shouted. She turned her attention back to the road just too late: great yellow lights seemed to rear up at her through the fog, and a large van, driving in the middle of the road, exactly as she was, rode relentlessly into her. There was the awful noise of screeching brakes, breaking glass, crunching metal: and then silence.

'Oh, Christ,' she said, getting out.

'Stupid bloody woman,' shouted the driver, 'sitting in the middle of the bloody road.'

'You were in the middle of it too,' said Cassia, surprised by her calm, 'and I'm very sorry, but I've got a woman in the back of my car, who'll die if we don't—'

'Dr Fallon!' It was Nurse Hampton. 'I'm a little concerned.' That was code for desperate.

Cassia went over to the car; Barbara Perkins appeared unconscious.

'She's just vomited. She's in severe shock. Blood pressure's down again. And her abdomen is becoming extremely rigid.'

It was years since Cassia had been involved in a medical emergency; but the absolute concentration on the moment, the consideration of nothing else, the total lack of emotion, the clear insight into what had to be done, returned to her now with a thud of recognition.

'Nurse Hampton, you run to the hospital. It's not more than five minutes away by foot. Tell them she'll need immediate surgery, say there's internal haemorrhaging. Get them to bring a stretcher. I'll stay here with her. You go down there, first left, then it's straight ahead of you. Good luck. And you—' she said to the man—'if you can't be useful and go and ask anyone in any of these houses for some towels and pillows, just sit down in your van and be quiet. I'll buy you a new van, I'll buy you two new vans if you like, but just stop shouting at me and making a bad situation worse.'

Whether it was hearing the magic word 'Doctor' or her tone, or the sight of Barbara Perkins, apparently very close to death, the man set off obediently towards the nearest front door. Cassia took Barbara's blood pressure again: seventy over fifty. Barbara's eyes flickered open suddenly, looked into hers. Cassia managed to smile.

'You're going to be fine,' she said, and, there being nothing else left to her to do, decided to try prayer.

*   *   *

Prayer worked. Less than ten minutes after Nurse Hampton had left the car, she first heard, then saw the miracle: a stretcher on wheels being pushed at a run by two orderlies, then a doctor and a nurse, followed by Nurse Hampton, breathing very hard.

'Quick,' said Cassia, 'she's very, very bad, needs plasma immediately, emergency surgery, ectopic pregnancy, ruptured, I'm sure, pulse now failing, blood pressure seventy over fifty, severe rigidity of the abdomen—'

'Fine,' said the doctor, 'absolutely fine. We've alerted Theatre. Now if we can just lift her out . . . We've got plasma with us, if we can get a vein up. Excuse me, please,' he said with surprising courtesy to the van driver, who was standing, his arms holding what must be, Cassia thought, at least a dozen towels, and as many pillows, his face a mixture of fascination and horror as they lifted Barbara Perkins out of the car and settled her on to the stretcher.

'You'd better come with us,' Cassia said, 'and I'll write you a cheque for the van once my patient is safely in hospital. And you might as well bring those towels. We could still need them.'

*　　　*　　　*

There was another thread being drawn towards the others in this particular weave that afternoon: Harry Moreton's chauffeur, Arthur Manning, decided that what he needed before what threatened to be a difficult evening, was a piece of Cook's pork pie and a cup of tea. He went down to the kitchen where Cook was having her afternoon nap, and found the kettle simmering on the stove and a large piece of pie on the table. He was halfway through it when Nancy the kitchen maid came in and said she wouldn't really advise eating the pie, Cook had said it was off and was going to give it to next door for their dog. Manning said cheerfully that it tasted fine to him, and continued to eat it enthusiastically.

Cassia was drinking a cup of coffee in the waiting room when a tiny, rather stern-faced woman doctor came over to her.

'Dr Fallon? I'm Monica Gerard, consultant obstetric surgeon here.' Of course: it was Miss Gerard's hospital. She'd forgotten.

'Is she going to be all right?'

'Yes, she is. Very dicey at one point, and she needed a lot of blood, but everything's steadying now. Ectopic, as you said, ruptured, and we've had to sever the tube, but yes, fine. That was clever of you. Not easy to spot. As for getting here in this fog . . .'

'Yes, it wasn't too good. You should see my car.'

'Oh dear. Well, you did better than a lot of ambulances. And I hear your lass arrived on foot.'

Hearing the redoubtable Nurse Hampton described as a lass made Cassia smile. 'Yes. She was marvellous.'

'I know your name, and can't think how.'

'I suggested a friend of mine came to you. Edwina Moreton.'

'Ah yes.' The small stern face softened. 'Mrs Moreton. Is she quite well now?'

'Quite well.'

'Good. So where do you work?'

'Oh? nowhere much,' said Cassia, 'just a couple of birth control clinics and the new postnatal at St Christopher's. I trained there.'

'Did you? Why aren't you doing a decent job somewhere?'

'Well, I got married and . . .'

'Foolish woman.' Monica Gerard almost smiled. 'Terrible thing to do, you know, wasting all that training.'

'I know,' said Cassia humbly. 'So I was told in no uncertain terms. By Mr Amstruther, you know?'

'I do indeed. Old friend. So you trained under him, did you?'

'Yes, I did. I wanted to do obstetrics but . . .'

'Hmm. So you're fitting lasses up with diaphragms all day. Dear, oh dear,' Miss Gerard looked at her watch. 'I must go. I've got a section to do—twins, one a breech. Look, we should talk some more. Ring my rooms and make an appointment.'

It clearly didn't occur to her that Cassia might not wish to talk to her. But then, thought Cassia, it wouldn't. And it shouldn't.

*   *   *

'I don't feel too good,' said Manning to Mrs Manning, falling on to his bed with a groan at one that morning, having delivered Harry Moreton safely and finally to his door.

'Well, you shouldn't have eaten all that cheese,' said Mrs Manning, 'it always gives you indigestion.'

'Wasn't the cheese,' said Manning, and then suddenly shot out of bed and into the small bathroom next door. He emerged five minutes later looking green, and then had to rush back again before he even reached the bed.

Mrs Manning sighed. It was obviously going to be a long night.

*   *   *

Edwina was just reflecting how wonderfully lucky it was that the fog had cleared in time for her photographic session in Hyde Park with the cars, when Bishop came into the dining room. Harry, whose temper could always be measured at breakfast by the amount he ate (worse meant more), was just buttering his third piece of toast.

Bishop cleared his throat. 'I'm very sorry, Mr Moreton, but Mr Manning will not be able to drive you today. He is indisposed.'

'Oh Jesus,' said Harry, 'what a bloody awful nuisance. Well, I'll have to use taxis, I suppose. Get me one, would you, Bishop? In about fifteen minutes?'

'Certainly, sir.'

'Harry,' said Edwina, 'you might at least think of me. I've got my photographic session with the cars today. How am I going to manage without Manning?'

'I have no idea,' said Harry. 'Do it another day perhaps?'

'I can't. The models have been booked, and the photographer. I'll just have to drive them myself, one at a time, and get taxis back. Or maybe—'

'Edwina, are you out of your mind? Do you really think I'm going to allow you to drive those cars through the streets of London?'

'What else can I do? I've got to have them. Simply got to. I shall be fired if I don't. Harry, please! It's so important. Look, it's not so far from your office, is it? Couldn't you drive one at least, the Hispano, and then get a taxi? And maybe you could trust me with the Delage?'

'Oh God,' he said. 'Yes, all right, Edwina, I'll

drive the Hispano. But you're not driving anything. Bishop, you drive pretty well, will you follow me with Mrs Moreton in the Delage? To Hyde Park. And then hopefully Manning will have recovered later and will be able to collect the cars.'

'Certainly, sir. It will be a pleasure, sir.'

*　　　*　　　*

Cassia woke up late, and phoned the Queen Alexandra to enquire after Barbara Perkins. She was recovering, they said, but would not be able to go home for at least two weeks. Cassia, remembering the flushed, fleshy features of Mr Perkins scowling at her on the doorstep when she called to explain, clearly seeing Barbara's near death as something designed to inconvenience him, and her mother's whining voice saying she couldn't be expected to drop everything and look after their children just like that, felt a pang of pity for the Perkins children; and then, remembering her own, and the fact that Delia had been fractious the day before and that Janet had remarked, with a dazzling smile, that it looked as if she might be getting Bertie's chicken pox, telephoned Monks Ridge.

'Yes,' said Janet, as if she were imparting the news that Father Christmas had just arrived early, 'yes, she is poxy. And a tiny bit irritable. But nothing to worry about, Mrs Fallon, we're all absolutely fine here. No need to rush back.'

'Oh, well, if you really think so. And how was school for Bertie?' Bertie had resumed to his old school on that Monday. The first day had been fine, but she still worried about him.

'Splendid still. It's as if he'd never been away. Already back in the football team. And don't worry about Delia, she'll be fine. We're going to do lots of painting, take her mind off it.'

'Thank you. And Dr Fallon? Is he all right?'

'He's fine, Mrs Fallon, yes.'

'Well, tell him I'll see him tomorrow evening, would you?'

Cassia put the phone down feeling inadequate and depressed. Sometimes she wondered if it would matter if she never went back to the house at all, if indeed it might be better for everyone if she did not. She forgot everything these days, everything except her own problems and—oh God. She'd forgotten something else now. Edwina's photographic session. Well, there was no way she'd want her car now. But she should have told her.

She dialled the number. No, Mrs Moreton had left, and so had Mr Moreton, and Bishop with them, taking two of the cars to Hyde Park, near the Serpentine, Mrs Moreton had said.

'Oh God,' said Cassia. There was nothing else for it, she'd just have to go up there herself.

The car still went surprisingly well. It looked dreadful, with its lovely headlamps crushed and its radiator bent in, and its bumper broken in half, but it would be easier to drive it to Hyde Park—at least Edwina would be able to see for herself that it was unusable.

*   *   *

'Look, Edwina, I'm going now,' said Harry. 'Don't on any account move that car or let anyone else move it, apart from Bishop. All right?'

559

'Yes, all right,' said Edwina crossly. The morning so far was not going well. Justin was in a bad temper, the models were late, and one of the two borzoi dogs she had hired for the day had just slipped its leash and plunged joyfully into the Serpentine. 'But—Oh my God. Just look at Cassia's car. What on earth does she think she's doing? Oh, it's too bad.'

'Looks as if it's been used as a war ambulance,' said Justin. 'Really, darling, this is all we need.'

'I'm so sorry, Edwina,' said Cassia, hurrying over to them. 'Oh, hello, Harry. I didn't think you'd be here.'

'Neither did I,' he said shortly, 'nor do I want to be. I'm just leaving, in fact and—oh Christ, get off me, you filthy, fucking animal.' The borzoi had tired of the Serpentine and was leaping up at him, attempting to lick his face, its once luxuriously white, perfectly coifed coat slimy and matted, leaving a trail on Harry's camel-wool overcoat.

Cassia tried not to laugh and failed; then she met Harry's furious eyes and said, 'Sorry. I'm really sorry.' He said nothing.

'What on earth happened to your car?' said Edwina. 'I can't imagine how you could be so stupid.'

'Well, you see, I collided with a van yesterday, I had a woman in it, she'd collapsed in the clinic— she was desperately ill, we had to get her to hospital, and because of the fog the ambulances weren't getting through so—'

'So it was being used as a war ambulance!' cried Justin, clapping his hands. The story seemed to have completely cheered him up. 'How divine. I think we should use the car, Edwina. As a kind of witty aside. You know?'

'No, I don't,' said Edwina irritably. 'It's appalling, and look at the inside, God, it's disgusting, Cassia, really.'

'Well, I'm sorry,' said Cassia, finally indignant. 'I didn't do it on purpose, Edwina, and I forgot till this morning—'

'You forgot! My photographic session! Cassia, how could you?'

'Edwina, you really are monstrous,' said Cassia. 'You might spare a moment's thought for me—and my patient, come to that. Since you're so very concerned, I have to tell you she survived emergency surgery. Performed by Miss Gerard, as a matter of fact. Although she nearly died, and would have done without my war ambulance. Well, I'll take it away. I'm so very sorry to have inconvenienced you.'

'Oh, don't be so ridiculous,' said Edwina. 'Of course I'm glad the wretched woman didn't die, but it's just so—well, so difficult for me.'

'It was quite difficult for me as well,' said Cassia. 'And I did love this car, and just look at it.' She sighed, and patted the bonnet of the Jaguar tenderly.

'It hardly matters, though, does it?' said Harry Moreton suddenly. His voice was extraordinarily hostile: even Justin turned to look at him. 'I mean you can buy another one, after all, can't you? You can buy a dozen more if you want to. Edwina, I'll see you later, no doubt.' And he turned on his heel and walked away from them.

*   *   *

561

It wasn't the hostility that had made Cassia realise—she was growing used to that—it was the bitterness, the awful, naked bitterness on his face as he'd said she could buy a dozen cars if she wanted. It had been curiously personal, that bitterness, it had come from his heart, an emotional plaint; it had shaken her, shocked her even. And finally decided her, after all, that she could not let matters rest.

CHAPTER THIRTY-ONE

'Cecily, you look wonderful. Doesn't she, Justin?'

'Beautiful!' said Justin, taking Cecily's hand and kissing it.

'Of course I don't,' said Cecily. 'I look frightful. But at least I'm thin. For now, anyway. I'm eating like a pig.'

'Cecily,' said Justin severely, 'you could never look frightful. Not with those eyes. Could she, Edwina?'

'Absolutely not. So Cecily, when are you leaving here?'

'I've promised Fanny to come to your show,' said Cecily, 'so I suppose that means in a week. I'm— well, I'm a bit frightened. To tell you the truth.'

'Frightened!' said Edwina. 'What on earth about?'

'I know exactly what,' said Justin. He smiled at her. 'You've been in here, safe and sound, for a long time.'

'Yes.' She stared at him, surprised at his understanding. 'Yes, that's right, but—'

'You'll be fine,' he said. 'We'll all look after you, won't we, Edwina? It would be marvellous to have you there on Saturday, seeing your lovely little daughters in their moment of glory.'

'Yes, I know,' said Cecily.

It formed a wonderful bridge, the show, spanning the gulf between her and Fanny, easing them back into closeness; she was almost herself again now, this small, beloved daughter of hers, although a little thin, and still, it had to be admitted, a little wary of her; and Cecily knew she had to find the courage to go, to see her, that that would close the gulf completely.

'Anyway,' Edwina was saying now, 'we have another full rehearsal on Sunday, with all the clothes this time, if Leon de Rosay has managed to finish the bridesmaids' dresses, all the girls are coming, the professionals are doing the rehearsal for nothing, which is sweet of them, don't you think, and—Cecily, are you all right?'

'Yes, I'm fine,' said Cecily, wiping her eyes on a rather inadequate handkerchief. 'Sorry, it was just hearing Leon de Rosay's name reminded me of— well, it was a bit of a bad evening, that one. That's all.'

'Poor you,' said Justin. He produced a very large handkerchief. 'Here you are, this is clean, I promise. The worst thing about what you've been through is that every single occasion, or place, or piece of music, or anything, is a memory. Everything hurts, life's a minefield.'

'Well,' said Edwina, looking at them, half amused, 'I think I might leave you two together. I've got an awful lot to do. Cecily, if you need any help getting home or anything, I can always send

Manning.'

'Thank you so much,' said Cecily, and giggled. Her emotions were so raw still, so mixed up, that laughter followed on tears with hideous ease.

'I can't see why that's funny,' said Edwina, bending to kiss her. 'Anyway, lovely to see you out of bed. You need a few new clothes, don't you, though? That's really not very flattering, so baggy, although I suppose you'll grow into it again. Bye, then. Justin, are you really sure you want to stay here on your own?'

'Yes,' said Justin, 'yes, I'm quite sure. I'll see you tomorrow, darling.'

As Edwina left, they looked at one another and laughed.

'She really is a monster,' he said. 'She thinks not only the world, but the universe, centres around her. But one has to like her, goodness knows why. Now, shall I ring for some more tea, and biscuits? We have to feed you up a bit.'

'Oh, yes please!' said Cecily. 'But I'll have to stop eating like this soon—I'll be the size of a cushion again in no time.'

'Nonsense. You looked lovely before. I get very tired of these stick insects of ladies. I'm sure your husband didn't want you to look like them.'

'Oh, I don't know,' said Cecily. 'I don't know what he wanted—from me at any rate,' and burst into tears again.

Justin wiped her eyes tenderly on the handkerchief again. 'Another minefield exploded,' he said. 'It's important to talk about him, you know, remember him properly. When my wife left me—'

'Your wife!' said Cecily.

'Yes. She left me for some rather unpleasant Italian, and I was very unhappy for a very long time. But in the end I learnt that I had to remember the happy times, otherwise all those years were wasted, thrown away. You must do the same. It's—' The door opened and a smiling student nurse came in with a heavily laden tray. 'Oh, my goodness, now what do we have here? Warm scones, how wonderful. And cream! Cecily, come on, let's eat mountains of it all.'

* * *

After he had gone, she sat looking out at the cedar tree and wondering about his marriage. Presumably his wife had left him for all the reasons she had nearly left Benedict. It was very odd that she found him such good company, so extraordinarily soothing and comforting. Odd and really very nice.

* * *

Miss Gerard's brisk voice said, 'Dr Fallon, nice to see you again. Your young woman is recovering very well. And when I told her she would be almost certainly unable to have any more children, she appeared about to leap out of her bed and embrace me. I'm recommending a ligature of the remaining tube, just in case.'

'Good,' said Cassia. 'I'll go in and see her if I have time.'

'Do. She was very complimentary about you. As was Horace Amstruther when I spoke to him. Two pretty good recommendations, I'd say.'

565

'Well, both a bit prejudiced, I'm afraid.'

'My dear girl,' said Monica Gerard, 'if you think it is easy to prejudice Horace Amstruther in your favour, you have him very wrong, I assure you. Never was a man more monstrously prejudiced against women. Or men, for that matter, should they happen in some minute way to fall out of his rather exacting standards. So well done. Now then. Proposition for you.'

Cassia's heart lurched. A proposition! The most, the very most, she had hoped for had been a few words of advice and just possibly encouragement.

'I'm enlarging the department at Alex's, recruiting a new team. I'm looking for young, talented people, surgeons, women preferably. I get a strong gut instinct about the sort of people I want to work with, and you're one. I'd like you to come on board.' Cassia sat staring at Monica Gerard, felt her face flush, felt tears rising behind her eyes. She blinked them hastily away; she was sure those fierce dark eyes had not harboured tears, except possibly of exhaustion, for several decades. She felt as if someone had come into the room and tossed the moon into her lap, told her she could keep it, yet felt at the same time quite calmly confident, as if she had been coming to this moment all her life. She forgot about Harry, about Edward, even about her children. She knew only the same sense of fierce concentration and single-minded purpose so long forgotten and brought back to her the week before as she had steered Barbara Perkins through her crisis. Her response did not mirror this sensation.

'But I never even did a house job,' she said.

'I'm perfectly aware of that,' said Monica

Gerard. 'You can do it here. Providing you can square your domestic arrangements, I see no reason why not. Then you can move straight on to registrar status. All right?'

'I—well . . .'

'Oh, now come along,' said Miss Gerard, a touch of impatience in her voice. 'Surely you can sort out a few children? Horace Amstruther said you weren't short of money. You'll have to live in, of course, but you should be able to get home fairly regularly. A good nanny, surely, a London house . . .'

Her mind was racing, veering about now, contemplating the children, Edward, resiting Janet, resiting all of them, hauling their lives around, contemplating possibilities, assessing probabilities. 'Well, I suppose—'

'Good,' said Miss Gerard briskly, holding out her hand. 'Splendid. We can get you in after Christmas, that should give you plenty of time. I must ask you to leave now, I'm afraid. I've a frightfully demanding woman coming in, seven months pregnant, prima gravida, big baby as far as I can establish, tiny pelvis, refusing a section, so far at any rate. Anyway,' she stood up, held out her hand, 'delighted. Keep in touch, let me know when you've sorted yourself out.'

Cassia walked out into Harley Street not sure if she was in heaven or in hell.

*　　　*　　　*

'Our marriage is over,' said Edward. 'That's one thing I am sure about.' He looked at Cecily rather helplessly. He was not usually given to personal

567

revelations, but she had been through so much herself, it suddenly seemed rather easy.

He had been to see her on an impulse; he had volunteered as a member of the Sussex branch of a committee being organised to study the proposals for the National Health Service and the reaction of GPs to it, and there had been a committee meeting that morning. Cassia was at her fashion show rehearsal with her friends and Janet had taken all the children to visit an aunt in Hastings; he had no wish to sit alone at Monks Ridge reflecting upon the wreckage of his marriage.

Cecily smiled at him, and reached forward, patted his hand. 'I don't think you should feel that. It's much too early to say. And if it's all this nonsense about her and Rupert . . .'

'Oh it's not that. I don't give a toss about that. I don't like the man very much, but I don't actually believe all this stuff about them having an affair. I do mind that she is so close to him, tells him everything.'

'That's not his fault,' said Cecily mildly. 'Cassia is a very special person, you know, very special. She is headstrong and self-centred at times, of course she is. But she is brave and clever and an extraordinarily loyal friend. As of course you are: I owe you a great deal for taking Fanny in when I was so ill.'

'It was nothing, really,' said Edward, thinking remorsefully of the complaints he had made about Fanny, about having her to stay.

'It was a lot. And you have to remember,' she added, leaning forward and in her earnestness taking his hand, 'it can't have been easy for Cassia, coming into all that money. It sounds like a dream

568

come true, but actually it's also a nightmare. Very hard to handle. For you, of course, but also for her.'

Edward stared at Cecily; her hand in his was very gentle and warm and her eyes sweetly sympathetic. He felt as if he had been tossing about on a bed of barbed wire and someone had come along and said, look, if you just shift over here a bit, it's softer and quite warm and you'll be a lot more comfortable.

'I've been a terrible husband to her,' he said suddenly, 'really terrible, but it was so hard, when she—oh God.' He felt tears rising behind his eyes, swallowed hard, horrified at himself.

'Of course you haven't. Well, sometimes no doubt you have. As I was sometimes a terrible wife. But I've learnt—well, I'm learning,' she corrected herself hastily, 'to admit it and to admit the good things too. You must do the same, otherwise it's not fair on anyone.'

Edward left her shortly after that, and drove back to Sussex feeling much happier. He was still quite sure that his marriage was over, but he no longer felt quite so bitter about it. Or so self-reproachful.

*   *   *

'Well, thank God for the myth about dress rehearsals,' said Rupert finally, collapsing into a chair in Francis Stevenson-Cook's rather grand office on the corridor below the photographic studio. He had made it available to the cast for the evening, and it had become an unofficial green room, set with bottles of wine and glasses and

Thermos jugs of coffee and tea. It was after ten and the last model had departed, and Francis and Edwina had gone off with several of the non-professional models to calm their nerves, as they put it, at the KitKat Club.

'Do you think it is a myth?' said Cassia. 'About dress rehearsals, I mean?'

'Oh, darling, I'm afraid so. I've been to some magnificent dress rehearsals which have become magnificent shows, and some terrible rehearsals which have become terrible shows. It's actually quite rare for the opposite case, but it keeps people calm. Now, Cassia, let's get drunk.'

'Don't let's,' said Cassia. 'It caused rather a lot of trouble last time.'

'Oh, darling, I'm so desperately sorry about that.'

'Rupert, let's not talk about it, please. I can't bear it and I have other problems, much worse ones.'

'Tell me about them,' said Rupert, leaning forward, wiping away a tear that was trickling down her face. Things had eased between them recently, mostly, he knew, because of an increase in his own self-confidence: he no longer felt obsessed with his failure in every possible direction—even with women.

'No, honestly, it won't help.'

'Very well. Let's talk about me, then. Such a very agreeable subject. Bookings are now solid up to March. Isn't that wonderful?'

'It is wonderful, Rupert. And I've really enjoyed being involved. It's been very exciting.'

'Well, you obviously have an eye for a good play. You should back some more. This one is going to make you very rich.'

'Oh, don't talk about being rich,' said Cassia. 'I don't think I'm very good at it, not very good at all.'

He looked at her curiously. 'You've stopped spending it, haven't you?' he said. 'No new cars or frocks or houses even for ages. Why? Nothing more you want?'

'Oh, no. Lots of things, actually. It's just that . . .' She smiled at him; her old shaky, reluctant smile. He knew that smile very well: it preceded confidences of some magnitude. This was no exception. 'I've stopped spending it because I think—well, I think I might have to give the money back.'

Rupert stared at her.

'Give it back! Cassia, darling, who on earth to?'

'I'm not sure,' she said, 'but if it's come from where I think it has, I'm not keeping it. Not any of it.'

'And where do you think that might be?' he said, determinedly keeping the conversation light. 'The Bank of England?'

'No,' she said simply. 'Harry Moreton.'

The room froze into a silent stillness.

'Cassia,' he said gently, 'I'm a simple fellow. I need to have things explained to me very clearly. Could you please tell me why Harry Moreton should suddenly have handed over half a million pounds to you, and pretended it came from Leonora?'

'He likes to be in control of people,' she said, her voice very low, 'and he wanted my marriage to fail. I think he thought this way he might manage that.'

'But, darling, how, for God's sake?'

'Well, he has managed it. If it was him. The

571

money has wrecked my marriage. It's over, Rupert, absolutely. Isn't it?'

'Here,' he said, handing her his handkerchief, putting his arms round her. 'Cry, if you want to, but then listen to me. You've got to stop blaming yourself for all this. Your marriage has failed because you and Edward are basically unsuited, not because you suddenly came into a lot of money.'

'Rupert, if I hadn't had that money, I'd still be with Edward. I think Harry knew what would happen.'

'I still don't see why Harry should have done such a thing. I know there was always a lot of animosity between you, but that seems a little extreme.'

'It's not really animosity,' Cassia said finally, 'it's something quite different. The one thing I've never told you.'

*   *   *

He had never even suspected it: that was what hurt most. That he had thought he knew her so well, and this thing, so central to her, had remained a secret, too important to entrust even to him. 'Well,' he said finally, his voice carefully light, 'I had no idea . . . Lucky old sod, that's all I can say.' It was probably the most difficult speech he had ever had to deliver, and there had been no rehearsal for it. But he got through it, and clearly successfully: he saw her relax suddenly, smile.

'Well, not really lucky. Not any more. We've quarrelled.'

'Darling, you've been quarrelling all your lives. I can't remember a time when you weren't.'

'No. This is different. Final. Let's not talk about it.'

She was keeping something from him still; he decided to leave it for now, managed to smile at her again, say still in the same, light voice, 'I'm sorry, darling, but I don't think much of your plot. If Harry had wanted to manipulate you, he could have done it far more easily—and cheaply, I would have thought. And do you really think even he is rich enough to cast such an enormously expensive piece of bread upon the waters? And that Leonora would agree to such a piece of connivance? Of course she wouldn't. Honestly, darling, your imagination has been galloping away with you.'

'I can see it sounds insane, although you're wrong about Leonora: she was a great mischief-maker, dearly as I loved her. And I still don't see how the money can have come from her. Every bit of evidence I've got seems to show that she and Rollo were in financial difficulties.'

'But darling, Leonora was always in financial difficulties. She'd have been in them if she'd been married to Midas. And what evidence, anyway?'

'Oh, various things. I told you about the pawn tickets, then Miss Monkton found Leonora living in extremely difficult circumstances in Paris. All alone and ill. I'm quite sure it was Harry who rescued her from that, not Rollo at all.'

'Have you asked him?'

'Yes, and he denied it. Obviously. But he's so clever, so devious.'

'Yes, well, you should stick to simple chaps. Like me,' he said. The pain was beginning to worsen. She looked at him, he saw concern in her eyes.

'Rupert, the way I feel about Harry has nothing

573

whatever to do with how I feel about you. Nothing. I still love you terribly, you are my dearest—'

'Friend,' he said, no longer trying to disguise the bitterness, the sense of rejection he felt. 'I suppose that's all we ever were. I thought perhaps—the other night . . .'

'Oh, Rupert, darling! How many times have we said the other night was a sort of madness? A lovely, happy madness, that shouldn't have happened, that nearly spoilt everything between us.'

And because he did love her so much, because he could see that this was the moment, the turning point, when he could either lose her for ever or have her back as a loving friend, he managed to smile again, to say, drawing warmth, tenderness into his voice, 'Yes, of course we have. And it was. I regret it as much as you do, lovely as it was. I've hated that it spoilt things between us.'

'Not just between us,' she said.

'You and Edward?'

'No. Funnily enough, it didn't seem to bother him very much.'

'Was this the reason for the quarrel, then?' he said suddenly. 'This final quarrel between you and Harry? Was that what you wouldn't tell me before?'

'Yes,' she said quietly. 'Yes, it was, I'm afraid. He accused me of being a whore.'

'You mean you told him?'

'Not exactly, but he's very good at getting the truth out of people.'

'Oh dear, Cassia,' he said, half amused, half shocked, 'your honesty will get you into trouble one of these days.'

'It already has,' she said, trying to smile. There

was something wrong in this account; he felt, something illogical; but he couldn't quite think what it was.

'Well, I'm terribly sorry,' he said eventually, still struggling to keep his voice light. 'I certainly would not have wished to come between you and the love of your life.' Suddenly he couldn't bear it any longer, any of it. 'Look, I'm awfully tired, and so are you. Shall we call it a night?'

'Yes, I'm sorry. Thank you for listening to me, Rupert. As always, I feel better. Much better.'

*   *   *

They went out into the street, found taxis, kissed one another goodnight. Rupert went home to his small, lonely room and lay awake for a long time, thinking that for the first time in his life he could empathise with Edward Fallon. He was deeply, horribly jealous of Harry Moreton too.

*   *   *

'I really should go home,' said Edwina, 'it's almost midnight.'

'Don't go home,' said the man sitting next to her, whose name was St John Vincent. 'Our little gathering will be greatly diminished if you do, and I was going to ask you to join us at a small party.'

'Well, sweet of you to say so. But I have to go to work in the morning, don't I, Francis?'

'Indeed you do. As do I.' He smiled at her rather indulgently, almost as a father would. 'And we've both been working today, not pursuing pleasure idly as I'm sure you have.'

'You don't look as if you've been working. Not tired at all,' said St John Vincent slightly irritably.

'Then our looks belie us,' said Francis.

'You need a small fillip,' said Vincent. 'Come along, just for an hour or so. Janine has one of her gatherings going on. Myrtle, darling, do tell Francis and this perfectly divine creature that they absolutely must come to Janine's with us.'

Edwina had taken rather a dislike to Myrtle. She was dressed with enormous splendour in a heavily sequinned and embroidered robe and a beaded turban. Her face was dramatically made up, her eyes ringed with kohl, her lipstick almost black, and she smoked constantly through a very long cigarette holder. She seemed to have a somewhat proprietary relationship with Francis and kept stroking his face. She looked at Edwina now and said, 'St John, if she wants to go home, then she should. Never try to corrupt virtue. Isn't that right, Francis?'

'I thought you knew nothing about virtue, Myrtle,' said Francis.

'I don't, actually. Only that it's boring,' said Myrtle.

Edwina met her black-rimmed eyes and smiled recklessly. 'Well, I'd hate you to think me that. All right, I'd love to come. Francis, what about you.'

He hesitated, looked at her for several moments, clearly trying to establish something in his mind, then apparently resolved it. 'Yes, very well,' he said, 'just for an hour or so.'

It was Monday night, and they had been sitting in a night-club that was new to Edwina, called Jack's, for a while. Francis had phoned her in the office, told her he wanted to discuss various aspects of the fashion show, and suggested dinner. Harry was at the White City with friends, and she saw no reason to refuse. They had had an extremely nice evening at Daphne's in Sloane Avenue and Francis had suggested they moved on 'just for a short while. There are some people there who might amuse you.'

They did, and the people had amused her hugely. Two men, both undoubtedly homosexuals, and three women—two of them rather vulgar, but great fun, and the exotic Myrtle. Edwina had drunk a great deal of champagne, danced with all three men, and told a couple of extremely filthy jokes, which had been received with great enthusiasm. She would never, she realised, with a slight sense of shock, have done such a thing in public before: with her intimates perhaps, both Harry and her mother had a penchant for dirty jokes, but never with people she did not know.

She wondered if she was changing in other ways, and decided she was. She certainly felt different, quite different, quite a lot of the time: freer, not just in what she did, but in what she thought. She felt on the brink of some vast discovery about herself, and she looked back at the person she had been only a few months before, concerned only with the running of her household, the conduct of her social life, with something close to contempt.

She smiled at St John Vincent and said, 'Come on, then, let's go.'

Janine lived in Chelsea, in a very pretty house just off Cheyne Walk. They went down in Francis's car, all six of them; there was not enough room and she sat on St John Vincent's knee and became aware suddenly of his hand moving smoothly and very confidently along her thighs, and wondered if she had perhaps been wrong about his sexual orientation.

A tiny, sliver-thin woman opened the door to them herself, dressed in a pair of wide silk trousers and a very long silver sweater. 'Darlings, how lovely! Lovely, lovely to see you.' She kissed them all, then stood studying Edwina. 'And St John, who is this nice new friend?'

'This is Edwina,' said St John Vincent, 'a friend of Francis's.'

'Francis, you do find the most wonderful-looking people. Do you work on one of his magazines? You must do, you have that look about you.'

'What sort of look?' said Edwina, laughing.

'Oh, as if you had something to say, perhaps? Which I'm sure you do. Anyway, welcome.' She reached out and took Edwina's hand. 'The main thing is, Francis never brings anyone boring. Come and meet some people.'

The house was quite wonderful, Edwina thought, very, very modern; the drawing room particularly was exquisite: white walls, white curtains, white carpets, white sofas, chrome-framed mirrors, chrome wall lights. There were some very fine modern pictures on the walls. She recognised a couple of the artists, fashionable and immensely expensive: Otto Dix, Paul Klee—Harry had some of their work—and a huge Alberto Sarinio, the Surrealist, with his extraordinary animal heads on human bodies.

The room had perhaps two dozen people in it, all extremely well dressed, the men in dinner or smoking jackets, the women in evening dress or the new palazzo pyjamas; someone was playing the piano rather well, a few people were dancing. Edwina realised, with a stab of something half shock half pleasure, that two of the couples were women.

Janine took her hand, 'Let's get you a drink. Now, let me see, who can you meet . . .? Ah, yes, now this is Marcia Bryanston, and this is her brother, Ivor. Well, more than her brother, of course, as you can see, her twin. Ivor, darling, do go and get some more cigarettes, would you? Turkish, if you can find them.'

Edwina could indeed see they were twins, the likeness was extraordinary—two tall, blond, rather androgynous creatures, their hair identically cut in slightly long Eton crops, straight noses and very brilliant blue-green eyes. Ivor, like Marcia, seemed to be wearing mascara. And how sensible, thought Edwina suddenly, when his eyes are so amazing and it suits him so well. He looked, if anything, the more beautiful of the two. He was wearing a black velvet jacket and a very large loosely knotted tie, which exactly matched his eyes; Marcia's dress, long and very narrow, was the same colour. It was very clear, from the nipples etched clearly against the crepe fabric, that she had nothing on underneath it.

Janine put her arm round Marcia's shoulders. 'Marcia, this is Edwina, Francis brought her, Edwina . . . sorry, I didn't catch your surname.'

'Moreton,' said Edwina, but she found it odd saying Harry's name. She felt it suddenly no longer hers, felt, for some reason that she could not have explained, that she had shed it, shed her old life, indeed, as she walked into this room.

'Marcia paints,' said Janine, 'dreadfully naughty

579

nudes mostly. Do be careful, she'll try and persuade you to model for her.'

'I've never been painted,' said Edwina. 'I'd rather like it, I think.'

'Well, now is your chance. But I do warn you, not for your drawing room.'

Marcia stood studying Edwina for a moment, and then smiled at her. It was a brilliant, strangely seductive smile. 'Come and sit down,' she said. 'I want to know all about you.'

*　　　*　　　*

'You're beautiful. So beautiful.'

Edwina shivered, shuddered with pleasure; the tongue in her mouth was very gentle, exploring it, the fingers encircling her nipples intensely skilful. Delight shot, spread through her body; she shut her eyes, forcing herself to concentrate absolutely on the moment and its pleasures. They were in another room now, upstairs, a dark room full of people and throbbing music; she could not quite remember getting there, only a long conversation with Marcia, intriguing, enthralling, then dancing with Ivor, slowly, languorously, aware that Marcia was watching her, watching every move she made, and liking that fact, excited by it, and then Marcia joining them, dancing with them, and finally Marcia's hand taking hers, leading her away from her brother, out of the white room.

The music seemed to have taken possession of her, its rhythms become her own. This was more than dancing: not yet sex, but a strange amalgam of the two, smooth, fluid, absolutely compelling. She moved her own hands slowly down the body pressed against hers, lingering on the stomach, feeling for the mound below it, moved her hands round the narrow hips, felt for the slender buttocks. They were high and firm; she stood there, feeling them, kneading them, excitement hot, liquid, flooding her, her breathing very fast and hard, and then the voice came again: 'Oh my God, you're so beautiful.'

It was strange, so strange, to feel this intense sexual pleasure and desire, and then in the midst of it, the tumult, to hear a female voice.

*   *   *

Later, she looked for Francis. He was sitting in the drawing room, a little apart from the rest, talking to Janine. Edwina was momentarily anxious, that this might seem an aberration to him, that he had in some way not known, might even be shocked, in spite of bringing her here; but he smiled at her, almost imperceptibly blew her a kiss, and continued his conversation. Whatever she was doing clearly did not matter to him.

Marcia had left and Ivor was dancing with her now. She found his likeness to Marcia confusing and erotic; the same full, sensual mouth kissing her, the same brilliant, amused eyes looking at her, his hands moving on her in the same skilful way.

Later St John joined them, danced with them, kissed them both, caressed them both; a confusion of pleasures, of sound, of touch, of taste, possessed her. She wanted them both, she could have them both; she felt love, warmth, an intense happiness. Sexual pleasure, sexual excitement had taken hold of her brain; she felt drunk, drugged, and knew she was neither.

Next to her two women danced, kissing, caressing, and somewhere dimly beyond her consciousness she saw another couple still; a man and a woman—how strange, she thought, how very strange—were moving into yet another room, the room where she and Marcia had lain and discovered one another's soft, sweet, pliant bodies, had moved and moaned and cried out with pleasure, seeking out, knowing precisely what the other had wanted, where the delights lay.

She had no real idea where she was, or where she should have been, she could hardly have told anyone her own name, but an energy possessed her, a new warm, vivid energy; she felt strong, safe, inviolate.

*   *   *

At some point later, she was dancing with Janine and noticed the clock: it was almost five. The night had vanished, consumed itself in a confusion of pleasure. She looked for Francis again; he had gone. Anxiety stabbed at her.

Janine read the anxiety and smiled. 'Don't worry about Francis. He said to say goodbye, that he'd see you tomorrow. He seldom stays for long. He just likes to see us all, to feel part of us. We're a very happy little group.'

'So I see,' said Edwina.

*   *   *

She arrived home at six thirty, removed her shoes on the doorstep, fled up the stairs, praying she would meet no one, and fell into bed, fully dressed. She lay there, wide awake, in a state of wonderment, marvelling that she could have lived without such pleasures for so long.

CHAPTER THIRTY-TWO

Cassia's hand, holding the telephone receiver, was wet, slippery with sweat. The room seemed to be rather dark, and there was a pain somewhere tight in her chest. She wondered if she might be having a heart attack, even hoped that she was. It would solve a lot of dilemmas, save so much anguish.

'Yes? Miss Gerard's secretary speaking.'

'Oh, is she there, please? It's Cassia Fallon.'

'No, Mrs Fallon, I'm afraid she isn't. She's operating this morning.'

'Oh, I see.' Relief flooded her, sweet, soothing, the room lightened. Execution had been stayed. 'I'll ring back.'

A very brief reprieve, then, before she was branded as incompetent, unreliable, probably in Miss Gerard's eyes contemptible, before she had to set aside, and be seen to be setting aside, what she wanted so much that it was a bodily hunger, a physical pain, before she had to face finally that success in her career was not to be hers, that she was condemned to a professional lifetime of compromise, of dissatisfaction.

There was no real decision to be made: Cassia knew that. She had three small children, one of whom had already suffered a considerable trauma, and all of whom were about to have to endure the pain of seeing their parents' marriage come to an end. For that really was indubitable; there was no alternative to it. They needed to part: he, as well as she, would be happier and stronger for it.

The children, however, would be wretched, torn in their loyalties; they would need absolute security and endless attention if they were to begin to recover, not a mother who came home once a week, exhausted and self-obsessed. No, she had no choice; but Monica Gerard would not see it that way, and her scorn, both personal and professional, would be hard to bear.

* * *

It was Wednesday; she had hours to kill before she started her clinic. She went out and bought a newspaper, sat reading it. There was much discussion of the position of the King, not in his relationship with Mrs Simpson, on which the press with extraordinary restraint was still remaining silent, but with Parliament and the country; what some saw as a simple desire to help the less advantaged of his subjects, others read as a conscious rift with his ministers—the same men who might stand between him and his personal happiness. And how, thought Cassia, would the King finally decide? Would he choose personal happiness or professional duty? The thought of the two of them, herself and her King, struggling with moral dilemmas, amused her, quite cheered her up.

Later she went to see Cecily. She found her looking very much better, still thin, still a little frail, but quite cheerful.

'Cecily, can I ask you something about

Leonora?' She took herself by surprise with that question, had not thought it was currently in the forefront of her mind.

'Yes, of course.'

Cecily said that, yes, she had heard from Benedict that Leonora had been in financial difficulties at one point, that she had kept it from him, from all of them, that Harry had told him about it. 'He went immediately over to Paris to see her.'

'Harry,' said Cassia. 'Are you sure it was Harry who told him?'

'Yes of course. I remember him telling me about it, Benedict, I mean.'

'And when was that, can you remember?'

'Oh . . . the spring before she died.'

'And where was she living then?' said Cassia.

'In a very nice apartment, apparently, one of those ones with a *porte cocherie*, you know, built round a lovely courtyard garden.'

'And Gresham was back?'

'I don't know if he was actually back, but he'd certainly arranged for her to have some more money, and for medical care and so on.'

'You didn't ever visit her, those last few months?' said Cassia.

Cecily flushed. 'No, I didn't, and I do feel ashamed about it, but well, you know, I always had a rather difficult relationship with Leonora. I was jealous of her, she was always so close to Benedict. And she knew about his—his problems, of course, knew why he'd married me. I found that very difficult to cope with. I knew I should have gone, but I kept putting it off . . .'

Cassia drove back to her own house feeling

585

thoughtful. Her conversation with Rupert had eased her worries, shifted them—her carefully constructed theory about Harry did now seem a little foolish—but she was still very far from happy.

She decided to go to Paris: to do some research for herself.

*   *   *

Edwina was reading American *Vogue*, so engrossed she didn't consciously hear the pounding footsteps on the stairs, the same footsteps moving along the corridor, only her own door wrenched violently open, and Harry's voice telling her he wanted to talk to her.

She put her magazine aside with exaggerated patience. 'Yes, Harry?'

'Edwina, you are to give that damnfool job up. Immediately.'

'Don't be ridiculous. Why should I?'

'Because I wish it, that's why you should.'

'Well, I'm sorry, Harry, but I don't wish it. I enjoy my job, in fact I love it.'

'Yes, so I see. And your relationship with that—creature Stevenson-Cook, and some other fairly unpleasant characters as well, it seems.'

'I don't have a relationship, as you put it, with Francis Stevenson-Cook.'

'Of course you do. You dine with him night after night, you've been seen at night-clubs with him, you could at least have the grace to employ a little discretion. And don't start telling me he's a homosexual, because I know at least two women personally who have had affairs with him. Whether or not you've actually been to bed with him is of no

586

interest to me but I will not be publicly cuckolded—I will not have my wife linked in London gossip with such a person.'

'Such a person!' she said. 'Harry, you sound like Edward Fallon. I'm surprised at you.'

'At least Edward Fallon has a moral code of sorts,' he said, 'which is more than can be said of you.'

Edwina felt her cheeks begin to burn, felt fear, an icy trickle somewhere deep within her.

'I know where you were the other night,' he said. 'I heard about it, and your behaviour. With Marcia Bryanston and that twin brother of hers. Edwina, how could you?'

'Very easily,' she said, her courage up as always when she was cornered. 'I liked them both, they were interesting and amusing.'

'No doubt. And degenerate and decadent. Her paintings are pure pornography, and he sleeps with every homosexual and bisexual in London. They are both cocaine addicts. And those are the sort of people Stevenson-Cook numbers among his friends. I will not have it, Edwina, I really will not.'

'And how,' she said, leaning back in her chair, 'will you stop it?'

He came over to her then, leant on the arms of her chair, put his face quite close to hers. She could feel the rage in him, smell it. 'I have endured a great deal from you,' he said. 'Your lack of affection, your lack of interest in everything I do, your rendering yourself sterile—'

'Who told you that?' she said, too shocked to be careful.

'Nobody told me. I worked it out for myself. But of course it's true. I thought it must be.'

She felt a new, violent rage herself. 'That was a filthy trick. Trying to trap me.'

'With every justification, it seems. So here I am, denied my right to children, and now the foolish centre of a storm of very unpleasant gossip. I don't like it, Edwina, and I will not endure it. Either it stops or you will find yourself the guilty party in a very ugly divorce suit. You can make your own mind up, it is entirely up to you. But I have no intention of letting things go on in this way.'

* * *

Edwina sat in her room after he had left, and tried to decide what to do. She wondered who had told him about the other night, at Janine Sobel's house. It had been foolish of her to behave as she had, foolish of Francis to take her; she wondered idly why he had, whether he had had some kind of ulterior motive. She didn't trust him; she didn't trust any of them. She just liked them, wanted to be . . . well, if not quite one of them, to be accepted by them.

The world for Edwina had shifted totally on its axis that night at Janine Sobel's. A process that had begun when she had started work at *Style* had been completed in those hours. The person she had thought she was no longer existed; in her place was a stranger, stronger, cleverer, bolder. She felt she had been freed, that night, from the constraints of her old life; she had walked through a series of doors and found herself in a dazzling new landscape and she could not and would not go back.

Harry did not love her, he had no real interest in

her; she saw every reason to behave in a way that would redress those facts, and no reason at all to protect him and their increasingly unsatisfactory relationship. If she wanted to spend her solitary evenings with her own friends, doing what interested and amused her, then she felt she had a right to do so.

*   *   *

She said all this to Francis Stevenson-Cook next day over lunch in his office—for she dared not be seen in public with him, she really was too frightened of Harry for that—and he listened to her carefully, then smiled and refilled her glass.

'I was right,' he said with great satisfaction. 'I read you exactly right.'

Manipulative so-and-so, she thought with a mixture of amusement and irritation. She was under no illusions about Francis. He picked people up and played with them for a while and then tired of them and set them down again. She had realised that finally the other night at Janine's, watching him surveying the scene with that strange indulgent detachment. The danger was in not realising it: but she did, and he knew she did, and therefore she was safe.

*   *   *

That same afternoon in London another woman had found herself confronted with a new angle on her marital dilemma: Mrs Wallis Simpson, lunching at Claridges with Esmond Harmsworth, son of Lord Rothermere, owner of the *Daily Mail*, was

589

asked if she had ever considered the possibility of a morganatic marriage. Within this framework, Mr Harmsworth explained, she could marry the King but would not take his rank, and nor would any children have the right of succession. It could provide a solution of sorts: might she suggest it to the King?

*   *   *

'Good God,' said Edward.

Cassia looked at him across the kitchen; he was reading a letter, was rather pale. The hand holding the letter was shaking. 'What? Is something wrong?'

'No,' he said slowly, 'no. Just—well, a bit of a shock. That's all.'

'Can I see?'

'Yes, of course.' He handed it over. They had, in the calm of their tacit decision to separate, become more friendly, more able to communicate; rage, resentment, jealousy even, seemed to have left them, leaving only a great sadness and regret that was easier to bear.

'Oh, Edward,' said Cassia, and she felt her eyes filling with tears, saw the words '. . . able after all to offer you a place as registrar as from next year, and we understand you will be doing your MRCS.' She took in the name of the hospital: St Mark's, Clapham, a good teaching hospital. 'Edward, I'm so pleased. You will accept this one, won't you?'

'Yes, of course I will.'

She moved forward, put her arms round him. For the first time for months he didn't shy away, but returned the embrace, and then said, 'I think

590

we should talk, don't you?'

They talked for a long time: agreed that they should part, that they were no longer remotely able to make one another happy; that he at least could not bear the imbalance of their relationship, knowing she did not love him; that they should, could hopefully, remain friends.

'I'm so truly happy for you,' she said, kissing him gently on the cheek. 'Nothing could please me more.'

'I know,' he said, 'I can see that. Thank you.'

He would be living in at the hospital; there was no question of him doing anything else. It would make the transition for the children far easier, would help to explain his absence. They agreed the practice should probably be sold, that the family also should move to London, that Cassia should buy a large house there.

'But we still have to tell them,' he said, 'we can't pretend. Oh dear,' he said, and sighed heavily, 'it's all so sad, isn't it?' He dashed his hand across his eyes suddenly. 'Sorry. Bit emotional.'

'Me too,' she said, and looked at him; saw suddenly not the Edward who was sitting there now, his eyes heavy with the hurt of it all, but the Edward she had seen that first day in Casualty, young and hopeful and happy, his brown hair flopping over his face as he bent over her ankle, bandaging it with slow and infinite care, and then sitting back on his heels, smiling his slow, sweet smile at her for the first time. She burst into tears and cried, cried for a long time.

When Peggy came out to find them and tell them it was lunchtime, Edward was sitting with his arm round her.

'They seem much happier,' she said to Mrs Briggs later. 'I think maybe they've come to their senses after all.'

* * *

Cecily was waiting for the car to take her home that Thursday afternoon, feeling sick. The thought of being away from the doctors and nurses who had cared for her for so long was terrifying. She saw a taxi coming in the gate; someone visiting some fortunate patient, one who could stay a little longer. And then watched in amazement as Justin Everard got out of it.

'I thought you would need company,' he said, walking over to her, giving her a kiss, 'company to lend you courage. Come along, give me that case. Oh, look, here is your wonderful car now. I shall never forget our journey down to Devon in that car, with your little girl being sick all over Edwina's bag. So enchanting.'

'It didn't seem very enchanting to me,' said Cecily, laughing.

Justin held her hand all the way home, telling her funny stories about sessions he had been on, the fashion show, the dreadfulness of Edwina; she forgot all about her nervousness.

The children and Nanny were waiting outside on the steps of the house, holding a big white banner that read 'Welcome Home'. Mrs Forbes stood behind them weeping openly. As they walked into the hall, her arms round the two girls, the first thing Cecily noticed was the smell of flowers, and then she looked about her and laughed with pure pleasure: vases of roses, of lilies, of freesias, stood on every conceivable surface; glorious white and scarlet azaleas filled the jardinières; trailing greenery was draped over the doors.

'It's wonderful,' she said, 'simply wonderful.'

'Justin did most of it,' said Fanny.

'Did you really?'

'Well, I and a few underlings,' he said modestly. 'Edwina helped as well.'

'You are so kind to me,' said Cecily, 'so very very kind, I can't think why.'

'I'm very fond of you,' he said simply. 'I think you're wonderful.'

*   *   *

Later she phoned Edwina to thank her.

'Oh, it was all Justin really,' she said. 'He absolutely adores you.'

'It's rather comic, isn't it? Since he's—well, he's . . .'

'Cecily,' said Edwina, amused, 'you really are ridiculous.'

'I am not ridiculous,' said Cecily. Weariness and emotion had brought her near to tears. 'I think he's wonderful too. I'm terribly fond of him. But I don't think I could cope with—'

'Cecily, if you mean he's a fairy, of course he's not. I really thought you understood that. He puts it on because people expect it of him, in his profession, but he's one of the biggest wolves in London.'

'Oh,' said Cecily. 'Oh, yes, I see.'

*   *   *

'What's the matter, Rupert?' said Eleanor Studely. They were having a glass of wine after the performance as they often did; he had hardly spoken.

'Oh nothing. Just a bit low.'

'Come on,' she said, 'tell me. A trouble shared and all that.'

'Oh, I'm being ridiculous. A foolish old man. As usual. I shall get over it, no doubt, but this one was rather special.'

'Oh, I see.' She sounded amused. 'Real love, was it, this time?'

'Eleanor,' said Rupert, 'I don't want to be rude, but if my misery is so amusing, then perhaps we should end this discussion.'

'Rupert, don't be silly. Of course I don't find it amusing. It's just that I've known you quite a long time, and I've seen you tumble in and out of love so many times.'

'I'm afraid this is rather different,' said Rupert coldly. He knew he was being unpleasant, but he couldn't help it, that most unattractive of qualities, self-pity, distorting his judgement and his behaviour. 'Perhaps you have forgotten how it feels to be rejected, Eleanor. By someone you really care about.'

The minute he'd said it, he was horrified at himself; he looked at Eleanor, saw high colour flash into her face, saw her eyes dangerously brilliant, saw the shake of her hand as she put down her glass.

She stood up. 'I think I will go home now,' she said. 'I'm very tired. Goodnight.'

'Eleanor,' he said, 'I'm so desperately sorry. Do forgive me. Christ, I don't know what came over

594

me.'

'Whatever it was, I would rather not hear any more of it,' she said, opening the dressing-room door. 'Goodnight, Rupert.'

This was the woman, he thought, who had watched her much-loved husband die from tuberculosis while being forced to carry on working in order to support all three of them for six desperate months; who had, in the three years since, managed to care for her daughter, all on her own, without the benefit of any family whatsoever. And who, most remarkably, had managed to remain positive, generous and tranquil. Who had had the courage to risk coming into their funny, dangerous little project. Whose gaiety and perseverance had seen them through many dark hours. And he had shown her in return bad temper and meanness. All because his pride had been hurt. He ought to be put up against a wall and shot.

* * *

'Mummy,' said Bertie, 'can we come and watch you all on Saturday? Please?'

'Bertie, you'd hate it,' said Cassia firmly. 'Lots and lots of ladies just walking up and down in silly frocks.'

'But we'd still like to see you, wouldn't we, William?'

'Course we would.'

'It's out of the question,' said Edward sharply. 'You'd be bored to tears after five minutes and someone would have to look after you.'

'You could look after us,' said Bertie. 'You're coming, aren't you?'

'No,' said Edward. 'No, I'm afraid I can't.'

They both stared at him. 'But don't you want to see Mummy on the stage thing?' said Bertie finally. 'With Aunt Edwina and everyone? And Fanny and Stephanie dancing?'

'Yes, and Rupert's doing something for it, too,' said William, 'and you wouldn't let us see his play, you've got to let us come to this.'

'Perhaps Janet could take them?' said Edward. He looked at Cassia with an expression that was close to desperation.

'Well,' she said thoughtfully, 'I think that's a very good idea. I'm sure Janet would love to see the fashion show, and as long as Peggy and Mrs Briggs could look after Delia, then that's the answer. Janet, would you like that?'

'Oh, I'd love it,' said Janet, her face flushed with pleasure. 'Thank you very much, Mrs Fallon.'

'Good,' said Edward, 'that's settled, then. You must excuse me now, I've got things to do.'

He walked out of the room, and Cassia went after him. 'Edward, it's time we told them. I think it's a good moment.'

'There's never a good moment.'

'All right, but it's as good as any.'

Afterwards she had no idea whence had come that panic-stricken conviction, or the courage to see it through, but he gave in, agreed with her, and they did it, somehow, they got through it. They sat on the sofa by the fire, holding hands, Cassia's arm round Bertie, Edward's round William, and told them first that Edward had a very exciting new job which meant living in a hospital all the time for two or three years, and then that after that she and Edward would not live together all the time.

'You see, we don't seem to make each other happy any more,' said Cassia, wiping the tears that were rolling silently down Bertie's face.

'Don't you like each other?'

'Yes, of course we do. Very much. But we disagree about so many things, we keep quarrelling, you know we do, you've heard us, and if we don't live together all the time, then we think we can stop quarrelling and just be friends.'

'When we quarrel you tell us not to be so silly,' said William. 'Why can't you stop being silly?'

'It's very hard to explain,' said Cassia with a sigh. 'It's different when you're grown up: you need to live with someone you don't quarrel with.'

'So are you going to live with different people?' said William warily.

'No,' said Edward, 'of course not. Well, I am, but only other doctors. In the hospital. And I shall come and see you lots, every weekend that I'm not working.'

'We'll get a new big house in London,' said Cassia, 'and—'

'In London? Why not here?'

'Well, we'll be nearer Daddy in London, and—and my work. I won't be away three days a week any more.'

'No,' said William, 'I like it here, and what about Buffy?'

'Buffy can come too. We'll have a garden, a big garden.'

'No. I like it here.' His small face was working, his eyes filled with panic. 'This is our house, I don't want to leave it.'

'No,' said Bertie, 'I won't leave it, not ever, whatever you say, and you said we could have ponies, we can't have ponies in London.'

'All right,' she said soothingly, aware that she was making life still more difficult for herself, desperate to soothe the panic, ease the pain, 'we don't have to go to London, we can stay here. If that's what you want, if that will make you feel happier about it. And have ponies.'

Bertie was sucking his thumb, watching them warily. 'And will you stop going to London to work?'

She hesitated, then said quietly, 'If you like, yes.'

'So it'll be like now really, only the other way round? You'll be here all the time and Daddy won't.'

'Well, sort of like now, yes. But, Bertie, you must understand that—'

'And you won't be shagging anyone else? Not either of you?'

'Bertie!' said Edward. His face was rather pink.

'It's all right, Edward. He picked that particular expression up at school. I explained it meant being someone's girlfriend. Or boyfriend.'

'Oh. Oh, I see. No, Bertie, certainly not.'

Bertie looked up at them both, an expression on his face that Cassia had never seen before. Analysing it, she realised with something of a shock that it was cunning. 'So you really are still friends?'

They looked at each other.

'Yes,' said Cassia firmly, 'we're still friends. Very good friends.'

'Want to prove it?'

'Yes,' said Edward.

'You come to the show thing as well on Saturday, then. Come and see Mummy. Otherwise I won't believe you.'

598

Finally Edward said, 'Yes. Yes, all right.'

'We can't tell Janet she can't come now,' said Cassia firmly.

'No, that's all right. We'll all go.'

'Good,' said Bertie. He smiled at his father rather uncertainly.

Cassia wasn't so foolish as to think it was over; she knew there would be many tears, much grief yet, and that the small piece of cunning Bertie had exhibited was only the beginning. They had lost security, her children, in that hour in the sitting room, lost a degree of innocence; but if she did what she had said, if they both did, if they kept their promises to them, they would recover, they would survive. And as she sat there, trembling, still holding Edward's hand, she suddenly realised what she could just possibly do now and found in it some consolation for herself at least.

CHAPTER THIRTY-THREE

Rupert had scarcely slept at all, so deeply ashamed of himself did he feel. Every time he closed his eyes he saw Eleanor's face first flushed with anger, then white and drawn with pain. He realised that only one thing was going to begin to explain his behaviour, and that was making Eleanor understand the depths of his misery and humiliation—the misery that had driven him to make his remark. And it must be done quickly: he must not put it off. Eleanor's hurt had been too severe to be left untreated for a minute more than necessary.

Sitting in his taxi on the way to her small house in Balham, a large bunch of flowers in his hand, he reflected not for the first time how unfortunate it was that Eleanor was in no way the type of woman to whom he was attracted; nothing could have been more convenient, more suitable, than for him to be in love with his leading lady, moreover a leading lady who was beautiful, intelligent, interested in what interested him, caring about all the things that he cared about. But life was not convenient, or suitable; if it was, he would have spent less time in the company of dizzy young blonde things who had no interest in him whatsoever beyond his ability to provide them with a good dinner, a few bunches of flowers, possibly the odd bit of jewellery—and very occasionally a sexual experience which they probably found at best moderately satisfying. These days he increasingly yearned for a proper home and a family of his own.

He spoke of this yearning to Eleanor, as they sat drinking some very good coffee in the kitchen of her enchanting little house, after he had made his stammering explanation and she had accepted it with a grace and generosity that he knew he did not deserve.

'I do know,' she said, 'that in spite of everything, I am very blessed. Portia gives my life a stability and a meaning that it would not otherwise have. And I did love Walter very much, so I have very happy memories to see me through as well. We were very happy, in a strange way during those last few months; we said all the things we wanted to one another, all the misunderstandings were cleared up . . . Rupert, are you all right? What is it?'

It was the word misunderstanding that did it: it made Rupert suddenly see what had been wrong with the explanation Cassia had given him about Harry's anger with her, about their brief liaison. Harry had misunderstood: not about *what* had happened, but *when*. He stood up suddenly, pushing his chair back.

'Eleanor, I'm so very sorry, but you must excuse me. I've just realised I've been rather stupid. Well, not just I, Cassia also. Do please forgive me, I have to go and see someone urgently. Thank you for your generosity. I'll see you later, at the fashion show. Goodbye. So sorry, so very sorry.'

After he had gone, Eleanor cleared away the coffee cups and took them into the kitchen, staring out at the grey November day. She did feel better: much better. She had appreciated Rupert's self-abasement while being more than a little aware that he was giving what amounted to a very good performance of a self-abasing man—but nothing was going to ease the much deeper pain she was experiencing: that of unrequited love. She had fought it for a long time, knowing it was hopeless, recognising Rupert's golden charm for the dangerous thing it was. However, she had now stopped fighting it and had given in to it, admitted it. And it hurt. It hurt a lot.

*　　　*　　　*

Harry Moreton was staring down into the street from his study when he saw a taxi pull up outside and Rupert Cameron get out of it. As Rupert was the last person in the world he wished to speak to, he called out to Bishop that he was not to be

601

disturbed under any circumstances and slammed the study door very firmly shut. Rupert was neither deterred nor deceived by Bishop's announcement that Mr Moreton was unavailable, and, indeed, Rupert stood in the hall saying so quite loudly—so loudly that the sound reached Edwina who was in her sitting room.

Edwina's nerves were stretched very taut; she ran downstairs and told Bishop that of course Mr Moreton was available and that he was to show Mr Cameron into the study immediately.

'It really is too bad when I'm trying to work and have so much on my mind. Rupert, he's in there, although why you or anyone else should wish to speak to him, I cannot imagine. Now can I please have some peace and quiet?'

Harry scowled as the door opened and Rupert Cameron came in, an apologetic and nervous Bishop behind him.

'Cameron,' he said, 'I have nothing to say to you whatsoever.'

'You don't have to say anything,' said Rupert, 'but I'd be really awfully grateful if you'd listen.'

*　　　*　　　*

Cassia had an appointment at Leon de Rosay's salon at eleven for a final fitting of her dresses. She had intended to get up early, but she had fallen into an exhausted sleep at four, having lain awake until then, fretting over the children, thinking about Harry and what they'd shared.

For as long as she lived now, everything that happened to her, every emotion she experienced, would be set against it, judged by it. It still hurt, the loss of him, the pain was frightful; it was in everything she did, everywhere she went. But at least now she had her new idea, her new scheme, consolation of a sort. If only she could persuade Edward, make it work . . .

*   *   *

She woke in a panic, to brilliant daylight. Ten o'clock. She felt confused, heavy with sleep; it was hard to hurry. She looked at herself in the mirror, at her pale drawn face, her eyes dark ringed. Hardly the face of a mannequin; she wasn't going to do much for Edwina looking like this. God, she was dreading this thing: if only she could get out of it. But she couldn't; short of a heart attack there was no excuse.

She thought of Amstruther's rather beady joke that the first symptom of heart disease was often sudden death and then it was usually too late . . . God, what would he say if he knew she'd turned down yet another opportunity? Well, no doubt he would know—he and Miss Gerard were friends.

She pulled on the dress she had worn the day before; there was no time to do anything about her face. She even had smudges of mascara under her eyes from not cleaning it off properly the night before; she licked her finger, tried to rub it off and made it worse. She dragged a comb through her hair, pushed her feet into her shoes, realised she had laddered one of her stockings. Well, what did it matter?

She grabbed her handbag and her keys and ran out of the front door, down the steps and into her car; it had come back from the garage, pristine and gleaming, quite restored to its original beauty. If only she could do the same for herself, she thought.

She set off down Walton Street with a screech of tyres. She was dimly aware that another car was coming up behind her; as she braked at the bottom of Walton Street it hooted at her, hard. Some bloody man, no doubt, irritated by the sight of her car, by the fact it was being driven by a woman, it happened quite often. Deliberately not so much as looking into the mirror, she pulled out and roared down Draycott Avenue. The car followed, still hooting.

'Oh shut up,' she shouted irritably into her driving mirror. The car was a black Bentley; whoever owned it clearly felt he should have the road to himself. She turned right into the King's Road, drove down much too fast. The car was still behind her, continued to hoot. What was the matter with him? Ah, thank God, there were some traffic lights ahead, just changing. She could shoot through them, leave him stuck behind, with a bit of luck. Then she was practically at Leon's. She put her foot down, shot the lights; they were just changing. Good.

'Oh God,' she said, as the Bentley followed her through; she had been so engrossed in his behaviour she had not been concentrating on what was in front of her, had to swerve to avoid another parked car. Another hoot—was he a maniac or something? The Bentley suddenly accelerated, shot past her, pulled in sharply in front of her and stopped; she almost ran into it.

She sat for a moment, breathing rather hard, shaking violently, then got out of the car on legs that could scarcely hold her, walked towards the

Bentley. The King's Road rang with hooting horns, people shouting.

'Are you completely mad?' she shouted, as the door opened and a large frame began to emerge from it.

'Yes,' said Harry, 'probably. My God, you look dreadful, Cassia, what on earth have you been doing? And why aren't you wearing my pearls?'

*   *   *

At Fort Belvedere that same day, Mrs Simpson was with the King, enjoying briefly the eye of the storm that they had created, the King having only a few days previously informed his mother and his brothers that he was prepared to 'go out quietly' if a way could not be found to enable him have the wife he so desperately wanted.

Meanwhile in London in the homes of the King's ministers and the Lords of the press, the arguments raged as to the advisability or indeed feasibility of the morganatic marriage proposal, which Mrs Simpson and consequently the King favoured and which was now the subject of formal discussion. And still the press was held silent.

*   *   *

Cecily had already changed into three different dresses and was trying to decide whether she should consider a fourth, when Justin arrived at the house.

'Oh dear,' she said, hearing the door-bell peal, 'that's Mr Everard, I had no idea it was so late.'

'It isn't late at all,' said Susan, who already had

done her hair, and stood proffering dresses, expressing the opinion that each was even prettier and more suitable than the last. 'I should go for the blue,' she added, 'it always did suit you.'

'That's just the point, I've worn it a lot. I want to feel confident, look really nice. No,' said Cecily, suddenly decisive, 'I'll wear the cream. And that means the pearls, Susan, the double string, I think, that Mr Harrington gave me for our tenth wedding anniversary.'

She was very surprised she had managed to say that: surprised and proud. It was the sort of thing an ordinary woman might have said, a confident woman who had nothing to be ashamed of, nothing to fear from what lay ahead of her, a woman who was looking forward to an evening with old friends who would almost certainly be pleased to see her, would not turn their backs on her, not shun her, not treat her like some sort of a pariah.

She was still managing to retain this mood of optimism and courage—albeit with some slight difficulty—when she went into the drawing room to greet Justin. Expecting one of the ecstatic greetings that she had come to expect from him, she was taken aback by him being clearly impatient.

'I did say you should be ready,' he said. 'I've left the rehearsal to come and fetch you.'

'Well, you didn't have to,' said Cecily. 'I'm perfectly capable of getting across a mile of London on my own.'

'I wanted to,' he said, his voice not quite its warm, charming self, 'but I didn't want to be long, that's all. I'm taking pictures at this thing, and—'

'I'm sure they can wait ten minutes for you to get back,' said Cecily. 'Now I've got some champagne on ice for us, and we can—'

'Cecily, darling,' said Justin, the 'darling' coming out with a clear effort, 'I do not have time for champagne. I've left my assistant in charge of a very tricky sequence and I must get back to it.'

'Well, it's a pity you didn't send your assistant for me,' said Cecily sharply, 'and I want some champagne, so you'd better just go back without me. Go on, Justin, I'll follow. And you needn't worry that I won't come, I have far more pressing reasons for being at this thing than arriving with you.'

She wasn't looking at him as she delivered the last bit of this speech, so she didn't see the hurt in his eyes; but she heard the drawing-room door slam behind him as he walked out and felt a stab of pain herself. She sat down in a chair and rang for Adams, thinking that Justin had not even told her how nice she looked, and irritation disposed of the pain again.

However busy Benedict had been, he had always had time to compliment her, was never in too much of a rush to take a glass of champagne with her if she wanted one before they went out . . .

*　　　*　　　*

Justin sat in his taxi, shaking quite literally with rage. To think he had left one of the most important sessions of his life, risked it going wrong, just to find himself on the receiving end of a lot of upper-class nonsense from a spoilt, over-indulged woman. How could she possibly not realise how crucial it was? How could she not appreciate him tearing himself away from it, just to collect her?

607

Of course it was hardly surprising she was spoilt; her husband had been one of the richest men in England. Well, he wasn't going to spoil her. Either she accepted him for what he was, appreciated the limitations of his job and lifestyle, or their relationship was over. Then he realised that their relationship existed only in his hopeful imagination and that, in actual fact, it had no future whatsoever.

*   *   *

'Oh, Cassia, there you are. I do think you could have got here earlier. I could have done with someone to help me sort out the seating arrangements.'

Cassia looked at Edwina across the ballroom of the Dorchester, the chaos of the room: men up ladders fixing lights, more men fixing trailing cables, more men still putting a red baize cover on the vast catwalk that extended two thirds of the room's width; various models drifting about in dressing robes; a young man with long brown hair shouting at one of the models; a pianist playing what was clearly supposed to be soothing music and which was having no effect whatsoever and the wife of her lover glaring at her across the chaos. All these things seemed to go some way towards restoring her to reality.

Until then, she had not felt herself rooted in reality at all. She had experienced in the course of the day a flow of such extraordinary and violent emotion that she was by then utterly spent. She had managed to collect the dresses from Leon de Rosay half an hour earlier, to thank him for them, to say, yes, they fitted beautifully now. Was he able to tell, she wondered, as he studied those dresses on her, could he see by looking at her, what had been happening to her in the hours between the morning appointment and the evening, the hours that his seamstresses had spent feverishly unpicking and restitching, the hours that she had lain in her bed in her house in Walton Street with Harry?

Could he tell that the body on which he now studied his creations had arched, thrust, throbbed, soared into pleasure, not just once, but again and again, as morning became afternoon and afternoon evening. Could he tell that the voice that assured him with courteous calm that the dresses were perfect now, quite perfect really, had cried out repeatedly, loudly, with wild primitive pleasure, that the ears in which he pinned first this style of earring, now that, had heard words so extraordinarily, so powerfully carnal that merely remembering them made her body clench with delight?

And perhaps the most extraordinary words of all, given that they were on Harry's lips, were, 'I'm sorry,' not once, but again and again.

*   *   *

'I'm sorry,' he had said, as she stood there scowling at him, still shaken from the near crash, 'I was only trying to catch you, attract your attention.'

'And quite possibly kill me, yourself and several other people besides into the bargain,' she said. 'Really, Harry, you are cretinously stupid. You'd better talk to that man, the one in the Riley, I think he's going to hit you.'

'I'm sorry,' he said to the man in the Riley, the bonnet of which was virtually enfolding a lamp-post, 'frightfully stupid of me, of course you must allow me to pay for any damage, here is my card.'

And 'I'm sorry,' he said to her, as she sat in the Bentley, still scowling, 'sorry I said you looked dreadful, but you—well, you do. Did you sleep in that dress or something?'

'No,' she said.

'Well, it looks like it. And laddered stockings,' he said, tracing the snaking shape of it with his thumb, from her knee down to her ankle. 'Really, Cassia!'

'Well, I'm sorry you find it all so shocking,' she said irritably, while noticing and trying not to notice that even the simple fact of his thumb moving idly up and down her leg caused reverberations in other places in her body, invisible, horribly responsive places.

'Not shocking, just surprising,' he said, and then, 'I'm sorry, Cassia. I'm sorry I misjudged you. Leapt to conclusions. About—about Cameron.'

And while she sat there, staring at him, amazed at this most extraordinary and unexpected of all his apologies, he said, clearly with excessive difficulty, 'I do tend to be slightly hasty. At times. And I'm not going to pretend I don't care about it. I do. But I can live with it. I don't care about it enough to stop loving you.'

Happiness flooded her, drenched her; she stayed very still, afraid to speak further, afraid even to move.

'Good chap, Cameron,' he said, sitting back in the driving seat, looking rather distantly out of the window. 'Very good. Good friend to have come to see me, you know. No, of course you don't. This morning. To explain.'

'Oh, I see,' she said. 'So what—what did he tell you?' she said nervously.

He looked at her consideringly for a moment, then half smiled. 'Oh, now,—' he said, 'here is a pretty situation. I have the opportunity to hear your evidence and set it against his. Shall I do that, Cassia, would you like to give me your version of what he told me? Might it be different in any way, do you think?'

'You are monstrous,' she said, anger rising in her, 'absolutely monstrous. I will tell you what happened, not to gain your bloody approval, Harry Moreton, but because I want you to know.'

'Don't be ridiculous,' he said, reaching over. 'I wasn't serious. I can't help being jealous of the bastard, Cassia, but I can live with it. I've said I'm sorry, for fuck's sake, what more do you want?'

She looked at him and smiled. Everything seemed very simple suddenly.

'You,' she said, 'I want you and as soon as possible.'

*   *   *

For Edwina the entire evening had blurred. Somehow the chaotic room cleared into order, the music began, the pianist running through his repertoire of Gershwin, Cole Porter, Irving Berlin. The models arrived one by one, the amateurs excited and chattery, the professionals languid. The children appeared for her approval, transformed from rather ordinary little girls into a myriad of befrilled and beribboned bridesmaids.

The gilt chairs began to fill; peering through a

gap in the curtains Edwina saw countless friends, saw Cecily enter alone, looking terribly nervous, then saw first one, then another, then a crowd of people go over to her and greet her (but where was Justin, for heaven's sake? He had promised to look after her). She saw Francis arriving, with Aurora Le Page and Drusilla Wyndham; saw Edward Fallon with the two little boys and an extremely pretty, dark girl who Cassia said was their nanny; saw the Whittakers settle themselves, Lady Whittaker looking interestingly nervous; her own parents, her mother looking quite wonderful in beaded black; saw Leon de Rosay slip into the back row, having driven everyone in the dressing room completely crazy; saw Justin appear from behind the scenes and set up his camera on a tripod next to Leon; and then time really took a rush forward, and she had made her announcement, welcomed everyone, and then it was starting and the first girls were gliding in the most professional manner along the catwalk, even Venetia Hardwicke, who had two left feet, and then . . .

'Silence!' said Francis Stevenson-Cook. 'Pray silence for Mr Rupert Cameron, who will read aloud from tomorrow's newspaper, which through my unrivalled contacts with Fleet Street I have managed to acquire. It says it all.'

Rupert stood up, smiling, waving a copy of the *Daily Sketch*, and began to read from it in excessively dramatic tones.

'Huge Success at Charity Fashion Show. The cream of London society and the fashion and theatrical world met last night in the new ballroom in the Grosvenor House Hotel where a

fashion show in aid of St Christopher's Hospital was staged by Mrs Edwina Moreton, a fashion editor on Style magazine' very loud cheers.

Edwina felt thankful that neither Aurora Le Page nor Drusilla Wyndham were at this party, organised by Francis at the Dorchester.

'Seats for the show were totally sold out, and guests staying in the hotel who did not have tickets were prepared to stand and watch for its hour and a half duration. Many of Mrs Moreton's friends, including Mrs Cassia Fallon, a doctor at St Christopher's Hospital—' loud cheers and wolf whistles—*'modelled the clothes, which were by London's top couturiers, along with a large number of professional mannequins.*

'The finale of the show was a wedding sequence, including a children's ballet choreographed jointly by Madame Evelyn Brunel of the well-known Brunel Academy and Mr Rupert Cameron, the actor, star of the new hit play Letters—' this to deafening applause. *'One of the very pretty bridesmaids was ten-year-old Portia Studely, the daughter of Mr Cameron's co-star, Eleanor Studely.*

'The evening raised over £1,000 for the hospital, and Mr Stevenson Cook, the publishing director of Style Publications, who presented the cheque to Mrs Mary Whittaker from the hospital committee, paid tribute to all Mrs Moreton's hard work—' cries of 'well done, Edwina'—*'and said he was proud to have Style magazine associated with the show.'*

613

A few people were not at the party: Edward Fallon had returned to the house in Walton Street with Janet Fraser, saying (with perfect truth) that the boys must be got home, they were exhausted and needed to go to bed. He and Janet then spent the rest of the evening drinking cocoa and playing canasta.

Edward was surprised, as he drifted off to sleep, by how much he had enjoyed the whole occasion; for some reason the foolishness of Cassia's friends, the strain of contact with them, had been eased by Janet's smiling, sensible presence, her occasional sharp comment. And she was wonderful with the children (who had been swiftly bored, asking at regular intervals and in loud whispers when it would be over), reminding them firmly how much they had wanted to come, feeding them boiled sweets at regular intervals from a seemingly bottomless paper bag in her pocket; he really had been very impressed by that. And by her insistence that Cassia went to the party afterwards, and her tactful recognition that he, Edward, would love to escape it, 'but maybe if Daddy could come with us, that would help me a lot'.

It had all been very impressive.

*   *   *

Cecily had not been at the party, and nor had Justin; they had returned to the house in Eaton Place together (having apologised to one another almost in unison in the interval of the fashion show) and had drunk a bottle of the champagne she had had put on ice for their earlier

614

consumption. She had then gone up to bed, pleading a genuine tiredness, but very happy none the less, and resolved to try to understand the demands of a life hitherto unimaginable to her, and he had walked all the way home to his flat in Clapham, scarcely noticing the distance and equally resolved to try to understand the effect of a life equally unimaginable to him, and its power to spoil even the sweetest and most unselfish of people.

*   *   *

Eleanor Studely was also not at the party; she had insisted that she and Portia, who had a nasty headache, should go home to the peace and quiet of Peckham. Eleanor sat drinking a strong cup of tea and tried to tell herself that being at the party, watching Rupert Cameron flirting with the enormous number of pretty young women who would be there, would be more painful than sitting here all alone, thinking about it. She was not terribly successful.

CHAPTER THIRTY-FOUR

'Cecily—' Cassia's voice was urgent, oddly excited on the telephone. 'Do, you speak French?'

Cecily struggled into a sitting position. 'Yes,' she said, 'yes, I do.'

'Good. I want to ask you something . . .'

*   *   *

Three days later, as Cassia lay in their twin cabin in the Golden Arrow, as it made its way through the dark stretches of northern France, she felt a strange mixture of elation and terror. Making Cecily her accomplice had been a stroke of genius, she thought; desperate to go, completely incapable of thinking of any excuse to present to her family and, indeed, Harry for doing so, the inspiration had come to her as she lay on the sofa at Walton Street after the party. And it had worked beautifully; Cecily had been excited, intrigued, had promised absolute discretion, had completely understood her reasons for wanting to go (presented more as a mild curiosity as to Leonora's situation in the last few months of her life than a burning, desperate need to understand it), had suggested they present the trip as a treat for Cecily and a chance to buy the new clothes she so desperately needed.

*   *   *

They were staying at the Ritz. 'My treat,' said Cassia firmly, 'it's the least I can do. We're going to have some fun as well.' And as they sipped their drinks, studied the absurdly elaborate menu for luncheon, she wondered why she had not indulged herself more in the time since she had become rich.

There had, of course, been the requirement for tact with Edward, a requirement she had scarcely fulfilled, she reflected with a stab of misery, but there was, of course, something else, something which initially had not been a factor but increasingly now was: a sense of unease about it, a sense that it was not properly hers, that she had no right to it.

Perhaps the trip would give her the right to it, but she was very much afraid it wouldn't.

* * *

After a lunch of lamb noisettes so tender they seemed quite literally and in the approved manner to melt in the mouth, they walked out into the brilliant streets of pre-Christmas Paris.

Cecily knew Paris well, she had spent six months there just before she had done her London season, and she acted as guide. It was like a celebration of fashion, that walk: they bought clothes, perfume, hats for themselves, presents for everyone else; stopped every hour or so for lemon tea, hot chocolate piled high with *crème chantilly*, and, to restore their flagging energies, wonderful pastries, fruit tartlets, chocolate eclairs.

They took a taxi back to the hotel at seven and collapsed exhausted into hot baths; having changed and re-energised themselves with cocktails, they went out to dine in the art nouveau splendour of Maxims and sat happily weary, eating lobster thermidor and observing chic Paris at play.

'The thing about Paris,' said Cecily thoughtfully, 'is that everybody is much more self-confident than they are in London. So they're not worrying about what everybody else thinks all the time. Oh, I am enjoying myself, this was such a lovely idea.'

* * *

They took the Metro next morning to Porte d'Auteuil. Cassia had half expected to find herself in the middle of a slum, a sort of Parisian

617

Whitechapel, and was relieved to find a district that, although not beautiful, was still quite respectable. The chief difference was in its colour: where the Paris she knew was all shades of white and golden stone, the Auteuil was drab, uncompromising grey with new apartment blocks rising on every corner.

She stood in the street, imagining Leonora arriving here completely alone, ill and anxious, from the glorious tree-lined sweep of the avenue Foch and felt sick.

The apartment block in which Leonora had lived was a vast rectangular concrete structure, built in the new functional style, extending a full block about a dozen storeys tall, set with small, square windows; there was a door leading straight off the street every thirty yards or so, each one firmly locked. 'She was number one hundred and ten,' said Cassia, 'it must be about halfway along. How on earth are we going to get in? There's no central door, no porter.'

'We'll just stand there,' said Cecily. 'Someone's bound to come out sooner or later. Then we can simply walk in.'

Not for the first time since they had arrived in Paris, Cassia looked at her with a certain admiration.

They had to wait almost half an hour. Eventually an old man emerged, a cigarette adhering to his bottom lip; he glared at them and tried to pull the door closed. Cecily gave him a dazzling smile, put out her arm quickly and stopped him.

'*Bonjour, Monsieur. Comment allez-vous? Nous visitons notre grandmère au cinquième étage.*'

The old man glared at them, but he let them

through.

Inside, the building was clean, but incredibly ugly. The apartment was on the fourth floor.

'Think of hauling your shopping up here,' said Cecily. 'And she was ill when she had to do this, and no lift. I can't bear it.'

They knocked on the door of 110; no answer, nor to those on either side of it, nor the two doors opposite. The silence was somehow threatening; the only sound the echoes of their knocking.

An old woman came slowly up the stairs towards them, breathing heavily, carrying a very full shopping basket. Cecily went down to meet her, held out her hand for the basket and said, *'Puis-je vous aider, madame?'* The old woman looked at her suspiciously for a moment, then grunted and handed the bag over. *'Dans quel apartement est-ce que vous habitez?'*

'Numéro cent sept.' She set off along the corridor. *'Là bas.'* She spoke very fast, and rather gutturally: Cassia thanked God once again for Cecily and followed meekly.

Numero 107 was quite a long way down the corridor from 110; when they got there, Cecily set down the basket while she fumbled for her key, and then said, *'Madame, est-ce que vous connaissez la femme qui habitait dans cet apartement-là? Numero cent dix? Une femme Anglaise?'*

'Non,' said the old woman very firmly indeed. *'Non, je ne l'ai jamais connu.'* She turned away from them, walked into her apartment; Cecily put a small, elegant foot against the peeling door.

'Vous étes sûr? Lady Beatty? Ou peut-être vous la connaissez comme Madame Gresham?'

'Non, mademoiselle. Pas du tout. Non.' She

slammed her door on them with a final glare.

'Oh dear,' said Cecily. 'Sorry, Cassia.'

'She must have known her,' said Cassia. 'Cecily, tell her who we are. Tell her Leonora has died, that we're trying to find out who looked after her when she was here, so that we can thank them. Or even—' inspiration struck her—'reward them. Here, write that old woman a note, push it under her door. Saying what I told you to. I bet it'll work.'

It did work; five minutes later they were sitting in the old woman's apartment, being poured large cups of very bitter black coffee from a tin jug.

*   *   *

The apartment was very basic: one fairly large room and a kitchen and bathroom leading off it. It was dark, the only small windows looking out from the living room on to another huge block directly behind it: and it was cold. Cassia tried to imagine Leonora living there, Leonora with her extravagant tastes, her love of luxury, her beautiful clothes, tried to imagine what desperation must have brought her there—and failed.

It was a strangely frustrating experience, sitting there, asking Cecily to ask questions, important questions, not sure if she had asked exactly the right one, not sure if she had interpreted its answer correctly. But a story did emerge; Leonora had moved into the apartment just after Christmas, and had stayed only a few weeks. So that part of the story at least was true. She had been unwell, a doctor came two or three times, then no more.

A young man who had lived next door had befriended her, done some shopping for her, the old woman herself had taken soup in from time to time. She had been visited by an English lady, Miss Monkton, Cassia supposed, then shortly after that a friend had come and taken her away and they had not seen her since, although she had written to thank them both, herself and the young man.

'Ask her—' Cassia felt sick suddenly, sick and shaky—'ask her if it was a man or woman. The friend.'

'It was a woman. A young woman. A French woman, she thought, anyway, she spoke perfect French.'

Relief, absurdly, flooded Cassia, blessed warm relief.

The young woman had been tall, blonde, very slim, it seemed. Nice legs; well dressed. Obviously well off. The old woman cackled with laughter, made a cupping gesture with both hands. Cecily smiled.

'She had a rather large bosom, apparently.'

'But she doesn't know her name?'

'No.'

'Cecily, ask her why she didn't want to talk to us.'

The old woman's face became guarded, then she spoke at some length, in staccato sentences.

'Apparently, Leonora was frightened of people finding she was here. She owed money, madame thinks. In the end, she couldn't even pay the doctor, that's why she stopped calling him.'

'What was the matter with her? Does she know?'

Another long exchange. There were gestures, a hand on the abdomen, the breast. 'She says she thought women's troubles. Quite bad. And something else as well, perhaps, but she wasn't

621

sure.'

'Oh, God. Poor Leonora. Does she know the doctor's name?'

The doctor's name was Bertillon, his surgery in the rue Chanez.

'And this young woman, she came for Leonora when?' Before Easter: that was the most accurate date they could get.

She stood up. 'Cecily, ask her what she would most like from us in the way of thanks for what she did for Leonora—food, wine, money . . .'

The old woman looked disdainful. 'She doesn't want anything. She said Leonora was her friend, that it was a pleasure.' The old woman was talking again, her dark eyes gleaming; Cecily listened, then laughed. 'She says perhaps a bottle of Benedictine would be very welcome.'

Dr Bertillon was a charming, rather handsome young man with dark eyes and dark curly hair; he even spoke rather halting English. He was not, however, able to be of very much help to them, since the Dr Bertillon who had treated Leonora was his father, at that time away on a visit to relatives in Tours.

'Thank you, Dr Bertillon,' Cassia said. 'Perhaps I could telephone your father when he gets back next week?'

'But of course, madame. I am sure he will be pleased to speak to you.'

*   *   *

The apartment in Passy was, as everyone had told her, beautiful. In fact, everything was exactly as everyone had told her, she thought, and wondered why that irritated her. It was on the top floor of a most lovely eighteenth-century house, set high above the Trocadero Gardens, its entrance through a *Porte cocherie*, and with an exquisite central courtyard that even in the cold December light had a golden summery quality. The porter's wife took them up to the apartment adjacent to the one Leonora had lived in—hers, it seemed, was occupied—so that they could admire the view, both over the courtyard at the back and out on to the Luxembourg Gardens at the front.

The porter's wife said something to Cecily in French. 'Apparently, Leonora used to like to walk in the Trocadero Gardens when she first came here. Then later, she couldn't get down, was confined to the balcony, she spent all that spring and summer until she died lying out there.'

'Who visited her? Does madame know?'

More rapid French: then, 'Several gentlemen and a very nice, kind elderly English lady.'

'And who brought her here? Ask her that.'

Cecily asked the woman. 'A French woman, quite young. You see, it all seems to be true. Cassia, let's go and have lunch, I'm starving.'

'Yes, of course,' said Cassia, 'but I want to know if there's anyone still living here who knew Leonora? Who I might talk to?'

There was: a lady who had lived on the floor below, a Madame Christophe. They had become quite good friends. She was out for the day, would be back that evening. 'And she speaks English. Cassia, please can we get some food? I'll faint soon.'

After lunch, Cassia told Cecily to go back to the hotel to rest, and when she had seen her into a taxi, turned back up the boulevard Montparnasse. She had another reason for coming to the area.

*　　　*　　　*

The Montparnasse Cemetery was where Leonora was buried; walking along gravelled paths, half amused half impressed by the elaborate tombs and effigies, she wondered why it had been chosen for Leonora. There was a cemetery in Passy: why bring her here? She recognised several famous names, Baudelaire, Maupassant, Saint-Saëns, smiled at a sculpture of a couple in bed on one, a copy of Rodin's *Kiss* on another.

She found Leonora's grave finally, marked with a simple white marble cross, carved only with her name, and the dates of her birth and death: June 1886–May 1935.

There were some dead flowers lying beneath the cross; she wondered who could have put them there, wished she could thank them, placed the bunch of small white roses she had purchased on her way next to them.

It was very cold; she pulled her coat up round her neck, and stood there, thinking of Leonora lying there beneath the hard frosty earth, in the cold she had hated so much, trying to recall her as she had known her first, before the shadows had gathered about her, lovely, charming, amusing, adored by her husband, loved by her friends . . .

Madame Christophe offered Cassia pastries and coffee, more than happy to talk about Leonora. She was pretty, plump, well dressed, wearing a lot of jewellery; she had been widowed very soon after she had moved to the apartment, which was one of the things that had drawn her to Leonora; they had both been lonely, both living in their pasts.

'She was so brave, so very brave. She was in much pain and yet she never complained. Except she hated to see people from her past; she said they would find her ugly.'

'I wish I had seen her, wish I'd known how ill she was. She must have thought so badly of me.'

'Oh no, madame.' Her face was shocked. 'She loved you. She would talk about you for hours, you and your *maman*, the fun she had with you, when you were a debutante, and she was so proud of you, of your success as a doctor. She thought you were wonderful.' She smiled. 'She and her cousin, Monsieur Moreton. He admired you greatly too. I think Lady Beatty would have wished that you and he had married. He was here a great deal during those last few weeks.'

'Really?'

'*Mais oui!* He was so good to her, so gentle, so *tendre*. And when she was dying, he sat by her bed for thirty-six hours, never left her for more than a few moments until she was *sauve*. She was very afraid of dying, of being put in the cold. She hated the Passy cemetery being so near, it's just down there, you know, behind the gardens. She used to say, "Soon I shall be down there unable to escape", and in the end she made Monsieur Moreton promise that she would be taken somewhere else, that this would be a place where she was only alive, not lying still and cold.'

So that was why she was at Montparnasse, thought Cassia. Madame Christophe wiped her eyes, smiled weakly. 'He was so very good to her. When she was still well enough to go out, she liked

625

to go down the steps into the gardens, he would take her, walking with her so patiently, and towards the end he would carry her back up the stairs in his arms. I'm sorry, this upsets you.'

'No,' said Cassia, 'don't be sorry, I like to hear these things.' She thought of Harry, so arrogant, so impatient, walking slowly through the gardens, carrying the sick Leonora up the stairs, sitting with her through the long hours as the death she feared so much became inescapable, giving her courage, and realised what a capacity he had indeed for love, thought how strange that was when he had known so little, what an extraordinary and complex person he was.

'Madame Christophe, did you meet a young woman, a Frenchwoman? Tall, blonde? It was she who brought her here in the first place.'

'No, I never met such a person, but in the early days there were quite a few visitors. I did not know Lady Beatty so well then.'

'What about her brother, Mr Harrington, did you meet him?'

'Yes, I did. A charming man. He was not here as much as Monsieur Moreton, but still he made many visits.'

'And did you meet Mr Gresham?'

A long, agonising silence, then: 'Ah, yes,' she said at last. 'A big man, yes? Very big, very—what do you say, jolly?'

'Yes, I suppose so. So you did meet him?'

'I did, but only once. And then only in the *vestibule*, with another gentleman, an Englishman, a business compatriot, as I understood it.'

'Oh, I see,' said Cassia. She wondered who that might have been: a lawyer probably. Well, it wasn't important. 'I'm surprised you didn't see more of him, I thought he was here quite a lot.'

'Perhaps he was here more than I thought, madame. Time is *compliqué*, is it not, our memory plays tricks with it. He was not so friendly toward me as the other two gentlemen. Perfectly pleasant, *bien sûr*, but . . .' She shrugged.

'Yes, I see. But he wasn't with Leonora when she died?'

'No, madame, no one was with her then, except her doctors and Monsieur Moreton. I went in, to bid her farewell, and so I know that.'

'And did she speak well of Mr Gresham?'

'Oh, yes, madame. She had nothing but good to say of him. That he had always cared for her, left her well provided for. I think she was very sad that they had decided to part, *mais c'est la vie, n'est-ce pas?*'

'Yes,' said Cassia absently. *'C'est la vie.'*

* * *

She took a taxi back to the Ritz; she felt tired and curiously discouraged. She had learnt nothing that day to indicate that things were not as she had been told: perhaps it was time to bury her anxieties, let them rest . . .

* * *

'I'd like to get the divorce proceedings set in motion as soon as possible,' said Harry. 'I presume that will be acceptable to you.' He spoke casually, as if he were discussing taking her out to tea, and smiled at her almost benignly.

Edwina smiled back, slightly uncertainly. His mood had changed again so totally that it was unnerving. All his rage, his animosity towards her, seemed to have gone; he was relaxed, cheerful, albeit distant. Maybe he had someone else: maybe the whole thing, all the fuss about having children, his rage at her going around with Francis Stevenson-Cook, and even her indiscretion at Janine Sobel's, had been an elaborate cover-up. The thought gave her a stab of alarm. It was one thing to walk away from a marriage because it no longer held any interest for her, quite another to appear foolish: the deceived, unwitting wife.

'I'm perfectly happy to provide grounds,' he said, 'of course, so I'll speak to Geoffrey Partington, shall I? Get things moving?'

'Well . . .'

'Naturally, I wouldn't argue about money. I have no desire to see any wife of mine in straitened circumstances. I'd want you to have a nice little house and an allowance which I don't think you could find ungenerous.'

'The thing is,' she said, 'I haven't actually quite made my mind up yet. I mean about your ultimatum. About giving up my job and so on.'

She had, but she wasn't going to hand it to him on a plate. Making grandiose gestures and statements was one thing; putting them into practice, walking out of a marriage that had, however she looked at it, considerable advantages, in terms of wealth and status, suddenly seemed very much another. At worst, she intended to walk out with a great deal more than she had walked in. And if there was someone else in his life, which suddenly seemed rather likely, it might be easier to

628

ensure a really generous settlement—misbehaving at a party hardly constituted grounds for divorce. The case would go in her favour and if he was anxious to become free as soon as possible, she could make a great deal of capital from that. Capital being the operative word, she thought.

'Well,' he said, his eyes blank, 'do make your mind up soon, Edwina. I don't enjoy the present situation very much at all. As I explained to you.'

'Well, that's unfortunate for you, Harry,' said Edwina, 'but I must ask you to endure it a little longer, I'm afraid. I'm sure you wouldn't want me to end our marriage lightly.'

*　　　*　　　*

'And how was Paris?' said Justin Everard. 'I've missed you a lot.' He had suddenly turned up on her doorstep the day after her return, said he had been working at a studio in Chelsea and could she give a poor artisan a cup of tea?

'It was wonderful, we had the best fun and I've brought you something I think you'll like.' It was an antique camera she had found in one of the small streets off the rue de Rivoli, wooden with brass fittings, absurdly expensive, very beautiful.

Justin was overcome by it, kept turning over and over, stroking it as if it were some kind of beloved animal. 'I adore it. How lovely, how generous you are.'

'Just wanted to say thank you,' she said simply, 'for everything.'

'You do that by simply being. Now, you have missed a lot of wonderful gossip. Have you seen the *News Chronicle*?'

No,' said Cecily, 'only *The Times*, which I could hardly follow, and the *Telegraph*, which was very firm on the matter. Said the King must put duty first and give Mrs Simpson up.'

'Quite right. Terrible woman. Well, the *Chronicle* has this extraordinary story that he should be allowed to marry her but she shouldn't be queen. Did you ever hear such nonsense?'

'Oh, I don't know,' said Cecily, 'I do feel sorry for him. He obviously loves her.'

'Darling Cecily, you're such a romantic. Which is why I adore you so much. I agree he loves her, but he can't have it all ways. Now look, I came to see you for two reasons: one, because I missed you, and two, to ask you to have dinner with me.'

'What, tonight?' said Cecily.

'Don't sound so frightened. Tonight or tomorrow night or the next night. Whenever it suits you. I am at your disposal. I just want you to come.'

'Well, I don't know,' said Cecily. She felt genuinely alarmed by his invitation. Being visited by him at the nursing home, chatting and laughing with him at the fashion show—that was all right, she could cope with that. But dinner: dinner was quite different, dinner was a statement, it had a sexual content, it was . . .

'All right,' he said, laughing, oddly able to read her thoughts, 'suppose it was lunch. Would that frighten you less?'

A rush of affection, of gratitude to him, flooded Cecily. His ability to understand her fears, to read her thoughts, and, moreover, to sympathise with them, still amazed her. And Justin was, despite his rather absurd manner—which now Edwina had explained it to her, she quite enjoyed—formidably

630

straightforward. After twelve years of tension and secrets, his company was, to Cecily, like walking out into the sunshine. And then he was such fun, so full of gossip and jokes, and he seemed to find everything she said amusing or interesting or both. That in itself was a novelty.

And on top of all that, she had to admit, he was rather good-looking, in a slightly effete way, with his heavy brown hair and soulful dark eyes. She could not imagine what he could possibly find attractive about her. Maybe she was just a novelty. Maybe she was just charity work. Maybe once he was satisfied she really was better, he would disappear from her life. Anyway, in the meantime, she should just enjoy it; it was all very morale-boosting.

'No,' she said, 'no, not lunch, I'd like to have dinner with you very much. Thank you.'

'Splendid. Tomorrow, then? Friday is always a nice night. Somewhere quiet, I thought, I'll find somewhere. Bye, darling.'

She couldn't simply be charity work, Cecily thought, he didn't have to buy her dinner, tell her he adored her, call her darling. He could just have gone on coming to call. She smiled rather foolishly in the mirror at herself and started fretting over what she should wear.

*   *   *

'I suppose,' said Harry, running his finger idly down the length of Cassia's abdomen, lingering tenderly in her pubic hair, 'I suppose we should think about telling people soon. Otherwise the rumours will begin.'

631

He had sent her a telegram to the Ritz: IMPERATIVE YOU RETURN TO WALTON STREET EARLIEST STOP, it said. URGENT BUSINESS NEEDS YOUR ATTENTION STOP. CONFIRM TIME OF ARRIVAL FRIDAY. MORETON.

She had cabled back, saying, MEETING IMPOSSIBLE, and another had come within the hour saying, REPEAT, WALTON STREET MEETING IMPERATIVE STOP. ALTERNATIVE VENUE MONKS RIDGE STOP. PERHAPS WITH DR FALLON STOP. MORETON.

She had given in then, as of course he had known she would, had cabled back again saying, WALTON STREET MIDDAY STOP. VERY ANGRY ABOUT TERMS STOP.

She and Cecily had arrived to a London alive with excitement about the King and Mrs Simpson; now that the silence of the press had finally broken, nobody talked of anything else. She remarked on this to Harry who threw up his hands in mock horror.

'None of that, please. I have severe *ennui* on the subject.' He was waiting for her, sitting naked in bed, a bottle of champagne on ice beside him and a basket of roses in the fireplace so huge it dwarfed the room.

'Hurry up,' he had said, as she stood there, half laughing half angry with him still at the danger of his peremptory telegrams. 'I want you in here beside me, with absolutely no clothes on, in less than thirty seconds. We've wasted quite enough of our lives already.' This was a constant cry of his.

'Harry, of course we can't tell people,' she said

632

now, sitting up in her alarm. 'Tell them what, anyway?'

'That I love you. That you love me. That we're going to—what are we going to do, Cassia? Get married? Live in splendid sin?'

'Neither,' she said, 'not for a long time, anyway.'

'Why in the name of heaven not?'

She took his hand in hers, kissed it, said, 'Harry, I do love you. I love you more than I ever thought possible, but we can't do anything about it yet. I have the children to worry about.'

'The children! I thought you and Edward had agreed to part. I intend to institute divorce proceedings immediately, why can't you?'

'Have you really?' she said, appalled at the speed with which he was acting.

'Yes, of course. I can't see the slightest point in waiting. Although Edwina is behaving with sudden and rather suspicious loyalty. No doubt with her lovely eyes on my bank account. But I've agreed to provide grounds, as a gentleman should.'

'Naming me?'

'Of course not you. With some floozy in a Brighton hotel. Like poor Mrs Simpson. I see she has fled the country, by the way.'

'I thought you were bored with the subject. Well, yes, Edward and I have agreed to part. But we haven't actually even agreed to divorce. We have to let the children get used to the idea, they'll hate any notion of him being replaced, they adore him.'

'They'll adore me,' he said carelessly. 'Children always do.'

'Harry, you are unbelievably arrogant. These are another man's children. They'll be jealous, wary, resentful. It'll be very hard for them. Do you know what Bertie said to me the day I rescued him from that terrible school? He said he'd rather go back there even than Edward and I got divorced, that there was a boy in his dorm whose parents were divorced and he cried every night.'

'Poor little sod.'

'Yes, well, there you are. You've got to understand that.'

'Oh yes, I do,' he said, suddenly agreeable. 'I'm prepared for all sorts of difficulties, of course. Just the same, they do like me already. That has to be a help.'

'They like you now. They won't when they know. Honestly.'

'Well, all right. We'll begin our marriage with three difficult, hostile children. A small price to pay, to my mind. Under the circumstances. Any more objections?'

'Well, yes,' she said slowly, 'there might be. I can't tell you yet. It's a bit complex. It might not come to anything.'

'But if it does, it would affect you and me?'

'No. It would affect me.'

'Well, then, it would affect me too. Everything to do with you affects me Cassia, it always has. Surely you realise that. You don't seem to understand the nature of love very well.' He looked at her and smiled, then said, 'What was it exactly you were doing in Paris?'

'I told you, shopping, Christmas shopping mostly. Cecily asked me to go with her and I thought it was the least I could do. I have something for you by the way, it's a—'

'Cassia,' he said, 'I hope that's all you were doing.'

CHAPTER THIRTY-FIVE

I can't actually be doing this, thought Cassia; I can't really be lying here on the floor, the floor of an office, without any clothes on, it just isn't possible—and then she lost sight entirely of what might or might not be possible as Harry launched an assault on her senses that wiped out any kind of thought, any kind of reason, any notion of where she was, where she should have been, indeed.

It was his office they were in, and it was after midnight; she had allowed herself to be persuaded by him to go out to dinner despite her reservations, her fear that they would be seen—the talk would start, the rumours begin to spread—and she had allowed it because she wanted it so much.

'But not here, Harry, because I've offered Eleanor Studely a bed for the night, and somewhere very quiet, very discreet, not the West End, for heaven's sake.'

'I'm not very good at discretion,' he had said, 'but I'll do my best.'

He had phoned her back in half an hour. 'You are to come here, to the office,' he said, 'at eight o'clock. I have a very nice restaurant in mind. It's all right, it's totally discreet, you're not to worry about it.'

When she arrived, nervous, he opened the door to her himself; there was no porter on duty.

'I have given him the night off,' Harry said, taking her hand. 'Poor fellow, he was looking very tired. It is almost Christmas, after all. Come along upstairs.'

'Harry!' she said, beginning to suspect. 'Harry, whatever have you—'

'Be quiet,' he said, 'wait and see.'

She followed him up to the first floor, along the corridor, into his office; and then laughed aloud, for there, laid out on the floor, complete with cloth and wicker hamper and some bottles of wine, was a picnic.

'I did it all myself,' he said proudly. 'I phoned Fortnum's, and ordered all this. And here—' he went to a cupboard, opened it, brought out an ice bucket and some champagne—'can't have a picnic without champagne, and then to follow we have some very delicious-looking pastries. Really, Cassia, do stop shaking your head, you should be congratulating me on my originality and domestic skills. Not to mention my sense of occasion. Now take your coat off, and your shoes, and sit down on the rug. That's right. In a little while, you are to take your dress off as well, and then your stockings and so on. I have it all planned, you see. I see a sort of intramural *Déjeuner sur l'herbe*. Champagne?'

She sat down laughing on the rug, took the glass he handed her.

'You look very beautiful,' he said, his face suddenly serious. 'I do like it, that you are so beautiful.'

'Harry, I'm not beautiful. I'm quite ordinary really.'

'Oh no;' he said, sitting down beside her, leaning across to kiss her, 'there is nothing ordinary about you, Cassia. Nothing at all . . .'

*   *   *

636

It was two o'clock when they left the building; she was exhausted, sated with pleasure. She had looked down at her body, as she finally dressed, again, looked at its neat lines, its slender self-containedness, and marvelled that it could break into such tumultuous disorder, so many splintered fragments of piercing near-pain, could take leave of itself and its normal duties to behave with such absolute unpredictability, that all its parts could merge, fuse, become one, an absolute concentration of delight: and then reassemble, become itself again, something that could stand and walk and have clothes hung upon it, something over which she had control.

She looked up at him as he closed the door on to the street and smiled; he looked back at her, in a moment of absolute intent, and then bent and kissed her, gently, lightly, put his arm round her shoulder, and she turned her head, kissed his hand as it lay there: and thus they walked along the street to where she had parked her car.

*   *   *

Justin Everard, coming back from a long and exhausting session in his darkroom, saw them and realised he was not actually very surprised.

*   *   *

'Edward, may I talk to you? After surgery this evening, perhaps?'

He looked up at Cassia, clearly surprised. 'Yes, all right,' he said, 'but I may be quite late, and I may have to go out if there are any calls—Maureen has gone for an interview.'

He looked tired, she thought, and very strained; it was hardly surprising, of course, but he had seemed rather more cheerful lately.

'You ought to have a break,' she said, 'before you start your new life. It will be very hard to cope with if you're worn out before you start.'

'Yes,' he said with a sigh, 'yes, that's what Janet said.'

'Janet!' She would not have been more surprised if he had said he had discussed his situation with Sylvia Fox-Ashley.

'Yes,' he said shortly, avoiding her eyes, 'She obviously knew about it, and with people coming to see me about the practice—well, she was very understanding about it. And interested.'

'Edward, I thought you couldn't stand Janet.'

'You misunderstood me,' he said, 'as always. I didn't like the idea of having a nanny for the children. I thought you should have looked after them yourself. I always found Janet perfectly pleasant and, indeed, extremely good with them. And I have to say that in your frequent absences she does run things here extremely well.'

'Oh,' said Cassia. She felt rather put out suddenly. 'Well, I'm delighted, Edward. Anyway, do think about taking a break. If you can.'

'Yes, well,' he said, 'it all depends on when I can get someone. I haven't seen anyone I liked sufficiently yet.'

She went and asked Peggy to make shepherd's pie for supper: Edward's favourite. She wanted him to be in the best possible mood for their discussion.

*　　　*　　　*

638

Later that afternoon Harry phoned her. 'I found your gold neck-chain on the floor of my office. I can't imagine how it came to be there.'

'No,' she said, and the room was suddenly brilliant with memory of pleasure, 'no, I can't either.'

'I expect you'd like it back. I have to go to Paris for a few days. I'll leave it with Miss Murray, you can pick it up if you're passing.'

'Thank you. Thank you very much. Have a good trip. I mean, *bon voyage.*'

Saying that reminded her of Dr Bertillon. He would be back the next day, she would phone him. Or perhaps she wouldn't. There really didn't seem very much point.

*   *   *

Fleet Street was in turmoil that afternoon; it had received a statement issued by Mrs Simpson from Cannes, in which she stated that she would be willing, 'if such action would solve the problem, to withdraw from a situation that has been rendered both unhappy and untenable'. The ambiguity of this statement, implying as it did that this was a decision removed from the personal sphere and into the constitutional, fuelled rumours of the 'King's camp' led by Winston Churchill, and the Beaverbrook-Rothermere press, of a government hostile to the King for reasons more sinister than that of his amour, of something approaching a coup from within the royal circle.

Mrs Simpson, banking on the King's popularity, had suggested the King take the country into his confidence, with a broadcast that was the equivalent of one of President Roosevelt's 'fireside chats', and that the people should then decide what might be done; that Baldwin had crushed this merely fuelled the talk of coups and camps.

Crowds began to gather outside Buckingham Palace, Downing Street and St James's Palace: but at Fort Belvedere, the King had summoned his brother, the Duke of York, to tell him of his decision.

*   *   *

After supper, at which Edward expressed pleasure both to Peggy and to Janet, who had contributed an excellent apple pie, they went into the sitting room. Cassia felt absurdly nervous. 'Coffee, Edward?'

'No, thank you,' he said, 'you know I don't drink coffee after supper these days. I have trouble enough sleeping as it is.'

'Do you, Edward?' she said. 'I'm sorry.'

'Well,' he said, 'there's a great deal to worry about. It isn't going to be easy, what I'm going to do.' The words 'without you' hung in the air. She tried to ignore them.

'No,' she said, 'but I know you're going to love it, Edward. And do terribly well.' It sounded patronising; she hated herself.

'And obviously I've been worrying about the children,' he said, 'as I expect you have. And then there's the practice.'

Cassia took a deep breath. 'Edward, that's what I wanted to talk to you about.'

*   *   *

'These are lovely, Justin,' said Cecily, smiling at him. 'Thank you. The one of Fanny is specially nice.'

'She's very photogenic. Like you.'

'I'm not photogenic, Justin, don't be silly.'

'Darling Cecily, you are immensely photogenic. The camera likes you, as they say. Look at you here, at the fashion show. Lovely.'

She had to admit she did look much nicer than she would have expected. She was talking to Edward, laughing; she looked carefree, young again, her eyes alive. Edward, by contrast, looked strained, awkward.

'Poor Edward. He does hate social gatherings.'

'I'm not surprised,' said Justin, 'he's very dull.'

'Justin, that's horrid. He's not dull; he's just quiet. Quiet and shy.'

'Well, we're all shy,' said Justin. 'I'm shy.'

'You!' said Cecily. 'Justin, that is the most ridiculous thing I ever heard. You're so self-confident, you love being the centre of attention . . .'

'Well, that's where you're wrong,' he said. 'I do get dreadfully nervous, quite often. But I've learnt to hide it. That's why I'm so noisy, it's camouflage. Don't look like that, it's true. If I let people see, I'd be done for. That's why I love you, my darling,' he added seriously, 'you make me feel safe, I can forget about myself. I don't have to put on my act with you.'

'Oh,' she said. She felt rather confused by all this, deeply touched and not quite sure if she believed it at the same time.

'No, shy is one thing,' said Justin firmly, 'not making an effort quite another. Edward Fallon doesn't make any effort at all. He had that pretty girl with him, the nanny, and he had those two dear little boys with him who obviously adored him. It wasn't as if he was there all alone. I'm sorry, Cecily, I really don't think very much of him. Maybe I'm just jealous. I can see you're very fond of him.'

'Don't be silly. I mean I am fond of him, but—well, not in that way.'

'What way? In the way you're fond of me, you mean? And how would you define that exactly? Oh, this is lovely fun.'

'Oh, Justin, don't tease me.'

'I'm not teasing you, I really want to know. I'm very very fond of you. As you must very well know. Is it absolutely one sided? Because if it is, I might go out and throw myself in the river. Oh, sorry, my darling, not tactful.'

'It's all right,' said Cecily, laughing. Nothing could have made her realise more clearly how much she had recovered from Benedict's death than that moment. She leant forward and gave Justin a kiss on the cheek. 'I'm very fond of you, of course I am, but you are wrong about Edward. I think it is especially hard for him. Cassia is so lovely and so self-confident these days, and—'

'And a little bit naughty, from what I've observed,' said Justin, 'and who could blame her?'

'What? Justin, what sort of naughty?'

He looked at her and smiled, a wicked, conspiratorial grin.

'Well, let's just say that if you'd been coming down South Audley Street the other night, or rather at about two o'clock in the morning, you'd have seen her and Harry Moreton. Coming out of a building. Kissing, cuddling, obviously having just

642

had a *very* nice time!'

'Cassia! And Harry! Good heavens! Are you quite quite sure?'

'Quite *quite* sure.'

'Good heavens,' said Cecily again. Her mind was whirling. Did Edwina know? She was sure she didn't. And Edward, poor, poor Edward, surely he couldn't.

'I'm sorry, Justin,' she said, 'this really has been rather a shock.'

'Darling, you'd better go and lie down,' he said, his face concerned. 'I'm beastly and thoughtless. I just assumed you wouldn't mind very much, I thought it would amuse you. Here, come along, I'll take you to your room. Where is it?'

Cecily gave him her hand, allowed him to take her upstairs, to settle her on her bed. He bent over, kissed her forehead tenderly. 'Shall I ask your maid to come up?'

'Yes, please.' She felt very foolish, very unsophisticated, reacting in this way; she supposed perhaps she was not as emotionally stable as she had thought. It was just that—well, Cassia! Cassia, whom they had all admired so much, looked up to for her independent views, admired for her cleverness—and considered so extremely virtuous. And now, she thought, what should she do: should she tell Edward and Edwina or not? Surely not, that would be terrible.

Who could she talk to about it? she wondered. Maybe it was a mistake, maybe they had just been fooling about. Justin didn't know either of them very well. Who would know, whom could she ask? And then she thought: Rupert. Rupert would know.

643

She waved rather feebly at Justin, who was standing at the door blowing her kisses, and reached for the telephone.

*   *   *

Maureen Johnson stood waiting slightly impatiently for Dr Fallon to finish his surgery; she needed to get away, she had a second interview for a junior partnership in a practice in Euston that afternoon, and was running late already. In the early days she had admired his patience, the long time he spent with everyone; now it had begun to irritate her. He had begun to irritate her altogether with his tendency to self-justification, to over-explanation; it was as well events were moving them apart.

'Ah, Maureen!' He came out and smiled at her. 'Time for a coffee? I can ask Peggy—'

'No, really, Dr Fallon, I have to get a train to London in half an hour, the taxi will be coming very shortly—'

'Of course. Do forgive me. Well, I'll be brief. I just wanted to discuss something with you.'

'Yes, Dr Fallon?'

'My wife has suggested—proposed to me rather, that she should take over this practice. When I take up my new post at St Mark's, Clapham. I wondered what your reaction to that would be.'

'Well . . .' Maureen hesitated. She disliked Cassia intensely; she had found her arrogant, condescending, self-interested from the first day she had met her, and nothing that had happened since had changed her mind.

'You're not sure?' he said, watching her

644

carefully. 'That's interesting, neither am I. Could you perhaps give me your reasons?'

'Well . . .'

'Let me give you mine. It's all about confidence, is it not, medicine? I feel the patients here trust me—and you, they know us as doctors, as respected, successful doctors. If they bring us a problem, they think we can solve it. They only know Mrs Fallon as my wife. The fact that she is herself a qualified doctor—'

'Yes, but that's all,' said Maureen quietly.

'I'm sorry?'

'She is qualified. She has passed her finals. Very well, I know. But she has no experience, apart from her London clinics. Of course they must have been very challenging, but—'

'Very limited in their range. Indeed. So you're saying she would need a period as an assistant, a junior partner at the very least, are you?'

'Well, yes, ideally. I would have thought it would be very difficult for her simply to begin to practise here, without any practical experience. But that would obviously be very hard to arrange—impossible, really, while she was here.'

'Yes, it would. Although she would be working alongside me for a couple of months. And then she is very familiar with the village, with the patients, with their histories. She has known most of the children here all their lives. And of course they know her, very well.'

'They do,' said Maureen, 'but, as you said, not as a doctor. And that is how they would need to see her. If they were to have any confidence in her at all. I don't see how they could have that confidence. Oh, dear, I do feel rather disloyal,

645

talking like this.'

He looked at her and smiled rather wearily. 'I'm sorry. I shouldn't have asked you, it's very difficult for you. But I think simply talking to you has helped me to make up my own mind. Thank you. You must go and get your train. In fact, is that your taxi now?'

'I think so,' said Maureen, 'yes.'

'Good luck this afternoon, then.'

'Thank you.'

If she hadn't been in such a hurry, she would have seen Bertie, home from school with a cold, who had been in the hall for some time, ostensibly doing up his shoelaces, but actually listening very attentively to the conversation through the just open study door.

*   *   *

'Ah, Mrs Fallon, good afternoon.' Margot Murray smiled at her graciously. 'Mr Moreton did say you were coming in.'

'Yes, I somehow managed to lose my necklace here, so stupid of me . . .' Her voice tailed away.

She felt confused, embarrassed, sure somehow that Miss Murray must know perfectly well what had been going on between her and Harry.

'Indeed, yes, it is here, in my desk, in an envelope. Here we are, I think you will find it in order, do check it, won't you?'

'I'm sure that's not necessary,' Cassia said hastily. 'Thank you so much, Miss Murray.'

'Please think nothing of it. Now I have something else for you, a note from Mr Moreton, if you could just bear with me while I get it from the file—oh, excuse me, Mrs Fallon, I'm so sorry.'

The phone had rung; Cassia smiled at her, picked up a copy of *The Times* which was lying on the low table, to show she was not troubled by the delay, started to read the personal column, as if she found it deeply fascinating.

She became aware that Miss Murray was speaking perfect French, absolutely perfect, perfect French . . . Cecily, Leonora, their trip to Paris . . . the old woman in the Auteuil describing the woman who had come for Leonora, taken her away . . . realising that Miss Murray was slim, tall, blonde, had good legs, did have a rather large bosom, actually . . . remembering the old woman gesturing with her hands, to describe such a thing . . .

'Mrs Fallon, are you all right? You look a little pale.'

Cassia smiled carefully. 'Oh, yes, yes, thank you. Just a bit—well, faint.'

'Do sit down,' said Miss Murray graciously. 'I will fetch you a glass of water. It is rather hot in here.'

She came back with the water, made Cassia drink it slowly, watching her rather severely. She would have made a wonderful matron, Cassia thought.

'Thank you, Miss Murray. I must go now. I'm working at St Christopher's Hospital at two, I run a clinic there, you know.' God, why was she telling Miss Murray all this? She must think she was completely demented.

'Oh, well, if you are sure you are well enough. I admire your attitude: punctuality, timing, is so important, I feel.'

Another memory, another French voice, time is

647

compliqué, our memory plays tricks with it . . . time, timing, this whole thing was about time, what happened when . . .

Margot Murray was speaking again, handing her something. 'Here is the letter from Mr Moreton, Mrs Fallon.'

'Thank you.'

Standing in the lift, she tore open the letter; it was a large sheet of paper, and simply said, 'I love you,' in Harry's sprawling writing. She found it surprisingly difficult to read, for some reason, and then realised as she got outside that she was crying.

*   *   *

Rupert was eating his lunch when Cecily phoned. She sounded very upset.

'Rupert, can I talk to you?'

'My darling, of course you can. Now? On the telephone? Tell you what, I have to be at the theatre in half an hour; do you want to come and talk to me there, in my dressing room, while I get ready? It's a very automatic process, you mustn't think I won't be concentrating on you.'

'If that would really be all right. Yes, thank you. I'll meet you there.'

Now, what could that be about? thought Rupert. Perhaps Fanny wanted to go on the stage: sweet little thing, she was. Definitely not an idea to be encouraged.

*   *   *

Fortunately, he was looking into the mirror when Cecily finally managed to ask him about Cassia and

Harry. Even so, he knew, his eyes flicked to meet hers, knew she had seen that; then he smiled at her quickly and easily.

'Darling, what a wonderful rumour. I wish I could help tell you it's nonsense, but I can't. I would have to do some detective work of my own.'

'I'd have thought,' said Cecily just a little coldly—she knows I know, he thought, she can tell—'I'd have thought you could just have asked her. I thought you and she told each other everything. And you suffered enough from rumours yourself, didn't you, a few weeks ago? I'd have thought you'd be rather sympathetic about getting such things scotched. If it's not true. It is true, isn't it?' she said suddenly. 'I can see it is, and I can see you knew. I'm surprised at you; Rupert, I really am.'

'Cecily, what was I supposed to do about it?' he said, realising there was no point in pretending. 'Tell Edwina, tell Edward? Of course not. That is for them to do, not me, it's their affair—literally. I can only be here if Cassia needs me.'

'Needs you to lie for her, you mean.'

'No, I don't mean that. Cassia would never ask that, anyway. She is very direct.'

'Oh, very,' she said.

'Cecily,' he said gently, 'don't be too hard on her. She—well, she's been very unhappy. For a very long time.'

'Oh, really?' said Cecily. 'Well, so was I. For a very, very long time. Most of the time I was married, actually. I didn't start having affairs with other people's husbands, though, to make myself feel better.'

Rupert sighed. 'Of course you didn't,' he said,

'but we all manage differently.'

'Yes, well, making other people unhappy doesn't seem a very good way of managing to me. I think it's awful, dreadful of her, poor gentle Edward, never hurt a fly . . . I think it's awful of you to defend her, I don't think she deserves defending. I'm going home. Oh, don't worry, Rupert, I won't tell anyone. But I'm going to find it very hard to be nice to Cassia in future. And Harry, for that matter.' She walked out of the dressing room, slamming the door after her.

Rupert sat staring at it. 'Oh dear,' he said aloud, 'oh very very dear.'

*   *   *

Cassia sat in the small drawing room at Walton Street, trying not to scream while the operator asked her to hold the line while she connected her to her Paris number.

A voice in French informed her she was speaking to Dr Bertillon's surgery; she asked if she might speak to him.

'Le Dr George Bertillon? Ou le Dr Pierre?'

'Le—le Pere?' said Cassia hopefully.

'Dr Pierre. Un moment, madame.'

Another wait: more clicks, then, *'Ici Pierre Bertillon. Bonjour.'*

'Bonjour,' said Cassia, and then, hopefully, 'Do you speak English?'

'A little, madame.'

'My friend and I came to see your son last week. Two English ladies.'

'Ah! Two beautiful English ladies. My son has told me how very *charmantes* you were, madame.'

'Well, thank you. So did he tell you what it was about?'

'Only a little. Lady Beatty, *n'est-ce pas*?'

'Yes. The thing is, I didn't realise how ill she was, what difficulties she was in until she died. If I had, I would have come over, helped her, I feel so terrible about it. Anyway—'

'Madame, forgive me, but you must speak *plus lentement*. I have only a little English.'

'I'm sorry. Well, there were two things, really. One, I do hope there are no medical bills of any kind outstanding, because if so—'

'No, madame, of course not.'

'I know—she told you to stop coming after a bit. Because she couldn't pay you.'

'Yes, madame, although I did call from time to time in any case. I was concerned for her, fond of her by then.'

'That was very kind of you,' she said. 'Thank you.' Something jarred here: what was it?

'But the gentleman, of course, he pay me. *Immédiatement*.'

'Oh, I'm glad. And you didn't look after her once she was in Passy, did you?'

'No, madame. The gentleman found another doctor. A more fashionable one.' He laughed. 'I do not mind. And in any case, it is better to have a doctor who lives near you, *bien sûr*.'

'Yes. Well, you were certainly very near her before.'

'The last few weeks, indeed, very, very near.' Something else. What was it? Probably just the French translating oddly. 'And of course the new doctor, he was a specialist. In her condition.'

'In the cancer?'

A long pause, then, sounding slightly awkward, 'Yes, madame. Yes, of course.'

'So you don't think she suffered too much?'

'I hope not, madame. I did my best.'

'Well yes, thank you. Thank you very much. For all you did. It must have been so hard for her, managing on her own, in an awful place like that.'

'Oh, it is not really so bad, madame. Not the rue Molitor. The other place . . . well! That was not good.' His voice seemed to be coming from rather far away.

'The other place?'

'Yes, madame. In the rue Cauchon.'

'I'm sorry. She was living in another apartment? Down there, in the Auteuil?'

'Yes, madame. You did not know?'

'No, I didn't. When was that?'

'For the whole year preceding. That was very, very bad. I was shocked to find her there. It was I who was able to secure the other apartment for her, in the rue Molitor. A patient of mine had died and—'

'Oh dear,' said Cassia. 'Oh dear.' It was all she could find to say, that inadequate little phrase, so deep was her shock.

'Pardon, madame?'

He must think her completely barmy; she struggled to come back to him, to explain. 'I'm sorry. You see, I thought she was only in difficulties for a couple of months. We all did.' (Didn't we, Harry, didn't we?)

'Oh, no, madame. Sadly, that was not the case. She first came to see me—let me see, in late 1933.'

'Oh God. But that means . . .' It all made sense now, the strange phrases about growing fond of

652

her, the references to 'the last few weeks'. Only the rest of it didn't make sense at all.

'Dr Bertillon, was it a Mr Gresham who paid you? Paid your bills?'

'No, madame. I do not recognise that name at all. It was a Monsieur Moreton who paid them all. I have the receipts here.'

*   *   *

Edwina had left three messages for Cecily that morning and was told she was out; when she rang a fourth time, and was told she was back but busy, she became exasperated.

'Please put me on to her, Adams. I just want to ask her if I can take a photograph in the drawing room, for my magazine, and I have to speak to her soon because she might put her Christmas tree up. Or is it up already?'

'No, madam. It is only the sixth of December, after all.' His tone was mildly reproachful.

Cecily came on to the line. 'Edwina?'

'Yes. What on earth have you been doing, Cecily? I've been trying to get hold of you all morning.'

'Sorry. I've been out.' She sounded odd, Edwina thought, strained.

'Oh, I see. Well, look, I need to use your drawing room for a photograph. Or rather your fireplace. I want to display some things on it. Under that divine mirror. I thought you wouldn't mind.'

'Oh, Edwina, I'd rather not.'

'Why, for heaven's sake? Justin will do the picture, I thought you'd be pleased. Only for God's sake don't put your Christmas tree up yet, this is

653

supposed to be March.'

'Well, I wouldn't be pleased,' said Cecily, 'and I'm sick of having my houses used as photographic backcloths. What's wrong with yours? And if I want to put up my own Christmas tree in my own house, I will.'

It was so totally unlike her to be rude that Edwina was shocked.

'Cecily,' she said, 'Cecily, are you all right?'

'Yes. No. Oh, I don't know.'

God, maybe she was going to have another breakdown, Edwina thought. 'Look,' she said, 'don't worry about the photograph. It doesn't matter, honestly. I can ask someone else. Um—are you sure you're all right?'

'Oh, Edwina, I'm sorry,' said Cecily. She sounded very contrite suddenly. 'I didn't mean to be rude to you. Of all people. Upset you. I'm just a bit upset.' And she burst into noisy tears.

'Don't worry about being rude to me, upsetting me,' said Edwina, anxious to divert her, to cheer her up, 'I'm quite used to it, I live with the rudest man in London, don't forget. And the most upsetting, I should think. Specially at the moment, do you know what he's—'

She had been about to regale Cecily with Harry's ultimatum, his insistence she should give up her job, purely to distract her from her own troubles, but, 'Oh, Edwina,' said Cecily, 'so you know, do you? I thought perhaps you must. I'm sorry. So sorry.'

'Know? Know what? Cecily, what on earth are you talking about?'

*   *   *

654

Mr Brewster was enjoying the quiet cup of tea and the two digestive biscuits he always had at four o'clock, when his secretary informed him that Mrs Fallon was on the telephone. 'She sounds rather distressed, Mr Brewster.'

Mr Brewster set aside the biscuits. Mrs Fallon did indeed sound very distressed and it took him some few minutes to ascertain exactly what she wanted, and even having ascertained it, was not able to respond immediately, but had to ask her if he might ring her back. This being apparently impossible, since she was working, she said she would ring him back within the hour.

'Will that give you long enough, Mr Brewster?' Mr Brewster said he hoped so, and set himself to the task.

When Mrs Fallon phoned back, sounding more agitated still, an hour and a half later, he was able to give her the information that the document by which Rollo Gresham had set up the Maple Trust and thus empowered Leonora to make her deed of settlement upon Cassia, had been dated 3 May, 1935. 'And the will, drawn up by me, in which she exercised her appointment, was signed a fortnight later.'

He told Mrs Fallon that he had not appreciated that there was any significance in the date of the first document, that it certainly held no legal importance of any kind, and tried to reassure her that there was no need for her to be anxious about it, but he could tell that he had failed.

*   *   *

Janet Fraser was trying to persuade William to eat the scrambled egg she had cooked for his tea when the telephone rang in the kitchen. She took the call herself; Peggy was not well, Maureen was out delivering a baby and Dr Fallon had gone to see old Joe Carter who had slipped on some ice and broken an ankle. It was Mrs Fallon. She sounded rather agitated.

'Janet, I'm so sorry to bother you, and I know you'll think I'm quite mad, but up in my room, in the bottom drawer of the chest of drawers, is an old copy of *Country Life*. Could you go and fetch it and tell me the date of it, please? Thank you.'

Janet found the magazine at once, and took it downstairs again.

'I have it here, Mrs Fallon, yes. Now the date is, let me see, yes, April thirtieth, 1935. Is that all you want to know? Good. No, everything is fine here, everyone perfectly happy. William has been practising his solo verse for the carol concert next week and it is simply beautiful, and Bertie's cold is much better. No, that's perfectly all right, don't worry at all about anything, and we shall see you tomorrow, shall we? Oh, good. Very well, Mrs Fallon, goodnight.'

As she put the phone down she heard the door open and Dr Fallon came in; he was very pale. He saw her looking at him and tried to smile.

'Hello, Janet.'

'Hello, Dr Fallon. Is everything all right?'

'What? Oh, yes. Well, no. Not really. Poor old Joe died; went into heart failure, died in my arms.'

He looked desperately upset, Janet thought; she felt a pang of concern for him. 'I'm so sorry,' she said, 'so very sorry. Do come in and sit down, I'll bring you a cup of tea.'

'That would be very nice,' he said, 'thank you. Silly to get upset, but I've seen him through so much—pneumonia, pleurisy, the arthritis—and then it's a broken ankle that gets him. I can never help being distressed by a death of a patient. I'm sorry.'

'Dr Fallon, please don't apologise. I can quite appreciate how very sad it must be. But at least you were there, you didn't arrive too late. I'm sure you eased his passing and, of course, his family must have found it comforting and helpful. I'll go and get that tea now.'

When she got back with the tea he was sitting at his desk, his head in his hands; he didn't hear her come in. She felt so sorry for him that, without stopping to consider whether or not it was acceptable for her to do such a thing, she put her arms round his shoulders. 'Don't be too distressed, Dr Fallon,' she said, 'it was surely time for him to go. As we say in my village.'

He looked up at her, half startled, half grateful, and she saw there were tears in his eyes. He managed a smile and patted one of her hands awkwardly.

'What a comforting thought, yes. Yes, indeed it was. It was just, as I said, having seen him through so much and . . . oh dear, you must think me rather a fool.'

'Of course I don't, Dr Fallon,' she said, 'I don't think anything of the sort. I think it's extremely nice that you should care so much about people. Extremely nice. Now drink your tea, and just let me know when you want supper. I've made a casserole, in Peggy's absence, so it's very flexible.'

'How nice,' he said, taking the tea, smiling again, and then, 'Whatever did we do without you, Janet? I really can't imagine.'

* * *

Cecily was pacing her sitting room, feeling very odd; her initial distress at discovering the affair between Cassia and Harry easing just slightly and making way for a rather more uncomfortable emotion, which, try as she might to deny it, she recognised as envy. For Cassia to be indulging in an illicit sexual relationship with a man like Harry Moreton Cecily found very shocking.

She also—and this was where the discomfort came in—found it strangely exciting; it had made her aware of her own long-dormant desires. She felt herself suddenly dull, sensually dreary, sexually deprived; she looked back on her sex life with Benedict, so unsatisfactory for the most part, and a surge of self-pity and discomfort rose in her. She had hardly known sexual pleasure; she knew of it, she had read of it, but had never experienced herself more than a flicker, an echo of it. And she wanted to, she wanted it very much; she had felt the longings, the physical yearnings in her body, never more than now, recovering from her unhappiness and remorse over Benedict, discovering pleasure, sexual awareness with Justin—she wanted it desperately.

She found Justin extremely attractive; she was surprised and even slightly shocked to discover how much she thought about him, not merely his company, his charm, his extraordinary gentleness and consideration towards her, but his tall, slender body, his beautiful hands, his rather oddly good-looking face, his brilliant eyes, his expressive mouth. Sometimes, as he had kissed her briefly, tenderly, on the lips—the full extent so far of their sexual encounters—she had longed for him to go further, to feel his mouth working on hers, his tongue exploring her, had even thought of taking the initiative—but shyness, delicacy, and a fairly strong conviction that she was very little more to him than a loving and loved friend, held her back.

Tonight, with sexual infidelity filling her head, sexual excitement strong in the air, she longed for Justin, longed for him not only to kiss her, but to go further, longed for his hands on her, his mouth moving over her, not only on her lips; longed for . . .

At this, this realisation she ran up the stairs to the nursery floor and endeavoured to occupy her thoughts and, indeed, her entire self with her children and the care of them. They were her future, her interest, her excitement now; she was a matron, a widow, and a failed wife, and she had not only no business but no right to be looking for anything more from life than their happiness.

'You look awfully pretty, Mummy,' said Stephanie, coming into the nursery bathroom, smiling at her, 'prettier every day. Justin said that, didn't he, yesterday? I wish I had a boyfriend like Justin.'

'He's not my boyfriend,' said Cecily, and, to her horror, burst into tears.

*　　　*　　　*

Rupert Cameron was eating his second light meal of the day, prior to leaving his flat for the evening performance, when Cassia telephoned him. She sounded almost hysterical.

'Rupert, I've got to talk to you.'

'Cassia, darling,' he said, 'has Cecily been on to you?'

'Cecily? Why ever should Cecily be on to me?'

'Oh, no matter,' he said quickly. 'What is it? What's the matter? Is it this business of taking over the practice? What did Edward say? I hope he didn't turn you down.'

'No, no, he seemed to quite like the idea.' She had forgotten about that, it seemed of absolutely no importance whatsoever. 'It's . . . oh, Rupert, I can't tell you on the phone. Can I come over now?'

'Come to the theatre. I'm going over there straight away.' If he didn't forget his lines tonight, he thought, it would be something of a miracle.

* * *

She was looking terrible: pale, tense, literally hollow eyed. She also looked as if she had been crying.

'Darling, sit down there, have a drink, I've got some perfectly foul sherry.'

'I don't want a drink, Rupert. I want you just to listen to me.'

'I'm listening,' he said.

'You know what I told you before? That I thought Harry had something to do with my money?'

'Ye-es.'

'I *know* he did now. Leonora was poor for a year and a half before she died, not just a few months. The awful place she was living in, I went to see it

660

when I went to Paris. Well, apparently, that was nothing compared to the one where she was before. And it wasn't a friend who rescued her finally, it was Margot Murray. Harry's secretary, you know?'

'I don't, but—'

'And then, Harry paid all her medical bills. Not Rollo at all.'

'Darling, none of this is exactly proof of anything. Simply that they couldn't find Rollo straight away. Don't you think?'

'No, no, I don't. Rupert, think, think, please.'

Tears of what seemed like fright were rolling down her face; he held out a handkerchief to her. 'Try to keep calm, darling.'

'Sorry.' She blew her nose, took a deep breath. 'The thing is, if she was short of money all that time, then Leonora had no money. There was no trust fund then, no interest.'

'Cassia—'

'No, I know there wasn't. The trust fund was set up just two months before she died, two weeks before she willed it to me.'

'But if Gresham had no money, then how could he do that anyway? I still think you're making no sense.'

'That same month, Rollo's house and estate here went on the market. Also he sold his house in Cannes that summer. I know that too. It's desperate stuff, not the action of a man who had so much money he could settle half a million pounds on his mistress, a month or so before she died. I don't think the money was his at all, Rupert, I still think it was Harry's.'

'Cassia, that is ridiculous. Honestly, you've been

reading too many novels.'

'I don't read novels. And Richard, even he knew she couldn't have had all that money: he looked utterly shocked when I told him, he would have known—'

'Cassia, you must calm down. You're in a state of panic.'

There was a knock on the door. 'Twenty minutes, Mr Cameron.'

'Oh God. I must start getting ready. Don't go away, Cassia, it's perfectly all right.'

She looked at him. 'Do you still really think so? That the money couldn't be from Harry?'

'Yes, I do. I think it's absolutely out of the question.'

'Well, where did this money come from suddenly? Why should Rollo Gresham suddenly hand it over, start selling all his assets?'

'I don't know. But there must be a reasonable explanation for it. There always is. Maybe he just wanted to get out of England, settle in—where is it, Marrakesh?'

'Yes, but why, if he was so hard up, and everyone knew that, why give Leonora money then? When she was dying? It's all mad.'

'Maybe he didn't know how ill she was. Maybe they thought she'd live much longer. I always had the impression it was something of a shock to everyone, not just you. Can't you ask Harry?'

'No. Well, I already have, about some of it at least, and he's lied to me, that's one of the things that makes me so suspicious still, and he'd just go on lying, of course he would.'

'Perhaps you should go and see Gresham,' said Rupert cheerfully, 'he'll put you straight. Don't look like that, my darling, it was only a joke. Anyway, what made you suddenly think of the dates on all these deeds and trust funds? Why didn't that come to light before?'

'It just didn't occur to me that it mattered. It was something a French woman said, someone who lived in an apartment in the same house as Leonora: she said time was complicated, that our memories played tricks with it. I was thinking this whole thing is about time, not *what* happened so much as *when* it did: when Leonora moved away from the avenue Foch, when she was rescued, when Gresham sold his houses, it all weaves together— and there are some great big holes in the cloth. Oh, Rupert, I hate this so much. If I'm right, if Harry has done this—' Tears stood in her eyes; she looked frightened, like a small child.

Another knock on the door: 'Ten minutes, Mr Cameron.'

'Darling, I'm sorry, but I'll have to start concentrating. Can you wait here? It's only an hour and a half, we can have dinner later. There's something else I want to talk to you about as well.'

'Yes, all right,' said Cassia, 'good idea. I'll go home for a bit, and then come back. Thank you, Rupert.'

But he could see, as she went out of the door, that she was distracted, not really concentrating on what he was saying at all. Perhaps not a night to warn her that Cecily had found out about her and Harry after all.

*   *   *

Half a mile away, in Mount Street, Edwina, having

663

tried and failed to get hold of Harry in Paris decided that she would speak to Cassia instead. There was no reply to the house in Walton Street; she decided to try Monks Ridge.

Edward answered the phone; he sounded tired.

'Oh, Edward. This is Edwina Moreton here. I'd like to speak to Cassia.'

'Good evening, Edwina. I'm afraid she's not here. She's in London.'

'No, she isn't. I've tried. So I thought she must be down there.'

'I'm sorry, Edwina. She isn't. She's away. As is so often the case.'

Edwina suddenly wondered if he knew. And saw life through his eyes, just for a moment, and with a flash of very rare imagination, saw how unsatisfactory for him it must be, married to Cassia, Cassia with all that money; Cassia living in London, free as a bird, the cover being her work. Her work! Well, he must be very naive, Edwina thought, and then realised she too must be naive to swallow it all, all that nonsense. Who needed a house in London; a conveniently small house, too small for her family, ideal for just one person, one independent person? Just so that she could work for a few hours each week at a hospital or a clinic or whatever it was Cassia was supposed to do. Maybe she wasn't doing anything, maybe the whole thing was a front, an elaborate cover-up for the affair with Harry. What a marvellous idea, and how they must have enjoyed it, the two of them, having duped their spouses.

It was suddenly borne very strongly in upon Edwina that she and Edward, whom she had always so despised, had been deceived in exactly the same way by exactly the same people: and she felt not only angry but extremely foolish. It suddenly became rather important to her to get hold of Cassia, to deliver a few extremely well-chosen words.

'So do you know where Cassia is?' she said. 'I mean, is she coming back tonight?'

'No,' said Edward, and he sounded exasperated now as well as tired, 'she won't. She's just phoned to say she won't be back until the weekend. Some panic or other at the hospital.'

'Oh, really?'

Harry also wasn't coming back until the weekend. It seemed not unreasonable to think that the two of them were together somewhere. In fact, it seemed very unlikely they were not. Edwina suddenly felt more foolish still: foolish and very, very angry.

'Edward,' she said, 'Edward, I wonder if you realised something . . .'

CHAPTER THIRTY-SIX

Cassia was not to be found. Not by her husband, who had phoned the house in Walton Street immediately (having put down the telephone on Edwina) and repeated the process every hour until midnight, when he had fallen exhaustedly asleep, and then recommenced his task at six a.m.; not by Rupert, who had also phoned the house several times and then tried Monks Ridge as well, to have the phone picked up by a hugely agitated Edward; not by Harry Moreton, who had telephoned her

665

from Paris almost as frequently through the night as her husband; not by Nurse Hampton, who had wanted her to start the clinic earlier than usual on the Thursday; not by the Dean, who wanted her approval on the press release he had prepared for the medical journals on the subject of her research Chair; and not by Edwina Moreton, who had decided the only thing that was going to make her feel better was a confrontation with Cassia, and the sooner the better.

All these people, or most of them, began eventually to telephone one another: and as the morning of Thursday 10th December wore on, it became apparent that the last person to have seen Cassia was Rupert. Rupert told all of them the simple truth: that she had come to see him the night before at the theatre and had then promised to return so that they could have dinner together, but that she had not done so. He began examining and re-examining his conversation with her for some clue as to what might have happened to her.

By the fifth call of the day, which was from Harry Moreton, the examination had led him to a remark he had made shortly before she had left, partly in jest: 'No, I would say almost entirely in jest,' he said to Harry, 'that she should go and see Rollo Gresham in Marrakesh. Of course I don't think she intended to do any such thing, but it seemed worth mentioning, that's all.'

'Sweet Jesus,' said Harry, 'surely she couldn't be so unutterably stupid.'

'She was very upset,' said Rupert carefully, 'and more than ready to be unutterably stupid.'

'What was she upset about? Come on, Cameron, you'd better tell me.'

Rupert told him.

*   *   *

In London that morning, the brief reign of Edward VIII ended, as the Instrument of Abdication was signed and witnessed by the King's three brothers.

Queen Mary, speaking probably for millions, remarked, 'To give up all this for that.'

The newly designated ex-King, no longer constrained by government, announced that he would broadcast to his people, as he had wished to do much earlier in the affair, the following night.

*   *   *

The plane was very noisy; much noisier, or so it seemed to Cassia, than Harry's small one, and seemed to be making rather lumbering progress, but proved actually astonishingly fast. They were in Paris by midday, at Le Bourget airport, where she and a handful of other passengers changed into a very different plane, a Dewoitine, the steward told her proudly, as if he might have built it himself, with only eight reclining seats and each with its own small table. They were to go on to Toulouse, where they would spend the night, reaching Casablanca at midday the following day.

'From there, you can take a train, or a car, of course, it's only about a hundred miles,' the nice young man at Thomas Cook had said, having entered rather thoroughly into the spirit of her adventure, and thinking how he was looking forward to telling his girlfriend about the beautiful young woman in the sable coat who had been waiting outside the door of their Knightsbridge office as they opened, and demanded to know how she could get to Marrakesh 'as soon as it's humanly possible, and, yes, I have my passport with me.'

'And if you want to stay in a hotel, then you must go to the Mamounia,' he had added. 'It's often described as the most beautiful hotel in the world. Winston Churchill often stays there. The gardens once belonged to royalty. I could send a cable if you like.' Cassia said she would like.

*   *   *

By the time they reached Toulouse she was completely exhausted. The noise of the aircraft, the constant juddering, the realisation finally of what she had done, in all its inescapable folly, overwhelmed her; she almost fell down the steps of the plane and into a bus, along with her fellow passengers, most whom seemed to be travelling in irritatingly jolly groups. She was borne through the darkness to a hotel, the standard and location of which was of no interest to her, so long as it provided her with a bed on a steady and silent floor. In the event it was modestly luxurious, the dinner served more than adequate, and the bed comfortable; she sent a telegram to Edward to tell him where she was going, and that she was quite safe—and then went to bed and slept dreamlessly.

She woke at five to the darkness, feeling very alone and very afraid, and half tempted to fly home again, and was only prevented by the thought of how much she would hate and despise herself if she did, and that she would forfeit for ever any chance of finding out the truth. And of course that she would have made several people extremely worried and angry to no purpose whatsoever.

*   *   *

In London that morning, Justin Everard also lay awake in the long dark winter dawn, reflecting upon his future and where Cecily Harrington might be placed in it.

He genuinely loved Cecily; he found her deeply attractive both physically and emotionally; he loved being with her, he enjoyed the atmosphere of warmth and caring in which she seemed permanently to move, and he found her far removed intellectually from her often vapid peers. She was intelligent, thoughtful and well read, her interests frequently coincided with his, particularly in the arts, and indeed he had noticed a pleasing and growing self-confidence in her own intellectual views, despite her still shaky emotional state.

Increasingly, over the past few weeks, he had found the thought of consummating a physical relationship with her immensely intriguing; her body, regaining now its lush plumpness, her full, lovely breasts, her surprisingly slender legs and neck, her large dark eyes and full mouth, her gleaming cloud of dark hair, were beginning to obsess him. And, aware though he was of Cecily's emotional vulnerability, the dreadful wrong he would be doing her should he disturb her, arouse her without proper consideration of the consequences, he had begun to plan, in the nicest, kindest possible way, her seduction.

Nevertheless, the events of the previous day had worried him. Was there really any future in a relationship between the two of them? Between two people, one of whom regarded the sexual frissons between people married to other people amusing and diverting (even while not approving of it for themselves), the other finding it shocking and distressing; between two people, one of whom moved in a world not only of sexual freedom, but sexual anarchy, and to whom homosexuality was a blithe accident of biology, potentially even a happy one, and the other to whom it was something abhorrent and who, having discovered it in her husband, had regarded it as a shameful sickness.

Two people, one of whom had come from a level of society that was modest, to put it mildly, and for whom the earning of a living was not only satisfying and pleasant but essential, and the other from its upper echelons and rich beyond the dreams of most of the population.

Could emotional concern, sexual fulfilment, even the most ardent love, possibly counteract all those difficulties? Or would there be, the first rapture having passed, resentment, unhappiness, discontent, disillusion?

Justin found no comfort in the answers that came to him.

*   *   *

Later, as Edwina sat at her dressing table, applying her make-up, Harry phoned.

'You,' she said briefly, 'are contemptible.'

'Really?' he said. He sounded rather cheerful, she thought.

'Yes. You and Cassia.'

'I see. And you and the Sobel crowd, the

Bryanston twins—I suppose that's something quite different.'

'Of course it's different. Cassia is my friend. Or so I had thought.'

'Well, at least we are equal now, Edwina. Anyway, I phoned to tell you I'm not coming home for a few days.'

'Good,' she said, 'and when you do, my solicitor will be waiting for you. Do give my regards to Cassia. Tell her she's very welcome to you.'

'She's not with—' he began, but she had slammed the phone down.

*   *   *

'Where's Mummy gone now?' said Bertie.

Janet looked at him thoughtfully; for the very first time he sounded plaintive, upset about the situation, about what must seem his mother's endless absences, what indeed *were* her endless absences, she thought rather sadly.

'She's got some very important work to do,' she said, 'terribly important. She can't just turn her back on sick people, any more than your father can. They're doctors, their patients' lives often depend on them.'

'She doesn't have to be a doctor,' said Bertie, 'she could just be a mother again, like she used to be. Then she wouldn't have to worry about her stupid patients.'

*   *   *

It was the smell that Cassia noticed first about Morocco, the strange, fierce, potent smell that

671

somehow fused with the heat; years later, discussing those few extraordinary days with someone who had visited Morocco frequently he said, 'Ah, yes! Woodsmoke, camel dung and incense, wonderful.' She wasn't sure about the wonderful, but she could, in memory, pick out all those elements.

And after the smell, the literally pressing proximity of bodies, of brown grinning faces, of people proffering, offering her things—lengths of fabric, jewellery, ornaments—a sense of panic, almost of claustrophobia, and then after that the relief and promise of order as her driver, the driver she had hired in Casablanca, shooed them contemptuously away as if they were little better than the mangy, scrawny dogs who ran everywhere, ushered her into the car and shut her away, briefly safe from it all.

He had driven her then along a hundred miles of painfully rough, red, sandy roads, through plains which seemed to her to be desert, through occasional squalid villages where they were stared at by children playing in the dust and watched morosely by wretched-looking donkeys, tethered in the blazing sun.

The heat was stifling, she had been feeling very sick, and the driver had started talking when they left Casablanca and was still talking when they arrived in Marrakesh and she became aware of the tall city walls, built with the red mud of the plains, the extraordinarily intricate roofline of domes and turrets and minarets, and carved out behind them in the blue sky, the unbelievable sight of the snow-capped Atlas mountains. They looked impossibly, tantalisingly near, those mountains, cool and reassuring, a note of clean sanity in what seemed to her the hot near-hell of these streets, filled with apparently starving animals, donkeys piled high with loads three times their own height, their bones jutting so sharply through their skin that it was painful to look at them, dogs and cats slinking in the gutters, close to death.

Cassia had sat shrinking into the corner of her car, absurdly fearful of what was outside, her mission almost forgotten, her only concern reaching some kind of civilisation that she could recognise as such, despising herself for her feebleness and her chauvinism.

And then her car pulled into the entrance gates of La Mamounia, and she smiled with pure pleasure, so lush it was, filled with palm trees and brilliantly flowering shrubs and grass, an oasis of calm, of peace, of green, wonderfully green, after the red of the mud and the dust.

The hotel itself was pale pink with a large curving courtyard in front of it, parked with a few extremely large and expensive-looking cars. Her driver picked up her one piece of totally-inadequate baggage and led her into the hotel, where it was so cool, so quiet, she could scarcely believe she was in the same country, never mind the same city, as the one outside.

They took her up to her room, with its vast bed, its balcony overlooking the gardens, its basket of fruit and huge vases of flowers, and left her there.

She could not possibly go down to dinner, she could see that—she had only the crumpled clothes she had been wearing since leaving London, and a simple black jersey dress which would certainly not serve for use in the extremely grand dining room, so she had a bath and then ordered a meal of smoked salmon and salad and fruit from room service, and ate it sitting in her bed, feeling slightly decadent and miraculously more cheerful.

She lay down then, wondering a little fearfully, but with a degree of intense excitement, what the next day might bring.

*   *   *

Other English guests in the hotel tried without a great deal of success to tune their radios to the BBC in order to listen to what was arguably one of the most historic broadcasts ever made: that of the ex-King of England, introduced now as His Royal Highness Prince Edward, speaking from Windsor Castle and telling his people that he had discharged his last duties as King and Emperor, and declaring his allegiance to the new King, his brother, the Duke of York.

*   *   *

The whole of England heard that broadcast. The country was almost entirely silent for its duration; families everywhere gathered round the wireless, some distressed, others surprised, all of them, whatever their views on the matter, deeply moved.

In Monks Ridge Edward Fallon sat with his arms round his two little boys, Janet Fraser opposite him in Cassia's chair, strangely subdued, and Peggy standing in the doorway, weeping openly, as they were told that the King found it impossible to carry the heavy burden of responsibility without the help and support of the woman he loved.

In London, Cecily Harrington sat in her drawing room, also with her children, thinking how desperately the King must have loved this woman, hoping that he had indeed been comforted by his mother and his family, as he was claiming he had been, feeling a pang of intense sympathy with him as he described the 'matchless blessing enjoyed by my brother and so many of you, and not bestowed upon me—a happy home with his wife and children'.

Rupert Cameron, who had also not had that blessing bestowed upon him, listened to the broadcast in his dressing room, his heart heavy, for he had always felt a certain empathy with his sovereign, had defended his right to follow his heart.

As he sat there, the door opened quietly and Eleanor came in. Her eyes were full of tears. She looked at Rupert and he at her, wondering in this moment of very raw emotion why he had never been more moved by her beauty, her gentleness, and, telling himself he was acting purely in friendship, stood up and took her into his arms, in order to comfort her.

Justin Everard, listening to the radio while he worked in his darkroom, found himself actually rather affected by the intense emotion of the moment and especially touched by this reference to the 'greatest kindness he had been treated with by all classes, wherever he had lived or journeyed through the Empire' and his gratitude for it.

And even Edwina Moreton, listening to it with Francis Stevenson-Cook; in his flat in Mount Street, felt a lump in her throat as the voice, clear and very strong now, wished the new King 'and his people, happiness and prosperity with all my heart. God bless you all. God save the King.'

At which point Francis poured them both a glass of champagne and raised his, echoing the last words himself.

But Harry Moreton, flying across southern Europe through the darkness, heard nothing of it at all.

CHAPTER THIRTY-SEVEN

Absurdly, Cassia found herself worrying as to what she should wear to visit Rollo Gresham. She had nothing remotely suitable for the situation and, more relevantly, for the climate either. She put the dress on as the slightly better option, and rang for breakfast; and then, because she could not possibly postpone it any longer, went down to the lobby and asked them to call her a taxi.

*   *   *

Justin did not often work on Saturday, but there was a general air of panic at Style House at the moment, and everyone who worked there, whether full-time or freelance, was in a state of acute tension; the Americans, who ran the sister company in New York and who were the overlords, were arriving for their annual visit at the beginning of January and there was an absolute need to get Style House in order by then. The Americans would expect to see dummy issues, work in progress, photographs, layouts clearly ready in plenty of time; this meant virtually doing two issues in the time they usually spent on one, which meant, in turn, a six- or even seven-day week.

Consequently Style House that Saturday morning was operating as if it were a weekday, and Justin was just leaving to go and take some photographs in Edwina Moreton's drawing room when the telephone rang, and his assistant told him that it was for him.

Suzanne, the secretary, looked up at him with a knowing smile. 'It's your rich lady friend,' she said, putting her hand over the mouthpiece. 'Keep in with her, Justin, and you'll be able to give up work altogether in a month or two.'

Justin scowled at her and took the phone.

'Hello?' he said cautiously.

'Justin, hello, it's Cecily. How are you?'

'I'm very well,' he said.

'It can't be much fun working on Saturday. I'm sorry.'

'Oh, it's all right,' he said, 'but we're all in a panic here. I'm about to rush off and do some pictures for Edwina, so I can't be long.' He sounded more impatient than he actually felt partly because he was irritated by Suzanne's remark and partly because his mind was actually fixed on the difficulties of the morning ahead and taking pictures of a drawing room that he knew to be the wrong location for the job. He had wanted something ornate, almost baroque, rather like Cecily's drawing room—Edwina's was contemporary in style and filled with her husband's aggressively modern pictures.

'Oh, I see. Yes. She wanted to use my house for those, but I refused, I'm afraid.'

677

'She did?' Damn. It was yet another pointer to the differences between them. Cecily would not wish her drawing room to be photographed; it would not be the sort of thing she would feel comfortable with, seeing it as somehow rather vulgar, commercial, an invasion of her privacy, not something that was to him absolutely everyday, part of his normal working life.

'Justin, if you'd rather use my house, I—'

'No, no,' he said shortly, 'it's all arranged now, it really doesn't matter at all.'

'Oh.' She sounded taken aback, then rallied. 'Well, I actually phoned to say would you like to come and have supper here tonight? Nothing formal, just me and the girls. A little—well, a little thank you. For everything.'

'Oh.' Justin hesitated. Nothing could have appealed to him more: but the uncomfortable conversation he had had with himself two nights ago, the conclusions he had been forced to reach, resurfaced; and he saw this as a rather clear turning point. If he and Cecily were not right for one another then the sooner he started to ease out of the relationship the better, however much it hurt him to do.

He took a mental breath and said, 'I'm sorry, Cecily. I'm busy tonight. Working in the darkroom, you know.'

'Oh, I see. Tomorrow perhaps?'

God, this was going to be difficult. 'No, not tomorrow either, I'm afraid. It's Sunday, I have to go and see my mama. Sorry. Maybe some time next week.'

'Yes,' she said, and he could hear the hurt in her voice, 'yes; all right. Maybe next week. Goodbye,

Justin.'

'Goodbye, Cecily,' he said, and hoped she couldn't hear the hurt in his.

*   *   *

Rollo Gresham lived in the part of Marrakesh known as the Ville Nouvelle, the area built under French colonial rule; off the avenue d'el Jadida, and very near the Marjorelle Gardens. Cassia had been told about those gardens by a helpful porter in the hotel as she waited for her taxi, told she must go and see them, that they were 'very very beautiful' and designed by the French painter Jacques Marjorelle in the 1920s.

Removed from the peace and tranquillity of the hotel grounds, and confronted again by the twin terrors of Rollo Gresham and Marrakesh in the raw, she began to feel very sick; she was about to vomit: she told him to stop, leant out of the door and threw up repeatedly. Mercifully, they were no longer in the crowds; they had already reached the Ville Nouvelle, and the street was wide, tree lined and almost deserted. The driver was surprisingly kind: he got out, held her head, passed her a handkerchief that was only slightly grubby, and offered to fetch her some water.

'No,' she said, 'no, really, it's all right. I'm so sorry. I'll be all right in a minute. Where are we?'

'Marjorelle Gardens through there,' said the drive, indicating a small side road. 'Avenue d'el-Jadida along street. Very very near.'

'Yes, I see. Thank you. I think I'll walk the rest of the way. I need some air. You go.' She gave him his fare and a tip worth twice as much.

He gazed at her, his wizened face still concerned. 'Will wait for you.'

'No, no, don't. It's perfectly all right. I might be hours. Please, I'll be fine. But thank you for everything. You were very kind.'

It was horribly hot in her jersey dress; the sun was beating on her unprotected head. She crossed the street slightly unsteadily, hoping she wouldn't be sick again, and walked down the street towards the avenue d'el-Jadida.

*　　*　　*

Harry Moreton taxied down the airfield in Casablanca in that combination of exhaustion and exaltation which seems almost hallucinogenic. He climbed out of his plane on legs which threatened to fail in their function, and walked across to the control tower with his papers. And an hour later was asleep in a surprisingly comfortable train.

*　　*　　*

'What earth is the matter with you, Justin?' said Edwina irritably; 'This whole thing should only have taken an hour or two at the most, and here we are, nearly lunchtime and we're still setting it up.'

'Oh, shut up,' said Justin. 'I get so bloody tired of editors telling me things should only take an hour or two. If the lighting was wrong, if the beastly pots didn't look right, you'd be the first to complain. It's very difficult in this room, you knew perfectly well I wanted somewhere that was basically darker, less modern looking.'

'Yes, well, at forty-eight hours' notice, that was a

680

little difficult to arrange,' said Edwina. 'If your girlfriend had been a bit more co-operative—'

'If you mean Cecily, she is not my girlfriend. Far from it. I never heard anything so absurd.'

'Really? Well, in that case, all I can say is you'd better stop leading her up the garden path, encouraging her. She's going to get frightfully keen on you, and it's not fair. And besides, it will come back to reflect on me if she starts getting serious about you and then you ditch her. I introduced you to her, after all.'

'That would be really serious, wouldn't it?' said Justin. 'I'd hate to mess things up in your perfectly organised life, Edwina. Anyway—Edwina, are you all right?'

'Yes, I'm fine,' said Edwina, dashing a hand impatiently across her eyes, pulling her cigarette case out of her bag, flicking at her lighter with a hand that shook.

'Are you sure you're all right, Edwina?'

'Yes, I think so,' said Edwina with a sigh. 'It's just that my life is very far from perfectly organised— it's in total chaos, and I don't quite know what to do about any of it.'

'Well, you're not alone,' said Justin. 'Tell you what, let's have supper together tonight, shall we? We can give each other lots and lots of perfectly terrible advice and—'

'Marvellous idea. But would you mind eating here? I really don't want to go out. I'll tell Cook to do something wonderful. Now, in the meantime, can we please get this thing going? Otherwise I'm going to start screaming. Very loudly indeed.'

*   *   *

Cassia had no way of knowing whether Rollo Gresham's house was that of a rich man, but it looked to her fairly modest, the size of a detached suburban villa in England. It was certainly a very pretty house, set back from the street, not a Moroccan-style street, but quite wide and lined with jacarandas. The house was deco in style, white stucco with curved lines and a flat roof, and the lovely front garden was overflowing with flowers. A man was watering the shrubs with a long hosepipe; he grinned at her as she walked in, showing the largely toothless mouth she was growing swiftly familiar with. She smiled uncertainly back.

'You want Monsieur Rollo?'

'Er, yes. Yes, I do.'

'I call Mehdi. You wait.'

She moved to the shelter of the arched porch and waited. She felt sick again.

Mehdi appeared, clearly a more important servant, better dressed, in white tunic and trousers, with more teeth. 'You want to see Monsieur Rollo?'

'Yes please.'

'Your name?'

'Mrs Fallon. Mrs Cassia Fallon.'

'Wait, please.'

Three children came out, two boys and a girl. They looked at her uncertainly, and the younger boy smiled, a glorious, beautiful smile. He was altogether beautiful: fairly light skinned, with dark shining hair, only a little taller than Bertie, but clearly older. The little girl looked younger, probably only about seven, clinging to his hand. She looked as if she had been crying.

Mehdi appeared, waved them away as if they were dogs, said something incomprehensible. The older boy said something back, nodded, then they all ran. Mehdi looked at her. 'You alone?'

'Yes,' she said, surprised at the question. 'Of course I'm alone. As you see.'

'Wait again.' He went back into the house, reappeared. 'Monsieur Rollo says come back in two hours, all right? Three o'clock.'

'Oh, yes. Thank you.'

He bowed, the garden boy bowed, grinned at her, and she went out into the street.

*   *   *

Yes, they told Harry at the Mamounia, Mrs Fallon had indeed checked in, but had gone out shortly after breakfast; she had said she might not be back for luncheon. Would Mr Moreton require luncheon, would he perhaps wait in case Mrs Fallon returned?

Harry went to the bar, ordered a large whisky, issued a short prayer that Mrs Fallon would indeed return and tried to decide what he should do in case she did not.

*   *   *

Cassia had thought she would return to the hotel for the intervening two hours, and then realised that she had no idea how to get there. There were certainly no black cabs, or their equivalent, she couldn't walk, certainly not in this heat, and if she didn't faint or throw up again, she was bound to get lost and probably be attacked or at best pestered

683

on the way. She couldn't stand around here for two hours. It was hideous. For a moment she panicked and then she remembered, with a thud of pleasure, the Marjorelle Gardens; she could go and sit there for a while.

She retraced her steps, paid her entrance money and went into the gardens. And immediately felt quite quite different, no longer in the least sick, but almost dizzy with visual delight. The gardens were quite extraordinary in themselves, incredibly lavish, thick with palms and bamboo, planted with nasturtiums, geraniums, bougainvillaea, set with pergolas, lily-covered pools and brilliantly coloured paths painted in pinks, lemons and greens. The air was also lush, rich with sound, the sound of water and birdsong, but the most extraordinary thing of all about it was the colour of the walls, the walls of the garden and of the main building within it, an amazingly brilliant, stinging mauvish blue, a blue she could never remember seeing ever anywhere before and which she thought she might never see again.

She sat down on a bench by one of the pools, feeling better now, soothed and excited at once by this place, which must, she thought foolishly, resemble the Garden of Eden, thought also it had been worth coming here simply to see it; and composing and recomposing her thoughts for the interview ahead. This was a much better idea than returning to the hotel.

*   *   *

Lunchtime by any stretch of the hopeful imagination having come and gone, Harry tried to decide what to do. Presumably Cassia was at Gresham's place; how she had got the address, heaven only knew. Not for the first time since this whole insane adventure had begun, he was filled with intense admiration for her. He could only think of one other woman in his acquaintance who would have embarked on such a trip on her own, and that was Edwina. He seemed to find himself attracted to extremely strong women, Harry thought, and found the thought amusing, ironic even, then returned to his dilemma.

There was no point in trying to get into Gresham's house: he would be thrown out if he so much as put a foot into the garden, probably shot. He could wait around outside, in the hope that Cassia had either not got there yet, or that when she came out she would not try to shoot him herself. After a few more minutes he decided that was the only course.

He called for a taxi, looked at his watch: two twenty-five. He wished to God now that he had gone straight there, not wasted time in the bar. If he'd missed her, if she got to Gresham first, things could get very nasty indeed.

*   *   *

Cassia decided to make her way back to avenue d'el-Jadida. It was ten to three; she didn't want to be late. Rollo Gresham might keep to a very strict timetable, might even be going out, might use her lateness as an excuse not to see her. She felt much better now, in command of herself and events. She stood up, straightened the increasingly unchic and unsuitable dress and set off towards the house. She would be five minutes early, but that wouldn't matter. She could wait in the street, just by his gates. Nobody would accost her there.

* * *

'*Yallah!*' said Harry, throwing himself into the taxi.

The driver was neither moved nor impressed by this Moroccan exhortation. 'Yes, boss,' he said, and proceeded towards the Ville Nouvelle at his normal rather sober pace. He had a new car; he wasn't going to risk it for anyone.

The roads were surprisingly clear; they would be there, Harry reckoned, in less than fifteen minutes, if only this fool would put his foot down a bit. He fumbled in his pocket for some notes to wave at the driver, pushed them over the man's shoulder, and said, '*Vite, plus vite.*'

The driver shrugged, increased his pace imperceptibly, just enough to indicate he might increase it further.

'For God's sake,' said Harry, fumbling for some more notes. The man half turned again to him, assessing their value: and then it happened.

A donkey, carrying what appeared to be the contents of an entire house on its back, and the tiny cart it was pulling, slithered suddenly on the road. Its small legs gave way beneath it, and it lay spread-eagled in the road, its owner flogging it and shouting at it uselessly. A car coming towards it in the opposite direction slammed on its brakes and collided with a horse-drawn cart, whose load of several dozen chickens escaped and ran clucking joyfully all over the road. In rather less than sixty seconds the entire street was impassable, resembling a disorderly farmyard.

Harry's taxi, pulling out, swerved to avoid the largest contingent of chickens, and struck a large rackety van coming in the other direction. Harry, who had been leaning forward, shouting at the driver, was thrown right forward, hitting his head very hard on the dashboard; the last thing he remembered before losing consciousness was a large chicken clambering in through the driver's open window.

＊　　　＊　　　＊

'Janet,' said Bertie, 'Janet, do you think Mummy will be back on Monday evening? For my carol concert? And to hear William's solo? She will, won't she? A patient couldn't matter more than that.'

Janet smiled at him brightly. 'Yes, of course she will. I'm *absolutely* certain. She wouldn't miss that. Not for all the patients in the world.'

'I hope not,' said Bertie.

Later, when he was outside playing, she went in to see Edward. He was in the study, scowling over some papers at his desk.

'Dr Fallon, I'm so sorry to trouble you, but Bertie is very anxious that Mrs Fallon might not be back by Monday evening. For the carol concert. It's very important to them both. I wondered when she would be back. What I could tell them.'

'God alone knows,' said Edward wearily. 'She's abroad, in some godforsaken city in North Africa, can you believe it. She says she's leaving again tomorrow, but God knows if she will.'

Janet received this information in characteristic

style, rather as if Edward had told her Cassia was in Leamington Spa. 'I'm sure if she says she will, she will,' she said cheerfully, adding, 'North Africa, how very interesting. My father lived in Algiers for a few years in the twenties and made a few forays down there. Delightful people. Well, Delia and I are off now for a walk. We'll see you later, Dr Fallon.'

Edward, watching her through the window as they set off down the lane, Buffy on the lead, Delia chattering up at her happily, thought that she would have created calm and order out of a hell as visualised by Hieronymous Bosch.

*   *   *

Rollo Gresham was obviously quite ill, Cassia thought, looking at him carefully; he was a bad colour, and clearly short of breath. He was also extremely thin, a shadow of the man she remembered. He had had her brought through to a terrace at the back of the house and ordered tea. He had greeted her with courtesy, expressed pleasure, kissed her hand; she wondered why he had ignored her letters.

He sat in a large, high backed wicker chair, with his feet on a stool, and she noticed that his ankles were puffy and swollen. Heart disease, clearly. He was wearing loose, light trousers and sandals, and at one point he pulled his leg up to swat a fly on his ankle; the trouser leg slipped up and she saw a dressing on his leg.

'So what do you think of Marrakesh?' he said.

'Oh, it's very . . . interesting.'

'It's an acquired taste. It becomes rather

fascinating when you know it. Have you been to the square yet, to the Djemâa el-Fna?' He gave it the Arab pronunciation.

She had no idea what he meant, but she shook her head. 'I've only seen the gardens. The ones near here.'

'Well, you must go to the square. It's incredible. You step back in time, hundreds, possibly thousands of years. Snake charmers, fire-eaters, preachers, whirling dervishes—it's truly marvellous. Go tomorrow.'

'I'm going back to England tomorrow,' said Cassia.

'A very fleeting trip.'

'Yes.'

A silence, then, 'So how long have you lived here?' she said.

'Oh, on and off for several years,' he said carefully. 'I like it. This does me well enough.'

'Yes,' she said politely, 'it seems very nice to me.' She thought of the house in England, the one advertised in *Country Life*, with its cottages and stables and parkland and woods, and tried to imagine how he must feel about it.

'Of course,' he said, 'it's hardly what I was used to. But one has to adjust. As, no doubt, have you. Learnt to adjust. I was thinking of going into politics in England, you know,' he said suddenly.

This was so absurd she found it hard not to smile. 'No, I didn't know that,' she said. 'How . . . interesting.'

'Yes, I felt it was something my talents were suited to. I always liked public speaking, that sort of thing. But of course I shall never get the opportunity now.'

'No, I suppose not.' She hesitated, then said, 'I'm sorry you are not well.'

'Oh, I'm perfectly well. Just a temporary indisposition, here—' he indicated the leg—'and of course in our old age we grow less . . . vital. I don't have the energy I used to. And this climate is not ideal, to put it mildly.'

'No, I can see that. Are you well cared for?'

'What do you mean?' he said, his face wary suddenly. 'What do you mean by that? If you mean the servants, they aren't much good, you know. They're two a penny here, everyone has them, it doesn't mean anything. It's not like having servants in England. When I think of my household there . . . well. They're not the same out here, not the same at all.'

She was puzzled by his change of mood, of direction. 'Actually, I meant medically, are the doctors good?'

'Not bad,' he said, 'not as good as English doctors, but they're cheap, of course.'

'Ah.'

'So why the hell are you here?' he said suddenly. 'Eh? Tell me that, why are you here?'

'Well, I—that is, I wanted—'

'Wanted what? More? I hope you don't think you can get any more out of me,' he said, sitting back, looking at her with an expression of odd bitterness on his face, 'because there isn't any. It's all gone. As you see.'

'I don't know what you mean,' she said, 'of course I don't want any more. Of anything.'

'Then what the hell are you doing here?' He put his cup down, leant forward, his expression harsh. 'Have you come to check up on me, to make sure

690

I'm well and truly done for, eh? Is that what this is about?'

'No. No of course not.' Was this normal anger, justifiable hostility? Or was this some kind of paranoia, a dementia?

'Did Moreton send you? Did he tell you to come and try again? Is that it? I bet he did, I bet this is what it's about.'

'No, Rollo, of course he didn't. He has no idea I'm here. And I've no idea what you're talking about. Please calm down. Please.'

He did then, he seemed to relax; he lay back in his chair, reached for a cigarette and lit it. His hand shook slightly. He reached up to swat another fly, one that was buzzing round his head. His hair had become very thin, she noticed; it had been thick in the old days, thick and very wavy.

She smiled at him awkwardly. 'Those children looked very sweet,' she said, by way of finding some safe, neutral ground.

'What children?' His eyes were angry again: not so safe, then.

'The children I saw here this morning. Three of them. Are they the servants' children?'

'Yes. Yes, that's right.' He seemed to have seized on the explanation gratefully. 'Yes, servants' children. They cost me nothing. Nothing at all.'

'No, of course not.' The same fierce obsession with money, with a need to impress her with his penury; it seemed bizarre.

'Well,' he said finally, 'what does bring you here, then?'

His voice was heavy, exhausted suddenly. He clapped his hands, the manservant, Mehdi came in; he spoke to him in rapid French. Mehdi left the room, came back with a tray of drink: brandy, whisky, soda, glasses.

'May I offer you a drink?'

'No, thank you.'

'Oh, come along,' he said impatiently, 'I have to drink alone most of the time. You could do that for me at least. Come along, Cassia, have a drink.'

She had once interviewed a seriously ill mental patient; she had found the mood swings, the sudden lurches into reason and then away from it again, and her need to accommodate them, to go along with them even, highly disorientating. She remembered and recognised that disorientation beginning in her now. She must be careful. 'Yes, all right, then. Thank you. I'll have a brandy.'

'A good choice, I will have the same. Soda? No, it wrecks a good brandy, much better on its own.'

He poured the brandies, very large ones, raised his glass to her. His hands shook, she noticed, wondered if he had Parkinson's disease as well as his other problems. He was clearly a very sick man. 'To you. You were always pretty,' he said suddenly, 'now you are beautiful. She would have been proud of you.'

'Thank you,' she said carefully. 'You mean Leonora?'

'I do mean Leonora. Yes. Perhaps we should drink to her. A little late but . . . to Leonora.'

'Leonora.' She drank, obediently.

'You still haven't told me why you're here.'

'I wanted to see you,' she said.

'I am flattered. It's a very long journey, however did you come?'

'I flew. With Air France. To Casablanca.'

'Very enterprising. And Moreton isn't with you?

692

Didn't send you?'

'No. No, really he didn't.'

'I hope not. Well, then. Tell me what you want.'

She decided to be at least partly honest. 'I have come here to clear up a mystery,' she said. 'I can't get the truth from anyone else.'

'A mystery?'

'Yes. About—well, about Leonora's circumstances, when she died.'

'When Leonora died she had a great deal of money,' said Rollo Graham, 'as you know. A great deal of money.'

'Yes, I do know. Which she then left to me.'

'Of course. Very neat. First she had it, and then you had it.'

'Yes,' she said, 'yes, that's right.'

'Not really,' he said, and his face was ugly again suddenly, 'not really right at all.'

'I'm sorry, I—'

'Oh, it doesn't matter. Look, I'm getting rather tired of this. Tell me what you want to know and then I must ask you to leave.'

He seemed to be growing hostile again.

She took a deep breath. 'What I want to know is—where the money came from. That Leonora left me.'

'Why do you want to know that?' he said.

'I want to know because I—I'm afraid it can't have come from her.'

'Oh, come along!' He was smiling suddenly, seemed almost amused. 'Of course it did. It was her money, wasn't it? You must have seen the papers.'

'Yes, but—'

'But what? I am finding this rather interesting, getting your view of events.'

693

'You see, I found out she was living in rather bad circumstances a year, eighteen months before she died. She was very hard up, and ill, of course, so how could she suddenly be so rich?'

'Yes, that is a mystery, isn't it?' he said, and smiled at her suddenly, a cunning, rather ugly smile. 'I can see you would find that intriguing. Well, who do you think it might have come from?'

'I don't know, you see. I didn't think it could have come from you . . .'

'Oh, indeed? And why not?'

'I thought that you were—well, not in possession of that sort of money. By then.'

'I see. And how do you know that?'

'I just heard some rumours.'

'Oh, you did? Dear me, what a lot of detective work you have been doing, Cassia, to be sure. I wish you would drink that brandy, isn't it good enough for you? That's better. Now tell me, where did you hear these rumours? In London, was it? Have they been talking about me there? Who did you talk to, who did you track down? And did anyone help you, I wonder, in this quest?'

'No,' she said firmly, 'nobody helped me. It was a chance meeting with Miss Monkton, she seemed to know—'

'Miss Monkton!' he said, sitting back and smiling again. 'Poor old Monk. With her wispy hair and her bad breath. What a dance Leonora led her. Leonora and I.' He stopped smiling, his face darkened again. 'How the hell did she know what money I had and hadn't got, eh? Was she spying on me too?'

'Rollo, neither of us has been spying on you. It was just that she had found Leonora living

694

somewhere rather wretched, and Leonora told her.'

'Told her what?' he said, his voice suddenly loud. 'What did she tell her? Eh?' He reached forward, grabbed Cassia's wrist; his face was very close to hers. His breath was foul, hideous.

She tried to smile at him, not to turn her head away. 'Just that you'd lost a lot of your money,' she said steadily.

'And nothing else?'

'No. Nothing else. Really.'

He sat back, seemed to relax. 'Oh, I see. Just that. Well, she was quite right. I had. A great deal. Leonora helped me lose it, what's more. She had a great talent for that: losing money. I hadn't realised quite how much.'

'And so I just didn't understand how Leonora could have had so much money to leave to me. I couldn't see where it might have come from.'

'But you have an idea, don't you?' he said, his eyes glittering. 'I can see you have an idea. Do you want to tell me what it is?'

'No,' she said, oddly frightened now. 'No, really, I don't have an idea. That's why I'm here. I thought you might know.'

'Didn't you see the document?' he said, releasing her suddenly. 'The deed of settlement?'

'Yes, I did, but—'

'Well, then. You do know. It came from me.'

'But did it? Did it really?'

'Well, if not from me, then whom?' he said impatiently. 'Who else could it have come from?'

She was silent.

'Come along, Cassia. Who, in your clearly crazed imagination, could have, would have handed over

695

half a million pounds to Leonora, if it wasn't me? Who, who, who?' His face was thrust into hers now, he was breathing heavily. She felt trapped, terrified. 'Cassia, who do you think that money came from?' He raised his hand, and she thought he was going to hit her.

She decided to tell him: things could hardly get worse. 'I thought perhaps from Harry—Harry Moreton.'

'Harry Moreton! Dear sweet Jesus. That's very rich. Very rich indeed.'

He released her, sat back in his chair and started to laugh. He laughed for so long she was alarmed. It was hysterical laughter, totally uncontrollable, crazy, his face growing red, and then, finally, it turned to coughing, ugly coughing, then choking, a horrible fighting for breath. She watched him in alarm, then stood up, bent his body forward, banged him hard on the back. The coughing slowly eased; she poured him some water, held it to his lips.

'Thank you,' he said finally, sitting back, wiping the tears from his eyes. 'What a fine doctor you are. There was much talk of you and your medicine, I seem to remember.'

'Really?' she said.

'Yes. Leonora was very proud of you. And sad that you had not pursued your career.'

'Was she? I'm surprised, I always thought she found it a little puzzling. That I should want to do it.'

'Oh, no. It saddened her. Anyway, let us return to your idea. Your strange idea. No, my dear Cassia, the money did not come from Harry Moreton. Most unfortunately. It came from me.

696

That's why I'm living here in this stinking, flyblown hellhole of a place, far from home, from my friends; that's why I can't come home, why I have no home any more; that's why I'm going to die out here—because the money came from me. Not Harry Moreton, Cassia, although—'

He stopped, looked at her with such absolute hatred that she shivered. He noticed and smiled. 'You're not frightened, are you? Yes, I think you are. Good. I quite like the thought that you are frightened. I've been very frightened, quite often, out here.'

'I'm sorry,' she said, 'but I still don't understand—'

'Oh, for God's sake,' he said, 'just get out, will you? Leave me alone. You'd better ask your friend Harry Moreton if you want to know any more. He can tell you all about it. Although he promised not to, promised not to tell anyone. They both did.'

'Both?'

'Yes, the two of them. Thick as thieves, they were, those two. A very appropriate expression that, under the circumstances. Don't you think?'

'I don't know.'

'I often wondered about them, didn't you?'

'Wondered what?'

'Oh, come along. You can't be that naive. If they were lovers. What do you think, eh? It makes a sort of sense, doesn't it? What do you think, Cassia? I never could decide.'

She stood up then, lost in a new panic, literally shocked at the idea, felt herself, despite the shock, examining it. Was it possible, was it? It had never, in her wildest imaginings, even occurred to her: the implications were hideous.

697

'I really have no idea,' she said finally.

'Oh, I have an idea,' he said. 'It seems to me not impossible. Quite neat, as a matter of fact. Think about it. His devotion was very intense: Too intense to be filial, I would have thought.'

She thought of Harry, caring for Leonora in her last days, paying for her medical care, carrying her up to her apartment, out into the Trocadero Gardens, sitting with her as she died, and felt very sick. Then she steadied. She would have known; surely she would have known.

'I'm sure you're wrong,' she said, 'and now I must go. I'm sorry to have taken up so much of your time.'

'No,' he said, 'sit down again, Cassia, you haven't finished your drink.'

'I don't want it,' she said, 'thank you. I haven't been very well today.'

'Really? I'm so sorry to hear that. The heat, I expect, and the strange food. Would you like to lie down for a while? Should I call my doctor perhaps, ask him to see you? Here, let me call Mehdi . . .' He was suddenly his old charming self, almost the Rollo she remembered; again, as he swung into sanity, she felt herself descending into madness.

'No,' she said, 'no, really, I'd rather go back to the hotel.'

'Do you have a taxi waiting? You won't get one here, you know, they don't come passing by.'

'Well, no. Perhaps you could call me one.'

'Yes, of course. Or I could send you in my car. It's not much, I'm afraid, not what you would have expected me to have once. Has Moreton kept all those cars of his? The Bugatti? Does he race that still?'

698

'Yes. Yes, I believe so.'

'Well,' he said, 'I suppose he would. He would have everything still. His houses, his paintings, his cars. Very nice for him. I raced my cars, you know. I had a very fine Alfa Romeo. I was very successful.'

'Yes, I remember. I remember that day at Brooklands—'

'When I beat Moreton. Yes, that was a good day. I enjoyed that. Well, he's beaten me now. Well and truly.'

She longed to ask him what he meant, was too afraid. 'I'm sorry. Anyway, if you could ask your servant to get a taxi for me perhaps . . .'

'Yes, yes, I will.' Relief flooded her for a moment. Then he said, 'But I'd like you to stay for a while. Until you feel better. Have a meal with me, please.'

'No, Rollo, really, I—'

'Now come along,' he said, 'I think you owe me a little pleasure. When I have given you so much. Don't you? I have little enough these days.'

He went over to the door, called through it; Mehdi appeared, and Rollo spoke to him in Arabic. Mehdi bowed, backed away, and Rollo closed the door, stood against it, barring her way.

'I'm glad I had this idea,' he said. 'I think we can have a very nice evening together. I apologise for my earlier inhospitality. Now let us begin with another drink. More brandy? Cassia, do sit down, try to relax. I want you to enjoy yourself, I really do.'

CHAPTER THIRTY-EIGHT

Cecily had slightly reluctantly accepted a last minute invitation to supper with Venetia Hardwicke. She had been reluctant on two counts: first, that she was still upset about Justin's refusal of her own invitation, and second, she really didn't feel she could cope with a dinner party, but Venetia had persisted, and in the end it seemed churlish to continue to refuse.

In the event, it was a very pleasant evening: a simple supper, as Venetia had promised, in the Hardwickes' very pretty dining room in their very pretty house in Keat's Grove, Hampstead. Everyone was so nice to her, so kind, so clearly and genuinely pleased to have her with them; and to her great surprise and pleasure, she found herself chatting quite easily to them all. So high were her spirits that by the end of the evening she felt quite optimistic about Justin again, able to tell herself that he really was extremely busy, and he had after all proposed a meeting the following week. She really couldn't believe he had been just pretending to like her all this time.

By the time she took her leave of the Hardwickes she was extremely happy, and also rather drunk. She became a little sleepy as the car drove southwards, and woke with a start to hear Preston hooting loudly at something.

'Sorry, madam,' he said, 'two young gentlemen who seemed to feel the middle of the road was the best place to walk. Nearly home, madam.'

'That's all right, Preston, where are we?'

'Just coming into Lowndes Square, madam,' said Preston, and looking out of the window, as they drew level with the Moretons' house, she saw the door open and Justin coming out of it: he turned and kissed Edwina who had followed him on to the doorstep.

Had she not had such a good evening, had she not had, indeed, quite so much to drink, Cecily might have acted quite differently; in the event, outrage and a lack of self-consciousness filled her in equal measure and she told Preston to stop and got out of the car.

Justin and Edwina watched her in a frozen fascination as she stalked across the pavement and stared up at them.

'I do hope you've both had a nice evening,' she said. 'I wasn't aware you had a darkroom in your house, Edwina. Next time you prefer someone else's company to mine, Justin, I'd be grateful if you could be honest with me. I'm neither half-witted nor so emotionally broken that I can't cope with the truth. And in any case I can't imagine why you thought I'd mind so much. I suppose you thought I'd have another nervous breakdown. You flatter yourself, you really do. Goodnight.' With that, she turned and went back to the car.

Preston opened the door for her and then, clearly wishing to enter into the spirit of things, closed it again with something of a flourish and drove away with a rather firm piece of acceleration.

'My God,' said Justin, gazing after them, 'I had no idea she had so much style.'

*   *   *

Harry Moreton woke up in his room at the Mamounia to find one of the hotel staff and a uniformed nurse looking at him rather anxiously. He looked at his watch, which said nine thirty, and sat up suddenly, swinging his legs over the edge of the bed. Pain hit him ferociously, followed by nausea.

The nurse pushed him firmly back on to his pillows. 'Lie still, please,' she said, 'I must call the doctor.'

'The doctor! For God's sake, I'm not ill.'

'You are concussed,' she said, 'and I have instructions to call the doctor when you wake.' She moved over to the house phone, spoke to the operator rapidly in French.

'Concussed!' said Harry, glaring up at her. 'Of course I'm not concussed. I just dropped off to sleep for a moment. I've flown from England, I'm extremely tired. Now I have to go—'

'Monsieur Moreton, you had a very bad blow on the head, and although you were not unconscious for very long, you have been sleeping on and off for several hours.'

'Of course I haven't. I drifted off briefly, that's all. I do seem to remember some darnfool doctor at the hospital insisting on an X-ray, which was perfectly all right, apparently. I'm sorry, but I really do have to go.'

'Monsieur Moreton, please! The doctor will be here shortly.'

'I can't wait for any doctor. What I have to do is very urgent. Please let me go.'

The nurse stood back rather helplessly. Harry stood up cautiously, pushed his feet into his shoes, reached for his jacket—and then rushed for the bathroom. He emerged feeling very shaky and slightly foolish.

The doctor had just entered his room. 'Filthy head,' said Harry to him conversationally, 'but I feel much better now.'

'Good,' said the doctor, 'that is good. Please lie down again.'

'I can't,' said Harry, hearing the desperation in his own voice, 'I really can't, I have to be somewhere. Now, at once.'

'Monsieur Moreton, if you tell me what is the problem, I will try to help, but you must remain quite still and quiet for twenty-four hours.'

'Oh, don't be absurd,' said Harry. 'While I'm remaining still and quiet, my—' he hesitated, then said firmly, 'a woman is in serious danger. Now will somebody please help me out of this place.'

*   *   *

Cassia started to cry. She knew there was no point in it, that it would probably make things worse, but she couldn't ever remember feeling so alone: even in the moments of greatest crisis in her life, such as when her mother had died or when she had finally sent Harry away, or she had made the decision to give up her medical career, there had always been someone there, even if they didn't properly understand. Now there was no one: no one at all.

It was ridiculous, too, she told herself, to be quite so distraught: she was only lost. Only lost: in a strange and seemingly dangerous country, where she did not speak the language, where nobody knew her, and she knew nobody, where she could not ask directions or even find out where she was.

And worst of all, she had, of necessity, left her handbag behind at Rollo Gresham's house and had no money.

She took a deep breath, fighting down the tears and the panic, and tried to think what to do. She had been walking for at least two hours, and she seemed far from anywhere, wandering along a road which clearly was heading out of the city, rather than into it, cold now and utterly exhausted. And the worst thing was that if a car, or indeed a pedestrian, came in sight, she simply felt terrified, and tried to hide, either in a gate or doorway, or even behind a tree or a shrub.

She had, at one point, been hopeful that she had found the direction at least of the train station, having heard a train starting up not so very far away, but had clearly taken a wrong turn after that, for the sound had never come near again.

She should simply turn round and retrace her steps, but she had done that several times already, and got nowhere: no road seemed to run straight, they all curved confusingly about, leading back on themselves. Or so it seemed in the dark and the cold.

Escape had been simple by comparison: she had sat there, admirably calm, she thought, drinking with Rollo Gresham, watching him top up his own glass, sipping at her own with minuscule sips. He was talking about the old days, in the grandiose terms that alternated with the paranoia, talking of grand social connections with the highest in the land, telling her how a knighthood had been on the cards. She had sat listening, responding politely, and had finally asked if she might go to the lavatory. He had told Mehdi to show her the way, and she had followed him, carefully noting the location of the front door.

She had used the lavatory, flushed it, and then started running taps; leaving them running, she had come cautiously out. There was nobody outside; she had walked, rather than run, to the hallway and then simply carried on walking out of the front door.

The gardener was still at work although dusk was falling—that was a dangerous moment—but she smiled at him cheerily, waved even, and walked quite steadily to the gate and then out into the street. And then she had run, run and run until she was absolutely exhausted, dreading every moment to hear shouts, feet running after her—but they did not come.

A crowd of people were leaving the Marjorelle Gardens. She plunged into their midst, where she was camouflaged, but they then all climbed into a fleet of taxis and she was left alone and exposed once more.

*　　　*　　　*

Osman Jamal was very tired. It had been a very long day, and the American ladies he had taken to Asni that afternoon had been both ungracious and ungrateful. Now he was taking a couple back to the Mamounia after a very long wait for them and their guide outside the Medina where they had dined at the Yacout restaurant. All he wanted to do was go to bed; and indeed that was what he planned to do, but as he got back into his car, having said goodnight to the couple and expressed enormous gratitude for a very modest tip, one of the porters

705

told him that the English lady he had driven up to the Ville Nouvelle that morning had failed to return and that an English gentleman who had arrived was very concerned about her.

Jamal enquired why it was not possible for the Englishman to be out looking for her, and was told that he was confined to his room on medical orders, having been involved in a car accident that afternoon. Someone from the hotel had been sent to an address the Englishman had given, but she had not been there. A small party had been sent out looking for her; there was even talk of involving the police.

Jamal was concerned; the English lady had been charming and generous and unusually polite to him. He felt it his duty to go and look for her himself; he would not be able to sleep if he did not. He knew what she looked like at least, which most of the rescue party would not.

He swung his car out of the Mamounia courtyard and in the direction of the avenue d'El-Jedida.

*   *   *

Harry Moreton had phoned Rollo Gresham's house; had spoken to a servant, had been told that his visitor had left a couple of hours earlier. Monsieur Rollo was indisposed, the doctor had been sent for and he was under sedation: there was no question of him being disturbed. But the lady had been perfectly safe and well when she left, although she had left her handbag behind; if Monsieur Harry cared to come and collect it, he was very welcome, or it would be brought to the

706

hotel in the morning. For some reason, that above anything else convinced Harry that he was speaking the truth. But it didn't find Cassia for him.

*   *   *

Cassia was shivering violently with the cold when she heard footsteps behind her. She hastened her own just a little: and heard them hasten also. She slowed down: so did they. Otherwise the street—wide, empty, menacing, with nowhere to hide—was deserted. She felt fright rise in her throat, a physical presence, like bile.

The footsteps behind her were getting nearer.

She looked over her shoulder, saw a man in white djellaba and turban only about thirty yards behind her, and began to run. At first he continued to walk; then as she began to feel safe, to tell herself he was actually only walking home himself, he increased his own pace. She ran faster: so did he. She could hear him now, hear his breathing, then his voice, speaking incomprehensibly to her.

She turned to face him; said, stupidly in English, please leave me alone, and he grinned, the awful half-toothless grin of Morocco, and moved nearer still. She turned her head away, began to run again.

He followed her, lightly, easily, in his soft shoes; she, in her high-heeled English ones, was helpless. She bent down to take them off, and as she bent, she felt a hand on her back, below her waist. She screamed, turned, lashed out at him with her shoes, caught him in the face with them, and began to run again.

He caught her in moments, grabbed her, grabbed her wrists, swearing at her, grinning at the same time; there were no streetlights, but the moon was full and the white walls of the street reflected it. His eyes were glittering, under the turban, his face etched with deep lines, he could have been any age. He certainly wasn't old and he certainly was strong.

Cassia did the only thing left to her: she raised her knee swiftly and kneed him in the crotch. He cried out with pain and bent over, releasing her, and she was able to run then, faster than she had ever thought possible: and then, dear God, looking over her shoulder, she saw another man coming along, faster than her assailant even, overtaking him. There were two of them now, how could she survive this? Why had she ever come to this hideous, awful place, she would be raped, tortured, mutilated, murdered.

She turned to face this new attacker, raised her hands to ward him off, sank on to her heels, crying, whimpering with fear. And heard his voice, familiar, gentle, wonderfully kind saying, 'Madame should have let me wait. Come with me now. Come with me, Madame is safe.'

*　　　*　　　*

In the car Jamal had blankets, a bottle of water, a flask of tea; he wrapped her up tenderly, drove quickly in the direction of the Mamounia.

'However did you find me?' she asked.

Jamal shrugged. 'I want to find you,' he said simply, as if that explained everything. 'I will drive until I find you. Many many people worried.'

In that moment, her entire perception of Morocco changed.

708

They pulled in to the courtyard of the hotel to find a reception committee; she looked up to see not only the familiar pair of porters flanking the door, but behind them, pushing past them now, the manager, and following him, confusingly, a nurse in a rather dated uniform, and behind her again, a large, looming, slightly unsteady figure.

'How could you have been so abysmally, so criminally stupid?' said Harry Moreton's voice, and she looked at him and did not really find it in the least peculiar that he was there, it seemed no more or less surprising than anything else that had happened to her in the last few days, and everything seemed to polarise in that moment, and the entire reason she had come was focused in him, in what he might and might not have done, and because one of those things had become the most important, the most crucially important of all, and heedless of all the other people standing there, the staff and the uniformed nurse and a couple of curious guests: 'Harry, were you and Leonora lovers?' she said.

She did not hear his answer: he had collapsed with a groan on to the steps, his head in his arms.

*　　　*　　　*

'Did Gresham tell you that?' he said a lot later, when, distracted from her own shock, she had settled him into bed, had assured the nurse, who at the doctor's suggestion had taken the precaution of giving Harry a sedative, that she would personally see he stayed there, had drunk several cups of strong tea herself and wolfed down a large club sandwich and a bowl of exquisitely crisp, salty *frites*.

709

She found herself suddenly feeling rather cheerful and pleased with herself.

'He suggested it.'

'And what did you think of the suggestion?' he said, glaring at her.

'I didn't know. It seemed . . . possible. Suddenly. I'd never thought of it before.'

'Well, thank God for that at least. No, of course I wasn't her lover. What the hell do you think I am, that I'd behave like that?'

'I don't know what you are,' she said wearily, 'that's the whole point. I don't understand you, you won't tell me things.'

'What things? What won't I tell you?'

'You know perfectly well,' she said. 'You won't tell me about the money. All along, you've ducked my questions, laid false trails, told me half-truths—'

'Would you like to give me an example of these false trails, these ducked questions, that you speak of so graphically?'

'You told me you didn't rescue Leonora. From that awful place.'

He stared at her. 'I didn't.'

'No, but your secretary Margot Murray did. Didn't she, Harry?'

'All right. She did. You didn't ask me who rescued her, you simply asked me if I did. I didn't.'

'But you told her to. You sent her.'

'This is,' he said, turning fretfully away from her, 'a ridiculous conversation.'

'I quite agree.' She longed suddenly to hit him; the frustration was so awful, so strong.

'What do you really want?' he said suddenly.

'The truth. About the money.'

'Ah,' he said, 'that.' His eyes closed, then opened. 'And did you get that? The truth? From Gresham?'

'No, well, not all of it. He's a little mad, I think.'

'Cassia, he's absolutely mad.'

'No, not absolutely,' she said slowly, 'and I . . . Harry, you look terrible, are you all right?'

'No, I'm bloody well not all right,' he said. 'My head hurts like hell and I think I'm going to be sick again. And this inquisition of yours isn't helping.'

'Harry, it's hardly an inquisition.'

'It seems like it to me.' There was a pause, then he said, 'Oh, Christ. Help me to the bathroom would you, Cassia?'

Five minutes later, back in his bed, he was asleep. She looked at him and sighed. She clearly wasn't going to learn very much from him for several hours yet.

*　　　*　　　*

Cecily woke up early on Sunday morning, feeling dreadful. Her head ached, she felt sick and, worst of all, she was experiencing considerable humiliation and remorse. How could she have done that, made a scene in the street, shouting at Edwina and Justin? It was appalling. Whatever must they have thought of her, what must Justin particularly have thought of her? And to think that she had been sorry for Edwina, concerned about her husband's infidelity. That was a joke. Justin was clearly having an affair with Edwina. And all this time, all this time she had thought he liked her, found her attractive, possibly even might love her. Of course he and Edwina were far more suited to one another. No doubt they had been laughing about her, saying how dreary she was . . .

* * *

Justin woke up feeling also very wretched. The thought of the pain he had inflicted upon Cecily, the humiliation, hurt him terribly. How could he have been so stupid? She would probably never speak to him again now, certainly not wish to be with him. He had as little chance of re-establishing their relationship as—well, as of being asked to take the cover photograph of *Style*, an ambition so long held he sometimes felt he had been born with it. The very least he could do was say sorry.

Justin was nothing if not brave. He would try, he would go round, take her some flowers, and if she wouldn't see him, then he could leave them for her. And if she did agree to see him, and then proceeded to berate him, he would deserve it. And he might even get a chance to explain. The only thing was, where could he get flowers on a Sunday?

What else could he take her, then? What present was even remotely suitable? Champagne perhaps? He had a bottle of very nice champagne, Veuve Cliquot, that Francis Stevenson-Cook had sent him recently to say thank you for some photographs he had taken at incredibly short notice, of a set of evening dresses on the stage at the Royal Opera House against the set of *La Bohème*. He could take that to Cecily. Of course it wouldn't mean that much to her, but it would be a great deal better than nothing.

He spent over an hour writing a two-line note to accompany it, and then decided he would take it immediately before his courage failed him.

Just as he was leaving his telephone rang: it was Aurora Le Page.

'Justin, darling, sorry to bother you on a Sunday, but I thought you might like to know, I've just left Francis, and he and I both agree that one of these pictures at the Opera House would make a perfect cover . . . Hallo? Justin, are you still there?'

'Oh, yes,' said Justin, 'I'm still here, darling Miss Le Page, and I do like to know. I like it very much, in fact I can't believe it. Thank you very very much. And I'd like to tell you, I do see it as a most wonderful omen. Wonderful.'

'Most wonderful what?' said Aurora Le Page, but he had gone. She put the phone down and sat shaking her head at it. Photographers became more absurd every day.

*   *   *

Cecily stood in her bedroom, struggling to do up a skirt, with hooks which proved themselves just slightly unequal to the task. The skirt, bought only a few weeks earlier, was a little tight for her. All the new things she had bought were quite tight, and soon she would be back in her old clothes; she would be fat again, fat and matronly. She looked at herself in the full-length mirror, standing there in her chemise: there was no doubt about it, the old Cecily was coming back, the Cecily with the full breasts and the rounded hips and the dimpled thighs; her brief spell as a sleek, chic creature was over for ever.

It wasn't fair, she didn't eat that much and Edwina wolfed down whatever she wanted and remained sliver-thin. No wonder Justin preferred her, she thought wretchedly.

She tugged again at the hooks, and one of them bent, and the fabric next to it ripped slightly. She pulled it off and threw it across the room, near to tears. She felt absurdly, disproportionately miserable at the sight of it lying there, useless, hardly worn, bought only a month ago.

Dimly, she heard a taxi pull up in the street below, heard the bell ring, and then she heard Fanny's voice suddenly, ringing out, laughing, heard her saying, 'Just a minute,' heard her footsteps pounding on the stairs and along to her room, then the door opened and Fanny said, 'Mama, whatever are you doing? You look ever so funny.'

Cecily burst into tears; loud, noisy tears, and then was aware of Fanny looking at her in terror, backing away, her eyes huge, realised just a fraction of a second too late why, that she thought she was having another breakdown, rushed after Fanny as she ran hysterically downstairs, calling, 'Come, quickly, come to Mama's room, quickly,' and she stood there, shocked at what she had done to Fanny, not just then but in the past; and she cried harder, and went back into her room: and so Justin found her, standing flushed, huge eyed, tear streaked, her hair dishevelled, her skirt still hurled into the corner.

He stopped absolutely still in the doorway, gazing at her, his eyes moving over her, first concerned, then tender, and then there was something else in his eyes, something she was largely unfamiliar with, but recognised none the less as wonderfully, unbelievably welcome, recognised desire.

He turned to Fanny who was standing behind him breathing heavily, her small face ashen, and said, 'Fanny, she's fine, don't worry, she's absolutely fine, aren't you, Cecily?'

'Yes,' she said, 'yes, of course I am. I just pricked my finger badly on a pin in my skirt, it hurt me a lot,' and watched Fanny's face grow relieved, relax and then smile.

Justin said, 'I expect she'd like a cup of tea, though, and some biscuits, perhaps. Do you think you could go and ask Cook for that?'

And when Fanny had safely gone, running down the steps, lightly now, shouting happily to her sister that everything was all right, Justin moved forward into Cecily's room and pushed the door shut behind him, still staring at her, his eyes brilliant, and stood in front of her, staring at her as if he had never seen her before, and then he put out his hands and took her face in them, and began to kiss her, really kiss her, kiss her mouth, so that she felt invaded, in every inch of her body, with a flooding warmth and a sweet, curiously uncomfortable pleasure, kissed her on and on, over and over again, and then moved his hands down, very slowly, down her throat, over her breasts, feeling them, stroking them, caressing them, and bent his head and kissed them too.

'You are beautiful,' he said finally, standing up again, standing away from her, smiling into her eyes, 'very, very beautiful. And I love you.'

*   *   *

'I really don't know that we're in the best place for

715

this interview,' said Harry Moreton. 'It's much too pleasant.'

They were sitting on the terrace at the back of the hotel, under one of the striped umbrellas, drinking coffee which he professed strong enough even for his taste.

'It seems a very good place to me,' said Cassia, 'and why shouldn't it be pleasant? And anyway, I know what you're thinking: that you can postpone it yet again, and then again. I won't have it, Harry, I really won't.'

He sighed, leant his head back. Cassia looked at him sharply.

'I don't think you ought to drink that coffee,' she said. 'It's not good for you when you've been concussed.'

'Oh, for God's sake,' he said, 'stop nannying me. It's superb coffee and I shall drink what I like.'

'No doubt you will,' she said, and decided he was perfectly well enough. 'Now please, Harry, please tell me everything. Otherwise I shall go back to London and you will never see me again.'

'Very well,' he said, with a sigh, clearly resigning himself, 'I will tell you. Where shall I begin?'

'At the beginning. It seems a sensible place.'

'All right. Well, Leonora finally contacted me, that spring, shortly after Miss Monkton found her. She was too sick, too wretched to struggle on any longer.'

'So you hadn't been to see her that whole year, after she left the Avenue Foch?'

'Once or twice. I had no idea she was ill, and when I did go to Paris, she insisted on meeting me in restaurants. You know what she was like, a superb actress, she was always very gay, always full of stories about her life, what a wonderful time she was having. I could see she was thin, pale, but when I asked her if she was all right, she told me that of course she was, that when women reached a certain age they became less . . . robust. And I saw her in London, once, briefly, in the late autumn, she was staying at the Basil Street Hotel, she seemed pretty well.'

'That must have been when she came over to pawn what was left of her jewellery.'

'Yes, I suppose so. Anyway, when she did finally ask for help, I was in America. Margot cabled me, I sent her over to Paris, told her to sort things out, find an apartment for Leonora, and went to see her on the way back. It was pretty awful. What she'd been through. I felt very ashamed of myself.'

'As did I. Still do. But, Harry, what—what was it, what had happened?'

'Well . . .' He hesitated, sighed, then said, 'She had syphilis.'

'Syphilis! Oh my God.'

'Yes. She'd had it for three, four years, apparently. She had recurrent fevers, terrible joint pains, and the tissue destruction had begun.'

'Oh, Harry. So it wasn't cancer at all?'

'Oh yes, she had that too. Poor Leonora. Uterine cancer, spreading very rapidly.'

'Oh dear,' said Cassia. She looked down, fighting tears, filled with horror at what Leonora had endured.

Harry covered her hand with his. 'You all right?'

'Yes, I'm all right.' She felt angry suddenly, angry and ashamed. 'Why shouldn't I be? I've always been all right, we all have, and all the time poor Leonora was going through this . . .'

717

'Yes, I know. Anyway, she had contracted it from Gresham—who knew he had it and didn't tell her.'

'Oh God.'

'Yes, he's a charming fellow.'

She thought of him, as he had been the day before; it all made sense suddenly: the dementia a very specific form with syphilis, the delusions of grandeur, the tremors that she had thought might be Parkinson's, the skin ulcers, the signs of heart failure.

'Anyway, she found out when she first developed the symptoms herself. Then she challenged him and he told her. He'd got it out here.'

'But why did he come out here in the first place? I don't understand.'

Harry hesitated, then he said, 'He's a paedophile, Cassia. He likes little children. They cater for this sort of thing out here . . .'

'Oh, Harry. I can't bear this.' She thought of those children, the ones she had seen yesterday, so tiny, so pretty, being brought to the house for—

She tried to focus on the mountains, the palm trees, while her brain adjusted to this horror. A fly settled on her plate, got to work on the crumbs of her croissant; she looked at it, as it went about its disease-spreading task, and thought it seemed to symbolise everything she was hearing, this ugly, evil story. 'Go on,' she said.

'He told her then. She challenged him about the syphilis, and he told her—not about the children— he presented it as a bad-luck story, he was very good at that. She was horrified, of course, but she felt she had no choice but to stay: and she was still fond of him, in her own way.'

'Yes. Yes, I think she was.'

'It didn't emerge about the children until she opened a letter of his one day, by mistake, from a friend out here, and discovered what had been going on. She told him she was leaving, and he told her that she would get nothing from him if she did. He was losing money hand over fist anyway; and she was helping.

'Anyway, she left, moved out, sold what jewellery and so on she had. She was all right for a bit, then she got through that money, the illness began to resurface, and the cancer was making itself felt and—well, you know the rest.'

'No, Harry. I don't. And why on earth didn't she tell us?'

'Cassia, think. She'd run away from home, from her husband, to live with a man who turned out to be a sexual criminal. One minute she was ensconced in millionaires' row, the next in a hovel, suffering from a sexually transmitted disease. She had committed an unutterable, an unspeakable folly: would *you* admit to that?'

She was silent.

'Anyway, I went to see her, as soon as I got back, and finally she told me. I think I would have killed Gresham, if he'd walked in that first week. As it turned out, I think he's suffered more. I hope so.'

'What did you do?' Fear, cold and clammy, was heaving into her stomach.

'I tracked him down. Got him to Paris. I told him I knew about his filthy predilections, and what he'd done to Leonora, that I'd make sure everyone in England, in the world, knew about them. And he was terrified. It would have meant disgrace, imprisonment. And Leonora didn't want it. She didn't want the disgrace, and I'm afraid she still cared about him.'

'So what happened then?'

'He came slobbering in, said he'd do anything at all to make it up to Leonora, give her money, set her up in style again, he said he hadn't got a lot left, but he'd sell his house in England, give her the money from that, his house in France, anything. I just sat there listening to him, watching him sweating and shaking, and I realised it would hurt him more than anything, to do that.'

'Not as much as the disgrace, if people had known.'

'Perhaps not, but that would have hurt Leonora. It terrified her to think of people laughing at her, of her name dragged through every sort of dirt, even after she'd died. She made me promise never to tell, and I did promise. I never told anyone at all—except Benedict, of course. He had to know. It seemed important to me. Perhaps it was wrong of me, perhaps I should have had him arrested.'

'It would have saved some children, at least,' she said soberly.

'I know—and it tortures me, that. Of course he promised it would never happen again, and I swore that if it did I would see him in jail. I knew in my heart that I couldn't be sure, but . . . I don't break my promises, Cassia. I really don't.'

'Harry, I saw some children at the house yesterday.'

'Christ, did you?'

'Yes, I did. Something has to be done, Harry. I can't bear to think of that going on and on, with him—'

'It would be very difficult,' he said. 'They see things differently here, you know. The Pasha

720

himself delivers native children to his guests, as gifts, should they so desire. Along with hashish, opium, diamonds . . . Life is cheap.'

'That's no reason not to try! Anyway, go on.'

'So I just said, fine, but I wanted that money, all of it, for Leonora, and that I wasn't going to forget about it. I made him put the houses on the market, I made him keep me informed of progress—I made him sweat,' he said, looking at her with an expression of great self-satisfaction on his face.

'Yes, I see,' she said again, 'but Leonora was dying, you must have known she was dying.'

'She was dying. But nobody realised how quickly she would go. In the end it was very quick. It was partly the syphilis, it weakened her heart. But that wasn't the point. I wanted to get the money away from him: he deserved it, deserved to be brought down as low as he had brought her.'

'And then what happened? I mean, about the money. And me.' The last word came out very quietly.

'You.' He smiled at her. 'Well, that was the happy bit. For her. She sat there one night, and started crying—she was very frightened of dying, you know—and I was trying to comfort her. She said what should she do with all the money, having got it, how useless it was, in fact, that she hadn't really wanted it, didn't see the point. And I said there must be something useful she could do with it. We didn't have to think very long.'

'You thought of me.'

'Yes.' He smiled at her again, the same complacent, self-satisfied smile. 'We thought of you. We thought what it would do for you, how it would rescue you—shall we get some more coffee, it's really awfully good here—'

'Harry, for God's sake! I think this is rather more important than coffee. What do you mean, rescue me?'

'Rescue you from your lousy, dreary marriage, your wasted life, your frustrated ambitions.'

'Oh, I see. So the money was from her, after all? From Leonora? Or so you would like me to think?'

'Yes, of course it was. She loved the idea of giving it to you. She saw it as a way of making things right.'

'For her.'

'And for you, surely?'

'I don't know,' said Cassia slowly, 'that it has.'

'What on earth do you mean? It's done all the things we thought it might do for you. It's given you your life back. It's made it possible for you to have a career again. I've got you back.'

'Exactly. You've got me back, and all the other things you wanted, you thought were right for me, you and Leonora. Harry, I don't know how you see this, but I see it as a piece of appalling manipulation. The thought of the two of you sitting there in Paris, saying this will do it, this will break up her marriage, her family—'

'You're being ridiculous,' he said, slamming his glass down.

'Am I? Am I really?'

'Yes, you are. It was—is a legacy, that's all. Lots of people come into money, are left it by relatives, they don't start rambling on about manipulation . . .'

'This money isn't quite like an ordinary legacy, though, is it, Harry? In the first place, it's horrible money. I hate the thought of it, where it came from, and in the second it smacks of blackmail to

722

me. What you did.'

'Cassia, you really are crazy. Blackmail! That man helped to kill Leonora, abandoned her, continues to conduct his disgusting life, about which he begged me, literally with tears in his eyes, to remain silent.'

'Exactly. He bought your silence.'

'Of course he didn't. I kept silent for her sake, because I promised Leonora.'

'That's a matter of interpretation, I would have thought. Actually.'

'Well, this is rich!' he said. 'You'll be telling me next that he doesn't deserve such treatment, that you're going to go round there and mop his filthy brow and give him his money back.'

'I'm not going to mop his brow, but I shall probably give the money away. No, not to him, he should be locked up, I want him locked up, but—'

'But what? Now I've heard everything. Everything.'

'Harry, I don't want that money. The very thought of it now makes me feel sick.'

He sat looking at her, an expression on his face of such total bafflement that she almost laughed.

'You just don't understand, do you?'

'No, I don't.'

'Let me try and explain again. There you sat, you and Leonora, with this obscene amount of money to play with. Saying what shall we do with it. And then saying let's give it to Cassia, because she's unhappy, she's got her life all wrong, and we know how to make it all right again! We know what's best for her, we know what will happen, she'll leave her husband and go back to her career, and maybe come back to London and then might even embark on an affair with me, Harry Moreton—'

'Jesus, Cassia, you really are mad, you know.'

'I'm not mad. Didn't it enter that great arrogant ego of yours that I might be perfectly capable of taking charge of my own life? Didn't it? No, it wouldn't, because you don't really know me at all. You never really listen to me and you never really think about my life, you just think of what you want me to do, want me to be. Harry, if I'd really really wanted to change things or go back to medicine, I'd have done so anyway, without your interference.'

'No, you wouldn't,' he said, and he was starting to shout now. 'You were too bloody stupid and too much under the thumb of that pathetic, half-brained man you're married to.'

'Don't talk about Edward like that, Harry, please.'

'Oh, so you're becoming loyal all of a sudden, are you? I don't recall much loyalty when you lay in my bed and told me you loved me. When you moved back to London for days at a time. When you—'

'Shut up,' she said, 'just shut up.'

'I will not shut up. What did you want us to do, Leonora and I? Say look, Cassia, if you like we'll give you some money to play with?'

'There you are,' she said, 'you've just admitted it, that you were both giving me the money, the pair of you, plotting it together. That's what makes it so ugly. You cold-bloodedly discussed what the money might do to me and my life, and decided it was a good idea.'

'But what,' he said, and he was patently trying to be calmer, 'would you have liked us to do?'

'I'm not sure, but the very fact that it was all

724

surrounded in secrecy, in strange half-truths, proves that you felt guilty about it, that I wouldn't be happy with it—'

'That's a filthy lie. It wasn't surrounded in secrecy, it was a perfectly sound, legal arrangement. I felt it better, safer for the money to be in trust for Leonora, I had no idea how long she was going to live, how soon she was going to die, it was only because you developed this obsession—'

'Yes, and I was right. I'm sorry, but I can't accept any of what you say. Even if you believe it yourself, which I very much doubt. You and Leonora have made me a pawn in your perverted chess game and I don't like it. God, when I think of the appalling fuss you made about my one small indiscretion with Rupert—that really is pathetic. Well, I'm not going to play your game any longer. I'm going home, and I'm going to try and put things right there, and I shall be extremely grateful if from now on you excise me from your life, as I shall you from mine.' She stood up. 'Goodbye, Harry.'

He looked up at her and gave her a rather odd smile. 'I shouldn't bank on the doctor taking you back,' he said, 'letting you back into his house even.'

She stared at him. 'What do you mean? The marriage may be over, but I have my children to think about, and besides, I'm going to—' She was stopped by a gentle tap on her shoulder.

'Madame Fallon, your car is here. To take you to Casablanca. And we have your handbag in reception, Jamal went to collect it this morning for you. If you are ready, madame . . .'

'Yes,' said Cassia, 'I'm quite ready. Thank you. I've nothing left to do here.'

And she turned her back on Harry and stalked into the hotel.

CHAPTER THIRTY-NINE

Cecily lay in the large, soggy, slightly lumpy bed in Justin's house in Clapham and wondered how something so extremely physically uncomfortable should provide such extreme physical pleasure. She had spent several hours in it now, had gone to the house as soon as she had seen the girls off to school—and it was now, she realised, looking at her watch with a certain sense of shock, almost time for them to come home for tea.

'I shall have to go soon,' she said, reaching out her hand, pushing Justin's floppy hair out of his eyes; he caught the hand and kissed it.

'But you will come back?'

'Well, not today, but would you like to come to supper this evening?'

'No, my darling. Correction, I would like to, but I really do have to do some work. And not at Edwina's house, either, don't look like that. Tomorrow night perhaps?'

'Tomorrow night. The girls will be thrilled. It's nice you and they have such a mutual admiration society.'

'Not as great as the one you and I have, I hope.'

'Maybe not.'

'I love you,' he said simply, 'very much. And you are—well, magnificent.'

'Don't say that,' she said with a shudder, 'it sounds fat.'

'Cecily,' he said, leaning over her, kissing first one breast then the other, 'you must rid yourself of this obsession about being fat. You are perfectly, beautifully, sensuously divine. I adore your body, it's luscious and glorious and I drown in pleasure in it. I can't believe how wonderful you are, in every way. I can't believe I've found you.'

'Nor I you,' she said, and was silent, smiling at the unlikeliness of it all, of the unhappy, unfulfilled woman she had been, transformed into this joyful, easy creature who lay beneath her lover and cried aloud with pleasure: and perhaps more importantly still, who felt valued, desirable, and the absolute centre of someone else's life.

*　　　*　　　*

'Look, look,' shouted William, who had been at the window since lunchtime, 'it's Mummy, she's here, she's here,' and Bertie, so certain she would not come, threw his book down, slid down the banisters and into her arms, occupied already by William, with whoops of joy.

Edward, in the study, had heard the car, and the whoops, but refused to get up to go and greet her.

Janet put her head round the door. 'Mrs Fallon's back,' she said, smiling, 'so she'll be able to go to the concert with you. Isn't that good news?'

'I suppose so,' he said, 'yes, yes, of course it is. But you will come too, won't you?'

'Dr Fallon, I can't. Who will look after Delia?'

'Peggy can look after Delia,' he said firmly. 'You've kept this household going these last few days, and I want you to come.'

After a few minutes, the door opened and Cassia

stood there, an arm round each of the boys.

'Hallo, Edward.'

'Hallo,' he said shortly.

'Mummy's been to Africa!' said Bertie, his eyes shining with pride. 'On an aeroplane, isn't she clever?'

'Oh, extremely clever,' said Edward, standing up, stalking past them, not even looking at Cassia.

Bertie looked up at them, startled, his small face anxious; then he recovered, took Cassia's hand, dragged her into the sitting room saying, 'Tell me all about it. How big was the aeroplane? Were the people all black? What language did they speak? Could you understand them . . . ?'

Janet appeared. 'Welcome back, Mrs Fallon, we're so pleased to see you, and just in time too. Dr Fallon has asked me to come to the concert as well, and leave Delia with Peggy. Will that be all right with you?'

'Yes, of course,' said Cassia. She was too exhausted to wonder at the strangeness of Edward requesting Janet's presence anywhere.

*   *   *

William sang beautifully, the descant verse of 'Oh, Come All Ye Faithful', his sweetly rich voice reaching out and up into the darkness, the tallest reaches of the church. Cassia sat between Edward and Janet, watching him intently through rather blurred eyes, watching his face, fiercely serious, his eyes fixed on the organist, and thought how extraordinarily literal was the phrase 'lump in the throat'. Opposite him in the choir stalls, with the bigger boys, stood Bertie; equally serious, equally intent, but occasionally daring a glance at her, as if he could not be quite sure that she was really there, had not vanished again.

She sat absorbing this moment, this utterly English occasion, in the dark, cold, candlelit church, the great Christmas tree standing to the right of the choir stalls, the crib to the left of it, the organ playing carols, tunes as familiar as her own name, surrounded by smiling mothers and stiff-faced fathers and smaller siblings, unnaturally neat and well dressed, contrasting it with what she had left behind only yesterday—the heat, the smells, the dust, the dark faces, the flowing robes, and her own fear—and unable to believe very fully in any of it.

The solo, the whole concert ended; and the church emptied gradually, people shuffling out of pews, greeting one another, smiling, saying how hard it was to think it was Christmas again.

*   *   *

After supper—impossibly strained, with only Janet's cheerful, optimistic presence to ease it—the children went, protesting, up to bed, and Cassia said to Edward, 'May I talk to you?'

'What about?' he said, his face so angry that she was frightened.

'The future.'

'Oh, that,' he said.

'Yes. What we are going to do, whether you have made a decision about the practice yet—'

'Oh, that is easy at least. Of course you can't have it. I would no more dream of handing this practice over to you than to Bertie.'

'What? Edward, you seemed so receptive to the idea before—I don't understand. Look, I'm sorry about my absence, but it was crucial. I had to go—'

'To be with Moreton, I suppose. I don't think I want to have it explained.'

She felt as if she were falling, very fast, into some kind of deep swirling vacuum. 'You know about that?'

'Yes, Cassia, I know about that. I was informed by his wife, as a matter of fact. Very neat, don't you think?'

Why on earth hadn't Harry warned her, told her they all knew? God, how she hated him. 'Edward, I'd like to explain.'

'Look,' he said, 'I don't really want any explanation. You have lied, and lied to all of us, you have neglected your children, you have humiliated me beyond endurance. My dearest wish would be that I need never see you again. Sadly that cannot be, at least for the time being. We have the children to make arrangements for. But don't, please, insult me by pretending you can explain. You've been sharing his bed for months, years for all I know, all our marriage, while putting up your obscene front of self-righteousness, and I find it disgusting. Abhorrent.'

'Edward—'

'Be quiet!' he said, and she thought for a moment he was going to hit her. 'I don't want to hear from you. You've always been attracted to him, I knew that. You were in love with him when you were a schoolgirl even, certainly after you met me. I dare say it was part of your plan.'

'I didn't have a plan,' she said, hearing her own voice rising, cracking with rage, 'I did not have any kind of plan. I had nothing to do with Harry for years and years, all the time we were married—'

'How very virtuous of you!'

'Shut up!' she shouted, losing her own temper now. 'Shut up! I'm not trying to make excuses, I'm trying to tell you how wrong you are, I was not sleeping with Harry Moreton until—'

'Until when exactly? I'm so interested to know.'

'Until a few months ago,' she said, her voice very low, 'when I knew our marriage was over.'

'Oh, very commendable. Please forgive me for misjudging you.'

'But you do misjudge me!' she cried. 'I tried so hard for so long, while we were married, I tried to be good—'

'Oh, for Christ's sake!' he said. 'Please spare me this self-sanctification, Cassia. It is, of course, extraordinarily unusual and noble for a woman to be faithful to her husband, to try to be good, as you put it. Except in that hideous circle that your friends, like Harry Moreton, move in. And I'm sorry, incidentally, you should have had to try so hard. I imagined, foolishly that our marriage was happy, that there need not have been too much effort involved in it all. I was wrong, it seems. What a failure I have been, in every possible way.'

'Edward, please don't start that!'

'I don't have to start it,' he said, 'because it has always been so. I should never have had anything to do with you, Cassia, let alone married you. It was a disaster for me the day I met you. I hope you realise that.'

'And for me,' she cried, driven from patience finally, 'for me as well. You love to present yourself as the injured party, don't you, Edward, as the poor, oppressed husband, but it's utterly untrue. All those years you oppressed me. You wouldn't let me near this practice in any way, you kept me out of it, occasionally allowed me to mix up some glucose and water, or bandage a knee. You wanted it all for yourself, to be the great, the all-powerful doctor. You were afraid I'd show you up, be in some way your equal, not your superior even, but your equal. Are you really so surprised I went my own way, with my own friends, my own—'

'Your own lover, in your own bed, in your own house in London. You're little better than a whore, Cassia, a—'

'Stop it! Stop it, stop it!' It was Bertie, his face ashen, with two spots of high colour on his cheeks, his eyes wide, horrified as he looked up at them. 'It's horrible, I hate you both. You promised, you promised you'd be friends, that you wouldn't get divorced. Why did you say that if it wasn't true?'

'Bertie, Bertie, darling.' Cassia reached down to him, tried to take him in her arms, to comfort him; he pushed her away, his small chest heaving.

'Don't do that. Don't. It's true what Daddy says, you're always going away, always leaving us here. William was crying last night because he thought you'd miss the concert.'

'Bertie, I—' She dropped her arms in despair.

'Bertie, come here.' Edward reached out to him now, but Bertie turned on him like a small fury.

'No. I hate you too. You're horrible, not letting Mummy help you. Why can't she look after the practice, why not? Just because Maureen said she couldn't—'

'What?' said Cassia. 'What was that about the practice?'

'Nothing,' said Edward, 'not now, for Christ's sake.'

She accepted it, tried again with Bertie. 'Bertie, come along, darling, let's go and sit down and talk about this.'

'No. There's nothing to talk about.'

Edward put out his hand, tried to put it on Bertie's shoulders; he pushed it furiously away.

'Bertie.' A soft voice spoke from the doorway; it was Janet. 'Bertie, do you want to come upstairs with me?'

'No,' said Bertie sulkily, but he walked slowly towards the door.

Cassia and Edward looked at one another silently across the vast yawning gulf that had been their marriage. And then she turned and went up to the room that had become hers and lay down on the bed, fully clothed, and wept until she could weep no more.

*　　　*　　　*

'Cassia! Cassia, wake up, for God's sake.' It was Edward: she struggled to sit up. It was still dark. 'Bertie's gone. He's run away.'

'Run away! Oh, Edward, no, he can't have done, when, how—'

'I don't know,' he said. 'He was asleep when I went to bed, I checked on him.'

'Yes, and I did in the night.'

'What time was that?'

'Oh, about half past three.'

'What time is it now?'

'Just after six.'

They were to repeat these details many, many

times over the next few days.

*　　　*　　　*

Janet had discovered Bertie's absence. She had got up at five thirty, hearing Delia crying, had settled her and then gone to check on Bertie herself. But he wasn't anywhere in the house. After a few minutes she had woken Edward—Edward, thought Cassia, pain piercing her, why Edward, why not me, have I really become so much less of a parent?—and told him what had happened.

The three of them searched the house, the garden; Edward took out the car and drove down to the village, round the lanes, came back grim faced. It was still dark; that somehow seemed to make it worse.

'He can't have got far,' Cassia kept saying over and over again, 'not in the dark. There aren't any buses, nothing, and surely, surely . . .' Her voice tailed off, she was afraid to finish the sentence.

'He wouldn't have taken a lift?' said Edward.
'God knows.'

'Oh, Edward, I've always told him not to, never, ever to get in a car with anyone, go off with anyone he doesn't know.'

'I know. But . . .' But driven by misery, by desperation, children did anything.

'Oh God,' she said.

'We'd better tell the police.'

It was a terrible phone call: it seemed to make the whole thing darker, official; Bertie had ceased to be a little boy who had run away, had become a missing child, possibly abducted.

Bertie approached the gates of St John's, the gates he had been driven through that last time by his mother, with feelings of such intense relief; the lights of the school were on, everyone must be having supper. He wasn't quite sure now why he had come, but he had just felt that if he was here, if he could make himself remember exactly how unhappy he had been, how desperate, it might make the new trouble seem less awful. He remembered vividly sitting on his mother's knee, warm and safe and comfortable for the first time for weeks, when she brought him home—and telling her he would rather come back here than she and his father were divorced. He'd thought he would just go in, wander round a bit, and try and think how bad it had been—and then he'd phone home and tell them where he was, ask them to collect him.

He was very cold now, though; very cold indeed. Where could he shelter just for a bit, while he thought, tried to decide what to do? Maybe the chapel: yes, that was an idea. He'd go in there, sit for a bit; and then—well, then maybe he'd just go home anyway. He didn't need reminding about the misery: he could see already that it had been even worse than his parents quarrelling.

Bertie slipped in through the door—it seemed almost warm inside—and sank into one of the pews. He was very, very tired; he'd been walking all day, except for that one bus ride he'd spent his last threepence on; it'd be nice to sit down, have a rest. He lay down, on his side, pulled his legs up on to the seat. Just for a few minutes, only a few minutes.

They had phoned everyone they knew in the area, everyone Mrs Briggs and Peggy knew, every parent of every child at the school; and then started on everyone they knew in London.

Rupert seemed a possibility; Bertie had adored him. They asked Cecily, of course, Fanny and Bertie had become great friends, 'Fanny might have heard from him, even,' Cassia had said, but Fanny hadn't. They even phoned Edwina, for Bertie had seemed to rather like Edwina at Laurence's christening, had pronounced her pretty—but all in vain. None of them had heard from or seen Bertie.

*   *   *

He wouldn't panic, Bertie had told himself, when he heard the key turning in the chapel door, when the caretaker had not seemed to heed his hammering and his cries; they would be back in the morning to unlock it for morning prayers, and then he could escape. He could pile the choirboys' cassocks on to him to keep warmer, and get through the night somehow. It was dark and a bit scary, of course, frightening shadows and funny noises, a sort of scuffling that made him jump and want to scream at first, until he realised it was the mice. There were lots of mice in the organ loft, it had been one of his few happier memories at the school: boys in the choir, Bertie among them, had taken bits of cheese down to feed them; nothing to be frightened of there.

And there was a tap in the little vestry; he could get a drink if he was thirsty: yes, he'd be absolutely fine till the morning. And then he could get out and ask if he could phone his parents. It would be all right. Of course it would.

* * *

The police had begun to search for Bertie in earnest on Tuesday morning. The first day, they had simply been circulating his picture, showing it to stationmasters, guards, bus conductors, professing a certain confidence; now on the second they were clearly more worried, searching the woods, barns, the riverbank, were talking of diving in the local gravel pit. When they said that, Cassia only just got to the lavatory in time; she came out, green and shaking, to find Edward in the hall, looking for the first time since she had come back from Morocco almost friendly.

'Are you all right?' he said.

'Yes. No. Oh, I don't know. This is so dreadful, Edward, and I did it, it's my fault.'

'No,' he said, quite sharply, 'no. We both did it, we are both to blame. Come along, come and sit down, you look all in.'

Astonished, she followed him into the kitchen and let him make her a cup of tea.

* * *

By lunchtime on Tuesday, Bertie's fists were raw with beating on the great door of the chapel, and his voice hoarse with shouting. He was also extremely hungry.

He had woken when it was still dark, waited for the light to come, shaking with terror; his only companion, his only comfort, his watch, with its luminous dial and nice, comforting tick, given to him by Edward when he first went away to school. He stared at it, taking in the time, five o'clock, thinking how long it would be before it was time for prayers, when he would be released, and only stopped himself screaming with a huge effort. Later he wondered if screaming might have helped; someone might actually have heard him in the still darkness.

As light came, he felt better, calmer: told himself it was after all only a matter of hours now before they came. And later, much later, heard the cars arriving endlessly . . . and then leaving again, and as the day wore on, a terrible, dreadful silence.

*   *   *

Cassia sat by the telephone all day, occasionally sleeping briefly. Edward would take out the car every two or three hours, and drive round, in an ever increasing radius, simply looking for him. 'I know it's probably quite useless,' he said, 'but I feel I have to do something.'

Very late on Tuesday evening, as she woke from some fitful half-sleep, the phone rang. She snatched it up; it was Harry.

'Cassia?'

'Yes. Yes, hello, Harry.'

'I just got back from Morocco. Edwina told me about Bertie. Have you found him yet?'

'No. No, we haven't.'

'I'm so sorry,' he said, 'so terribly sorry. Is there

738

anything I can do?'

'Only find him,' she said, and burst into tears and put the phone down.

*   *   *

Bertie was so cold now he could hardly think; he tried to keep warm, he knew that was important; he remembered that Scott of the Antarctic, whom he had read about recently, had stressed you must not get too cold, or you just fell asleep, and he kept stomping round the chapel, beating his hands against his sides at regular intervals all morning, but as it grew dark again he began to despair and crawled into his pew, covering himself with his cassocks; so hungry it hurt.

He realised now that it was possible that no one might come until after Christmas and that he would by then be quite dead; but he tried very hard not to think about it. He knew you could live for a long time just on water, that however hungry you were, you didn't die while you had water, but on the other hand, he thought he might die of the cold.

Prayer seemed the best thing, and God must surely listen more attentively to someone in a church than anywhere else. He couldn't think of many prayers, so he just said the Lord's Prayer over and over again, and in between, a more desperate 'Please, please, God, let someone find me soon'. He finally fell asleep, but he had forgotten to wind up his watch and had no idea what the time was when he woke again. And that did make him cry, and he really did feel alone.

*   *   *

On the Wednesday morning, there was a police message on the wireless, asking for information that might help them find a small boy called Bertram Fallon—answering to the name of Bertie—'three foot nine inches, brown hair, brown eyes, last seen at his home at . . .'

Cassia, listening to the description, began to feel herself going mad.

She was quite sure now he was dead; she saw his body, lying cold and still in some ditch or barn, had come to regard death indeed as the better option, better than the alternative, than abduction, sexual—what was the official phrase?—sexual interference. Her mind created and veered away from and then re-created hideous visions of small, trusting Bertie, lured into an alliance, subjected to some hideous abuse, from which even if he was rescued he would never recover.

She lay down and fell asleep, waking again to hear the phone ringing; it was the police, someone had seen a child answering Bertie's description in Birmingham.

'Birmingham! But how, why? Oh God, oh my God—' The policeman was gentle with her. 'Don't take too much notice of it madam, this happens with a radio appeal, it's doubled edged. That's why we postpone it for a while. People ring in all the time. The calls all have to be followed up, obviously, and nine times out of ten it's someone quite different, but yes, the Birmingham police will be alerted.'

It happened three more times: Bertie had been seen in Oxfordshire, hitching a lift on a farmyard

740

lorry; in Glasgow, going into a bus shelter; in St Ives, running along the beach.

For some reason, these calls broke Edward's spirit; Cassia went into the study halfway through the morning and found him weeping at his desk. She had no emotional reserves left to help him, and went out again quietly, closing the door behind her.

He came out after about an hour, tear stained and pale. 'You wouldn't come for a walk, would you?' he said. 'I feel I need some fresh air.'

'Edward, we can't both go out,' she said sharply.

Janet stood up and said, 'I agree with that, but would you like me to come with you, Dr Fallon? I would quite like some fresh air myself.'

'Yes,' he said, 'yes, that would be very nice, thank you.'

Watching them leave the house together, Cassia experienced, for the first time since Monday morning, an emotion that was nothing to do with Bertie. She wasn't sure, but it seemed to be hope; and why, she certainly could not imagine.

*   *   *

Bertie had more or less given up trying to keep warm now; he was so hungry it seemed easier just to lie still. A rather nice feeling was beginning to take him over, a sort of dreaminess. He had done a bit more praying, but he was beginning to give up hope in God as well now.

*   *   *

Maureen was taking all the surgeries; she was clearly upset and glad to be able to do something to help. Cassia looked at her as she rushed off that day in the middle of a very snatched meal to visit a toddler whose mother had phoned up hysterically with reports that he had swallowed some bleach, and wondered why she had disliked her quite so much.

When Maureen came back, she said tentatively, 'Was the baby all right?'

'Oh, yes. It wasn't bleach, it turned out to be gin. And only a bit. I think she thought if she said that on the phone I wouldn't come. People are very strange.'

'Yes, they are. And that woman is a nightmare; always leaving stuff out where her children can get at it. It was some aspirin tablets once before, poor little thing had to be stomach-pumped. What did you give it, lots of milk?'

'Yes.' She looked at Cassia warily. 'I'm so sorry, Mrs Fallon, about Bertie. Still no news?'

'No, no news.'

'Mrs Fallon . . .'

'Yes, Maureen?'

'There's something on my conscience. Something I feel very bad about. I shall say this to Dr Fallon as well, but I feel I must say it to you. Dr Fallon asked me if I thought he should let you have the practice, when he goes to do his membership. I'm afraid I said I didn't think it was a very good idea.'

'Yes, I rather gathered that from Bertie. Why not, Maureen?'

'I was being very small minded, I'm afraid. And I'm sorry, very sorry. I think you'd be marvellous. I'll tell Dr Fallon so.'

'Thank you, but don't worry about it. I really

can't care about anything at the moment.'

'Well, it's very nice of you to be so generous.'

*   *   *

As it began to grow dusk again, Bertie lost hope and stopped trying. He didn't even bother with the water any more. Better just to lie still, and let the dreaminess take over. He couldn't shout any more, he wasn't strong enough, nor could he beat on the door: the cuts and bruises on his hands were hurting quite a lot, and anyway, it wasn't worth it, nobody was going to hear. He was going to die here, alone with God. God and the mice.

He lay, curled up on his pew, and thought about his mother, whom he loved so much, who was so warm and loving and so much fun. She always listened to him seriously, never dismissed his worries as foolish, his stories as boring. Even if she did go away a lot working, it seemed worth it when she came back. And the last things he had said to her had been so terrible: he had said he hated her, that she was horrible.

He didn't mean it, or about his father: he loved them both, he wanted to see them again more than anything in the world. It was very, very sad that they couldn't be together, but if they couldn't and if he could only see them separately, tell them he loved them both, that would do. Nothing was worse than the thought of dying here alone, and never seeing them again, never telling them he loved them both, that he was sorry he'd said such awful things. They were saying awful things too, to each other, but they could all say they were sorry, sort something out, start again. But you couldn't start again if you were dead.

* * *

There were three more sightings of Bertie that afternoon: then at about four the phone stopped ringing. The thought of another hideous night, with all its attendant visions, filled Cassia with horror. It was very cold and had started to sleet; surely no child could survive out in this, she thought, not for a third night, a child dressed only in school shorts and a raincoat. She sat staring out at the gathering darkness, listening to the wind shrieking, shrinking from it all, from what Bertie must be going through. She put her head down on her arms, as Edward had done earlier, and started to cry: and having started, became hysterical, unable to stop.

Dimly through her sobbing, she heard the phone ringing, on and on, nobody answering it. Where were they all? What were they doing? Finally she hauled herself on to shaking legs and dragged herself to it, fearing, knowing it was yet another useless call, another false sighting. She picked it up, unable to say anything, simply sobbing uselessly down the line.

'Cassia? Cassia, it's Harry. Listen, I've had an idea. Where was that school Bertie went to?'

* * *

She knew it was absurd, impossible, but it was an idea at least, something to pursue. Shaking, shuddering, she phoned the school, the headmaster's house. There was no reply. Well, they would have broken up, of course, there wouldn't be

744

anyone there. So he couldn't be there. Could he?
But he might.

*   *   *

It seemed a very long thirty miles, in the dark and
the sleet. She only saw half a dozen other vehicles
all the way; everyone was very sensibly staying at
home. As she drove on, the sleet turned to snow;
the road became slithery, dangerous.

She had no idea why she was pursuing this rather
wild idea so fervently: common sense told her it
was almost certainly a wild goose chase, but there
was a glimmer of logic in it that gave her hope. And
anything was better than sitting by the telephone.

And then, wonderfully, she saw in front of her
the lights of the caretaker's lodge. She slammed on
her brakes, skidded on the icy ground, jumped out
of her car and ran, shouting, towards the door.

*   *   *

'Well, I haven't seen a boy,' said Mr Worthington,
slightly crossly, as if such a thing would have been
rather distasteful, 'not since they all went home.'

'Can we look, though? Can we go over to the
school?'

'Oh, I don't know,' said Mr Worthington. 'I'd
have to get the headmaster's permission, of course,
and—'

'Mr Worthington, my little boy has been missing
for three days. Anything is worth a try, now can we
please go over to the school?'

*   *   *

Bertie had seen the car lights: they swung briefly through the darkness of the chapel. He had been asleep and had woken just before they came. He lay there, stupefied with cold, wondering if he should do some more shouting and screaming, as he had each time he had heard a car before, and decided he couldn't be bothered. He pulled the cassocks back over his head, and tried to go to sleep again.

*   *   *

The headmaster had been out to a cocktail party, and was not pleased to see her on his return, associating her as he did with trouble and the confrontation of his school's shortcomings. He had heard about Bertie's disappearance, he told her, on the wireless, pointed it out with some kind of strange satisfaction, as if it confirmed his belief that Bertie had always been troublesome, that it had been him, not the school, at fault.

It was quite impossible, he said, that Bertie was anywhere on the school premises, the cleaners would have found him, the school had been cleaned from top to bottom at the end of term.

'I don't care how clean it is, I want to go over it. Now.'

He looked at her and recognised his defeat; they toured classrooms, dormitories, lavatories: no Bertie.

*   *   *

'You see, I did tell you,' he said, 'he couldn't have

been here.'

'Outside, outbuildings?'

'Only the cricket pavilion.'

'Let's look there.'

'Mrs Fallon—'

'Let's look.'

The cricket pavilion was empty; so was the lavatory block by the playing fields.

'You see, Mrs Fallon, he isn't here, it's really quite impossible.'

'Yes, well, thank you for looking.'

'I'll escort you back to your car.'

She felt he was doing it more to make sure she had left the premises than to be courteous. They walked back to the car in silence.

'Well,' he said, holding out his hand, 'I hope you find him. I'm sure you will, he's probably just being naughty.'

She had forgotten how much she disliked him until that moment; but she had no strength left to argue with him. 'I hope so,' she said, getting into the car, starting the engine.

'Happy Christmas, Mrs Fallon.' He hesitated, then clearly feeling he should say something pleasant, 'We missed Bertie at the carol service. He has a lovely voice.'

She smiled at him, unable to speak, swung the car away from the house, towards the gates.

*   *   *

Bertie heard the car leaving again, driving off, and burrowed deeper into the cassocks. He had been right not to try: whoever it was would never have come.

A quarter of a mile down the lane, Cassia suddenly heard the headmaster's voice again, took in his words. The carol service! The carol service. In the chapel. She had forgotten the chapel, set back, halfway up the drive, they all had. Was it worth trying there? Probably not. And it meant more arguments, more pitting her exhausted will against other people's strongly resistant ones, but . . .

She felt shocked at herself. How could she possibly give up on Bertie, fail him, while there was the faintest drift of hope? She braked violently, turned the car in the road, and drove back.

*   *   *

'He couldn't be there,' said Mr Worthington.

'Why not?'

'Well, I locked it up before the end of term,' he said, as if that made perfect sense. 'The night before.'

'I'm afraid,' said Cassia, 'that doesn't seem to me a reason at all. Come along, Mr Worthington, let's go.'

'I'll have to ask,' he said, glaring at her, 'have to ask again, and it's late, tomorrow would be easier.'

'And tonight would be safer. Bertie might be starving in there. Do you want to have his . . .' she paused, brought the dreadful words out . . . 'his death on your conscience?'

Mr Worthington looked at her, reached for his keys.

Janet was just trying to persuade William to eat his supper when she heard the phone. She took a deep breath and went out to the hall and picked it up.

*   *   *

Edward, returning from his patient, walking heavily into the hall, saw Janet standing by the phone, saw her replace it very gently in its cradle; saw that she was crying, tears streaming down her face.

'He's dead, isn't he?' he said. 'Bertie's dead.'

'No,' she said, 'no, he isn't, he's alive, Mrs Fallon's got him, he's all right.'

'Oh God,' said Edward, and because it seemed the most natural, the most inevitable thing in the world, walked forward to where she stood and put his arms round her. 'Shush,' he said, 'don't cry, it's all right. Everything's going to be all right now.'

*   *   *

Edwina was working at the desk in her sitting room when the phone rang; she went down to Harry in his study, and said, her voice most unusually trembly, 'It's Cassia, she wants to speak to you. Bertie's been found.'

She heard Harry saying, 'I just went over and over in my head everything I knew about Bertie, and it seemed it might be possible,' and, 'I do listen to you, Cassia, you see, I do think . . .' There was a silence, and then his voice, very quietly, 'I love you too,' before she closed the door.

EPILOGUE

12 May, 1937

Trafalgar Square did not look quite its staid self as dawn broke on the morning of 12 May, 1937; quite apart from the flags flying proudly from all the buildings set around it, and the bunting draping every conceivable and drapable space, it was lined from edge to edge with people in sleeping bags, most of them already awake, many of them drinking tea from Thermos flasks, waving Union Jacks at anyone who came past, and the more determinedly lively of them already singing. They were in one of the best possible places in the country that morning, those people, had the perfect view, for through Admiralty Arch they could see right down The Mall, and would be able not only to watch the coronation procession as it came along Whitehall, but then to make their way towards the palace when the royal family returned and came out on to the balcony.

Peggy and Mr and Mrs Briggs were in that crowd, had travelled up the night before, since the family were all in London, and only Maureen Johnson remained, minding the practice. She was very sniffy about the coronation, Peggy remarked to Mrs Briggs, had said to Mrs Fallon, or rather Dr Fallon, she never could remember to call her that even now, that she had not the slightest interest in any of them, and would be pleased to be on call.

'She's got no fun in her, that one,' she said, and Mrs Briggs said she'd often thought the same herself, but it had been very good of her to turn down her new job, in order to ease the new doctor in for six months or so.

'Not that I can think of her as the doctor, least of all the new one, but there you are, she seems to be making a wonderful job of it, everyone's very happy with her. I wouldn't have thought she'd want Dr Johnson there, but still, they seem to get on quite well most of the time.'

*   *   *

Edward Fallon, who had been up most of the night dealing with several emergencies, decided he would go to bed and sleep through the coronation. Like Maureen Johnson, he felt no interest in any of the people concerned, but at nine o'clock the phone rang in his small room with a message to call a Miss Fraser as soon as possible.

Edward sighed, although fairly happily, and went to phone Janet Fraser, who was sounding extremely cheerful and lively and told him that her new employers, a very nice family in The Boltons, had given her the day off, that she would really like to try and catch a glimpse of the procession, and was Edward free that day, as he had thought he might be, having completed a seventy-two hour stint on Casualty.

Edward said that he was, but that he was very tired and really had very little interest in the procession, and Janet said she was sorry, but that neither of those excuses seemed very acceptable to her, and if Edward really wished their relationship to flourish, then he must try to be a little more positive about everything; and then added, laughing into his rather indignant silence, that she was only teasing, and she wanted to see him anyway, but if he was too tired then she'd have to find someone else to go with her.

'I'll come and watch the beastly thing,' Edward said, hastily, and Janet said she didn't want to hear him telling her how beastly it was all the way through, she wanted him to enjoy it, and as she always told all her charges, enjoying things was simply a matter of determination.

'All right, I'll come and enjoy the beastly thing,' said Edward, 'but can I have a couple of hours' sleep first?'

'As long as it's only a couple. Would you like me to come and wake you up? I think I can find that nasty little room of yours by now.'

Edward said he would like that very much indeed.

*   *   *

Cecily and the girls were going to watch the procession from a balcony in Whitehall, outside the office of an erstwhile colleague of Benedict's. Cecily, who was not feeling very well that morning, was less enthusiastic about it than she had expected, but the girls were very excited, particularly at the prospect of seeing the little princesses riding in the coach.

'It'll be just like the end of the pantomime, won't it?' said Stephanie. 'You remember, when we went to see Rupert at Brighton, when he was Buttons?'

'I wish Justin could come with us,' said Fanny. 'He makes things so much more fun always.'

'Yes, he does,' said Stephanie, 'I love Justin. I

wish you'd marry him, Mummy, then it would be fun all the time. Why won't you? Then we could be bridesmaids, we've never been bridesmaids . . .'

'I am not going to marry anybody just so you two can be bridesmaids,' said Cecily firmly.

'You don't have to marry anybody, you've got to marry Justin. Why won't you? I know he wants to marry you.'

'How do you know that?'

'Well, he's always kissing you and calling you his darling.'

'There's more to marriage than that,' said Cecily slightly primly.

*   *   *

Justin was setting up a rather difficult shot in the blissful peace of the studio in a Style House rendered utterly still and quiet by the national holiday, when Cecily phoned. He was surprised; he had thought she would already be on her balcony, as he called it.

'Hello, my darling. Why aren't you helping the King and Queen to be crowned?'

'It's not time to go just yet.'

'I'm sorry I can't come,' he said.

'It's all right. Honestly. I'm sorry I was cross about it. I was being silly. Of course it's a good opportunity for you.'

'It is. And then I can enjoy you this evening with a clear conscience.'

'Yes. Justin?'

'Yes, Cecily?'

'Fanny and Stephanie were just telling me they want to be bridesmaids. At a wedding. Soon.'

'Oh, really?' he said, slightly absently. 'Whose?'

'Ours.'

There was a long silence, then he said. 'But, Cecily, you said—'

'I know what I said. But maybe I was wrong. And two years seems a rather long time suddenly. Also I've just got a feeling I might be bursting out of any frock I had to wear soon.'

'What? Darling, we're not back to the fat phobia again, are we? I thought we'd got that well and truly behind us.'

'Well,' said Cecily, 'there's fat and fat. And I've got something else to tell you, Justin, I was sick this morning. And yesterday.'

'Poor darling. I'm so sorry. Why do you think— Oh, Cecily. Oh, my God! Oh, heavens above. Look, go and lie down immediately and wait for me, I'll find a taxi and come over, straight away.'

'You'll do no such thing,' said Cecily severely, 'you must finish your photographs. Otherwise I'll think they were an excuse, to get you out of watching the coronation. I'm perfectly all right now, honestly. I have experienced this sort of thing before. But a June wedding might be rather nice, don't you think?'

'Divine,' said Justin, 'absolutely divine.'

* * *

Edwina Moreton was watching the procession from an office in Trafalgar Square, in the company of Francis Stevenson-Cook and a few other close friends. Later that evening she was giving a dinner party at her very chic new house in Cheyne Walk; much of the *beau monde* of London would be

755

there, all hoping that they, or their clothes or their houses, might find a mention in the dazzling new column she had launched in *Style* magazine called 'Talk About . . .', a wonderful blend of gossip and fashion, a microcosm of the magazine itself, as she had explained it to Francis when first proposing it. She had become very well known very quickly, on the strength of that column, photographed, quoted, in demand everywhere. That was not only an inevitable but a most fortunate result of it, supplying her as it did with an ongoing source of material. So much admired was the column, indeed, that there was talk of it being launched in American *Style* in the autumn, and she had been invited to New York to meet the social editor there.

'Edwina, darling, you look marvellous.' It was an old friend from her debutante days, rushing at her from across the room. 'Lovely to see you, haven't seen you since you became so frightfully famous. Is your gorgeous husband here?'

'Not really my husband any longer,' said Edwina cheerfully. 'We're getting divorced as soon as is humanly possible.'

'Oh, darling, I'm so sorry . . .'

'No, no, don't be, it's the most amicable divorce ever, we're great friends still, see each other for lunch at least every two weeks, it's really much better all round, he's far nicer to me these days.'

'Oh, splendid,' said the woman, slightly uncertainly, 'I'm so glad. Well, I've often thought James and I would get on much better if we weren't married—perhaps we should follow your example?'

'Yes, good idea,' said Edwina, slightly vaguely, 'only I do warn you, you need a frightfully good lawyer, you have to make sure you're going to get

756

exactly what you want. Even Harry made a bit of a fuss about the house, it is rather large, but then I told him I needed a decent place if I wasn't going to regret the whole thing. Now you must excuse me for a moment, I'm needed over there . . .'

*　　　*　　　*

In a large Victorian villa on the outskirts of Dorking, known as Maple House, about a dozen young women were sitting listening to a very graphic account of the coronation procession on the wireless, and toasting the King and Queen and the little princesses from the bottles of sherry that had been supplied by the Fallon Trust for the occasion. The two or three dozen children who were staying in the house, as their mothers enjoyed what the trust described as a respite, were playing in the garden under the watchful eye of three of the five girls employed to help the mothers get the most out of their respite.

Later there was to be a party in the garden, and the tables were already set up, red, white and blue bunting hanging between the trees, and a Union Jack from every window. The older children were engaged in blowing up red and blue balloons which the younger ones were in their turn popping rather determinedly, and two of the mothers who had tired of listening to the wireless were carrying out the big gramophone through the French windows to provide music for the party.

There was great excitement because the local paper had come to interview Mr and Mrs Douglas, who were in overall control and ran the house for the trust; it had attracted a great deal of attention,

757

being the flagship in what was to be a series of similar establishments.

The official purpose of the charity, which was itself called Respite, was to provide a holiday for exhausted young women, overburdened with children, their bodies worn out with too much childbearing, their spirits worn down with caring for their innumerable offspring and their demanding husbands. The women, who had usually heard about Respite through the Birth Control Association, could apply for a week or sometimes even a fortnight's break there, with their children; a panel for the trust, appointed by Dr Cassia Fallon, assessed each case on its merits. It had only been going for a few weeks and there was already a long waiting list; so far, despite the most gloomy prognostications from a great many people, most notably Mrs Ada Forbes—who was nevertheless a most tireless chairlady of the charity committee of Maple House—only two of the hundred or so young women who had already been granted a stay there had taken advantage of the situation and helped themselves to more than the food, lodging, companionship and sensible advice which was offered to them. Most of them simply returned to their homes and their lives refreshed, although already a handful—to the great satisfaction of all those in charge, but especially Dr Fallon—had decided they would like to bring about some more dramatic change in their circumstances, and were doing such heady things as taking correspondence courses, looking into the possibilities of training as shorthand-typists, or even nurses when their children were a little older.

The reporter, having finished his interview and

taken some photographs, was invited to stay for the party in the garden, but refused, explaining that he had several street parties to cover that afternoon; but as he told Mr and Mrs Douglas, having thanked them for giving him his interview, he had been pleasantly surprised to find the atmosphere of Maple House most impressively cheerful and calm.

'Oh, they all expect us to be somewhere between the workhouse and Bedlam,' said Mrs Douglas cheerfully, 'we're quite used to it,' and she went out into the garden to lead a patriotic singsong, commencing with 'Rule, Britannia'. It was that sort of day.

*　　　*　　　*

Rupert Cameron had not been watching the procession because he was rehearsing. Jasper Hamlyn and James Piggott had both decided that *Letters* should be brought up to date, made absolutely topical to incorporate and capitalise upon coronation fever, and Piggott had written two more letters which Hamlyn was now insisting went into that night's performance; it didn't *sound* very complicated, as Rupert said plaintively, but it meant other adjustments throughout the piece, final phrases moved along, and it was actually very complicated indeed.

'Rupert, darling, don't be difficult,' said Jasper Hamlyn.

Rupert wasn't often difficult, but he was very tired and beginning to feel the strain of doing *Letters* eight times a week for eight months. Moreover, ever since the night of the abdication, when he found himself so surprisingly holding her

759

in his arms, he had found working with Eleanor an appalling strain. Unrequited love was a terrible thing in any case; sitting on the stage with her, speaking words to her of passion and regret, hearing her returning them, and then watching her hurrying off home to her own life as the curtain came down, her own emotions so clearly untouched, was a nightly torture.

He had regretted it so much, that moment; absolute madness. She had been so clearly embarrassed afterwards, had pulled away from him, said she must be getting home, had refused his offer of seeing her to her train even, and next day had been patently anxious to make it clear that she wished nothing more than that they should be friends again. He knew he was not the sort of man she was attracted to; she liked serious, intellectual people, not foolish, vapid ones given to extravagant chatter.

And, of course, she must think him such a fool; chasing after young girls; indulging in endlessly unsuitable love affairs. He had even embarked on one such relationship since that night, in an endeavour to cure himself of the new aching, tender longing for Eleanor; more swiftly disastrous even than usual, and of course she had known, had teased him about it.

She had not yet arrived for the rehearsal, and he had to struggle through the first of the new letters with Jasper Hamlyn reading in for her; by the time she arrived, flushed with excitement, having seen the whole procession, without planning it at all, from the corner of Parliament Square, he was very irritated indeed.

'I was walking through, you know, just on the

off-chance, and I saw the tiniest gap in the crowd and just worked my way forward, it was wonderful, I was overcome with patriotic zeal.'

'Really,' said Rupert severely, 'I thought you of all people would have regarded the whole thing as lot of hysterical nonsense.'

'So would I,' she said, looking at him rather seriously, 'but somehow, you know, seeing the wonderful coach and the pair of them in their crowns, and little princesses and the old Queen, so brave and imposing, suddenly you felt it was terribly important, a historic moment. Especially standing there, so near the Houses of Parliament. Sorry, Rupert.'

'Well, I'm very pleased for you,' he said, rather severely, feeling not pleased at all, 'but perhaps now we could get on with real life. We have a great deal to get through in very little time.'

'Yes, of course,' said Eleanor, coolly, taking off her coat, 'and then, when we break for lunch, I have some news for you all.'

She's getting married, thought Rupert; she's found some filthy intellectual to marry her, and felt extremely sick.

'You'd better tell us now,' he said, anxious to get it over, hearing his voice still irritable and hating himself for it, 'then we can get back to work. What is it?'

She looked at them slightly nervously, and then visibly took a deep breath. 'I'm leaving the play,' she said, less elated suddenly, 'just as soon as you can find someone else. I've had an offer of a film, in Hollywood, and my agent says I must accept.'

There was a very long silence, then, 'What film?' said Jasper and Rupert in absolute unison, and an absolute unison of tone, outraged disbelief .

'It's a version of one of Somerset Maugham's stories, "The Letter". I am to play the lead. I can't tell you more now, but they are prepared to pay for me and Portia to go out there, and that will be wonderful for her, of course.'

'Darling, that is simply wonderful,' said Jasper, going over to her and kissing her. 'I don't know how we shall manage without you, but of course go you must. How thrilling, how very clever of you.'

'Thank you,' she said, smiling at him, returning the kiss. 'Yes, it is exciting, and Portia is beside herself and already planning to find Fred Astaire and offer her services to him.'

And Rupert then, in a performance which he knew would have won him an Oscar, smiled too, said, 'How marvellous, darling, I am so terribly proud of you.'

And then they stopped even pretending to rehearse and went to the pub, where Jasper managed to procure a bottle of rather inferior champagne, and they toasted her and her success, in between toasting Their Majesties, along with all the other occupants, and then went back to the theatre 'just for the briefest run-through,' said Jasper, 'then you'll both have to improvise, oh, God, Rupert, how are we going to manage without her?' and Rupert, still doing his Oscar-winning, said he couldn't imagine, but it was so exciting, they couldn't begrudge it to her for a moment, and then finally at about half past three, she excused herself and went to her dressing room to find an aspirin, 'I've got a headache, too much champagne, so silly of me,' and was gone for rather a long time.

She came back looking rather pale, and fluffed

762

the same line three times. Rupert, running out now of Oscar-winning qualities, snapped at her, and told her she should try to remember she wasn't quite a Hollywood star yet and retakes were unfortunately impossible in the theatre. She stood looking at him in silence for a moment, her face flushed, and then ran out off the stage.

'You bastard,' said Jasper, 'you unutterable bastard. Go and tell her you're sorry.'

Rupert made his way to Eleanor's dressing room; he knocked on the door. She didn't respond; and he knocked again and then again, and said, 'Eleanor, I'm sorry, so sorry, it was a dreadful thing to say, please forgive me.'

Still no answer: he tried the door but it was locked. Half exasperated, half anxious now, he went down to the stage doorman's office and took the dressing-room pass key from the hook.

It was still difficult to open the door, the other key being in the other side, but it finally worked. He opened it carefully, cautiously, half expecting to receive a stream of abuse, and found her sitting silently in front of the make-up mirror, tears pouring down her face. Her reaction seemed rather extreme to Rupert, but a lifetime of working with women, falling in love with them, knowing them intimately, had taught him that logic seldom entered their emotional equations.

'I'm so sorry,' he said again, 'I shouldn't have said it, I ought to be put up against a wall and—'

He was unprepared for what happened next: a pot of make-up removing cream flew through the air and struck him on the side of the head. 'Don't say it!' she shouted. 'Don't say you ought to be shot, or strung up, I can't stand it.'

763

He yelped with pain, sat down, clutching at his head where the cream had landed; it felt damp, and he felt something warm trickle down his face. 'It's blood,' he said, staring rather stupidly at his reddened hand. 'You've cut me.'

'Good,' she said, 'I'm glad. I hope it hurts. I hope it hurts you as much as you've hurt me,' and then, as if suddenly hearing herself, clapped her hand over her mouth, and said, 'Oh, Rupert, I'm so sorry. Really so very sorry.' She reached for some cotton wool, started rather ineffectually dabbing at his head with it.

'If you really want to hurt me, you're doing well,' he said. 'That's making it much worse.'

'Good,' she said. 'I mean—oh, God, I don't know what I mean.'

'Why are you so angry with me?' he said. 'I don't understand, it's so unlike you.'

'Yes, it is, isn't it?' she said. 'Utterly unlike me, Eleanor, sweet, gentle, patient Eleanor, never being difficult, never making a fuss, just listening to you quietly, all your bloody troubles. Well, I've had enough, enough of the whole bloody thing, I'm worn out with it, months and months of it—'

'What bloody thing?' he said. 'I don't understand. I was so pleased for you, I'm sorry I said what I did, but I was tired and my head ached and—'

'Are you really pleased I'm going?' she said. 'Really, really pleased?'

'Yes,' he said carefully, back on Oscar-winning form, 'yes, of course I am, I'm delighted,' and then she sat down in her chair and burst into tears again.

And then Rupert understood.

'You,' he said a great deal later, after he had kissed her a great many times, and told her how much he loved her, had been told how much she loved him, had allowed her to clean up the cut on his head and give him some medicinal brandy, had told her she was on no account to go to Hollywood on her own, that if she was intent on going, he would come too, and *Letters* could take care of itself, had heard that she dreaded going, she had hated Hollywood the one time she had been there, that all she wanted to do was stay in London, and probably give up acting altogether, that, yes, she would be quite happy keeping house for an actor, that would be absolutely fine . . .

'You, Eleanor Studely,' he said, 'you should be put up against a wall and shot. Fancy not telling me all this earlier. Emancipated woman like you.'

*   *   *

'So how did you find the procession?' said Harry Moreton. They were having dinner at the Connaught, the dining room full of visiting dignitaries from overseas for the coronation.

Cassia had taken the children and Tessa, the new nanny, to see the procession and had left them eating fish and chips (out of newspaper, their chosen treat) in the kitchen at Walton Street. It had been a rather uncomfortable evening; Harry was in a strange mood, awkward, truculent even, interspersed with an almost aggressive cheerfulness.

'Wonderful. The King embodied virtue and

reliability, the Queen looked very beautiful, and the little princesses were enchanting.'

'Lucky King,' said Harry, scowling at her.

'What do you mean?'

'I mean he's managed to find a woman whose only ambition is to look after him and him alone, or him and his children, not hundreds of sick and depressing people. Aren't you tired of that practice of yours yet, Cassia?'

'No, Harry, I'm not, I'm blissfully happy. I'm sorry your plan has misfired so badly, but it's really very nice for me.'

'What on earth do you mean?'

'I mean that here I am, thanks to you and Leonora, running my own medical practice, and it's absolutely wonderful.'

'Yes, well, it might be wonderful for you. It's pretty hellish for me. I only get to see you about once a week, twice at the most, and then you're quite liable to rush off and deliver a baby or something. Will you come home with me tonight at least?'

'Harry, I can't. I have to be at Monks Ridge very early, to take morning surgery. I'm sorry.'

'So am I. Don't you want to come home with me, sleep with me?' His voice had risen slightly; the people at the next table looked at them interestedly.

'Yes,' she said quickly, 'yes, of course I do, but— well, I told you. I have to get back. We're driving down very early in the morning.'

'I really don't know how much longer I can stand this,' he said.

'Harry, I'm very sorry. I don't quite see what I can do about it, though.'

'No, so you keep saying. It seems very obvious what you can do about it to me. When I think of all the time you wasted, all those years we could have been together. Cassia, please, please will you marry me? Soon. Come and live with me. Please.'

'Live with you where?'

'In my house. Of course. Where else?'

'Harry, I keep telling you, I can't do that. I'm sorry. I can't give up the practice, and I certainly can't bring the children to London.'

'Well—' he hesitated—'suppose I moved to Sussex. Became a commuting man, God help me. Surely that would convince you, a sacrifice like that?' He heard her hesitation, pounced. 'That'd be all right, wouldn't it? You could still carry on looking after all those dreadful people. The children would like it. Bertie and William could have ponies. Bertie's dying to ride, we were talking about it the other day. I said I'd teach him to jump, take him hunting. We're great friends, you know, he and I, he's never got over the fact that it was me who thought of where he might be when he ran away.'

'Yes, I know you're friends,' she said.

'Well, then?'

She was silent; he sat watching her. She could feel him watching her. It was tempting, the thought of him being in Sussex. It might work. And she wanted it so much, to marry him, to be with him. But something still frightened her, held her back. And she knew what it was . . .

'What is it?' he said. 'I still don't understand why you won't give in, Cassia. What more can I do? I've—yes, what is it?'

The waiter had appeared beside them. 'Coffee,

Mr Moreton, sir? And any brandy, liqueurs?'

'Yes, coffee. And brandy. Cassia?'

She shook her head. The waiter went away.

'Right. How would that be? I can't tell you how the proposition horrifies me, but I'd do it. For you.'

She said nothing.

'Jesus. All right, then, how about this? I'll put some money into that bloody charity of yours. You can have a poorhouse in every town if you want to—'

'Don't call them poorhouses. And don't disparage it, Harry, my trust, it's so important to me, a way of putting the money to really proper use, you know that.'

'Sorry. I'm sorry. But surely you're impressed by the offer?'

'No, I'm not,' she said, her voice loud with desperation, 'I'm not, and that's exactly it: it's mine, the trust, not yours, you don't understand.'

'But I'm trying,' he said, 'I'm trying, for Christ's sake.' There was a silence, then he sat back in his chair and looked at her very seriously. 'You're making me very unhappy, you know,' he said. He looked unhappy: unhappy and very tired.

Go on, Cassia, tell him you'll change the situation, tell him you'll give up the practice, or at least some of it, tell him you'll marry him. But she wouldn't, couldn't; she actually opened her mouth to begin and then saw him again in the garden at the Mamounia, smiling complacently, telling her how he and Leonora had planned things for her, and the old rage and resentment rose in her and she sat silent, looking down at the table. It was too impossible to explain to him. She was still angry with him when she thought about it all

768

dispassionately, thought about him plotting, playing with her life. And somehow, whatever he said, whatever he promised, she couldn't quite believe he'd changed.

'You can't believe I've changed, can you?' he said.

'No, Harry. I can't. I'm sorry.'

'Or that I'm trying to change?'

She was silent again, staring at him.

He sighed. 'I don't know that there is any future for us after all, you know,' he said suddenly. 'I can't wait for ever, Cassia, waiting for some revelation to strike you on your own tortuous road to Damascus. I've done as much as I can. I truly believe that.'

She sat there, panic suddenly hitting her, but still she didn't speak. She couldn't. She didn't dare.

'Suppose . . .' he said suddenly, looking up at her. 'Suppose . . . yes? What is it?'

The waiter looked nervous. 'Mr Moreton, I'm so very sorry, but—'

'Yes. What is it, for God's sake? Is the place on fire or something?'

'Mr Moreton, owing to the enormous demand this evening—all the Americans, you know—we have only . . .' He finally brought the words out rather slowly: 'We have none of your favourite brand of coffee. Tonight. I'm so sorry, Mr Moreton.'

Harry looked at him, an expression of absolute incredulity on his face. God, thought Cassia, now there's going to be a scene. One of the famous Moreton scenes that had taken place in virtually every restaurant in London. She smiled reassuringly up at the waiter, could see the maitre d' hovering in the background, clearly ready to

769

move in if necessary. And then heard the words, the absolutely extraordinary words:

'I don't give a toss about the coffee,' said Harry Moreton. 'You can bring me coffee essence for all I care. I'm trying to have an important conversation here, and I most certainly don't want to be bothered about which bloody coffee I'm going to drink.'

'Yes, Mr Moreton. Sorry, Mr Moreton. Thank you.' He hurried away.

Cassia sat looking at Harry for a while in silence, and he looked back at her, scowling. Finally she smiled at him. He smiled rather uncertainly back.

'What did I say?' he said.

'Something very important,' she said, 'very important indeed.' Then she leaned across the table, took his face in her hands and kissed him on the mouth.

'I think perhaps I could work part-time, after all,' she said finally, 'and a house in Sussex would be simply lovely. Now let's go home to bed, shall we?'